big NATE'S GREATEST HITS

More

big NATE

adventures from

LINCOLN PEIRCE

Novels:

Big Nate: In a Class by Himself

Big Nate Strikes Again

Big Nate On a Roll

Big Nate Goes for Broke

Big Nate Flips Out

Big Nate in the Zone

Activity Books:

Big Nate Boredom Buster

Big Nate Fun Blaster

Big Nate Doodlepalooza

Comic Compilations:

Big Nate From the Top

Big Nate Out Loud

Big Nate and Friends

Big Nate: What Could Possibly Go Wrong?

Big Nate: Here Goes Nothing

Big Nate Makes the Grade

Big Nate All Work and No Play

Big Nate: Game On!

Big Nate: Genius Mode

Big Nate: I Can't Take It!

Big Nate: Great Minds Think Alike

Big Nate: Mr. Popularity

Big Nate: The Crowd Goes Wild!

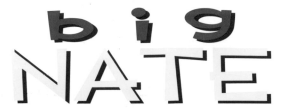

big NATE'S GREATEST HITS

by LINCOLN PEIRCE

Andrews McMeel Publishing

Kansas City • Sydney • London

IF YOU WANT TO IMPROVE AT "MONO-POLY," FRANCIS, YOU'VE GOT TO PLAY HARDBALL DURING THE NEGOTIATING PERIOD!

OKAY... I'LL GIVE YOU ORIENTAL AVENUE FOR ILLINOIS AVENUE AND PARK PLACE!

THAT SEEMS FAIR...

NO! NO, THAT'S **NOT** FAIR!

WANT ME TO THROW IN MARVIN GARDENS?

WAP!

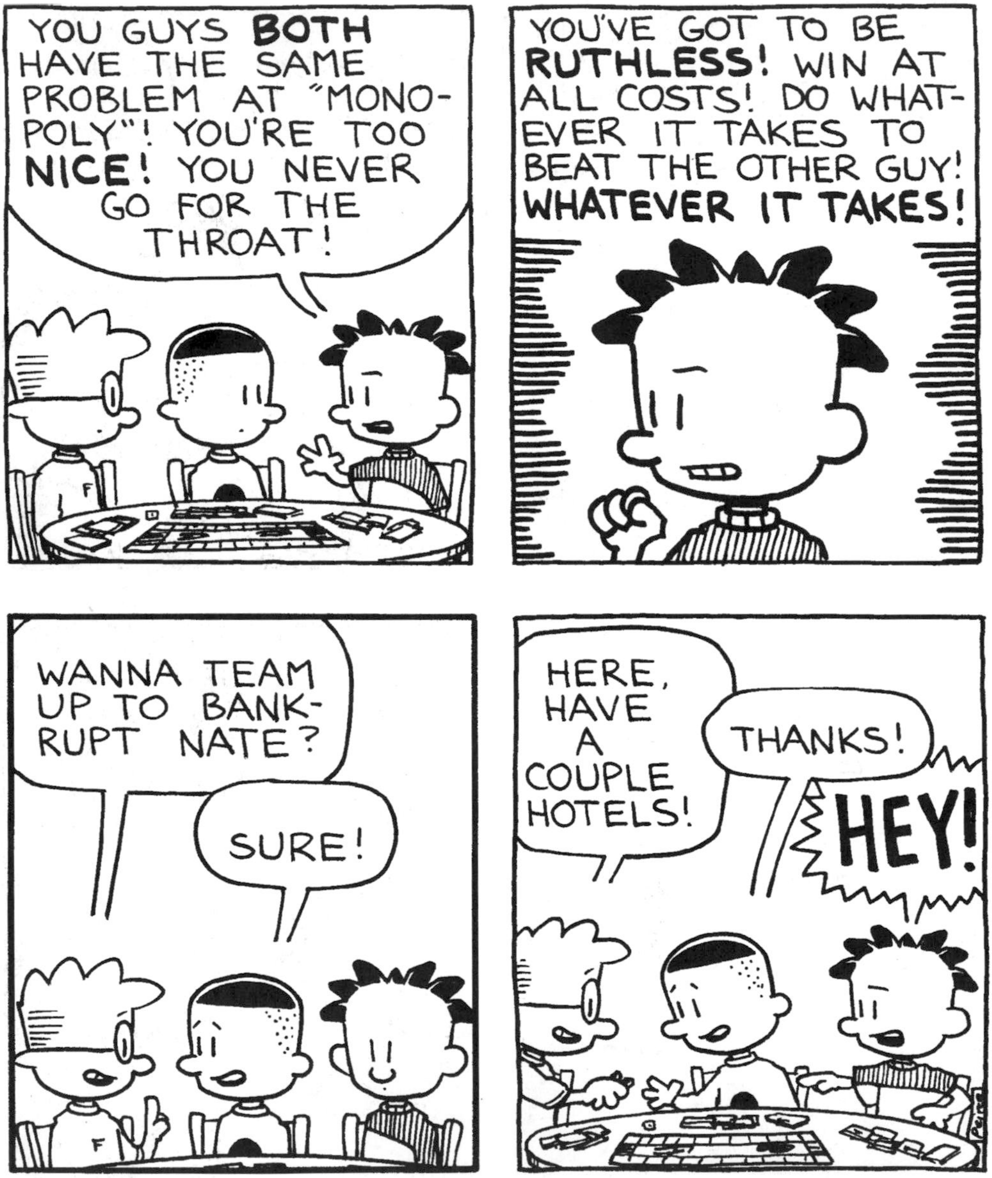
YOU GUYS **BOTH** HAVE THE SAME PROBLEM AT "MONO-POLY"! YOU'RE TOO **NICE**! YOU NEVER GO FOR THE THROAT!
YOU'VE GOT TO BE **RUTHLESS**! WIN AT ALL COSTS! DO WHAT-EVER IT TAKES TO BEAT THE OTHER GUY! **WHATEVER IT TAKES**!
WANNA TEAM UP TO BANK-RUPT NATE?
SURE!
HERE, HAVE A COUPLE HOTELS!
THANKS!
HEY!

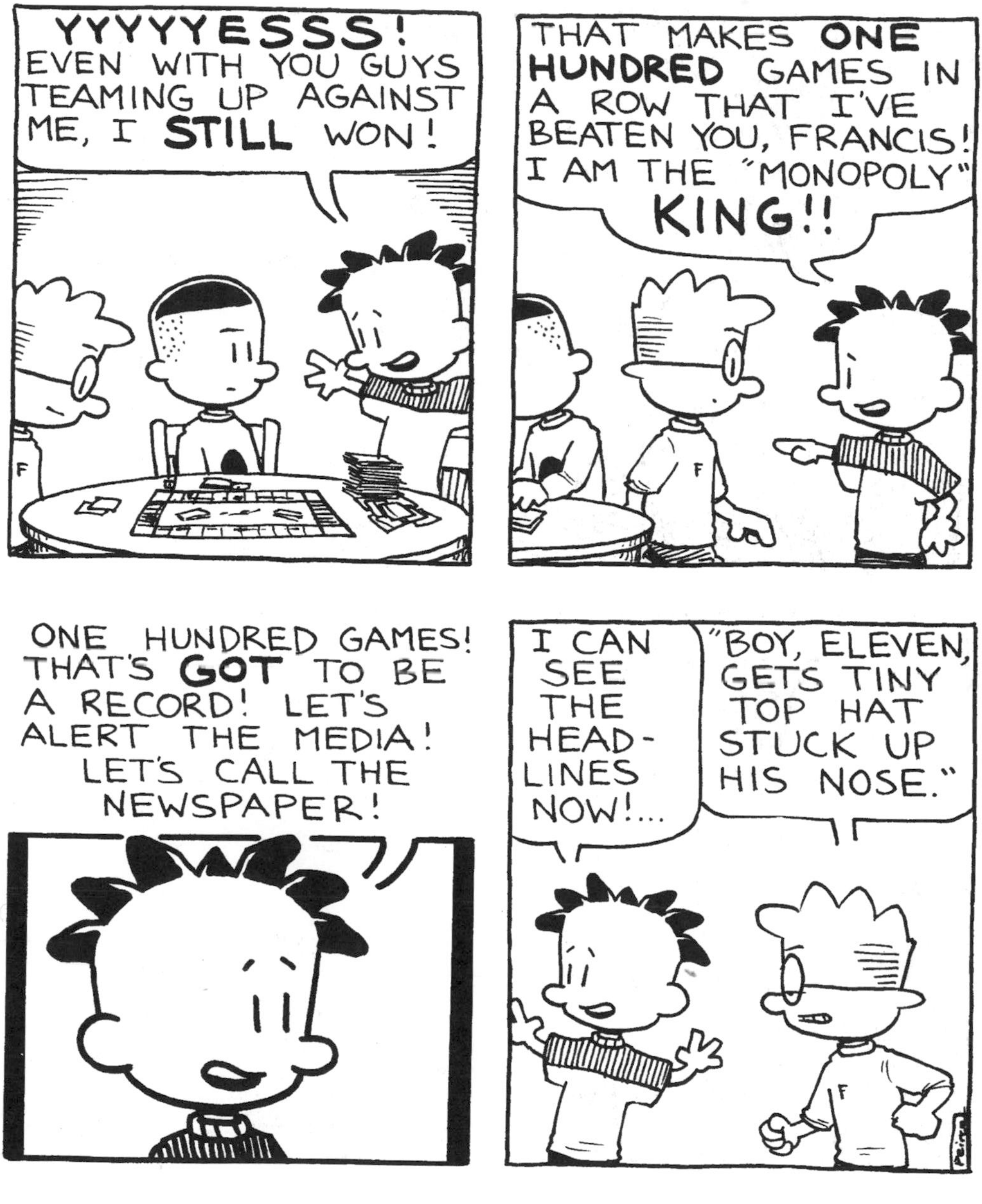
YYYYYESSSS! EVEN WITH YOU GUYS TEAMING UP AGAINST ME, I **STILL** WON!
THAT MAKES **ONE HUNDRED** GAMES IN A ROW THAT I'VE BEATEN YOU, FRANCIS! I AM THE "MONOPOLY" **KING!!**
ONE HUNDRED GAMES! THAT'S **GOT** TO BE A RECORD! LET'S ALERT THE MEDIA! LET'S CALL THE NEWSPAPER!
I CAN SEE THE HEAD-LINES NOW!...
"BOY, ELEVEN, GETS TINY TOP HAT STUCK UP HIS NOSE."
Peirce

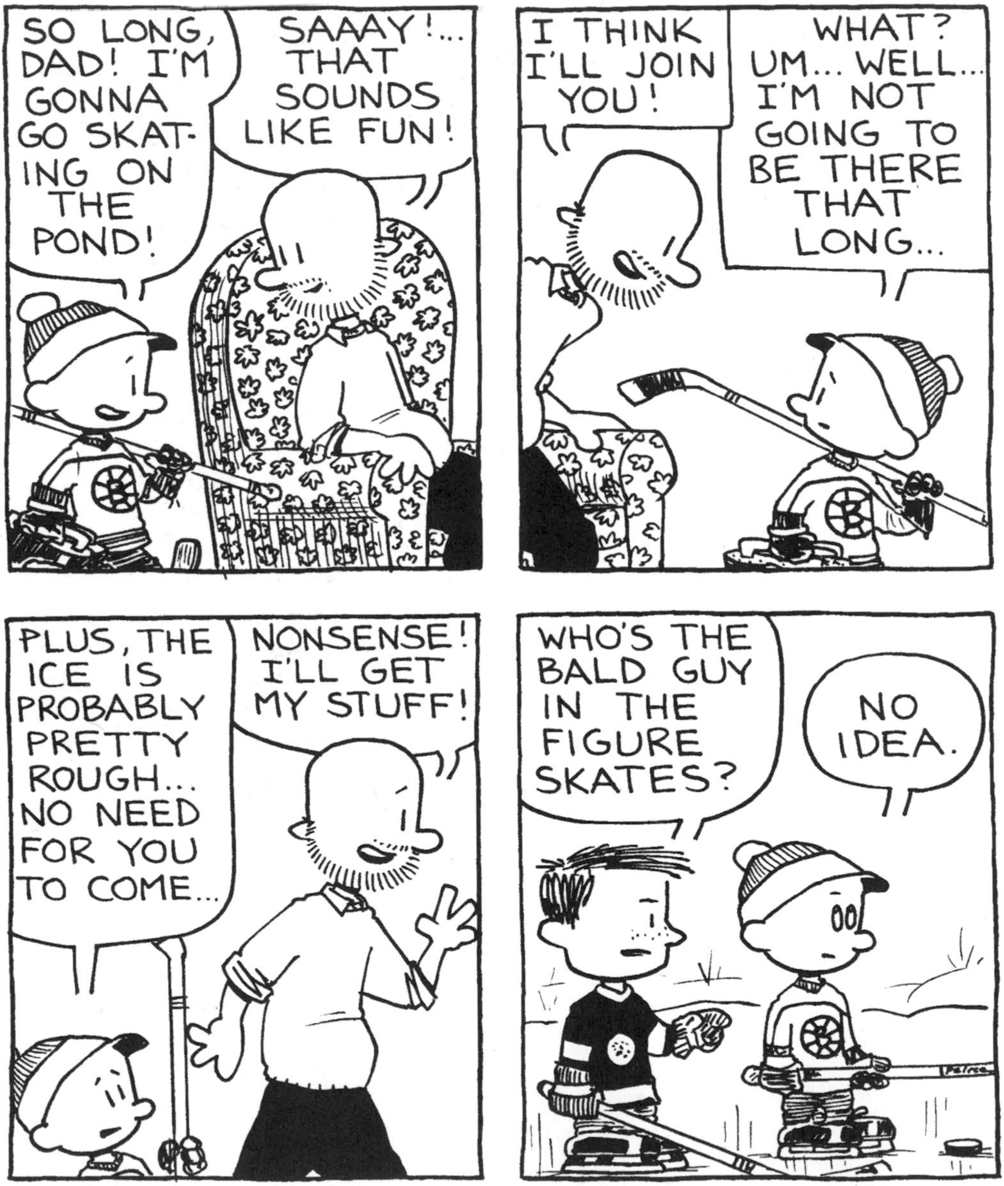
SO LONG, DAD! I'M GONNA GO SKAT-ING ON THE POND!
SAAAY!... THAT SOUNDS LIKE FUN!
I THINK I'LL JOIN YOU!
WHAT? UM... WELL... I'M NOT GOING TO BE THERE THAT LONG...
PLUS, THE ICE IS PROBABLY PRETTY ROUGH... NO NEED FOR YOU TO COME...
NONSENSE! I'LL GET MY STUFF!
WHO'S THE BALD GUY IN THE FIGURE SKATES?
NO IDEA.

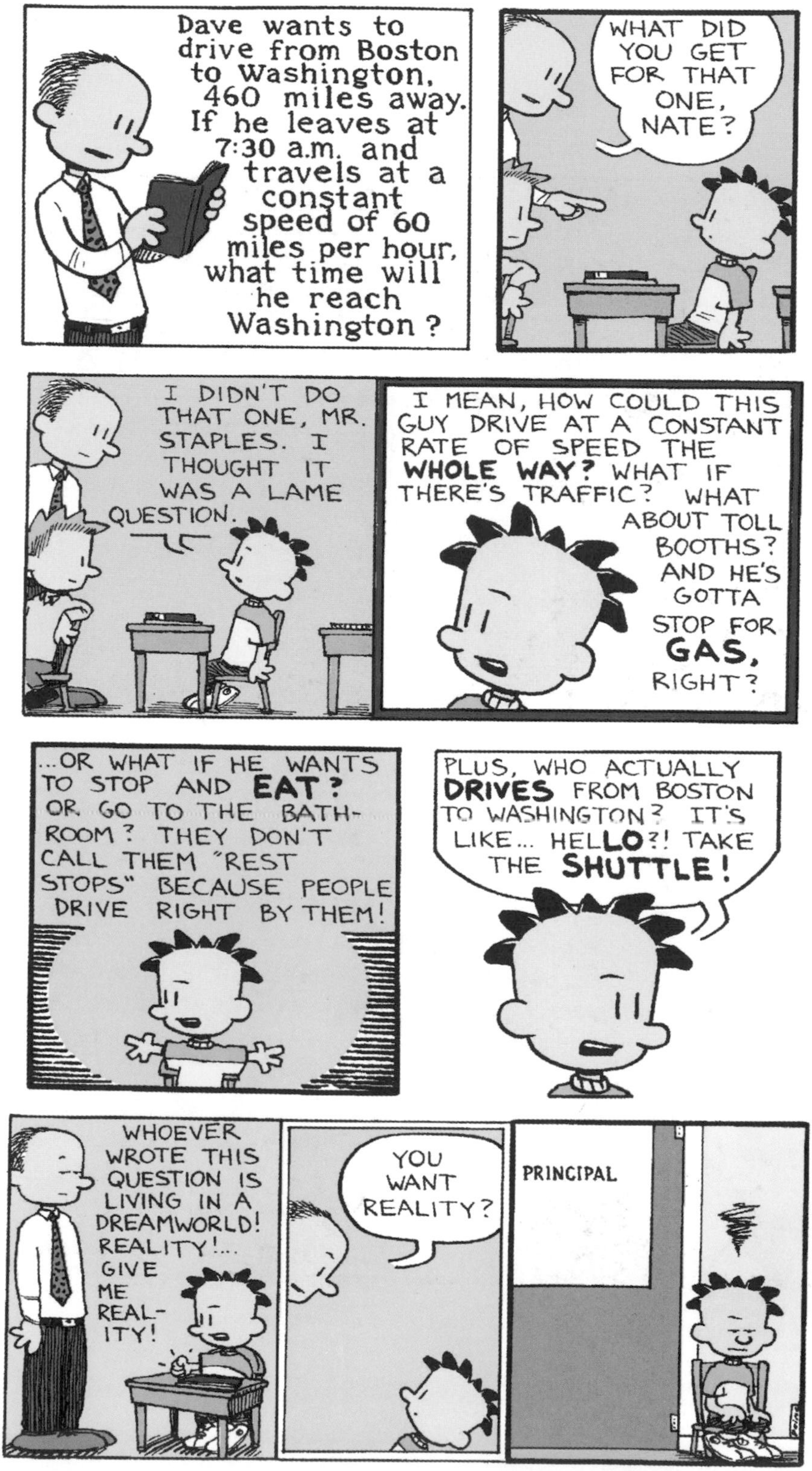
Dave wants to drive from Boston to Washington, 460 miles away. If he leaves at 7:30 a.m. and travels at a constant speed of 60 miles per hour, what time will he reach Washington?
WHAT DID YOU GET FOR THAT ONE, NATE?
I DIDN'T DO THAT ONE, MR. STAPLES. I THOUGHT IT WAS A LAME QUESTION.
I MEAN, HOW COULD THIS GUY DRIVE AT A CONSTANT RATE OF SPEED THE WHOLE WAY? WHAT IF THERE'S TRAFFIC? WHAT ABOUT TOLL BOOTHS? AND HE'S GOTTA STOP FOR GAS, RIGHT?
...OR WHAT IF HE WANTS TO STOP AND EAT? OR GO TO THE BATH-ROOM? THEY DON'T CALL THEM "REST STOPS" BECAUSE PEOPLE DRIVE RIGHT BY THEM!
PLUS, WHO ACTUALLY DRIVES FROM BOSTON TO WASHINGTON? IT'S LIKE... HELLO?! TAKE THE SHUTTLE!
WHOEVER WROTE THIS QUESTION IS LIVING IN A DREAMWORLD! REALITY!... GIVE ME REAL-ITY!
YOU WANT REALITY?
PRINCIPAL

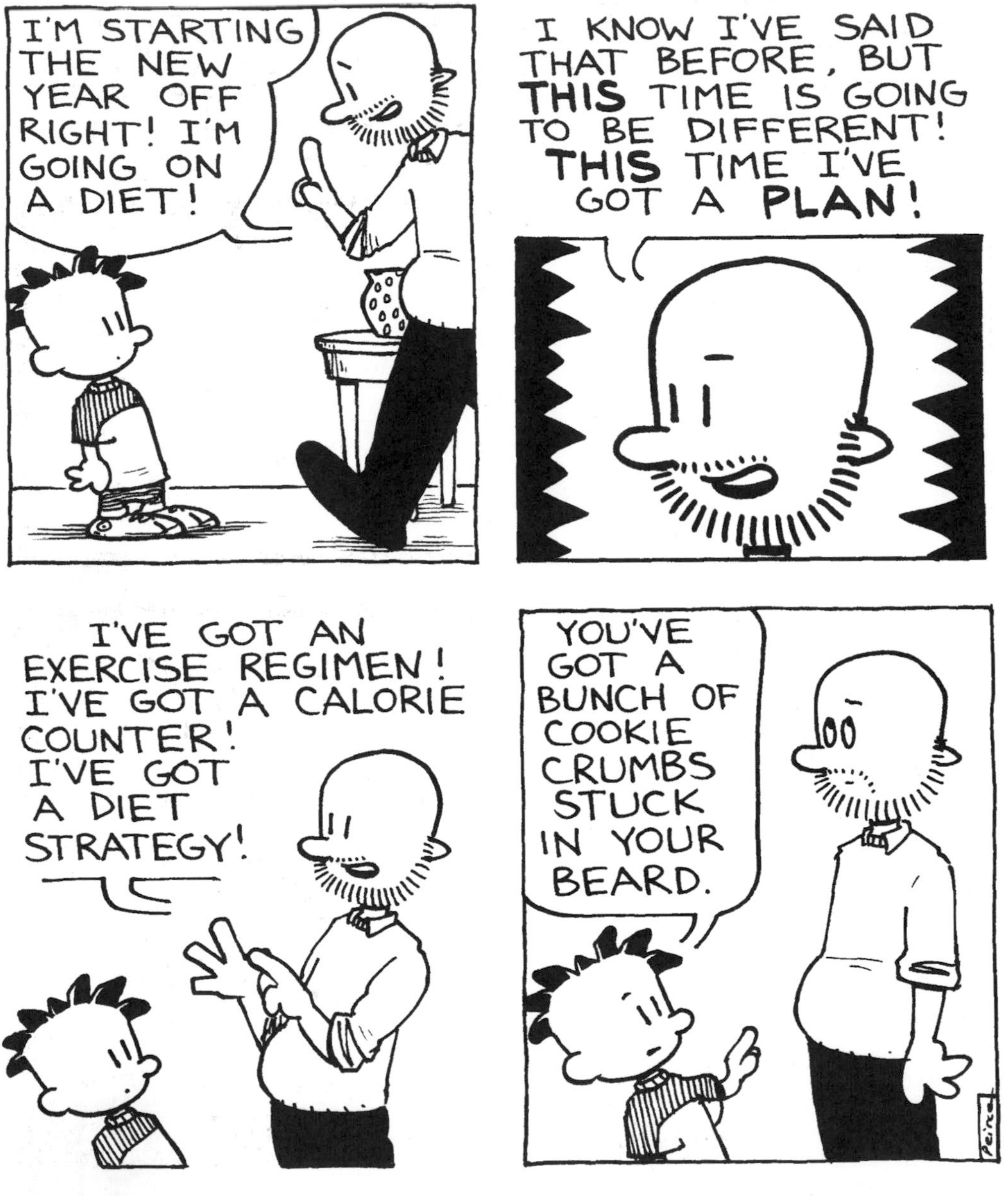
I'M STARTING THE NEW YEAR OFF RIGHT! I'M GOING ON A DIET!
I KNOW I'VE SAID THAT BEFORE, BUT **THIS** TIME IS GOING TO BE DIFFERENT! **THIS** TIME I'VE GOT A **PLAN**!
I'VE GOT AN EXERCISE REGIMEN! I'VE GOT A CALORIE COUNTER! I'VE GOT A DIET STRATEGY!
YOU'VE GOT A BUNCH OF COOKIE CRUMBS STUCK IN YOUR BEARD.
Peirce

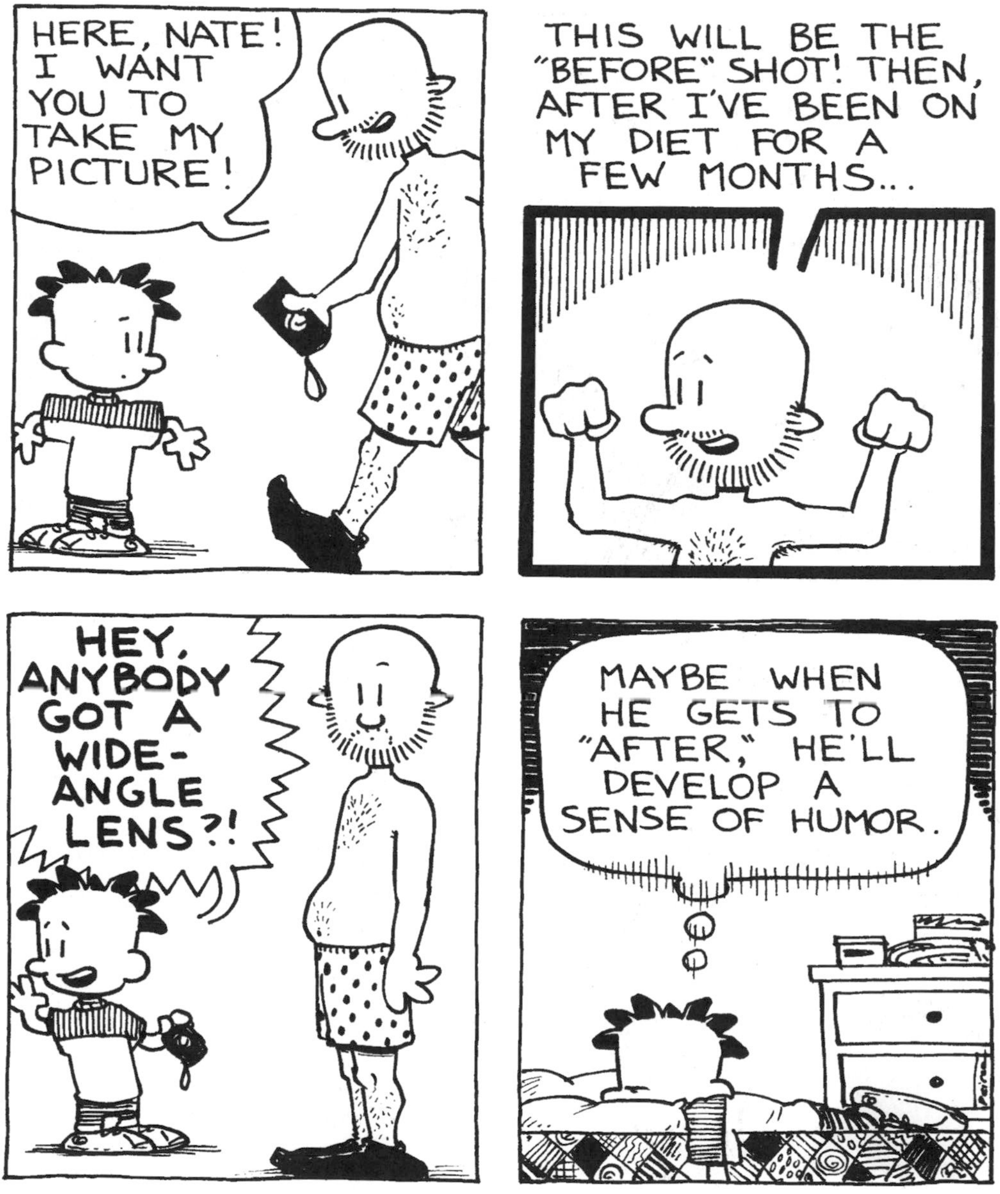
HERE, NATE! I WANT YOU TO TAKE MY PICTURE!
THIS WILL BE THE "BEFORE" SHOT! THEN, AFTER I'VE BEEN ON MY DIET FOR A FEW MONTHS...
HEY, ANYBODY GOT A WIDE-ANGLE LENS?!
MAYBE WHEN HE GETS TO "AFTER," HE'LL DEVELOP A SENSE OF HUMOR.

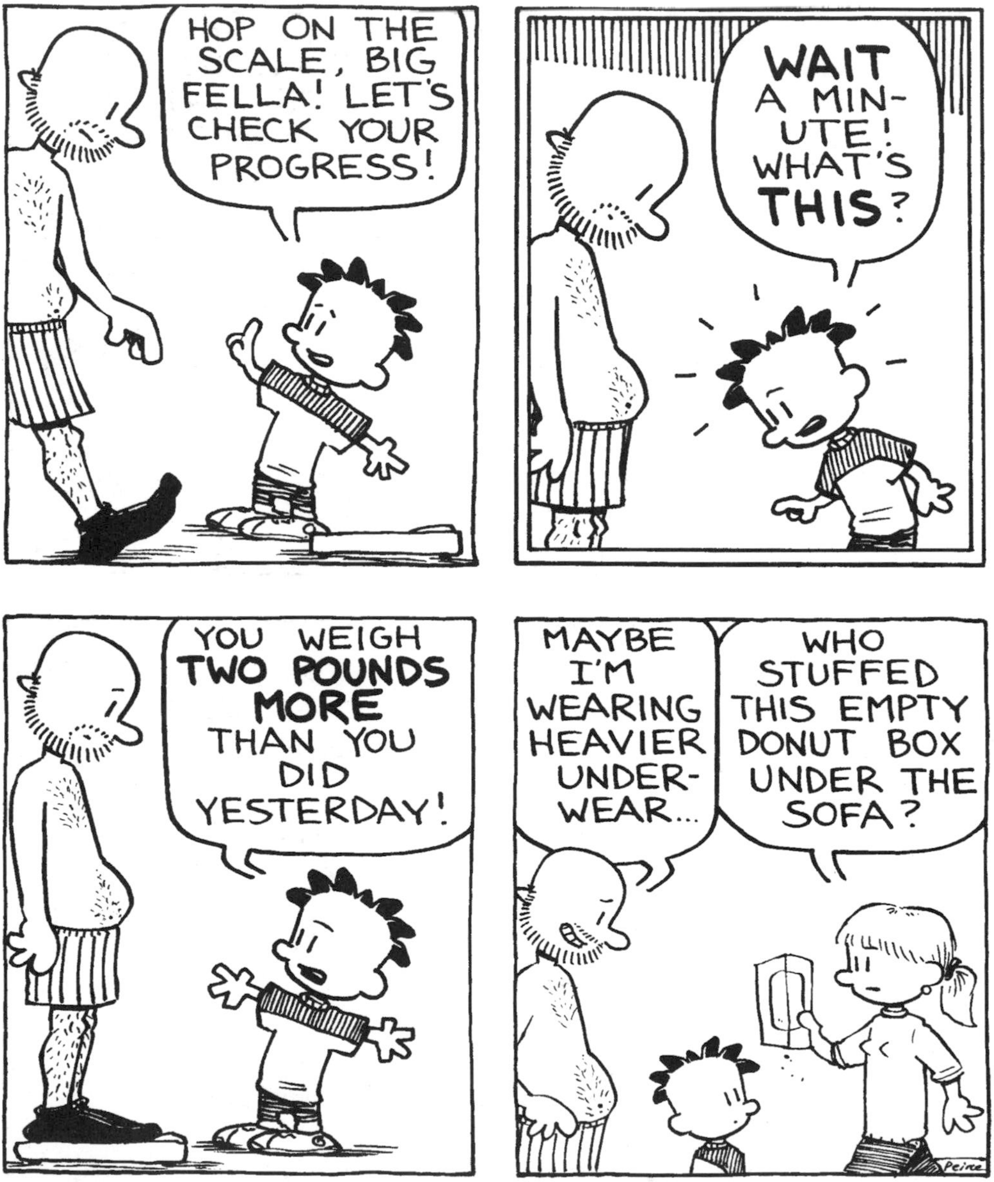
HOP ON THE SCALE, BIG FELLA! LET'S CHECK YOUR PROGRESS!
WAIT A MIN-UTE! WHAT'S THIS?
YOU WEIGH TWO POUNDS MORE THAN YOU DID YESTERDAY!
MAYBE I'M WEARING HEAVIER UNDER-WEAR...
WHO STUFFED THIS EMPTY DONUT BOX UNDER THE SOFA?
Peirce

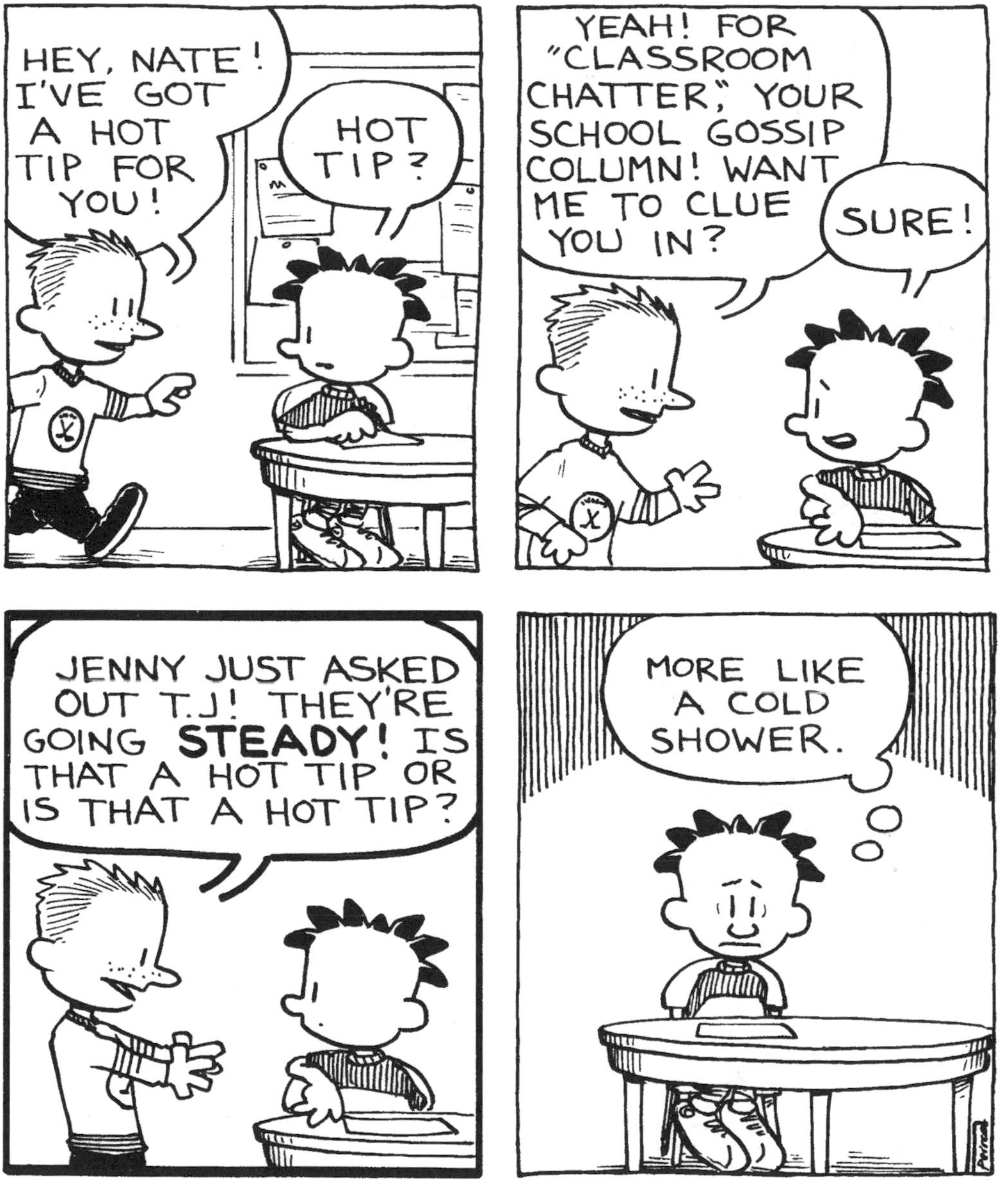
HEY, NATE! I'VE GOT A HOT TIP FOR YOU!
HOT TIP?
YEAH! FOR "CLASSROOM CHATTER," YOUR SCHOOL GOSSIP COLUMN! WANT ME TO CLUE YOU IN?
SURE!
JENNY JUST ASKED OUT T.J! THEY'RE GOING **STEADY**! IS THAT A HOT TIP OR IS THAT A HOT TIP?
MORE LIKE A COLD SHOWER.

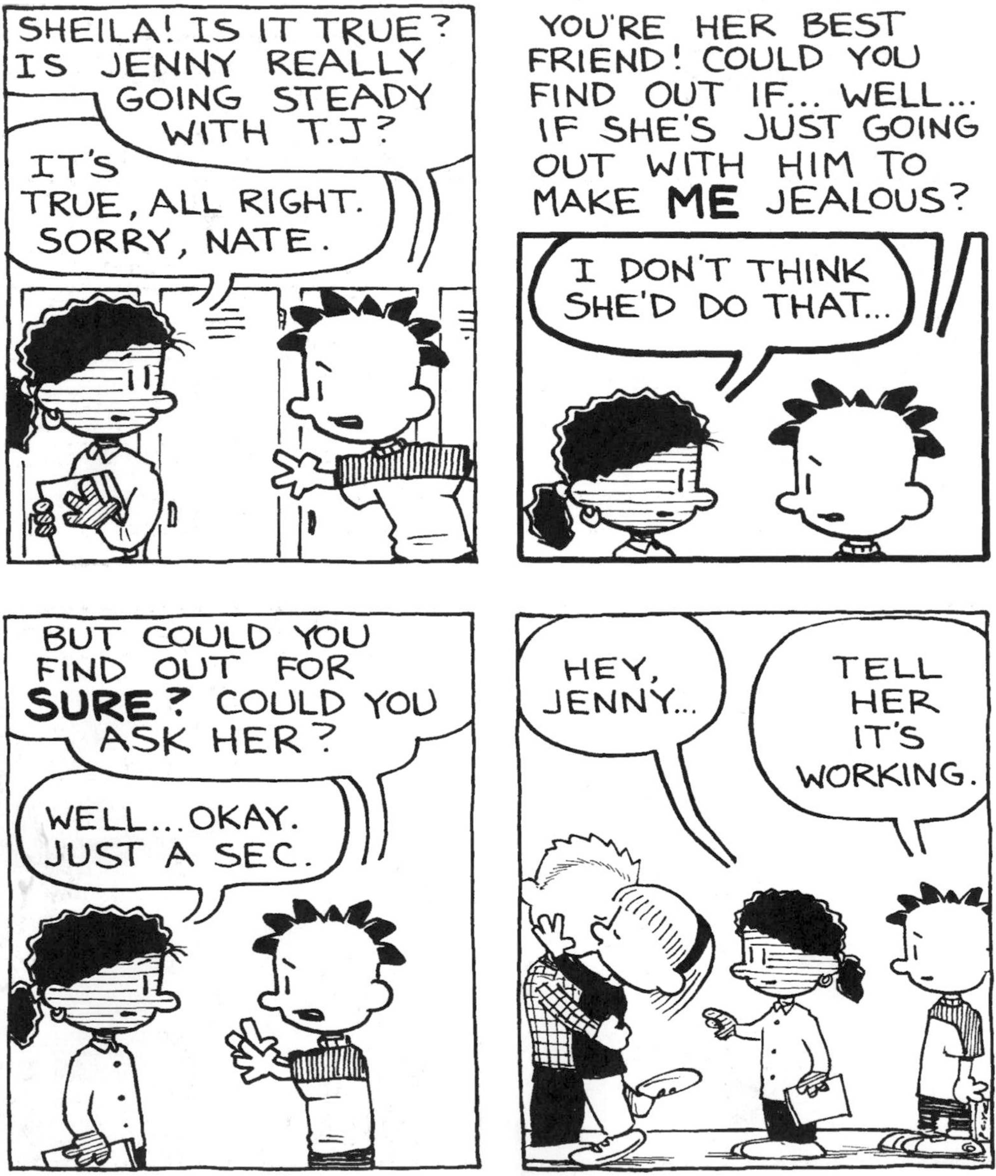
SHEILA! IS IT TRUE? IS JENNY REALLY GOING STEADY WITH T.J?
IT'S TRUE, ALL RIGHT. SORRY, NATE.
YOU'RE HER BEST FRIEND! COULD YOU FIND OUT IF... WELL... IF SHE'S JUST GOING OUT WITH HIM TO MAKE **ME** JEALOUS?
I DON'T THINK SHE'D DO THAT...
BUT COULD YOU FIND OUT FOR **SURE?** COULD YOU ASK HER?
WELL...OKAY. JUST A SEC.
HEY, JENNY...
TELL HER IT'S WORKING.

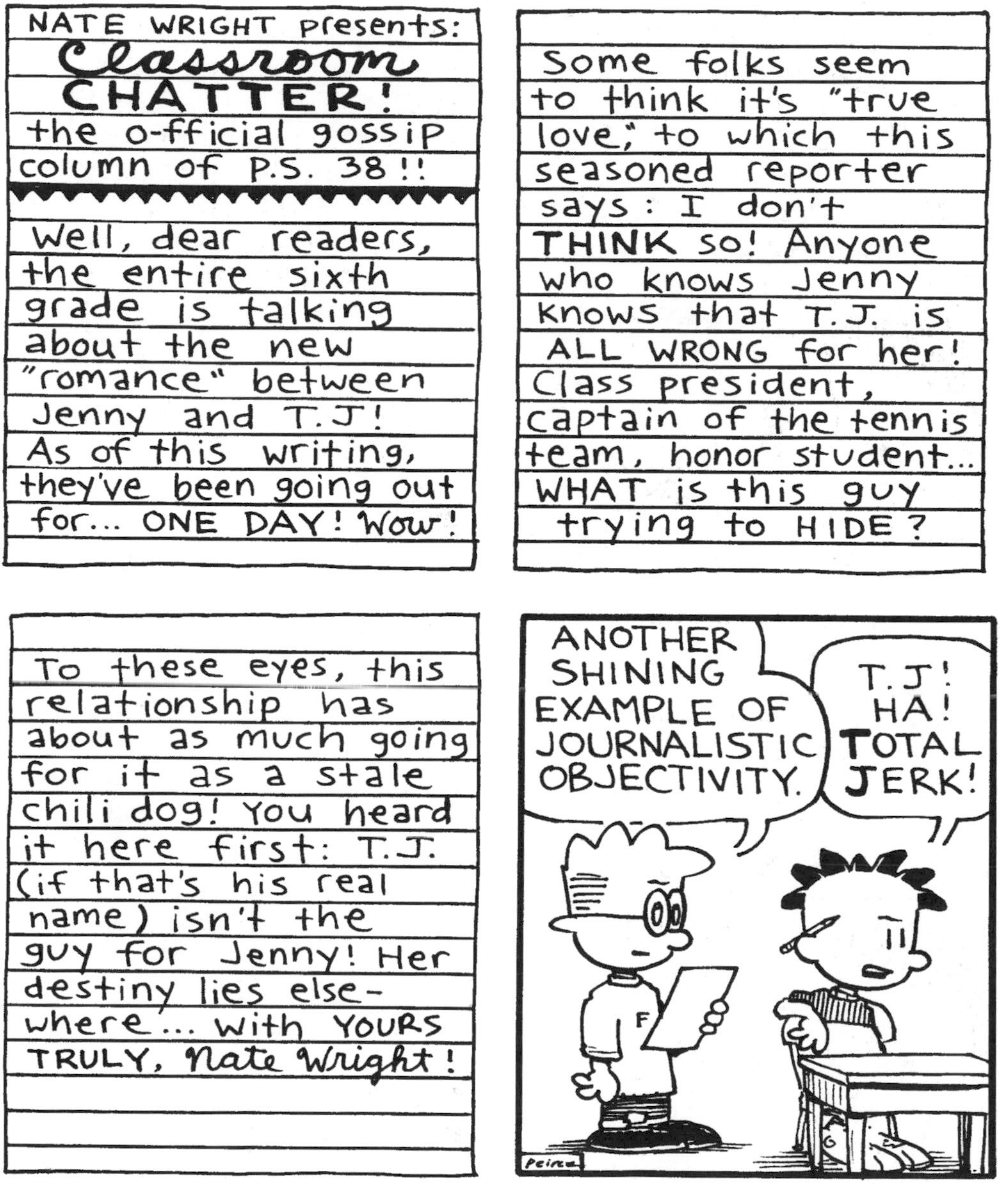
NATE WRIGHT presents:
Classroom CHATTER!
the o-fficial gossip column of P.S. 38!!
Well, dear readers, the entire sixth grade is talking about the new "romance" between Jenny and T.J! As of this writing, they've been going out for... ONE DAY! Wow!
Some folks seem to think it's "true love," to which this seasoned reporter says: I don't THINK so! Anyone who knows Jenny knows that T.J. is ALL WRONG for her! Class president, captain of the tennis team, honor student... WHAT is this guy trying to HIDE?
To these eyes, this relationship has about as much going for it as a stale chili dog! You heard it here first: T.J. (if that's his real name) isn't the guy for Jenny! Her destiny lies elsewhere... with YOURS TRULY, Nate Wright!
ANOTHER SHINING EXAMPLE OF JOURNALISTIC OBJECTIVITY.
T.J! HA! TOTAL JERK!

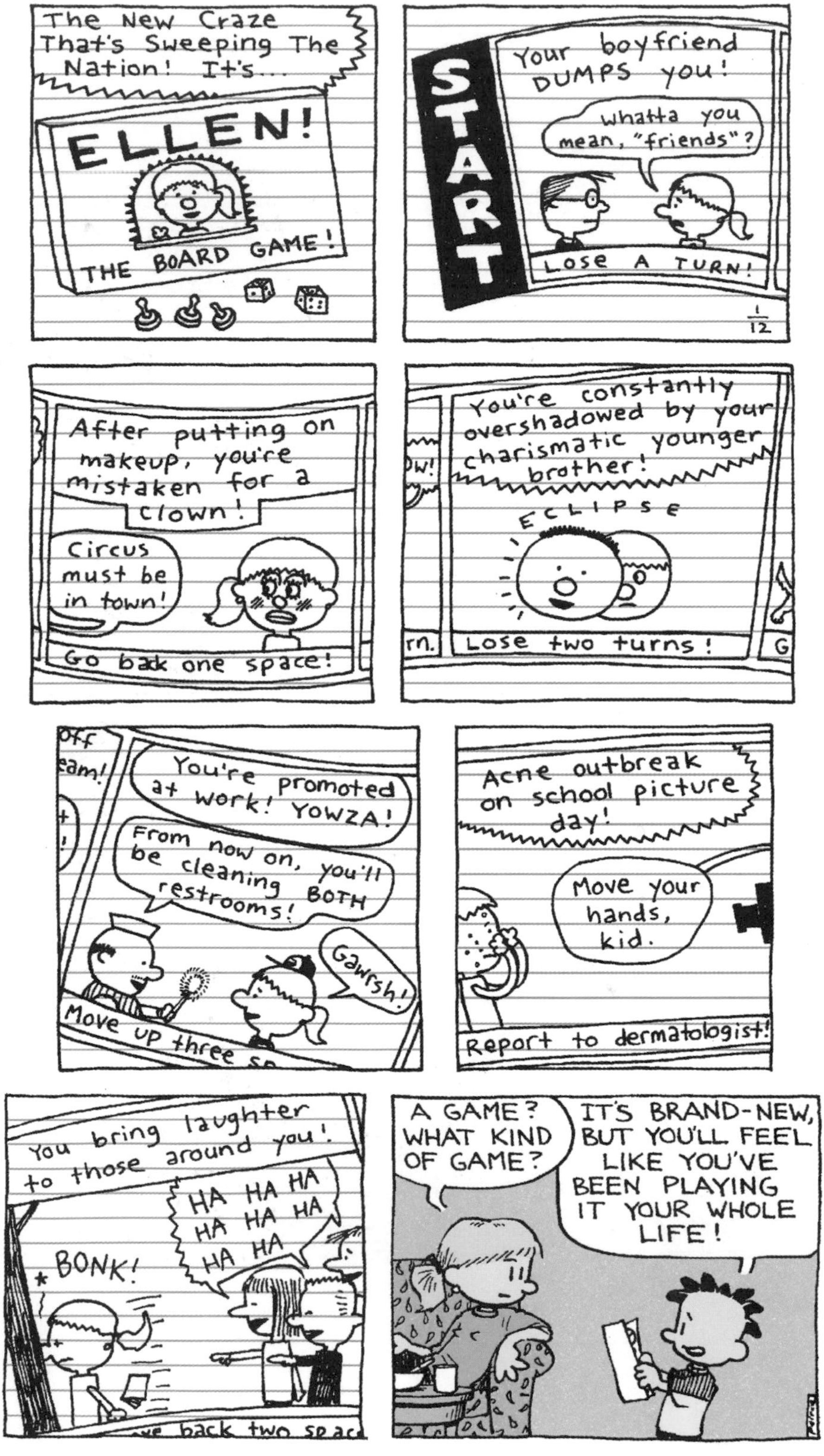
The New Craze That's Sweeping The Nation! It's...
ELLEN!
THE BOARD GAME!
START
Your boyfriend DUMPS you!
Whatta you mean, "friends"?
LOSE A TURN!
After putting on makeup, you're mistaken for a clown!
Circus must be in town!
Go back one space!
You're constantly overshadowed by your charismatic younger brother!
ECLIPSE
Lose two turns!
You're promoted at work! YOWZA!
From now on, you'll be cleaning BOTH restrooms!
Gawrsh!
Move up three s
Acne outbreak on school picture day!
Move your hands, kid.
Report to dermatologist!
You bring laughter to those around you!
HA HA HA HA HA HA HA HA
BONK!
ve back two spac
A GAME? WHAT KIND OF GAME?
IT'S BRAND-NEW, BUT YOU'LL FEEL LIKE YOU'VE BEEN PLAYING IT YOUR WHOLE LIFE!

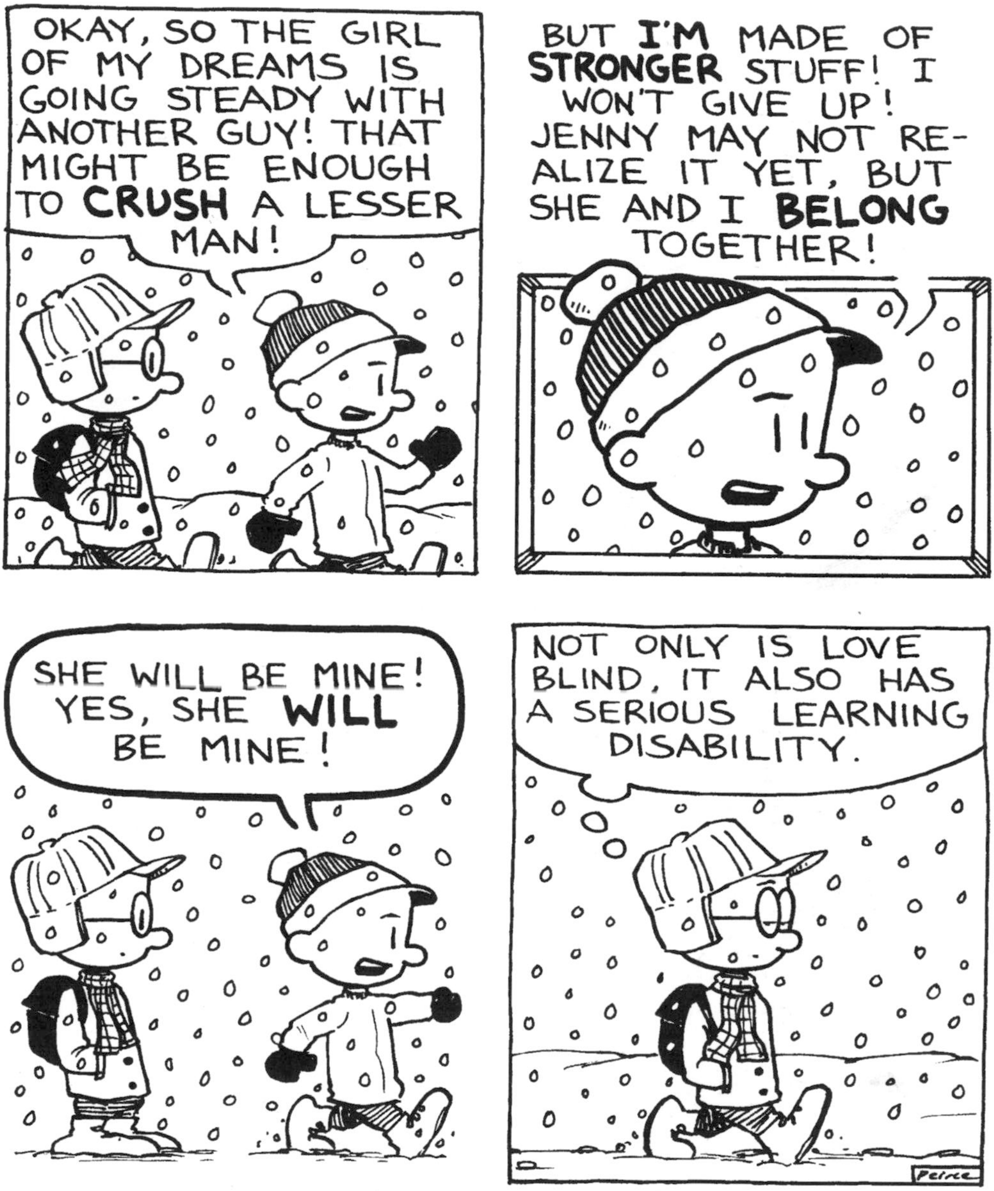
OKAY, SO THE GIRL OF MY DREAMS IS GOING STEADY WITH ANOTHER GUY! THAT MIGHT BE ENOUGH TO CRUSH A LESSER MAN!
BUT I'M MADE OF STRONGER STUFF! I WON'T GIVE UP! JENNY MAY NOT REALIZE IT YET, BUT SHE AND I BELONG TOGETHER!
SHE WILL BE MINE! YES, SHE WILL BE MINE!
NOT ONLY IS LOVE BLIND, IT ALSO HAS A SERIOUS LEARNING DISABILITY.
Peirce

THERE GOES T.J.... THE GUY WHO STOLE MY JENNY.
YOUR JENNY?
NATE, WILL YOU WAKE UP! SHE'S NOT YOUR JENNY! SHE WAS NEVER YOUR JENNY!
JENNY DOESN'T EVEN LIKE YOU, NATE! ACCEPT IT! SHE IS NOT YOUR GIRL-FRIEND!
NOT YET!..
AAARGH...
STAND BACK! I'M GONNA PUT ON SOME COLOGNE!
Peirce

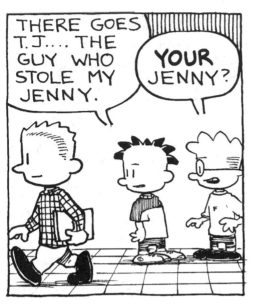

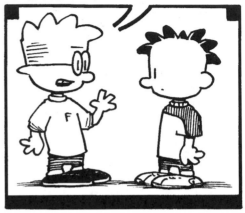

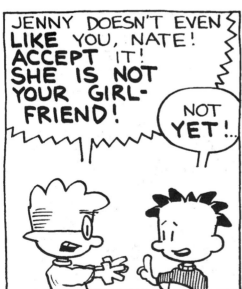

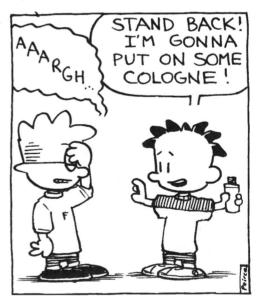

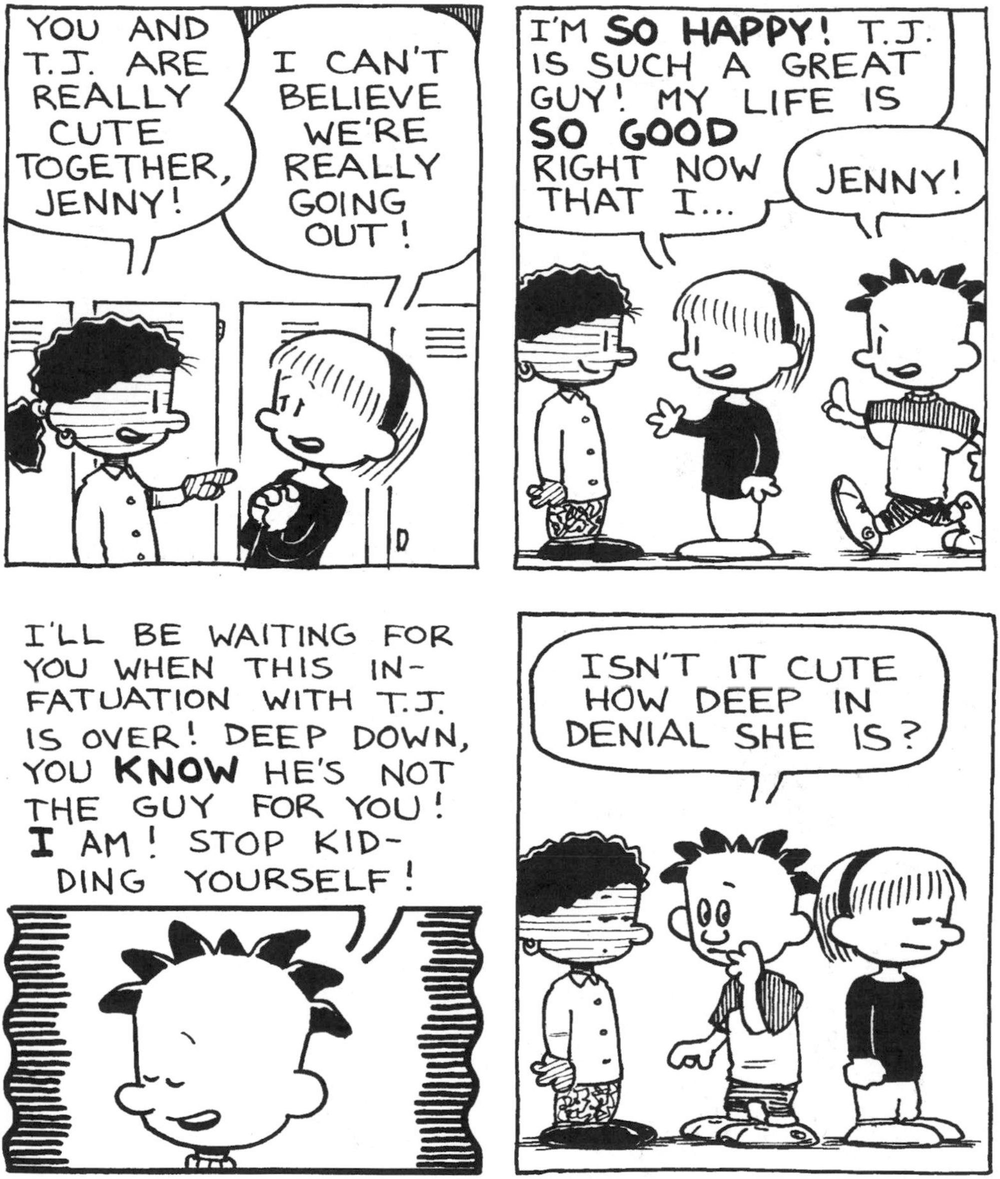
YOU AND T.J. ARE REALLY CUTE TOGETHER, JENNY!
I CAN'T BELIEVE WE'RE REALLY GOING OUT!
I'M **SO HAPPY**! T.J. IS SUCH A GREAT GUY! MY LIFE IS **SO GOOD** RIGHT NOW THAT I...
JENNY!
I'LL BE WAITING FOR YOU WHEN THIS IN-FATUATION WITH T.J. IS OVER! DEEP DOWN, YOU **KNOW** HE'S NOT THE GUY FOR YOU! **I** AM! STOP KID-DING YOURSELF!
ISN'T IT CUTE HOW DEEP IN DENIAL SHE IS?

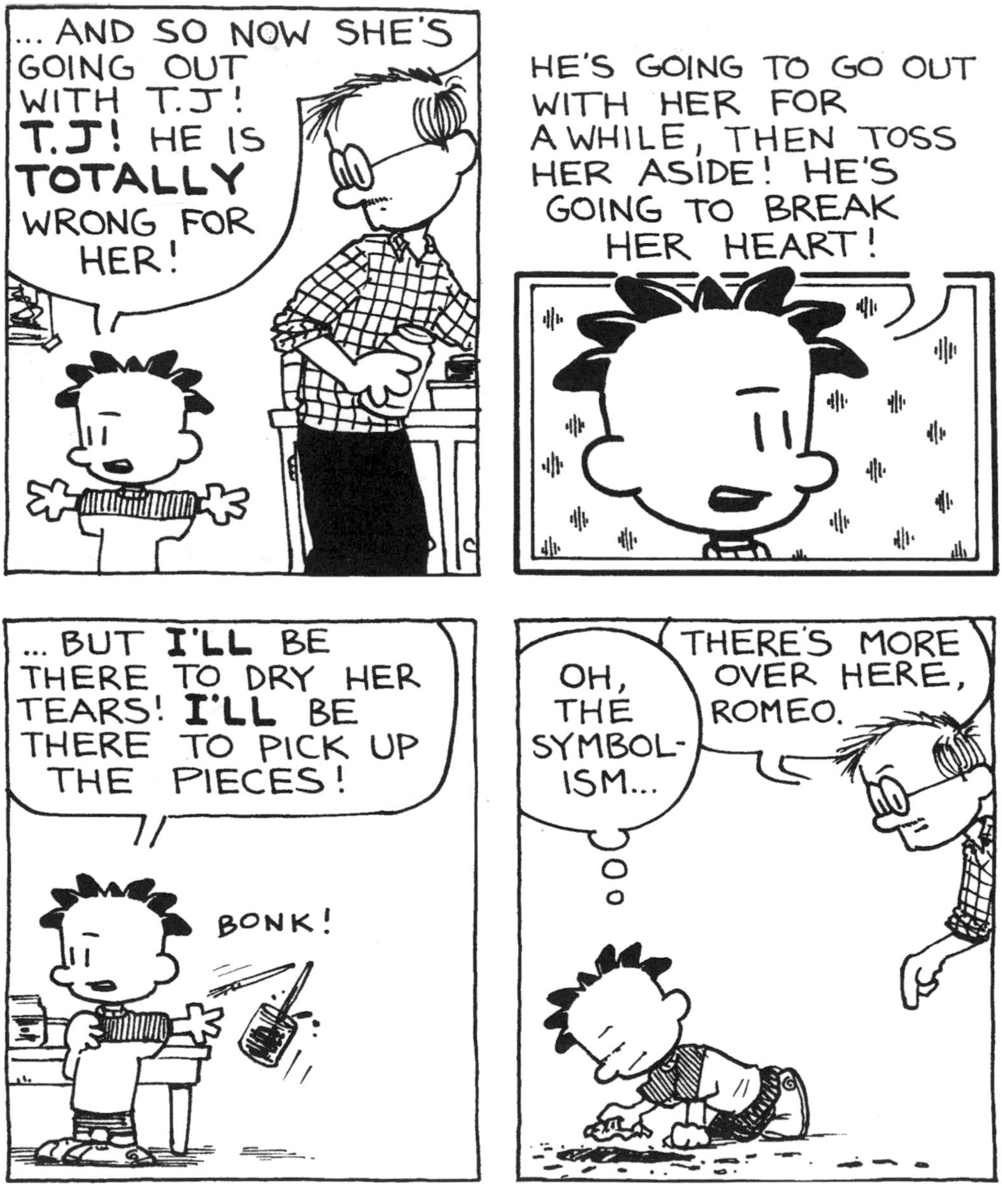

... AND SO NOW SHE'S GOING OUT WITH T.J! **T.J!** HE IS **TOTALLY** WRONG FOR HER!
HE'S GOING TO GO OUT WITH HER FOR A WHILE, THEN TOSS HER ASIDE! HE'S GOING TO BREAK HER HEART!
... BUT **I'LL** BE THERE TO DRY HER TEARS! **I'LL** BE THERE TO PICK UP THE PIECES!
BONK!
OH, THE SYMBOL-ISM...
THERE'S MORE OVER HERE, ROMEO.

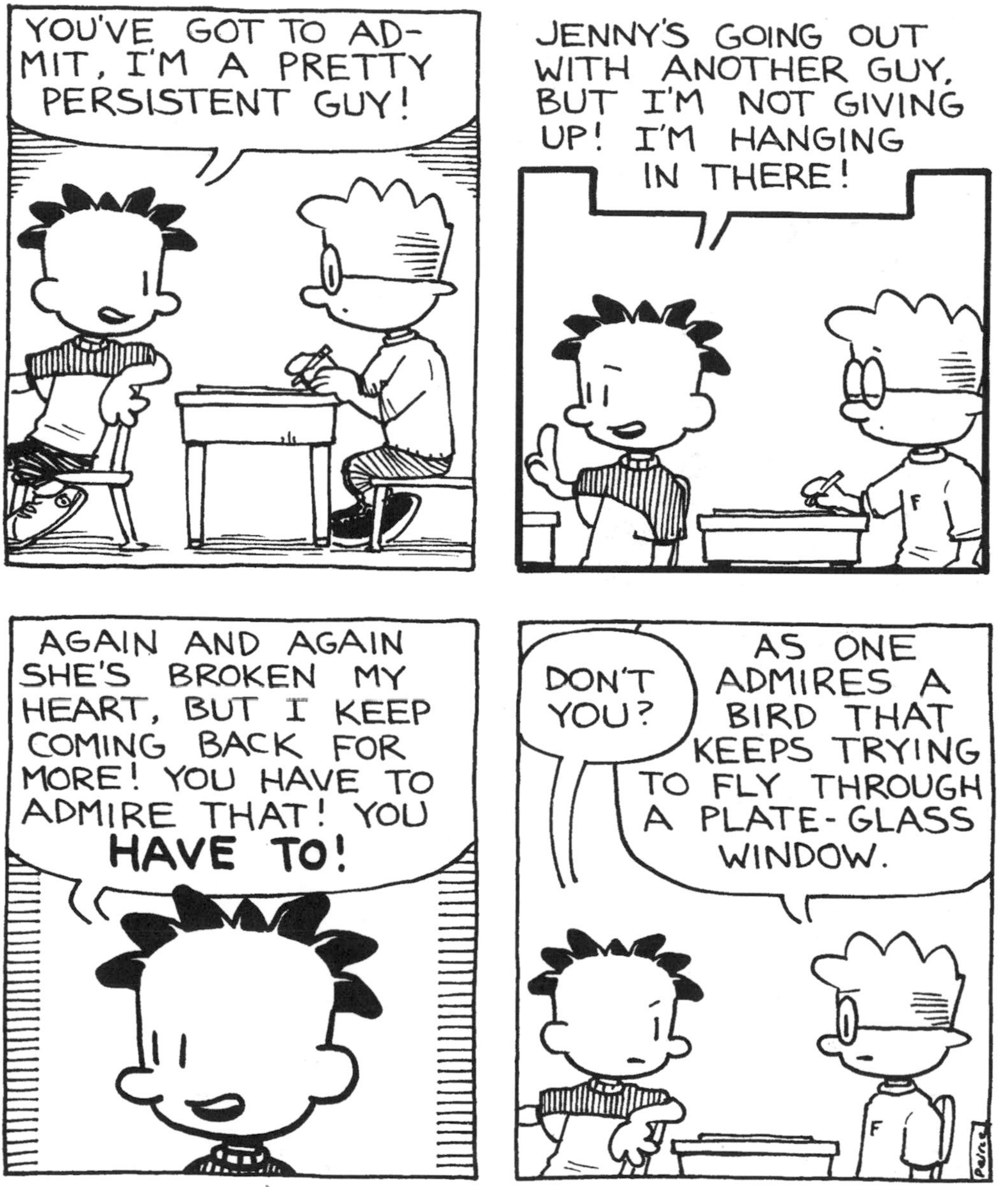
YOU'VE GOT TO ADMIT, I'M A PRETTY PERSISTENT GUY!
JENNY'S GOING OUT WITH ANOTHER GUY, BUT I'M NOT GIVING UP! I'M HANGING IN THERE!
AGAIN AND AGAIN SHE'S BROKEN MY HEART, BUT I KEEP COMING BACK FOR MORE! YOU HAVE TO ADMIRE THAT! YOU **HAVE TO**!
DON'T YOU?
AS ONE ADMIRES A BIRD THAT KEEPS TRYING TO FLY THROUGH A PLATE-GLASS WINDOW.
F
F
Peirce

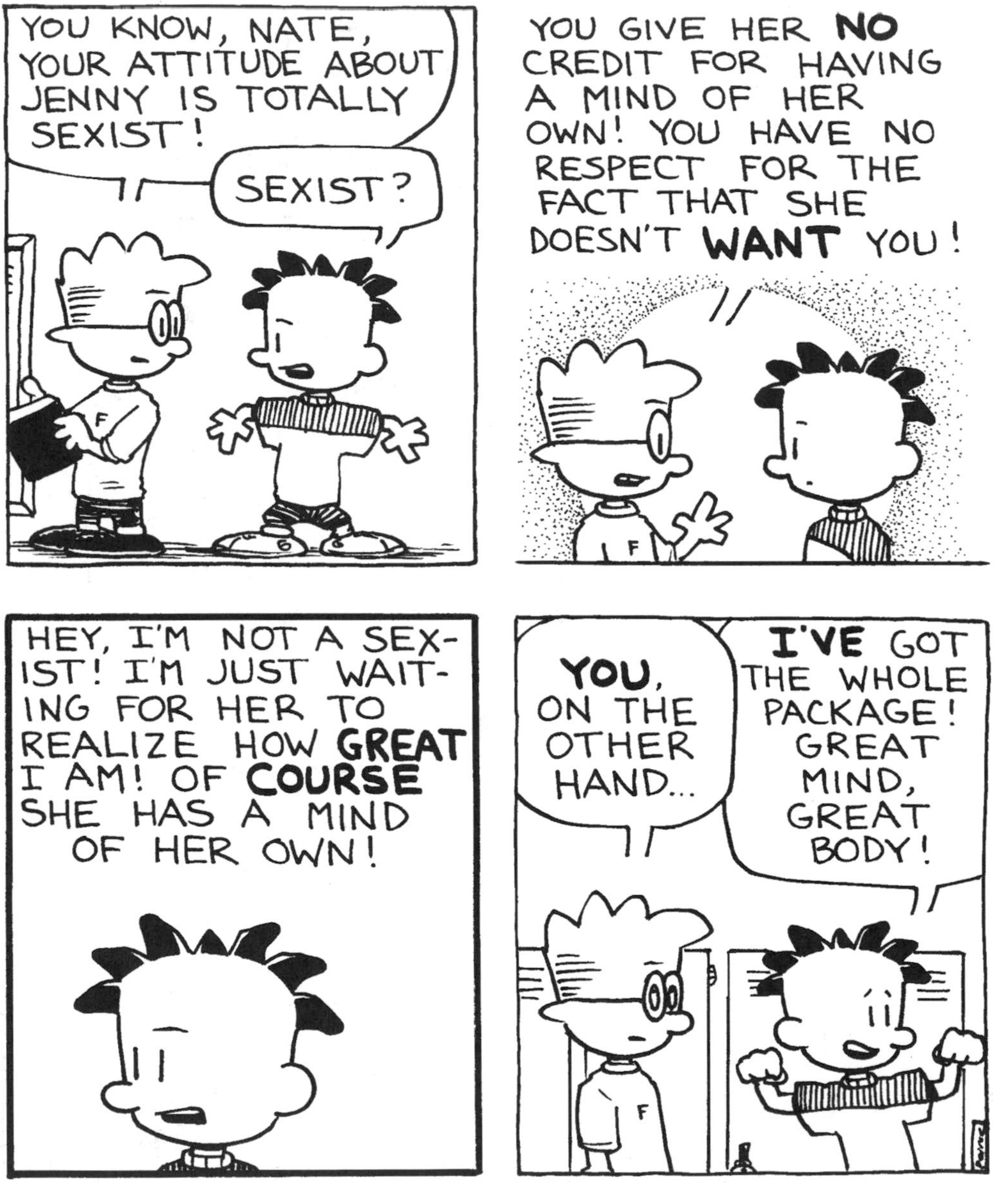

YOU KNOW, NATE, YOUR ATTITUDE ABOUT JENNY IS TOTALLY SEXIST!
SEXIST?
YOU GIVE HER **NO** CREDIT FOR HAVING A MIND OF HER OWN! YOU HAVE NO RESPECT FOR THE FACT THAT SHE DOESN'T **WANT** YOU!
HEY, I'M NOT A SEXIST! I'M JUST WAITING FOR HER TO REALIZE HOW **GREAT** I AM! OF **COURSE** SHE HAS A MIND OF HER OWN!
YOU, ON THE OTHER HAND...
I'VE GOT THE WHOLE PACKAGE! GREAT MIND, GREAT BODY!

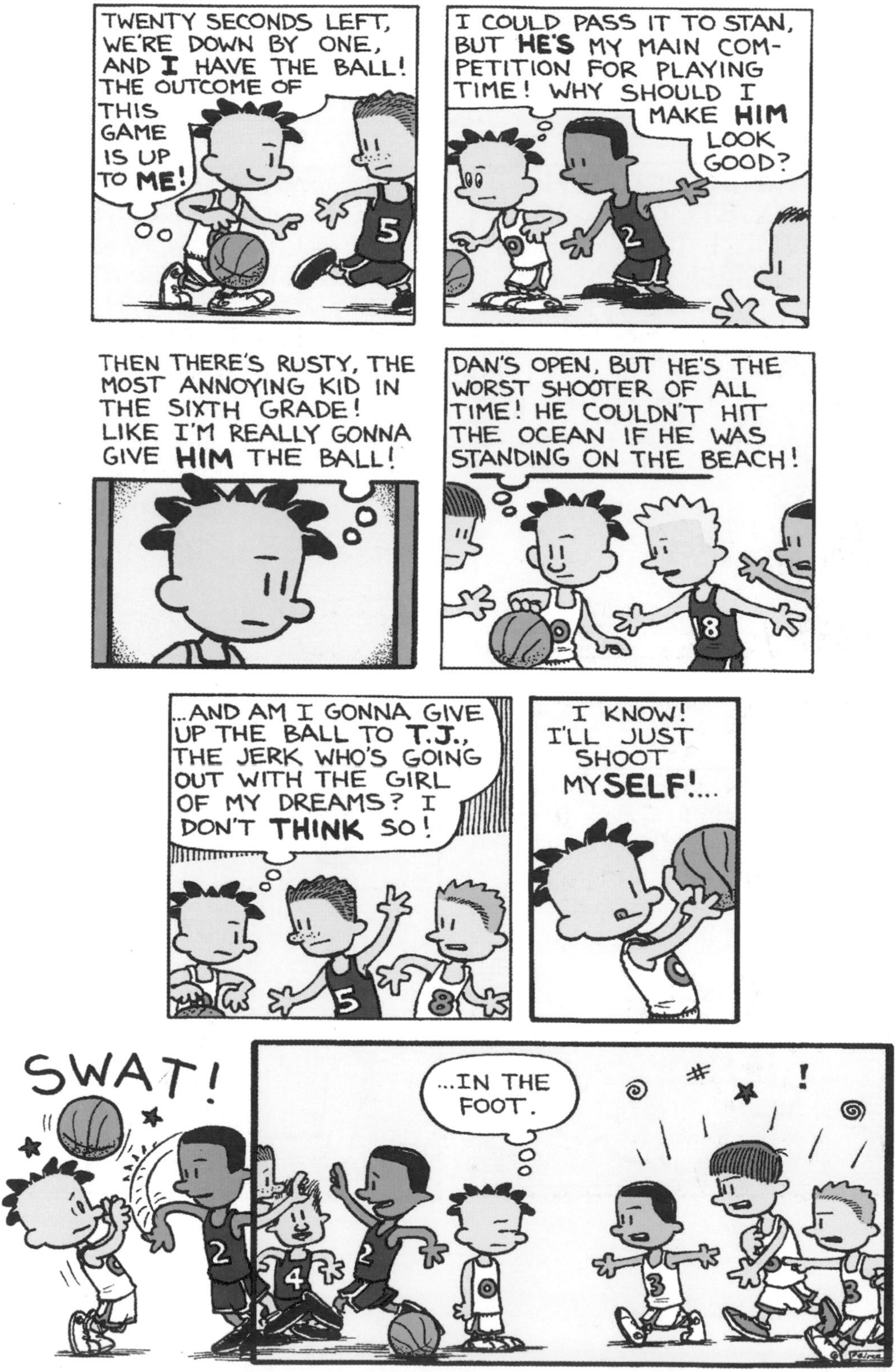
TWENTY SECONDS LEFT, WE'RE DOWN BY ONE, AND I HAVE THE BALL! THE OUTCOME OF THIS GAME IS UP TO ME!
I COULD PASS IT TO STAN, BUT HE'S MY MAIN COMPETITION FOR PLAYING TIME! WHY SHOULD I MAKE HIM LOOK GOOD?
THEN THERE'S RUSTY, THE MOST ANNOYING KID IN THE SIXTH GRADE! LIKE I'M REALLY GONNA GIVE HIM THE BALL!
DAN'S OPEN, BUT HE'S THE WORST SHOOTER OF ALL TIME! HE COULDN'T HIT THE OCEAN IF HE WAS STANDING ON THE BEACH!
...AND AM I GONNA GIVE UP THE BALL TO T.J., THE JERK WHO'S GOING OUT WITH THE GIRL OF MY DREAMS? I DON'T THINK SO!
I KNOW! I'LL JUST SHOOT MYSELF!...
SWAT!
...IN THE FOOT.

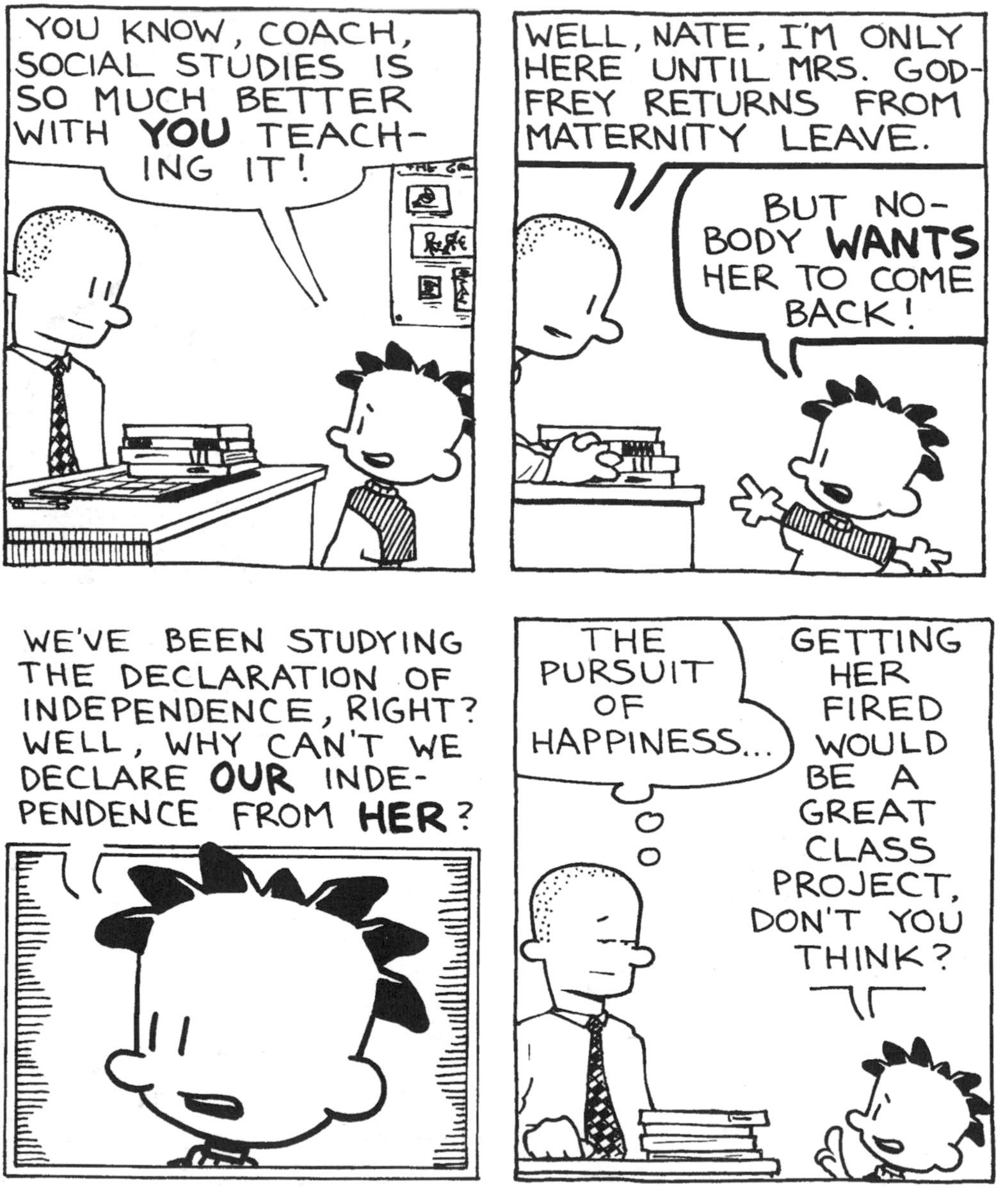
YOU KNOW, COACH, SOCIAL STUDIES IS SO MUCH BETTER WITH **YOU** TEACHING IT!
WELL, NATE, I'M ONLY HERE UNTIL MRS. GODFREY RETURNS FROM MATERNITY LEAVE.
BUT NOBODY **WANTS** HER TO COME BACK!
WE'VE BEEN STUDYING THE DECLARATION OF INDEPENDENCE, RIGHT? WELL, WHY CAN'T WE DECLARE **OUR** INDEPENDENCE FROM **HER**?
THE PURSUIT OF HAPPINESS...
GETTING HER FIRED WOULD BE A GREAT CLASS PROJECT, DON'T YOU THINK?

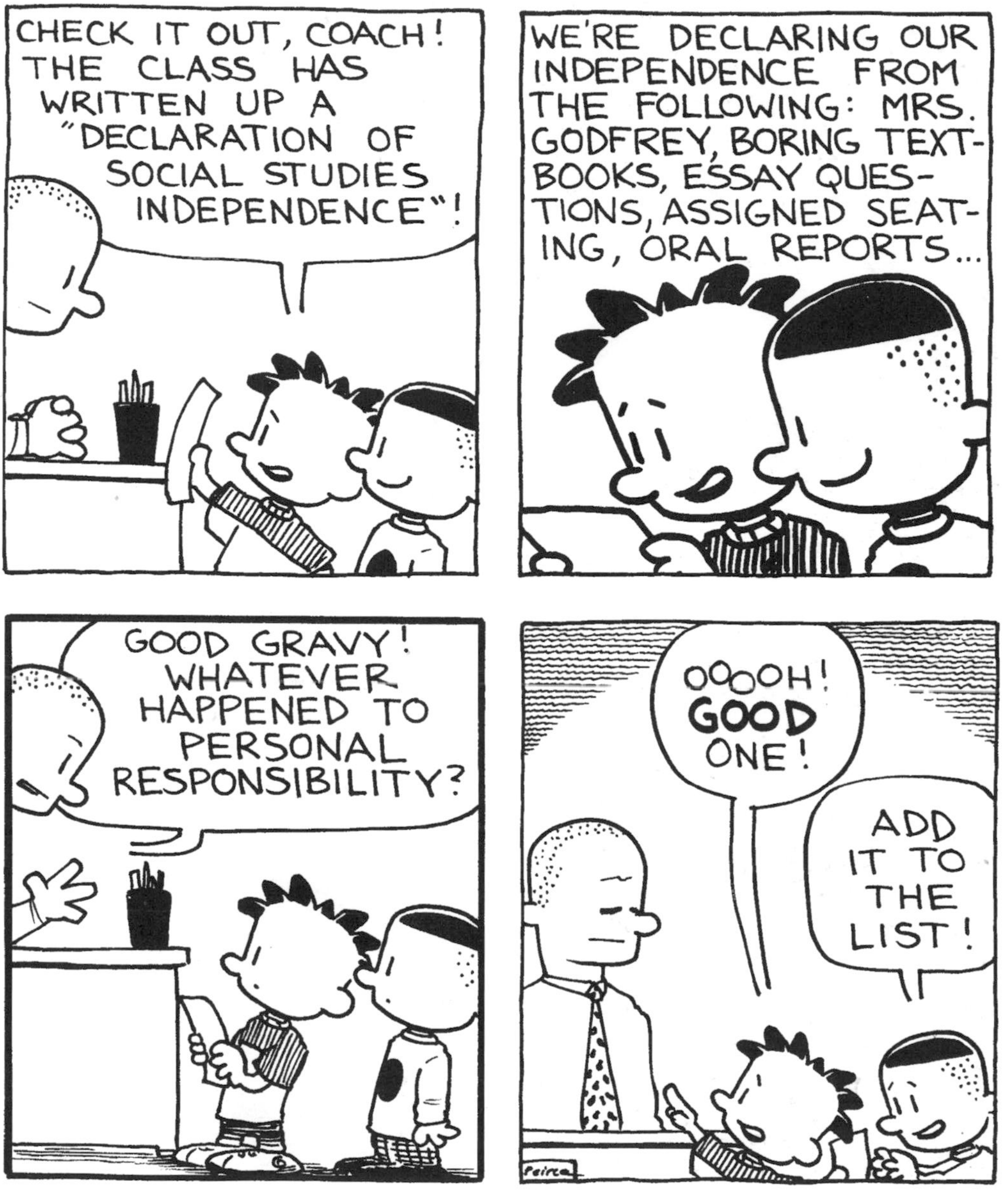
CHECK IT OUT, COACH! THE CLASS HAS WRITTEN UP A "DECLARATION OF SOCIAL STUDIES INDEPENDENCE"!
WE'RE DECLARING OUR INDEPENDENCE FROM THE FOLLOWING: MRS. GODFREY, BORING TEXT-BOOKS, ESSAY QUES-TIONS, ASSIGNED SEAT-ING, ORAL REPORTS...
GOOD GRAVY! WHATEVER HAPPENED TO PERSONAL RESPONSIBILITY?
OOOOH! GOOD ONE!
ADD IT TO THE LIST!
Peirce

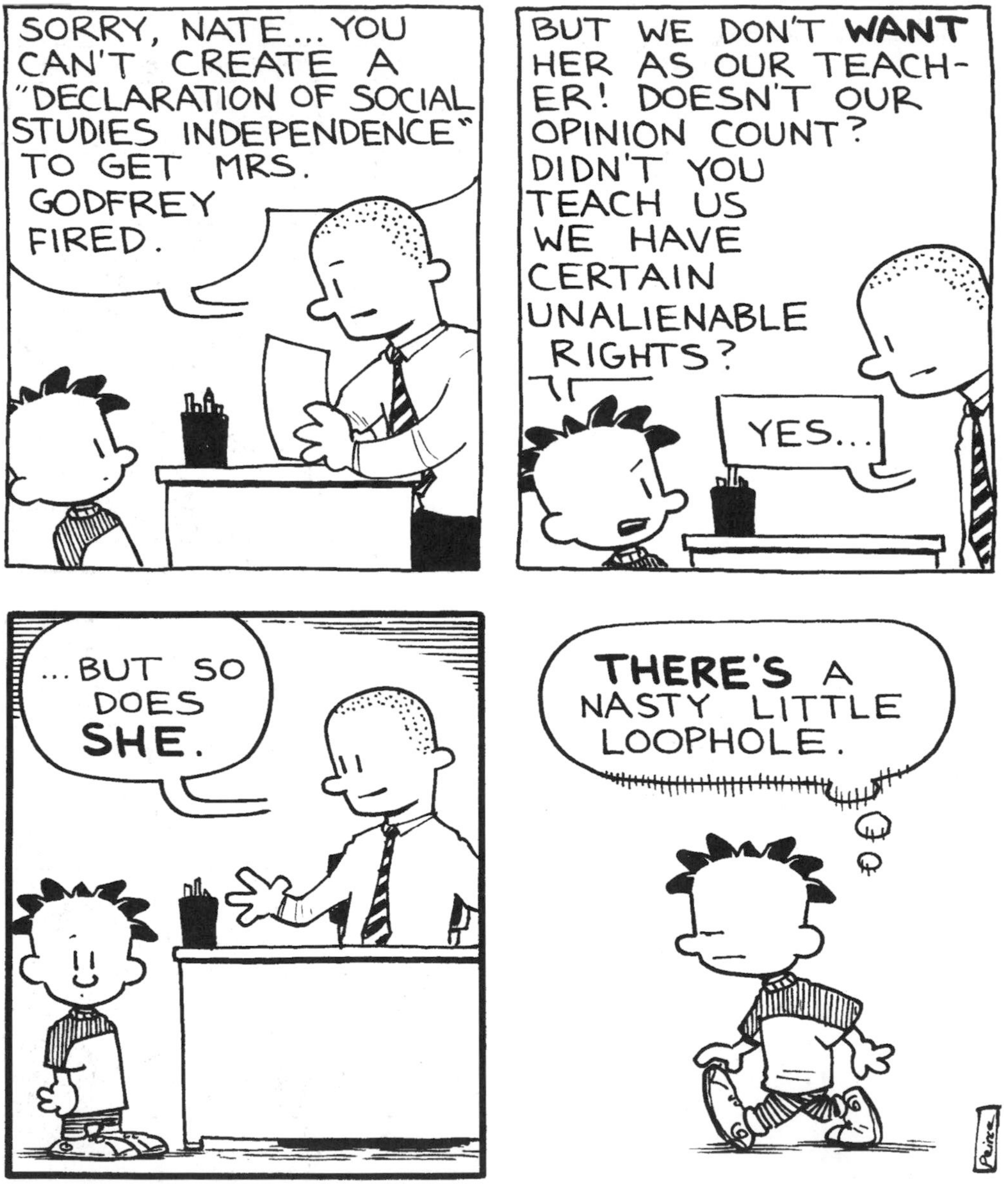
SORRY, NATE... YOU CAN'T CREATE A "DECLARATION OF SOCIAL STUDIES INDEPENDENCE" TO GET MRS. GODFREY FIRED.
BUT WE DON'T **WANT** HER AS OUR TEACHER! DOESN'T OUR OPINION COUNT? DIDN'T YOU TEACH US WE HAVE CERTAIN UNALIENABLE RIGHTS?
YES...
...BUT SO DOES **SHE**.
THERE'S A NASTY LITTLE LOOPHOLE.
Peirce

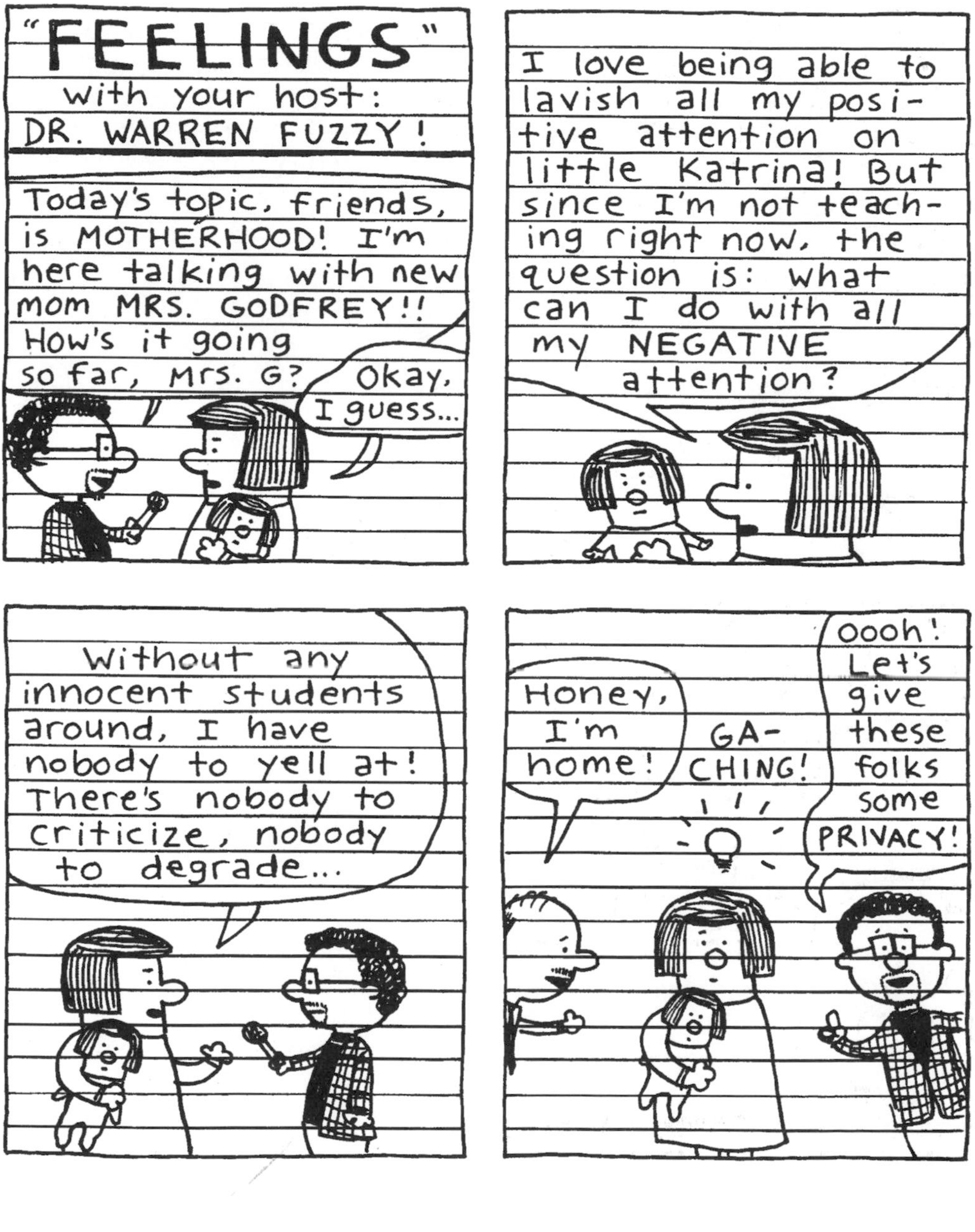
"FEELINGS"
with your host:
DR. WARREN FUZZY!
Today's topic, friends, is MOTHERHOOD! I'm here talking with new mom MRS. GODFREY!! How's it going so far, Mrs. G?
Okay, I guess...
I love being able to lavish all my posi-tive attention on little Katrina! But since I'm not teach-ing right now, the question is: what can I do with all my NEGATIVE attention?
Without any innocent students around, I have nobody to yell at! There's nobody to criticize, nobody to degrade...
Honey, I'm home!
GA-CHING!
Oooh! Let's give these folks some PRIVACY!

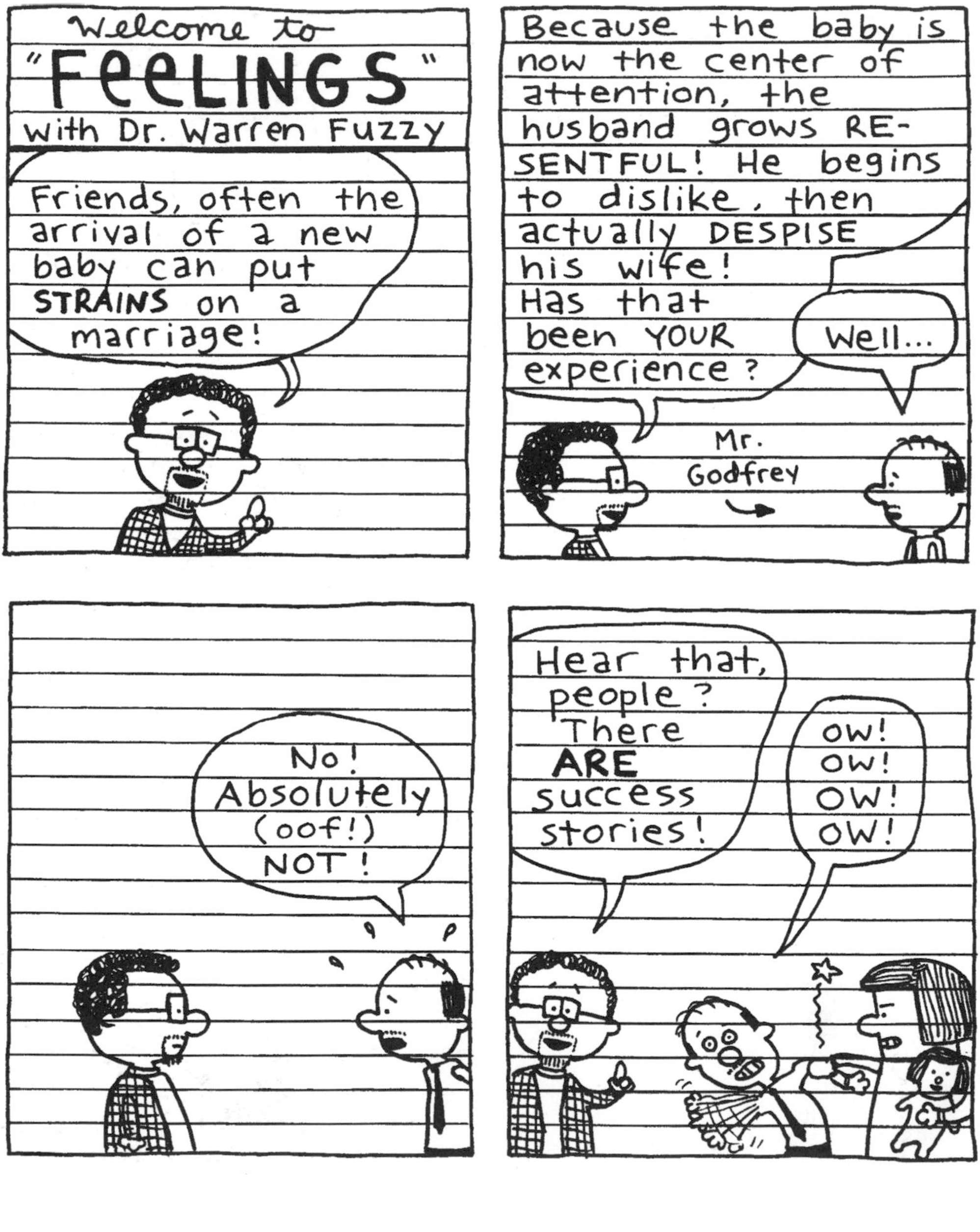

Welcome to "FeeLINGS" with Dr. Warren Fuzzy
Friends, often the arrival of a new baby can put **STRAINS** on a marriage!
Because the baby is now the center of attention, the husband grows RE-SENTFUL! He begins to dislike, then actually DESPISE his wife! Has that been YOUR experience?
Well...
Mr. Godfrey
No! Absolutely (oof!) NOT!
Hear that, people? There **ARE** success stories!
OW! OW! OW! OW!

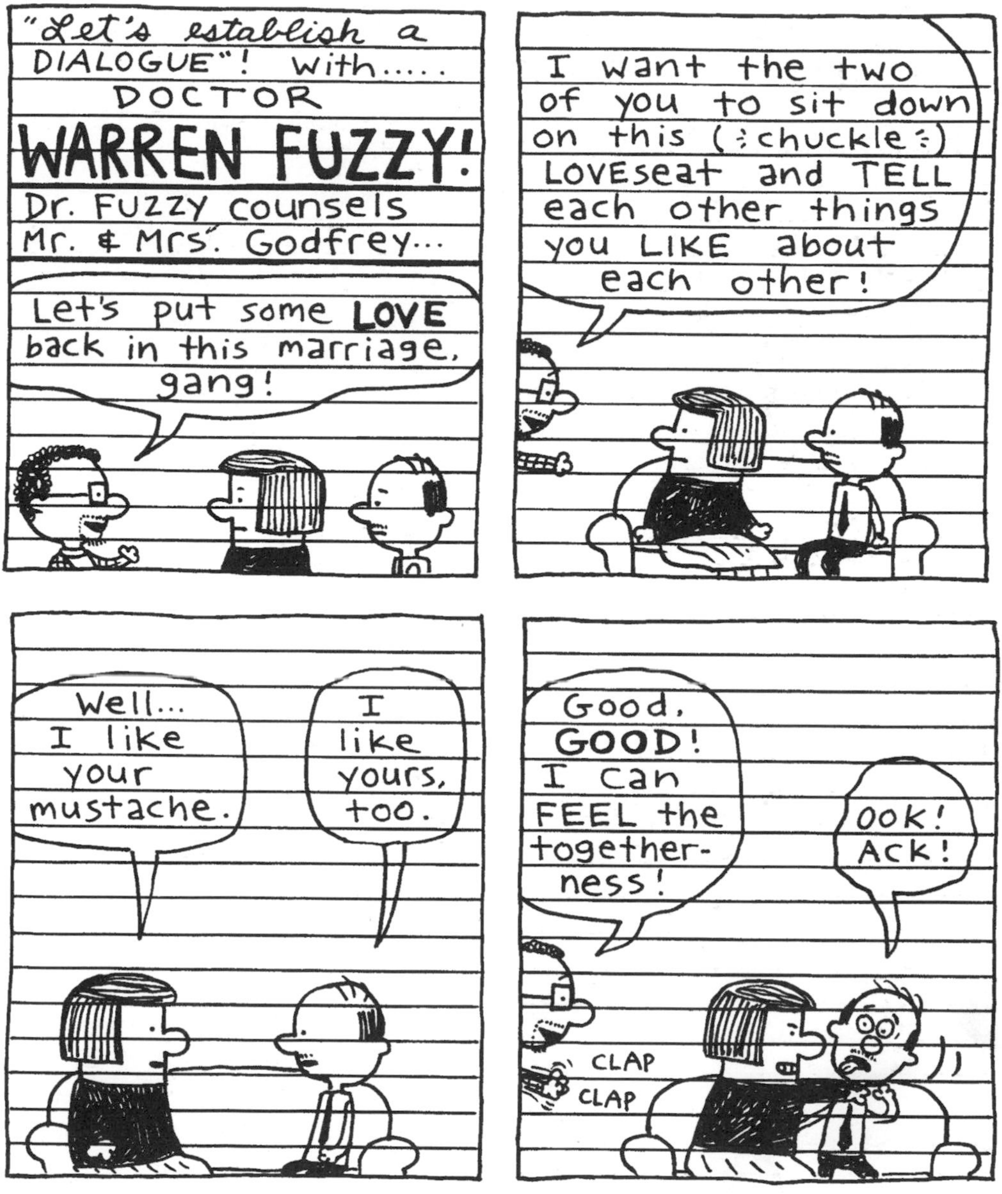
"Let's establish a DIALOGUE"! With..... DOCTOR
WARREN FUZZY!
Dr. Fuzzy counsels Mr. & Mrs. Godfrey...
Let's put some LOVE back in this marriage, gang!
I want the two of you to sit down on this (chuckle) LOVEseat and TELL each other things you LIKE about each other!
Well... I like your mustache.
I like yours, too.
Good, GOOD! I can FEEL the together-ness!
OOK! ACK!
CLAP
CLAP

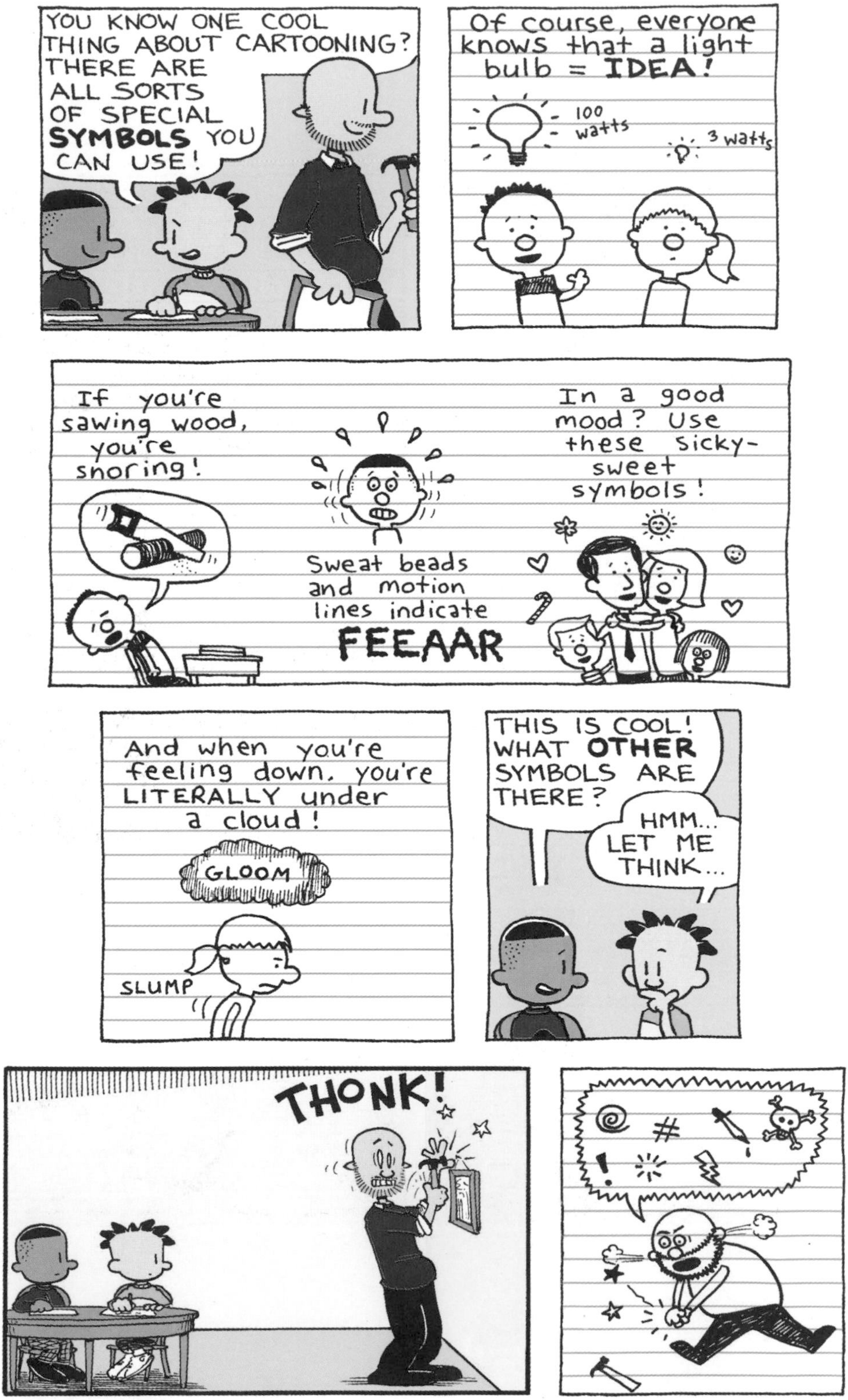
YOU KNOW ONE COOL THING ABOUT CARTOONING? THERE ARE ALL SORTS OF SPECIAL SYMBOLS YOU CAN USE!
Of course, everyone knows that a light bulb = IDEA!
100 watts
3 watts
If you're sawing wood, you're snoring!
Sweat beads and motion lines indicate FEEAAR
In a good mood? Use these sicky-sweet symbols!
And when you're feeling down, you're LITERALLY under a cloud!
GLOOM
SLUMP
THIS IS COOL! WHAT OTHER SYMBOLS ARE THERE?
HMM... LET ME THINK...
THONK!

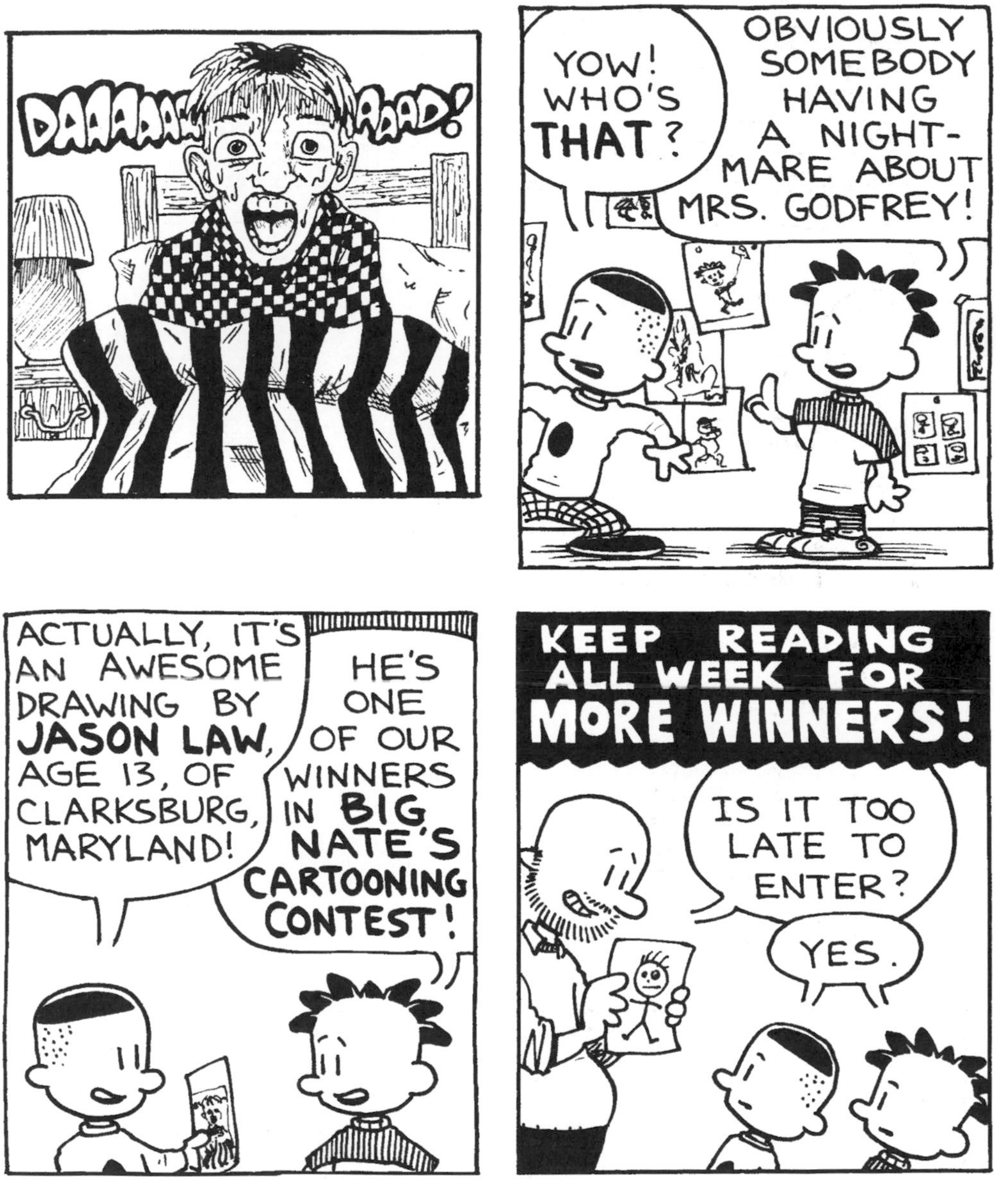
DAAAAAAAAAAAD!
YOW! WHO'S THAT?
OBVIOUSLY SOMEBODY HAVING A NIGHT-MARE ABOUT MRS. GODFREY!
ACTUALLY, IT'S AN AWESOME DRAWING BY JASON LAW, AGE 13, OF CLARKSBURG, MARYLAND!
HE'S ONE OF OUR WINNERS IN BIG NATE'S CARTOONING CONTEST!
KEEP READING ALL WEEK FOR MORE WINNERS!
IS IT TOO LATE TO ENTER?
YES.

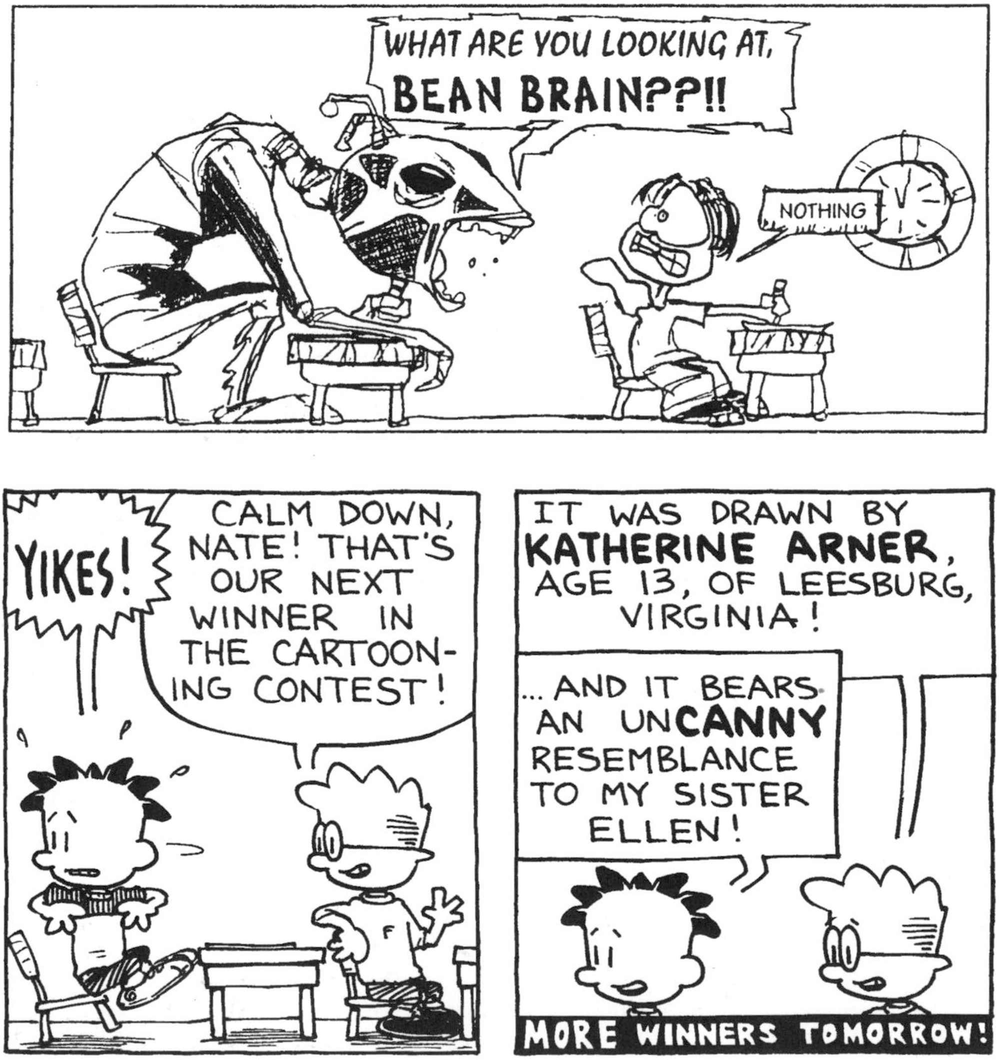
WHAT ARE YOU LOOKING AT, BEAN BRAIN??!!
NOTHING
YIKES!
CALM DOWN, NATE! THAT'S OUR NEXT WINNER IN THE CARTOONING CONTEST!
IT WAS DRAWN BY KATHERINE ARNER, AGE 13, OF LEESBURG, VIRGINIA!
... AND IT BEARS AN UNCANNY RESEMBLANCE TO MY SISTER ELLEN!
MORE WINNERS TOMORROW!

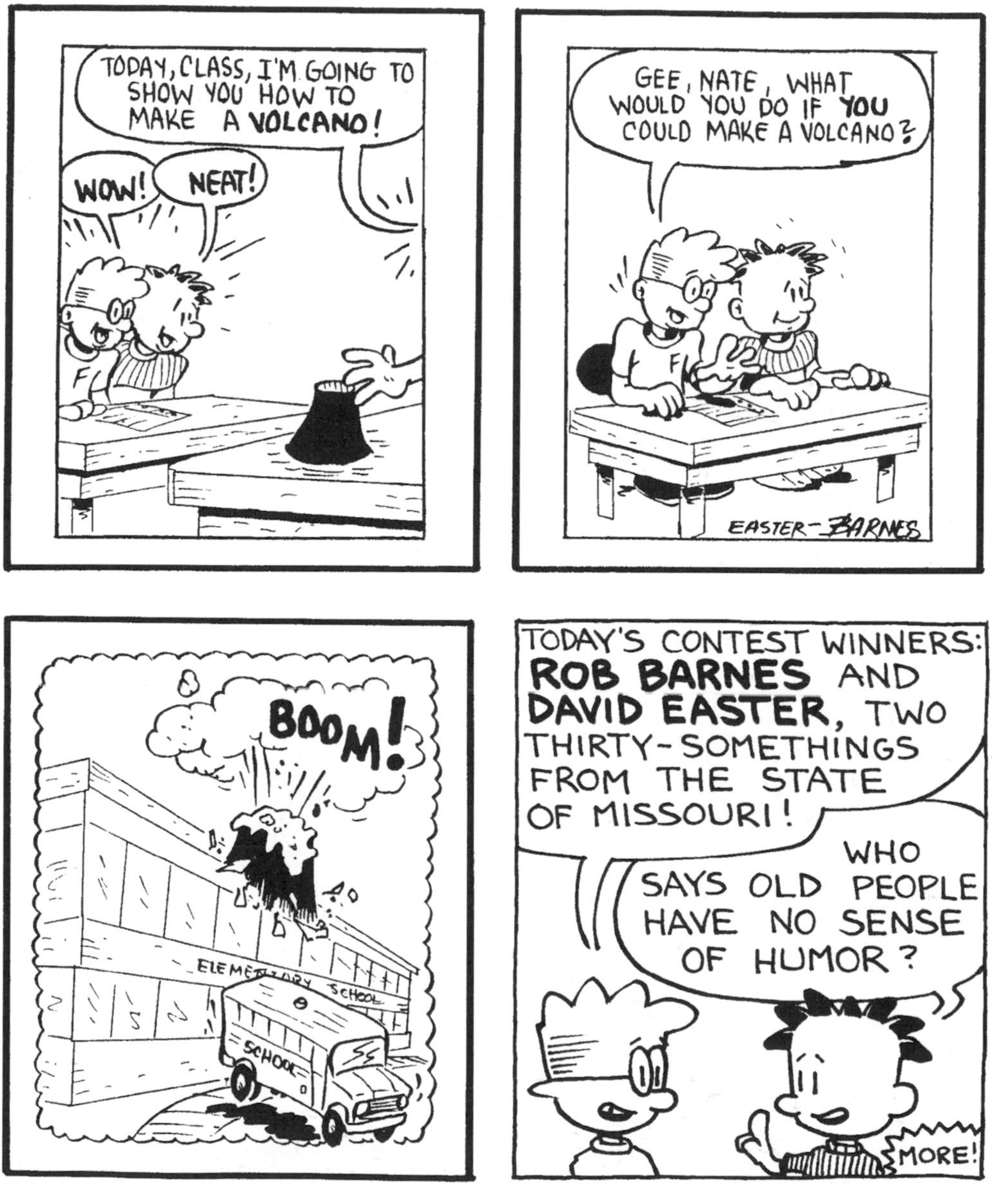
TODAY, CLASS, I'M GOING TO SHOW YOU HOW TO MAKE A **VOLCANO**!
WOW!
NEAT!
GEE, NATE, WHAT WOULD YOU DO IF **YOU** COULD MAKE A VOLCANO?
EASTER-BARNES
BOOM!
ELEMENTARY SCHOOL
SCHOOL
TODAY'S CONTEST WINNERS: **ROB BARNES** AND **DAVID EASTER**, TWO THIRTY-SOMETHINGS FROM THE STATE OF MISSOURI!
WHO SAYS OLD PEOPLE HAVE NO SENSE OF HUMOR?
MORE!

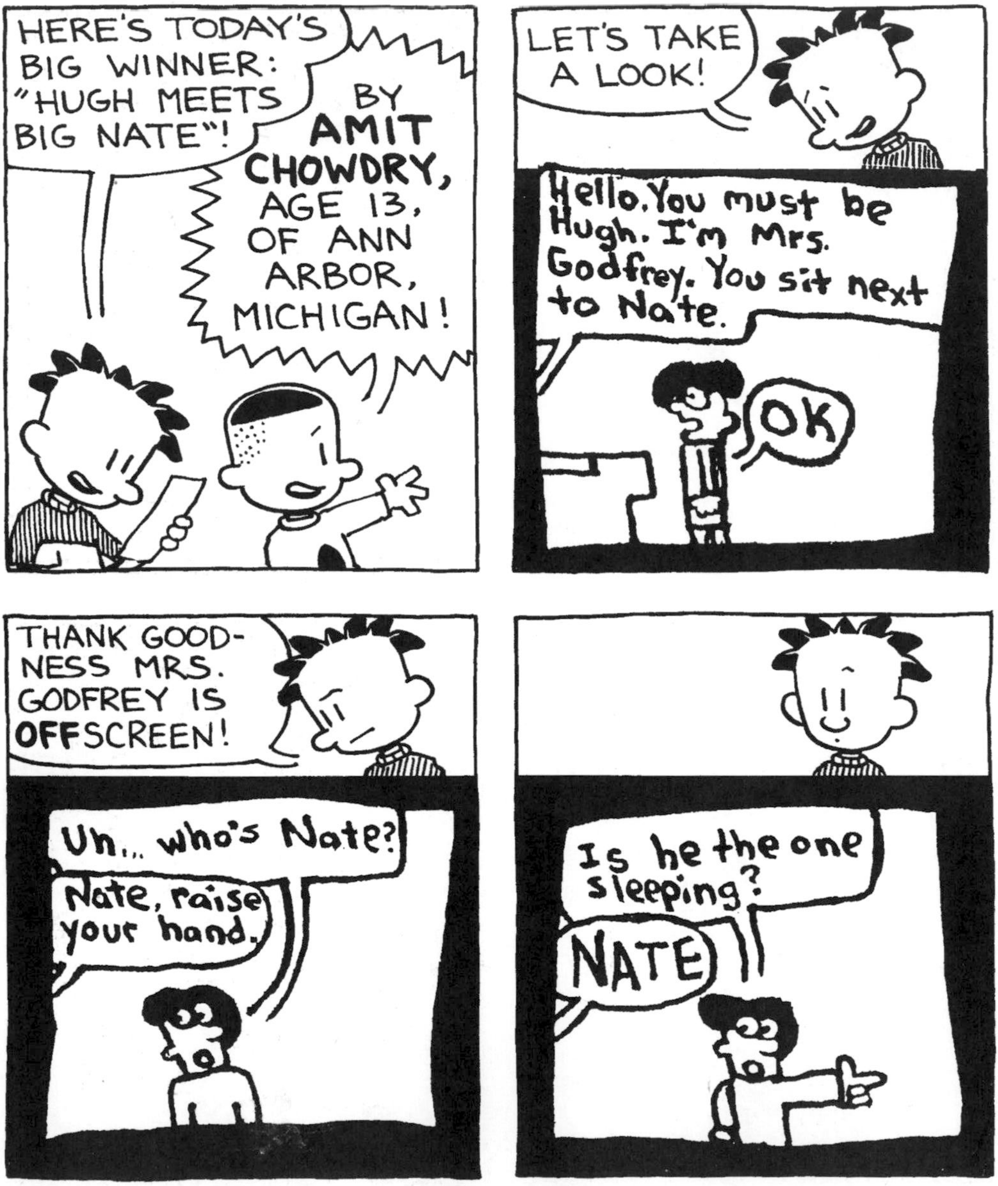
HERE'S TODAY'S BIG WINNER: "HUGH MEETS BIG NATE"!
BY AMIT CHOWDRY, AGE 13, OF ANN ARBOR, MICHIGAN!
LET'S TAKE A LOOK!
Hello. You must be Hugh. I'm Mrs. Godfrey. You sit next to Nate.
OK
THANK GOODNESS MRS. GODFREY IS OFFSCREEN!
Uh... who's Nate?
Nate, raise your hand.
Is he the one sleeping?
NATE

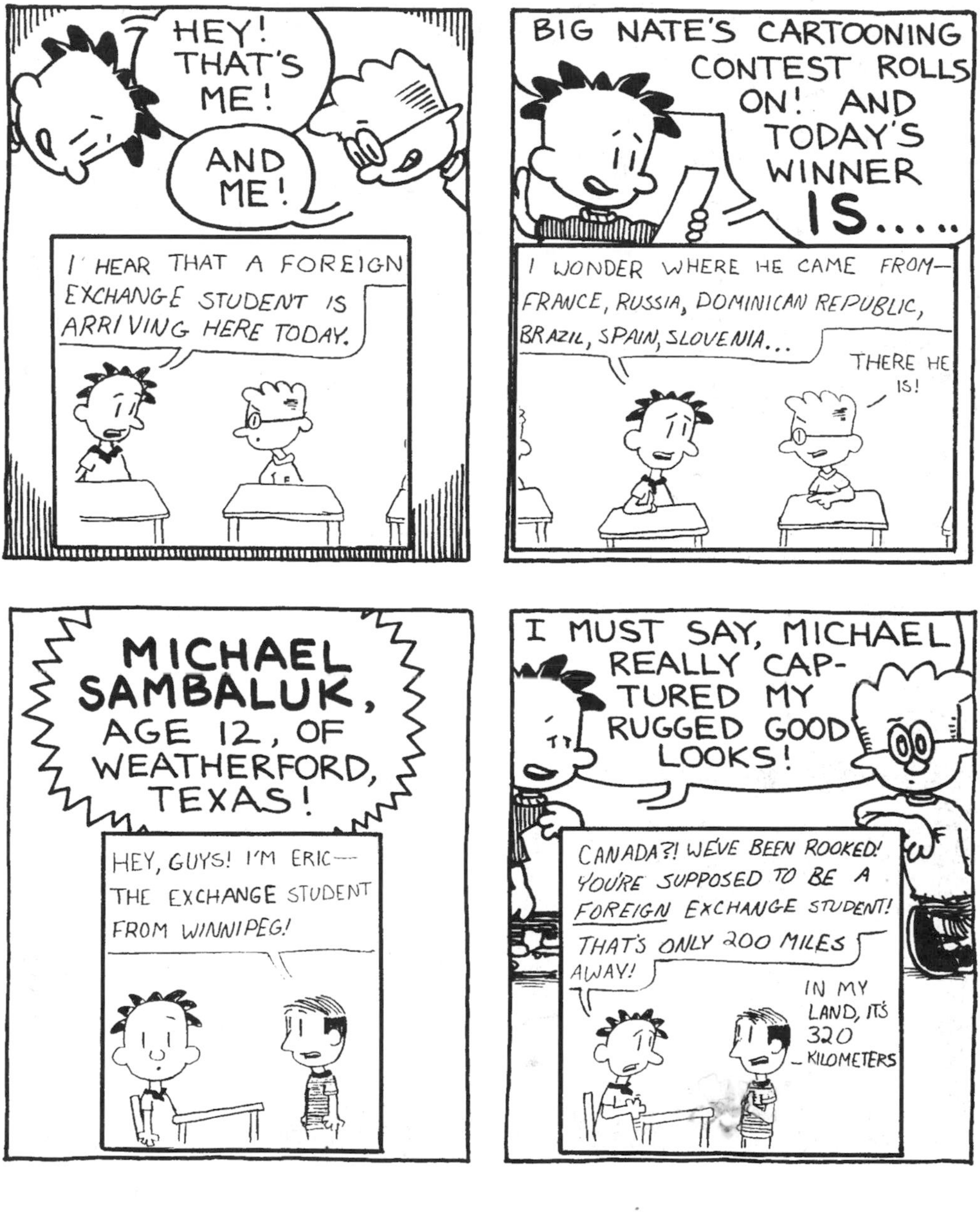
HEY! THAT'S ME!
AND ME!
I HEAR THAT A FOREIGN EXCHANGE STUDENT IS ARRIVING HERE TODAY.
BIG NATE'S CARTOONING CONTEST ROLLS ON! AND TODAY'S WINNER IS.....
I WONDER WHERE HE CAME FROM— FRANCE, RUSSIA, DOMINICAN REPUBLIC, BRAZIL, SPAIN, SLOVENIA...
THERE HE IS!
MICHAEL SAMBALUK, AGE 12, OF WEATHERFORD, TEXAS!
HEY, GUYS! I'M ERIC— THE EXCHANGE STUDENT FROM WINNIPEG!
I MUST SAY, MICHAEL REALLY CAPTURED MY RUGGED GOOD LOOKS!
CANADA?! WE'VE BEEN ROOKED! YOU'RE SUPPOSED TO BE A FOREIGN EXCHANGE STUDENT! THAT'S ONLY 200 MILES AWAY!
IN MY LAND, IT'S 320 KILOMETERS

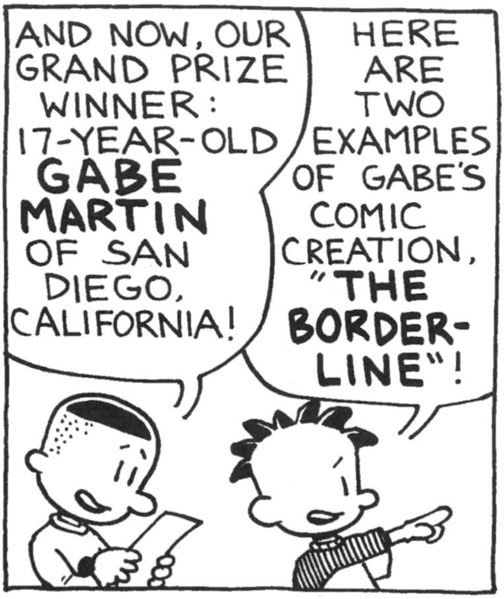
AND NOW, OUR GRAND PRIZE WINNER: 17-YEAR-OLD GABE MARTIN OF SAN DIEGO, CALIFORNIA!
HERE ARE TWO EXAMPLES OF GABE'S COMIC CREATION, "THE BORDER-LINE"!

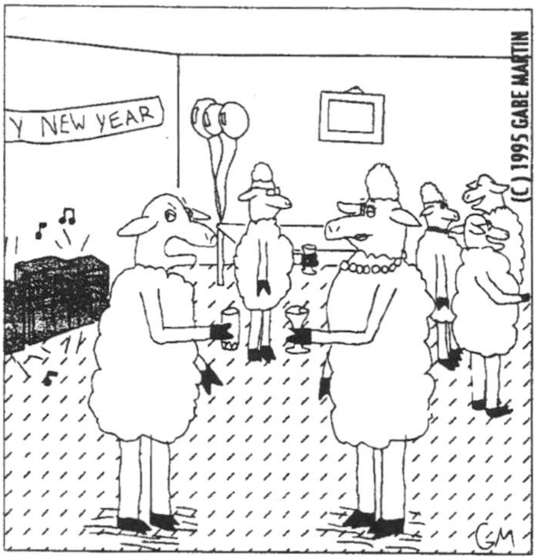
(C) 1995 GABE MARTIN
Y NEW YEAR
GM

" Oh for crying out loud! Not 'Barbara Ann' again! "

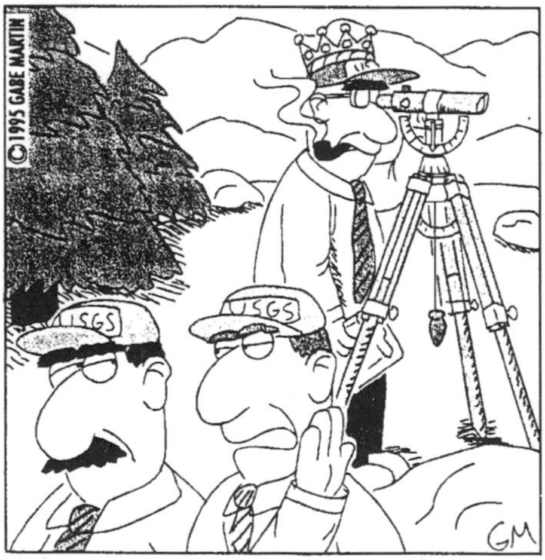
©1995 GABE MARTIN
USGS
USGS
GM

"There goes Lenny again–he thinks he's king of all he surveys."

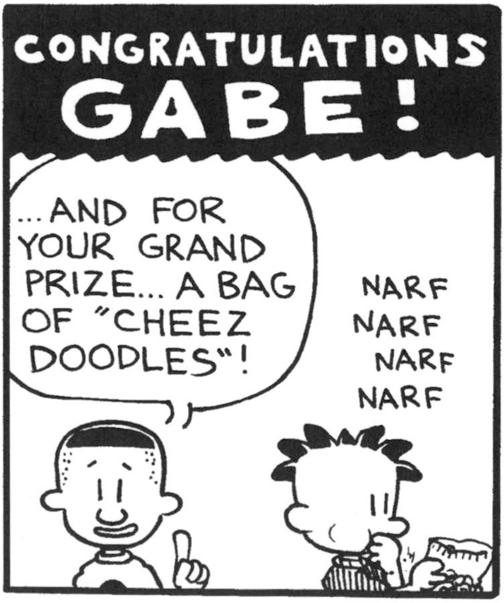
CONGRATULATIONS GABE!
...AND FOR YOUR GRAND PRIZE... A BAG OF "CHEEZ DOODLES"!
NARF NARF NARF NARF

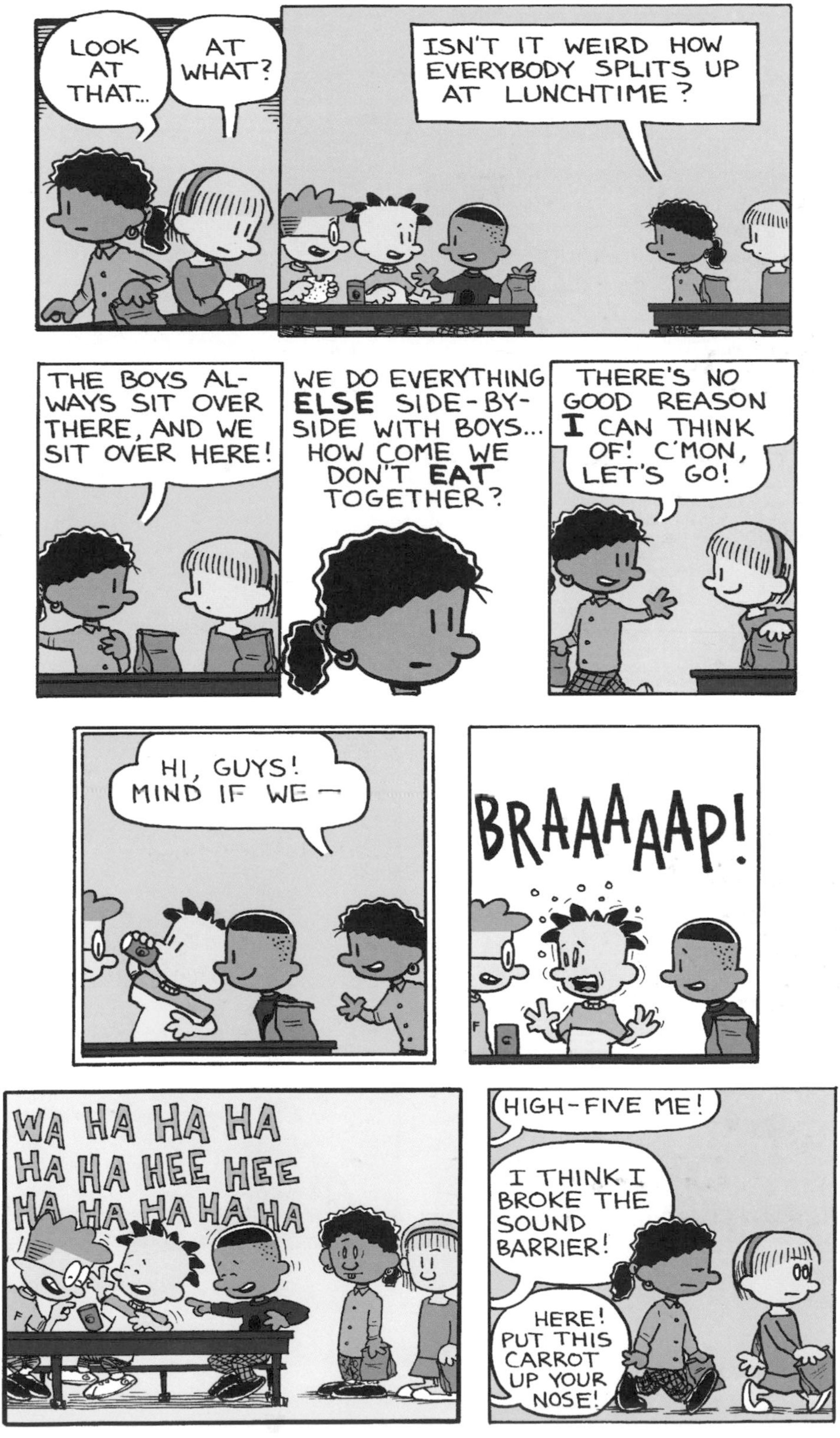
LOOK AT THAT...
AT WHAT?
ISN'T IT WEIRD HOW EVERYBODY SPLITS UP AT LUNCHTIME?
THE BOYS ALWAYS SIT OVER THERE, AND WE SIT OVER HERE!
WE DO EVERYTHING ELSE SIDE-BY-SIDE WITH BOYS... HOW COME WE DON'T EAT TOGETHER?
THERE'S NO GOOD REASON I CAN THINK OF! C'MON, LET'S GO!
HI, GUYS! MIND IF WE —
BRAAAAAP!
WA HA HA HA HA HA HEE HEE HA HA HA HA HA
HIGH-FIVE ME!
I THINK I BROKE THE SOUND BARRIER!
HERE! PUT THIS CARROT UP YOUR NOSE!

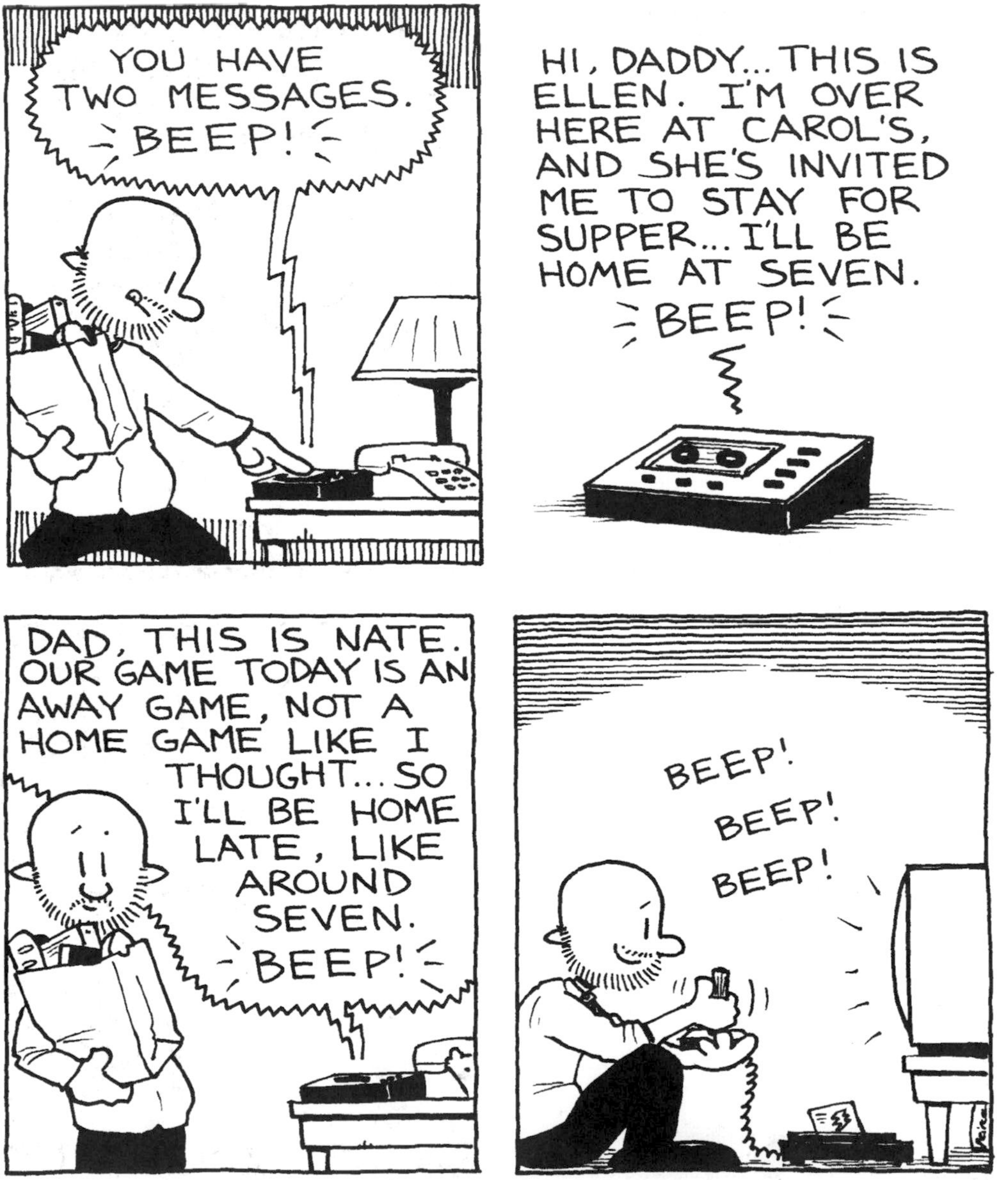
YOU HAVE TWO MESSAGES. BEEP!
HI, DADDY... THIS IS ELLEN. I'M OVER HERE AT CAROL'S, AND SHE'S INVITED ME TO STAY FOR SUPPER... I'LL BE HOME AT SEVEN. BEEP!
DAD, THIS IS NATE. OUR GAME TODAY IS AN AWAY GAME, NOT A HOME GAME LIKE I THOUGHT... SO I'LL BE HOME LATE, LIKE AROUND SEVEN. BEEP!
BEEP!
BEEP!
BEEP!

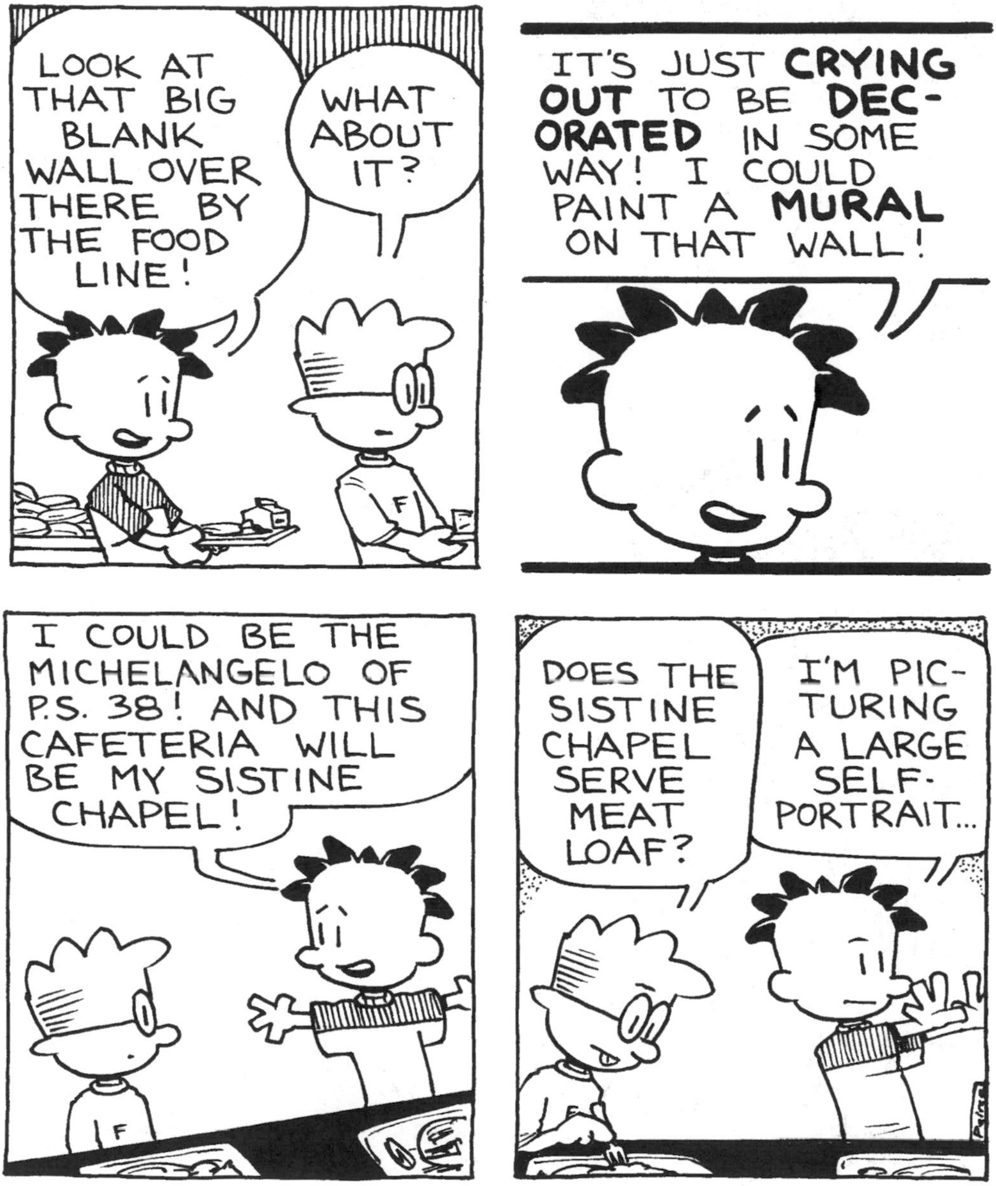
LOOK AT THAT BIG BLANK WALL OVER THERE BY THE FOOD LINE!
WHAT ABOUT IT?
IT'S JUST **CRYING OUT** TO BE **DECORATED** IN SOME WAY! I COULD PAINT A **MURAL** ON THAT WALL!
I COULD BE THE MICHELANGELO OF P.S. 38! AND THIS CAFETERIA WILL BE MY SISTINE CHAPEL!
DOES THE SISTINE CHAPEL SERVE MEAT LOAF?
I'M PICTURING A LARGE SELF-PORTRAIT...

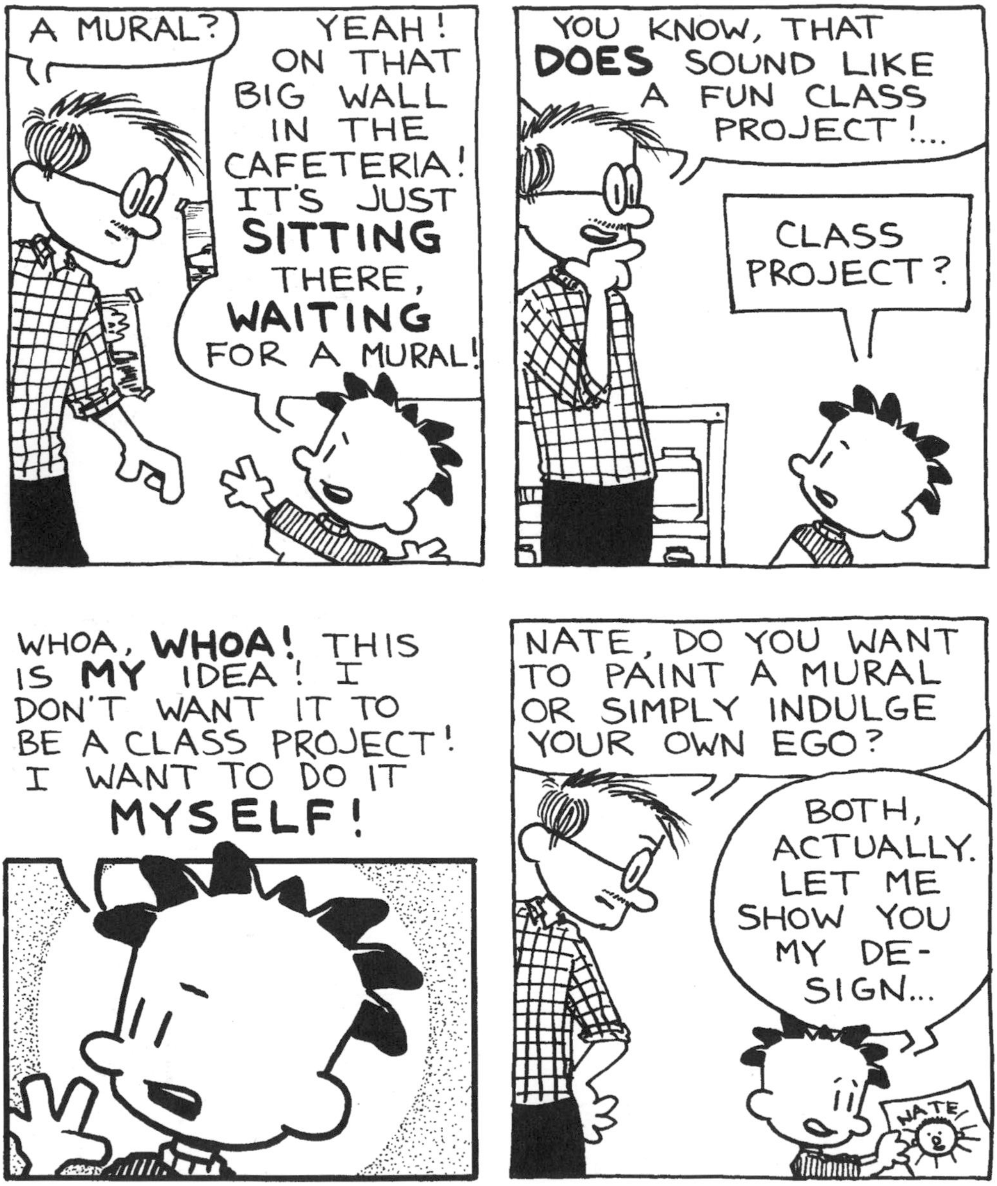
A MURAL?
YEAH! ON THAT BIG WALL IN THE CAFETERIA! IT'S JUST **SITTING** THERE, **WAITING** FOR A MURAL!
YOU KNOW, THAT **DOES** SOUND LIKE A FUN CLASS PROJECT!...
CLASS PROJECT?
WHOA, **WHOA!** THIS IS **MY** IDEA! I DON'T WANT IT TO BE A CLASS PROJECT! I WANT TO DO IT **MYSELF!**
NATE, DO YOU WANT TO PAINT A MURAL OR SIMPLY INDULGE YOUR OWN EGO?
BOTH, ACTUALLY. LET ME SHOW YOU MY DE-SIGN...
NATE

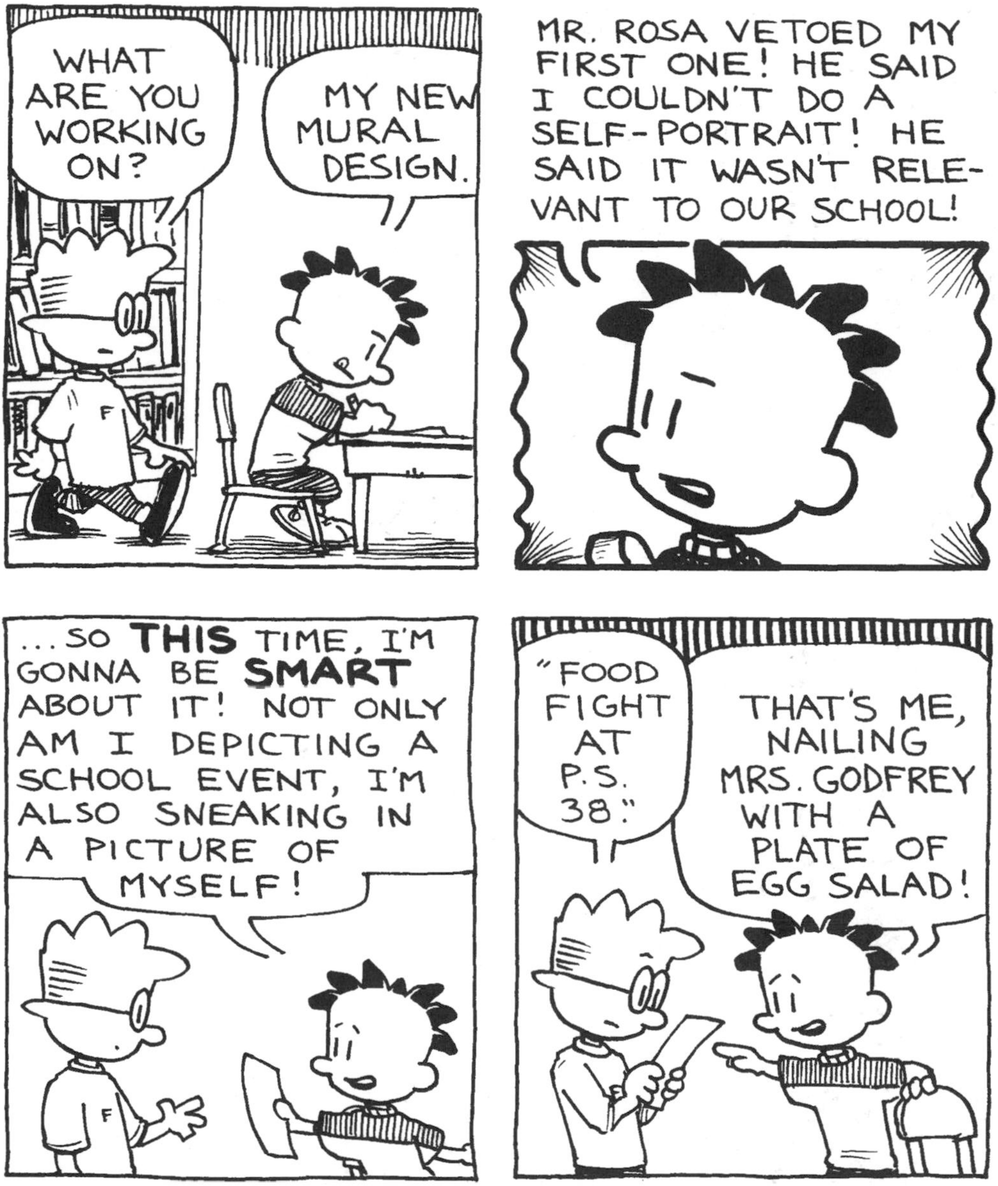
WHAT ARE YOU WORKING ON?
MY NEW MURAL DESIGN.
MR. ROSA VETOED MY FIRST ONE! HE SAID I COULDN'T DO A SELF-PORTRAIT! HE SAID IT WASN'T RELE-VANT TO OUR SCHOOL!
...SO **THIS** TIME, I'M GONNA BE **SMART** ABOUT IT! NOT ONLY AM I DEPICTING A SCHOOL EVENT, I'M ALSO SNEAKING IN A PICTURE OF MYSELF!
"FOOD FIGHT AT P.S. 38."
THAT'S ME, NAILING MRS. GODFREY WITH A PLATE OF EGG SALAD!

WHAT A REVOLTING DEVELOPMENT! 333

PAINTING A MURAL IN THE CAFETERIA WAS MY IDEA, BUT NOW MR. ROSA'S TURNED IT INTO A **GROUP PROJECT**! EVERY PERSON IN THE CLASS GETS TO CONTRIBUTE!

IT'S NOT **RIGHT**! THE POWER OF MY ARTISTIC VISION IS BEING **DILUTED**! I'M BEING FORCED TO WORK WITH **AMATEURS**!

DO YOU KNOW WHAT IT'S LIKE TO BE SURROUNDED BY MEDIOCRITY?

NOT SURROUNDED, EXACTLY, BUT IN CLOSE PROXIMITY.

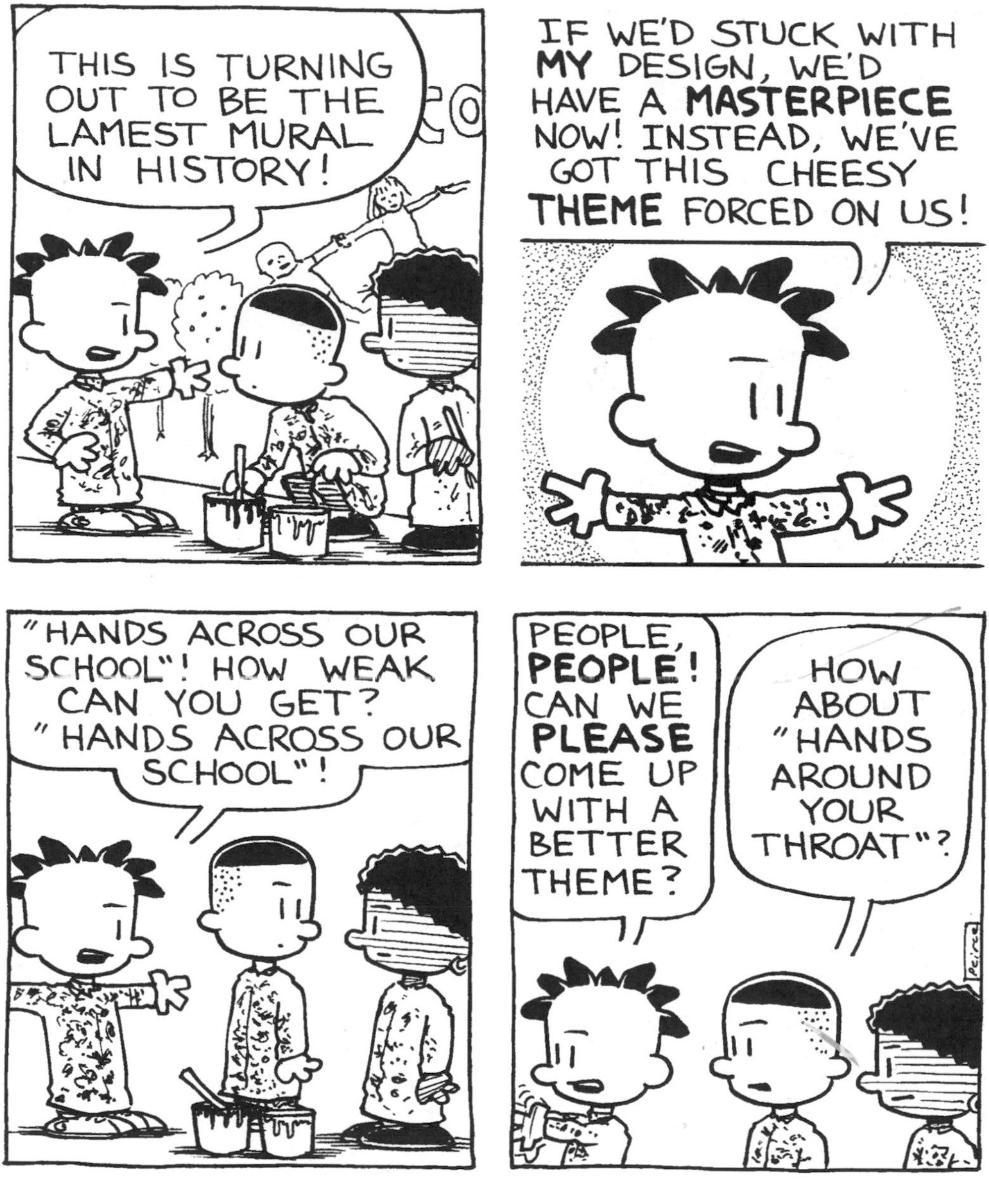
THIS IS TURNING OUT TO BE THE LAMEST MURAL IN HISTORY!
IF WE'D STUCK WITH **MY** DESIGN, WE'D HAVE A **MASTERPIECE** NOW! INSTEAD, WE'VE GOT THIS CHEESY **THEME** FORCED ON US!
"HANDS ACROSS OUR SCHOOL"! HOW WEAK CAN YOU GET? "HANDS ACROSS OUR SCHOOL"!
PEOPLE, **PEOPLE**! CAN WE **PLEASE** COME UP WITH A BETTER THEME?
HOW ABOUT "HANDS AROUND YOUR THROAT"?
Peirce

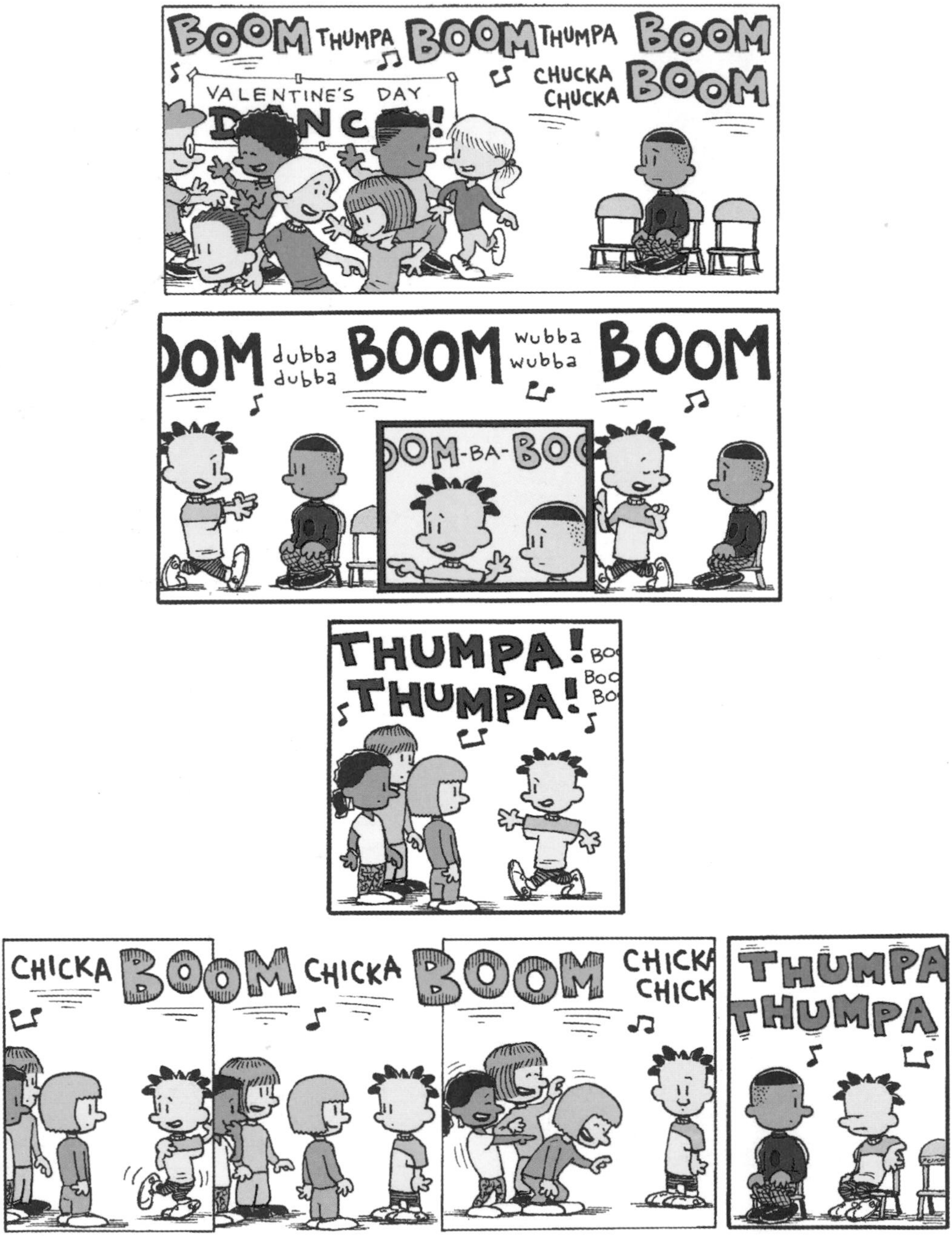
BOOM THUMPA BOOM THUMPA BOOM
CHUCKA CHUCKA BOOM
VALENTINE'S DAY
dubba dubba BOOM wubba wubba BOOM
THUMPA! THUMPA!
CHICKA BOOM
CHICKA BOOM
THUMPA THUMPA

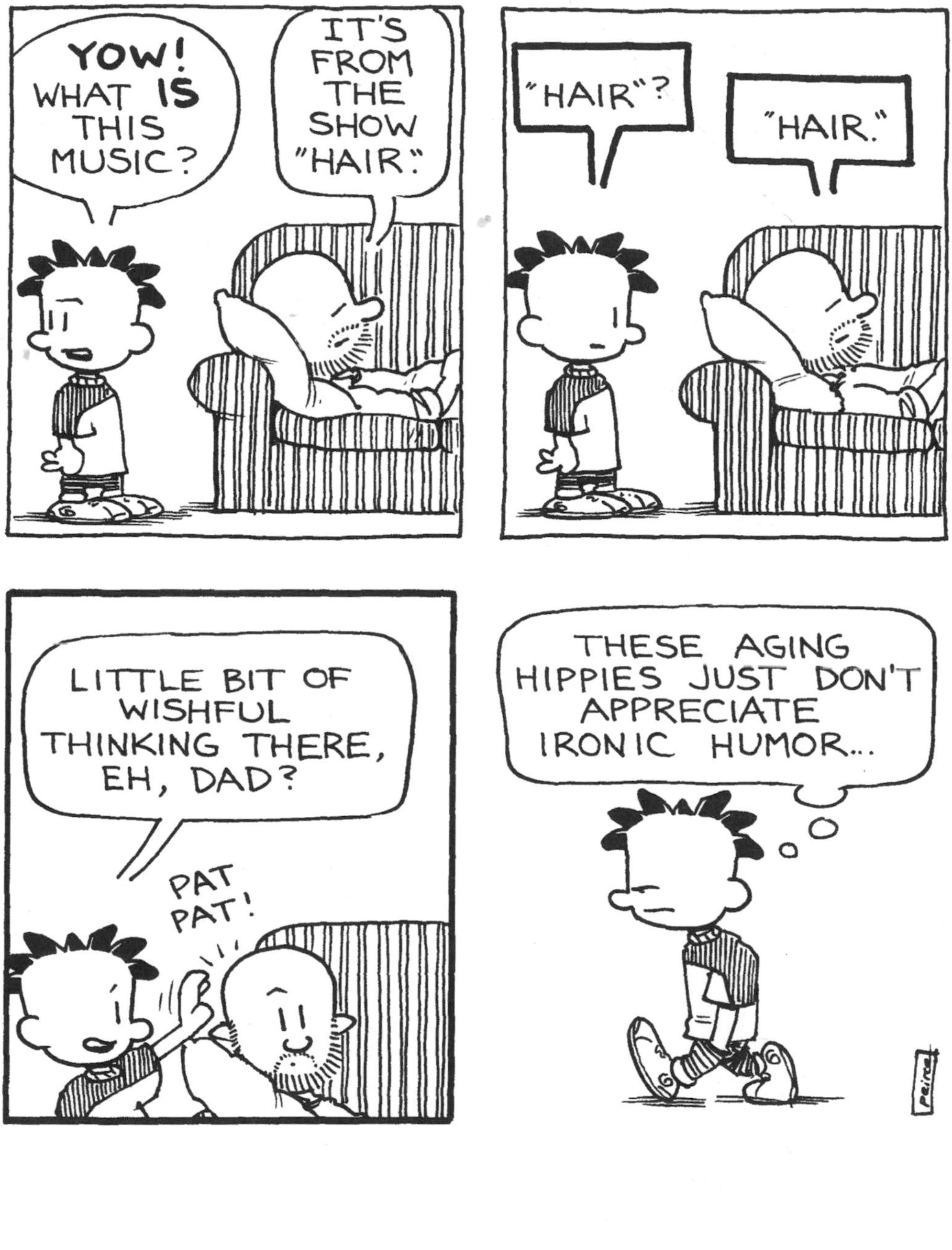
YOW! WHAT IS THIS MUSIC?
IT'S FROM THE SHOW "HAIR."
"HAIR"?
"HAIR."
LITTLE BIT OF WISHFUL THINKING THERE, EH, DAD?
PAT PAT!
THESE AGING HIPPIES JUST DON'T APPRECIATE IRONIC HUMOR...
PEIRCE

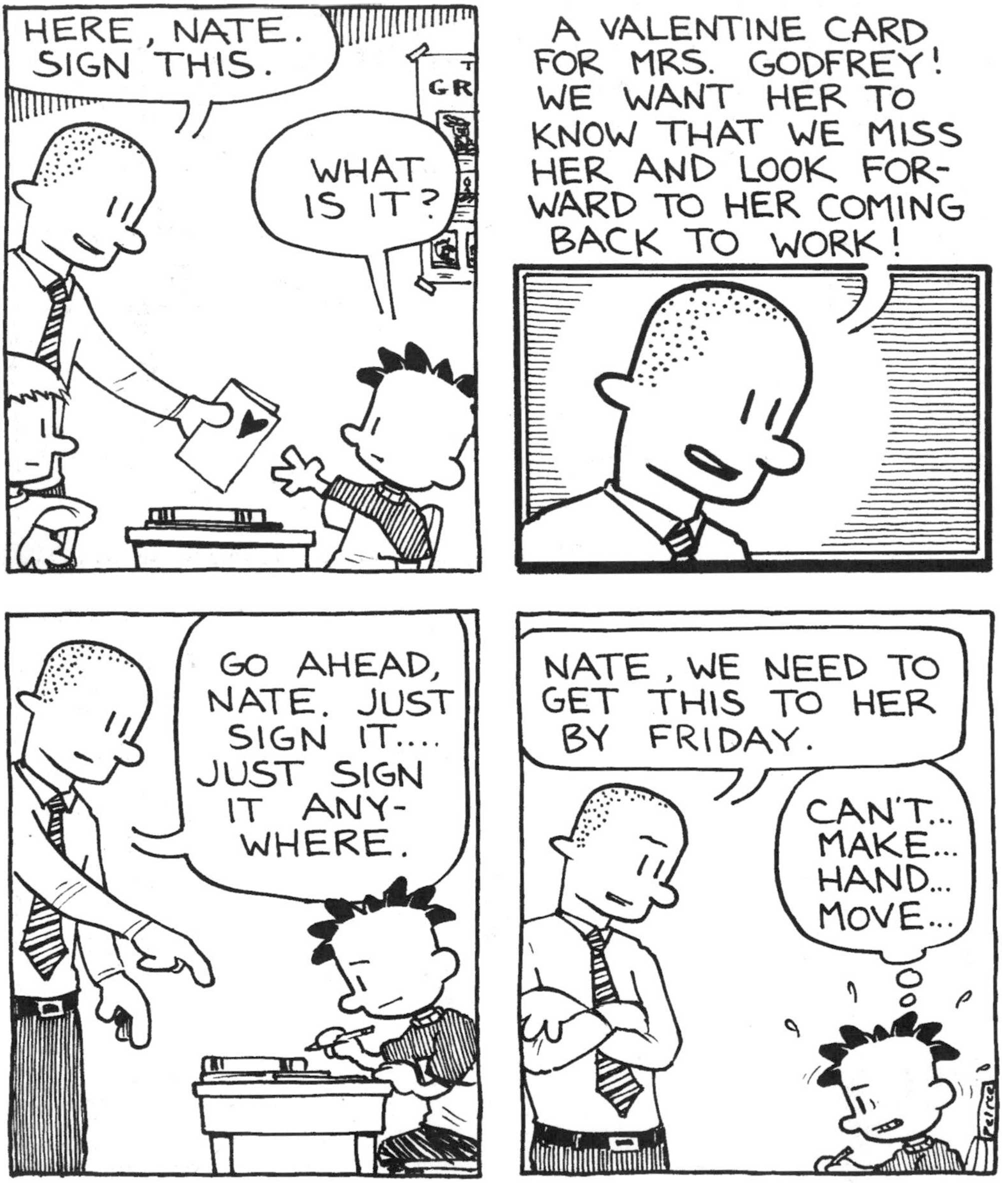
HERE, NATE. SIGN THIS.
WHAT IS IT?
A VALENTINE CARD FOR MRS. GODFREY! WE WANT HER TO KNOW THAT WE MISS HER AND LOOK FORWARD TO HER COMING BACK TO WORK!
GO AHEAD, NATE. JUST SIGN IT.... JUST SIGN IT ANYWHERE.
NATE, WE NEED TO GET THIS TO HER BY FRIDAY.
CAN'T... MAKE... HAND... MOVE...

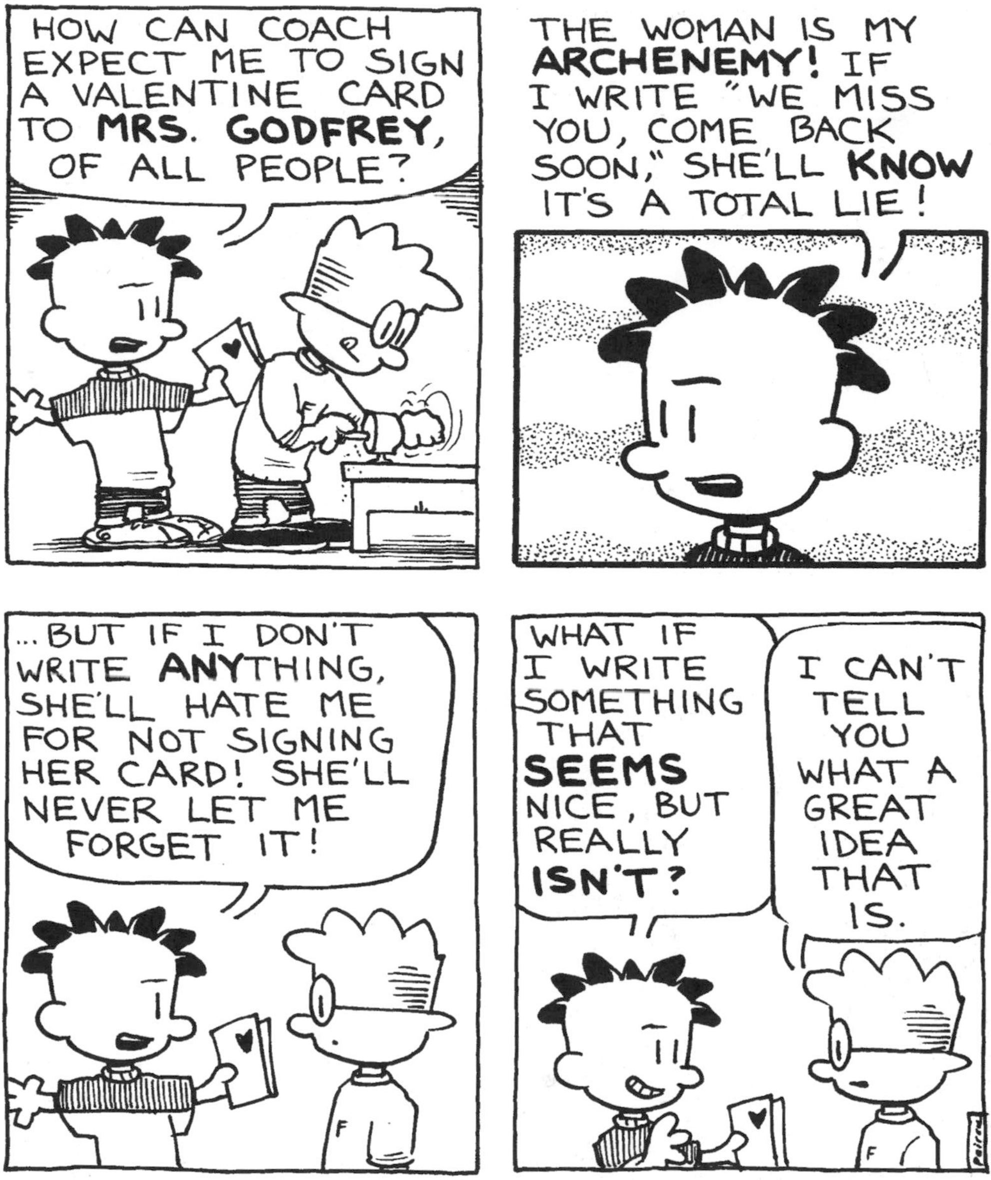
HOW CAN COACH EXPECT ME TO SIGN A VALENTINE CARD TO MRS. GODFREY, OF ALL PEOPLE?
THE WOMAN IS MY ARCHENEMY! IF I WRITE "WE MISS YOU, COME BACK SOON," SHE'LL KNOW IT'S A TOTAL LIE!
...BUT IF I DON'T WRITE ANYTHING, SHE'LL HATE ME FOR NOT SIGNING HER CARD! SHE'LL NEVER LET ME FORGET IT!
WHAT IF I WRITE SOMETHING THAT SEEMS NICE, BUT REALLY ISN'T?
I CAN'T TELL YOU WHAT A GREAT IDEA THAT IS.

I JUST DON'T KNOW WHAT TO WRITE ON THIS CARD TO MRS. GODFREY...
JUST WRITE ANY-THING! STOP MAK-ING SUCH A BIG DEAL OUT OF IT!
I'M NOT MAKING A BIG DEAL OUT OF IT!
YES, YOU ARE! YOU ALWAYS MAKE A BIG DEAL OUT OF EVERYTHING!
ME? I DO NOT! ASK ANYBODY! HECK, LET'S ASK THE WHOLE CLASS!
FOCUS GROUP, PEOPLE! DO I ALWAYS MAKE A BIG DEAL OUT OF EVERYTHING!?? LET'S SEE A SHOW OF HANDS!
CLAP
CLAP

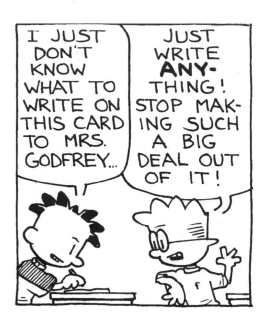

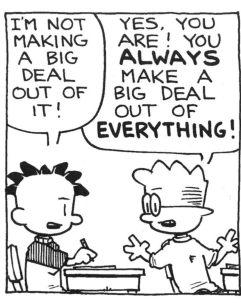

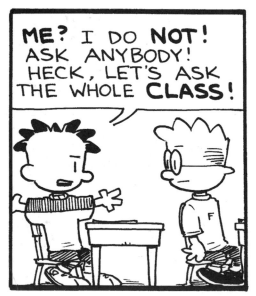

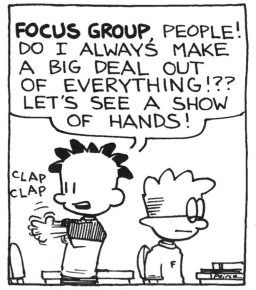

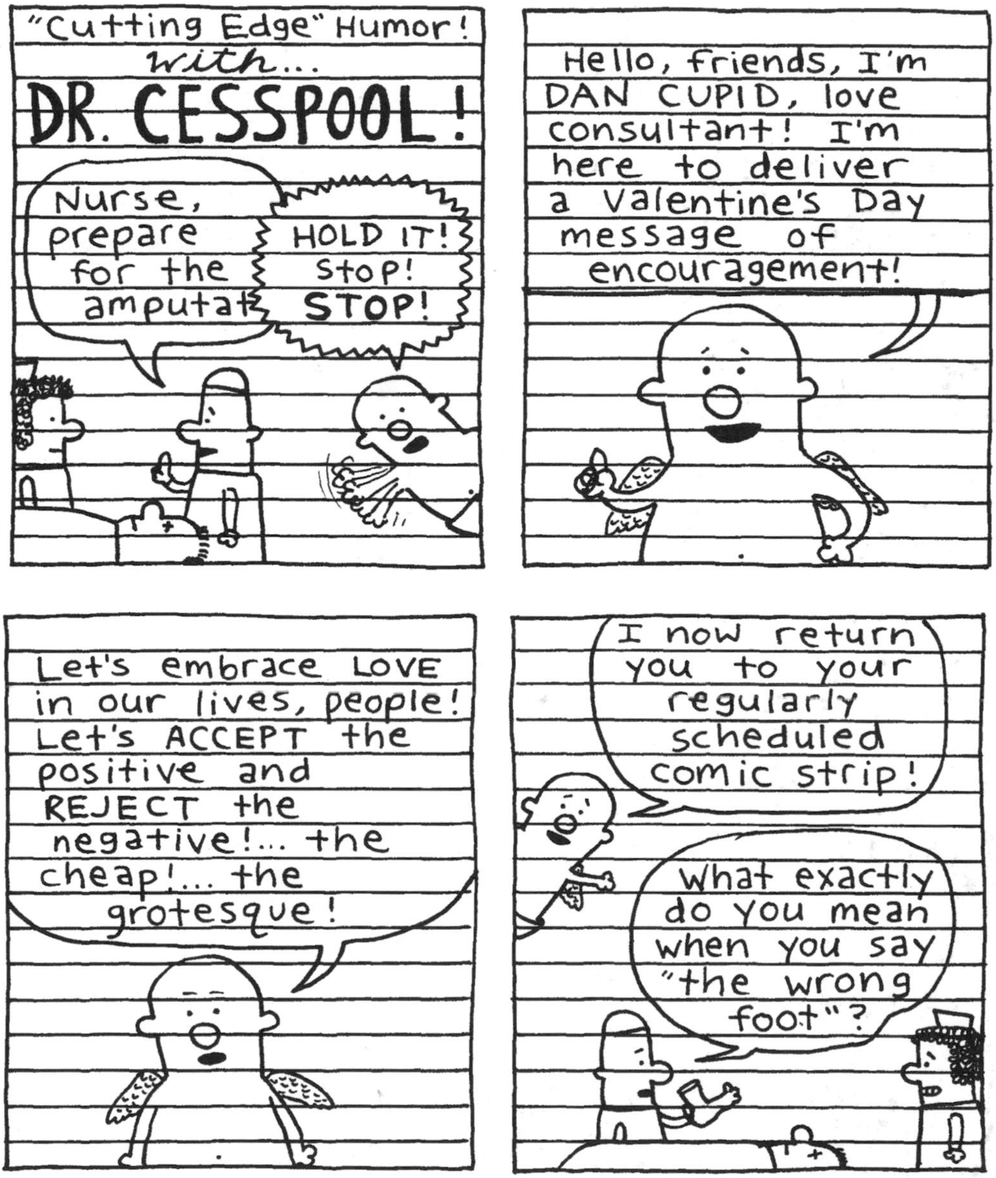
"Cutting Edge" Humor!
with...
DR. CESSPOOL!
Nurse, prepare for the amputat
HOLD IT! Stop! STOP!
Hello, friends, I'm DAN CUPID, love consultant! I'm here to deliver a Valentine's Day message of encouragement!
Let's embrace LOVE in our lives, people! Let's ACCEPT the positive and REJECT the negative!... the cheap!... the grotesque!
I now return you to your regularly scheduled comic strip!
What exactly do you mean when you say "the wrong foot"?

I DIDN'T GET ANY VALENTINES YESTERDAY! **ZIP! NADA!**

REALLY?

THAT'S SURPRISING. MOST PEOPLE GET AT LEAST ONE...

YES, THAT'S QUITE SURPRISING.

BELLCH!

ON SECOND THOUGHT...

WHAT ARE **YOU** LOOKING AT?

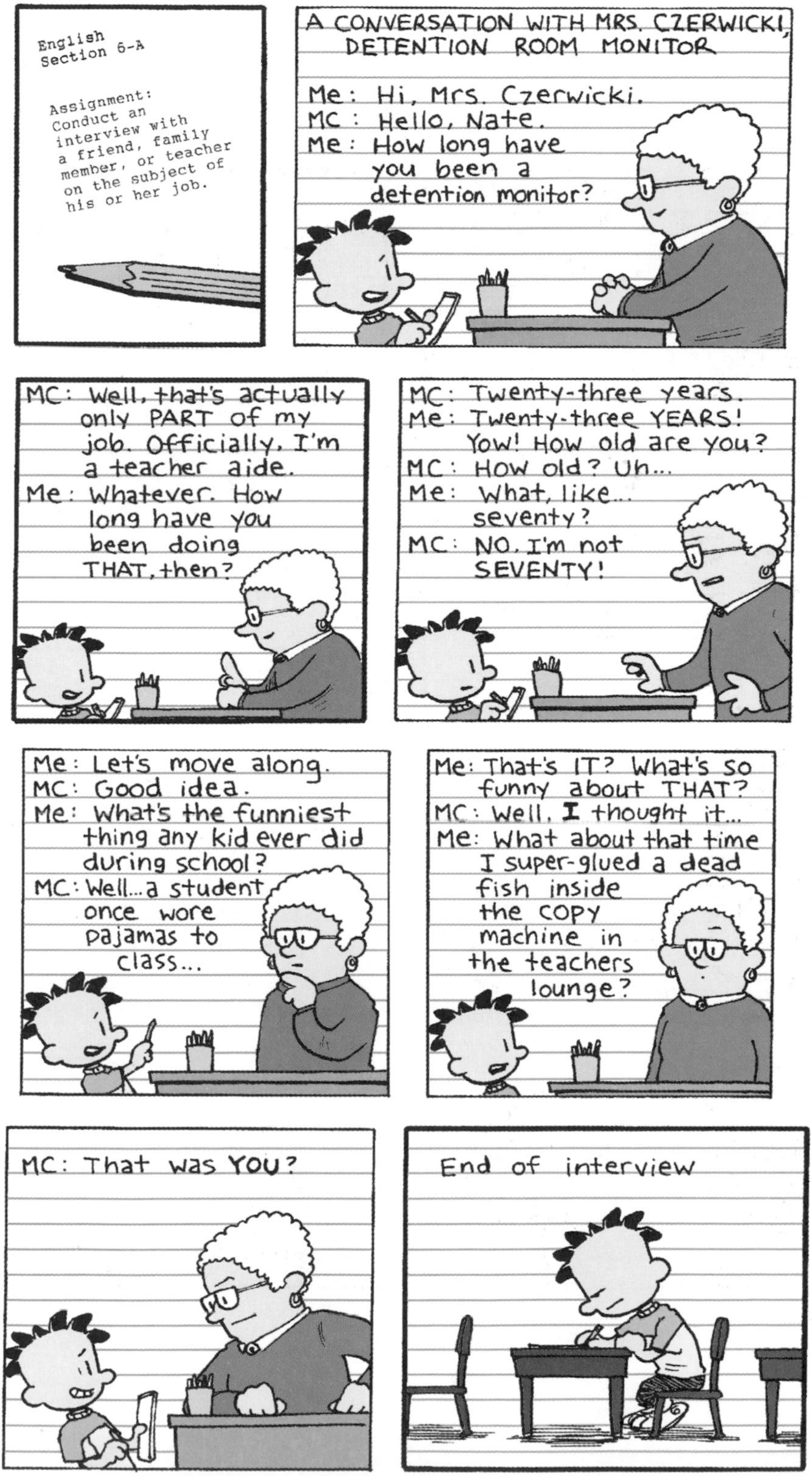
English
Section 6-A
Assignment: Conduct an interview with a friend, family member, or teacher on the subject of his or her job.
A CONVERSATION WITH MRS. CZERWICKI, DETENTION ROOM MONITOR
Me: Hi, Mrs. Czerwicki.
MC: Hello, Nate.
Me: How long have you been a detention monitor?
MC: Well, that's actually only PART of my job. Officially, I'm a teacher aide.
Me: Whatever. How long have you been doing THAT, then?
MC: Twenty-three years.
Me: Twenty-three YEARS! Yow! How old are you?
MC: How old? Uh...
Me: What, like... seventy?
MC: NO. I'm not SEVENTY!
Me: Let's move along.
MC: Good idea.
Me: What's the funniest thing any kid ever did during school?
MC: Well... a student once wore pajamas to class...
Me: That's IT? What's so funny about THAT?
MC: Well, I thought it...
Me: What about that time I super-glued a dead fish inside the copy machine in the teachers lounge?
MC: That was YOU?
End of interview

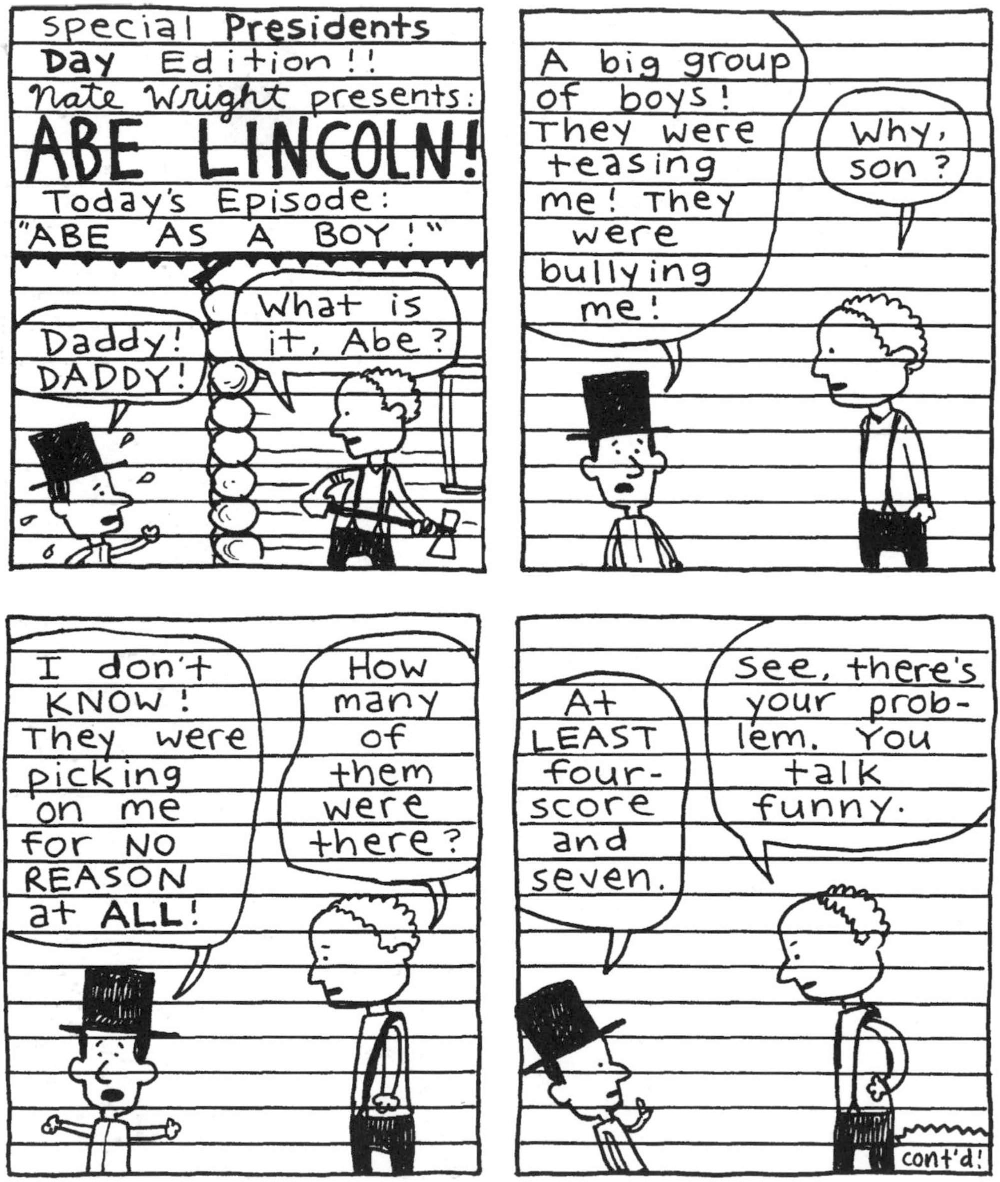

Special Presidents Day Edition!!
Nate Wright presents:
ABE LINCOLN!
Today's Episode: "ABE AS A BOY!"
Daddy! DADDY!
What is it, Abe?
A big group of boys! They were teasing me! They were bullying me!
Why, son?
I don't KNOW! They were picking on me for NO REASON at ALL!
How many of them were there?
At LEAST four-score and seven.
See, there's your problem. You talk funny.
cont'd!

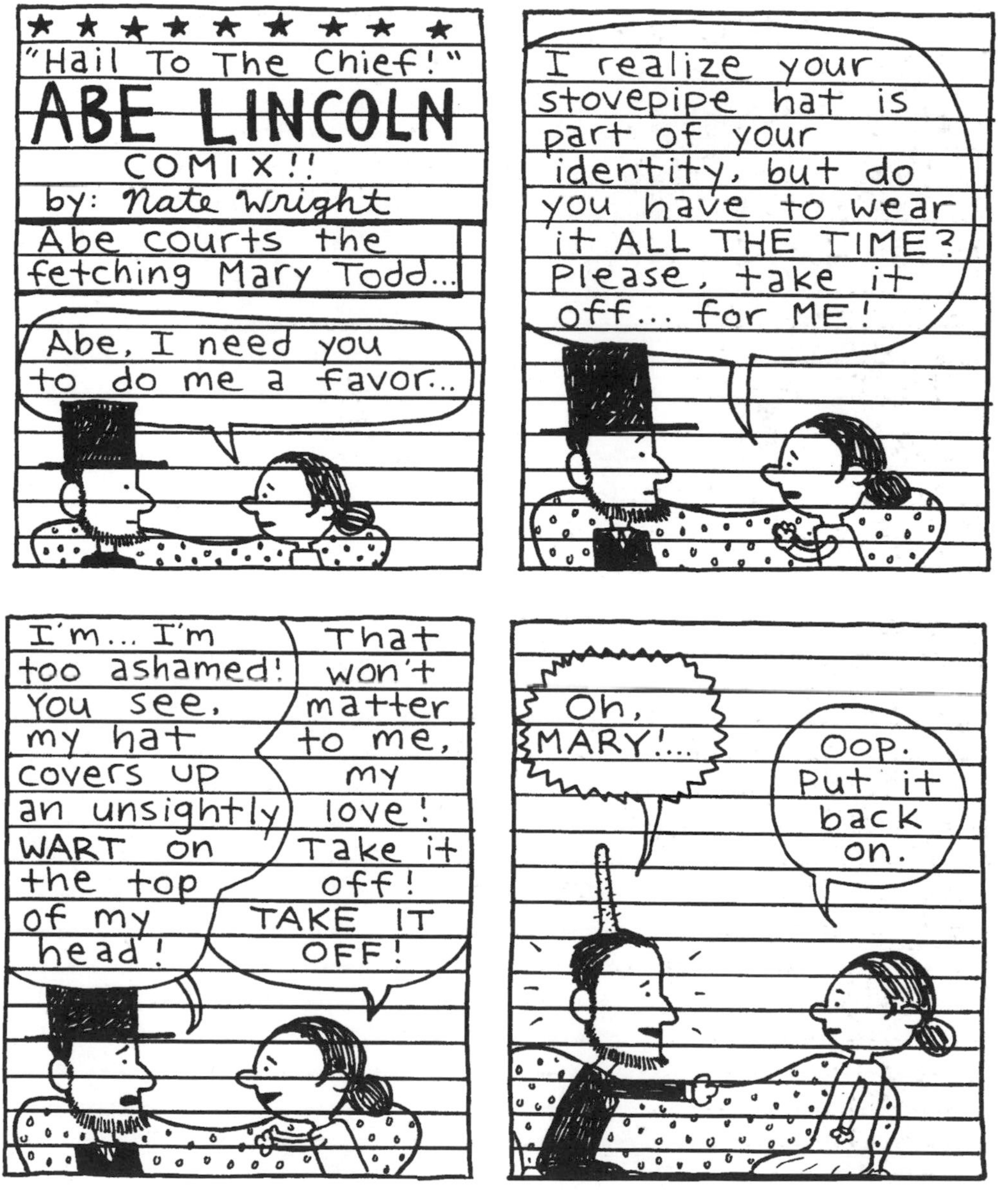

★ ★ ★ ★ ★ ★ ★ ★ ★
"Hail To The Chief!"
ABE LINCOLN
COMIX!!
by: Nate Wright
Abe courts the fetching Mary Todd...
Abe, I need you to do me a favor...
I realize your stovepipe hat is part of your identity, but do you have to wear it ALL THE TIME? Please, take it off... for ME!
I'm... I'm too ashamed! You see, my hat covers up an unsightly WART on the top of my head!
That won't matter to me, my love! Take it off! TAKE IT OFF!
Oh, MARY!...
Oop. Put it back on.

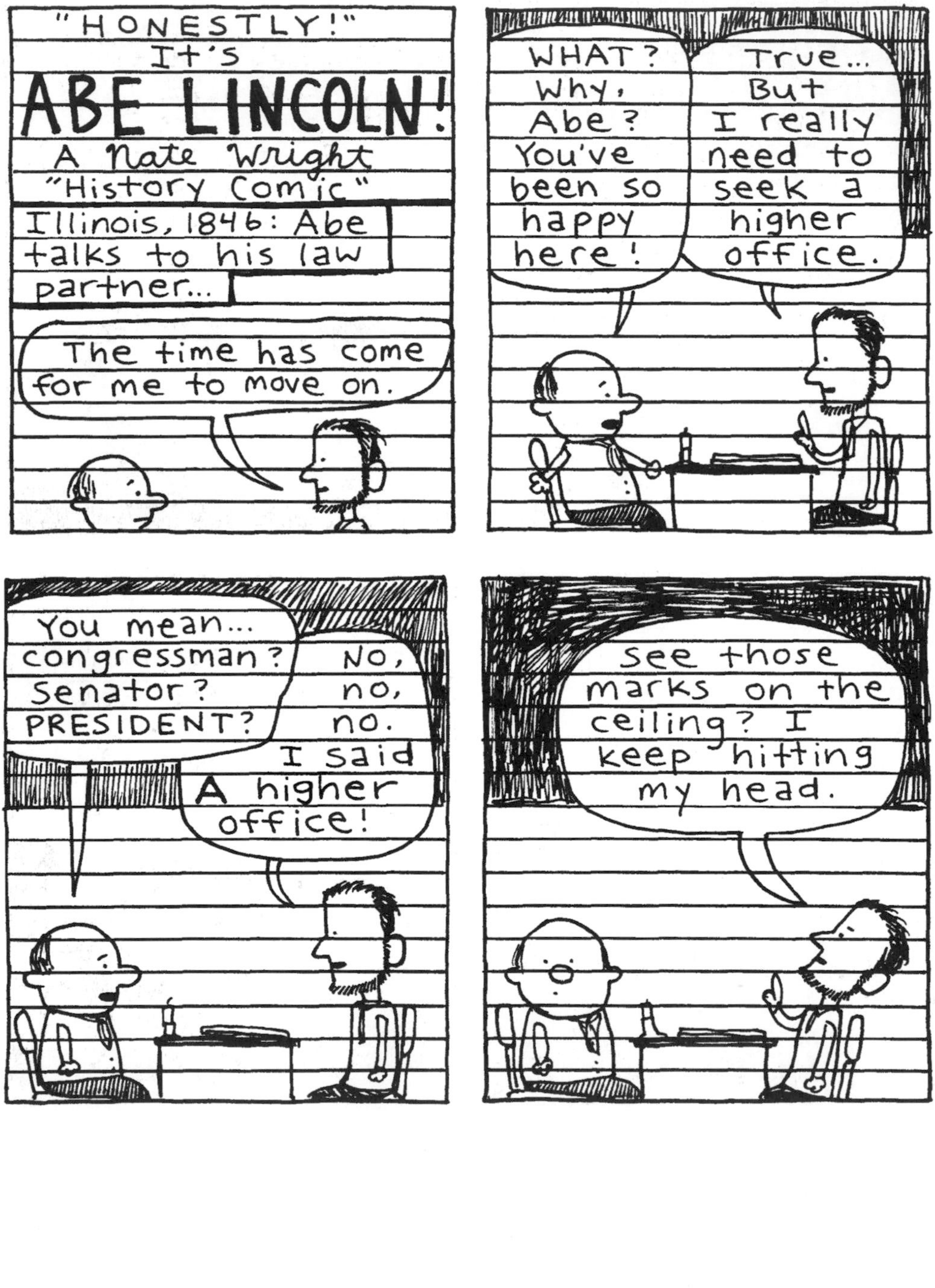
"HONESTLY!" It's ABE LINCOLN!
A Nate Wright "History Comic"
Illinois, 1846: Abe talks to his law partner...
The time has come for me to move on.
WHAT? Why, Abe? You've been so happy here!
True... But I really need to seek a higher office.
You mean... congressman? Senator? PRESIDENT?
No, no, no. I said A higher office!
See those marks on the ceiling? I keep hitting my head.

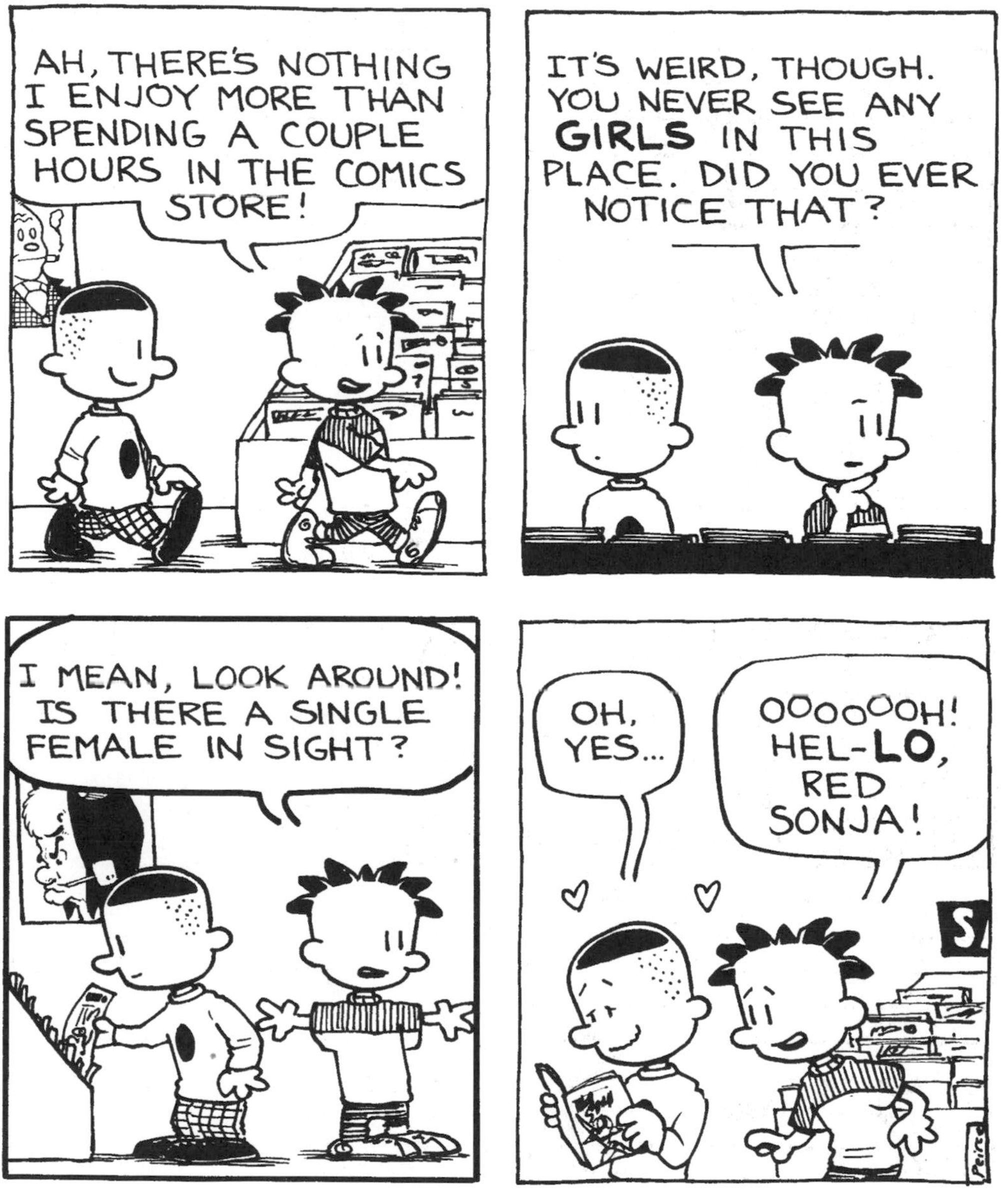
AH, THERE'S NOTHING I ENJOY MORE THAN SPENDING A COUPLE HOURS IN THE COMICS STORE!
IT'S WEIRD, THOUGH. YOU NEVER SEE ANY **GIRLS** IN THIS PLACE. DID YOU EVER NOTICE THAT?
I MEAN, LOOK AROUND! IS THERE A SINGLE FEMALE IN SIGHT?
OH, YES...
OOOOOOH! HEL-**LO**, RED SONJA!
PEIRCE

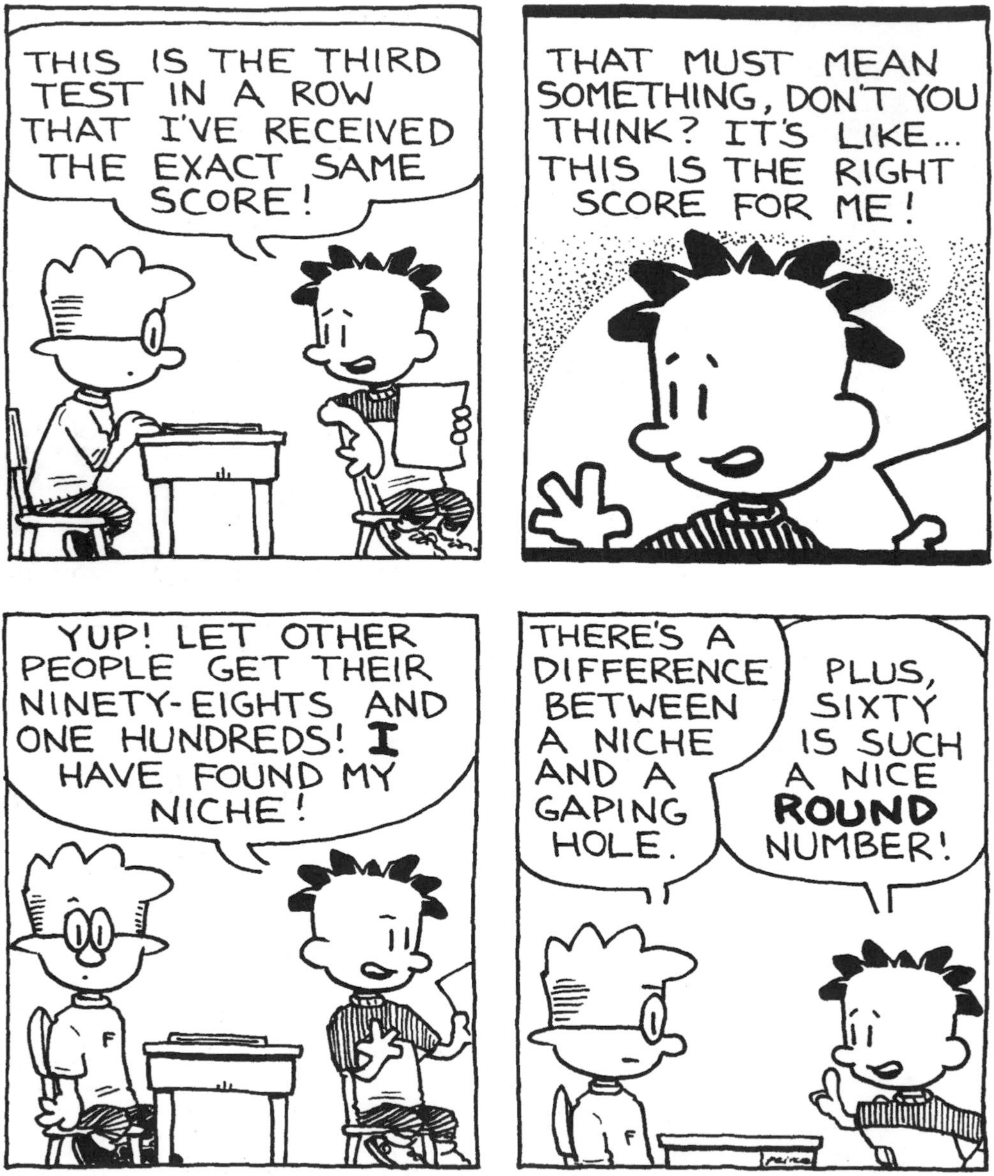
THIS IS THE THIRD TEST IN A ROW THAT I'VE RECEIVED THE EXACT SAME SCORE!
THAT MUST MEAN SOMETHING, DON'T YOU THINK? IT'S LIKE... THIS IS THE RIGHT SCORE FOR ME!
YUP! LET OTHER PEOPLE GET THEIR NINETY-EIGHTS AND ONE HUNDREDS! **I** HAVE FOUND MY NICHE!
PLUS, SIXTY IS SUCH A NICE **ROUND** NUMBER!
THERE'S A DIFFERENCE BETWEEN A NICHE AND A GAPING HOLE.

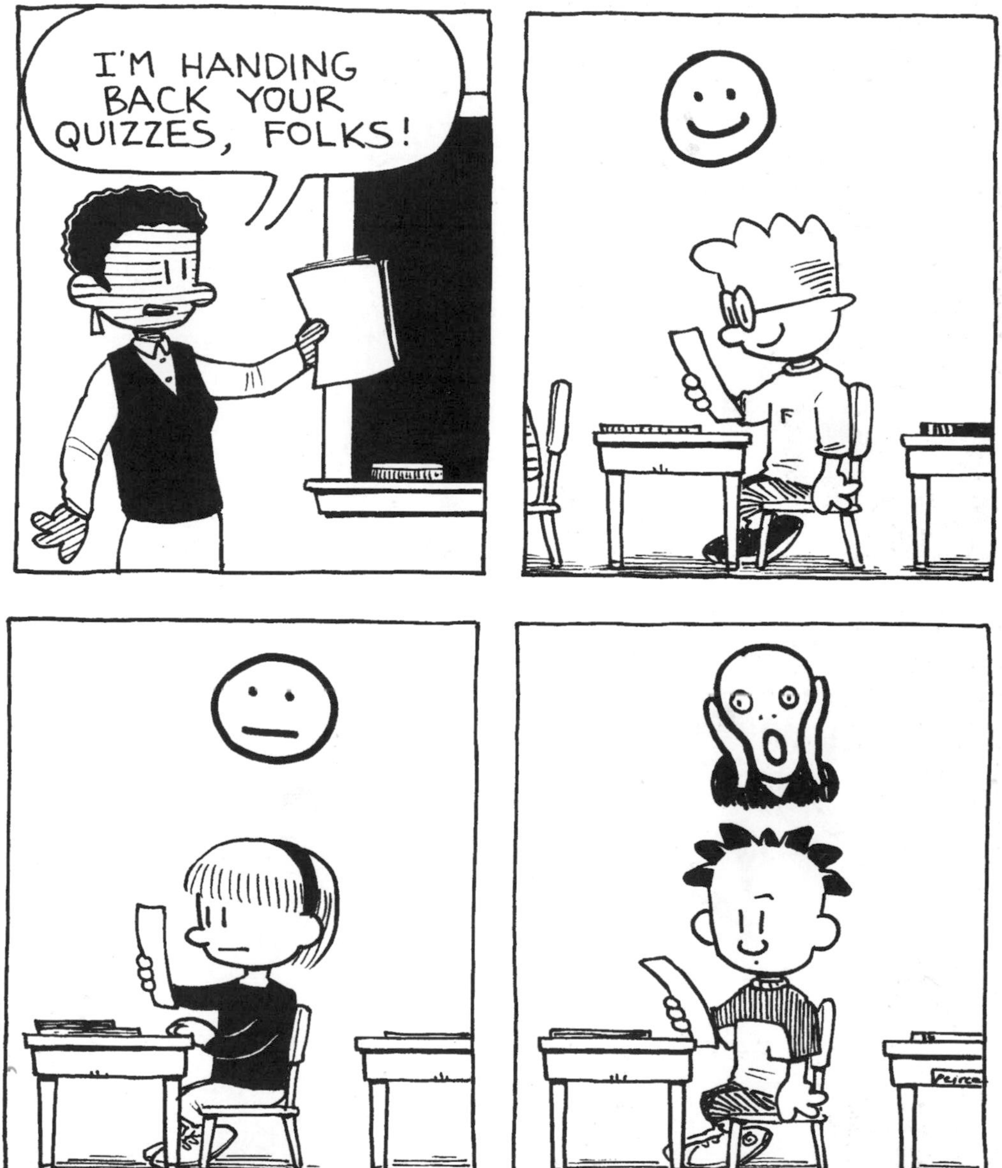
I'M HANDING BACK YOUR QUIZZES, FOLKS!

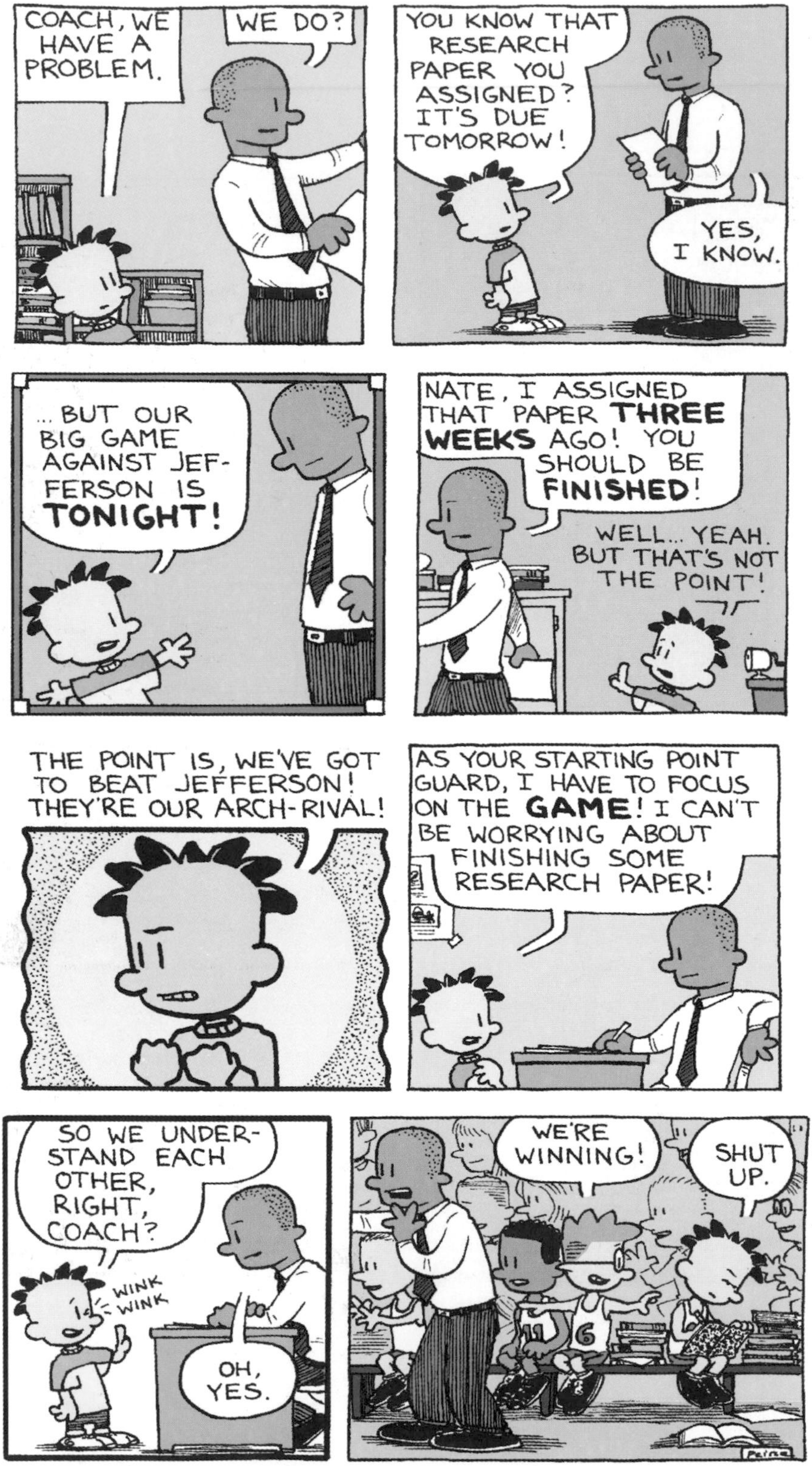
COACH, WE HAVE A PROBLEM.
WE DO?
YOU KNOW THAT RESEARCH PAPER YOU ASSIGNED? IT'S DUE TOMORROW!
YES, I KNOW.
... BUT OUR BIG GAME AGAINST JEFFERSON IS **TONIGHT!**
NATE, I ASSIGNED THAT PAPER **THREE WEEKS** AGO! YOU SHOULD BE **FINISHED**!
WELL... YEAH. BUT THAT'S NOT THE POINT!
THE POINT IS, WE'VE GOT TO BEAT JEFFERSON! THEY'RE OUR ARCH-RIVAL!
AS YOUR STARTING POINT GUARD, I HAVE TO FOCUS ON THE **GAME**! I CAN'T BE WORRYING ABOUT FINISHING SOME RESEARCH PAPER!
SO WE UNDERSTAND EACH OTHER, RIGHT, COACH?
WINK WINK
OH, YES.
WE'RE WINNING!
SHUT UP.

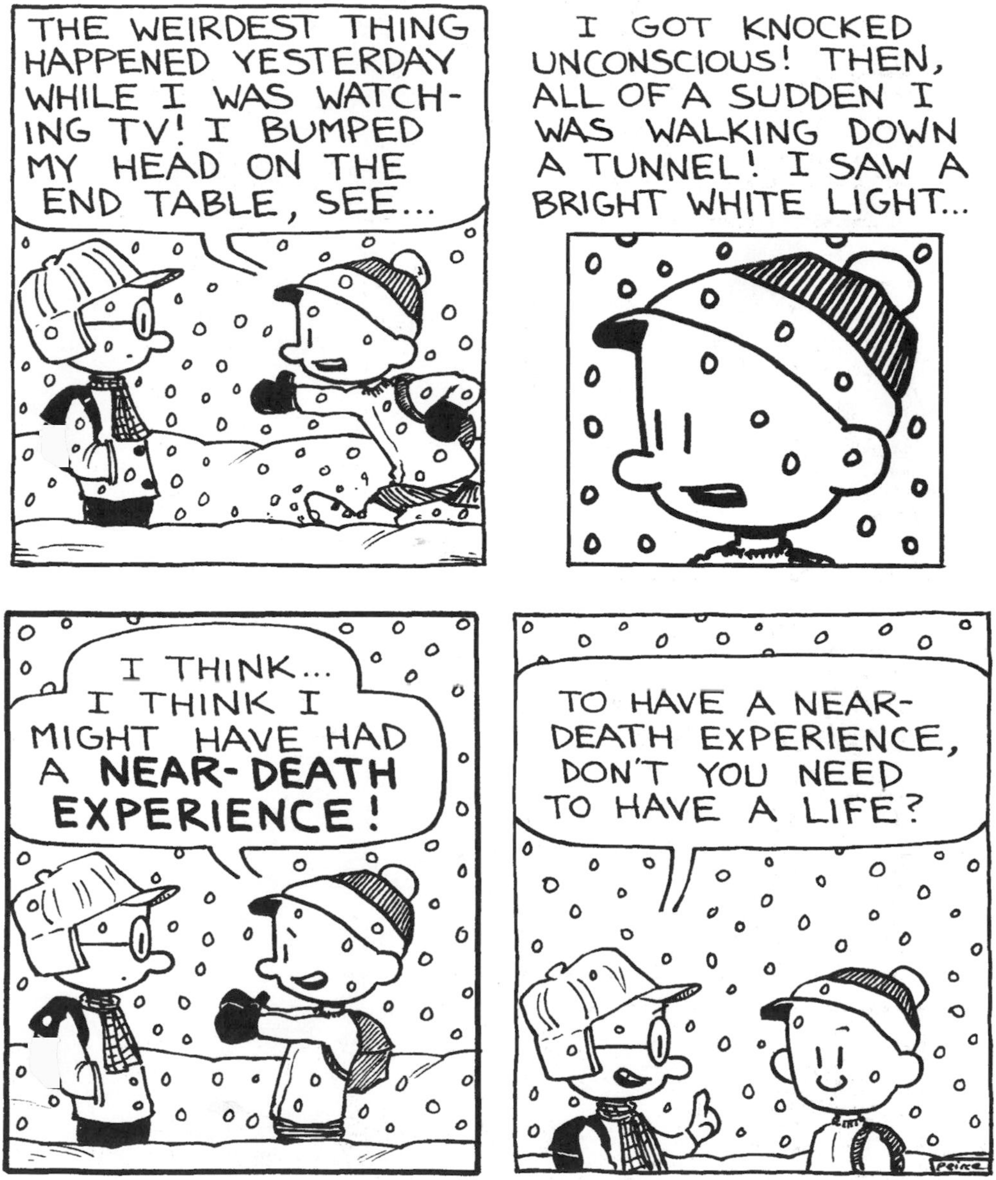
THE WEIRDEST THING HAPPENED YESTERDAY WHILE I WAS WATCHING TV! I BUMPED MY HEAD ON THE END TABLE, SEE...
I GOT KNOCKED UNCONSCIOUS! THEN, ALL OF A SUDDEN I WAS WALKING DOWN A TUNNEL! I SAW A BRIGHT WHITE LIGHT...
I THINK... I THINK I MIGHT HAVE HAD A NEAR-DEATH EXPERIENCE!
TO HAVE A NEAR-DEATH EXPERIENCE, DON'T YOU NEED TO HAVE A LIFE?
PEIRCE

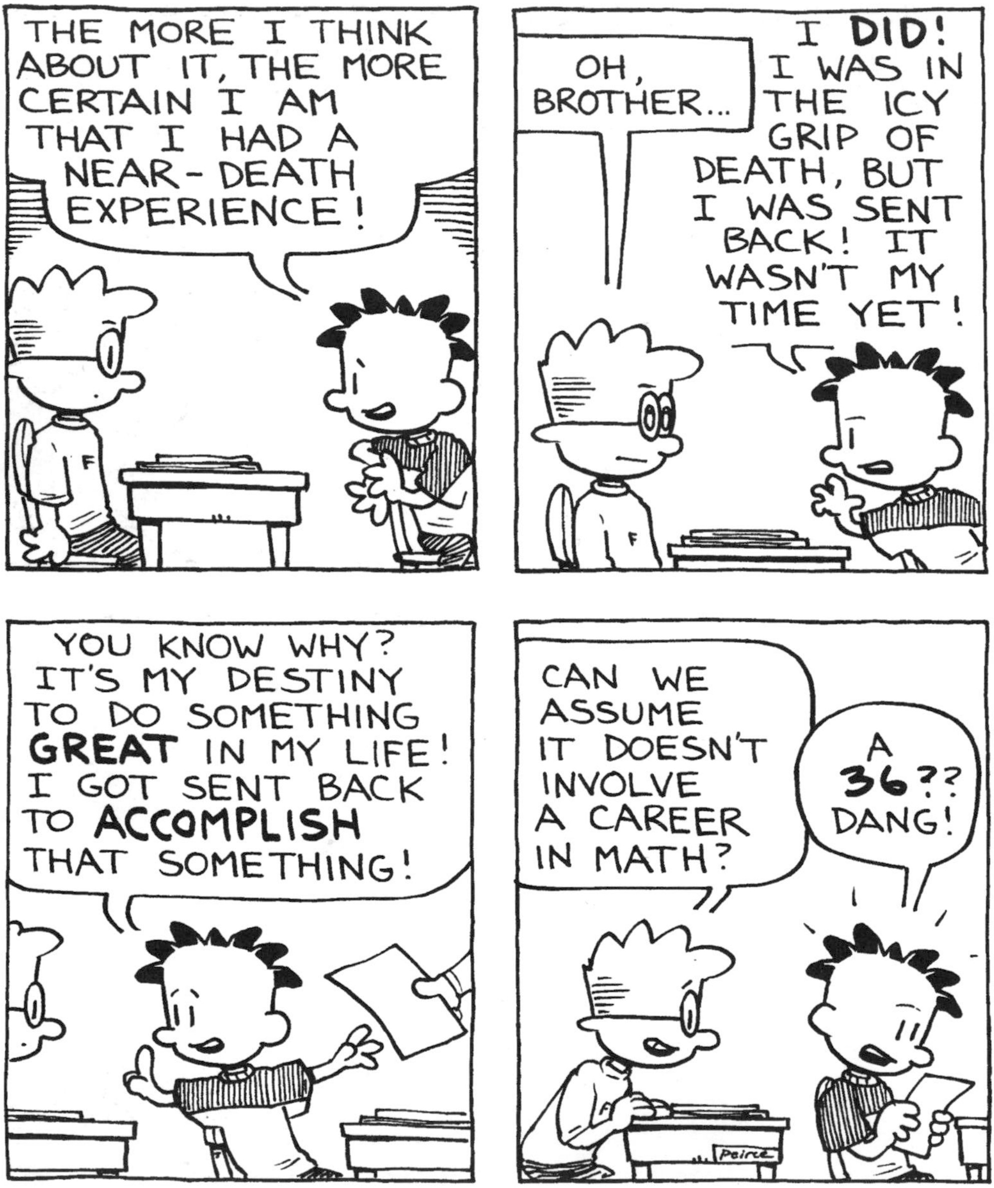
THE MORE I THINK ABOUT IT, THE MORE CERTAIN I AM THAT I HAD A NEAR-DEATH EXPERIENCE!
I **DID**! I WAS IN THE ICY GRIP OF DEATH, BUT I WAS SENT BACK! IT WASN'T MY TIME YET!
OH, BROTHER...
YOU KNOW WHY? IT'S MY DESTINY TO DO SOMETHING **GREAT** IN MY LIFE! I GOT SENT BACK TO **ACCOMPLISH** THAT SOMETHING!
A **36**??
DANG!
CAN WE ASSUME IT DOESN'T INVOLVE A CAREER IN MATH?
Peirce

...AND THEN I FLOATED OUT OF MY BODY! I WAS IN A TUNNEL, WALKING TOWARD A BRIGHT WHITE LIGHT!...

BUT THEN SOMETHING PULLED ME BACK! YES, I WAS YANKED BACK FROM THE ABYSS!

YAWNNN

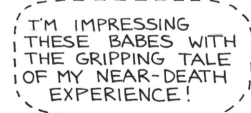

I'M IMPRESSING THESE BABES WITH THE GRIPPING TALE OF MY NEAR-DEATH EXPERIENCE!

WHAT ABOUT YOUR **BRAIN-**DEATH EXPERIENCE?

HEY, WHERE'D THEY GO?

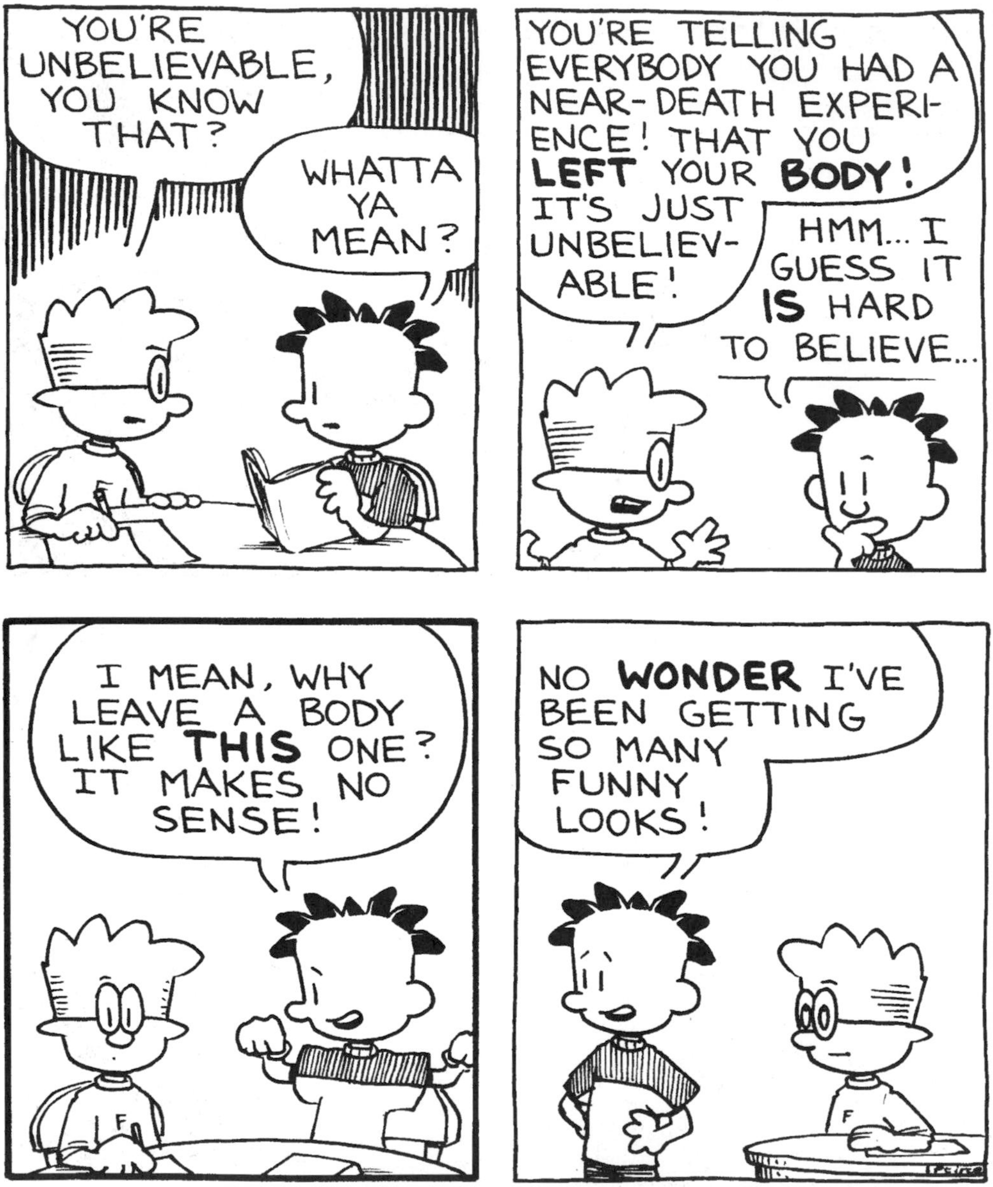
YOU'RE UNBELIEVABLE, YOU KNOW THAT?
WHATTA YA MEAN?
YOU'RE TELLING EVERYBODY YOU HAD A NEAR-DEATH EXPERIENCE! THAT YOU **LEFT** YOUR **BODY**! IT'S JUST UNBELIEVABLE!
HMM... I GUESS IT **IS** HARD TO BELIEVE...
I MEAN, WHY LEAVE A BODY LIKE **THIS** ONE? IT MAKES NO SENSE!
NO **WONDER** I'VE BEEN GETTING SO MANY FUNNY LOOKS!

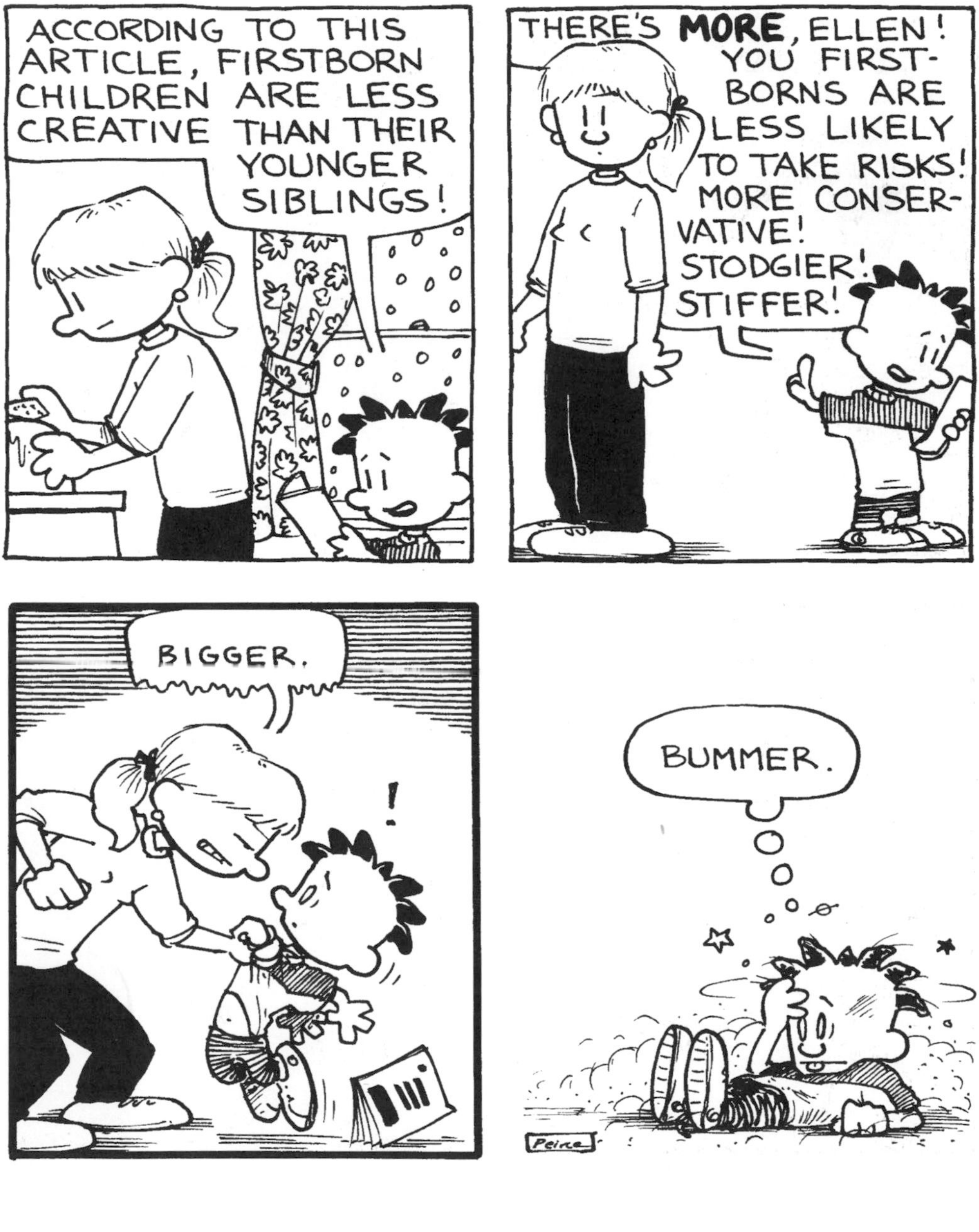
ACCORDING TO THIS ARTICLE, FIRSTBORN CHILDREN ARE LESS CREATIVE THAN THEIR YOUNGER SIBLINGS!
THERE'S **MORE**, ELLEN! YOU FIRST-BORNS ARE LESS LIKELY TO TAKE RISKS! MORE CONSER-VATIVE! STODGIER! STIFFER!
BIGGER.
!
BUMMER.
Peirce

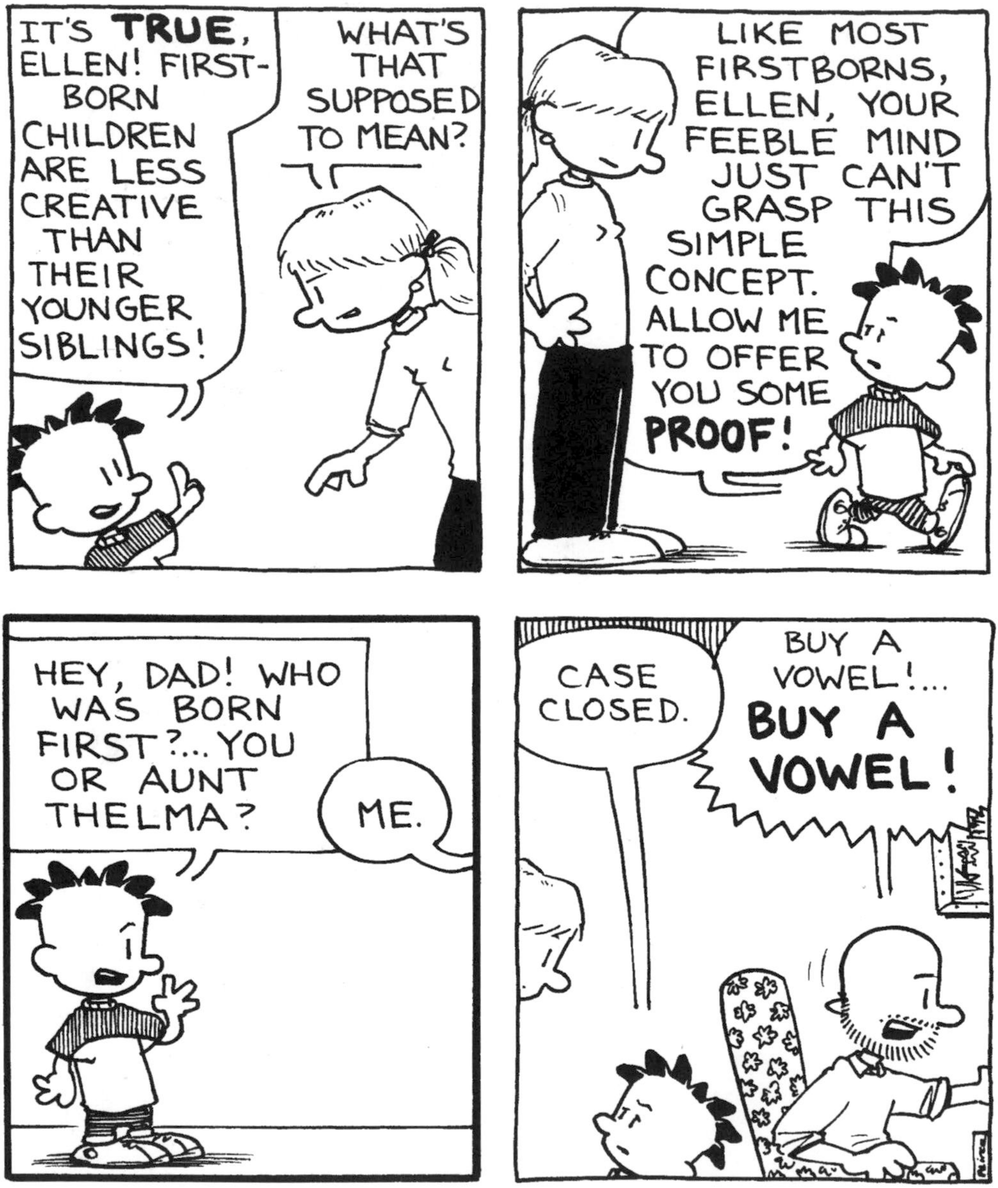
IT'S **TRUE**, ELLEN! FIRST-BORN CHILDREN ARE LESS CREATIVE THAN THEIR YOUNGER SIBLINGS!
WHAT'S THAT SUPPOSED TO MEAN?
LIKE MOST FIRSTBORNS, ELLEN, YOUR FEEBLE MIND JUST CAN'T GRASP THIS SIMPLE CONCEPT. ALLOW ME TO OFFER YOU SOME **PROOF**!
HEY, DAD! WHO WAS BORN FIRST?... YOU OR AUNT THELMA?
ME.
CASE CLOSED.
BUY A VOWEL!... **BUY A VOWEL!**

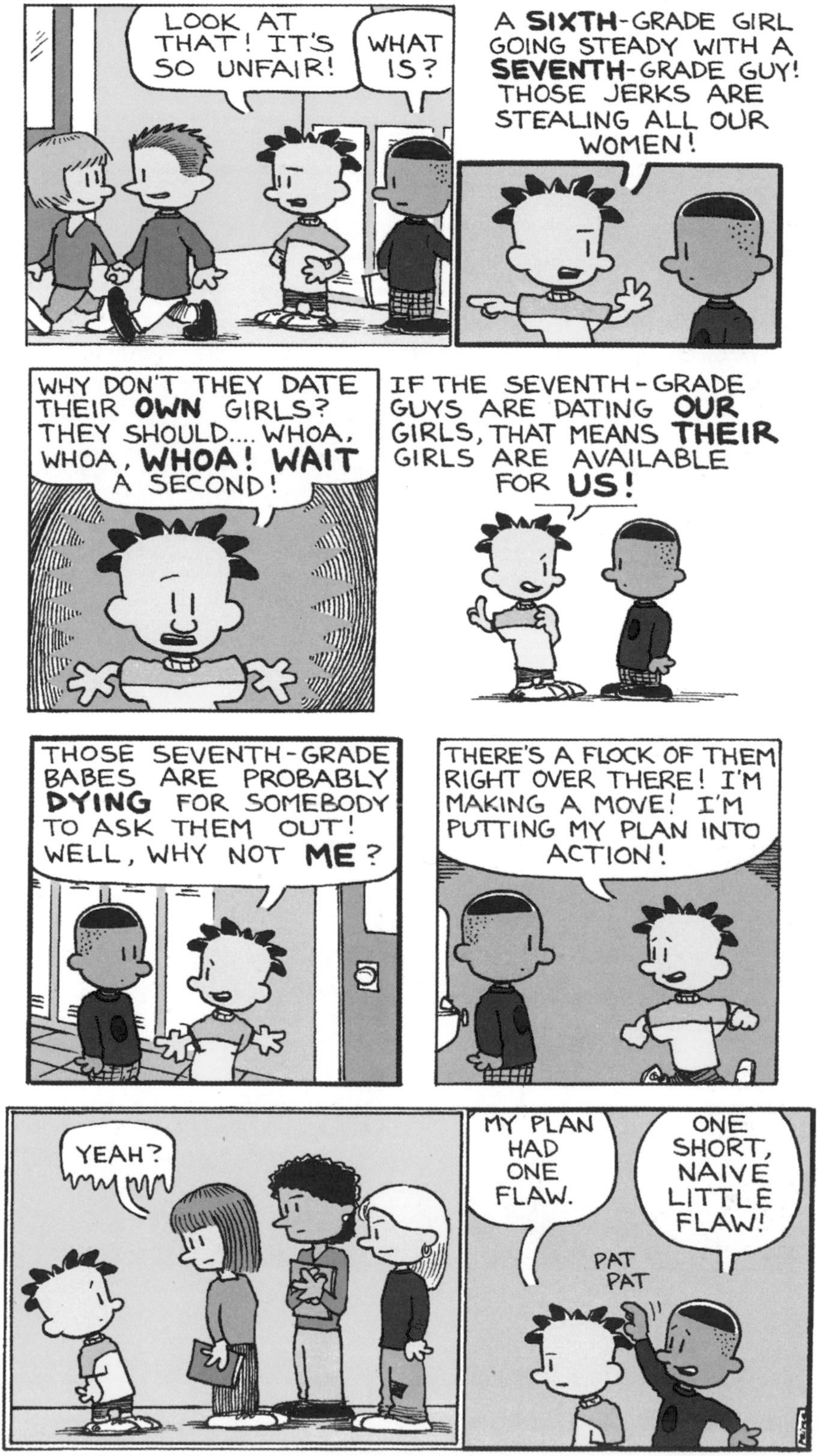

LOOK AT THAT! IT'S SO UNFAIR!
WHAT IS?
A **SIXTH**-GRADE GIRL GOING STEADY WITH A **SEVENTH**-GRADE GUY! THOSE JERKS ARE STEALING ALL OUR WOMEN!
WHY DON'T THEY DATE THEIR **OWN** GIRLS? THEY SHOULD.... WHOA, WHOA, **WHOA! WAIT** A SECOND!
IF THE SEVENTH-GRADE GUYS ARE DATING **OUR** GIRLS, THAT MEANS **THEIR** GIRLS ARE AVAILABLE FOR **US!**
THOSE SEVENTH-GRADE BABES ARE PROBABLY **DYING** FOR SOMEBODY TO ASK THEM OUT! WELL, WHY NOT **ME**?
THERE'S A FLOCK OF THEM RIGHT OVER THERE! I'M MAKING A MOVE! I'M PUTTING MY PLAN INTO ACTION!
YEAH?
MY PLAN HAD ONE FLAW.
ONE SHORT, NAIVE LITTLE FLAW!
PAT PAT

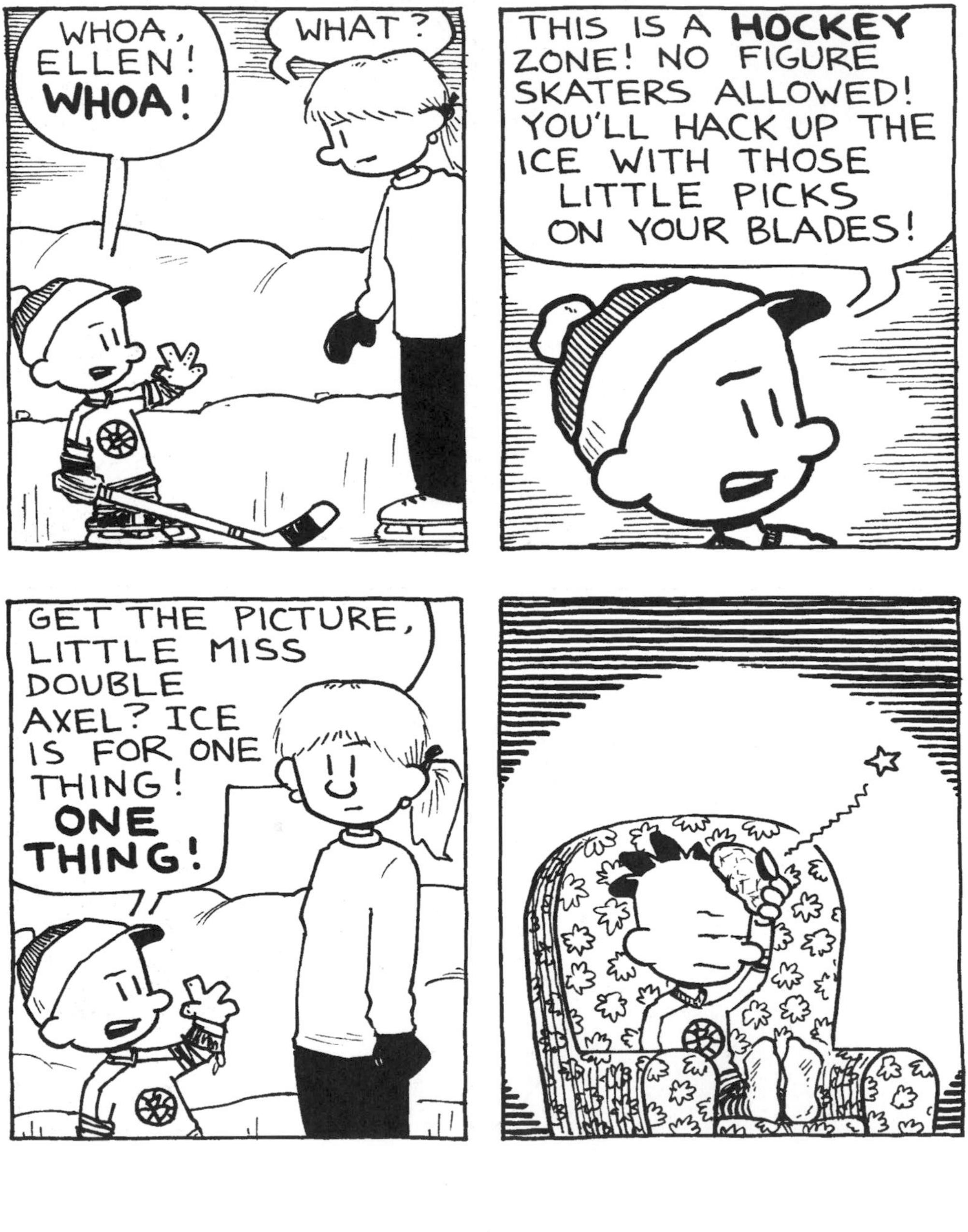
WHOA, ELLEN! WHOA!
WHAT?
THIS IS A HOCKEY ZONE! NO FIGURE SKATERS ALLOWED! YOU'LL HACK UP THE ICE WITH THOSE LITTLE PICKS ON YOUR BLADES!
GET THE PICTURE, LITTLE MISS DOUBLE AXEL? ICE IS FOR ONE THING! ONE THING!

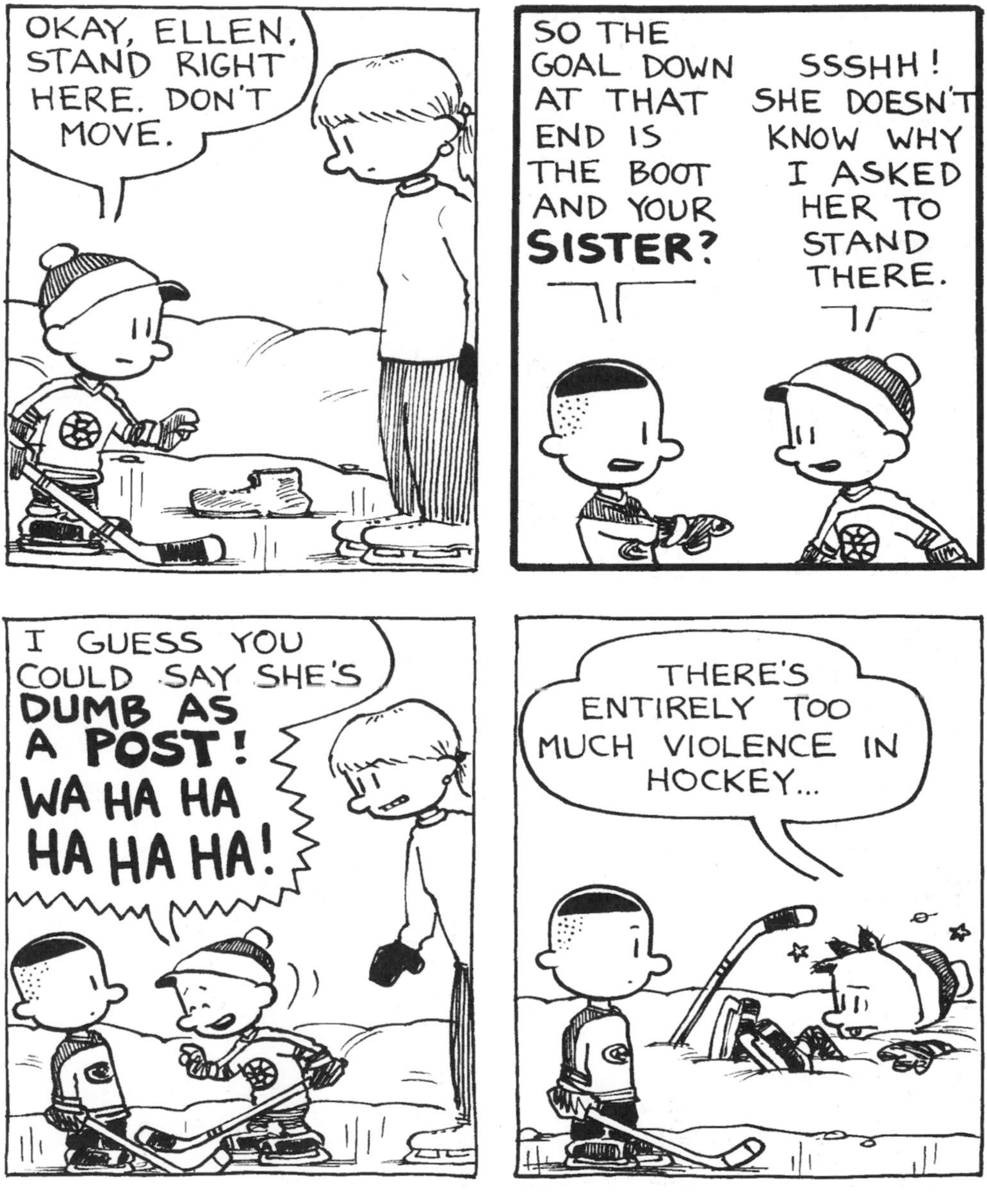
OKAY, ELLEN. STAND RIGHT HERE. DON'T MOVE.
SO THE GOAL DOWN AT THAT END IS THE BOOT AND YOUR SISTER?
SSSHH! SHE DOESN'T KNOW WHY I ASKED HER TO STAND THERE.
I GUESS YOU COULD SAY SHE'S DUMB AS A POST! WA HA HA HA HA HA!
THERE'S ENTIRELY TOO MUCH VIOLENCE IN HOCKEY...

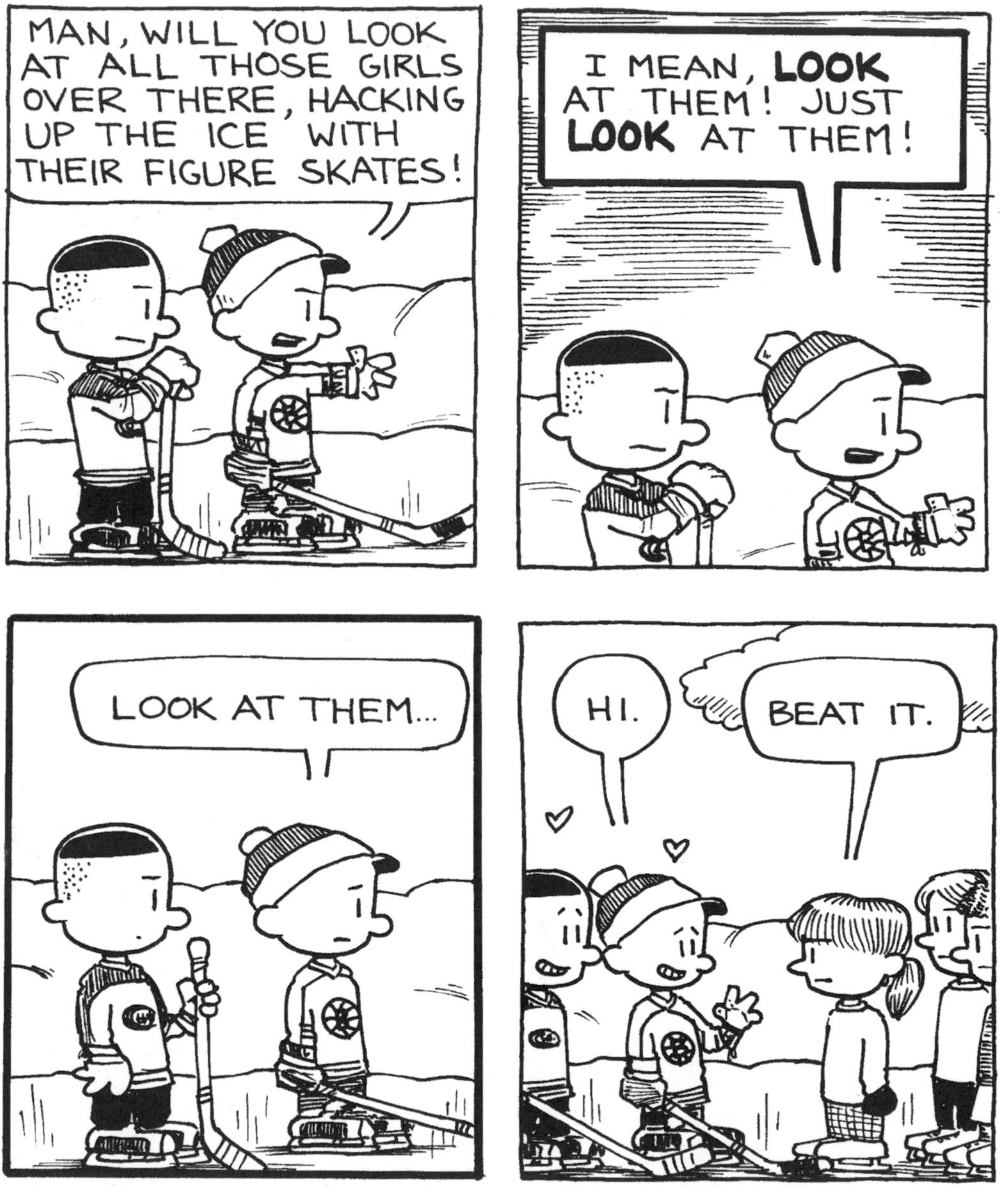
MAN, WILL YOU LOOK AT ALL THOSE GIRLS OVER THERE, HACKING UP THE ICE WITH THEIR FIGURE SKATES!
I MEAN, **LOOK** AT THEM! JUST **LOOK** AT THEM!
LOOK AT THEM...
HI.
BEAT IT.

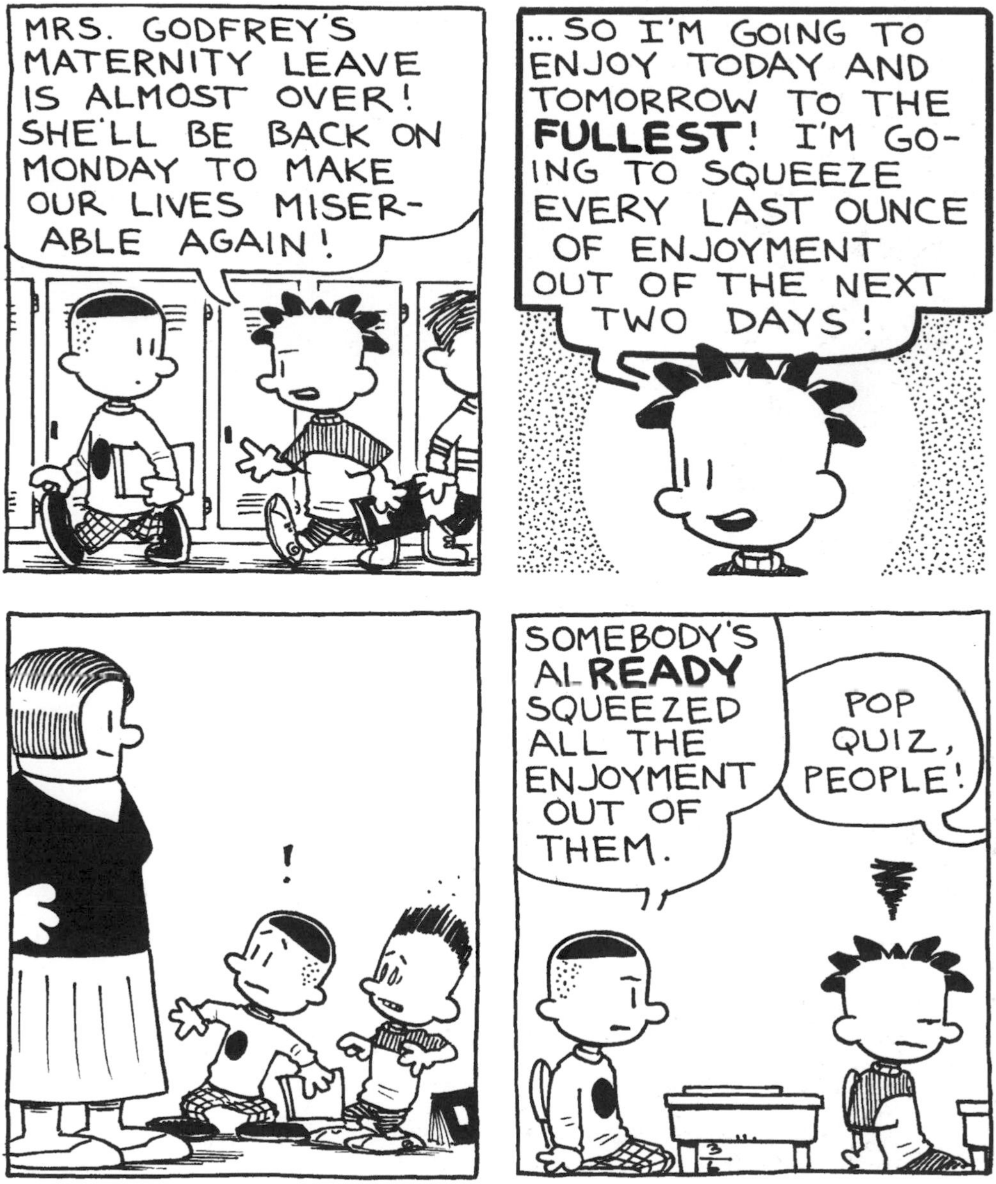
MRS. GODFREY'S MATERNITY LEAVE IS ALMOST OVER! SHE'LL BE BACK ON MONDAY TO MAKE OUR LIVES MISERABLE AGAIN!
...SO I'M GOING TO ENJOY TODAY AND TOMORROW TO THE **FULLEST**! I'M GOING TO SQUEEZE EVERY LAST OUNCE OF ENJOYMENT OUT OF THE NEXT TWO DAYS!
!
SOMEBODY'S AL**READY** SQUEEZED ALL THE ENJOYMENT OUT OF THEM.
POP QUIZ, PEOPLE!

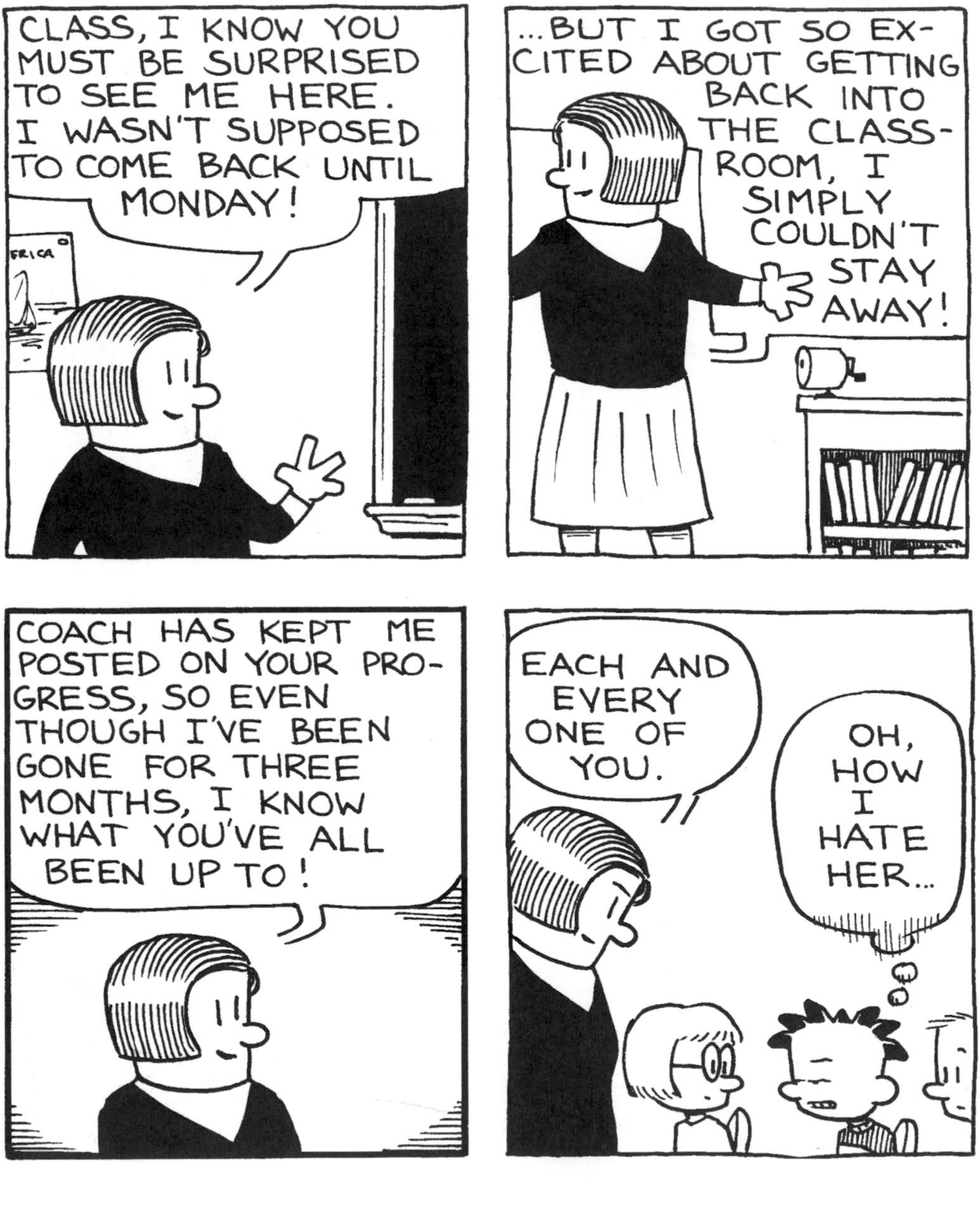
CLASS, I KNOW YOU MUST BE SURPRISED TO SEE ME HERE. I WASN'T SUPPOSED TO COME BACK UNTIL MONDAY!
...BUT I GOT SO EXCITED ABOUT GETTING BACK INTO THE CLASSROOM, I SIMPLY COULDN'T STAY AWAY!
COACH HAS KEPT ME POSTED ON YOUR PROGRESS, SO EVEN THOUGH I'VE BEEN GONE FOR THREE MONTHS, I KNOW WHAT YOU'VE ALL BEEN UP TO!
EACH AND EVERY ONE OF YOU.
OH, HOW I HATE HER...

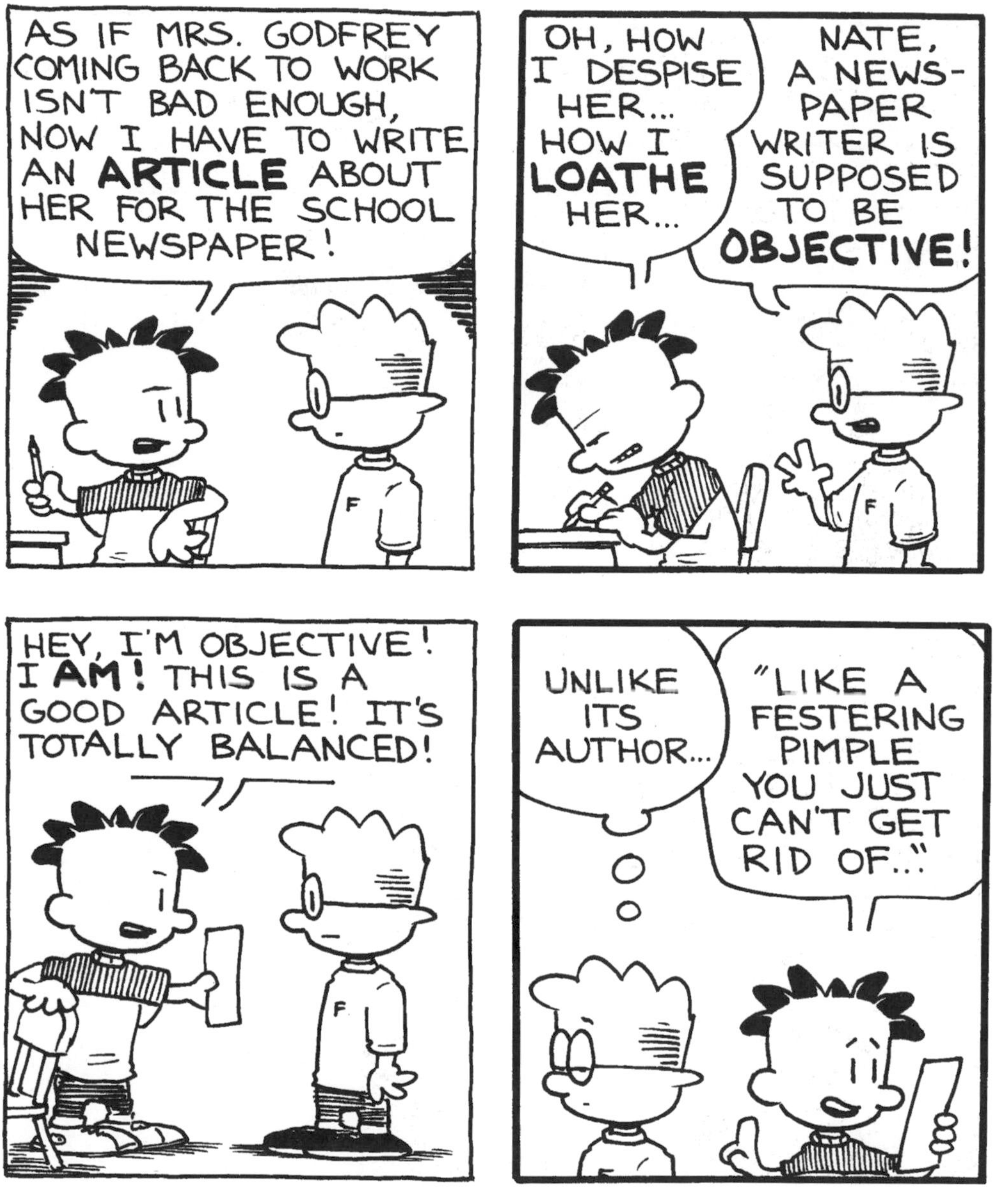
AS IF MRS. GODFREY COMING BACK TO WORK ISN'T BAD ENOUGH, NOW I HAVE TO WRITE AN **ARTICLE** ABOUT HER FOR THE SCHOOL NEWSPAPER!
OH, HOW I DESPISE HER... HOW I **LOATHE** HER...
NATE, A NEWSPAPER WRITER IS SUPPOSED TO BE **OBJECTIVE!**
HEY, I'M OBJECTIVE! I **AM!** THIS IS A GOOD ARTICLE! IT'S TOTALLY BALANCED!
UNLIKE ITS AUTHOR...
"LIKE A FESTERING PIMPLE YOU JUST CAN'T GET RID OF..."

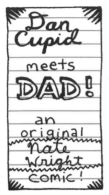

Dan Cupid meets **DAD!** an original *Nate Wright* comic!

Greetings, fellow fat bald guy!

Gawrsh! Dan Cupid!

You've been alone long enough, Dad! Let me pierce you with one of my "love darts"!

ka sproing!

NOW I'll go find a woman, hit HER with a dart, and BINGO! Instant romance!

Oh, THERE you are, Dan!

What's up, gang?

We're all headed over to Cloud Nine!

Yeah! There's a big party!

Ooh! I'm there!

HOURS LATER...

Come on, Dan! We're flying over to Hollywood to find a gal for Keanu Reeves!

Hmm...

What's wrong, Dan?

I just can't shake the feeling that I'm FORGETTING something!

COME HERE OFTEN?

GET LOST.

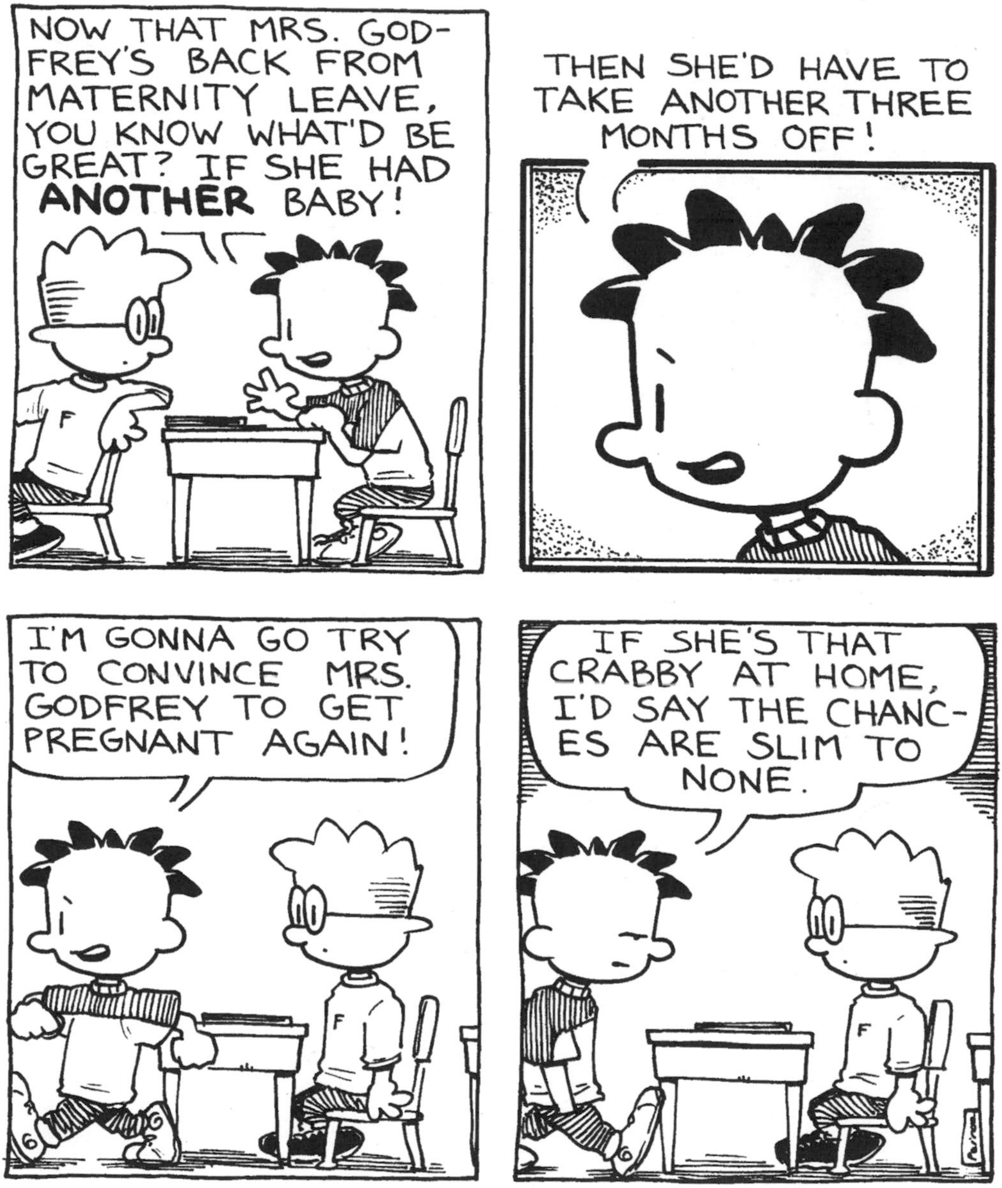
NOW THAT MRS. GODFREY'S BACK FROM MATERNITY LEAVE, YOU KNOW WHAT'D BE GREAT? IF SHE HAD **ANOTHER** BABY!
THEN SHE'D HAVE TO TAKE ANOTHER THREE MONTHS OFF!
I'M GONNA GO TRY TO CONVINCE MRS. GODFREY TO GET PREGNANT AGAIN!
IF SHE'S THAT CRABBY AT HOME, I'D SAY THE CHANCES ARE SLIM TO NONE.

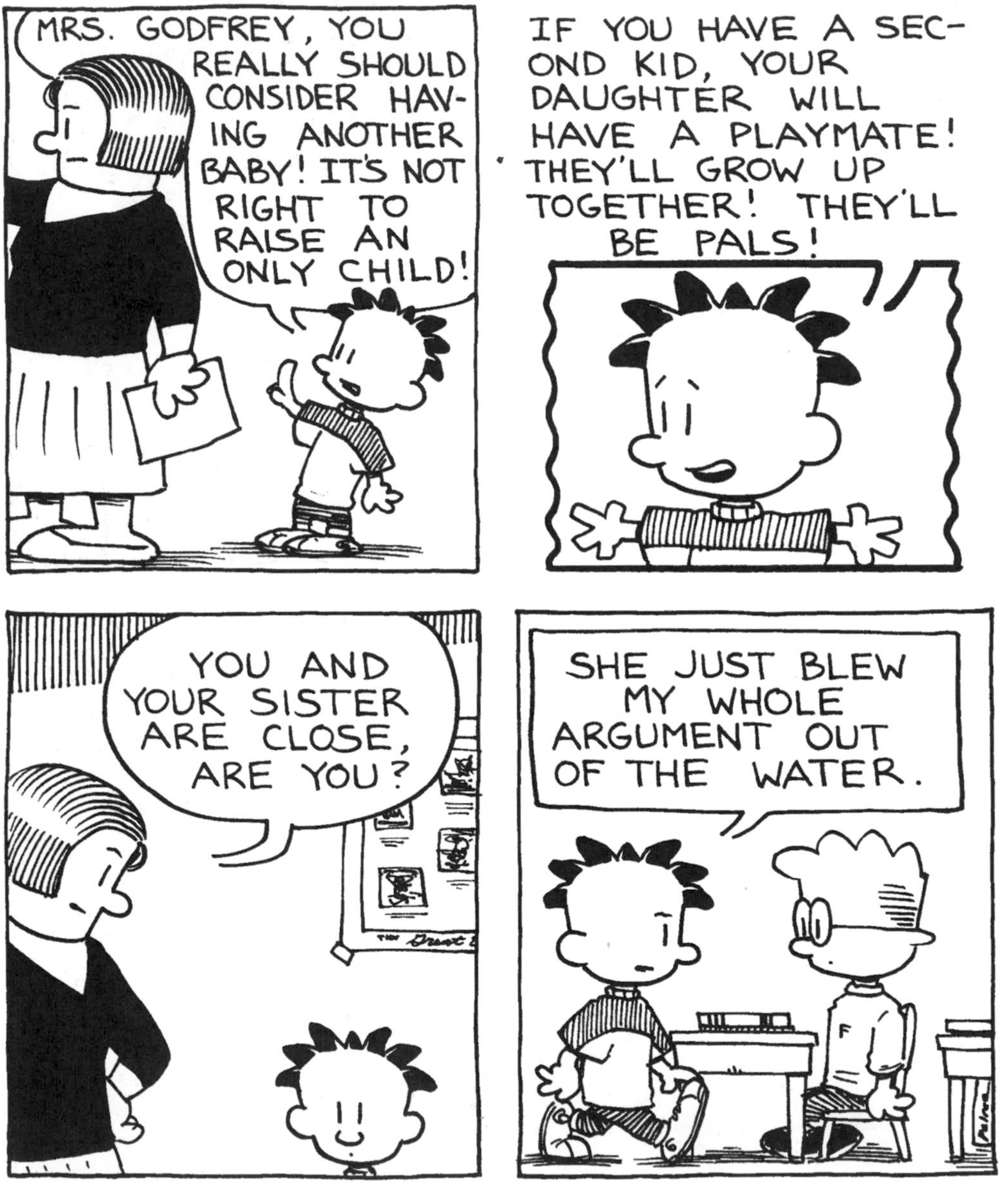
MRS. GODFREY, YOU REALLY SHOULD CONSIDER HAVING ANOTHER BABY! IT'S NOT RIGHT TO RAISE AN ONLY CHILD!
IF YOU HAVE A SECOND KID, YOUR DAUGHTER WILL HAVE A PLAYMATE! THEY'LL GROW UP TOGETHER! THEY'LL BE PALS!
YOU AND YOUR SISTER ARE CLOSE, ARE YOU?
SHE JUST BLEW MY WHOLE ARGUMENT OUT OF THE WATER.

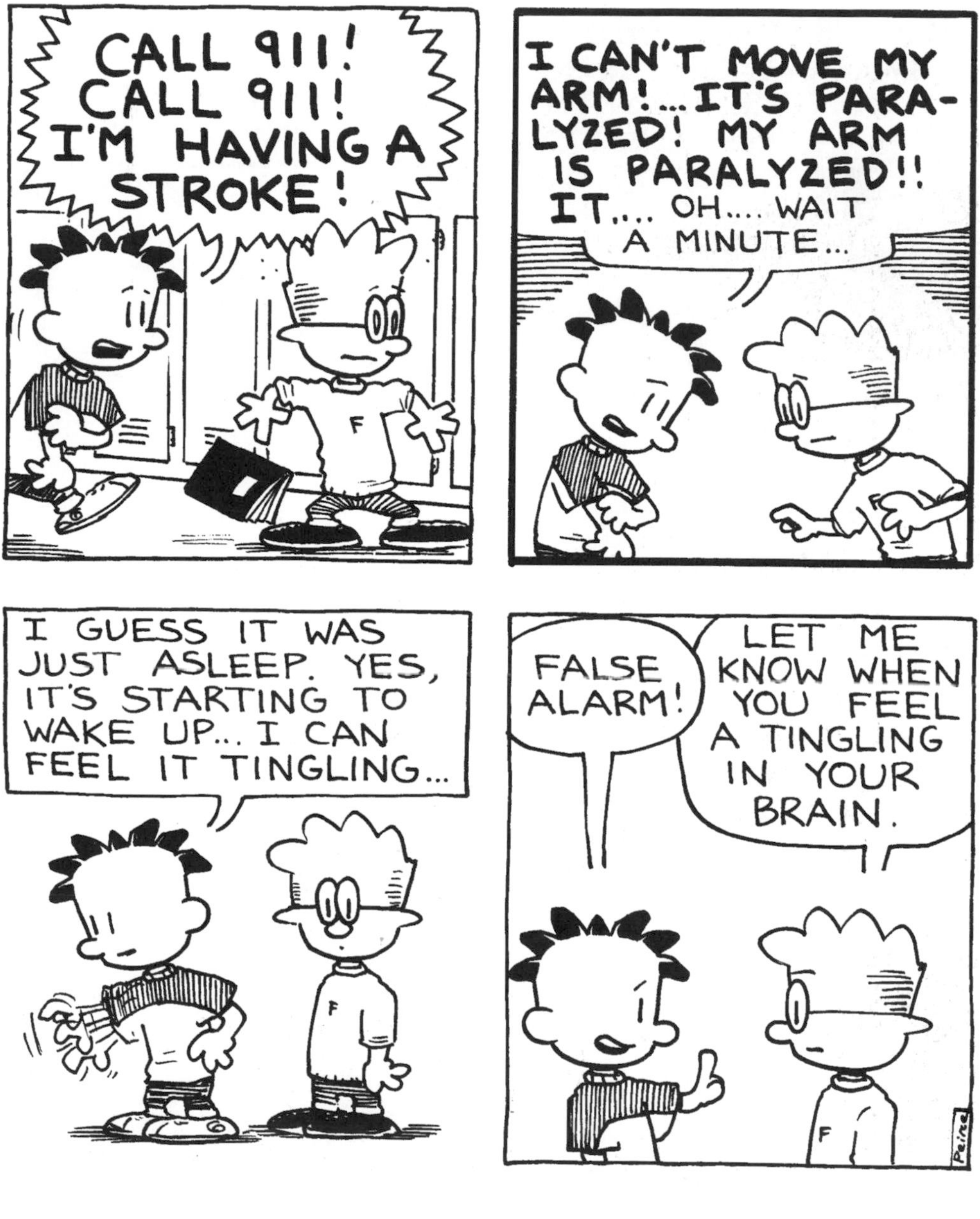
CALL 911! CALL 911! I'M HAVING A STROKE!
I CAN'T MOVE MY ARM!... IT'S PARALYZED! MY ARM IS PARALYZED!! IT.... OH.... WAIT A MINUTE...
I GUESS IT WAS JUST ASLEEP. YES, IT'S STARTING TO WAKE UP... I CAN FEEL IT TINGLING...
FALSE ALARM!
LET ME KNOW WHEN YOU FEEL A TINGLING IN YOUR BRAIN.
Peirce

...SO WHEN WE CONVERT FROM FRACTIONS, WHAT DO WE COME UP WITH? 1.333!
IF WE CONTINUED TO DO THE DIVISION, THOSE THREES WOULD GO TO INFINITY!
DO WE ALL UNDERSTAND THE CONCEPT OF INFINITY? OF SOMETHING THAT GOES ON AND ON FOREVER?
OOOOOOOOOH, YEAH.

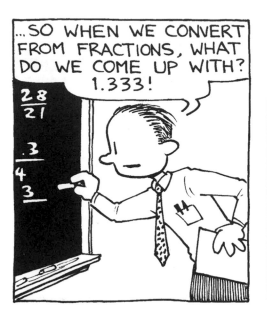

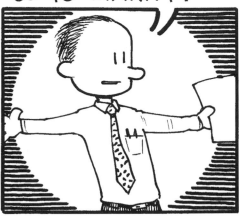

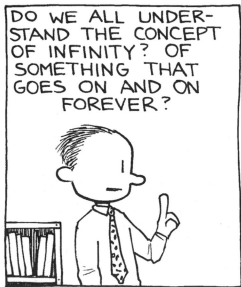

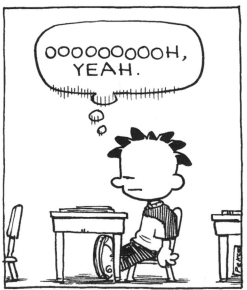

YOU MAY HAVE THE HIGHEST IQ IN THE CLASS, FRANCIS, BUT I AM A TRUE GENIUS!
REMEMBER WHAT EINSTEIN SAID: GENIUS IS 1% INSPIRATION AND 99% PERSPIRATION!
I THINK IT WAS EDISON WHO SAID THAT, ACTUALLY.
EDISON, EINSTEIN... WHAT'S THE DIFFERENCE? THEY'RE BOTH DEAD INVENTORS, RIGHT?
NOW HAND ME THAT DOO-HICKEY.
NO SWEAT.
Peirce

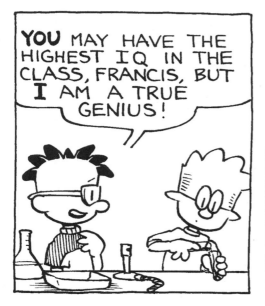

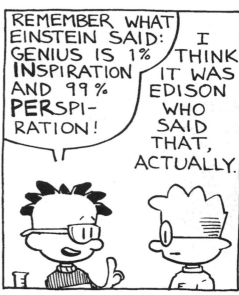

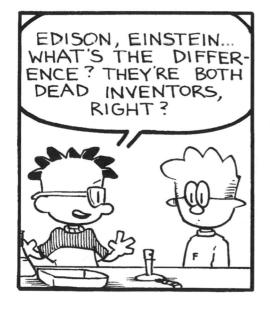

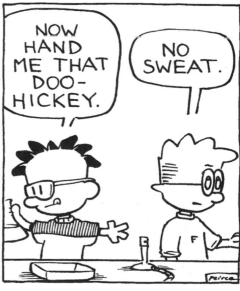

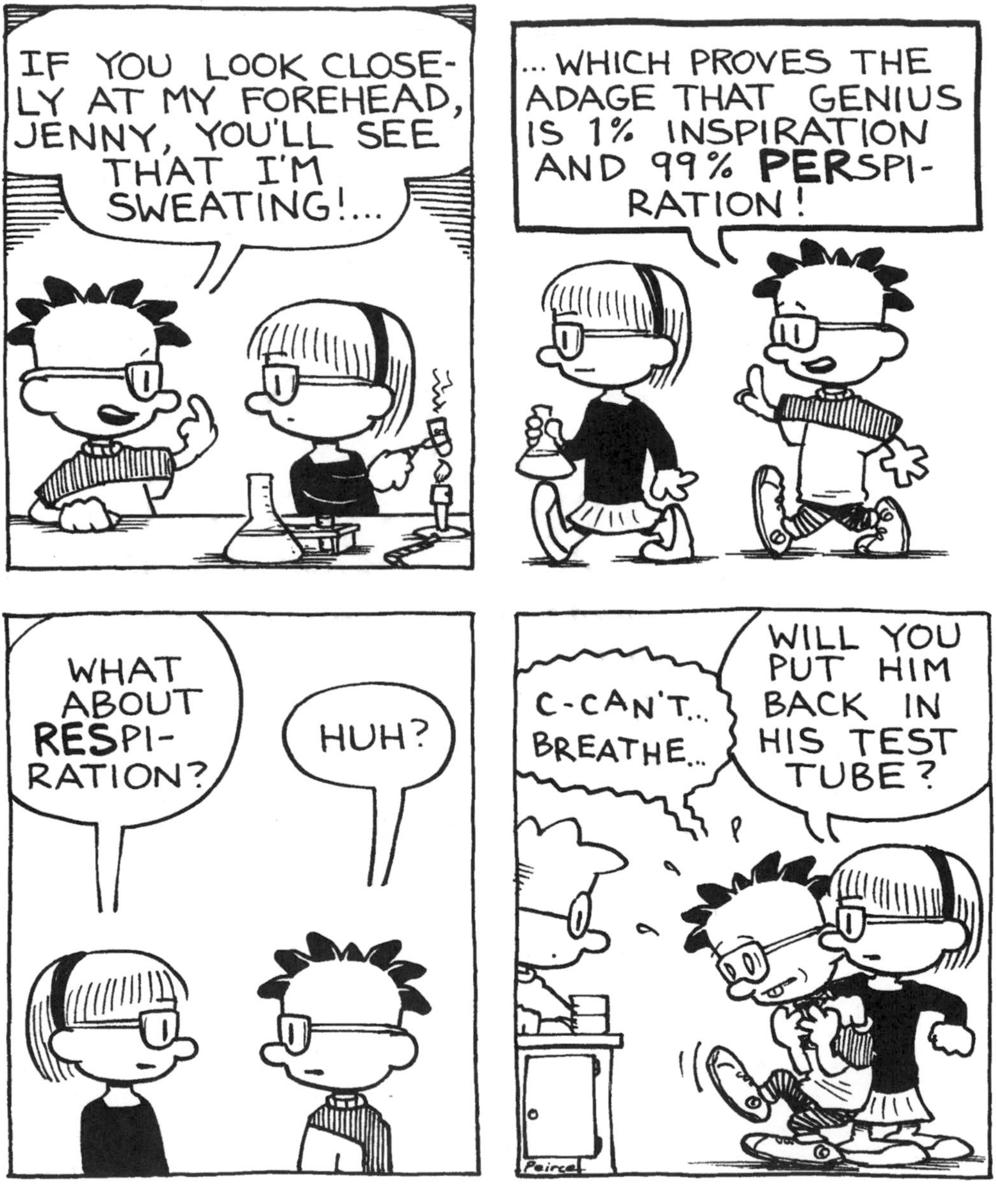
IF YOU LOOK CLOSE-LY AT MY FOREHEAD, JENNY, YOU'LL SEE THAT I'M SWEATING!...
...WHICH PROVES THE ADAGE THAT GENIUS IS 1% INSPIRATION AND 99% **PER**SPI-RATION!
WHAT ABOUT **RES**PI-RATION?
HUH?
C-CAN'T... BREATHE...
WILL YOU PUT HIM BACK IN HIS TEST TUBE?
Peirce

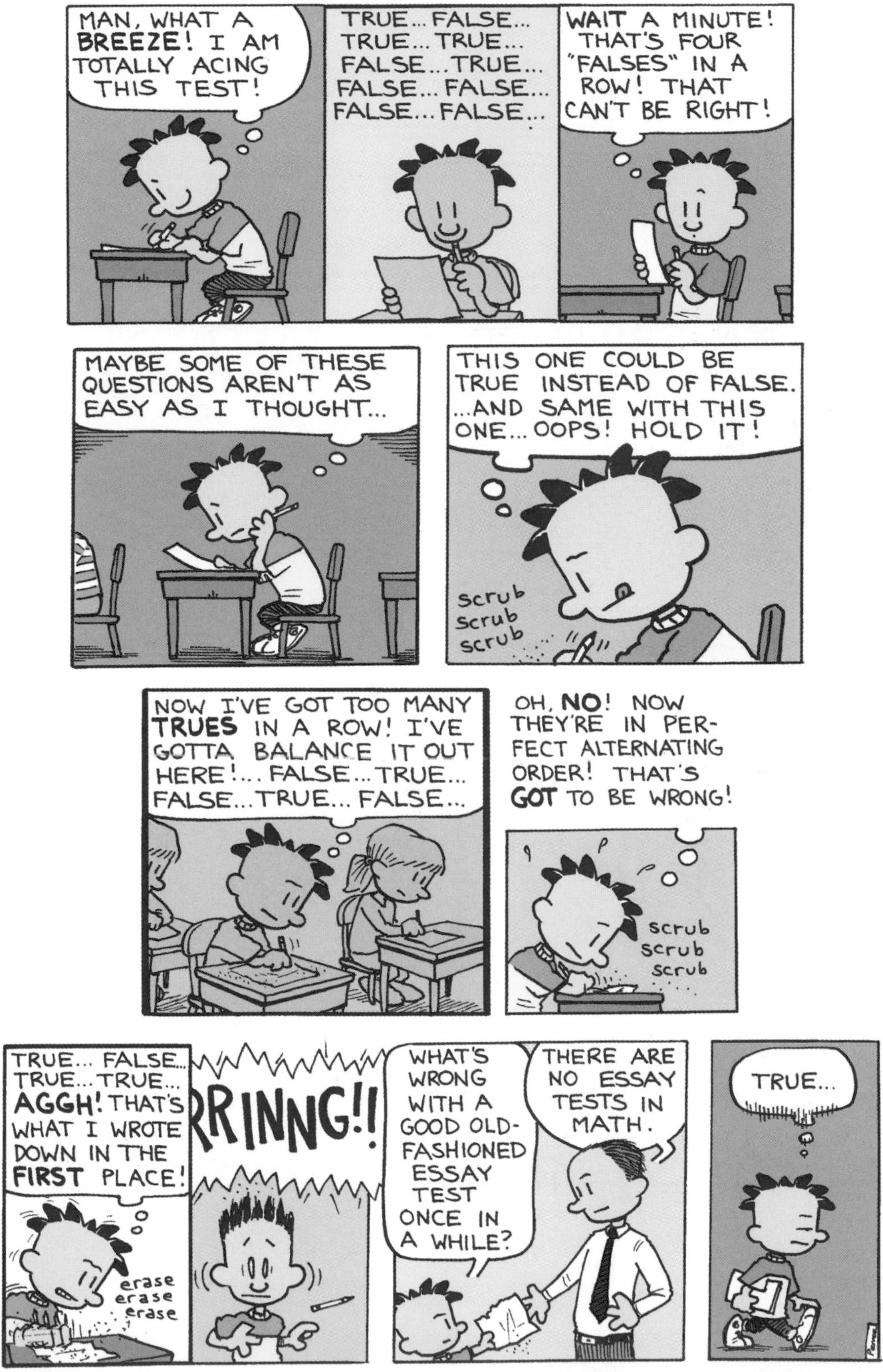

MAN, WHAT A BREEZE! I AM TOTALLY ACING THIS TEST!
TRUE... FALSE... TRUE... TRUE... FALSE... TRUE... FALSE... FALSE... FALSE... FALSE...
WAIT A MINUTE! THAT'S FOUR "FALSES" IN A ROW! THAT CAN'T BE RIGHT!
MAYBE SOME OF THESE QUESTIONS AREN'T AS EASY AS I THOUGHT...
THIS ONE COULD BE TRUE INSTEAD OF FALSE. ...AND SAME WITH THIS ONE... OOPS! HOLD IT!
scrub scrub scrub
NOW I'VE GOT TOO MANY TRUES IN A ROW! I'VE GOTTA BALANCE IT OUT HERE!... FALSE... TRUE... FALSE... TRUE... FALSE...
OH, NO! NOW THEY'RE IN PERFECT ALTERNATING ORDER! THAT'S GOT TO BE WRONG!
scrub scrub scrub
TRUE... FALSE... TRUE... TRUE... AGGH! THAT'S WHAT I WROTE DOWN IN THE FIRST PLACE!
erase erase erase
RRINNG!!
WHAT'S WRONG WITH A GOOD OLD-FASHIONED ESSAY TEST ONCE IN A WHILE?
THERE ARE NO ESSAY TESTS IN MATH.
TRUE...

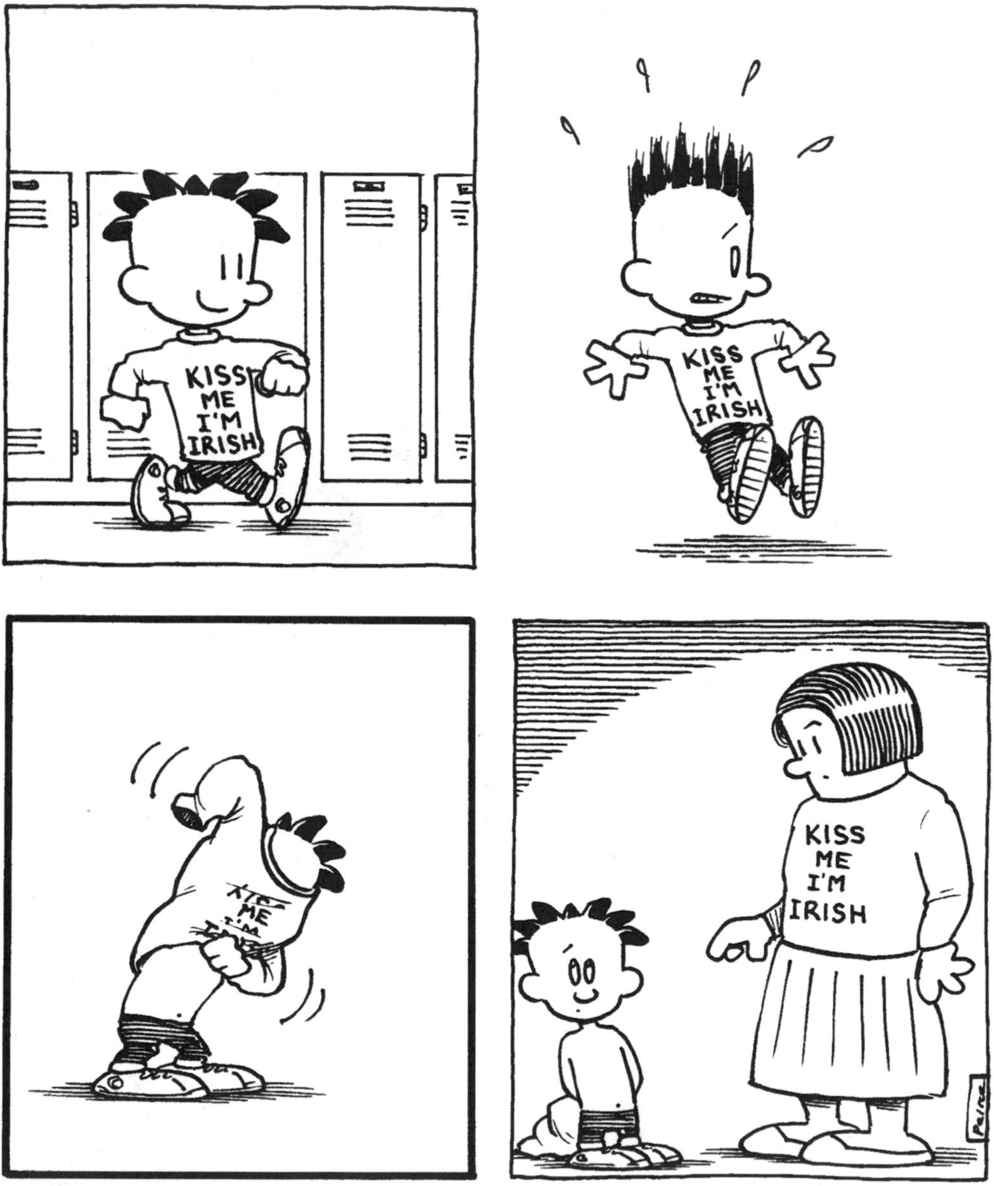
KISS ME I'M IRISH
KISS ME I'M IRISH
ME
KISS ME I'M IRISH

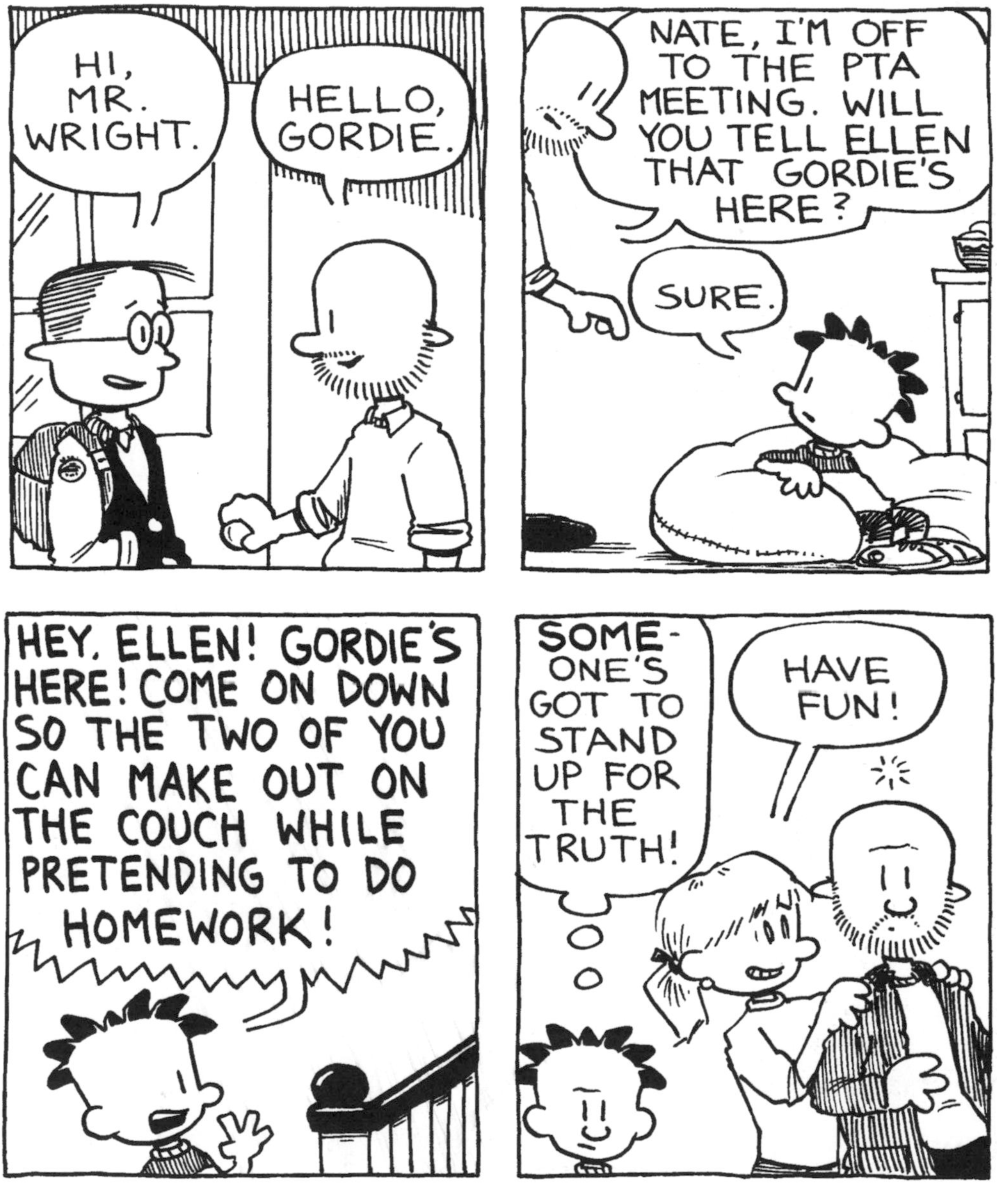

HI, MR. WRIGHT.
HELLO, GORDIE.
NATE, I'M OFF TO THE PTA MEETING. WILL YOU TELL ELLEN THAT GORDIE'S HERE?
SURE.
HEY, ELLEN! GORDIE'S HERE! COME ON DOWN SO THE TWO OF YOU CAN MAKE OUT ON THE COUCH WHILE PRETENDING TO DO HOMEWORK!
SOMEONE'S GOT TO STAND UP FOR THE TRUTH!
HAVE FUN!

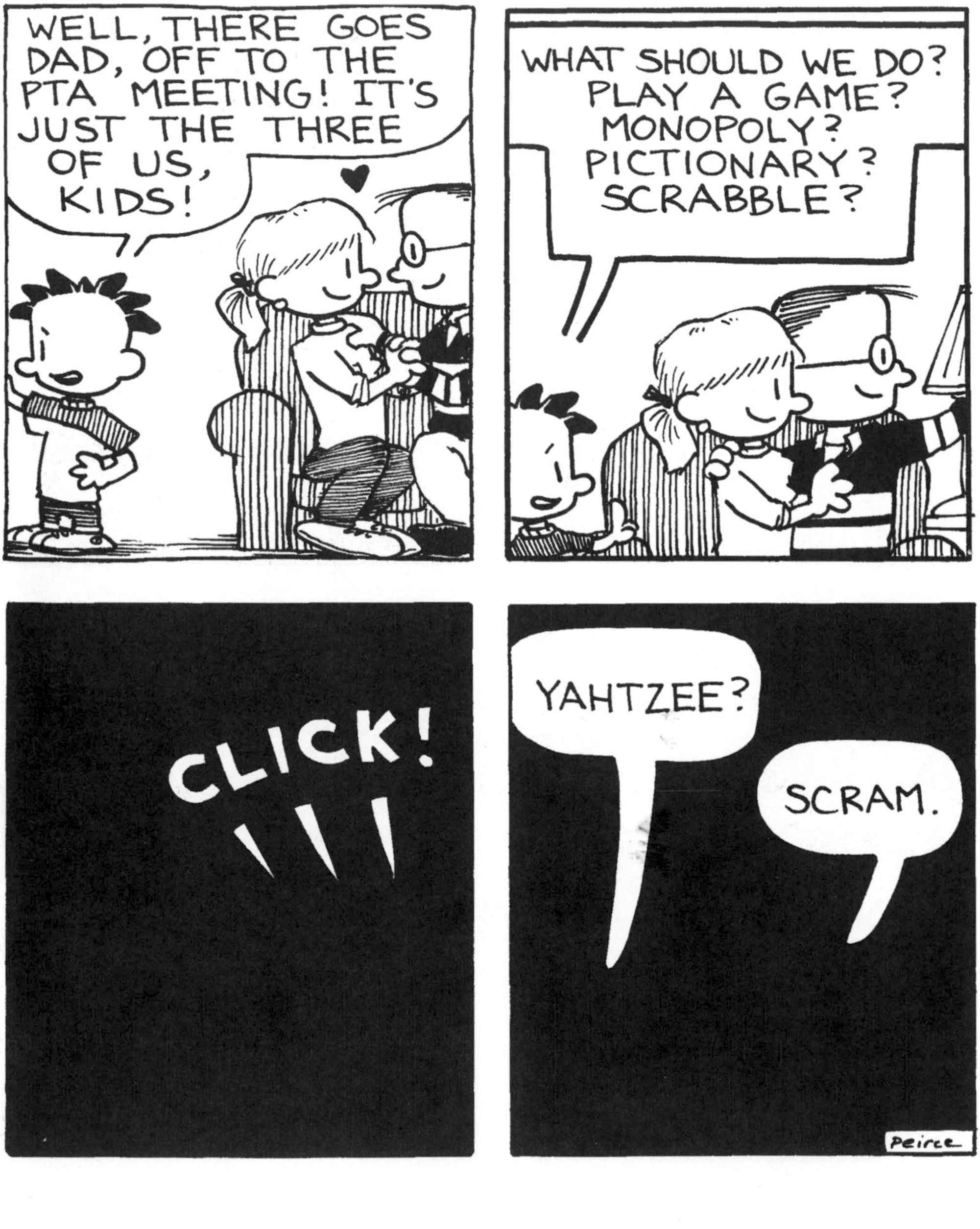
WELL, THERE GOES DAD, OFF TO THE PTA MEETING! IT'S JUST THE THREE OF US, KIDS!
WHAT SHOULD WE DO? PLAY A GAME? MONOPOLY? PICTIONARY? SCRABBLE?
CLICK!
YAHTZEE?
SCRAM.
Peirce

HELLO?
TEDDY! LISTEN TO THIS!
SMAK!... ♥ SMOOOCH! SMAK!... SMAK!
SMOOCH!... ♥ SMAK! ♥ SLURP! SMAK!
YOU SEE WHAT I HAVE TO PUT UP WITH?
HEY!

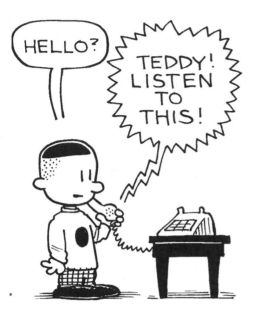

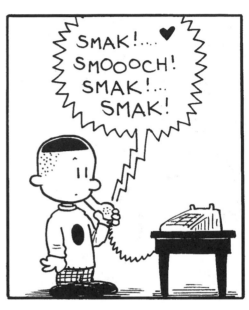

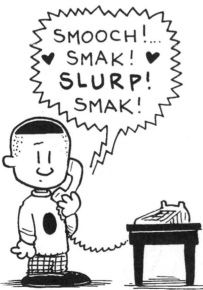

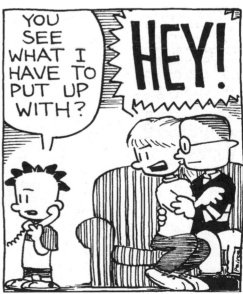

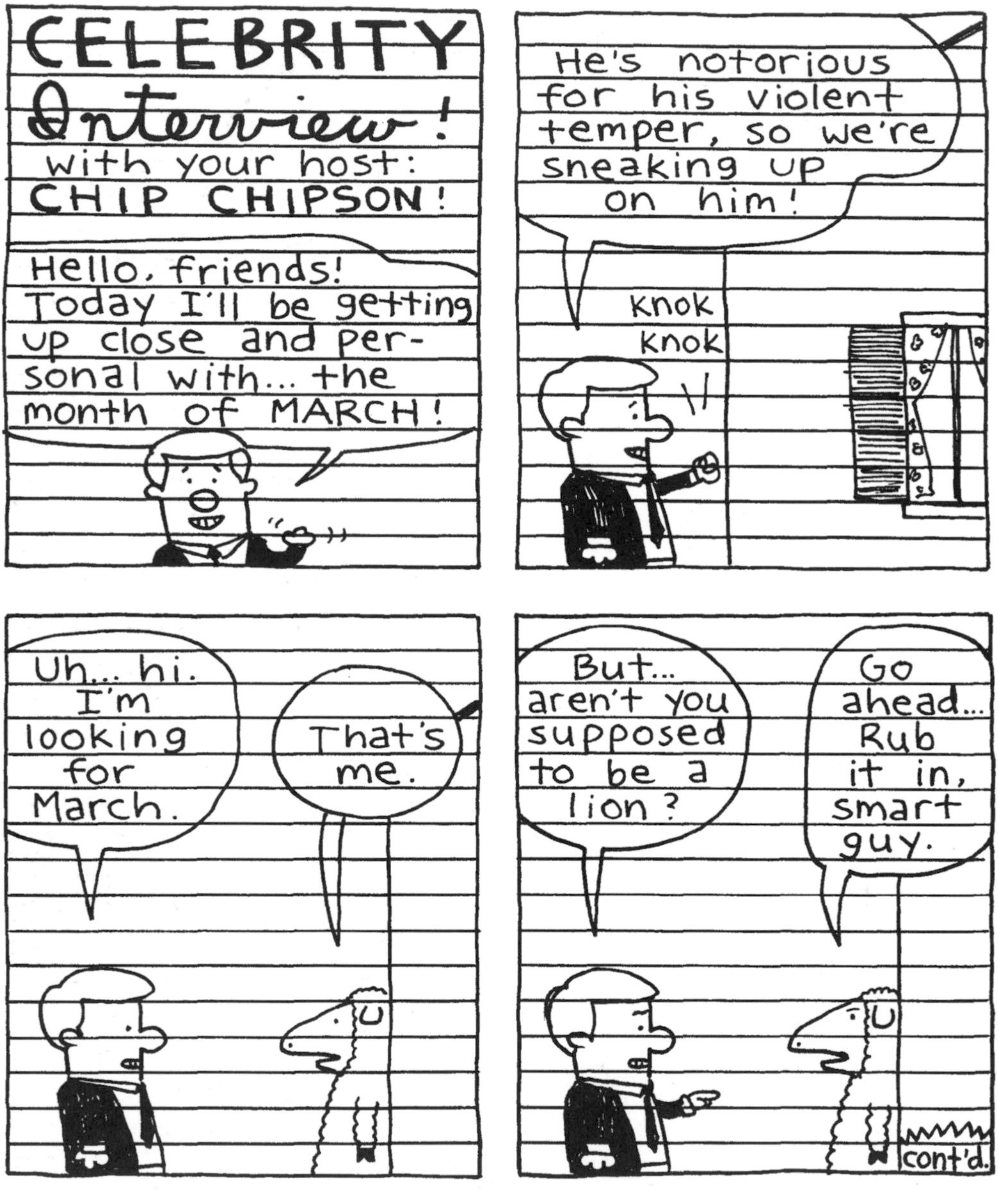
CELEBRITY Interview!
with your host: CHIP CHIPSON!
Hello, friends! Today I'll be getting up close and personal with... the month of MARCH!
He's notorious for his violent temper, so we're sneaking up on him!
KNOK KNOK
Uh... hi. I'm looking for March.
That's me.
But... aren't you supposed to be a lion?
Go ahead... Rub it in, smart guy.
cont'd.

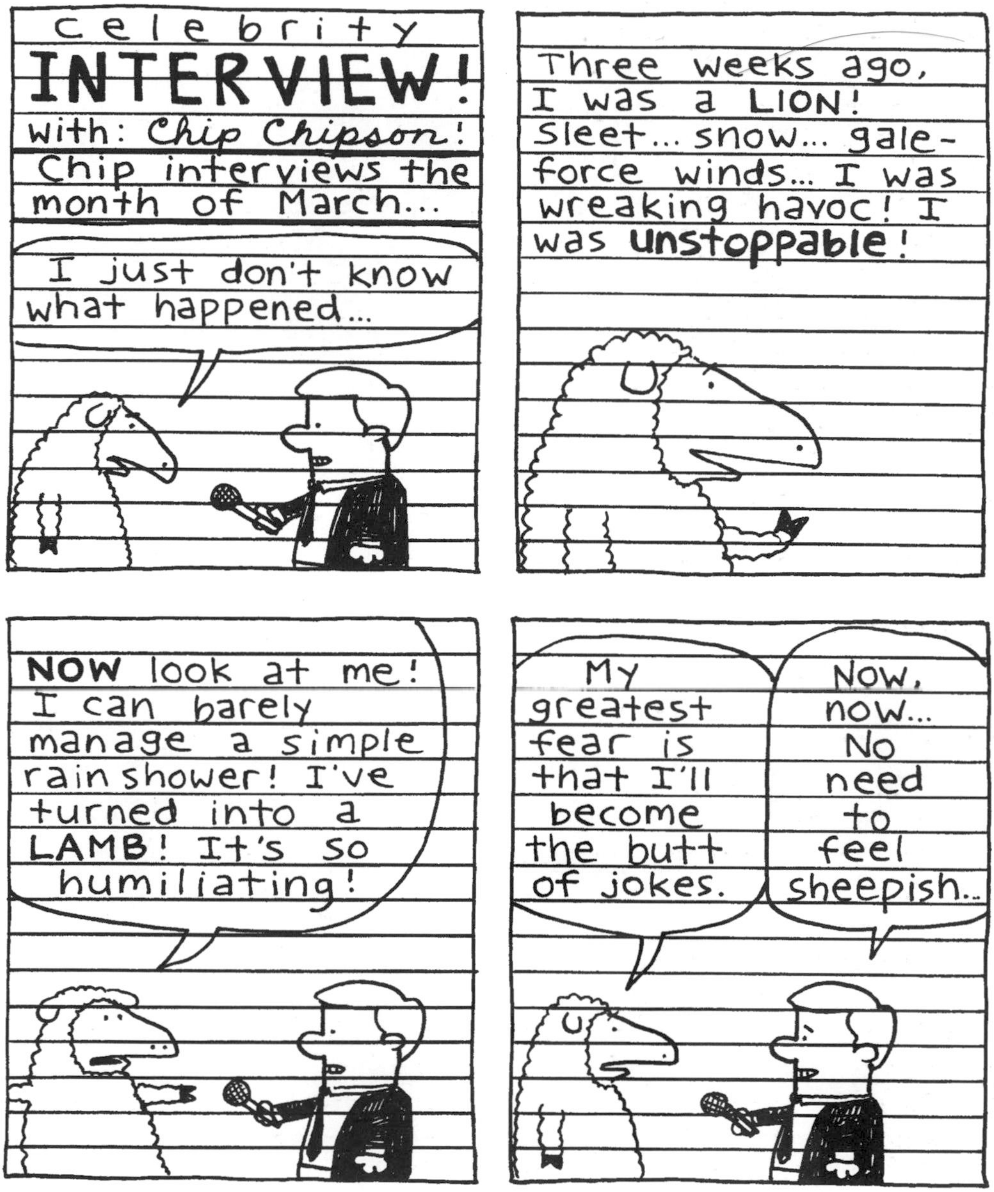

celebrity
INTERVIEW!
with: Chip Chipson!
Chip interviews the month of March...
I just don't know what happened...
Three weeks ago, I was a LION! Sleet... snow... gale-force winds... I was wreaking havoc! I was unstoppable!
NOW look at me! I can barely manage a simple rainshower! I've turned into a LAMB! It's so humiliating!
My greatest fear is that I'll become the butt of jokes.
Now, now... No need to feel sheepish...

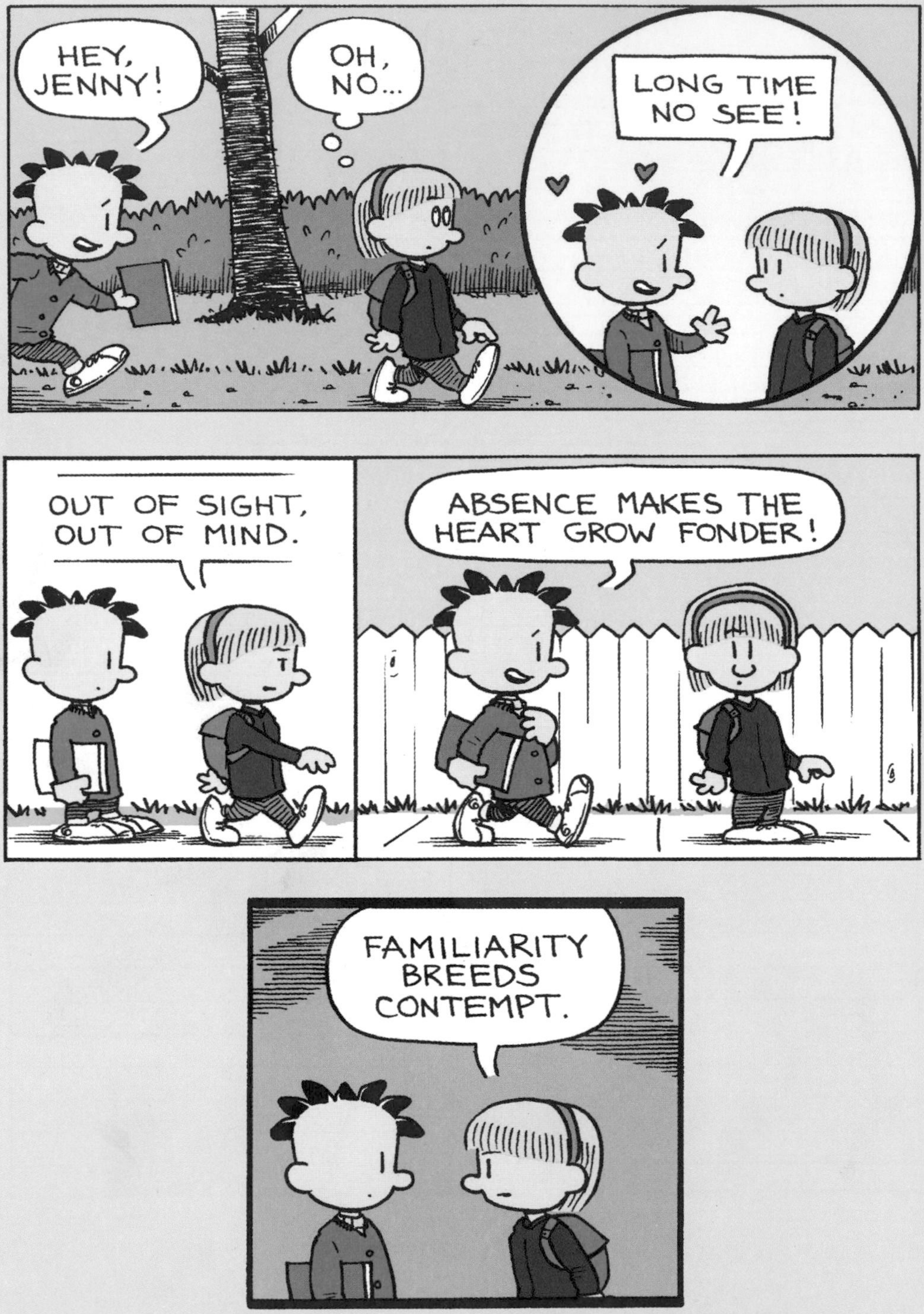
HEY, JENNY!
OH, NO...
LONG TIME NO SEE!
OUT OF SIGHT, OUT OF MIND.
ABSENCE MAKES THE HEART GROW FONDER!
FAMILIARITY BREEDS CONTEMPT.

IT'S A FINE LINE BETWEEN LOVE AND HATE!
WAKE UP AND SMELL THE COFFEE.
SHE OUT-CLICHÉD ME.
C'EST LA VIE.
Peirce

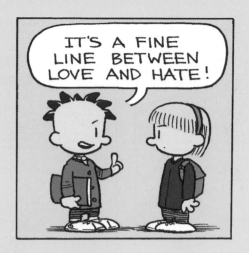

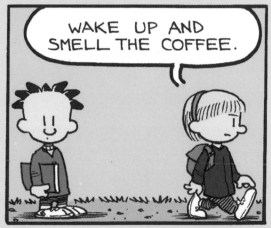

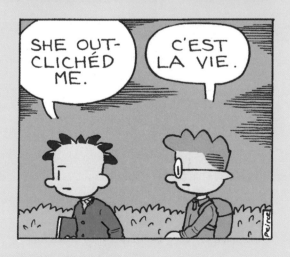

WRITE A POEM ABOUT **LOVE**? WHAT KIND OF LAME WRITING ASSIGNMENT IS **THIS**?
I THINK IT'S COOL!
BUT WHO AM I SUPPOSED TO WRITE ABOUT?
HEY, YOU DON'T HAVE TO WRITE ABOUT A PERSON! YOU CAN LOVE A TV SHOW!... YOU CAN LOVE A SPORT!...
YOU CAN LOVE A **FOOD**!
"ODE TO A CHEEZ DOODLE" BY NATE WRIGHT.
CRUNCH!
LEAVE US. I NEED TO BE ALONE WITH MY MUSE.
PEIRCE

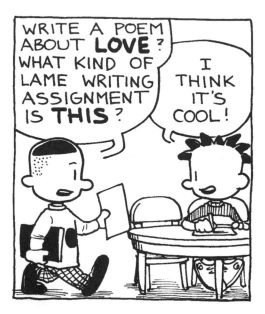

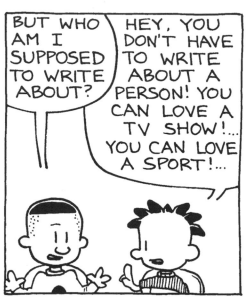

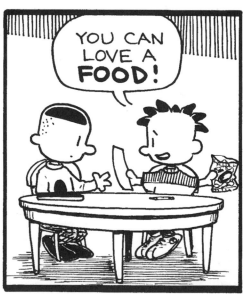

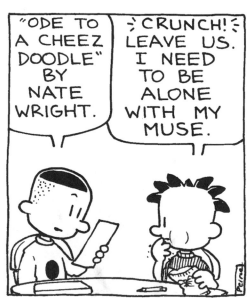

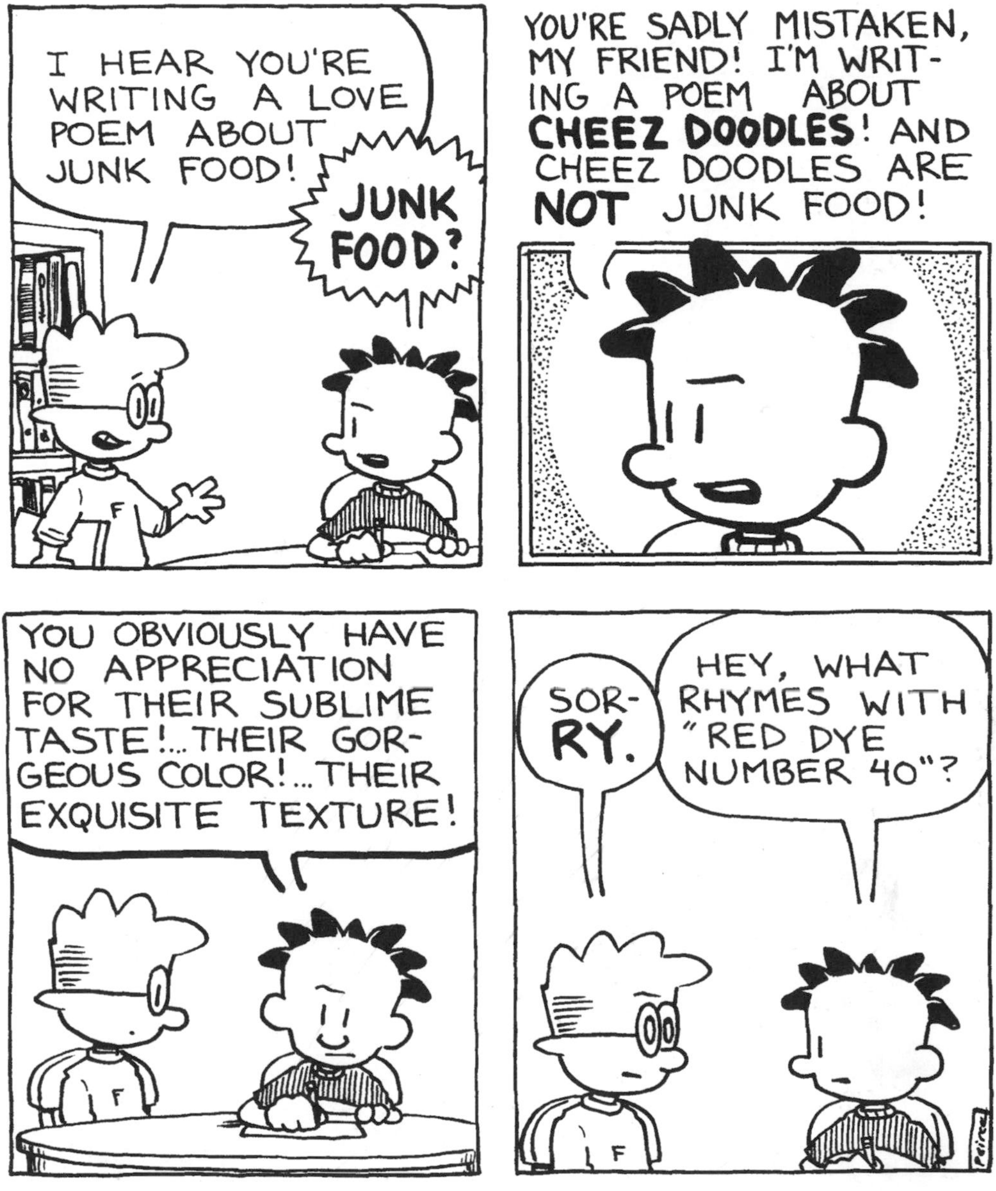
I HEAR YOU'RE WRITING A LOVE POEM ABOUT JUNK FOOD!
JUNK FOOD?
YOU'RE SADLY MISTAKEN, MY FRIEND! I'M WRITING A POEM ABOUT **CHEEZ DOODLES**! AND CHEEZ DOODLES ARE **NOT** JUNK FOOD!
YOU OBVIOUSLY HAVE NO APPRECIATION FOR THEIR SUBLIME TASTE!...THEIR GORGEOUS COLOR!...THEIR EXQUISITE TEXTURE!
SOR-**RY.**
HEY, WHAT RHYMES WITH "RED DYE NUMBER 40"?
Peirce

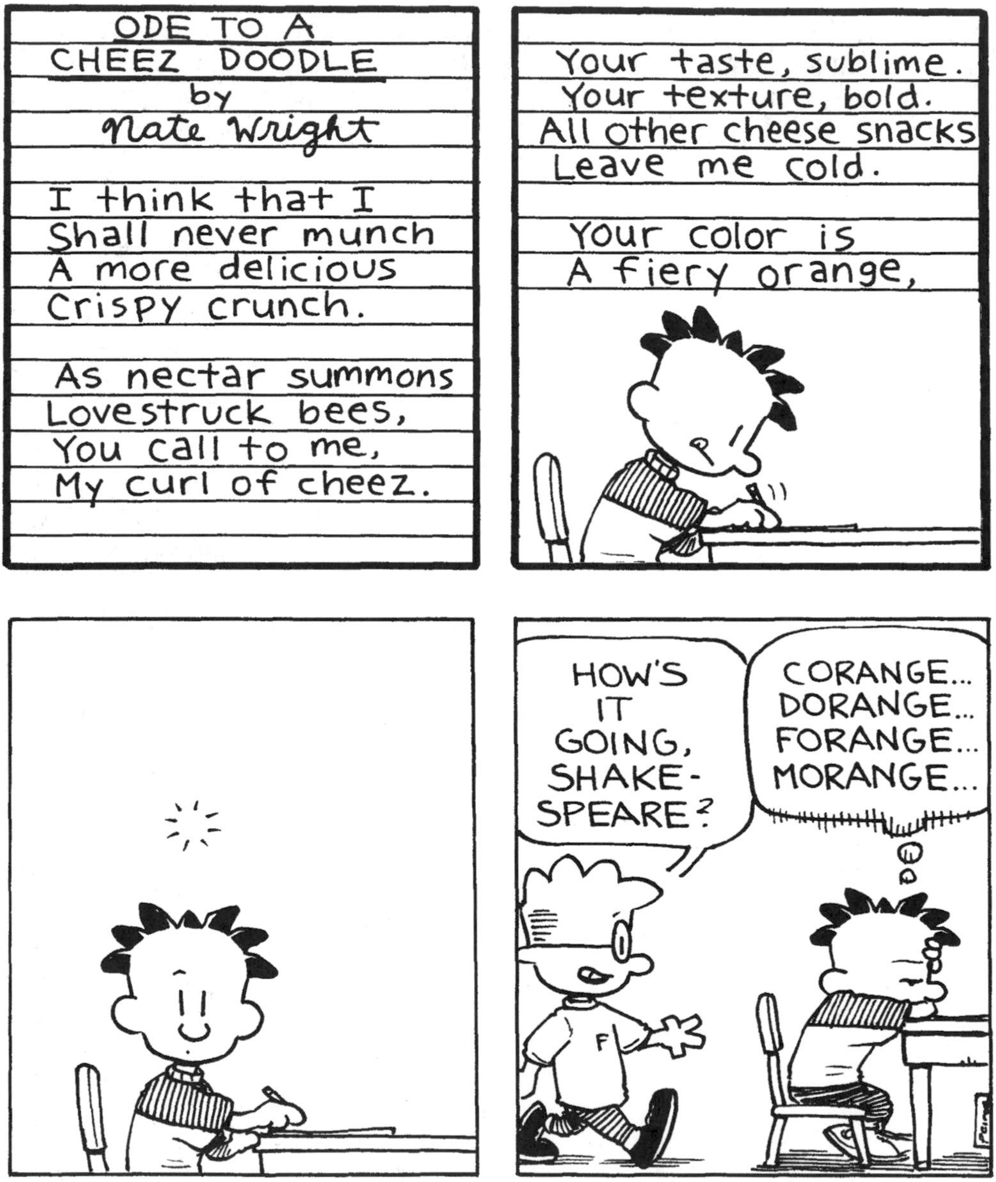
ODE TO A CHEEZ DOODLE
by
Nate Wright
I think that I
Shall never munch
A more delicious
Crispy crunch.
As nectar summons
Lovestruck bees,
You call to me,
My curl of cheez.
Your taste, sublime.
Your texture, bold.
All other cheese snacks
Leave me cold.
Your color is
A fiery orange,
HOW'S IT GOING, SHAKE-SPEARE?
CORANGE... DORANGE... FORANGE... MORANGE...

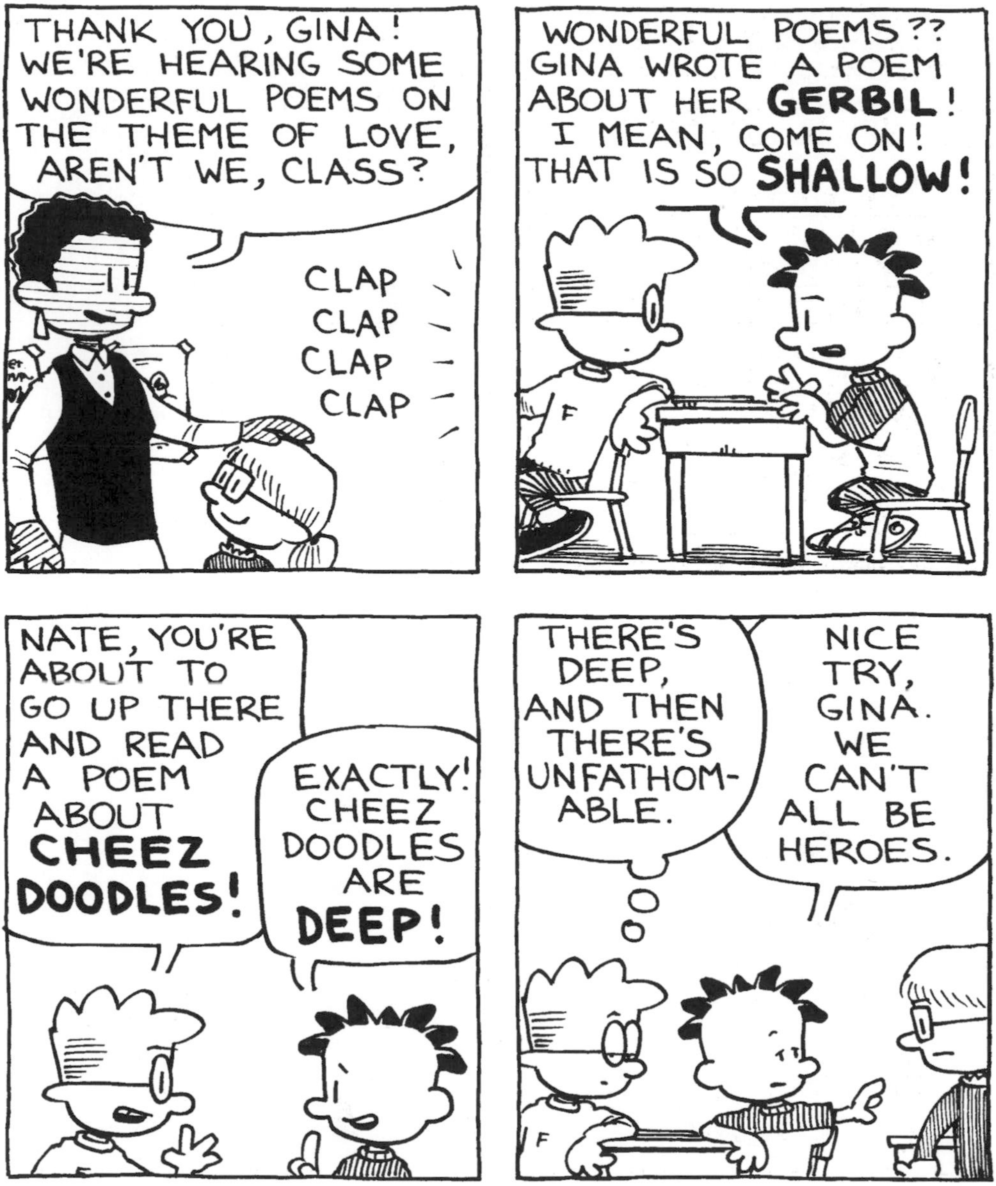
THANK YOU, GINA! WE'RE HEARING SOME WONDERFUL POEMS ON THE THEME OF LOVE, AREN'T WE, CLASS?
CLAP CLAP CLAP CLAP
WONDERFUL POEMS?? GINA WROTE A POEM ABOUT HER GERBIL! I MEAN, COME ON! THAT IS SO SHALLOW!
NATE, YOU'RE ABOUT TO GO UP THERE AND READ A POEM ABOUT CHEEZ DOODLES!
EXACTLY! CHEEZ DOODLES ARE DEEP!
THERE'S DEEP, AND THEN THERE'S UNFATHOM-ABLE.
NICE TRY, GINA. WE CAN'T ALL BE HEROES.

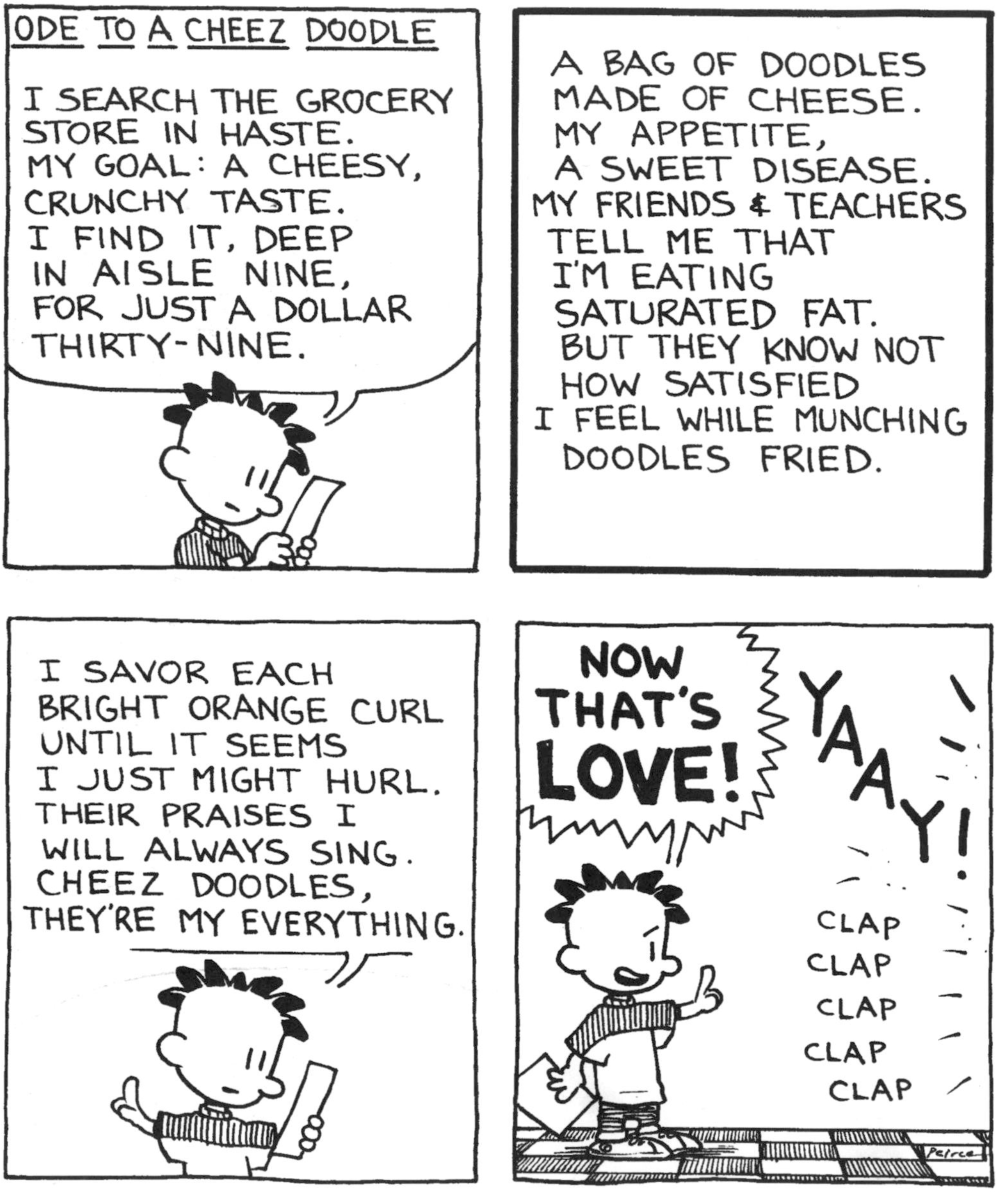
ODE TO A CHEEZ DOODLE
I SEARCH THE GROCERY STORE IN HASTE. MY GOAL: A CHEESY, CRUNCHY TASTE. I FIND IT, DEEP IN AISLE NINE, FOR JUST A DOLLAR THIRTY-NINE.
A BAG OF DOODLES MADE OF CHEESE. MY APPETITE, A SWEET DISEASE. MY FRIENDS & TEACHERS TELL ME THAT I'M EATING SATURATED FAT. BUT THEY KNOW NOT HOW SATISFIED I FEEL WHILE MUNCHING DOODLES FRIED.
I SAVOR EACH BRIGHT ORANGE CURL UNTIL IT SEEMS I JUST MIGHT HURL. THEIR PRAISES I WILL ALWAYS SING. CHEEZ DOODLES, THEY'RE MY EVERYTHING.
NOW THAT'S LOVE!
YAAAY!
CLAP
CLAP
CLAP
CLAP
CLAP
Peirce

MISS CLARKE! HOW COME I ONLY GOT A **B** ON MY CHEEZ DOODLE POEM?

I LIKED YOUR POEM A LOT, NATE... BUT YOUR ORAL PRESENTATION COULD HAVE BEEN BETTER.

YOU MUMBLED QUITE A BIT...

BUT I COULDN'T HELP IT! I HAD A MOUTH FULL OF CHEEZ DOODLES!

...WHICH BRINGS US TO THE ISSUE OF YOUR ORANGE TEETH...

I KNOW! ISN'T THAT A COOL SIDE EFFECT?

CELEB-
RITY
Chat!

with your
host:
BIFF
BIFFWELL!

Hello again, friends! I'm here with today's VERY special guest... HOPSY the Easter Bunny! Hi, Hopsy!

You the man, Biff.

Hopsy, you've been hiding Easter eggs professionally for YEARS! What's the secret of your success?

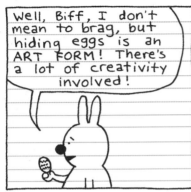

Well, Biff, I don't mean to brag, but hiding eggs is an ART FORM! There's a lot of creativity involved!

You want to hide the eggs in unique locations!... Places where folks wouldn't think to look!

It's no fun for people if they find the eggs too EASILY! You've got to make them WORK a little bit!

So the object is to provide people with a challenge?

That's ONE object. Occasionally I DO have another agenda.

And that would be?

Comic relief!

SPLURCH!

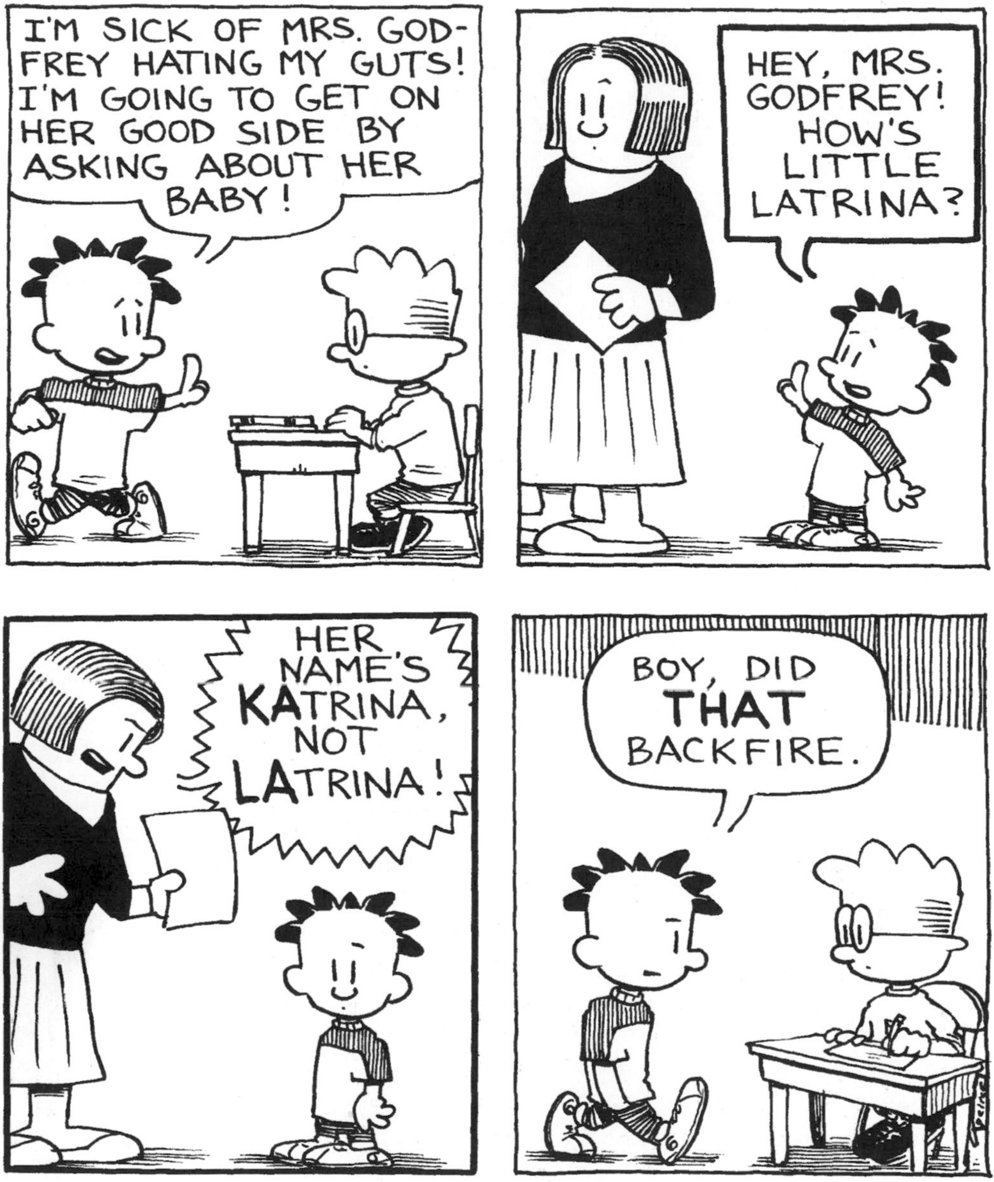
I'M SICK OF MRS. GODFREY HATING MY GUTS! I'M GOING TO GET ON HER GOOD SIDE BY ASKING ABOUT HER BABY!
HEY, MRS. GODFREY! HOW'S LITTLE LATRINA?
HER NAME'S KATRINA, NOT LATRINA!
BOY, DID THAT BACKFIRE.

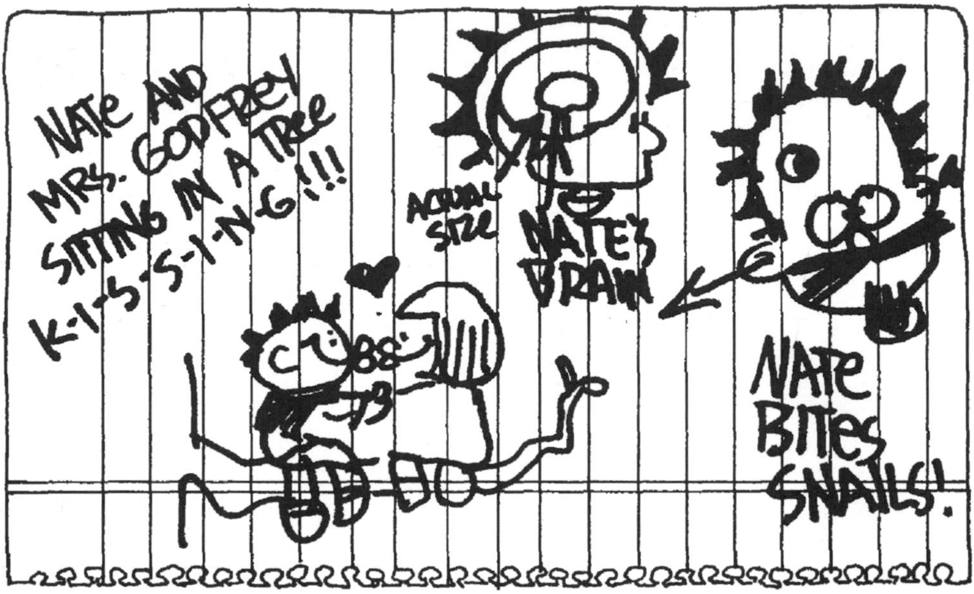
NATE AND MRS. GODFREY SITTING IN A TREE K-I-S-S-I-N-G!!!
ACTUAL SIZE
NATE'S BRAIN
NATE BITES SNAILS!

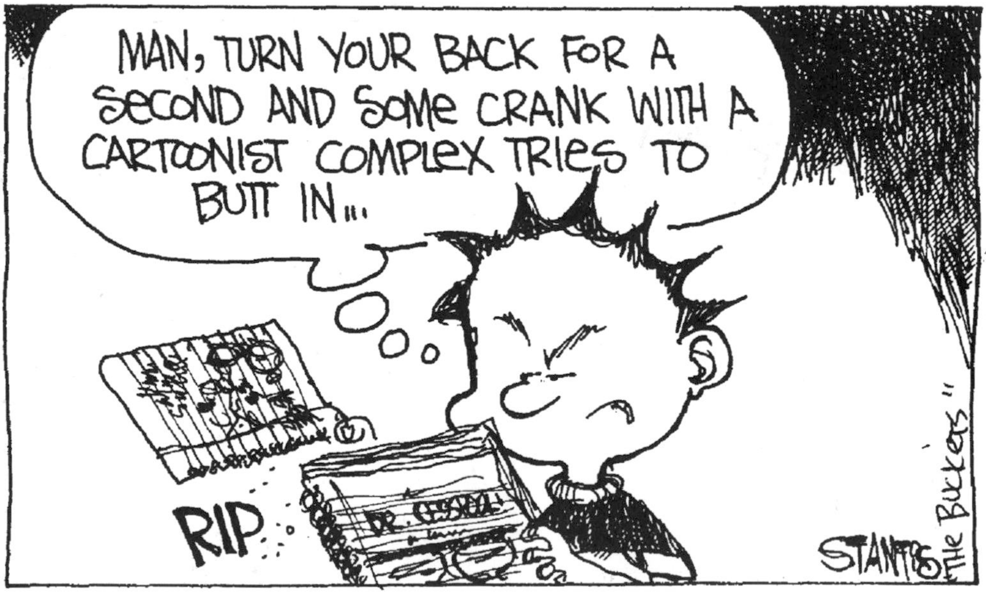
MAN, TURN YOUR BACK FOR A SECOND AND SOME CRANK WITH A CARTOONIST COMPLEX TRIES TO BUTT IN...
RIP
STAN '98
"THE BUCKETS"

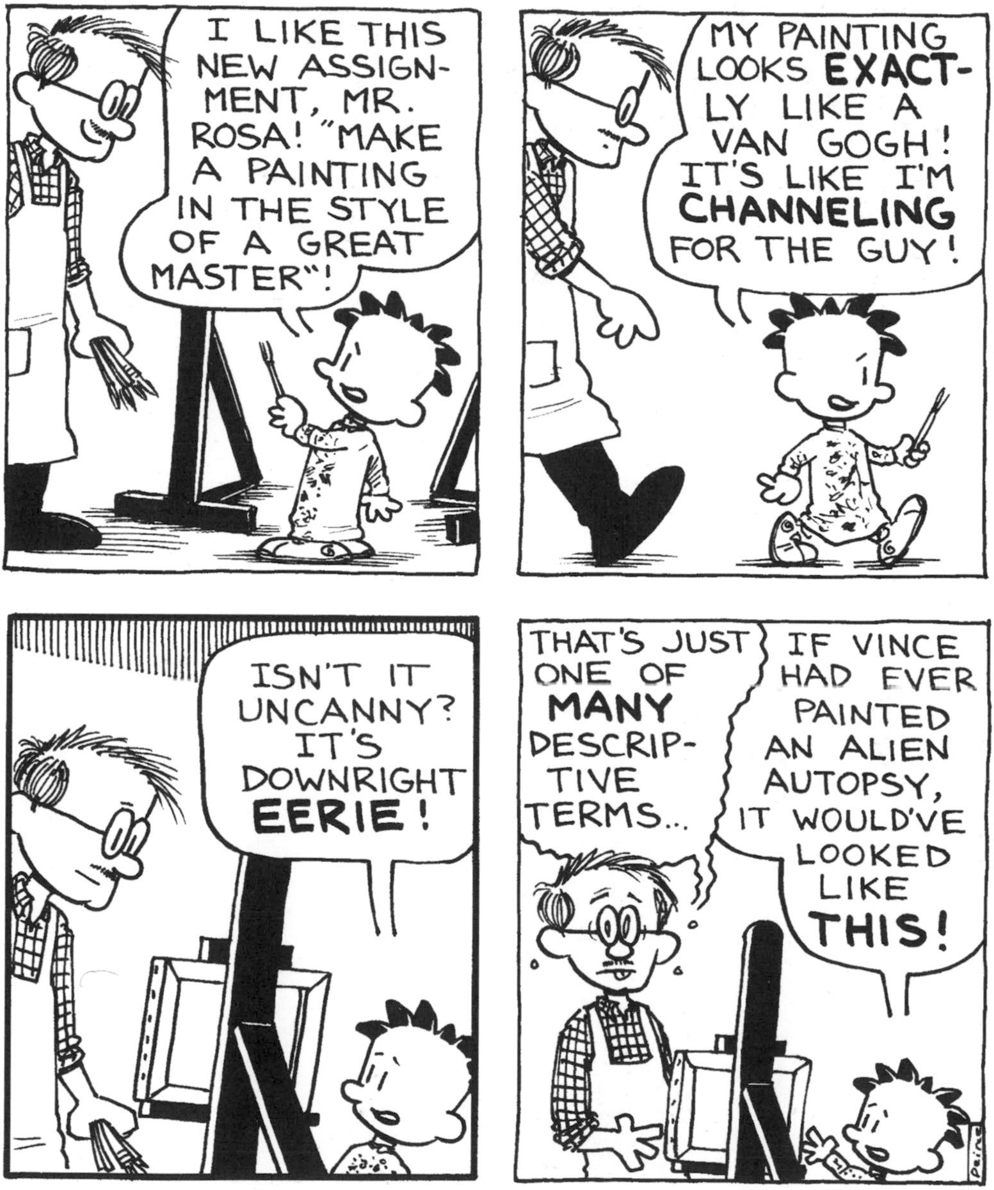
I LIKE THIS NEW ASSIGNMENT, MR. ROSA! "MAKE A PAINTING IN THE STYLE OF A GREAT MASTER"!
MY PAINTING LOOKS **EXACTLY** LIKE A VAN GOGH! IT'S LIKE I'M **CHANNELING** FOR THE GUY!
ISN'T IT UNCANNY? IT'S DOWNRIGHT **EERIE**!
THAT'S JUST ONE OF **MANY** DESCRIPTIVE TERMS...
IF VINCE HAD EVER PAINTED AN ALIEN AUTOPSY, IT WOULD'VE LOOKED LIKE **THIS**!
Peirce

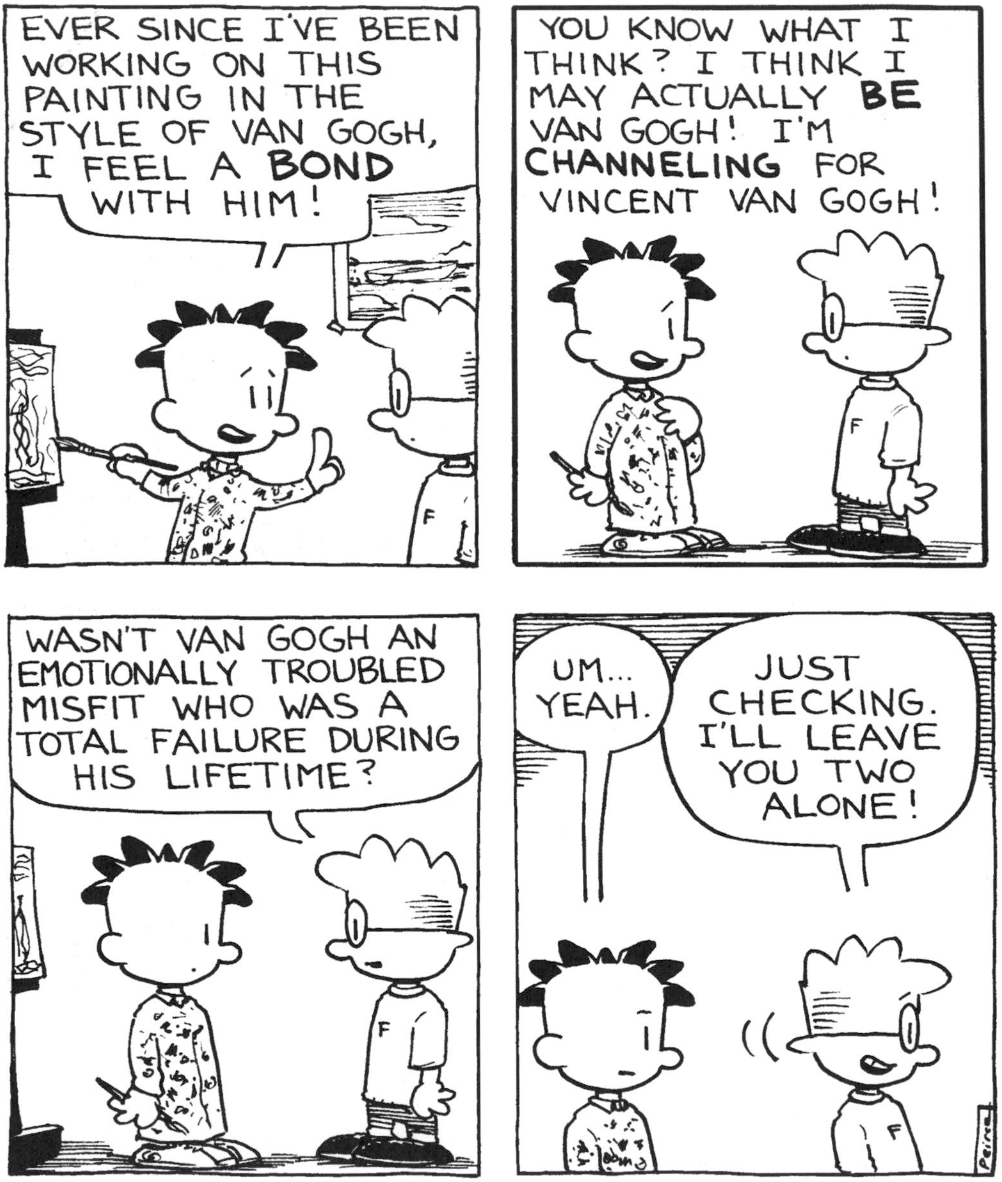
EVER SINCE I'VE BEEN WORKING ON THIS PAINTING IN THE STYLE OF VAN GOGH, I FEEL A **BOND** WITH HIM!
YOU KNOW WHAT I THINK? I THINK I MAY ACTUALLY **BE** VAN GOGH! I'M **CHANNELING** FOR VINCENT VAN GOGH!
WASN'T VAN GOGH AN EMOTIONALLY TROUBLED MISFIT WHO WAS A TOTAL FAILURE DURING HIS LIFETIME?
UM... YEAH.
JUST CHECKING. I'LL LEAVE YOU TWO ALONE!
Peirce

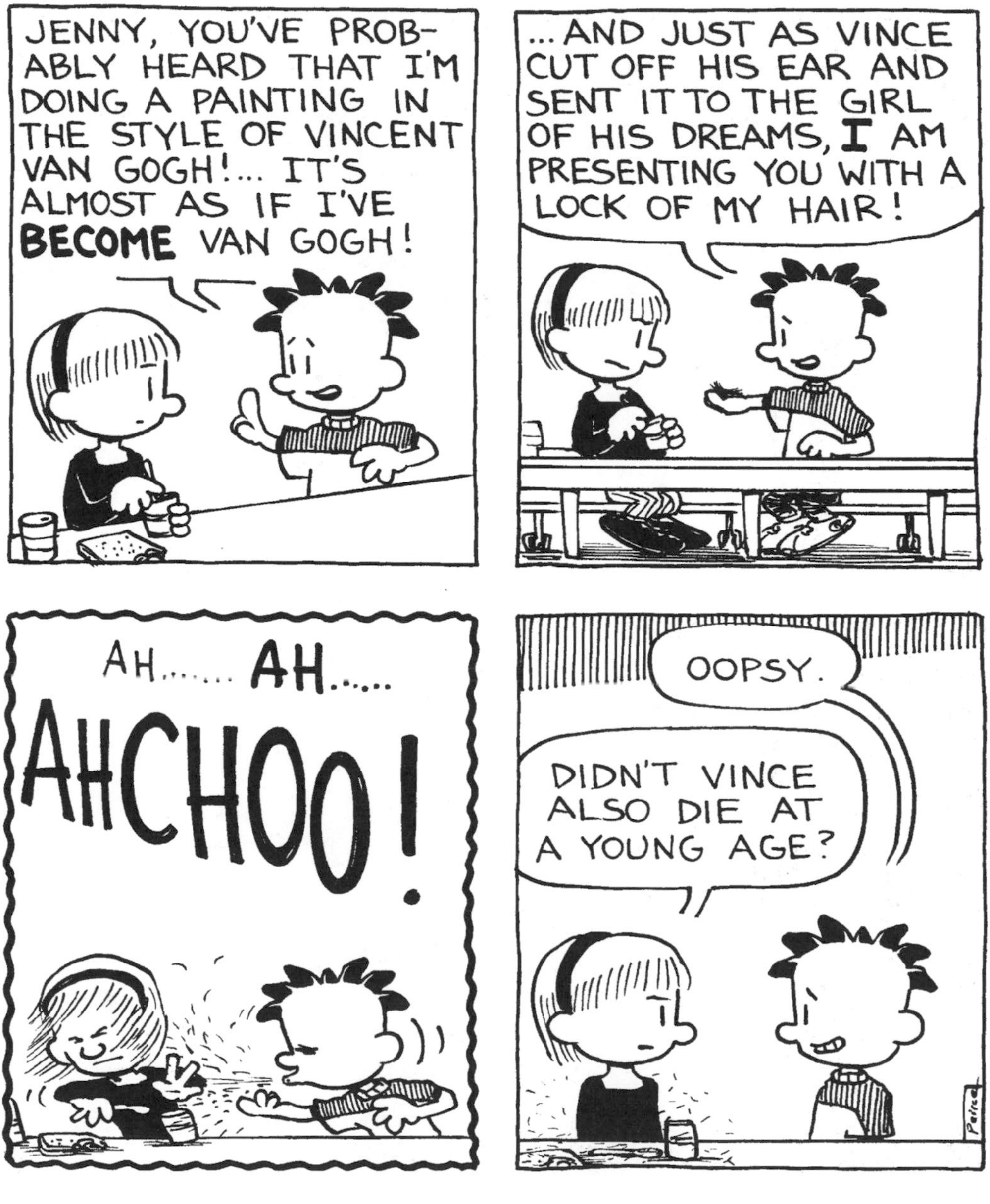
JENNY, YOU'VE PROBABLY HEARD THAT I'M DOING A PAINTING IN THE STYLE OF VINCENT VAN GOGH!... IT'S ALMOST AS IF I'VE **BECOME** VAN GOGH!
...AND JUST AS VINCE CUT OFF HIS EAR AND SENT IT TO THE GIRL OF HIS DREAMS, **I** AM PRESENTING YOU WITH A LOCK OF MY HAIR!
AH...... AH......
AHCHOO!
DIDN'T VINCE ALSO DIE AT A YOUNG AGE?
OOPSY.
Peirce

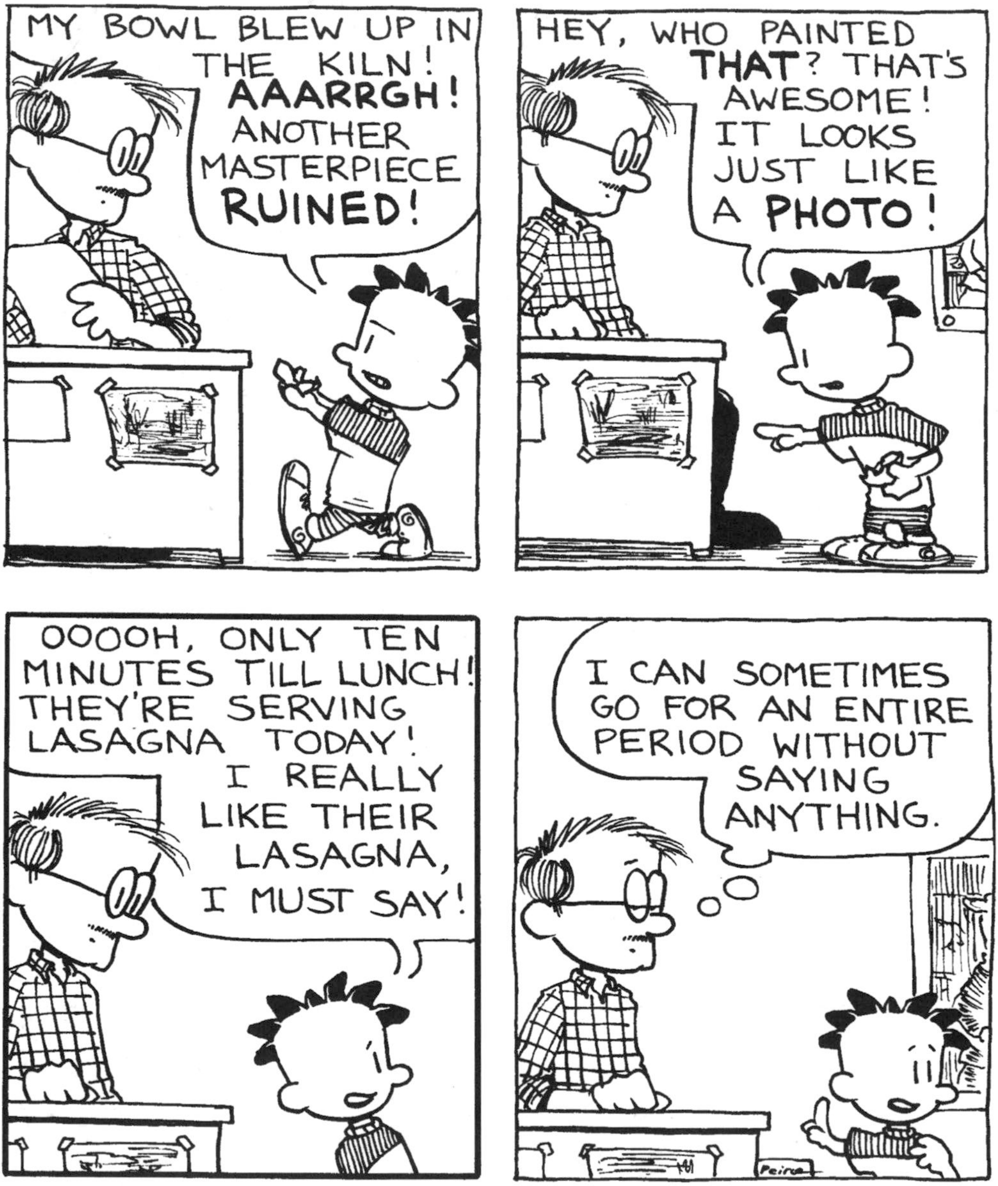
MY BOWL BLEW UP IN THE KILN! AAARRGH! ANOTHER MASTERPIECE RUINED!
HEY, WHO PAINTED THAT? THAT'S AWESOME! IT LOOKS JUST LIKE A PHOTO!
OOOOH, ONLY TEN MINUTES TILL LUNCH! THEY'RE SERVING LASAGNA TODAY! I REALLY LIKE THEIR LASAGNA, I MUST SAY!
I CAN SOMETIMES GO FOR AN ENTIRE PERIOD WITHOUT SAYING ANYTHING.
Peirce

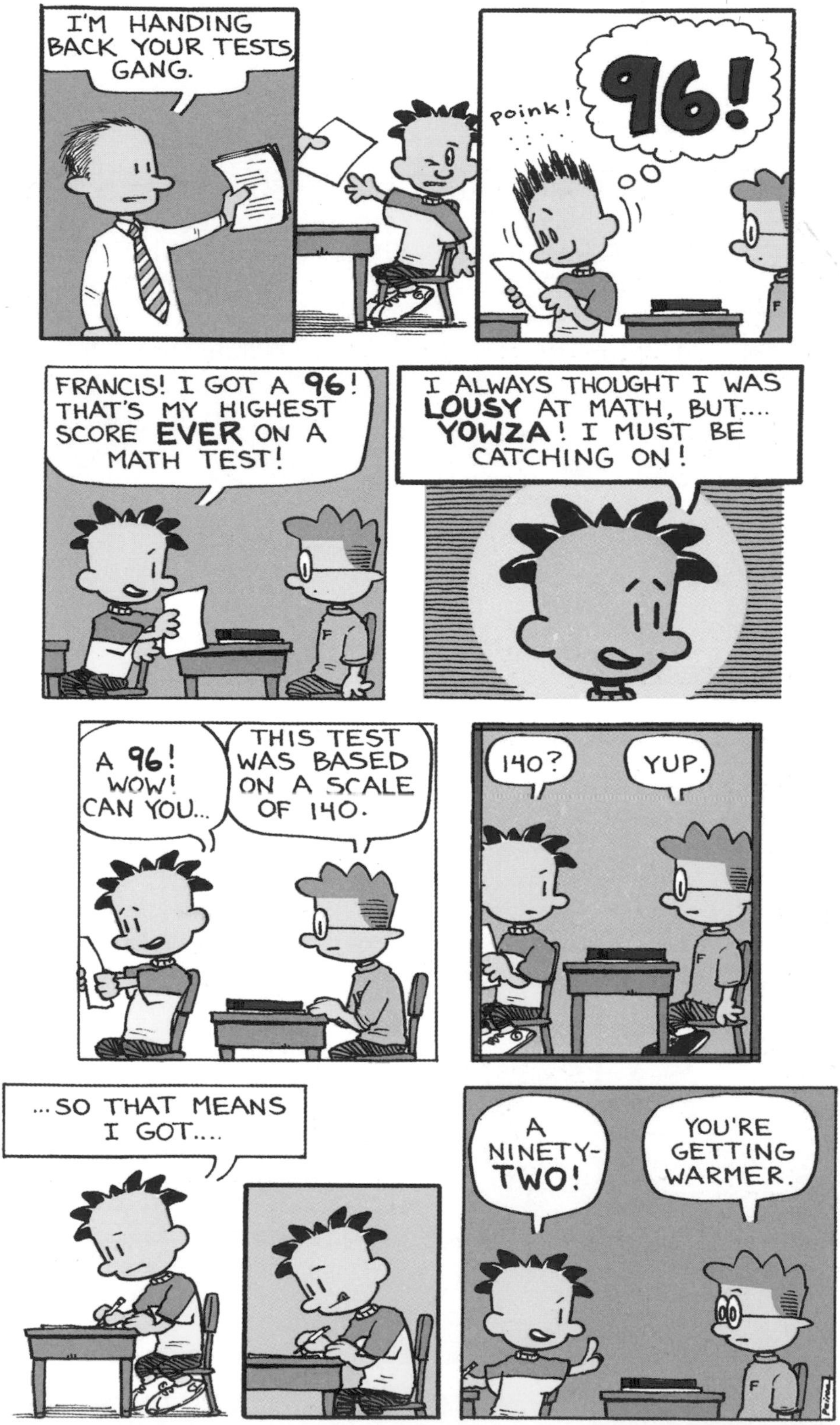
I'M HANDING BACK YOUR TESTS, GANG.
poink!
96!
FRANCIS! I GOT A 96! THAT'S MY HIGHEST SCORE EVER ON A MATH TEST!
I ALWAYS THOUGHT I WAS LOUSY AT MATH, BUT.... YOWZA! I MUST BE CATCHING ON!
A 96! WOW! CAN YOU...
THIS TEST WAS BASED ON A SCALE OF 140.
140?
YUP.
...SO THAT MEANS I GOT....
A NINETY-TWO!
YOU'RE GETTING WARMER.

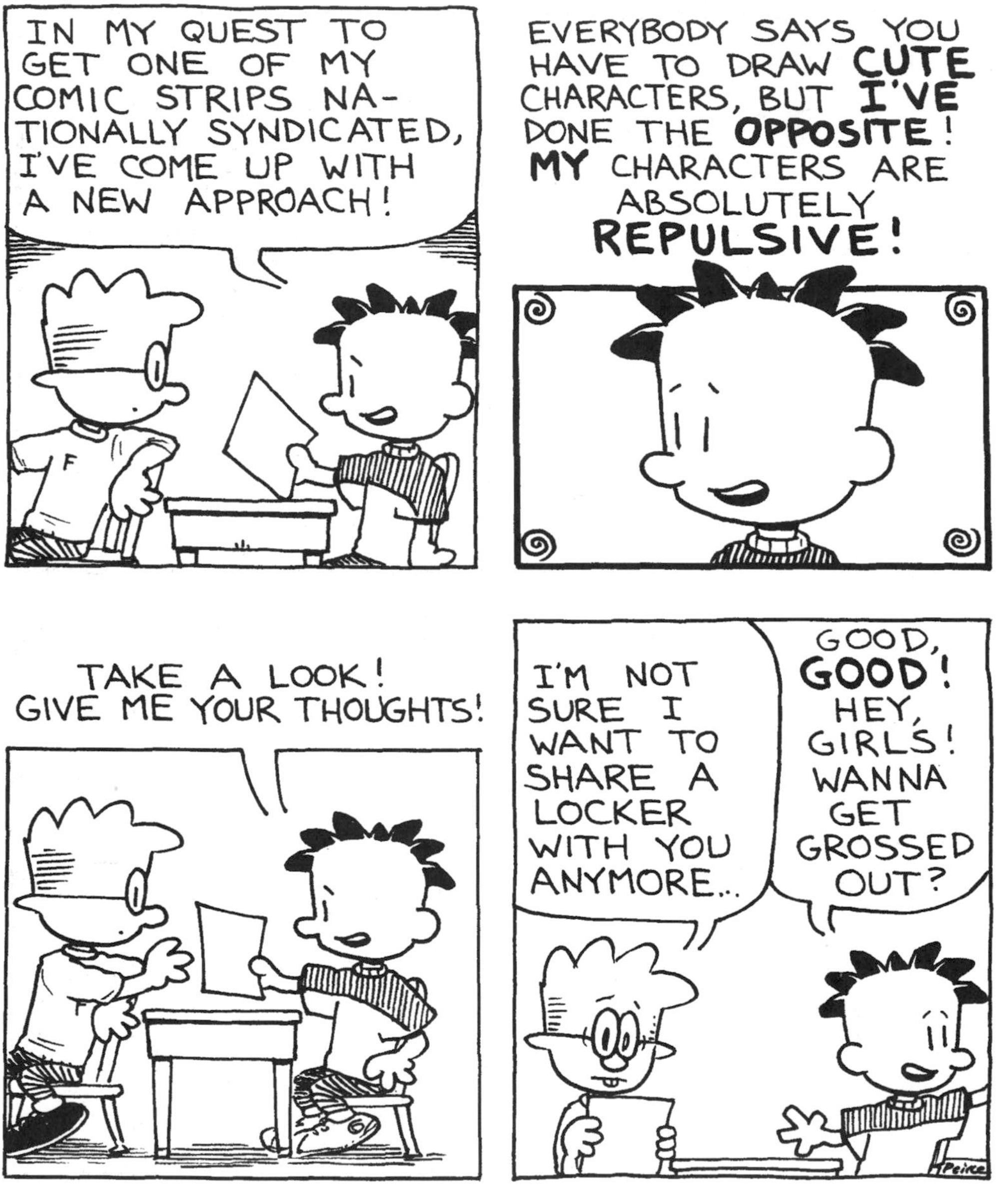
IN MY QUEST TO GET ONE OF MY COMIC STRIPS NATIONALLY SYNDICATED, I'VE COME UP WITH A NEW APPROACH!
EVERYBODY SAYS YOU HAVE TO DRAW **CUTE** CHARACTERS, BUT **I'VE** DONE THE **OPPOSITE**! **MY** CHARACTERS ARE ABSOLUTELY **REPULSIVE**!
TAKE A LOOK! GIVE ME YOUR THOUGHTS!
I'M NOT SURE I WANT TO SHARE A LOCKER WITH YOU ANYMORE...
GOOD, **GOOD**! HEY, GIRLS! WANNA GET GROSSED OUT?
F
Peirce

CHECK OUT MY LATEST CREATION, TEDDY!
IT'S THE WORLD'S MOST DISGUSTING COMIC STRIP! IT'S UTTERLY **REPULSIVE**!
IT'S A GREAT CONCEPT, DON'T YOU THINK? IT'S A NEW HIGH IN GROSS-OUT HUMOR!
SOMETIMES I AMAZE MYSELF WITH THE STUFF I COME UP WITH!
I'M ABOUT TO COME UP WITH SOMETHING MYSELF...

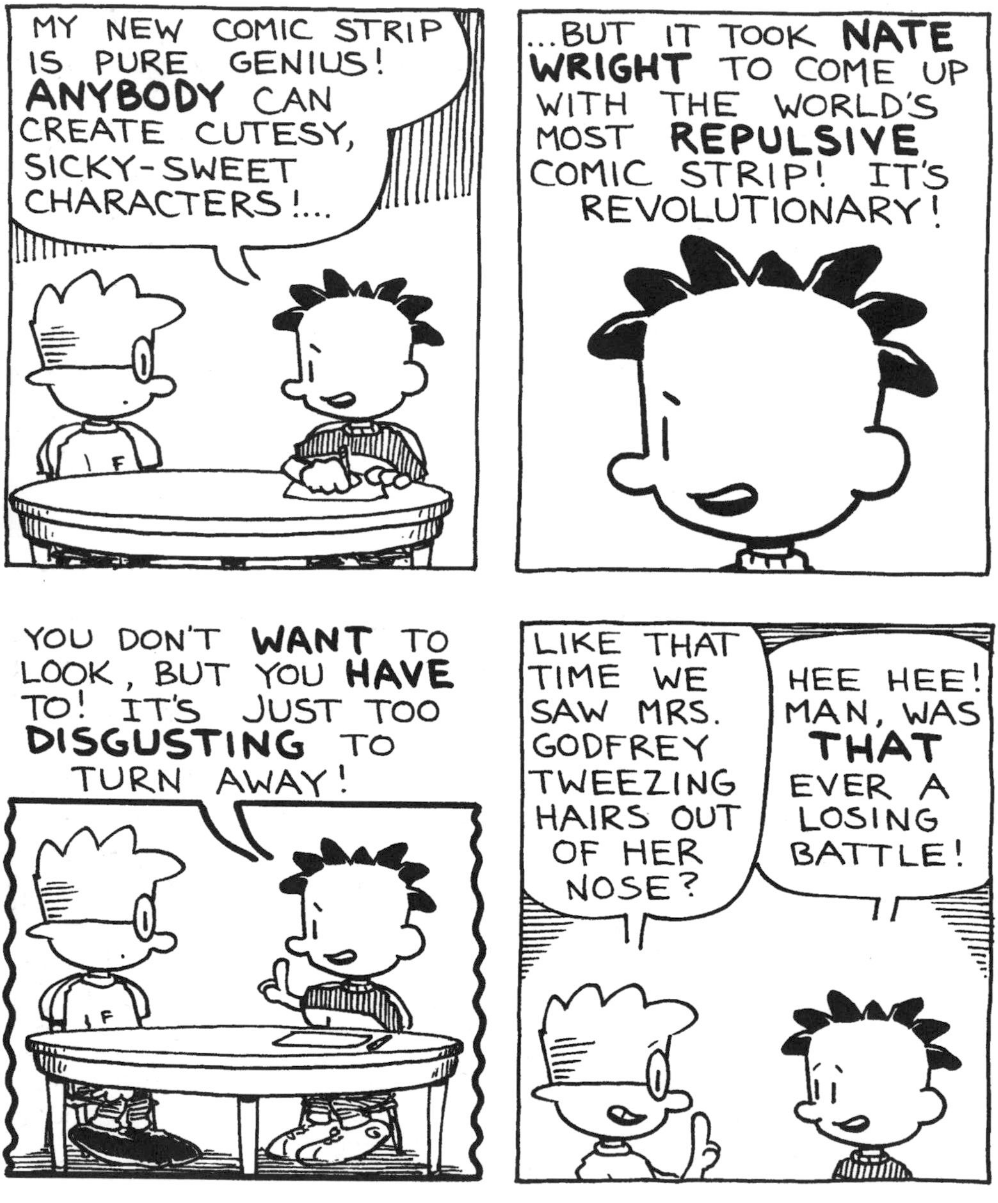
MY NEW COMIC STRIP IS PURE GENIUS! **ANYBODY** CAN CREATE CUTESY, SICKY-SWEET CHARACTERS!...
...BUT IT TOOK **NATE WRIGHT** TO COME UP WITH THE WORLD'S MOST **REPULSIVE** COMIC STRIP! IT'S REVOLUTIONARY!
YOU DON'T **WANT** TO LOOK, BUT YOU **HAVE** TO! IT'S JUST TOO **DISGUSTING** TO TURN AWAY!
LIKE THAT TIME WE SAW MRS. GODFREY TWEEZING HAIRS OUT OF HER NOSE?
HEE HEE! MAN, WAS **THAT** EVER A LOSING BATTLE!

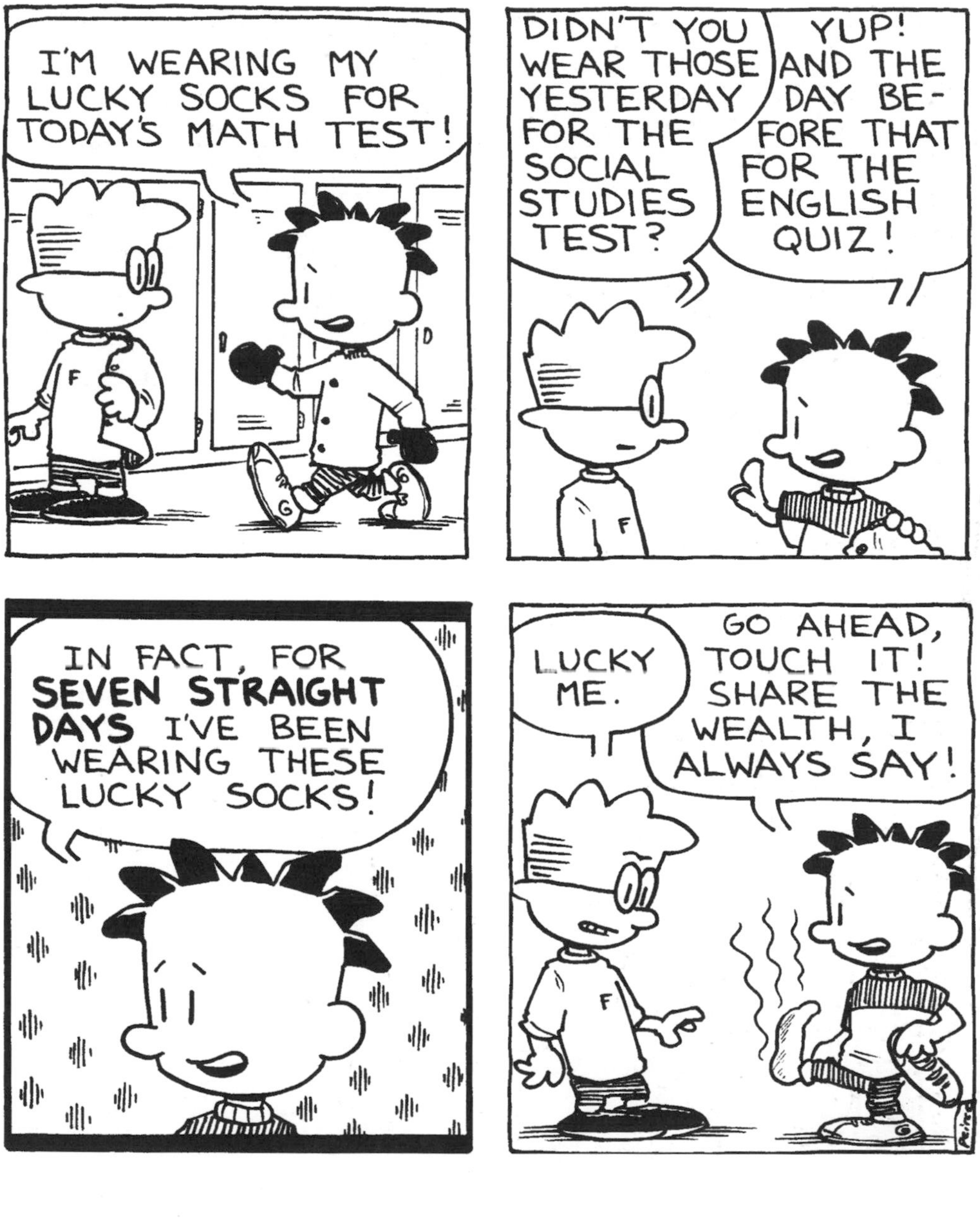
I'M WEARING MY LUCKY SOCKS FOR TODAY'S MATH TEST!
DIDN'T YOU WEAR THOSE YESTERDAY FOR THE SOCIAL STUDIES TEST?
YUP! AND THE DAY BE- FORE THAT FOR THE ENGLISH QUIZ!
IN FACT, FOR SEVEN STRAIGHT DAYS I'VE BEEN WEARING THESE LUCKY SOCKS!
GO AHEAD, TOUCH IT! SHARE THE WEALTH, I ALWAYS SAY!
LUCKY ME.
Peirce

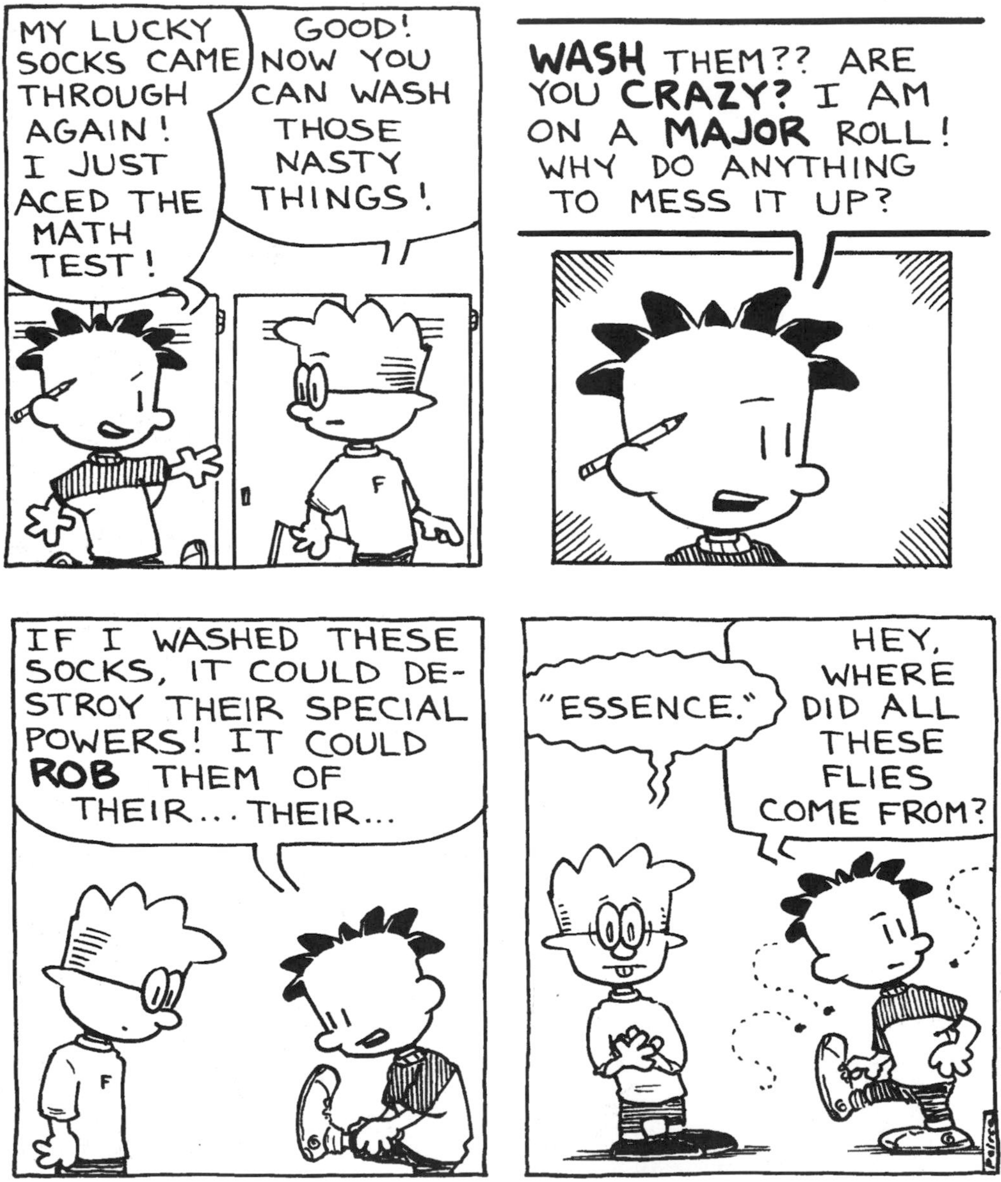
MY LUCKY SOCKS CAME THROUGH AGAIN! I JUST ACED THE MATH TEST!
GOOD! NOW YOU CAN WASH THOSE NASTY THINGS!
WASH THEM?? ARE YOU CRAZY? I AM ON A MAJOR ROLL! WHY DO ANYTHING TO MESS IT UP?
IF I WASHED THESE SOCKS, IT COULD DESTROY THEIR SPECIAL POWERS! IT COULD ROB THEM OF THEIR... THEIR...
"ESSENCE."
HEY, WHERE DID ALL THESE FLIES COME FROM?

MAYBE I'M CHARGING TOO MUCH...

YES, THAT MUST BE IT.

GOOD FORTUNE GUARANTEED! RUB MY LUCKY SOCKS 50¢

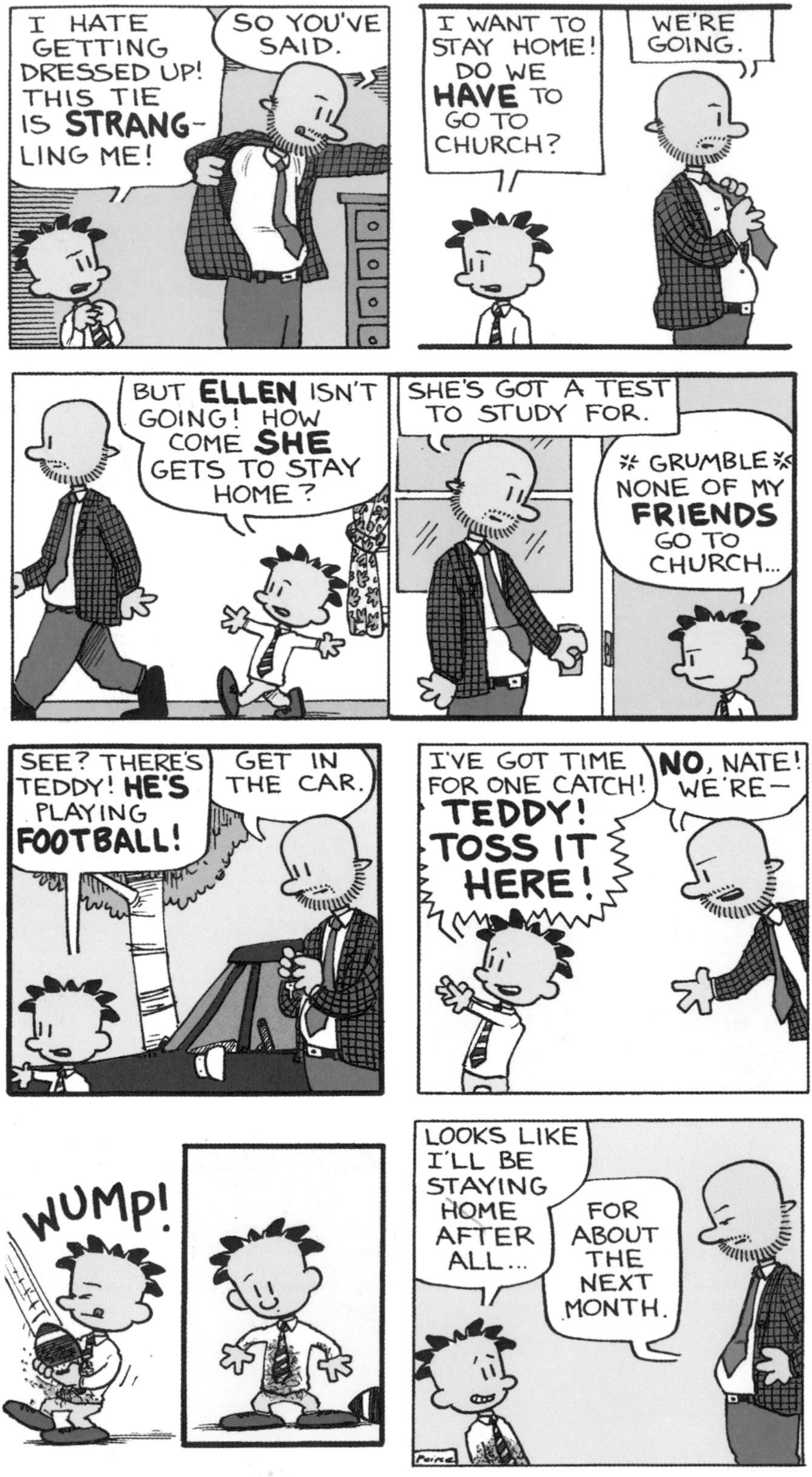
I HATE GETTING DRESSED UP! THIS TIE IS **STRANG-LING** ME!
SO YOU'VE SAID.
I WANT TO STAY HOME! DO WE **HAVE** TO GO TO CHURCH?
WE'RE GOING.
BUT **ELLEN** ISN'T GOING! HOW COME **SHE** GETS TO STAY HOME?
SHE'S GOT A TEST TO STUDY FOR.
GRUMBLE NONE OF MY **FRIENDS** GO TO CHURCH...
SEE? THERE'S TEDDY! **HE'S** PLAYING **FOOTBALL**!
GET IN THE CAR.
I'VE GOT TIME FOR ONE CATCH! **TEDDY! TOSS IT HERE!**
NO, NATE! WE'RE—
WUMP!
LOOKS LIKE I'LL BE STAYING HOME AFTER ALL...
FOR ABOUT THE NEXT MONTH.
Peirce

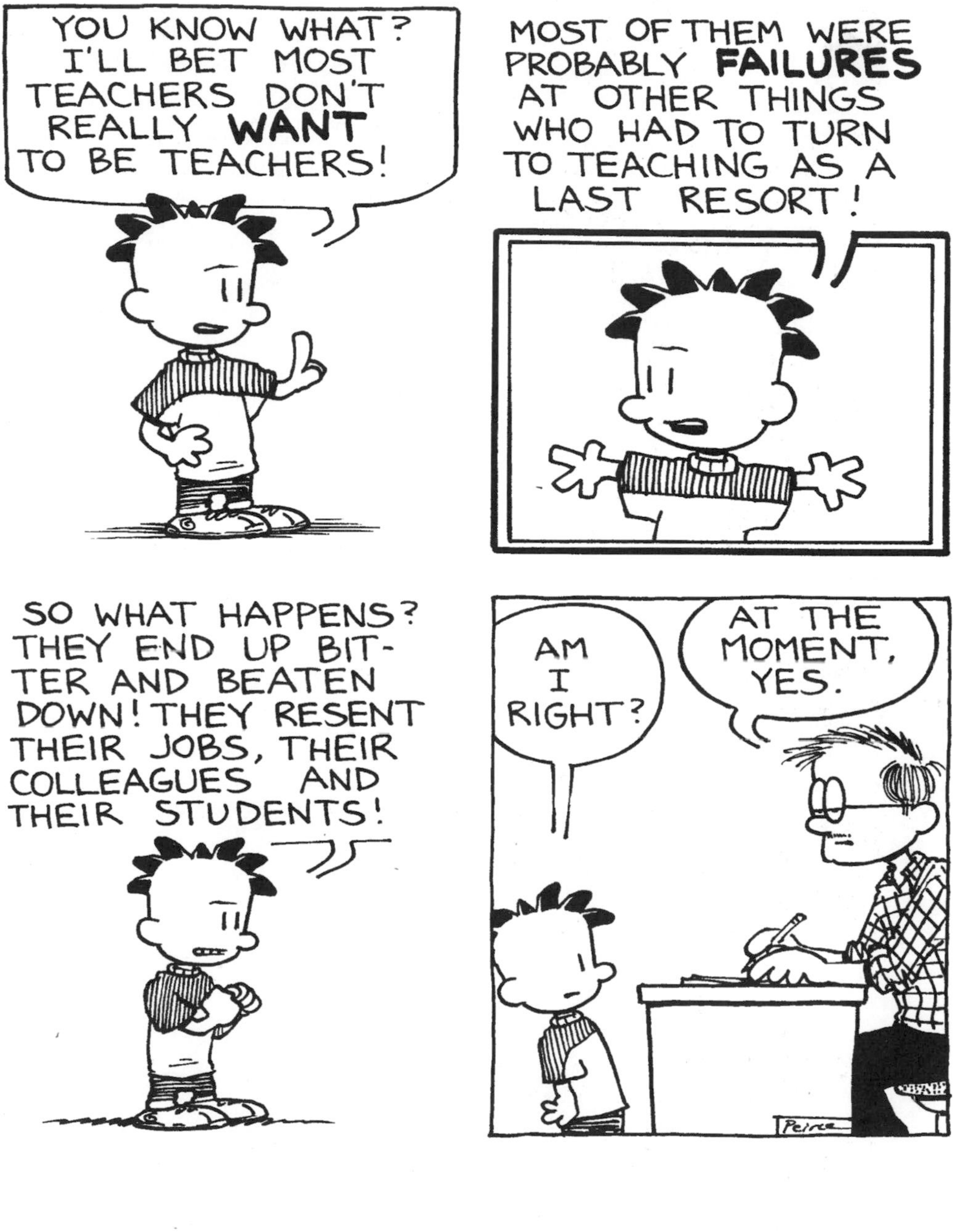
YOU KNOW WHAT? I'LL BET MOST TEACHERS DON'T REALLY **WANT** TO BE TEACHERS!
MOST OF THEM WERE PROBABLY **FAILURES** AT OTHER THINGS WHO HAD TO TURN TO TEACHING AS A LAST RESORT!
SO WHAT HAPPENS? THEY END UP BIT-TER AND BEATEN DOWN! THEY RESENT THEIR JOBS, THEIR COLLEAGUES AND THEIR STUDENTS!
AM I RIGHT?
AT THE MOMENT, YES.
Peirce

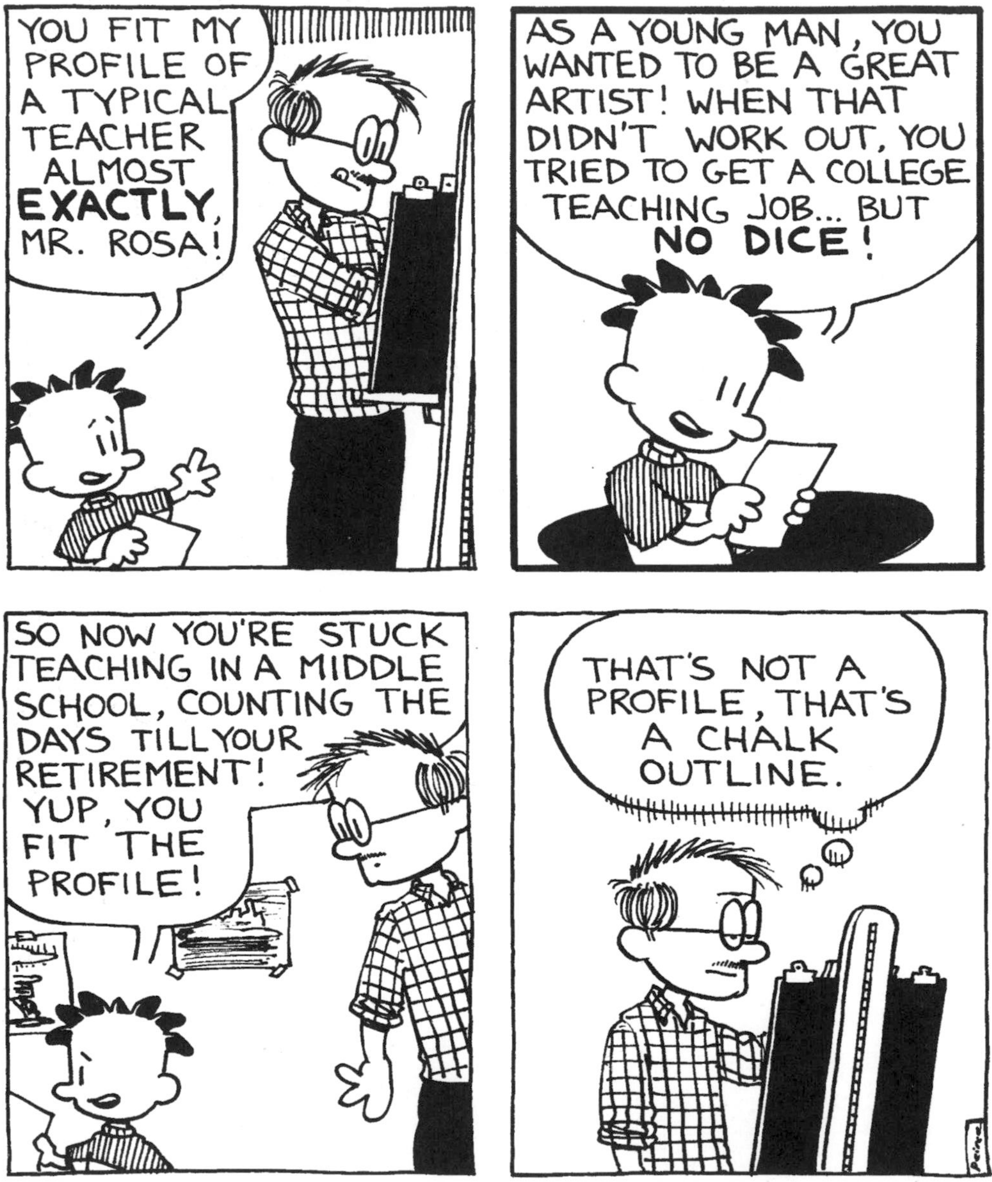
YOU FIT MY PROFILE OF A TYPICAL TEACHER ALMOST **EXACTLY**, MR. ROSA!
AS A YOUNG MAN, YOU WANTED TO BE A GREAT ARTIST! WHEN THAT DIDN'T WORK OUT, YOU TRIED TO GET A COLLEGE TEACHING JOB... BUT **NO DICE**!
SO NOW YOU'RE STUCK TEACHING IN A MIDDLE SCHOOL, COUNTING THE DAYS TILL YOUR RETIREMENT! YUP, YOU FIT THE PROFILE!
THAT'S NOT A PROFILE, THAT'S A CHALK OUTLINE.

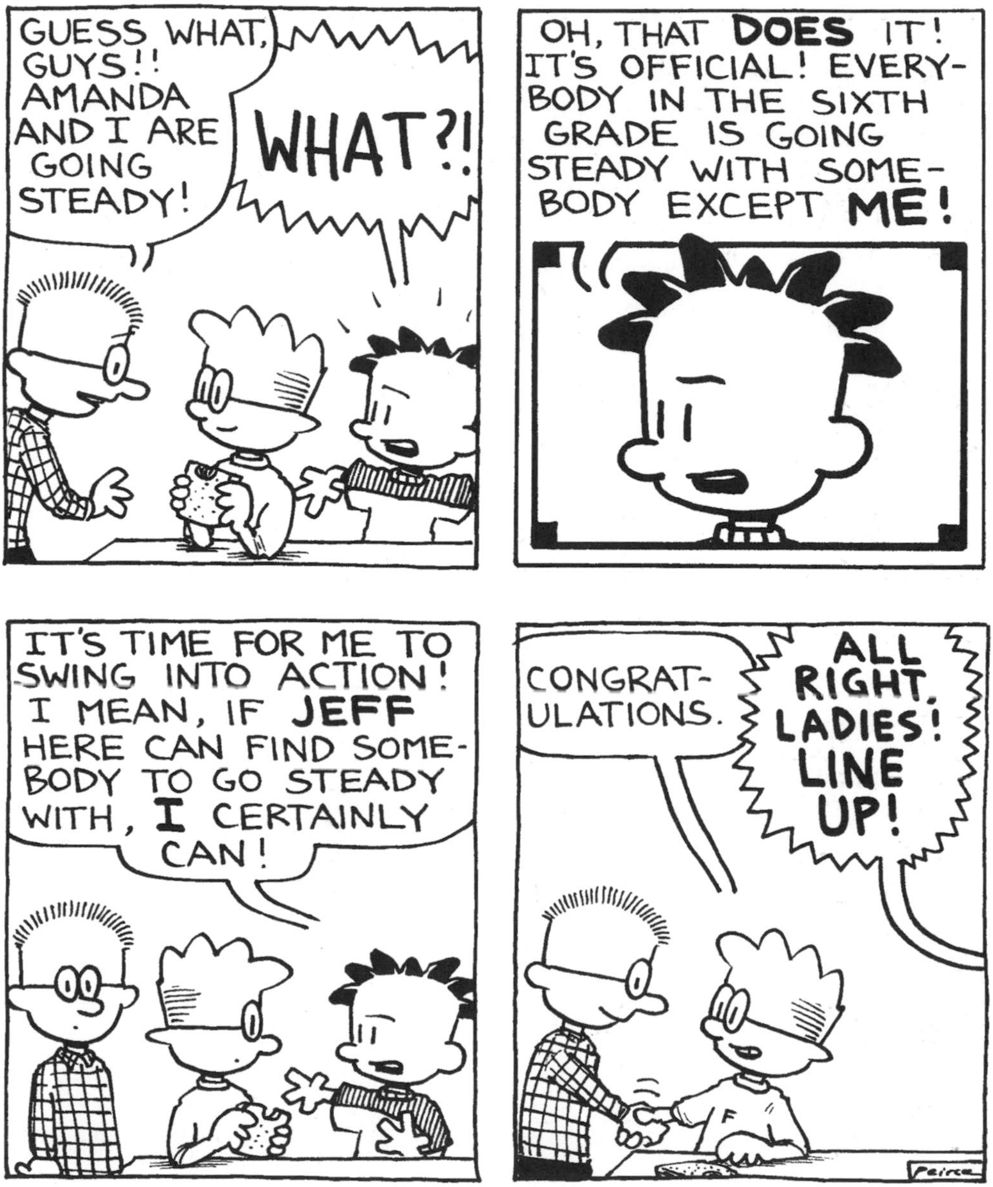
GUESS WHAT, GUYS!! AMANDA AND I ARE GOING STEADY!
WHAT?!
OH, THAT DOES IT! IT'S OFFICIAL! EVERY-BODY IN THE SIXTH GRADE IS GOING STEADY WITH SOME-BODY EXCEPT ME!
IT'S TIME FOR ME TO SWING INTO ACTION! I MEAN, IF JEFF HERE CAN FIND SOME-BODY TO GO STEADY WITH, I CERTAINLY CAN!
CONGRAT-ULATIONS.
ALL RIGHT, LADIES! LINE UP!
F
Peirce

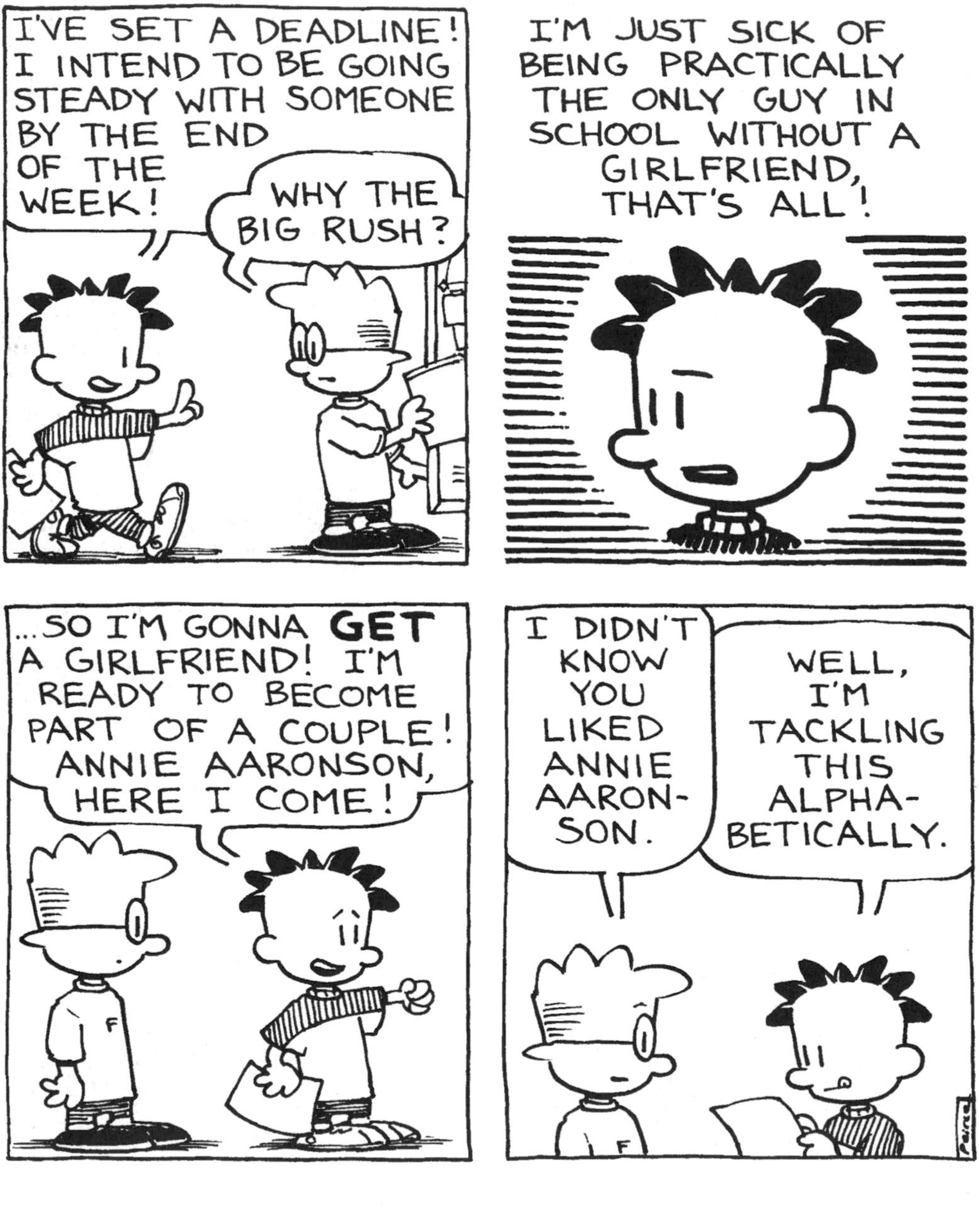
I'VE SET A DEADLINE! I INTEND TO BE GOING STEADY WITH SOMEONE BY THE END OF THE WEEK!
WHY THE BIG RUSH?
I'M JUST SICK OF BEING PRACTICALLY THE ONLY GUY IN SCHOOL WITHOUT A GIRLFRIEND, THAT'S ALL!
...SO I'M GONNA **GET** A GIRLFRIEND! I'M READY TO BECOME PART OF A COUPLE! ANNIE AARONSON, HERE I COME!
I DIDN'T KNOW YOU LIKED ANNIE AARON-SON.
WELL, I'M TACKLING THIS ALPHA-BETICALLY.
F
F
Peirce

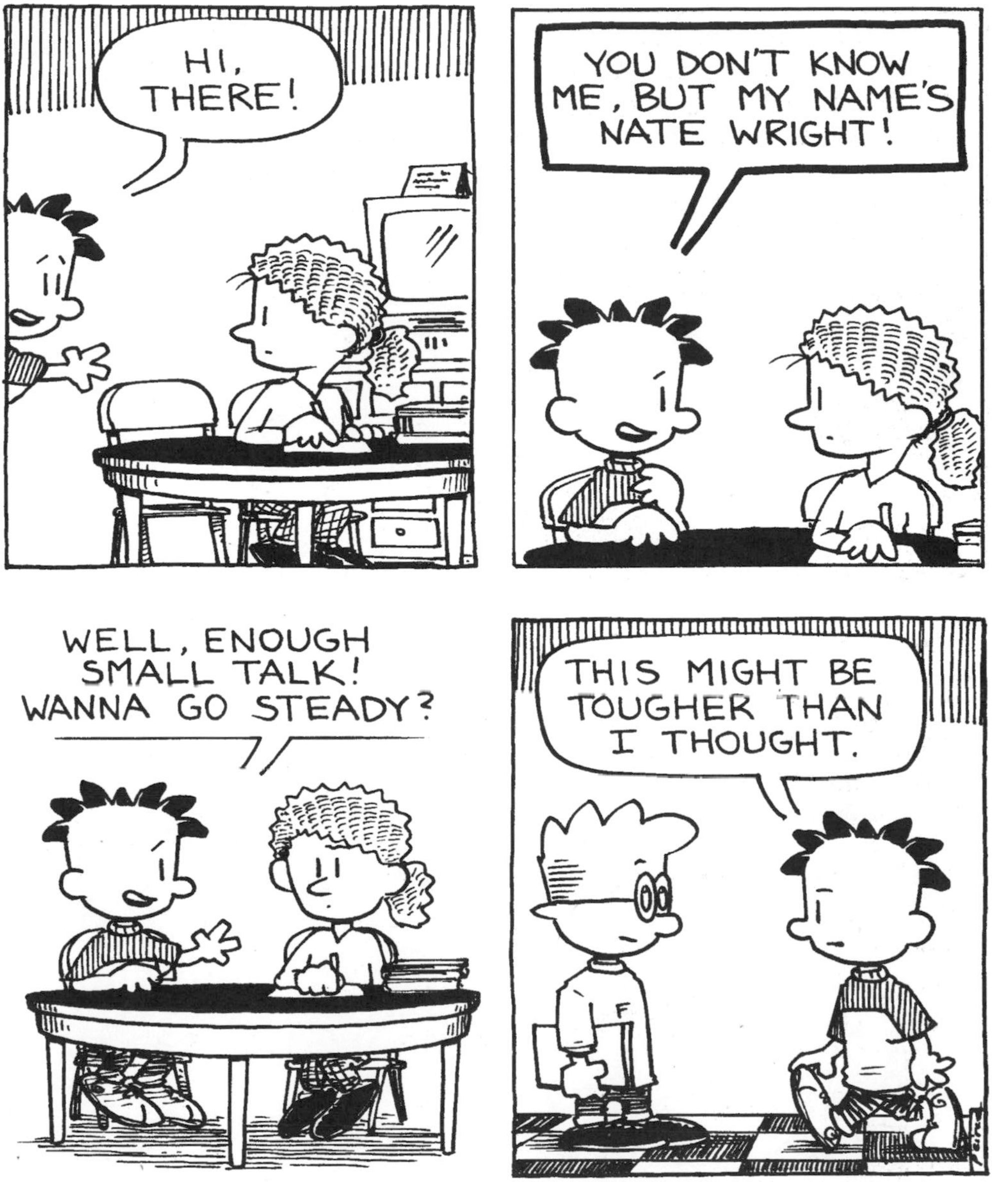
HI, THERE!
YOU DON'T KNOW ME, BUT MY NAME'S NATE WRIGHT!
WELL, ENOUGH SMALL TALK! WANNA GO STEADY?
THIS MIGHT BE TOUGHER THAN I THOUGHT.

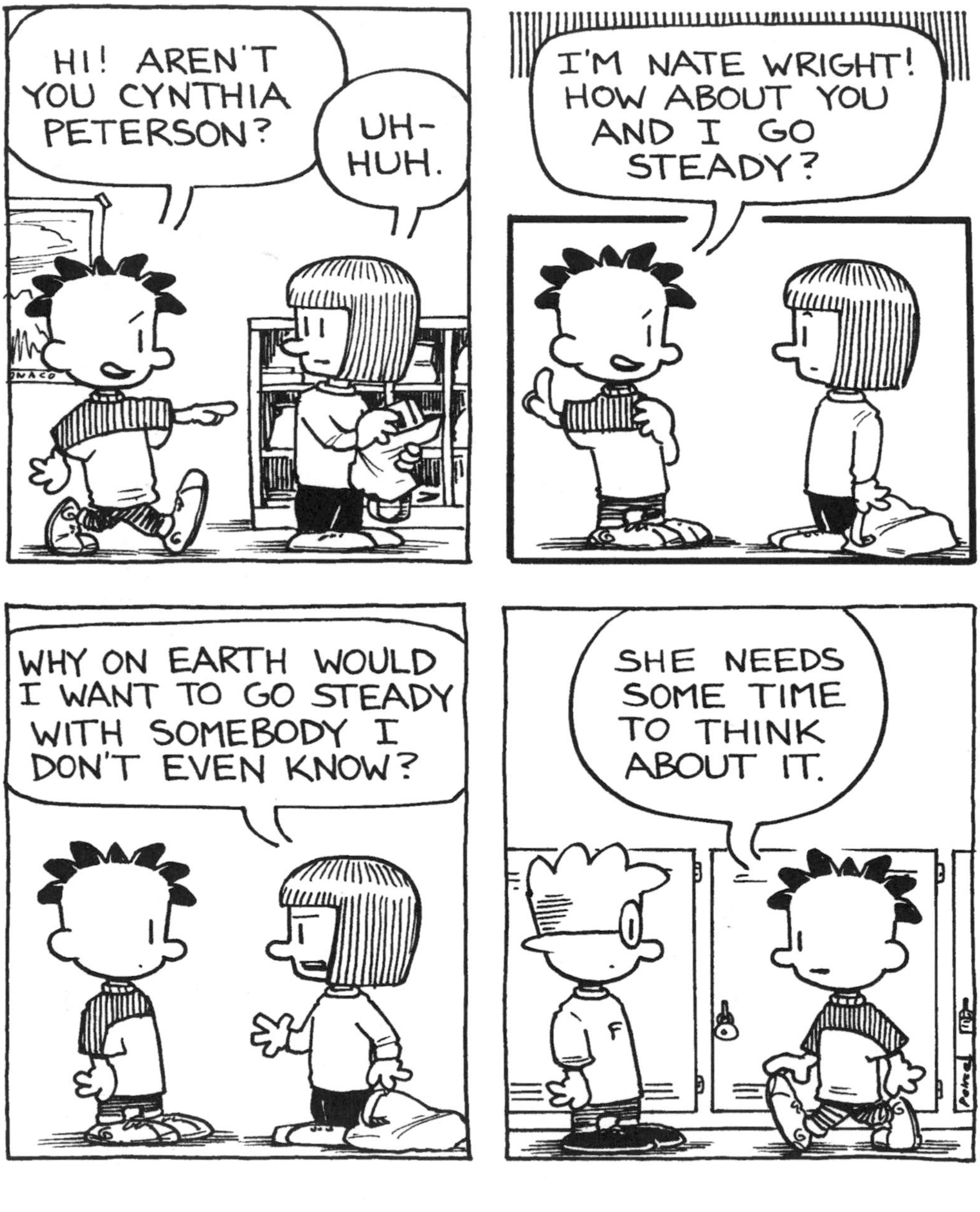
HI! AREN'T YOU CYNTHIA PETERSON?
UH-HUH.
I'M NATE WRIGHT! HOW ABOUT YOU AND I GO STEADY?
WHY ON EARTH WOULD I WANT TO GO STEADY WITH SOMEBODY I DON'T EVEN KNOW?
SHE NEEDS SOME TIME TO THINK ABOUT IT.

Dance FEVER!

with your "poet-in-residence":

DAN CUPID!

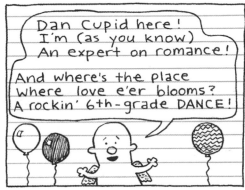

Dan Cupid here!
I'm (as you know)
An expert on romance!

And where's the place
Where love e'er blooms?
A rockin' 6th-grade DANCE!

A chaperone
Of sorts am I.
I float above the scene,
And watch the
Writhing bodies fueled
By sugar and caffeine!

There's Francis
Dancing clumsily
With Sheila. Ain't it sweet?

And Teddy's
pseudo-disco moves
Are really quite a "feet"!

trip!

The D.J.'s lame,
The music stinks.
But one thing can't
be missed:
The sight of
Clueless teachers
Trying hard to do
the "twist."

Here's how
to do it,
kids!

Then every head
Turns to the right
As in the door
Strolls NATE!

He's dashing!
Handsome! Debonair!
And fashionably late.

Ooooh!
Aaaah!

He saunters toward
A group of girls.
A young Adonis, he.

Let's listen
As he makes his move....

WHO WANTS TO DANCE?

NOT ME.

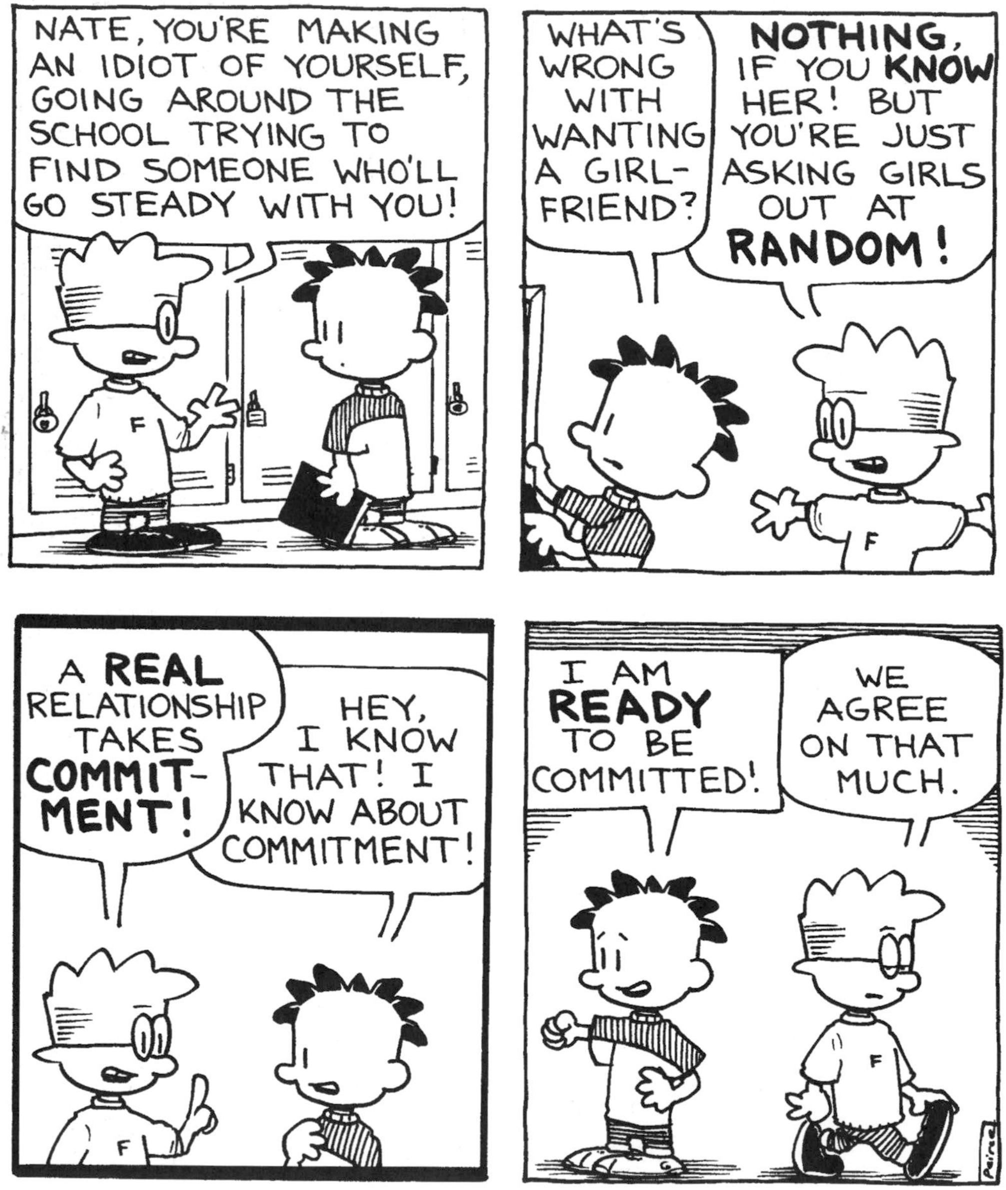
NATE, YOU'RE MAKING AN IDIOT OF YOURSELF, GOING AROUND THE SCHOOL TRYING TO FIND SOMEONE WHO'LL GO STEADY WITH YOU!
WHAT'S WRONG WITH WANTING A GIRL-FRIEND?
NOTHING, IF YOU KNOW HER! BUT YOU'RE JUST ASKING GIRLS OUT AT RANDOM!
A REAL RELATIONSHIP TAKES COMMIT-MENT!
HEY, I KNOW THAT! I KNOW ABOUT COMMITMENT!
I AM READY TO BE COMMITTED!
WE AGREE ON THAT MUCH.
Peirce

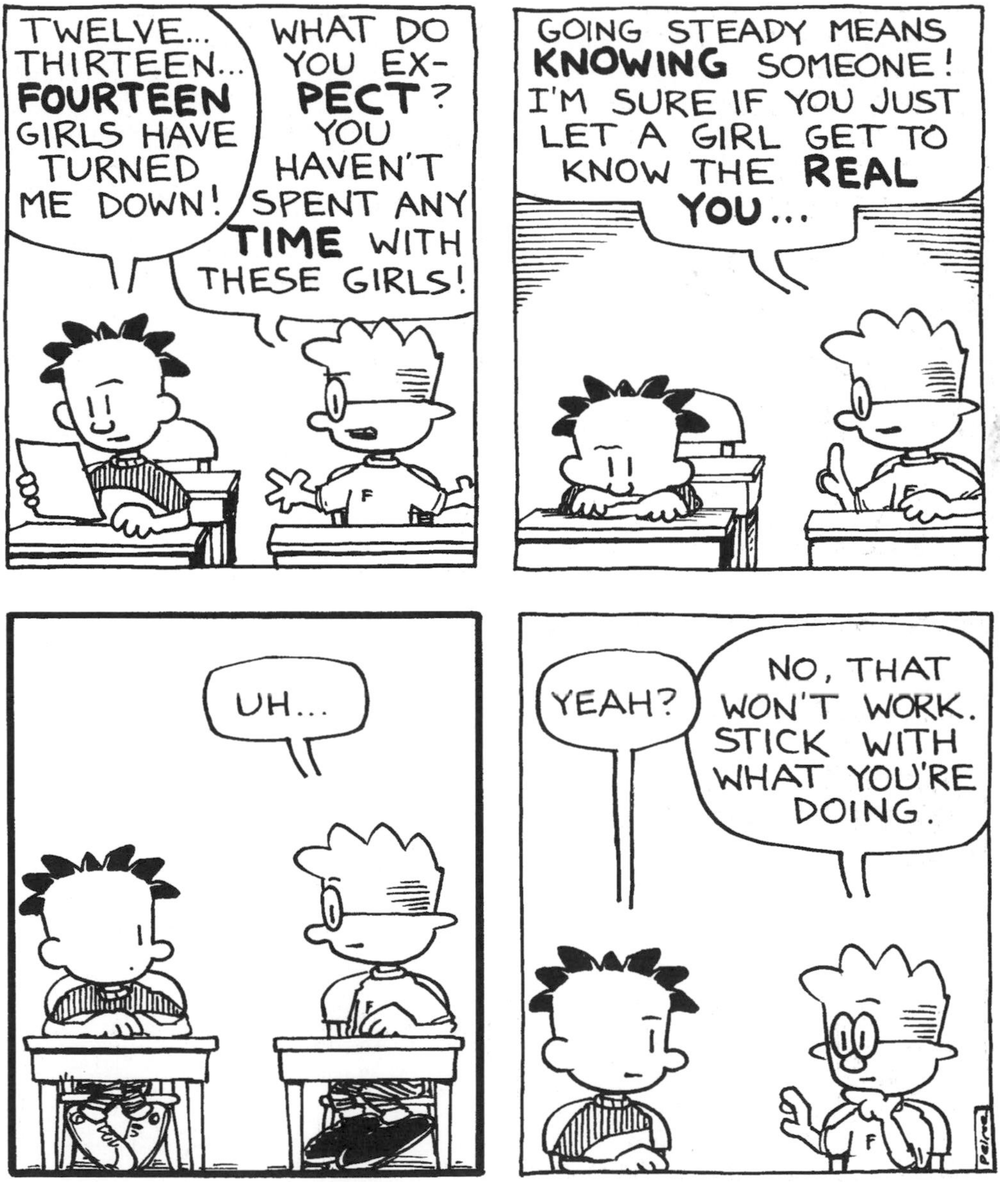
TWELVE... THIRTEEN... FOURTEEN GIRLS HAVE TURNED ME DOWN!
WHAT DO YOU EXPECT? YOU HAVEN'T SPENT ANY TIME WITH THESE GIRLS!
GOING STEADY MEANS KNOWING SOMEONE! I'M SURE IF YOU JUST LET A GIRL GET TO KNOW THE REAL YOU...
UH...
YEAH?
NO, THAT WON'T WORK. STICK WITH WHAT YOU'RE DOING.
Peirce

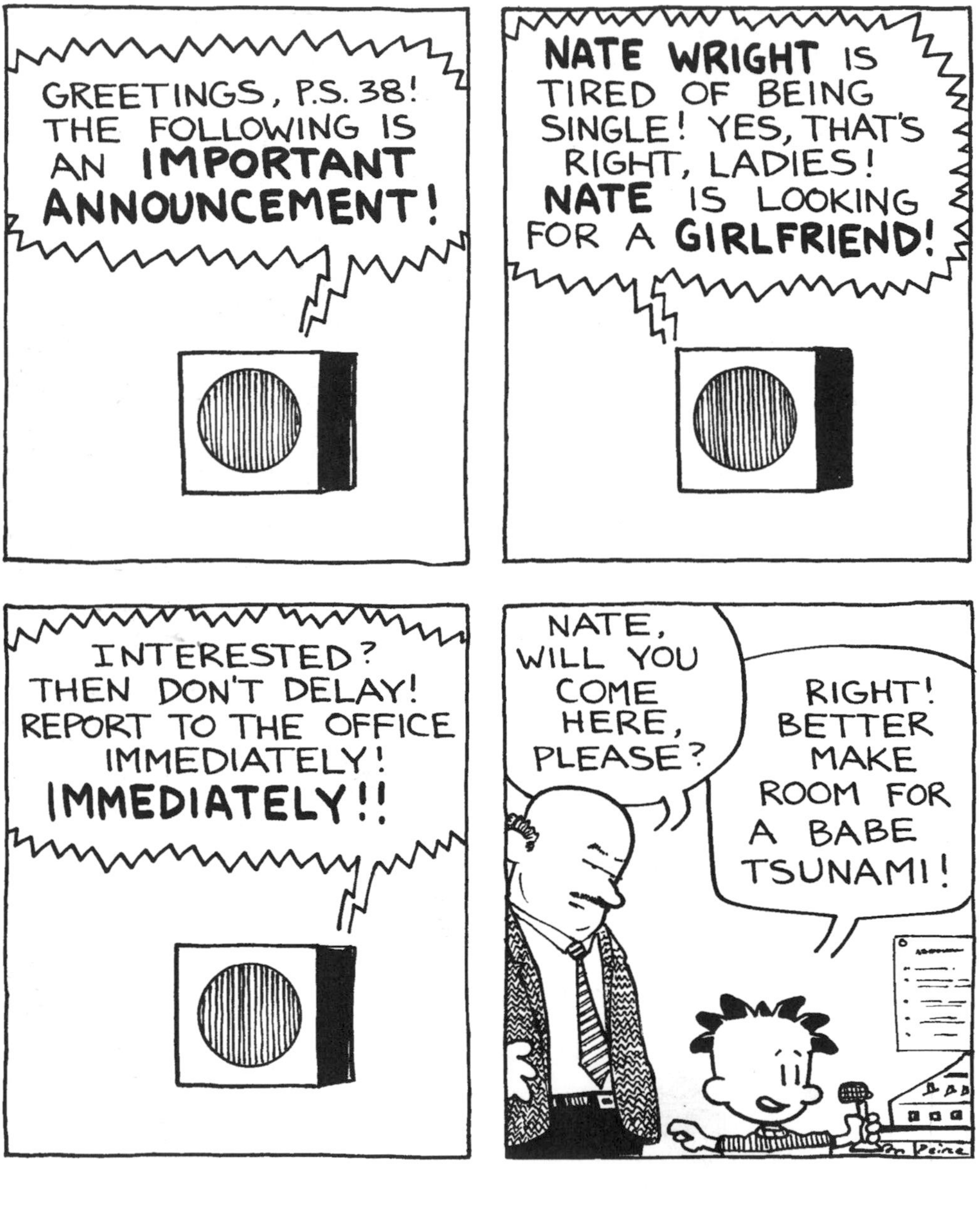
GREETINGS, P.S. 38! THE FOLLOWING IS AN **IMPORTANT ANNOUNCEMENT!**
NATE WRIGHT IS TIRED OF BEING SINGLE! YES, THAT'S RIGHT, LADIES! **NATE** IS LOOKING FOR A **GIRLFRIEND!**
INTERESTED? THEN DON'T DELAY! REPORT TO THE OFFICE IMMEDIATELY! **IMMEDIATELY!!**
NATE, WILL YOU COME HERE, PLEASE?
RIGHT! BETTER MAKE ROOM FOR A BABE TSUNAMI!

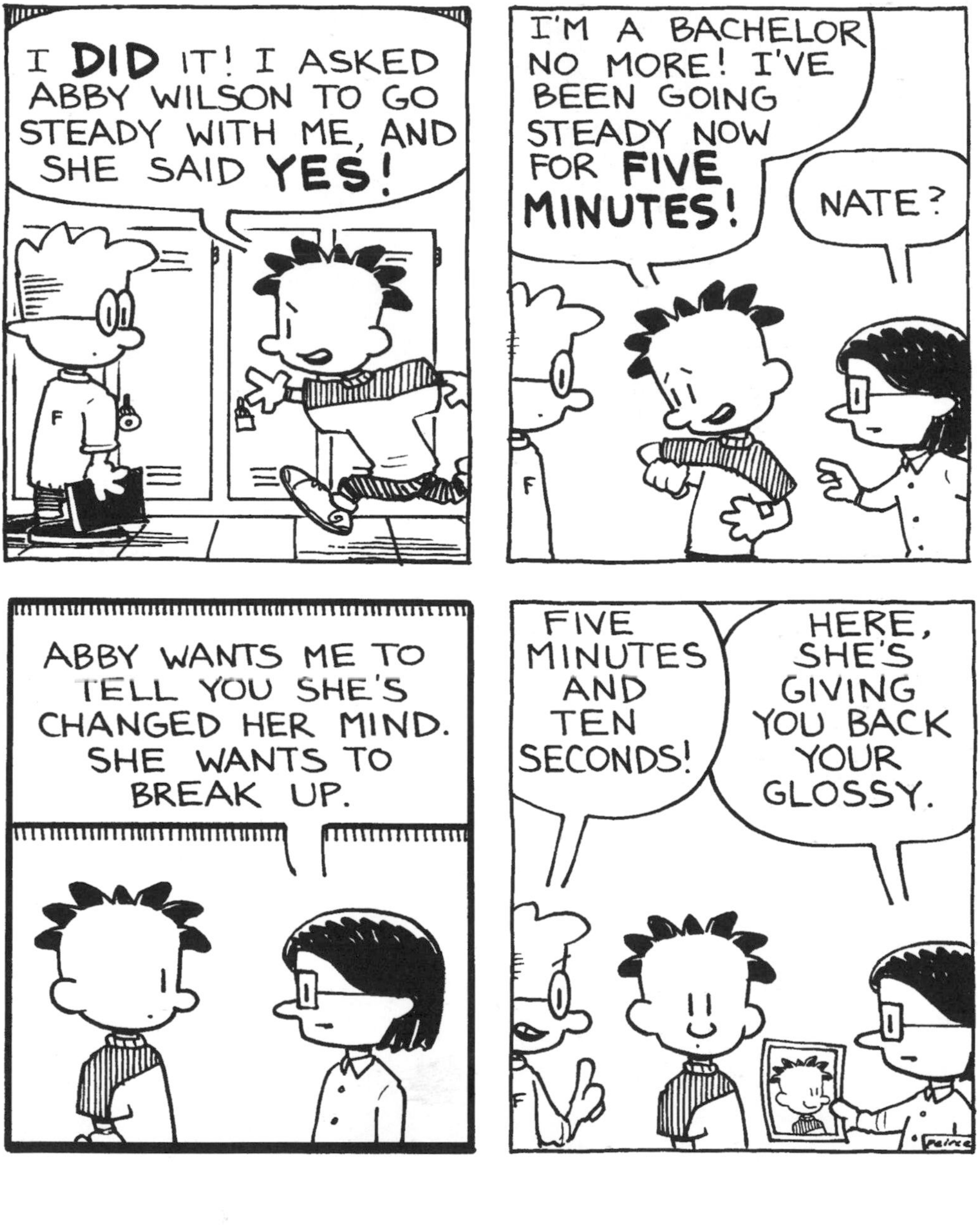
I DID IT! I ASKED ABBY WILSON TO GO STEADY WITH ME, AND SHE SAID YES!
I'M A BACHELOR NO MORE! I'VE BEEN GOING STEADY NOW FOR FIVE MINUTES!
NATE?
ABBY WANTS ME TO TELL YOU SHE'S CHANGED HER MIND. SHE WANTS TO BREAK UP.
FIVE MINUTES AND TEN SECONDS!
HERE, SHE'S GIVING YOU BACK YOUR GLOSSY.
F
F
F

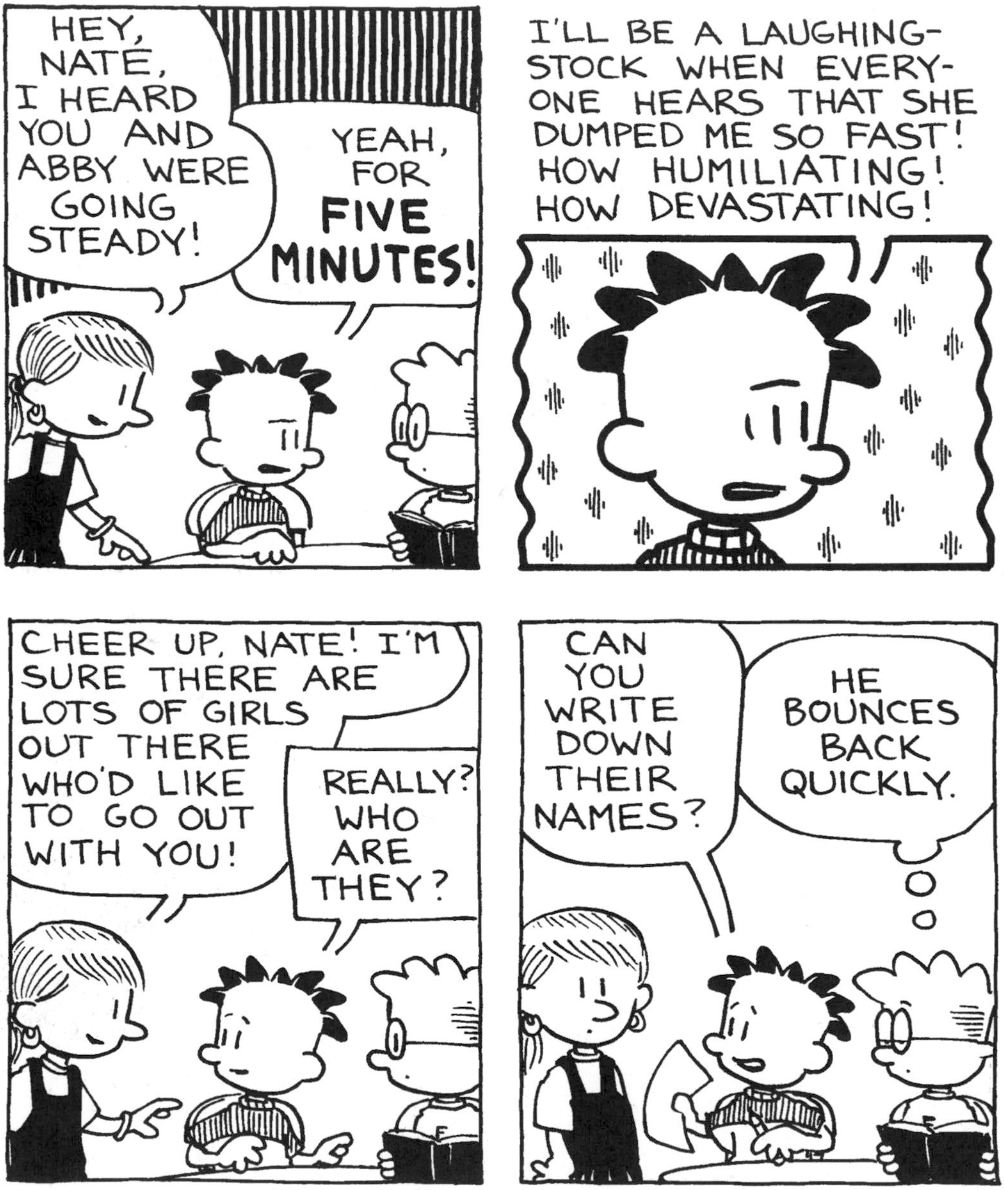
HEY, NATE, I HEARD YOU AND ABBY WERE GOING STEADY!
YEAH, FOR **FIVE MINUTES!**
I'LL BE A LAUGHING-STOCK WHEN EVERYONE HEARS THAT SHE DUMPED ME SO FAST! HOW HUMILIATING! HOW DEVASTATING!
CHEER UP, NATE! I'M SURE THERE ARE LOTS OF GIRLS OUT THERE WHO'D LIKE TO GO OUT WITH YOU!
REALLY? WHO ARE THEY?
CAN YOU WRITE DOWN THEIR NAMES?
HE BOUNCES BACK QUICKLY.

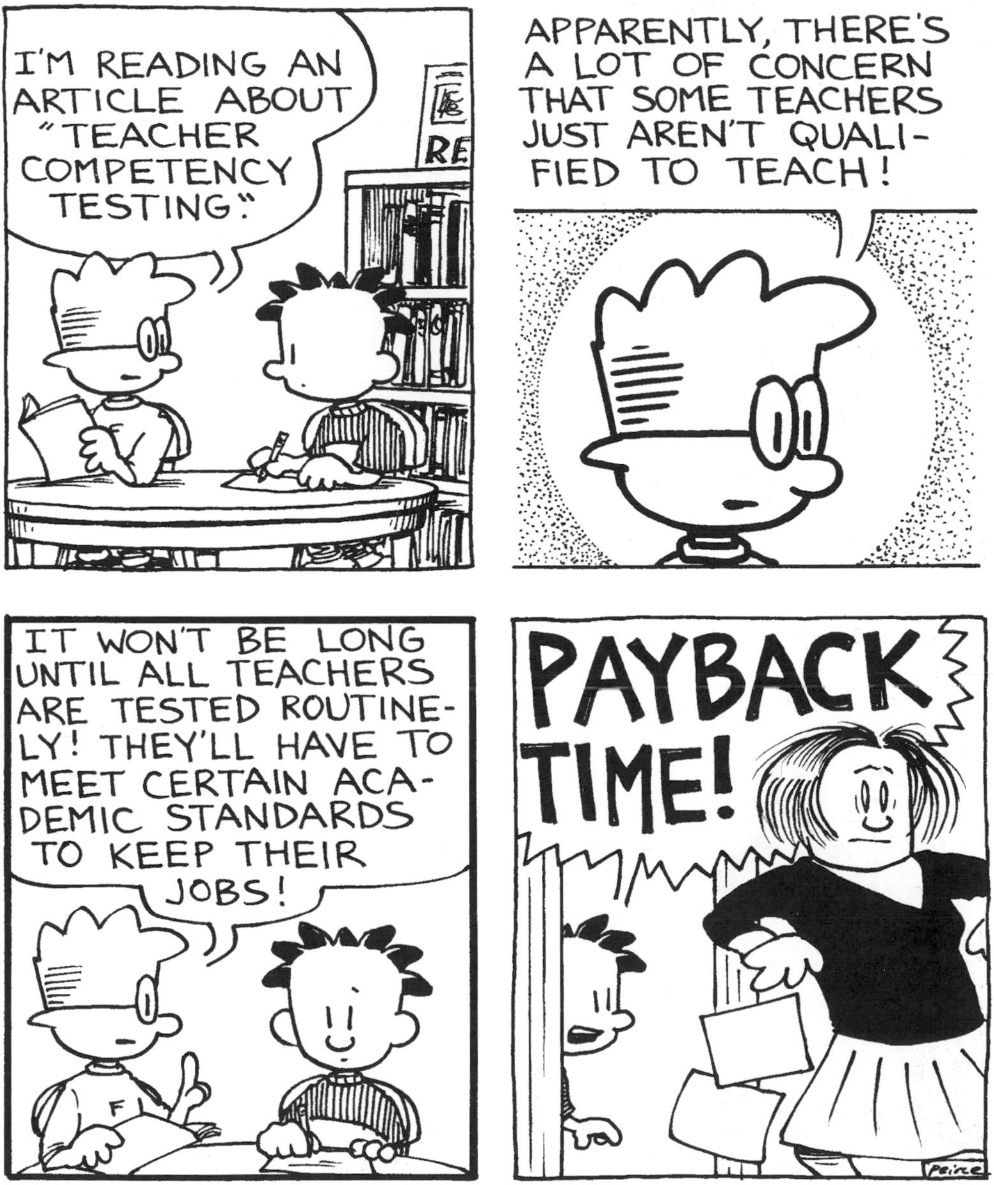
I'M READING AN ARTICLE ABOUT "TEACHER COMPETENCY TESTING."
APPARENTLY, THERE'S A LOT OF CONCERN THAT SOME TEACHERS JUST AREN'T QUALIFIED TO TEACH!
IT WON'T BE LONG UNTIL ALL TEACHERS ARE TESTED ROUTINELY! THEY'LL HAVE TO MEET CERTAIN ACADEMIC STANDARDS TO KEEP THEIR JOBS!
PAYBACK TIME!
Peirce

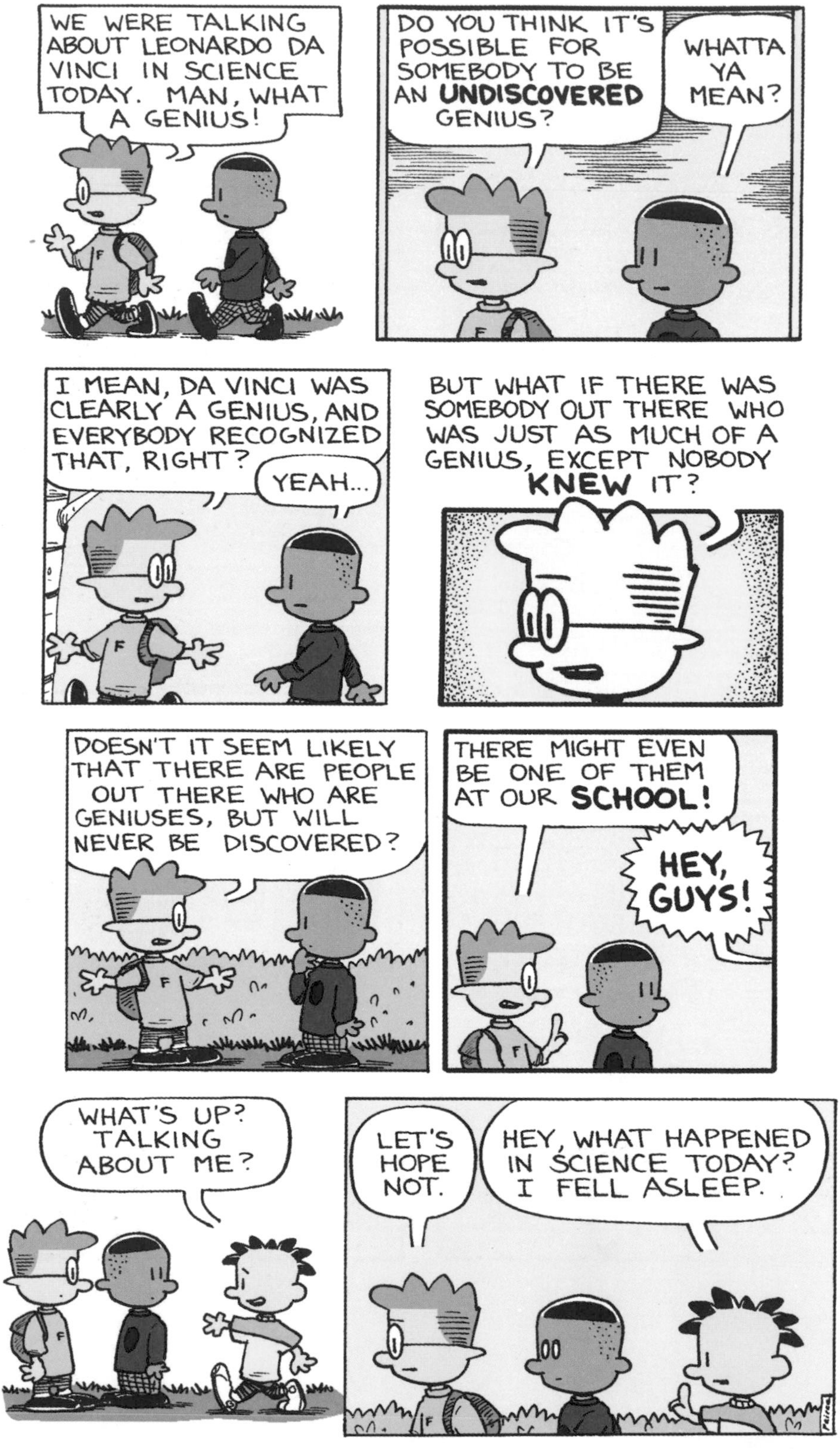

WE WERE TALKING ABOUT LEONARDO DA VINCI IN SCIENCE TODAY. MAN, WHAT A GENIUS!
DO YOU THINK IT'S POSSIBLE FOR SOMEBODY TO BE AN UNDISCOVERED GENIUS?
WHATTA YA MEAN?
I MEAN, DA VINCI WAS CLEARLY A GENIUS, AND EVERYBODY RECOGNIZED THAT, RIGHT?
YEAH...
BUT WHAT IF THERE WAS SOMEBODY OUT THERE WHO WAS JUST AS MUCH OF A GENIUS, EXCEPT NOBODY KNEW IT?
DOESN'T IT SEEM LIKELY THAT THERE ARE PEOPLE OUT THERE WHO ARE GENIUSES, BUT WILL NEVER BE DISCOVERED?
THERE MIGHT EVEN BE ONE OF THEM AT OUR SCHOOL!
HEY, GUYS!
WHAT'S UP? TALKING ABOUT ME?
LET'S HOPE NOT.
HEY, WHAT HAPPENED IN SCIENCE TODAY? I FELL ASLEEP.

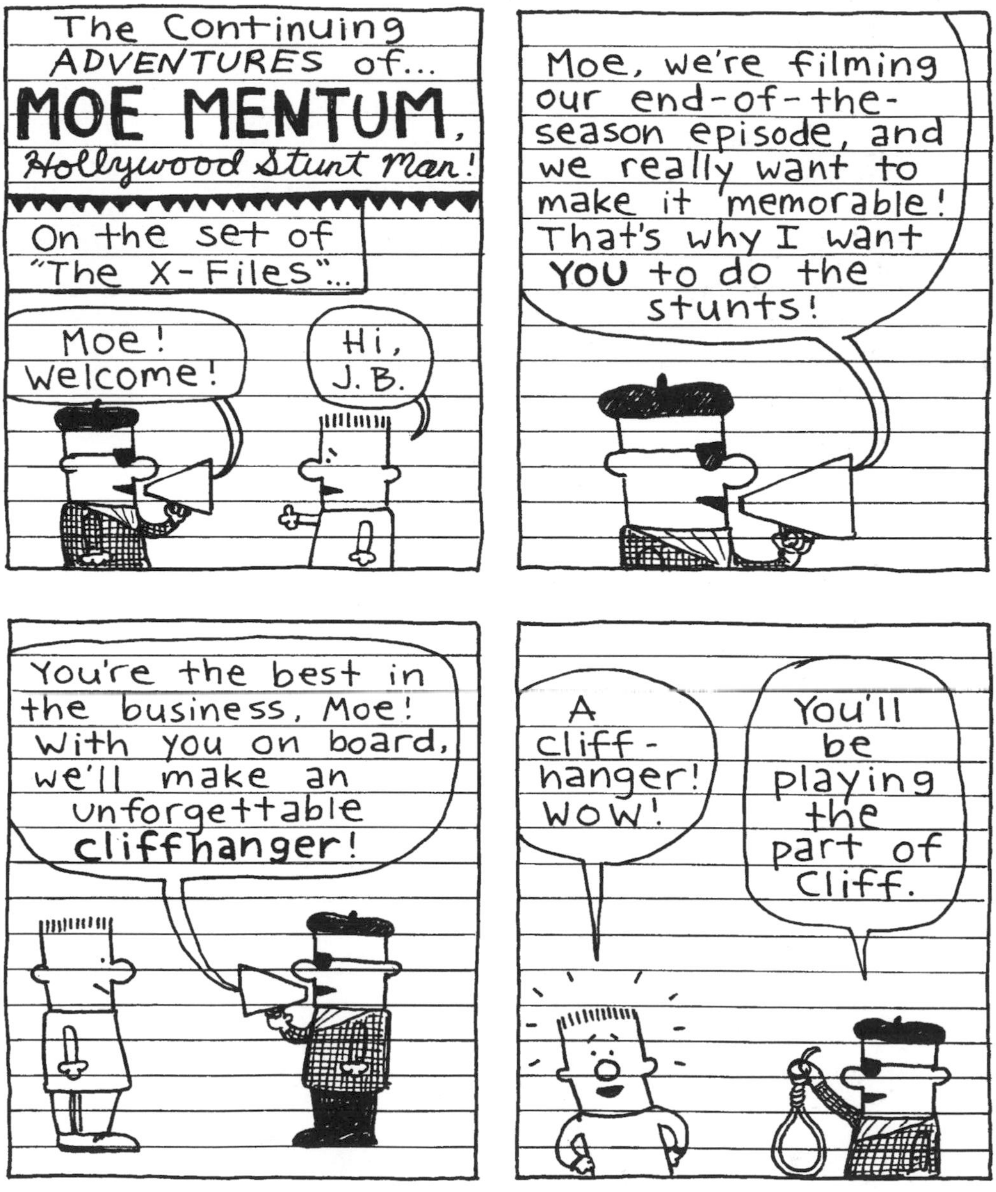
The Continuing ADVENTURES of...
MOE MENTUM, Hollywood Stunt Man!
On the set of "The X-Files"...
Moe! Welcome!
Hi, J.B.
Moe, we're filming our end-of-the-season episode, and we really want to make it memorable! That's why I want YOU to do the stunts!
You're the best in the business, Moe! With you on board, we'll make an unforgettable cliffhanger!
A cliff-hanger! WOW!
You'll be playing the part of Cliff.

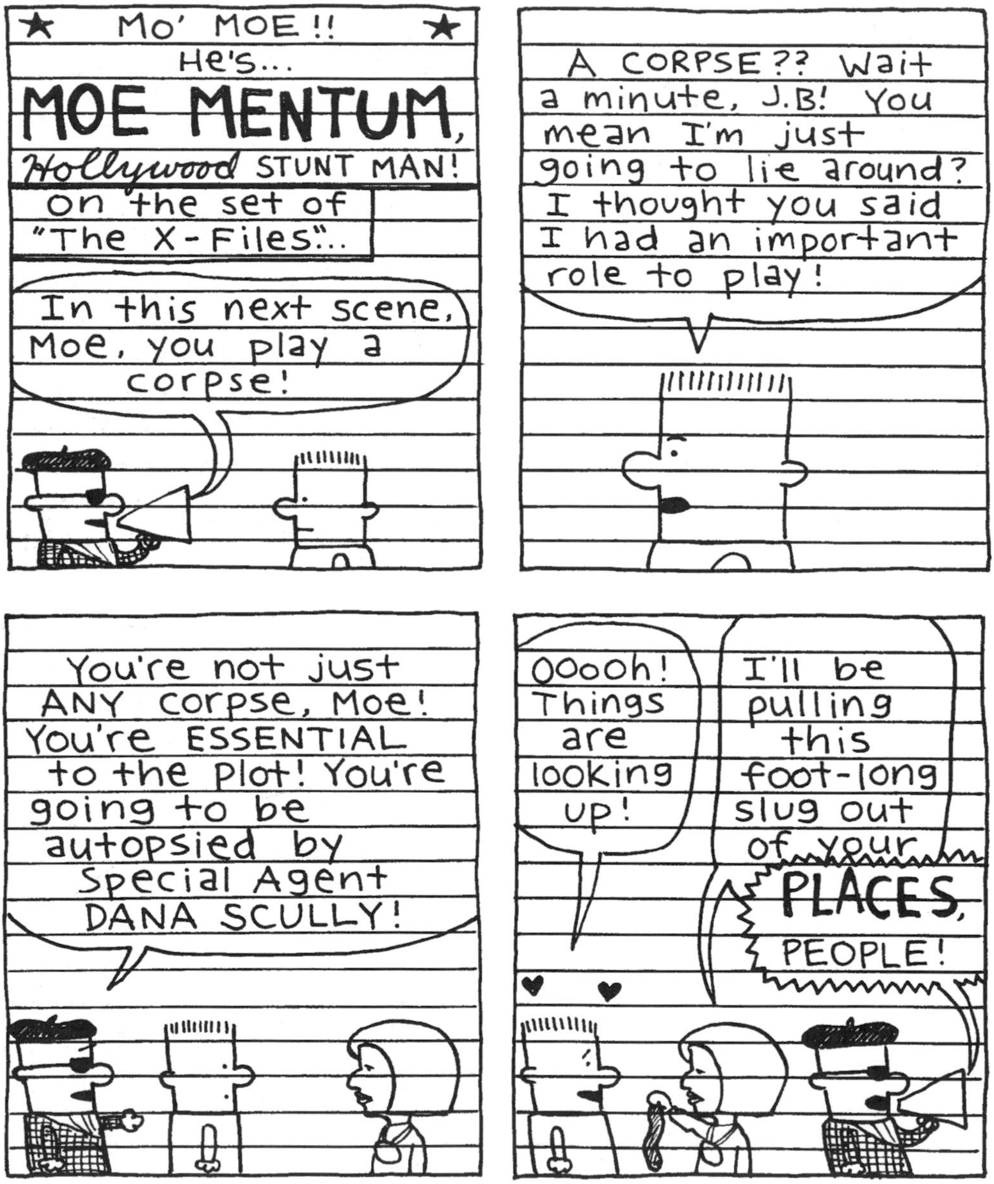
★ MO' MOE!! ★
HE'S...
MOE MENTUM,
Hollywood STUNT MAN!
on the set of "The X-Files"...
In this next scene, Moe, you play a corpse!
A CORPSE?? Wait a minute, J.B! You mean I'm just going to lie around? I thought you said I had an important role to play!
You're not just ANY corpse, Moe! You're ESSENTIAL to the plot! You're going to be autopsied by Special Agent DANA SCULLY!
Ooooh! Things are looking up!
I'll be pulling this foot-long slug out of your
PLACES, PEOPLE!

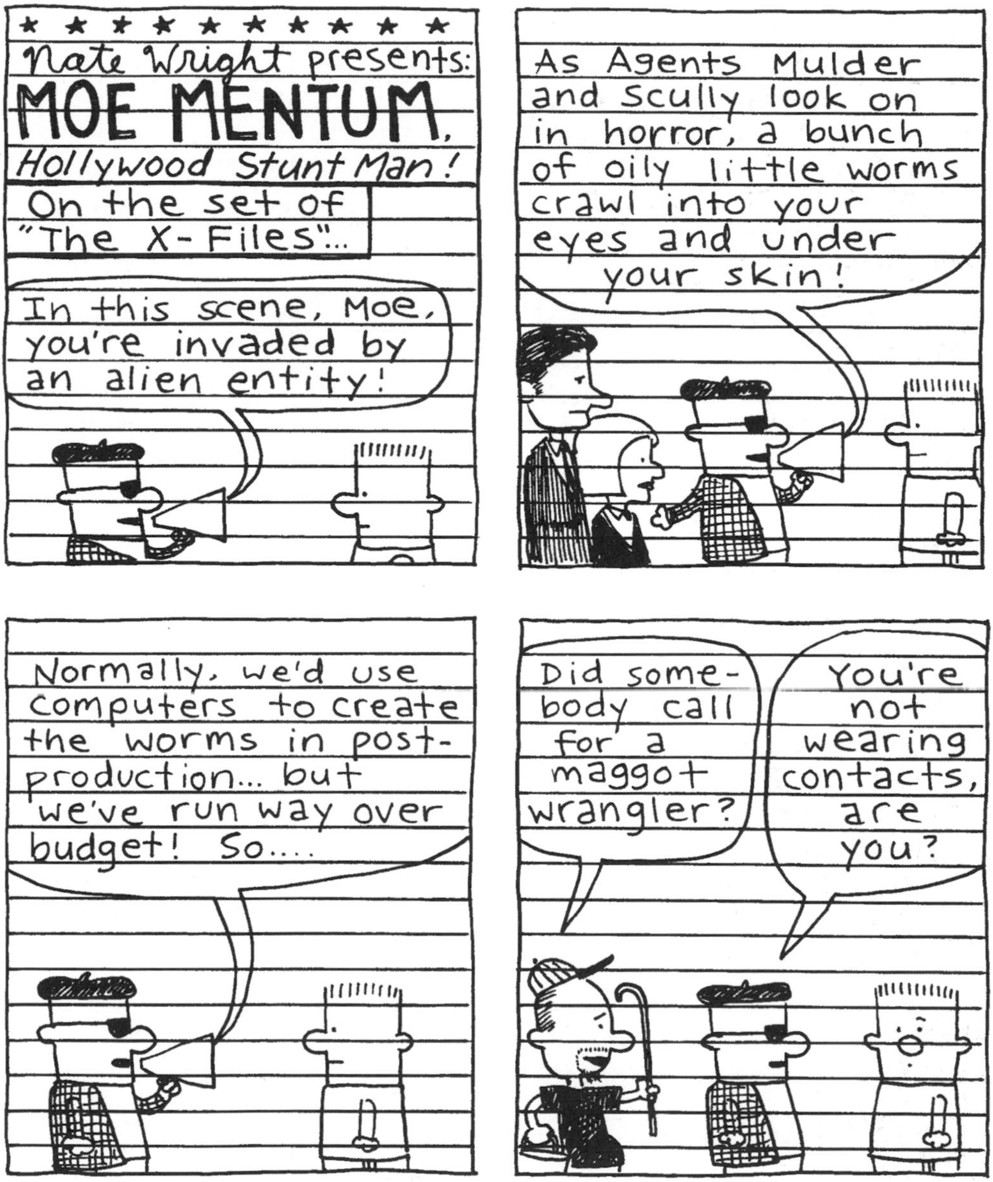
★ ★ ★ ★ ★ ★ ★ ★ ★ ★
Nate Wright presents:
MOE MENTUM,
Hollywood Stunt Man!
On the set of "The X-Files"...
In this scene, Moe, you're invaded by an alien entity!
As Agents Mulder and Scully look on in horror, a bunch of oily little worms crawl into your eyes and under your skin!
Normally, we'd use computers to create the worms in post-production... but we've run way over budget! So....
Did some-body call for a maggot wrangler?
You're not wearing contacts, are you?

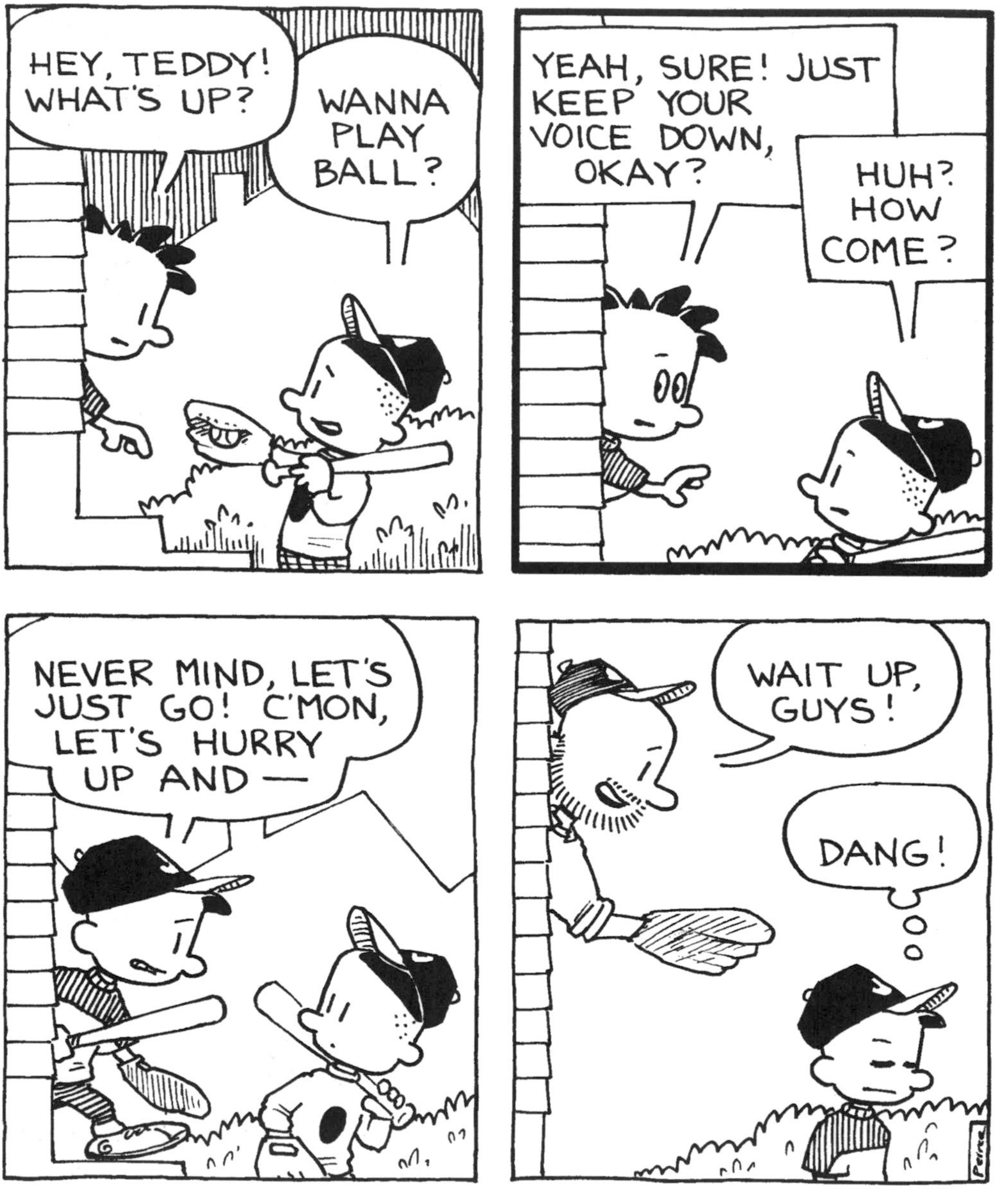
HEY, TEDDY! WHAT'S UP?
WANNA PLAY BALL?
YEAH, SURE! JUST KEEP YOUR VOICE DOWN, OKAY?
HUH? HOW COME?
NEVER MIND, LET'S JUST GO! C'MON, LET'S HURRY UP AND—
WAIT UP, GUYS!
DANG!
Peirce

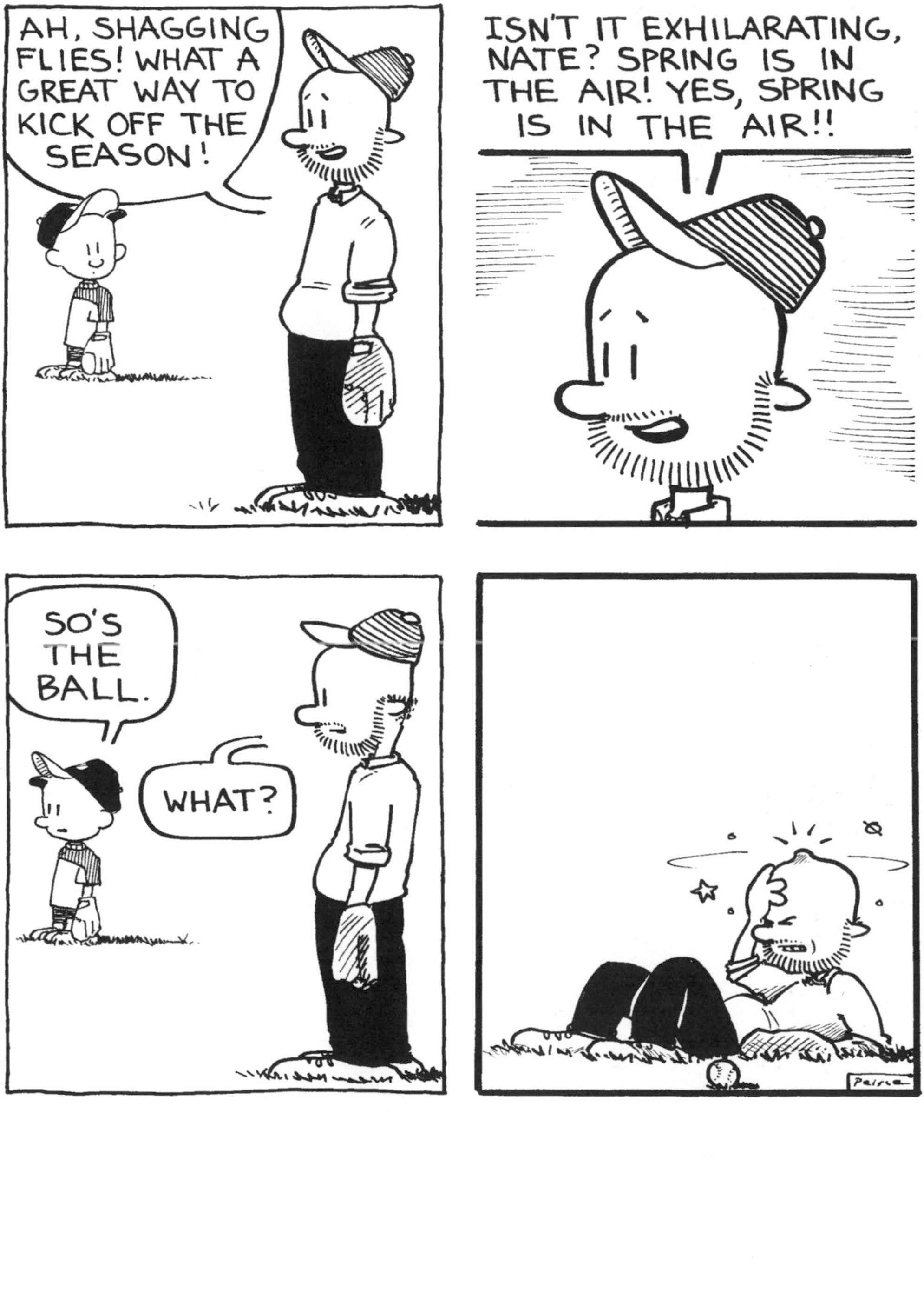
AH, SHAGGING FLIES! WHAT A GREAT WAY TO KICK OFF THE SEASON!
ISN'T IT EXHILARATING, NATE? SPRING IS IN THE AIR! YES, SPRING IS IN THE AIR!!
SO'S THE BALL.
WHAT?
Peirce

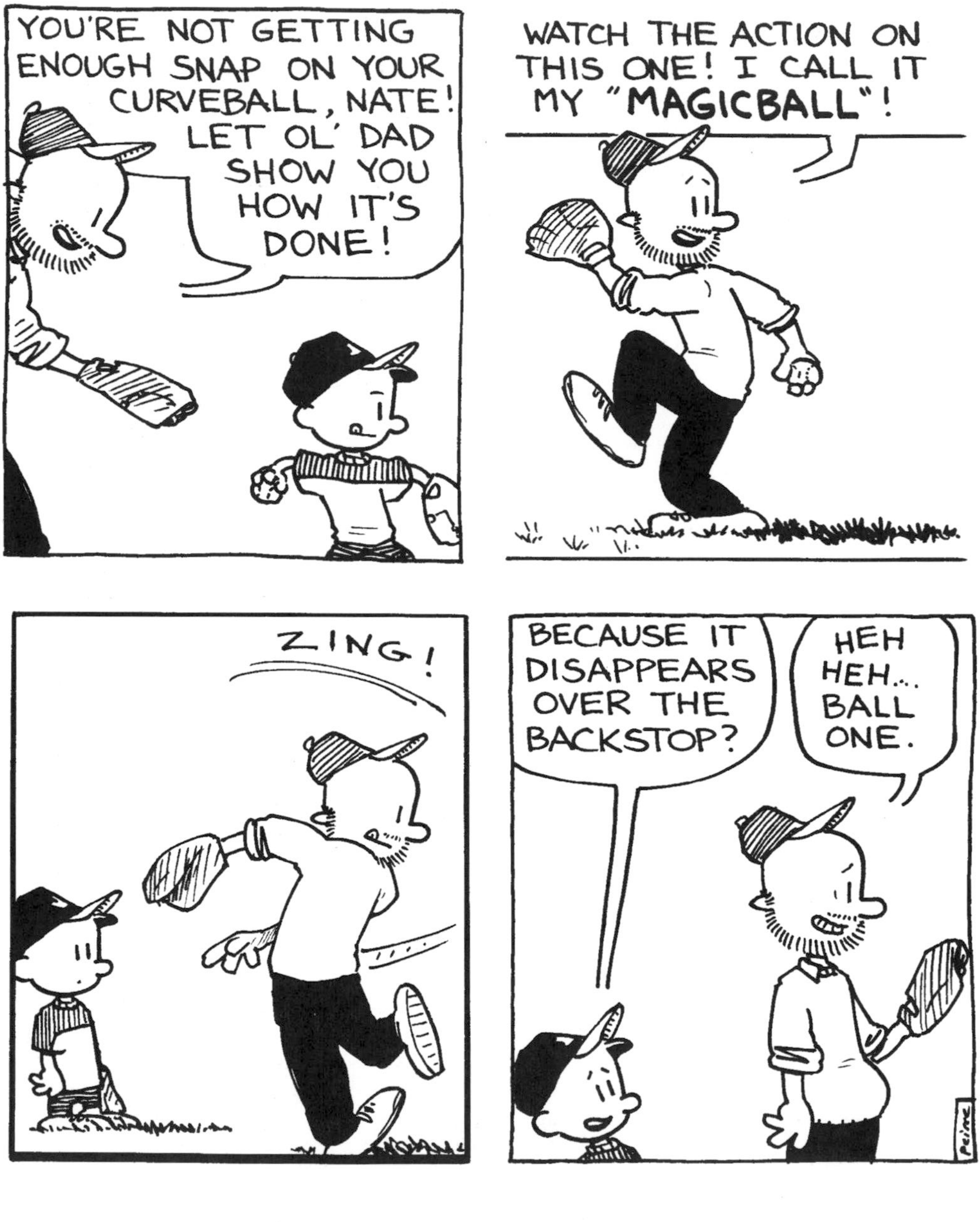
YOU'RE NOT GETTING ENOUGH SNAP ON YOUR CURVEBALL, NATE! LET OL' DAD SHOW YOU HOW IT'S DONE!
WATCH THE ACTION ON THIS ONE! I CALL IT MY "MAGICBALL"!
ZING!
BECAUSE IT DISAPPEARS OVER THE BACKSTOP?
HEH HEH... BALL ONE.
PEIRCE

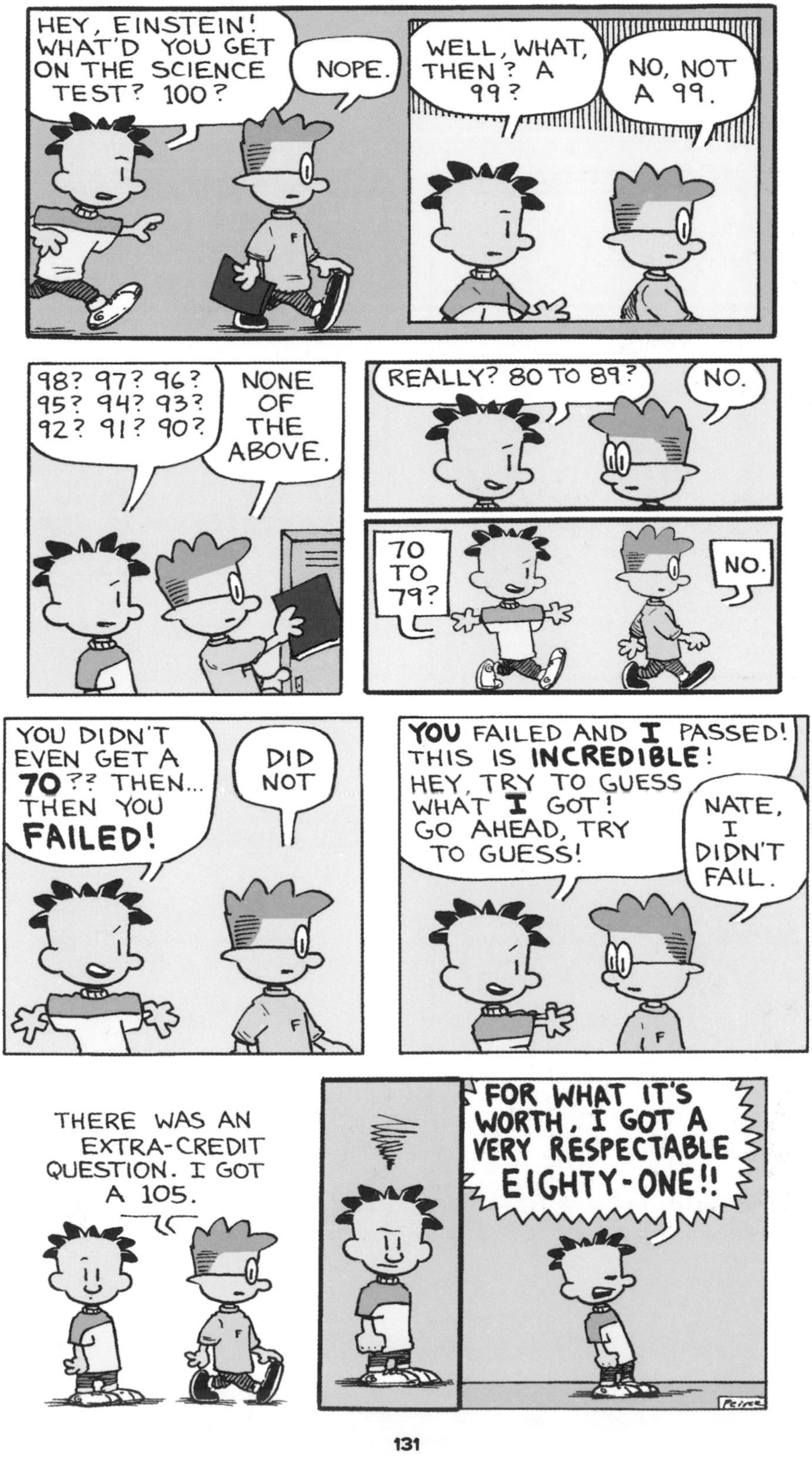
HEY, EINSTEIN! WHAT'D YOU GET ON THE SCIENCE TEST? 100?
NOPE.
WELL, WHAT, THEN? A 99?
NO, NOT A 99.
98? 97? 96? 95? 94? 93? 92? 91? 90?
NONE OF THE ABOVE.
REALLY? 80 TO 89?
NO.
70 TO 79?
NO.
YOU DIDN'T EVEN GET A 70?? THEN... THEN YOU FAILED!
DID NOT
YOU FAILED AND I PASSED! THIS IS INCREDIBLE! HEY, TRY TO GUESS WHAT I GOT! GO AHEAD, TRY TO GUESS!
NATE, I DIDN'T FAIL.
THERE WAS AN EXTRA-CREDIT QUESTION. I GOT A 105.
FOR WHAT IT'S WORTH, I GOT A VERY RESPECTABLE EIGHTY-ONE!!
Peirce

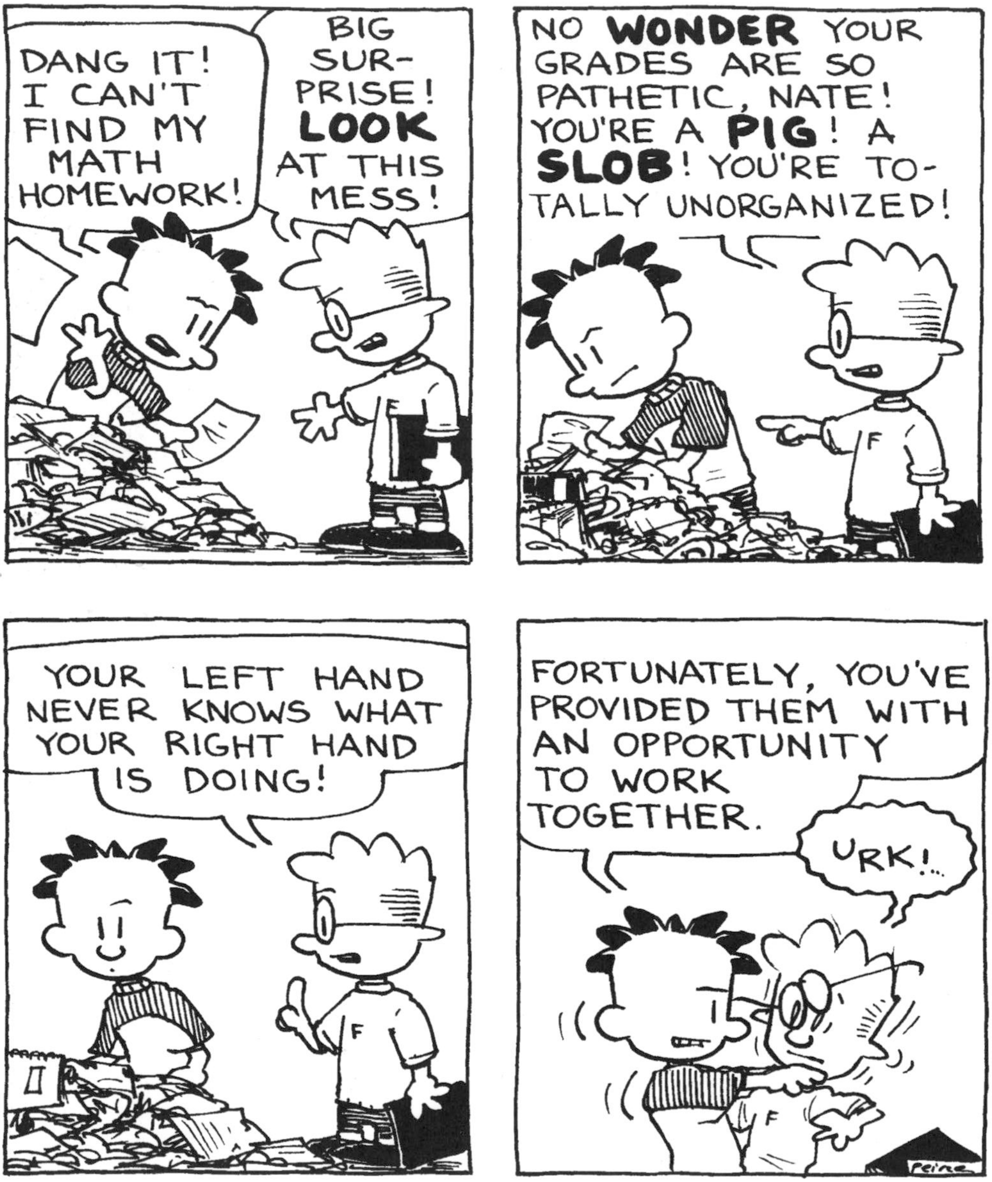
DANG IT! I CAN'T FIND MY MATH HOMEWORK!
BIG SUR-PRISE! **LOOK** AT THIS MESS!
NO **WONDER** YOUR GRADES ARE SO PATHETIC, NATE! YOU'RE A **PIG**! A **SLOB**! YOU'RE TO-TALLY UNORGANIZED!
YOUR LEFT HAND NEVER KNOWS WHAT YOUR RIGHT HAND IS DOING!
FORTUNATELY, YOU'VE PROVIDED THEM WITH AN OPPORTUNITY TO WORK TOGETHER.
URK!...

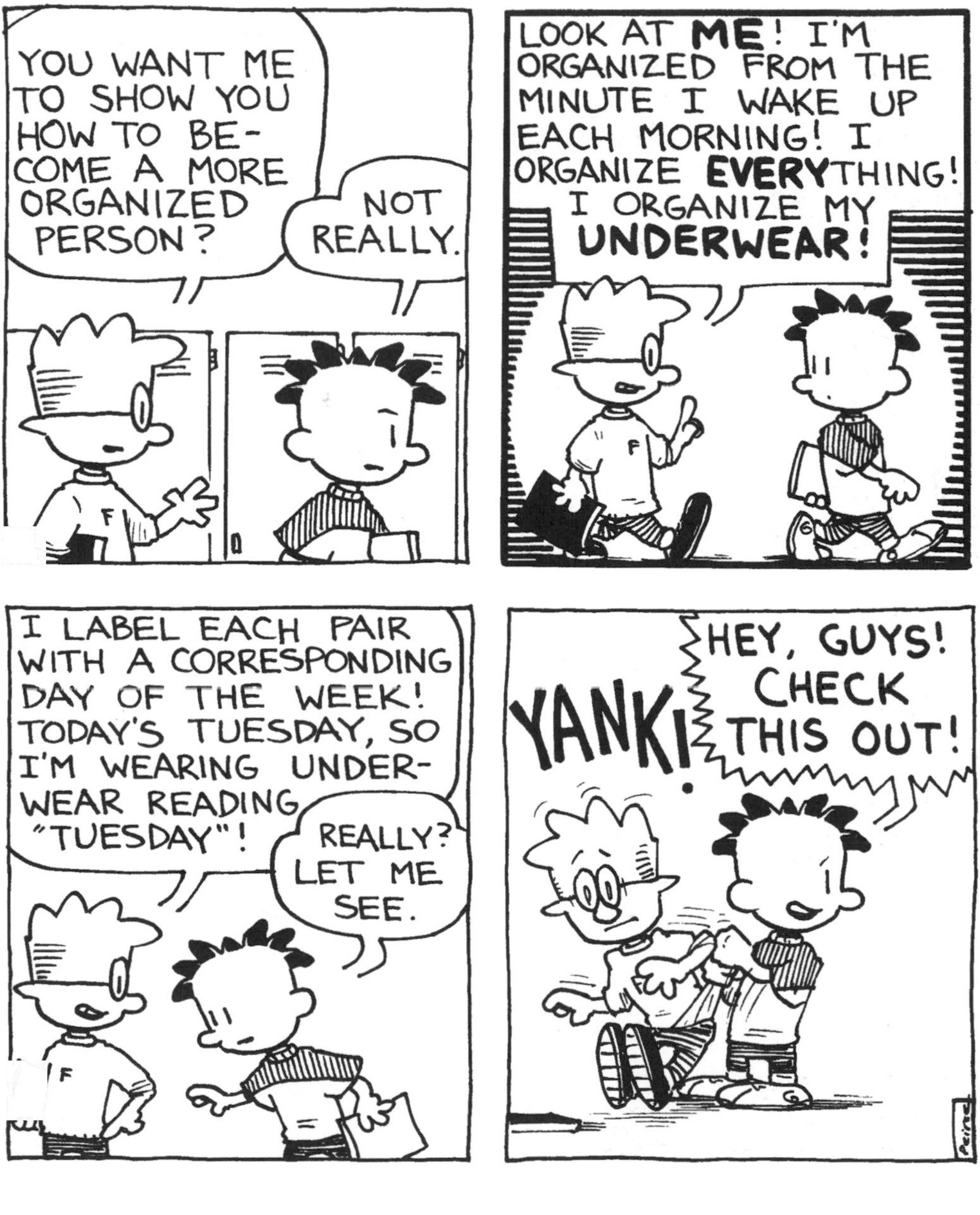
YOU WANT ME TO SHOW YOU HOW TO BE-COME A MORE ORGANIZED PERSON?
NOT REALLY.
LOOK AT ME! I'M ORGANIZED FROM THE MINUTE I WAKE UP EACH MORNING! I ORGANIZE EVERYTHING! I ORGANIZE MY UNDERWEAR!
I LABEL EACH PAIR WITH A CORRESPONDING DAY OF THE WEEK! TODAY'S TUESDAY, SO I'M WEARING UNDER-WEAR READING "TUESDAY"!
REALLY? LET ME SEE.
YANK!
HEY, GUYS! CHECK THIS OUT!
PEIRCE

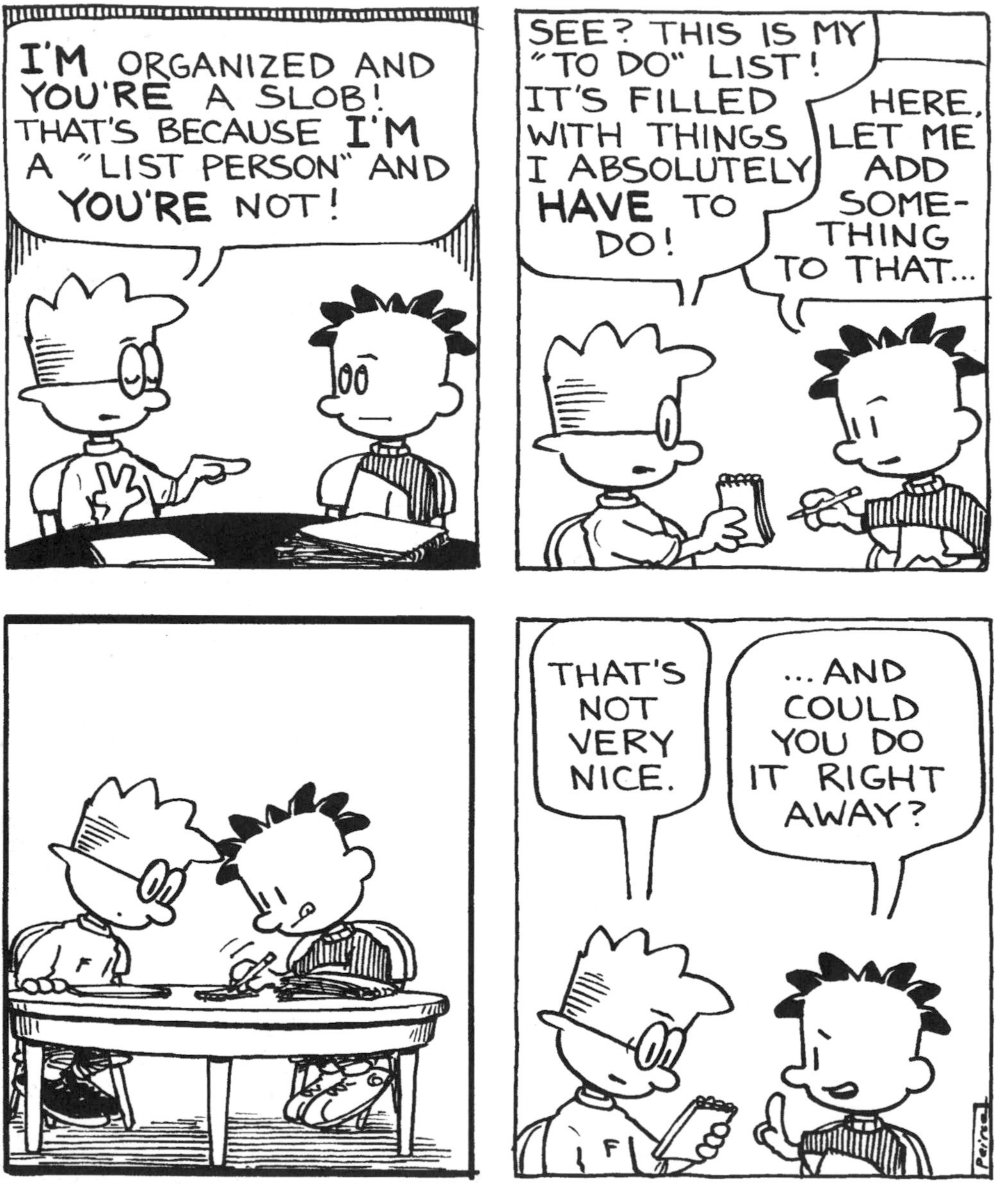
I'M ORGANIZED AND YOU'RE A SLOB! THAT'S BECAUSE I'M A "LIST PERSON" AND YOU'RE NOT!
SEE? THIS IS MY "TO DO" LIST! IT'S FILLED WITH THINGS I ABSOLUTELY HAVE TO DO!
HERE, LET ME ADD SOMETHING TO THAT...
THAT'S NOT VERY NICE.
...AND COULD YOU DO IT RIGHT AWAY?
Peirce

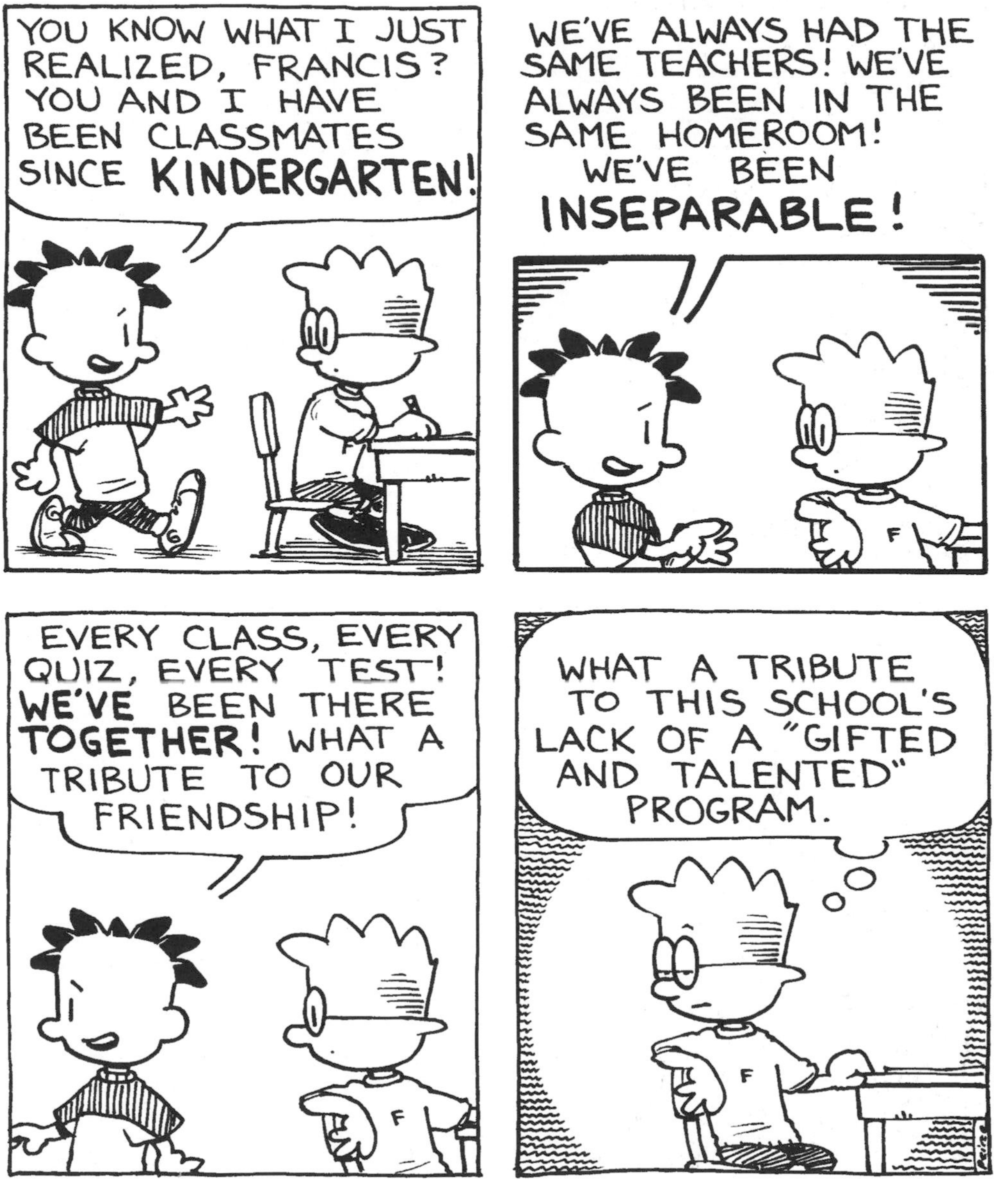
YOU KNOW WHAT I JUST REALIZED, FRANCIS? YOU AND I HAVE BEEN CLASSMATES SINCE KINDERGARTEN!
WE'VE ALWAYS HAD THE SAME TEACHERS! WE'VE ALWAYS BEEN IN THE SAME HOMEROOM! WE'VE BEEN INSEPARABLE!
EVERY CLASS, EVERY QUIZ, EVERY TEST! WE'VE BEEN THERE TOGETHER! WHAT A TRIBUTE TO OUR FRIENDSHIP!
WHAT A TRIBUTE TO THIS SCHOOL'S LACK OF A "GIFTED AND TALENTED" PROGRAM.

WE SHOULD KEEP OUR RECORD INTACT, FRANCIS! LET'S TRY TO MAKE SURE WE CONTINUE TO TAKE ALL THE SAME CLASSES!
YOU MEAN ALL THE WAY THROUGH HIGH SCHOOL?
BEYOND HIGH SCHOOL! LET'S GO TO THE SAME **COLLEGE**!
WHERE SHOULD WE GO?
WELL, I MYSELF PLAN TO END UP IN THE IVY LEAGUE.
WHAT'S THAT? SOME SORT OF BOTANY SCHOOL?
I'LL TRY TO KEEP IN TOUCH.

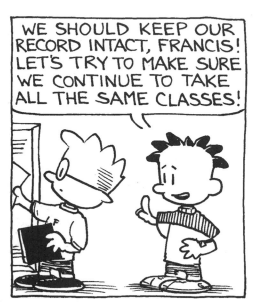

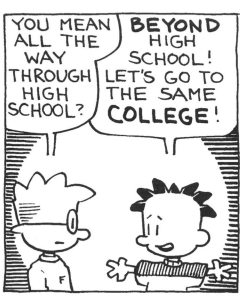

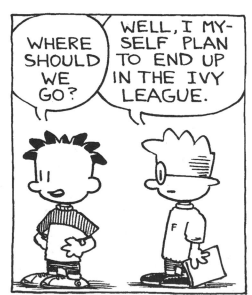

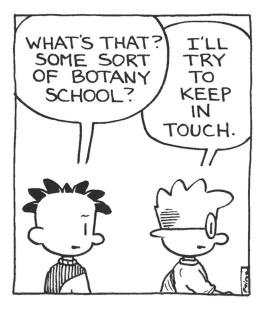

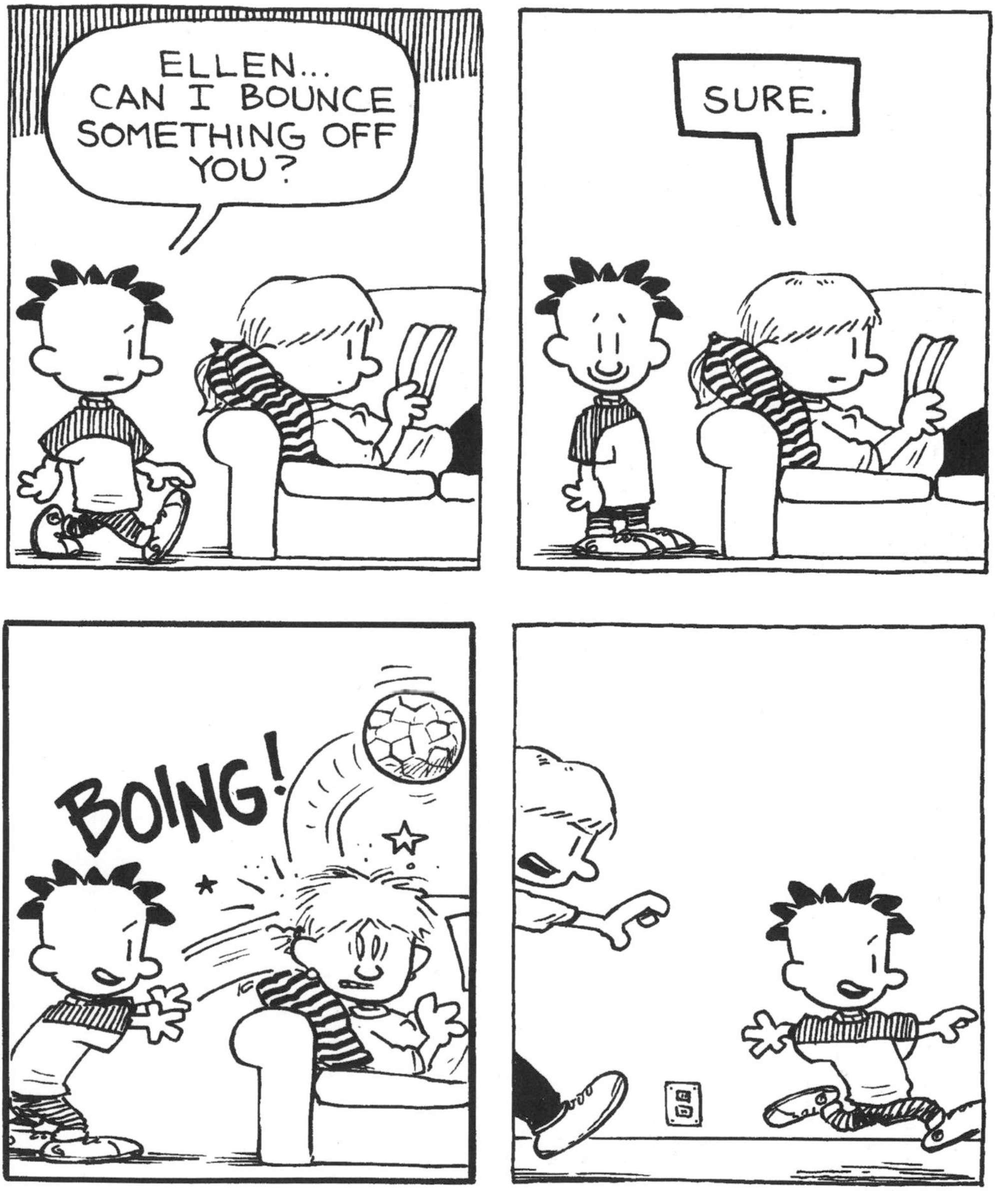
ELLEN... CAN I BOUNCE SOMETHING OFF YOU?
SURE.
BOING!

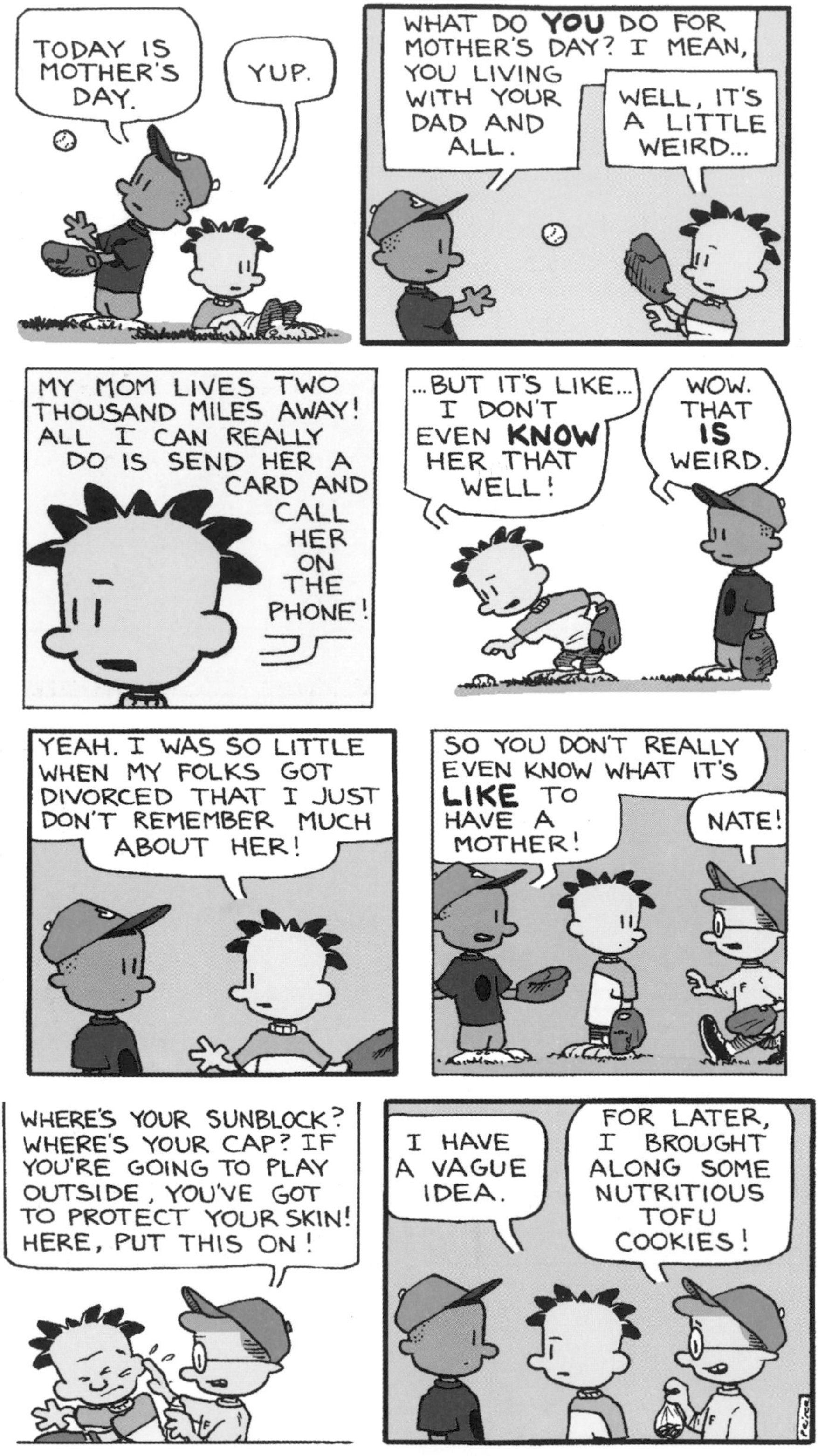
TODAY IS MOTHER'S DAY.
YUP.
WHAT DO YOU DO FOR MOTHER'S DAY? I MEAN, YOU LIVING WITH YOUR DAD AND ALL.
WELL, IT'S A LITTLE WEIRD...
MY MOM LIVES TWO THOUSAND MILES AWAY! ALL I CAN REALLY DO IS SEND HER A CARD AND CALL HER ON THE PHONE!
...BUT IT'S LIKE... I DON'T EVEN KNOW HER THAT WELL!
WOW. THAT IS WEIRD.
YEAH. I WAS SO LITTLE WHEN MY FOLKS GOT DIVORCED THAT I JUST DON'T REMEMBER MUCH ABOUT HER!
SO YOU DON'T REALLY EVEN KNOW WHAT IT'S LIKE TO HAVE A MOTHER!
NATE!
WHERE'S YOUR SUNBLOCK? WHERE'S YOUR CAP? IF YOU'RE GOING TO PLAY OUTSIDE, YOU'VE GOT TO PROTECT YOUR SKIN! HERE, PUT THIS ON!
I HAVE A VAGUE IDEA.
FOR LATER, I BROUGHT ALONG SOME NUTRITIOUS TOFU COOKIES!

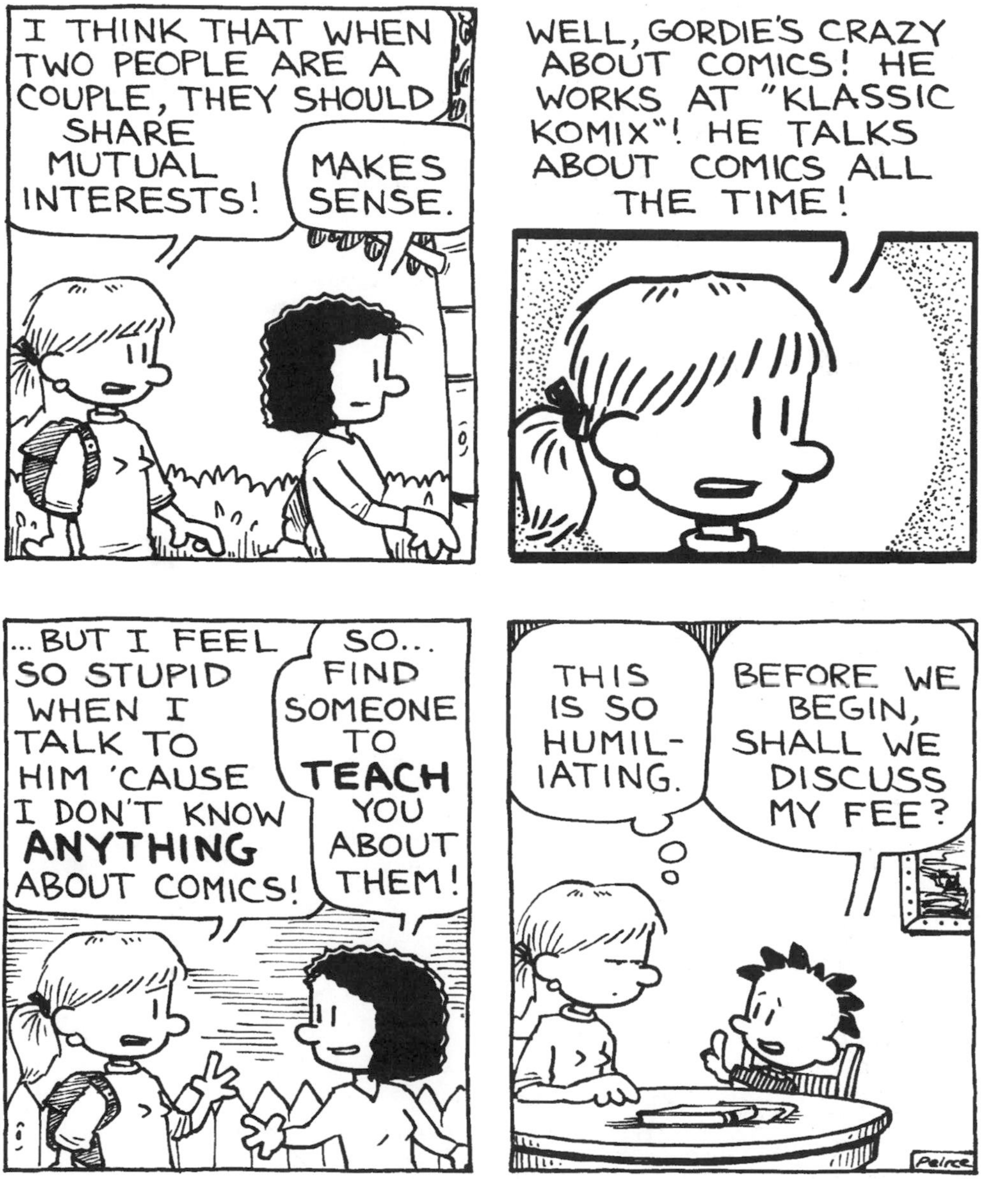

I THINK THAT WHEN TWO PEOPLE ARE A COUPLE, THEY SHOULD SHARE MUTUAL INTERESTS!
MAKES SENSE.
WELL, GORDIE'S CRAZY ABOUT COMICS! HE WORKS AT "KLASSIC KOMIX"! HE TALKS ABOUT COMICS ALL THE TIME!
...BUT I FEEL SO STUPID WHEN I TALK TO HIM 'CAUSE I DON'T KNOW ANYTHING ABOUT COMICS!
SO... FIND SOMEONE TO TEACH YOU ABOUT THEM!
THIS IS SO HUMIL-IATING.
BEFORE WE BEGIN, SHALL WE DISCUSS MY FEE?
Peirce

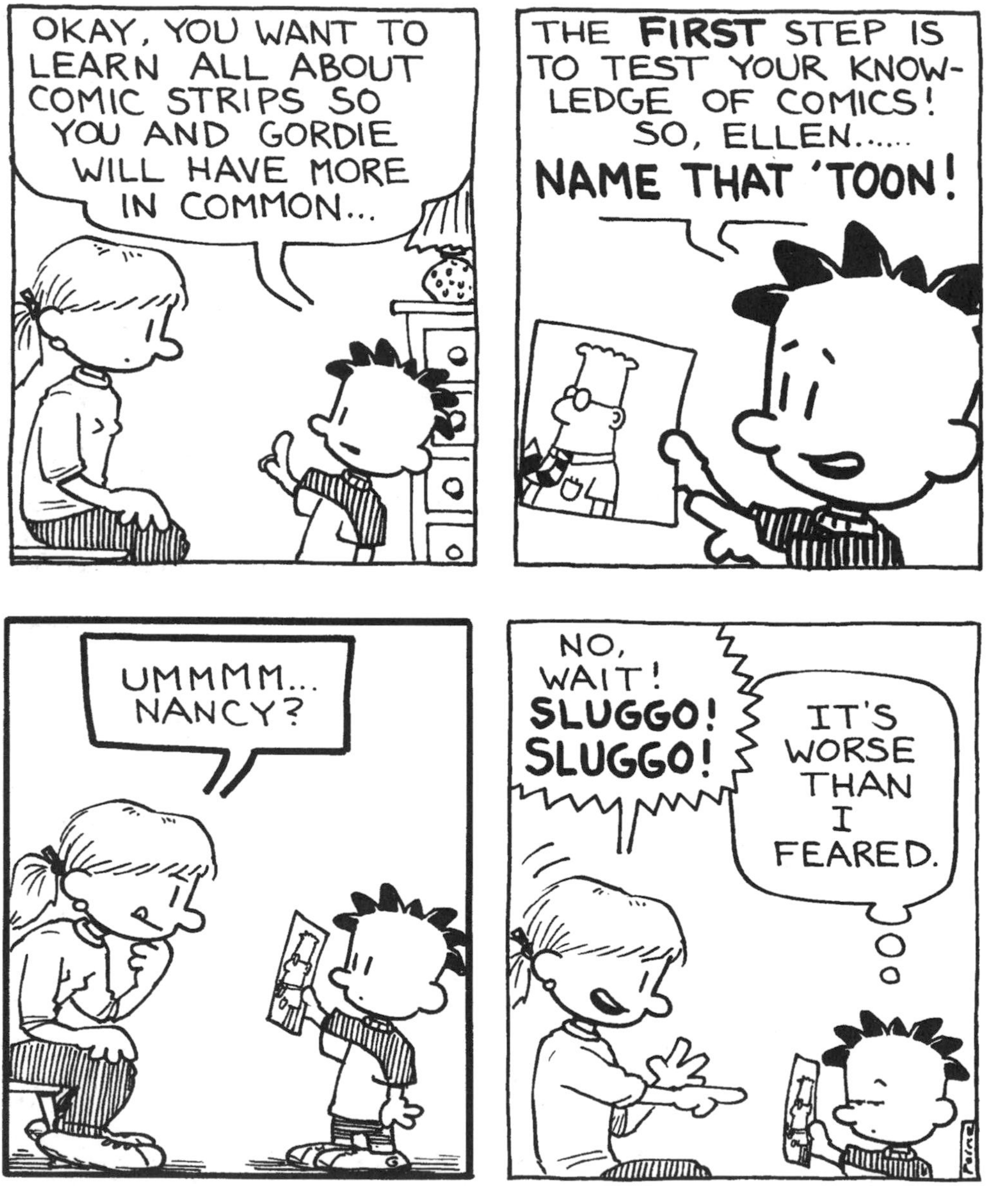
OKAY, YOU WANT TO LEARN ALL ABOUT COMIC STRIPS SO YOU AND GORDIE WILL HAVE MORE IN COMMON...
THE FIRST STEP IS TO TEST YOUR KNOW-LEDGE OF COMICS! SO, ELLEN...... NAME THAT 'TOON!
UMMMM... NANCY?
NO, WAIT! SLUGGO! SLUGGO!
IT'S WORSE THAN I FEARED.

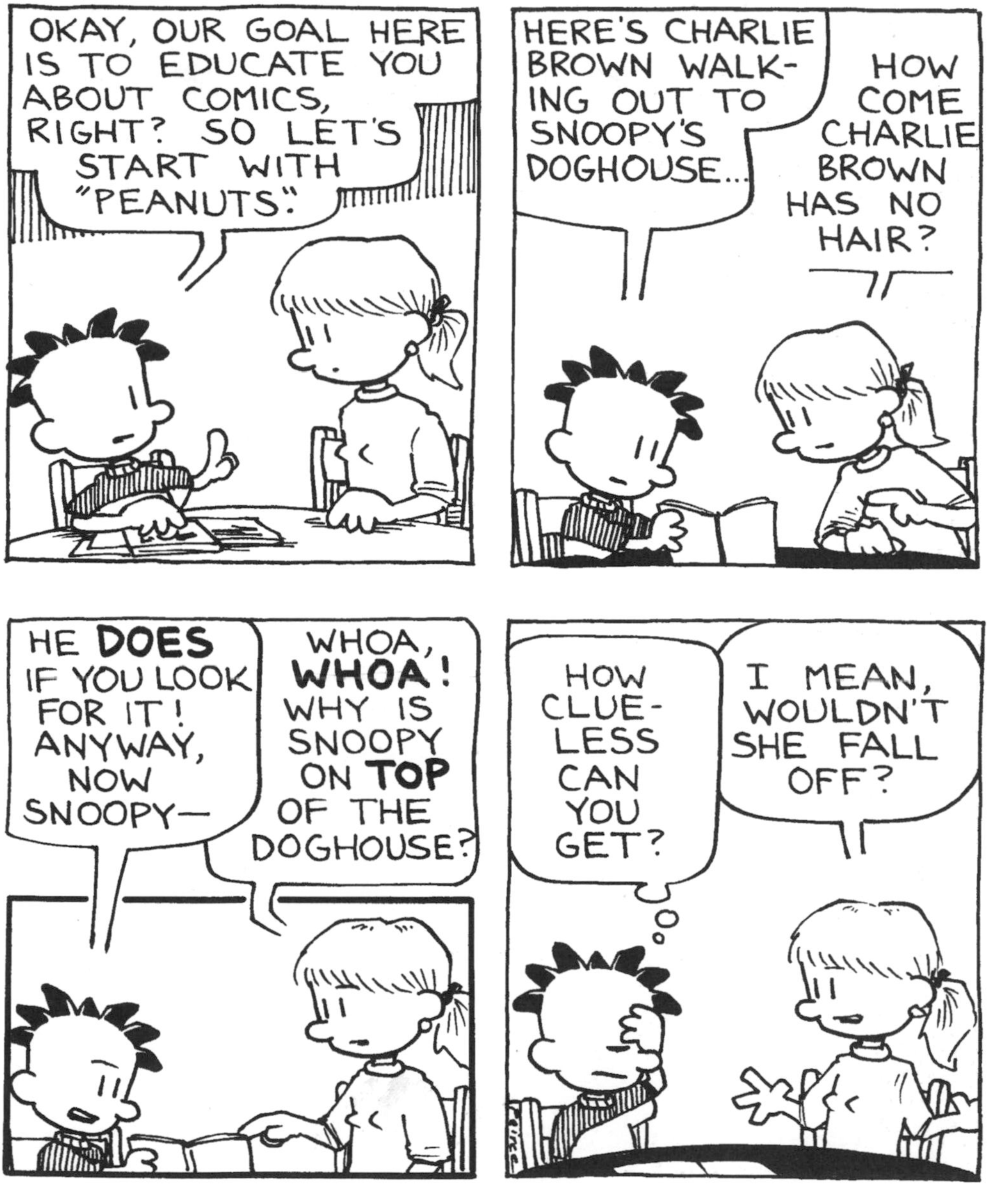
OKAY, OUR GOAL HERE IS TO EDUCATE YOU ABOUT COMICS, RIGHT? SO LET'S START WITH "PEANUTS."
HERE'S CHARLIE BROWN WALKING OUT TO SNOOPY'S DOGHOUSE...
HOW COME CHARLIE BROWN HAS NO HAIR?
HE **DOES** IF YOU LOOK FOR IT! ANYWAY, NOW SNOOPY—
WHOA, **WHOA**! WHY IS SNOOPY ON **TOP** OF THE DOGHOUSE?
HOW CLUELESS CAN YOU GET?
I MEAN, WOULDN'T SHE FALL OFF?

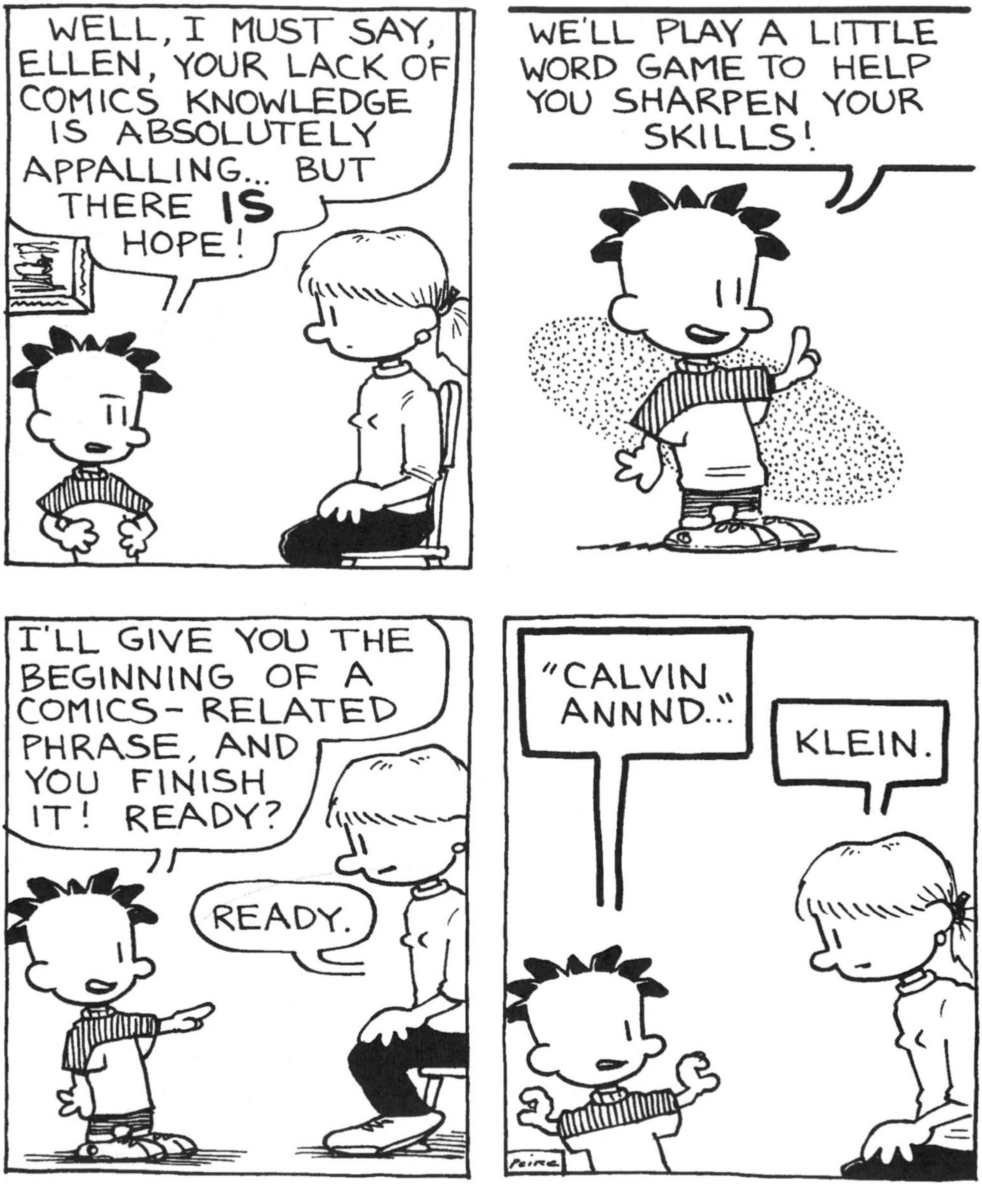
WELL, I MUST SAY, ELLEN, YOUR LACK OF COMICS KNOWLEDGE IS ABSOLUTELY APPALLING... BUT THERE **IS** HOPE!
WE'LL PLAY A LITTLE WORD GAME TO HELP YOU SHARPEN YOUR SKILLS!
I'LL GIVE YOU THE BEGINNING OF A COMICS-RELATED PHRASE, AND YOU FINISH IT! READY?
READY.
"CALVIN ANNND..."
KLEIN.

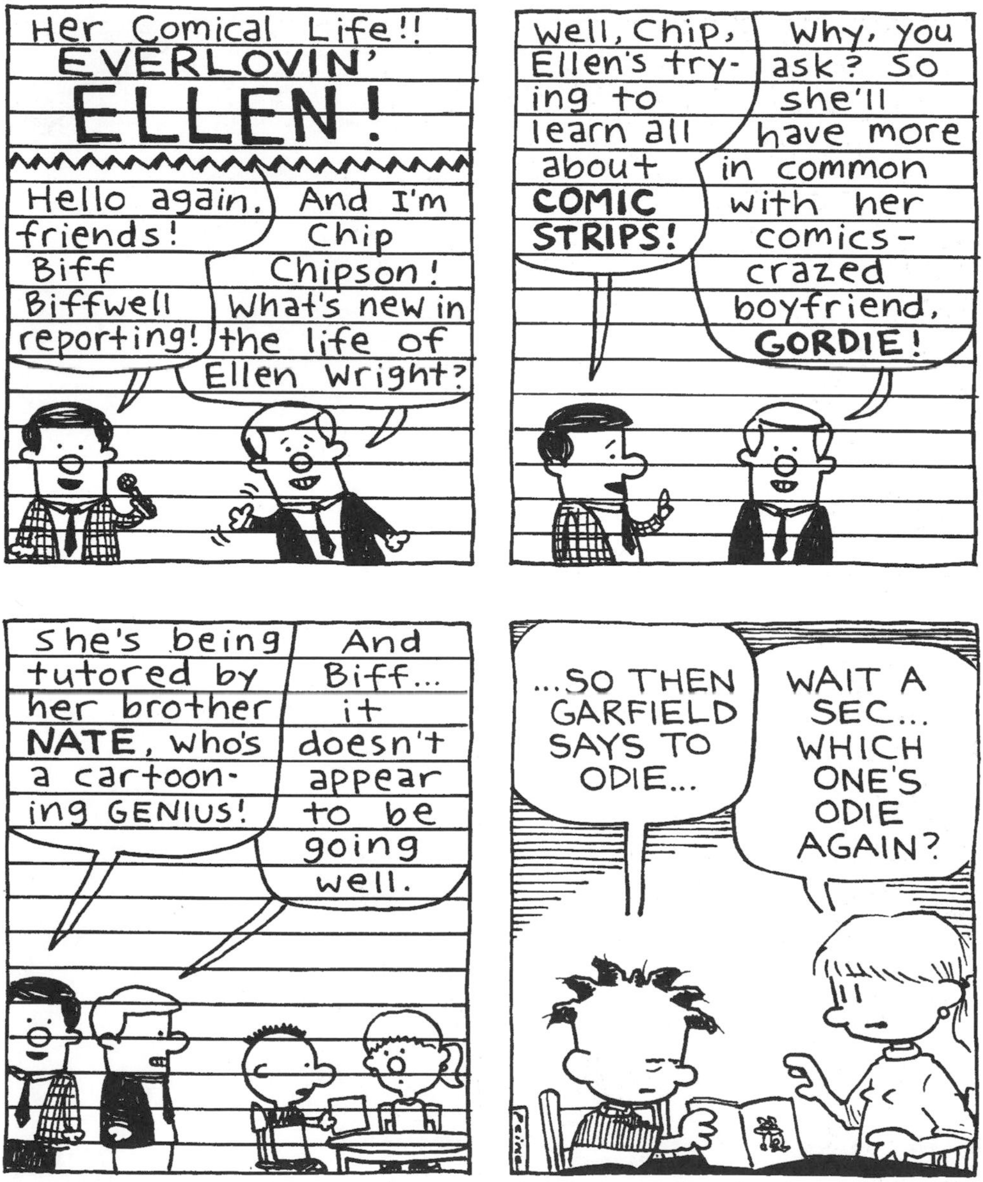
Her Comical Life!!
EVERLOVIN'
ELLEN!
Hello again, friends! Biff Biffwell reporting!
And I'm Chip Chipson! What's new in the life of Ellen Wright?
Well, Chip, Ellen's trying to learn all about **COMIC STRIPS!**
Why, you ask? So she'll have more in common with her comics-crazed boyfriend, **GORDIE!**
She's being tutored by her brother **NATE**, who's a cartooning GENIUS!
And Biff... it doesn't appear to be going well.
...SO THEN GARFIELD SAYS TO ODIE...
WAIT A SEC... WHICH ONE'S ODIE AGAIN?

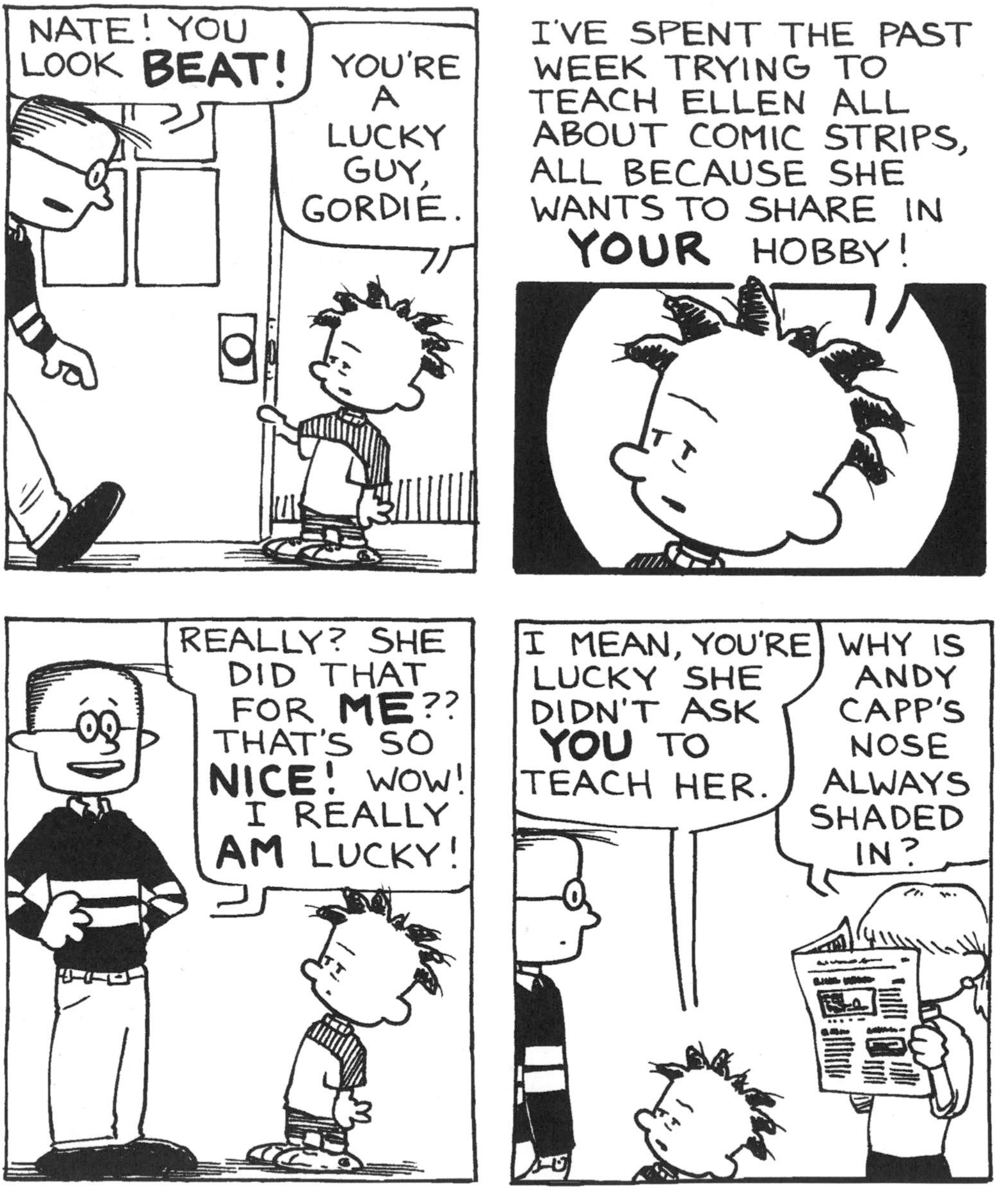
NATE! YOU LOOK BEAT!
YOU'RE A LUCKY GUY, GORDIE.
I'VE SPENT THE PAST WEEK TRYING TO TEACH ELLEN ALL ABOUT COMIC STRIPS, ALL BECAUSE SHE WANTS TO SHARE IN YOUR HOBBY!
REALLY? SHE DID THAT FOR ME?? THAT'S SO NICE! WOW! I REALLY AM LUCKY!
I MEAN, YOU'RE LUCKY SHE DIDN'T ASK YOU TO TEACH HER.
WHY IS ANDY CAPP'S NOSE ALWAYS SHADED IN?

The Continuing Adventures Of...

SUPERDAD!

The World's **ONLY** bald superhero with a slight paunch!

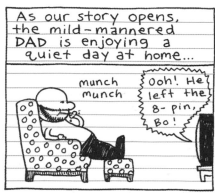

As our story opens, the mild-mannered DAD is enjoying a quiet day at home...

munch munch

Ooh! He left the 8-pin, Bo!

...when *SUDDENLY*, his solitude is shattered by a cry of...

HELP!

Hark!

With superhuman speed and grace, DAD transforms himself into SUPERDAD, defender of the defenseless!

Dad streaks to the scene, where he encounters an act of unspeakable horror!

HELP! HELP!

Gasp!

Will SUPERDAD intervene? Will he leap to the rescue?

HELP!

NO! SUPERDAD turns and walks away! Oh, the callousness! Oh, the indifference!

I SAID HELP!

NOOGIE NOOGIE NOOGIE

YOU'RE ON YOUR OWN.

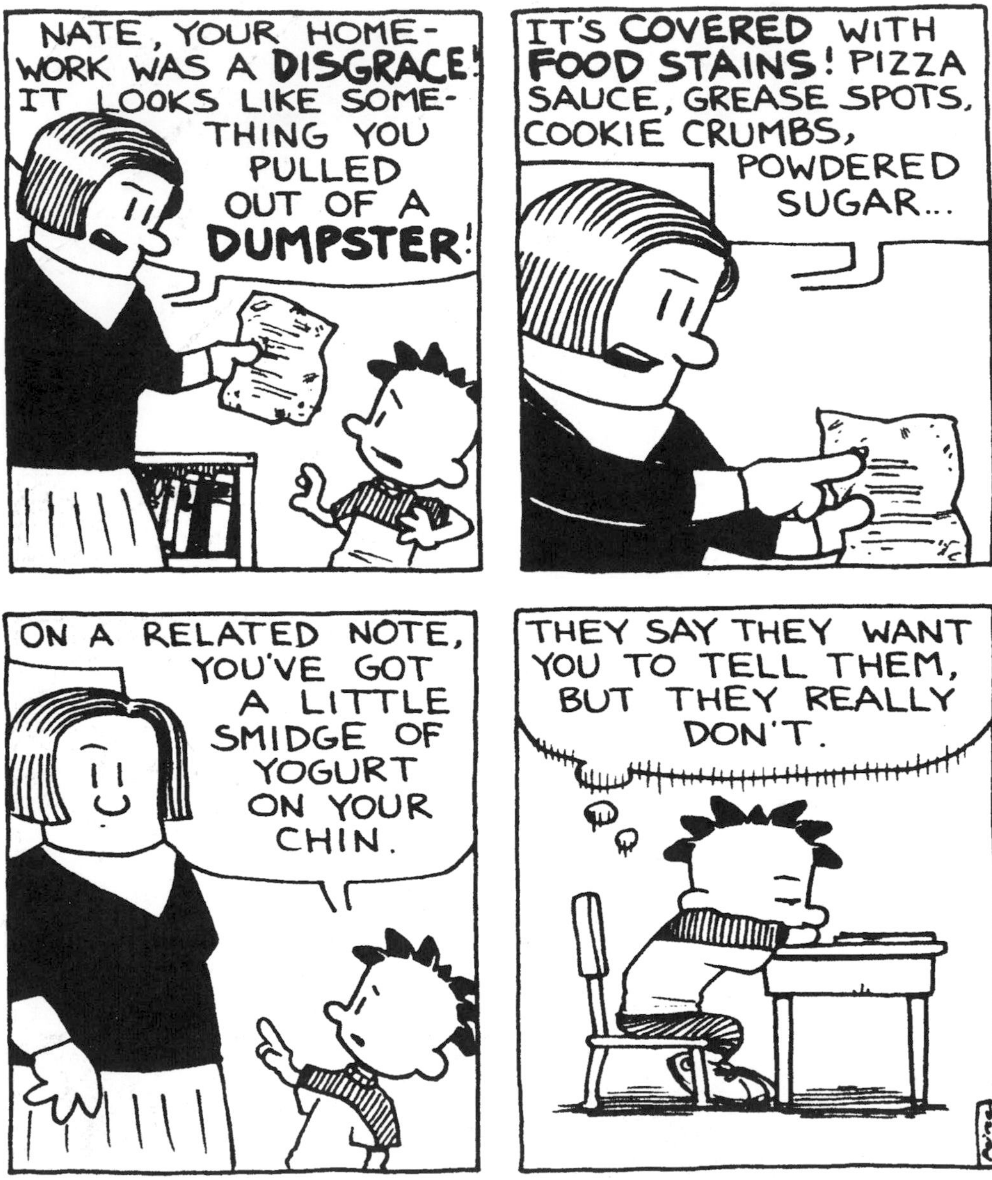
NATE, YOUR HOMEWORK WAS A DISGRACE! IT LOOKS LIKE SOMETHING YOU PULLED OUT OF A DUMPSTER!
IT'S COVERED WITH FOOD STAINS! PIZZA SAUCE, GREASE SPOTS, COOKIE CRUMBS,
POWDERED SUGAR...
ON A RELATED NOTE,
YOU'VE GOT A LITTLE SMIDGE OF YOGURT ON YOUR CHIN.
THEY SAY THEY WANT YOU TO TELL THEM, BUT THEY REALLY DON'T.

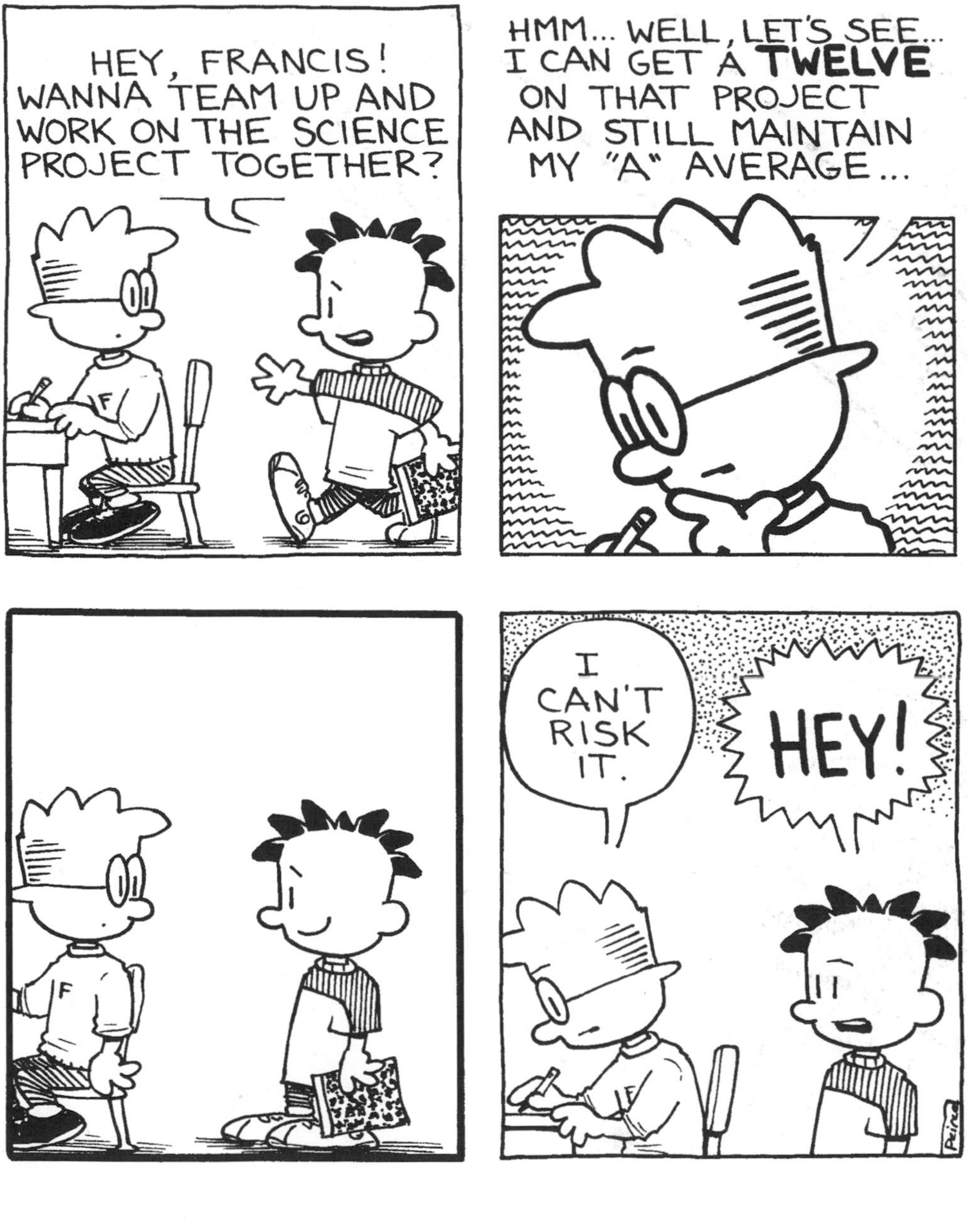
HEY, FRANCIS! WANNA TEAM UP AND WORK ON THE SCIENCE PROJECT TOGETHER?
HMM... WELL, LET'S SEE... I CAN GET A **TWELVE** ON THAT PROJECT AND STILL MAINTAIN MY "A" AVERAGE...
I CAN'T RISK IT.
HEY!

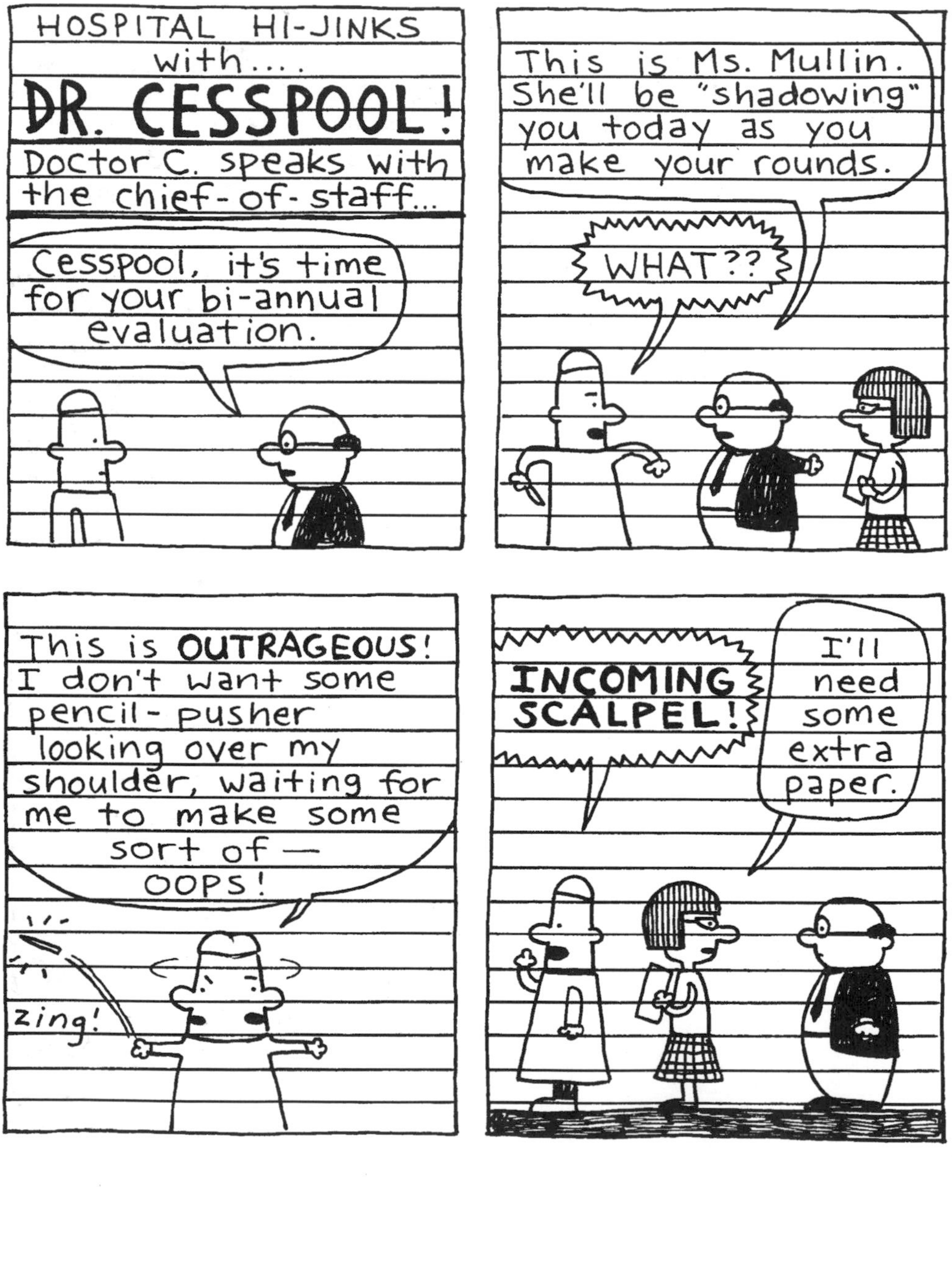
HOSPITAL HI-JINKS with.... DR. CESSPOOL!
Doctor C. speaks with the chief-of-staff...
Cesspool, it's time for your bi-annual evaluation.
This is Ms. Mullin. She'll be "shadowing" you today as you make your rounds.
WHAT??
This is OUTRAGEOUS! I don't want some pencil-pusher looking over my shoulder, waiting for me to make some sort of — OOPS!
zing!
INCOMING SCALPEL!
I'll need some extra paper.

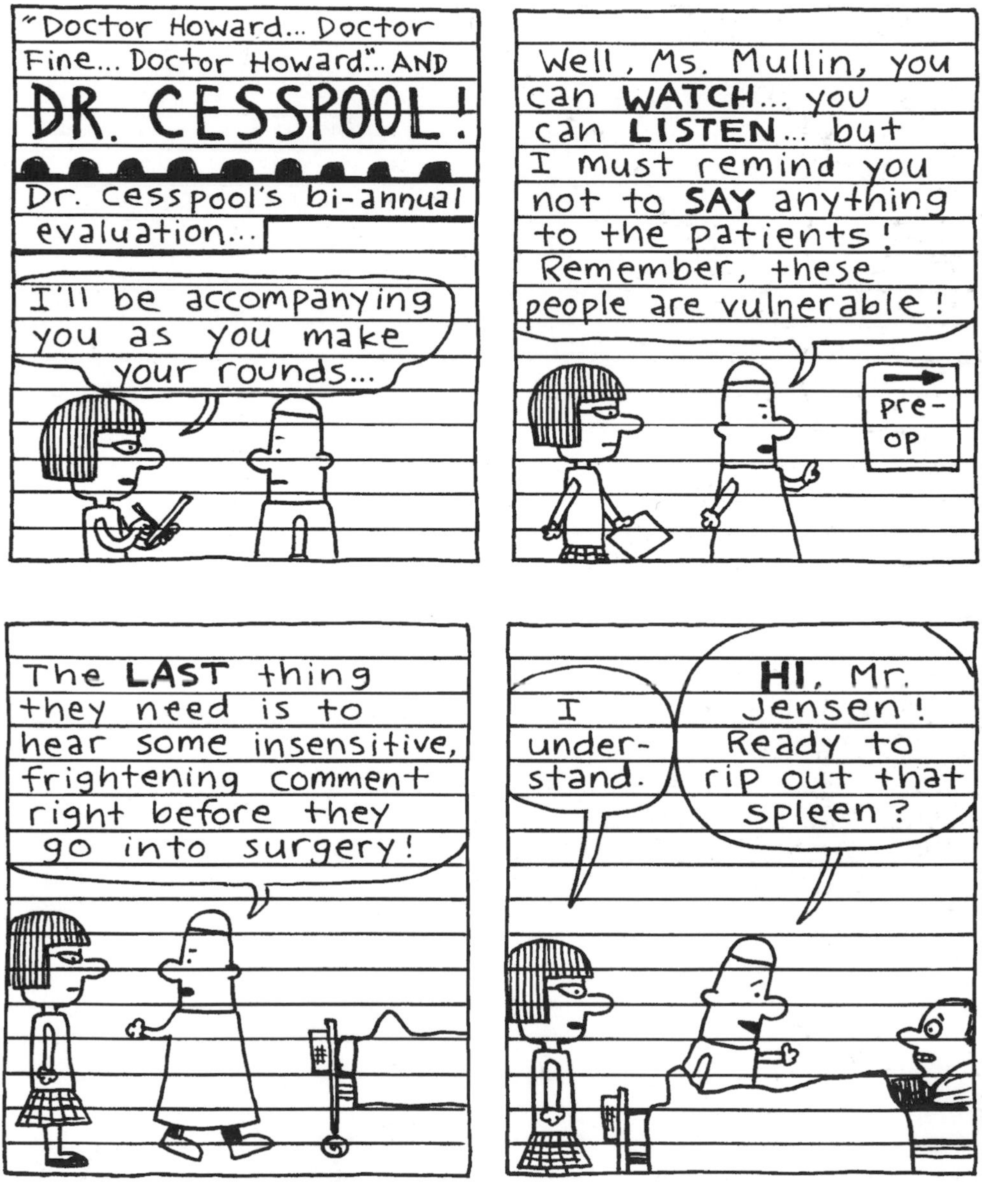
"Doctor Howard... Doctor Fine... Doctor Howard"... AND
DR. CESSPOOL!
Dr. cesspool's bi-annual evaluation...
I'll be accompanying you as you make your rounds...
Well, Ms. Mullin, you can **WATCH**... you can **LISTEN**... but I must remind you not to **SAY** anything to the patients! Remember, these people are vulnerable!
pre-op
The **LAST** thing they need is to hear some insensitive, frightening comment right before they go into surgery!
I under-stand.
HI, Mr. Jensen! Ready to rip out that spleen?

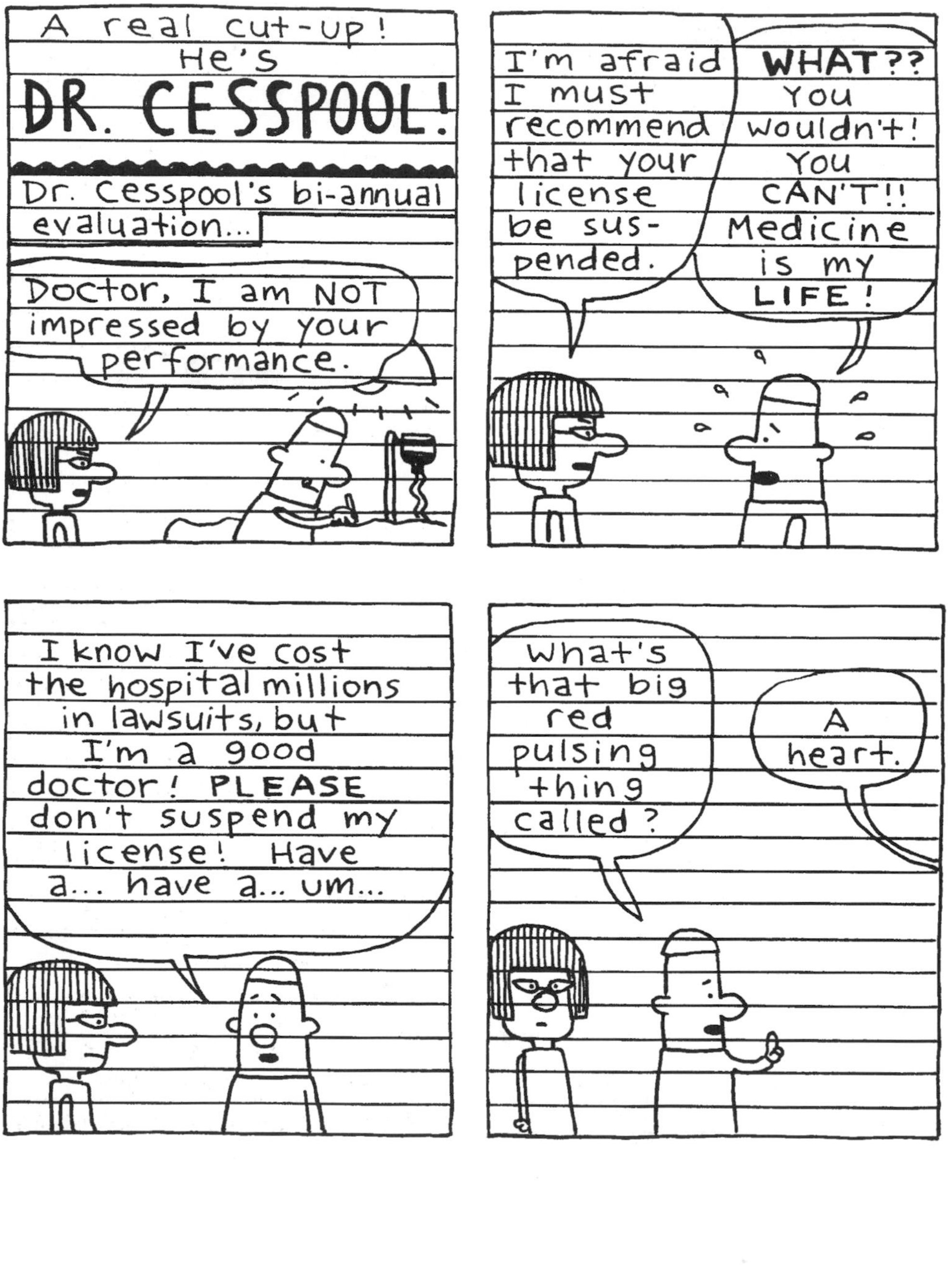
A real cut-up! He's
DR. CESSPOOL!
Dr. Cesspool's bi-annual evaluation...
Doctor, I am NOT impressed by your performance.
I'm afraid I must recommend that your license be suspended.
WHAT?? You wouldn't! You CAN'T!! Medicine is my LIFE!
I know I've cost the hospital millions in lawsuits, but I'm a good doctor! PLEASE don't suspend my license! Have a... have a... um...
What's that big red pulsing thing called?
A heart.

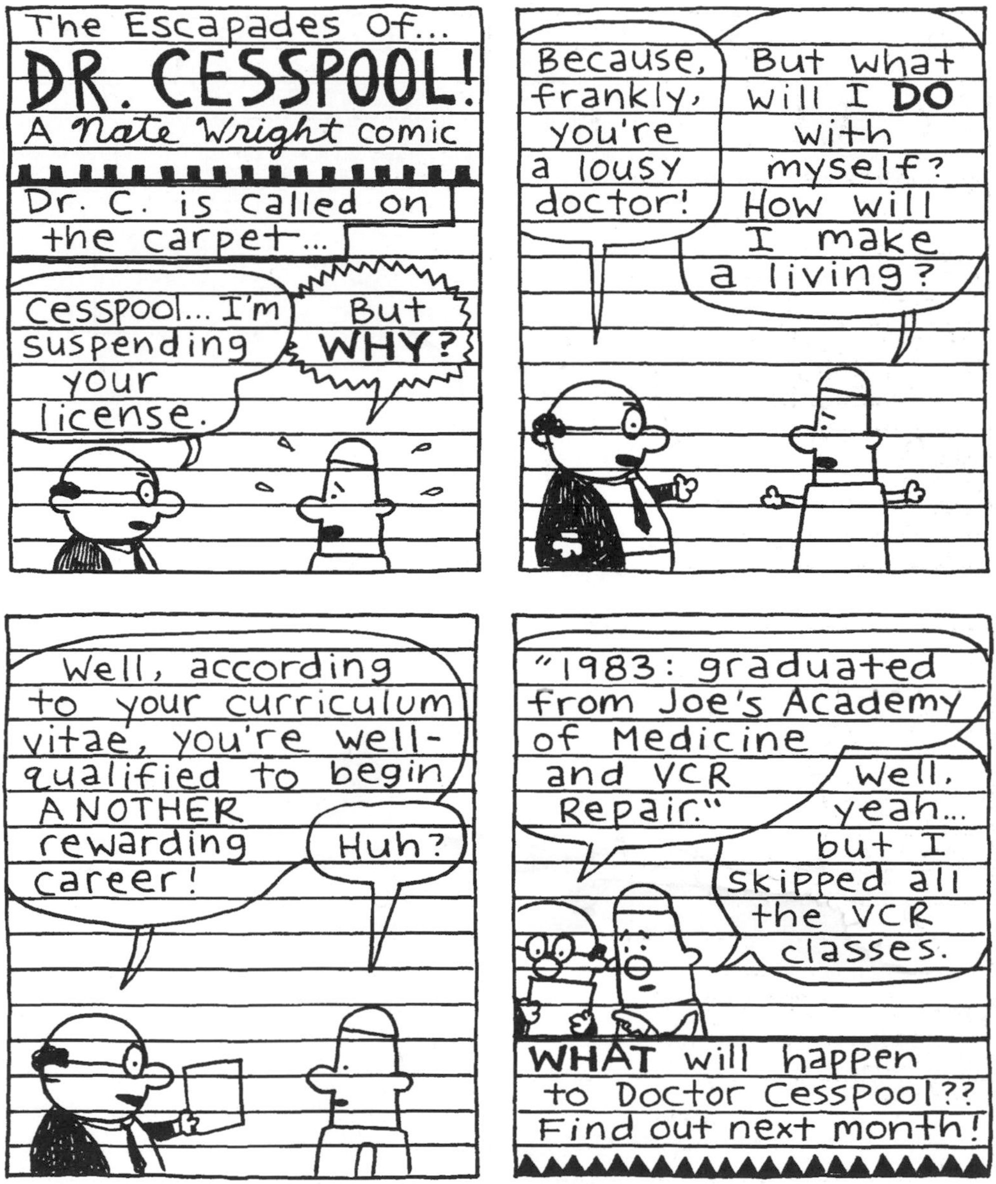
The Escapades Of...
DR. CESSPOOL!
A Nate Wright comic
Dr. C. is called on the carpet...
Cesspool... I'm suspending your license.
But WHY?
Because, frankly, you're a lousy doctor!
But what will I DO with myself? How will I make a living?
Well, according to your curriculum vitae, you're well-qualified to begin ANOTHER rewarding career!
Huh?
"1983: graduated from Joe's Academy of Medicine and VCR Repair."
Well, yeah... but I skipped all the VCR classes.
WHAT will happen to Doctor Cesspool?? Find out next month!

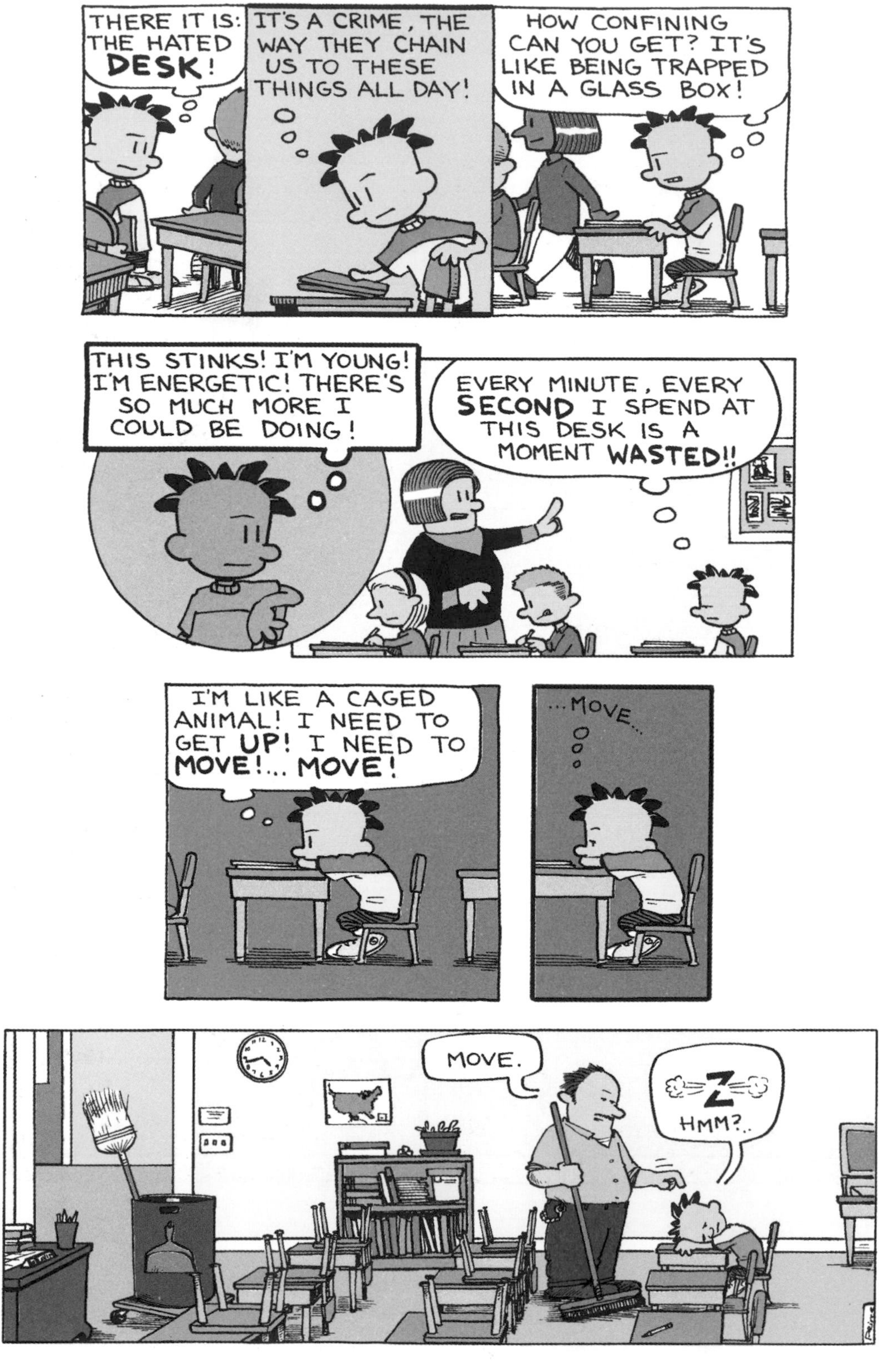
THERE IT IS: THE HATED DESK!
IT'S A CRIME, THE WAY THEY CHAIN US TO THESE THINGS ALL DAY!
HOW CONFINING CAN YOU GET? IT'S LIKE BEING TRAPPED IN A GLASS BOX!
THIS STINKS! I'M YOUNG! I'M ENERGETIC! THERE'S SO MUCH MORE I COULD BE DOING!
EVERY MINUTE, EVERY SECOND I SPEND AT THIS DESK IS A MOMENT WASTED!!
I'M LIKE A CAGED ANIMAL! I NEED TO GET UP! I NEED TO MOVE!... MOVE!
...MOVE...
MOVE.
Z
HMM?..

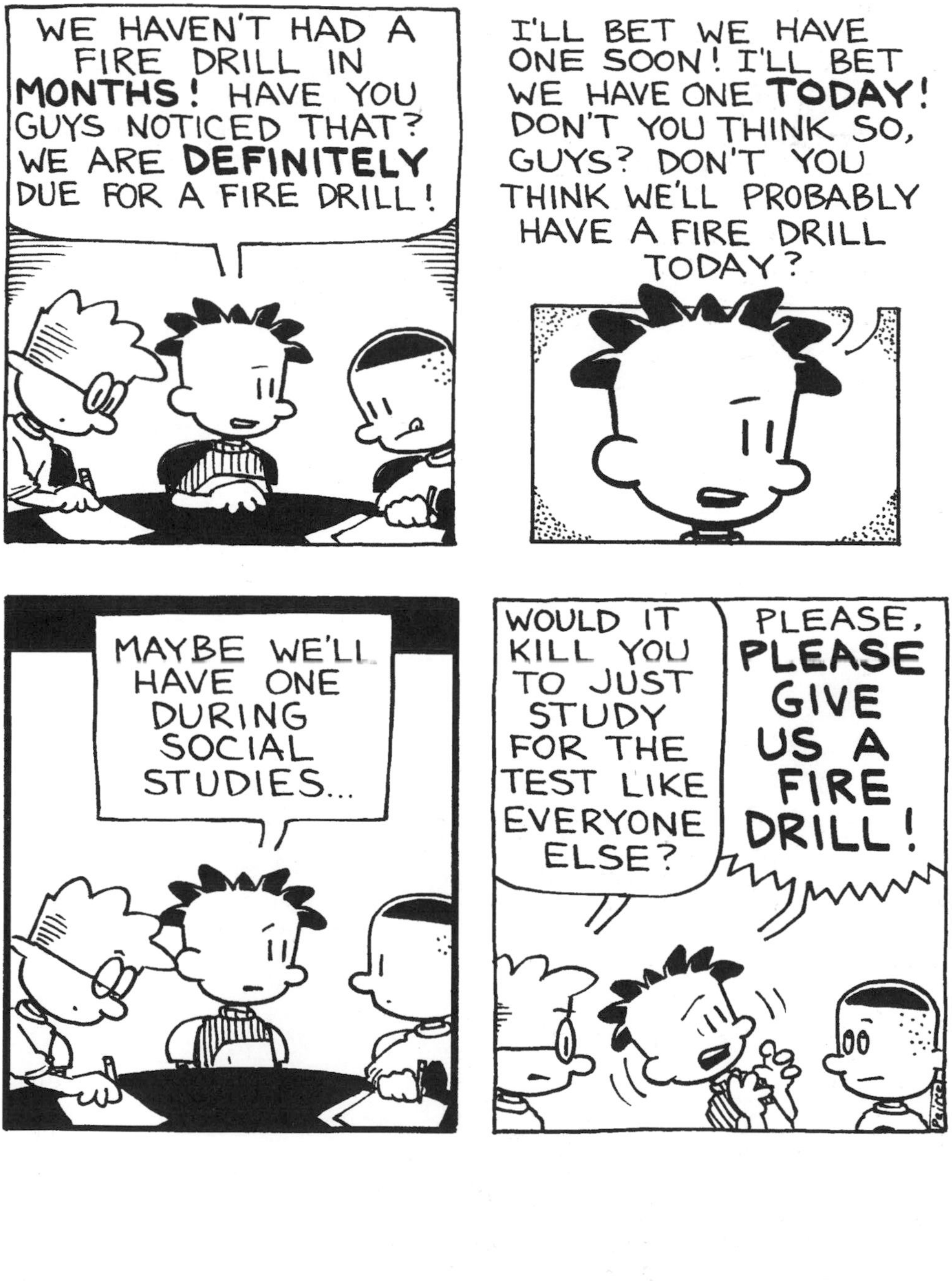
WE HAVEN'T HAD A FIRE DRILL IN **MONTHS**! HAVE YOU GUYS NOTICED THAT? WE ARE **DEFINITELY** DUE FOR A FIRE DRILL!
I'LL BET WE HAVE ONE SOON! I'LL BET WE HAVE ONE **TODAY**! DON'T YOU THINK SO, GUYS? DON'T YOU THINK WE'LL PROBABLY HAVE A FIRE DRILL TODAY?
MAYBE WE'LL HAVE ONE DURING SOCIAL STUDIES...
WOULD IT KILL YOU TO JUST STUDY FOR THE TEST LIKE EVERYONE ELSE?
PLEASE, **PLEASE GIVE US A FIRE DRILL!**

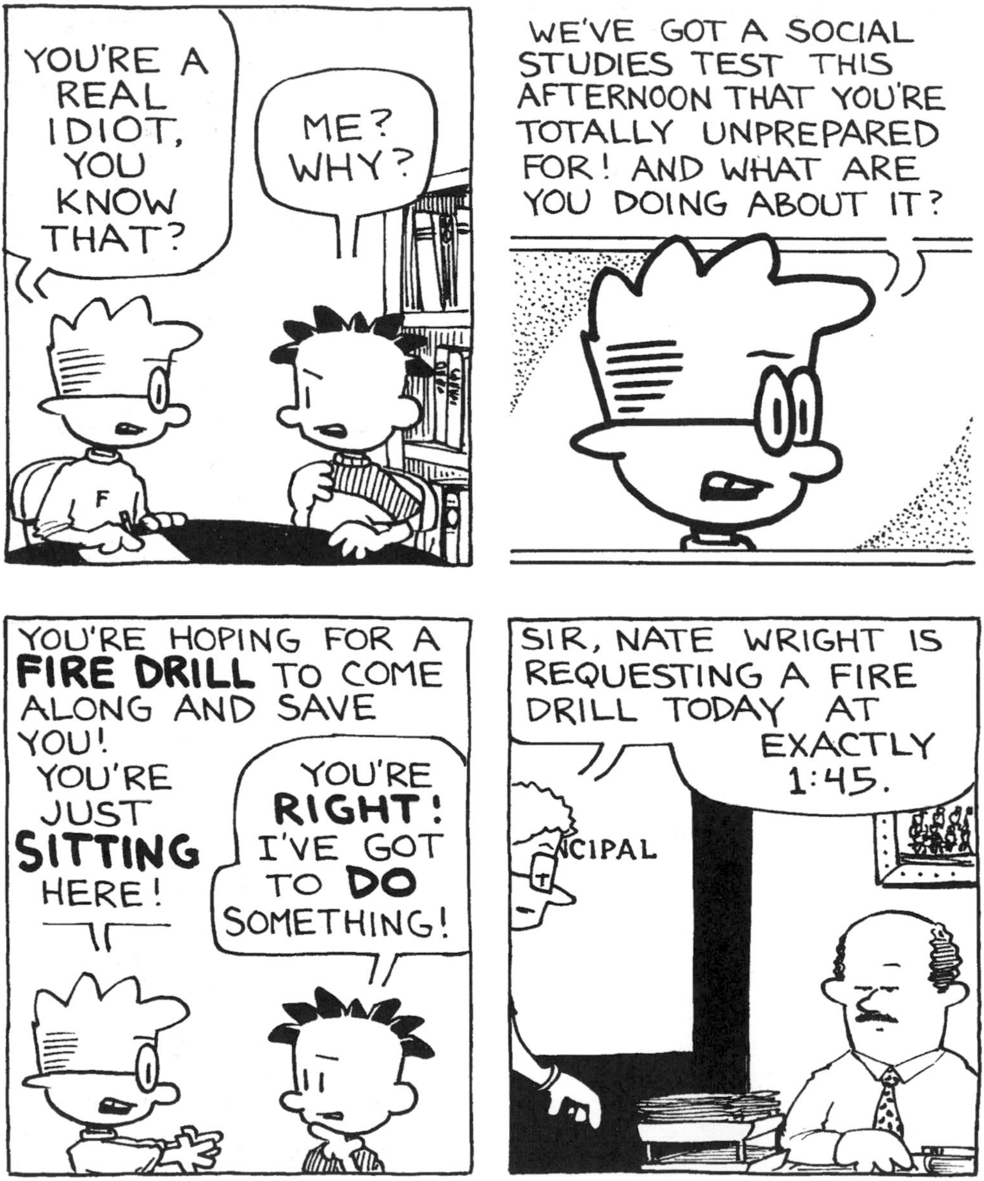
YOU'RE A REAL IDIOT, YOU KNOW THAT?
ME? WHY?
WE'VE GOT A SOCIAL STUDIES TEST THIS AFTERNOON THAT YOU'RE TOTALLY UNPREPARED FOR! AND WHAT ARE YOU DOING ABOUT IT?
YOU'RE HOPING FOR A FIRE DRILL TO COME ALONG AND SAVE YOU!
YOU'RE JUST SITTING HERE!
YOU'RE RIGHT! I'VE GOT TO DO SOMETHING!
SIR, NATE WRIGHT IS REQUESTING A FIRE DRILL TODAY AT EXACTLY 1:45.
F
NCIPAL

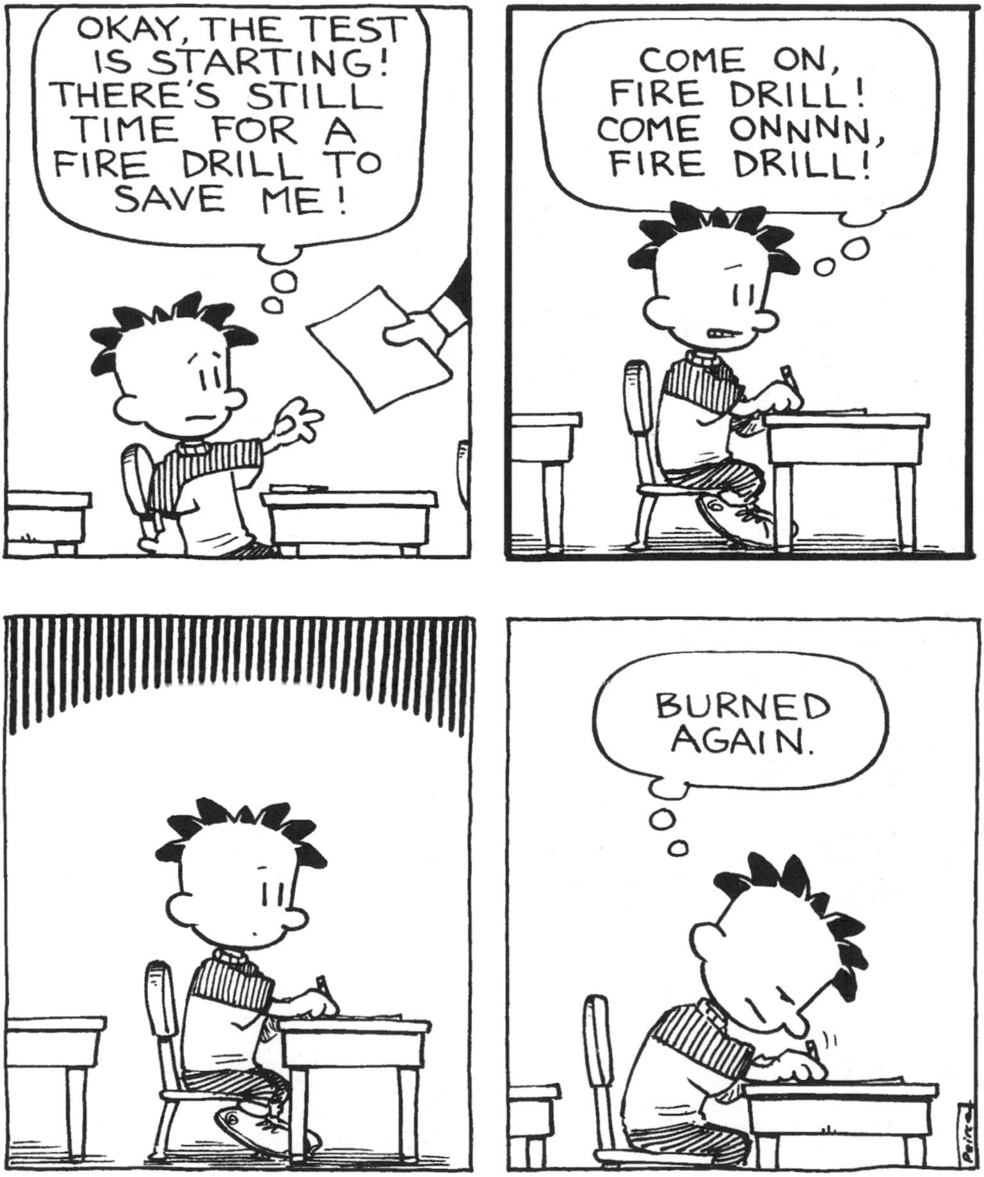
OKAY, THE TEST IS STARTING! THERE'S STILL TIME FOR A FIRE DRILL TO SAVE ME!
COME ON, FIRE DRILL! COME ONNNN, FIRE DRILL!
BURNED AGAIN.

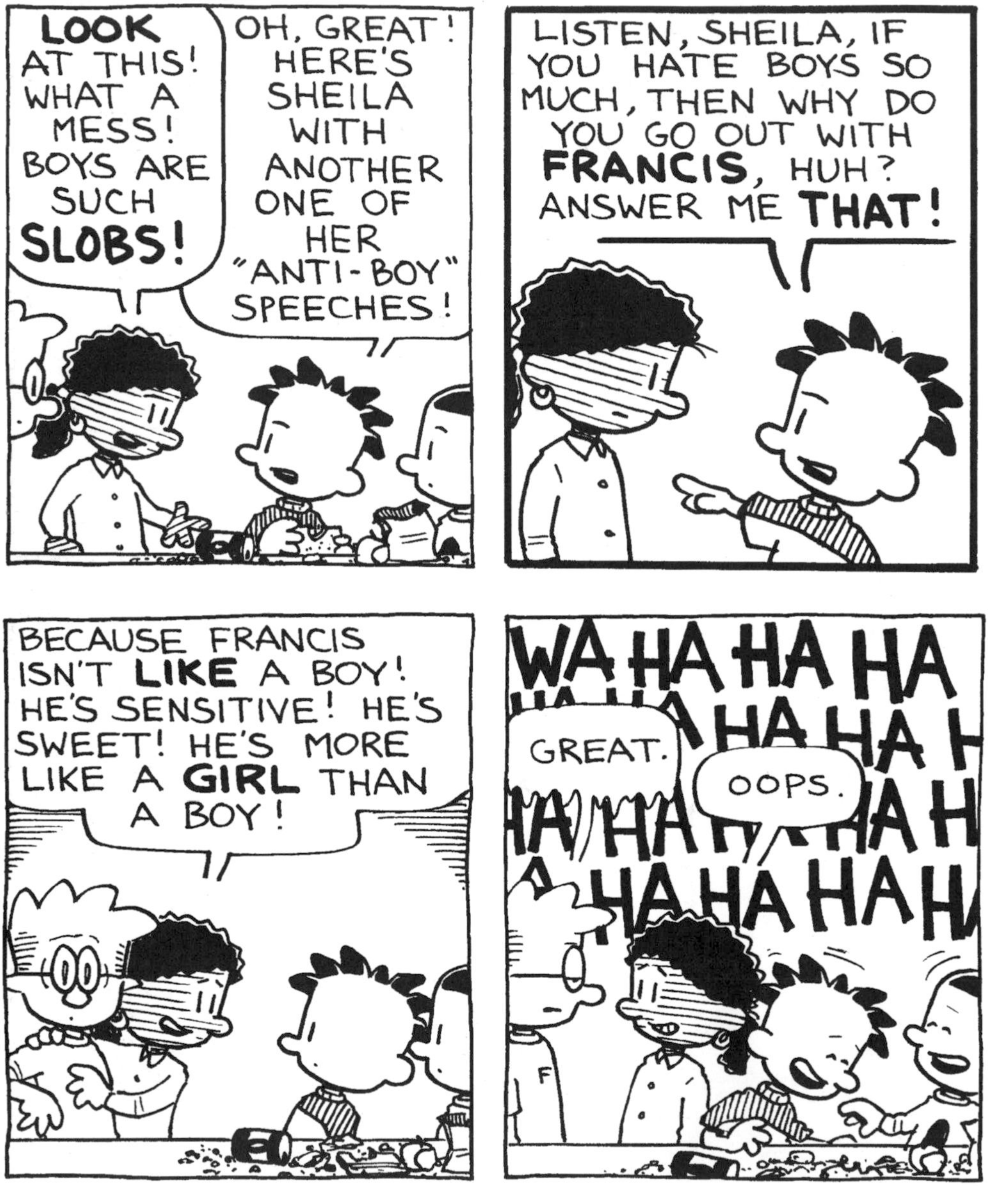
LOOK AT THIS! WHAT A MESS! BOYS ARE SUCH SLOBS!
OH, GREAT! HERE'S SHEILA WITH ANOTHER ONE OF HER "ANTI-BOY" SPEECHES!
LISTEN, SHEILA, IF YOU HATE BOYS SO MUCH, THEN WHY DO YOU GO OUT WITH FRANCIS, HUH? ANSWER ME THAT!
BECAUSE FRANCIS ISN'T LIKE A BOY! HE'S SENSITIVE! HE'S SWEET! HE'S MORE LIKE A GIRL THAN A BOY!
WA HA HA HA
GREAT.
OOPS.
HA HA HA HA

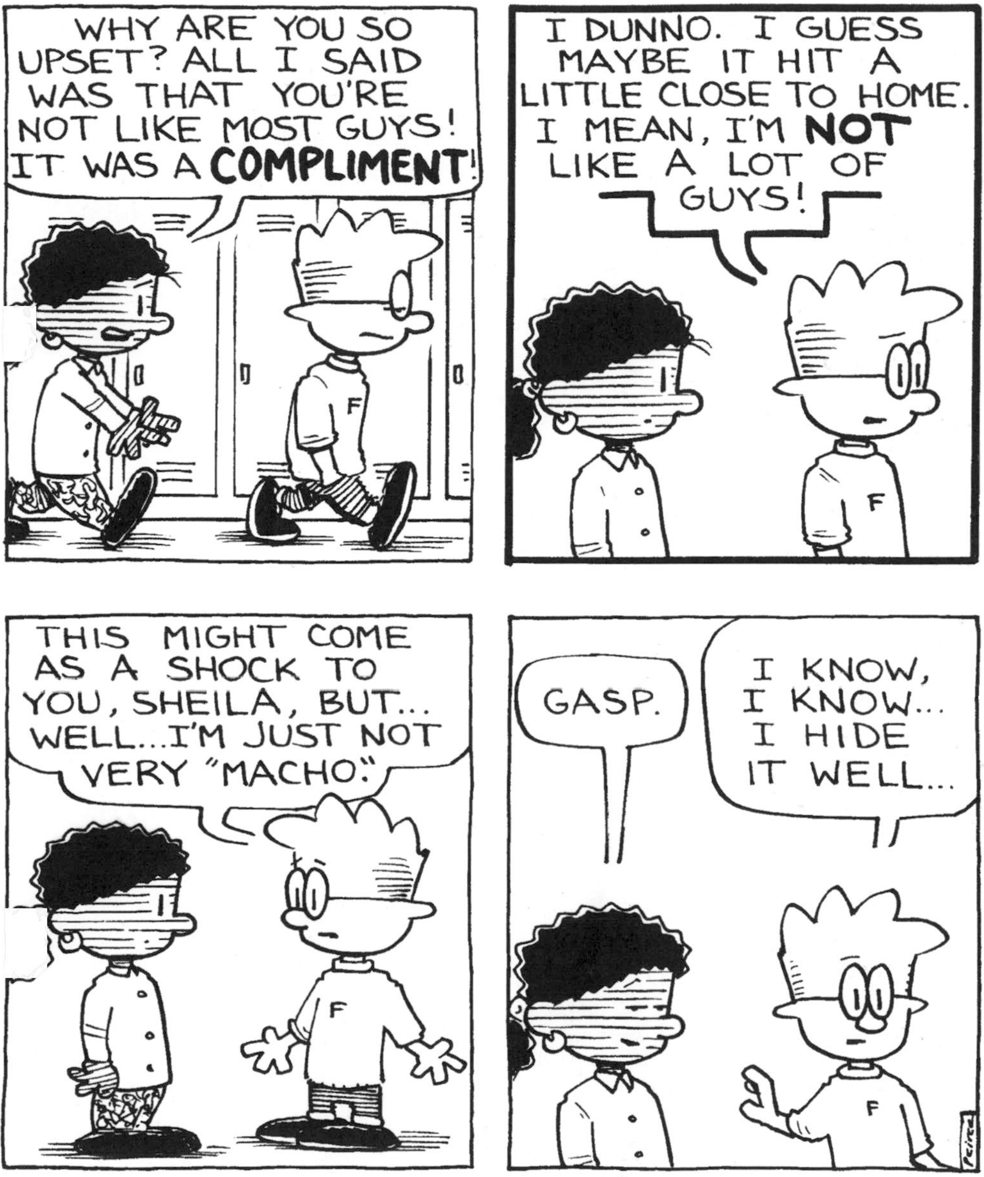
WHY ARE YOU SO UPSET? ALL I SAID WAS THAT YOU'RE NOT LIKE MOST GUYS! IT WAS A **COMPLIMENT**!
I DUNNO. I GUESS MAYBE IT HIT A LITTLE CLOSE TO HOME. I MEAN, I'M **NOT** LIKE A LOT OF GUYS!
THIS MIGHT COME AS A SHOCK TO YOU, SHEILA, BUT... WELL...I'M JUST NOT VERY "MACHO."
GASP.
I KNOW, I KNOW... I HIDE IT WELL...
F
F
F
F

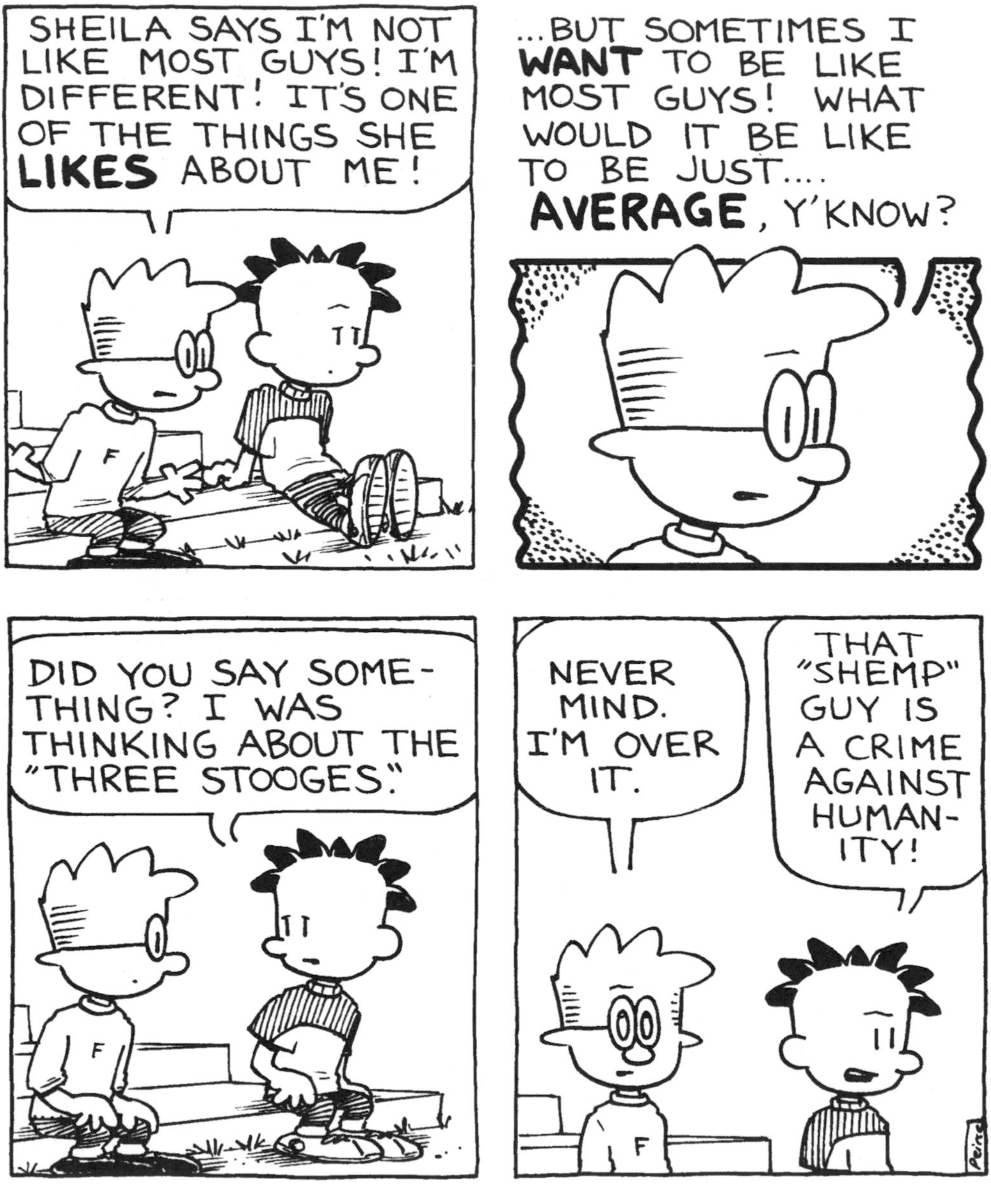
SHEILA SAYS I'M NOT LIKE MOST GUYS! I'M DIFFERENT! IT'S ONE OF THE THINGS SHE LIKES ABOUT ME!
...BUT SOMETIMES I WANT TO BE LIKE MOST GUYS! WHAT WOULD IT BE LIKE TO BE JUST.... AVERAGE, Y'KNOW?
DID YOU SAY SOME-THING? I WAS THINKING ABOUT THE "THREE STOOGES."
NEVER MIND. I'M OVER IT.
THAT "SHEMP" GUY IS A CRIME AGAINST HUMAN-ITY!
Peirce

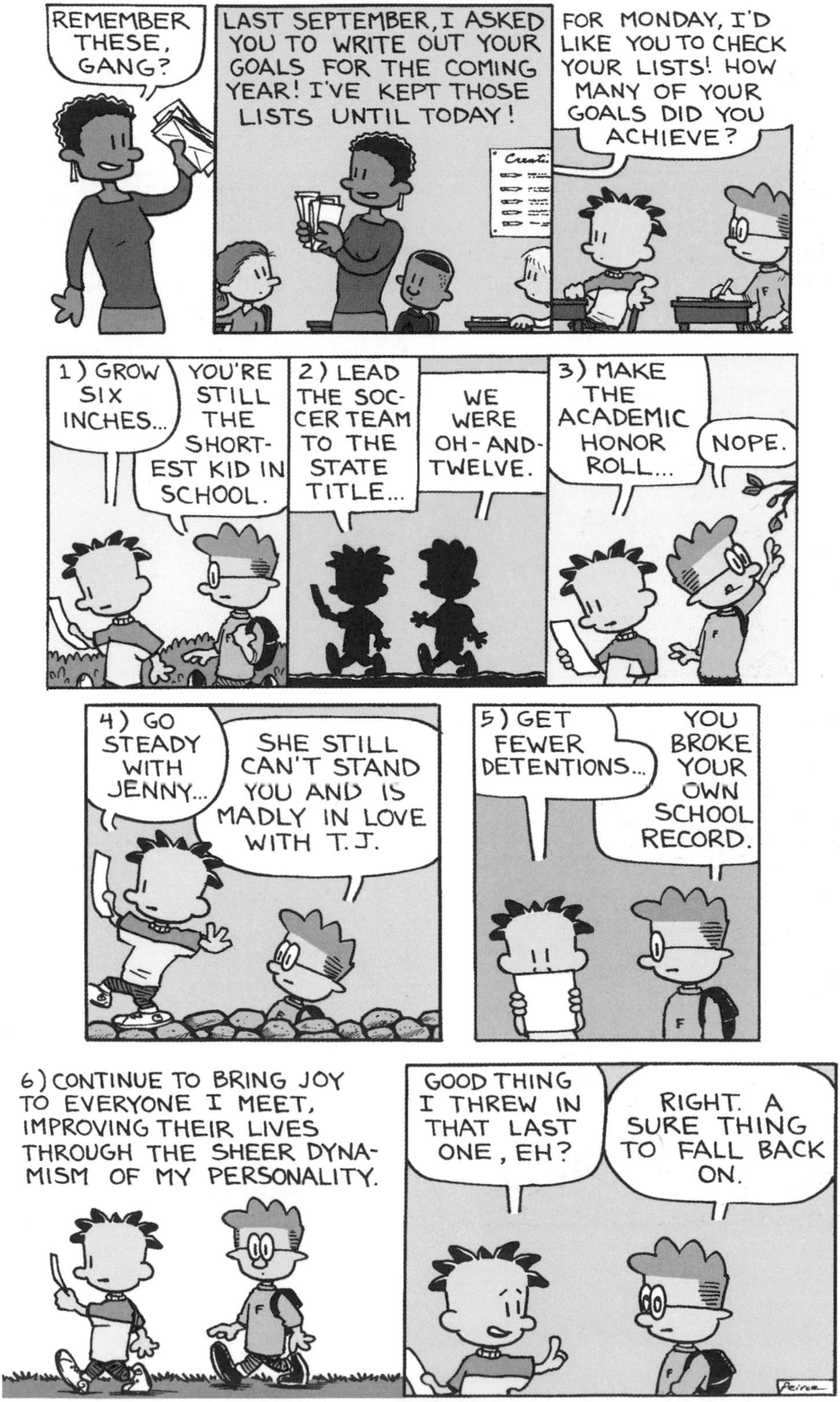
REMEMBER THESE, GANG?
LAST SEPTEMBER, I ASKED YOU TO WRITE OUT YOUR GOALS FOR THE COMING YEAR! I'VE KEPT THOSE LISTS UNTIL TODAY!
FOR MONDAY, I'D LIKE YOU TO CHECK YOUR LISTS! HOW MANY OF YOUR GOALS DID YOU ACHIEVE?
1) GROW SIX INCHES...
YOU'RE STILL THE SHORTEST KID IN SCHOOL.
2) LEAD THE SOCCER TEAM TO THE STATE TITLE...
WE WERE OH-AND-TWELVE.
3) MAKE THE ACADEMIC HONOR ROLL...
NOPE.
4) GO STEADY WITH JENNY...
SHE STILL CAN'T STAND YOU AND IS MADLY IN LOVE WITH T.J.
5) GET FEWER DETENTIONS...
YOU BROKE YOUR OWN SCHOOL RECORD.
6) CONTINUE TO BRING JOY TO EVERYONE I MEET, IMPROVING THEIR LIVES THROUGH THE SHEER DYNAMISM OF MY PERSONALITY.
GOOD THING I THREW IN THAT LAST ONE, EH?
RIGHT. A SURE THING TO FALL BACK ON.
Peirce

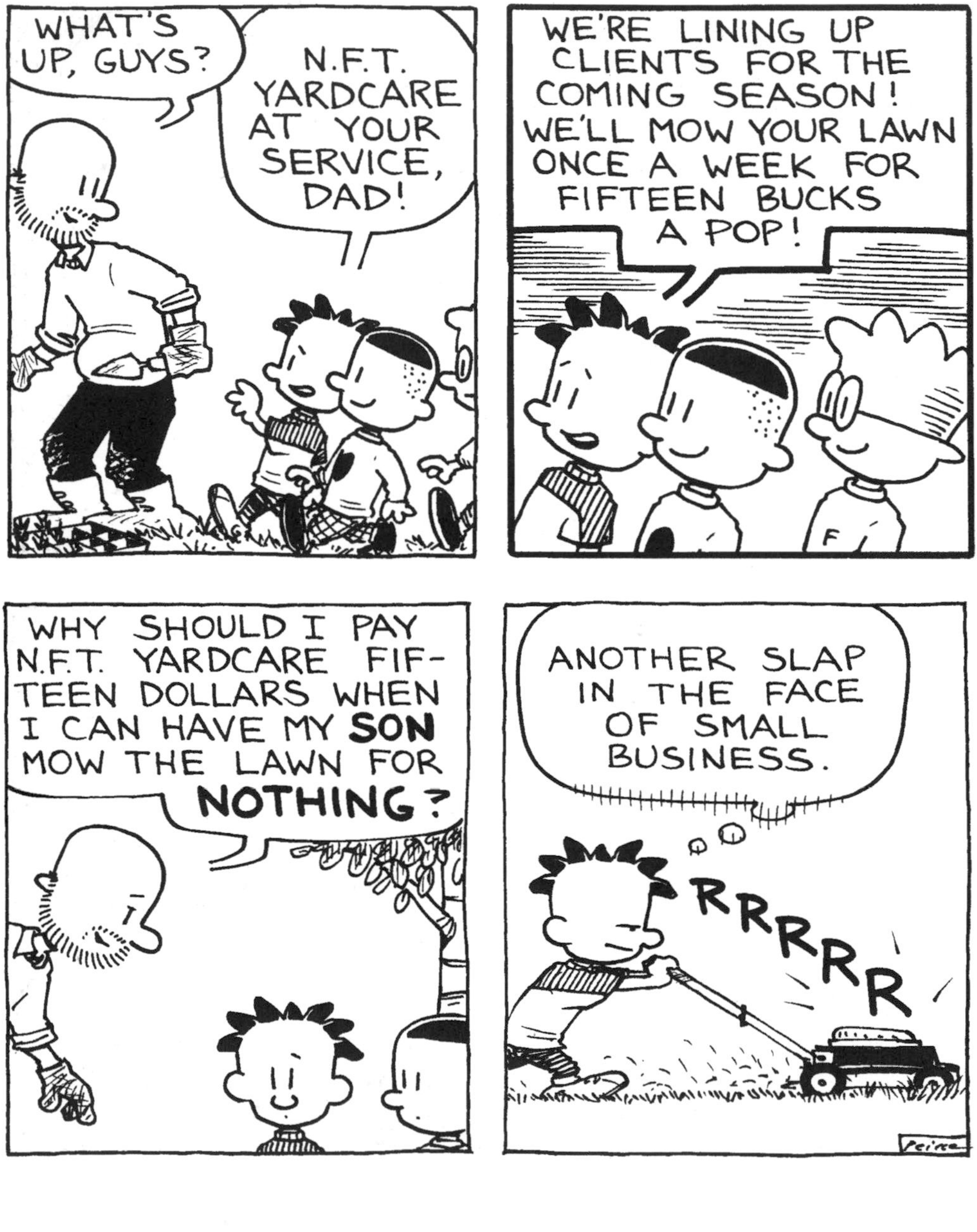
WHAT'S UP, GUYS?
N.F.T. YARDCARE AT YOUR SERVICE, DAD!
WE'RE LINING UP CLIENTS FOR THE COMING SEASON! WE'LL MOW YOUR LAWN ONCE A WEEK FOR FIFTEEN BUCKS A POP!
WHY SHOULD I PAY N.F.T. YARDCARE FIFTEEN DOLLARS WHEN I CAN HAVE MY SON MOW THE LAWN FOR NOTHING?
ANOTHER SLAP IN THE FACE OF SMALL BUSINESS.
RRRRRR
F

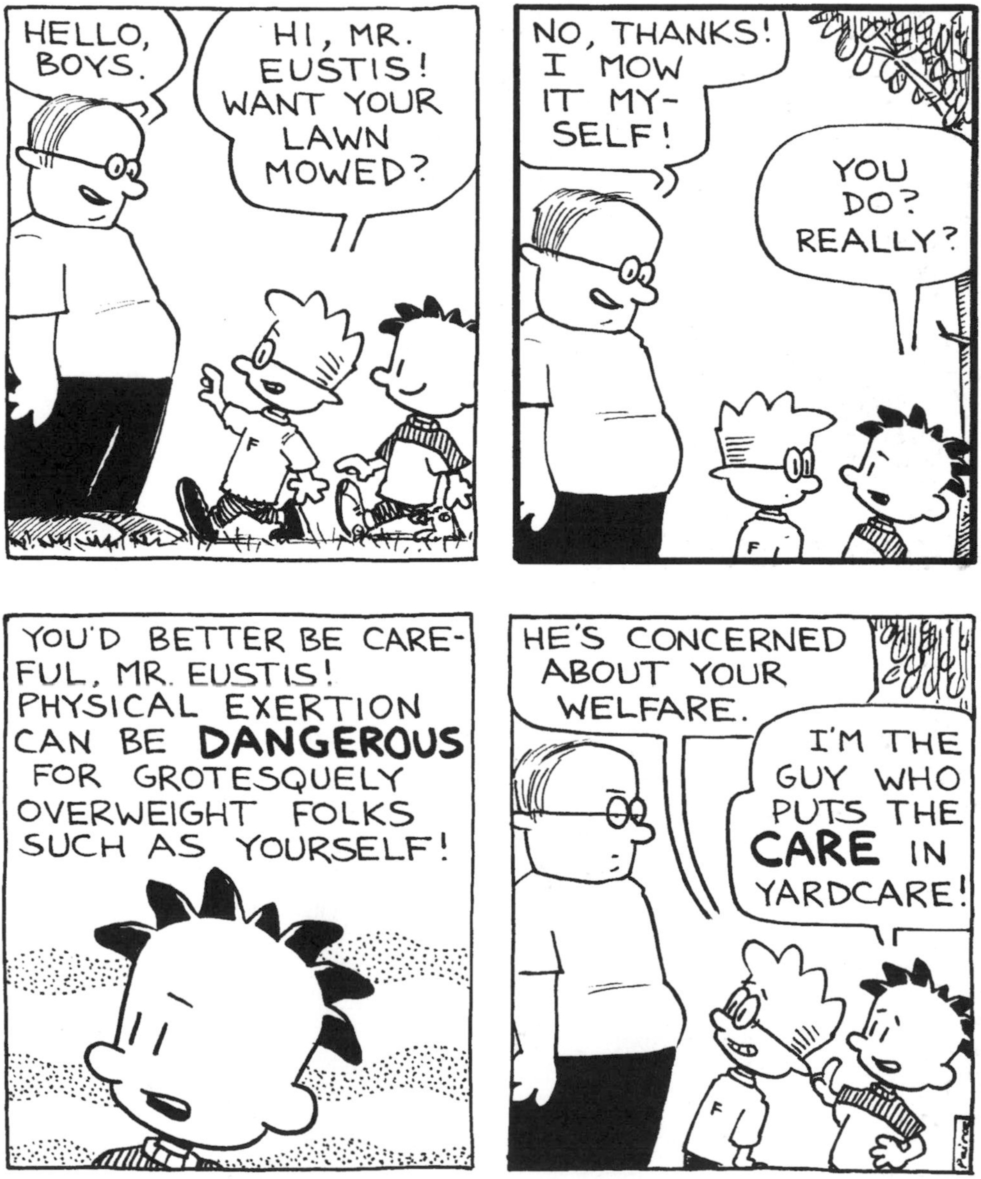
HELLO, BOYS.
HI, MR. EUSTIS! WANT YOUR LAWN MOWED?
NO, THANKS! I MOW IT MY-SELF!
YOU DO? REALLY?
YOU'D BETTER BE CARE-FUL, MR. EUSTIS! PHYSICAL EXERTION CAN BE **DANGEROUS** FOR GROTESQUELY OVERWEIGHT FOLKS SUCH AS YOURSELF!
HE'S CONCERNED ABOUT YOUR WELFARE.
I'M THE GUY WHO PUTS THE **CARE** IN YARDCARE!

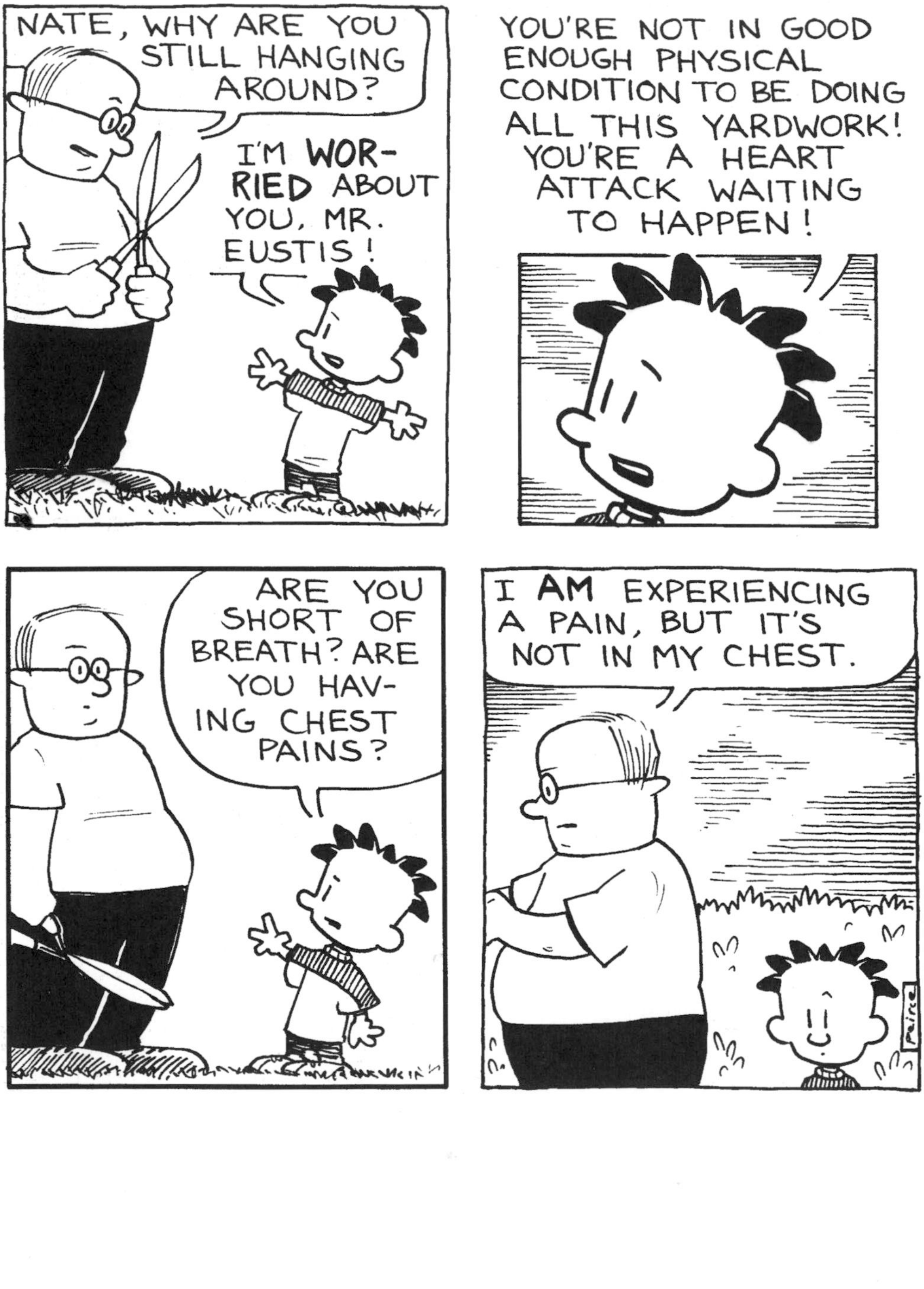
NATE, WHY ARE YOU STILL HANGING AROUND?
I'M **WORRIED** ABOUT YOU, MR. EUSTIS!
YOU'RE NOT IN GOOD ENOUGH PHYSICAL CONDITION TO BE DOING ALL THIS YARDWORK! YOU'RE A HEART ATTACK WAITING TO HAPPEN!
ARE YOU SHORT OF BREATH? ARE YOU HAVING CHEST PAINS?
I **AM** EXPERIENCING A PAIN, BUT IT'S NOT IN MY CHEST.
Peirce

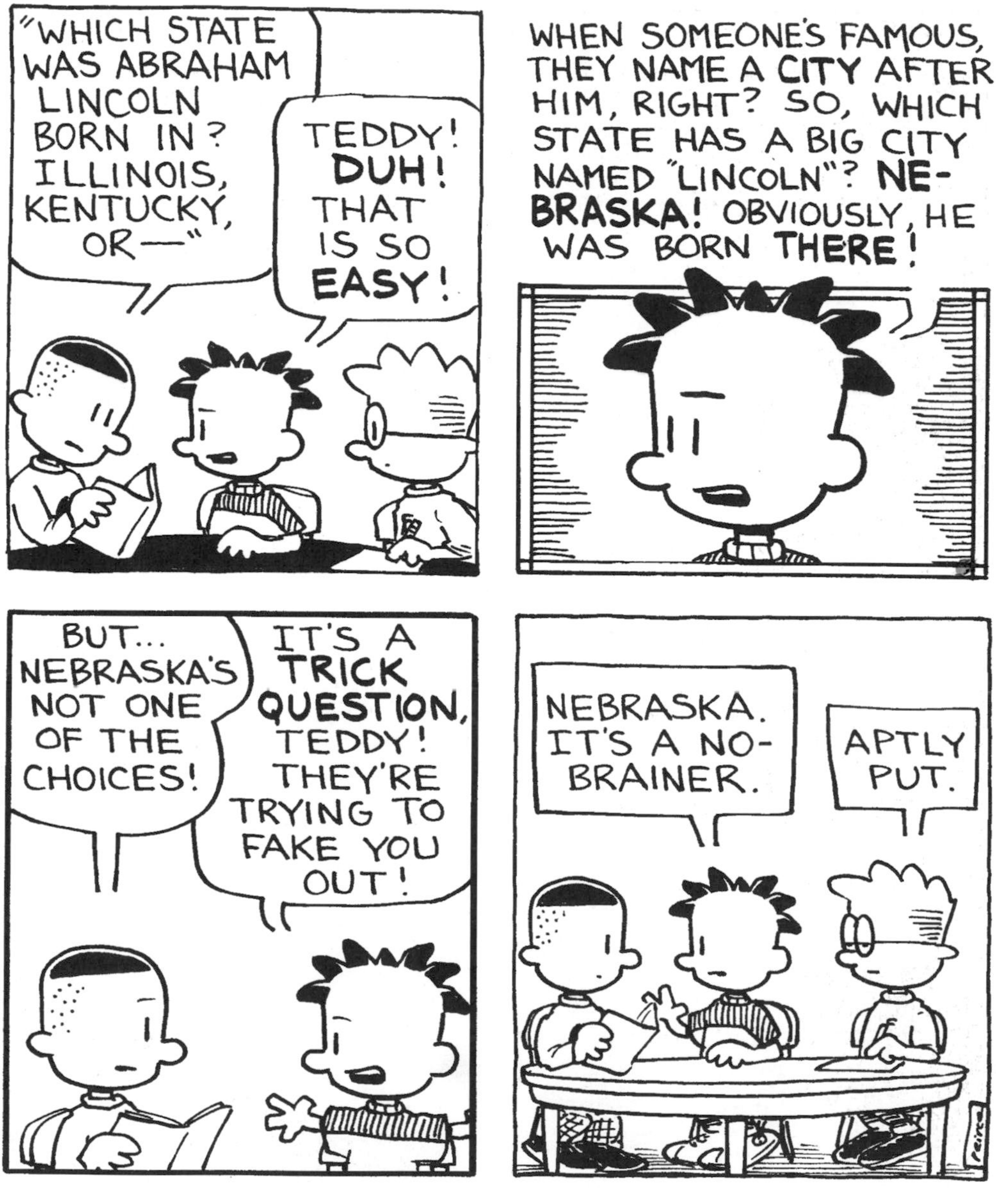
"WHICH STATE WAS ABRAHAM LINCOLN BORN IN? ILLINOIS, KENTUCKY, OR—"
TEDDY! DUH! THAT IS SO EASY!
WHEN SOMEONE'S FAMOUS, THEY NAME A CITY AFTER HIM, RIGHT? SO, WHICH STATE HAS A BIG CITY NAMED "LINCOLN"? NEBRASKA! OBVIOUSLY, HE WAS BORN THERE!
BUT... NEBRASKA'S NOT ONE OF THE CHOICES!
IT'S A TRICK QUESTION, TEDDY! THEY'RE TRYING TO FAKE YOU OUT!
NEBRASKA. IT'S A NO-BRAINER.
APTLY PUT.
PEIRCE

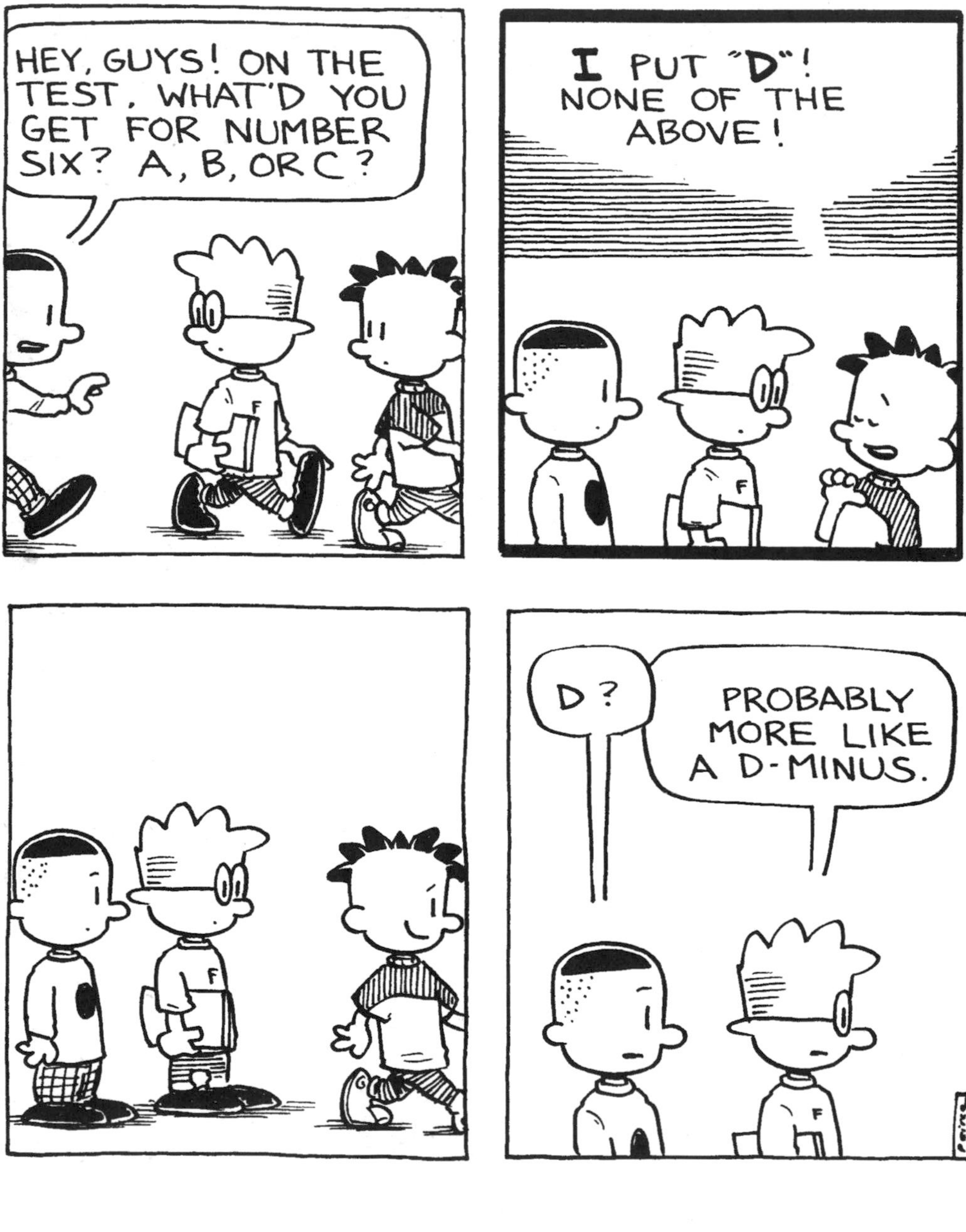
HEY, GUYS! ON THE TEST, WHAT'D YOU GET FOR NUMBER SIX? A, B, OR C?
I PUT "D"! NONE OF THE ABOVE!
D?
PROBABLY MORE LIKE A D-MINUS.

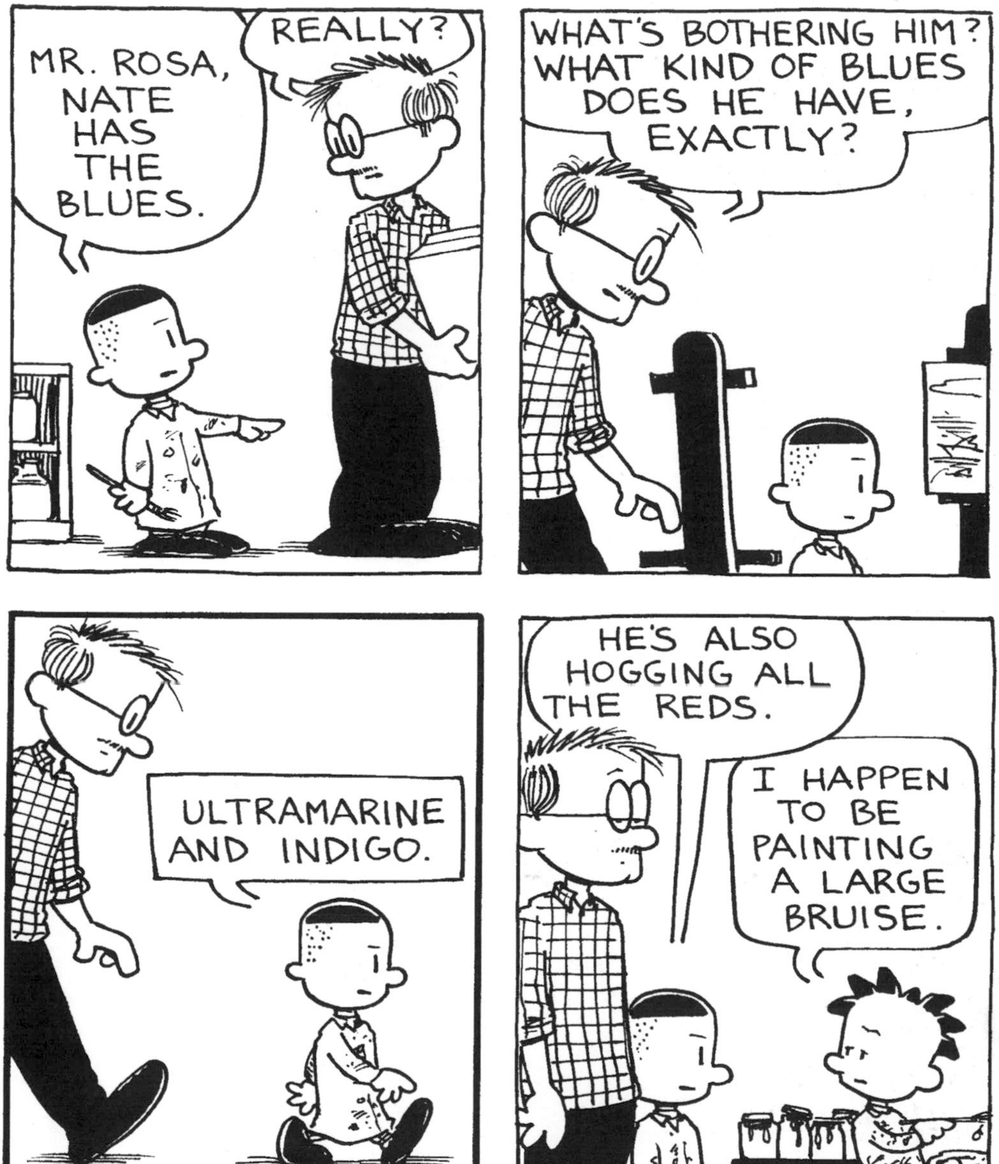
MR. ROSA, NATE HAS THE BLUES.
REALLY?
WHAT'S BOTHERING HIM? WHAT KIND OF BLUES DOES HE HAVE, EXACTLY?
ULTRAMARINE AND INDIGO.
HE'S ALSO HOGGING ALL THE REDS.
I HAPPEN TO BE PAINTING A LARGE BRUISE.

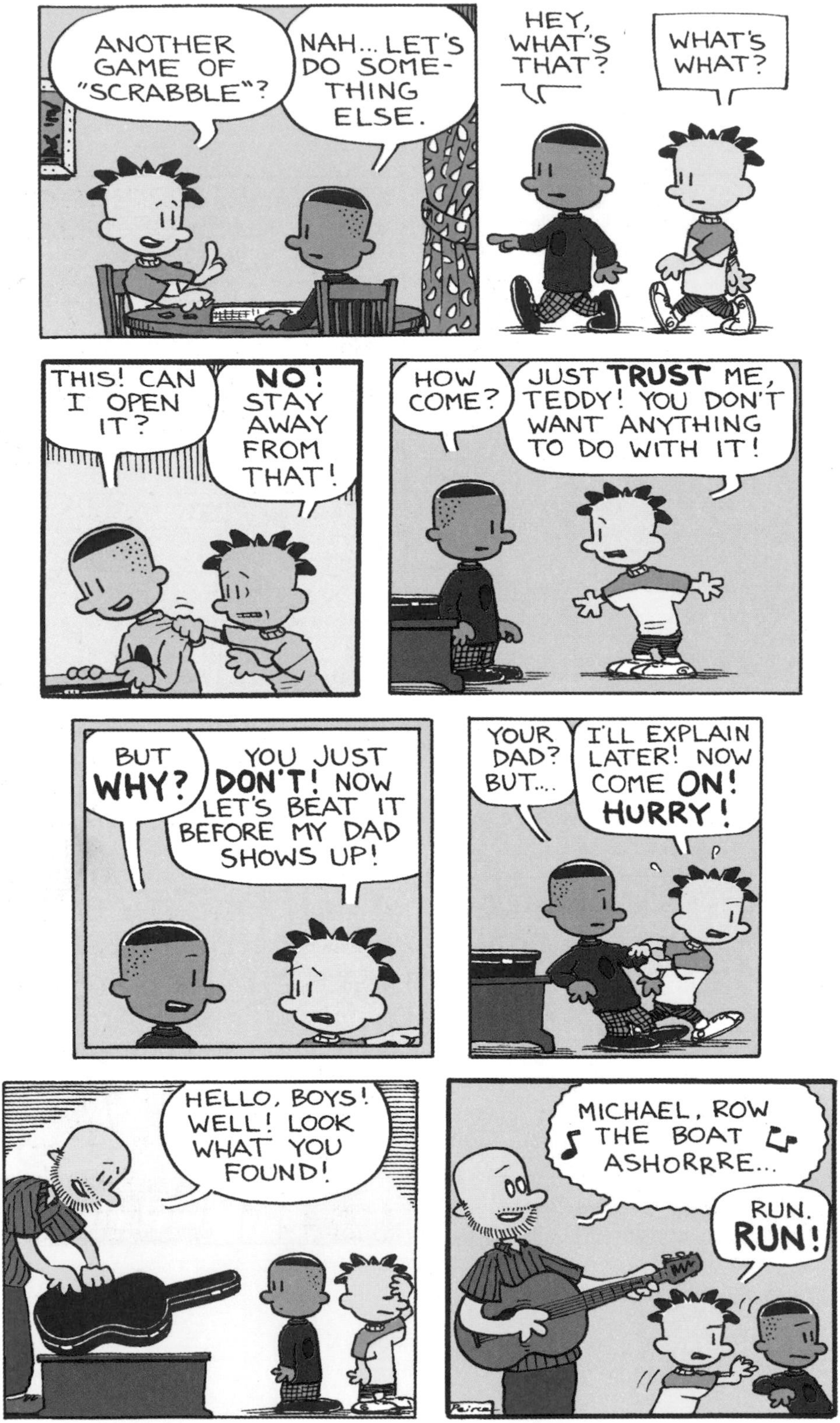
ANOTHER GAME OF "SCRABBLE"?
NAH... LET'S DO SOME-THING ELSE.
HEY, WHAT'S THAT?
WHAT'S WHAT?
THIS! CAN I OPEN IT?
NO! STAY AWAY FROM THAT!
HOW COME?
JUST TRUST ME, TEDDY! YOU DON'T WANT ANYTHING TO DO WITH IT!
BUT WHY?
YOU JUST DON'T! NOW LET'S BEAT IT BEFORE MY DAD SHOWS UP!
YOUR DAD? BUT....
I'LL EXPLAIN LATER! NOW COME ON! HURRY!
HELLO, BOYS! WELL! LOOK WHAT YOU FOUND!
MICHAEL, ROW THE BOAT ASHORRRE...
RUN. RUN!

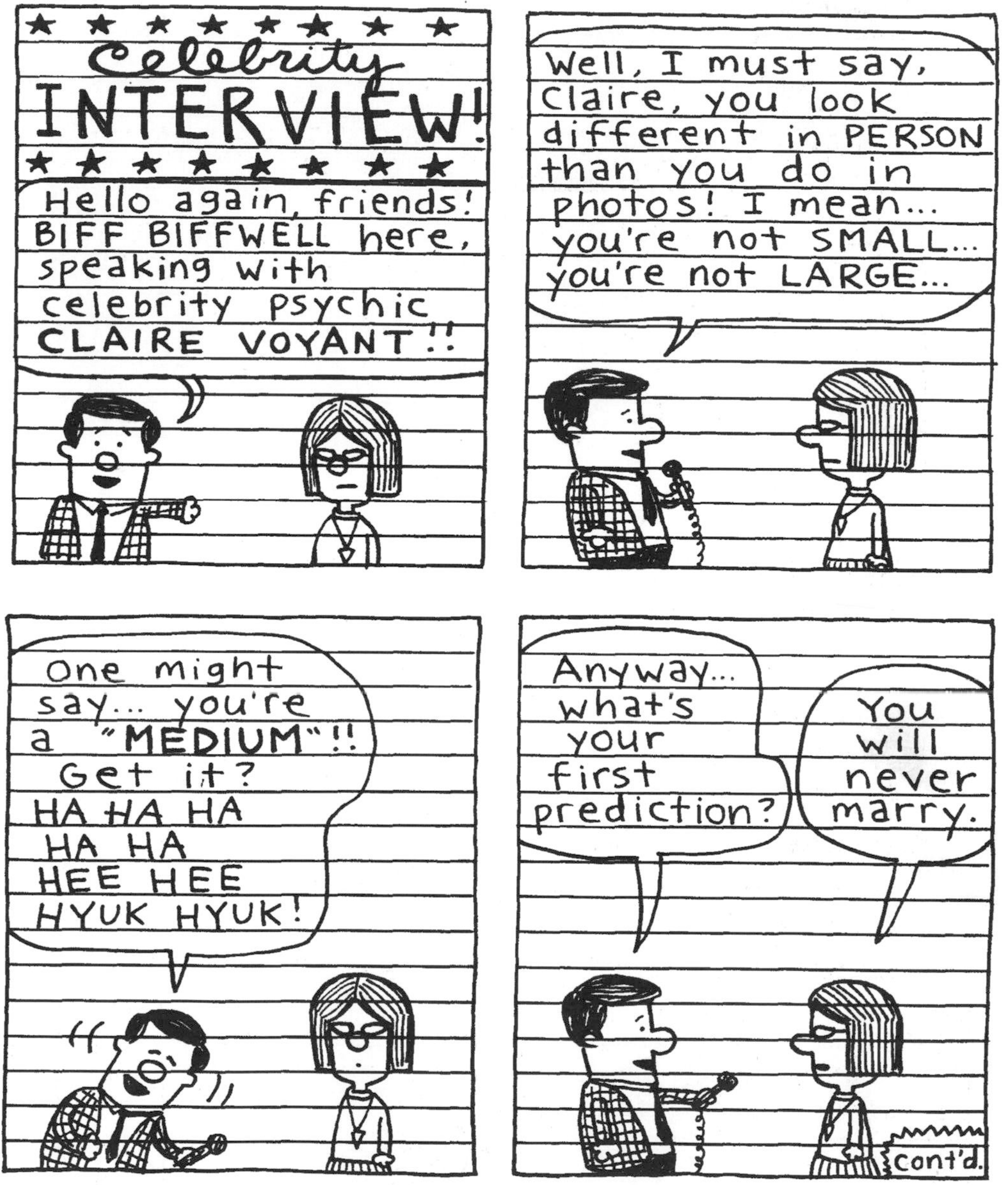
Celebrity INTERVIEW!
Hello again, friends! BIFF BIFFWELL here, speaking with celebrity psychic CLAIRE VOYANT!!
Well, I must say, Claire, you look different in PERSON than you do in photos! I mean... you're not SMALL... you're not LARGE...
One might say... you're a "MEDIUM"!! Get it? HA HA HA HA HA HEE HEE HYUK HYUK!
Anyway... what's your first prediction?
You will never marry.
cont'd.

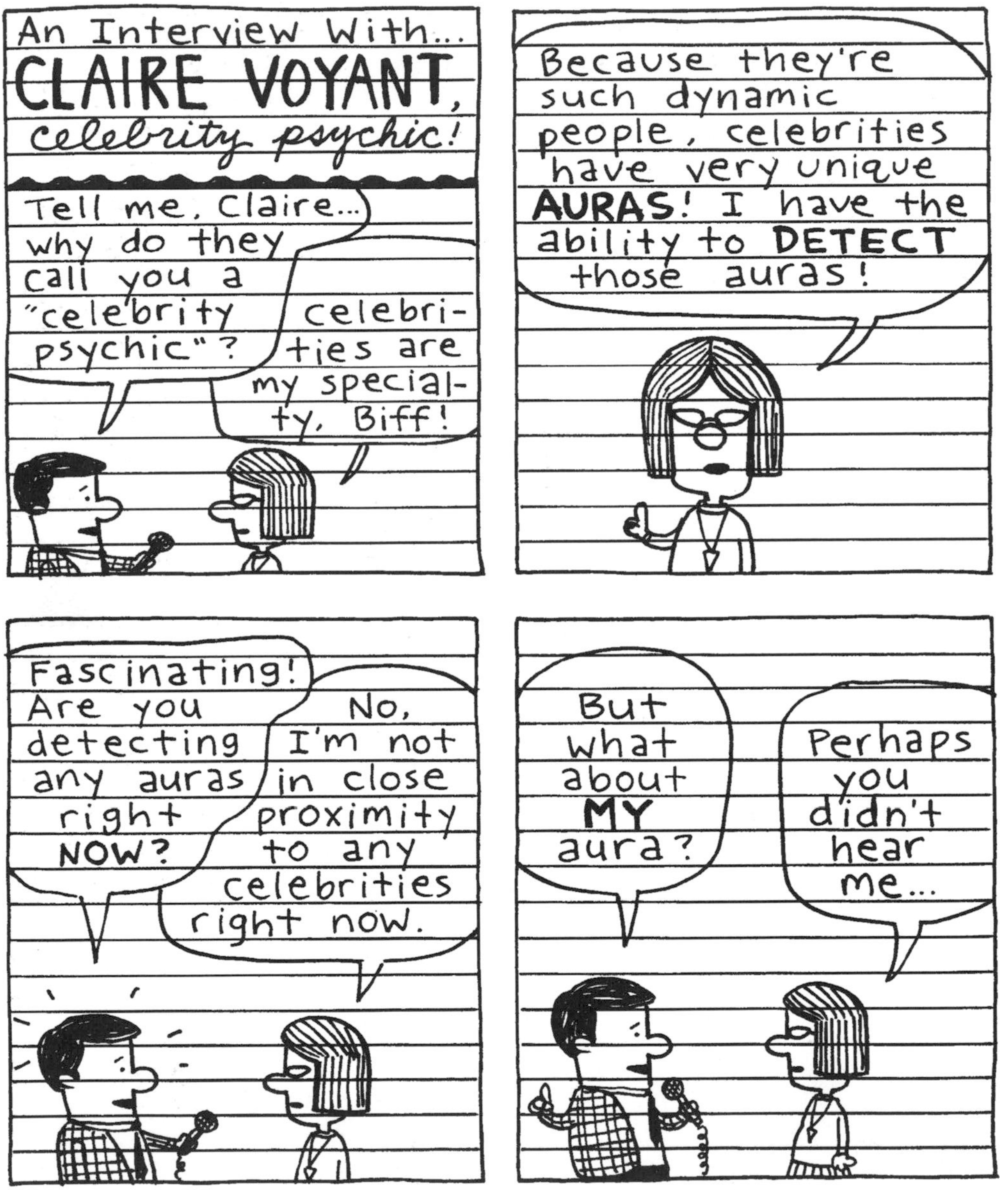
An Interview With...
CLAIRE VOYANT,
celebrity psychic!
Tell me, Claire... why do they call you a "celebrity psychic"?
celebrities are my specialty, Biff!
Because they're such dynamic people, celebrities have very unique AURAS! I have the ability to DETECT those auras!
Fascinating! Are you detecting any auras right NOW?
No, I'm not in close proximity to any celebrities right now.
But what about MY aura?
Perhaps you didn't hear me...

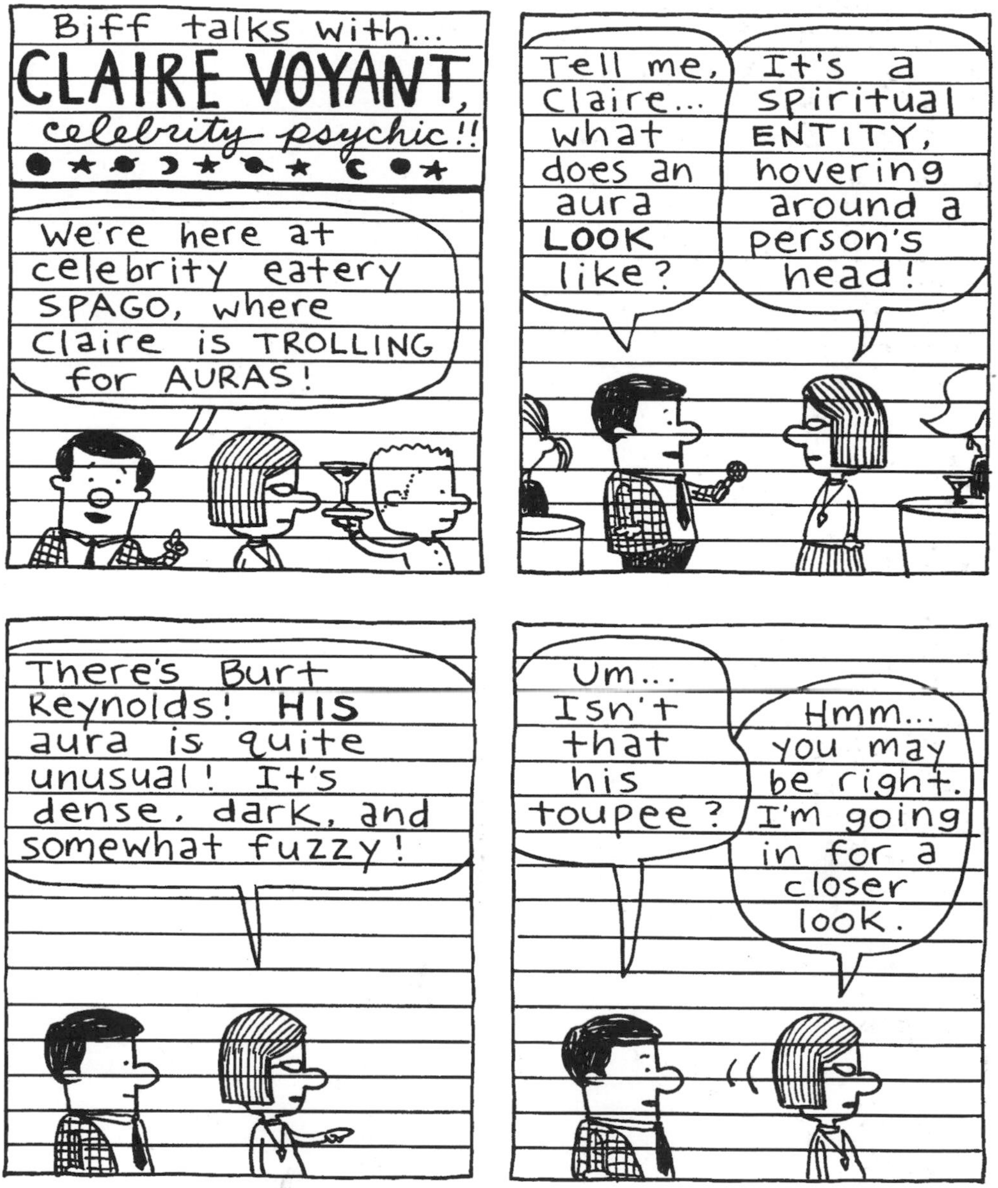
Biff talks with...
CLAIRE VOYANT, celebrity psychic!!
We're here at celebrity eatery SPAGO, where Claire is TROLLING for AURAS!
Tell me, Claire... what does an aura LOOK like?
It's a spiritual ENTITY, hovering around a person's head!
There's Burt Reynolds! HIS aura is quite unusual! It's dense, dark, and somewhat fuzzy!
Um... Isn't that his toupee?
Hmm... you may be right. I'm going in for a closer look.

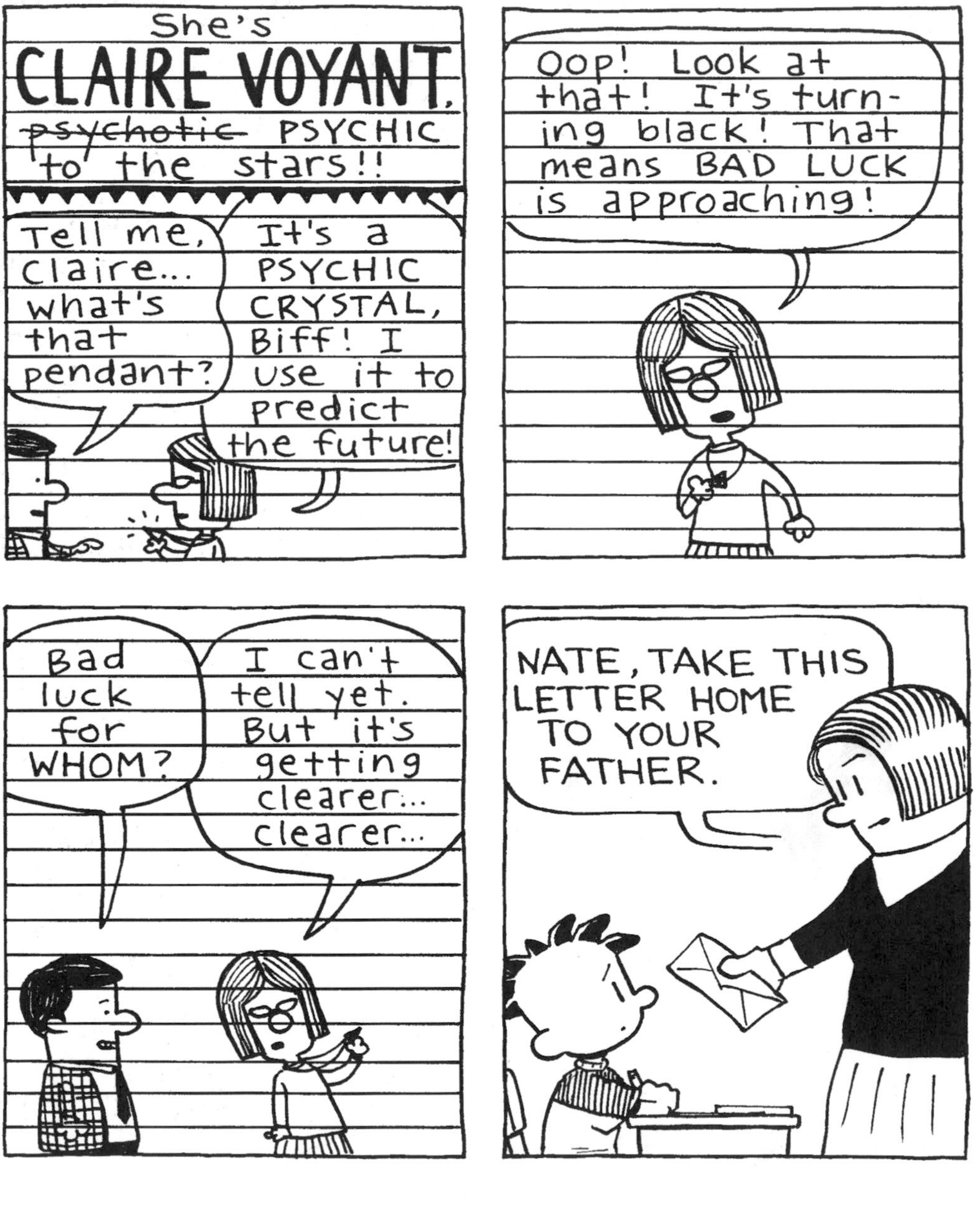
She's CLAIRE VOYANT, psychotic PSYCHIC to the stars!!
Tell me, Claire... what's that pendant?
It's a PSYCHIC CRYSTAL, Biff! I use it to predict the future!
Oop! Look at that! It's turning black! That means BAD LUCK is approaching!
Bad luck for WHOM?
I can't tell yet. But it's getting clearer... clearer...
NATE, TAKE THIS LETTER HOME TO YOUR FATHER.

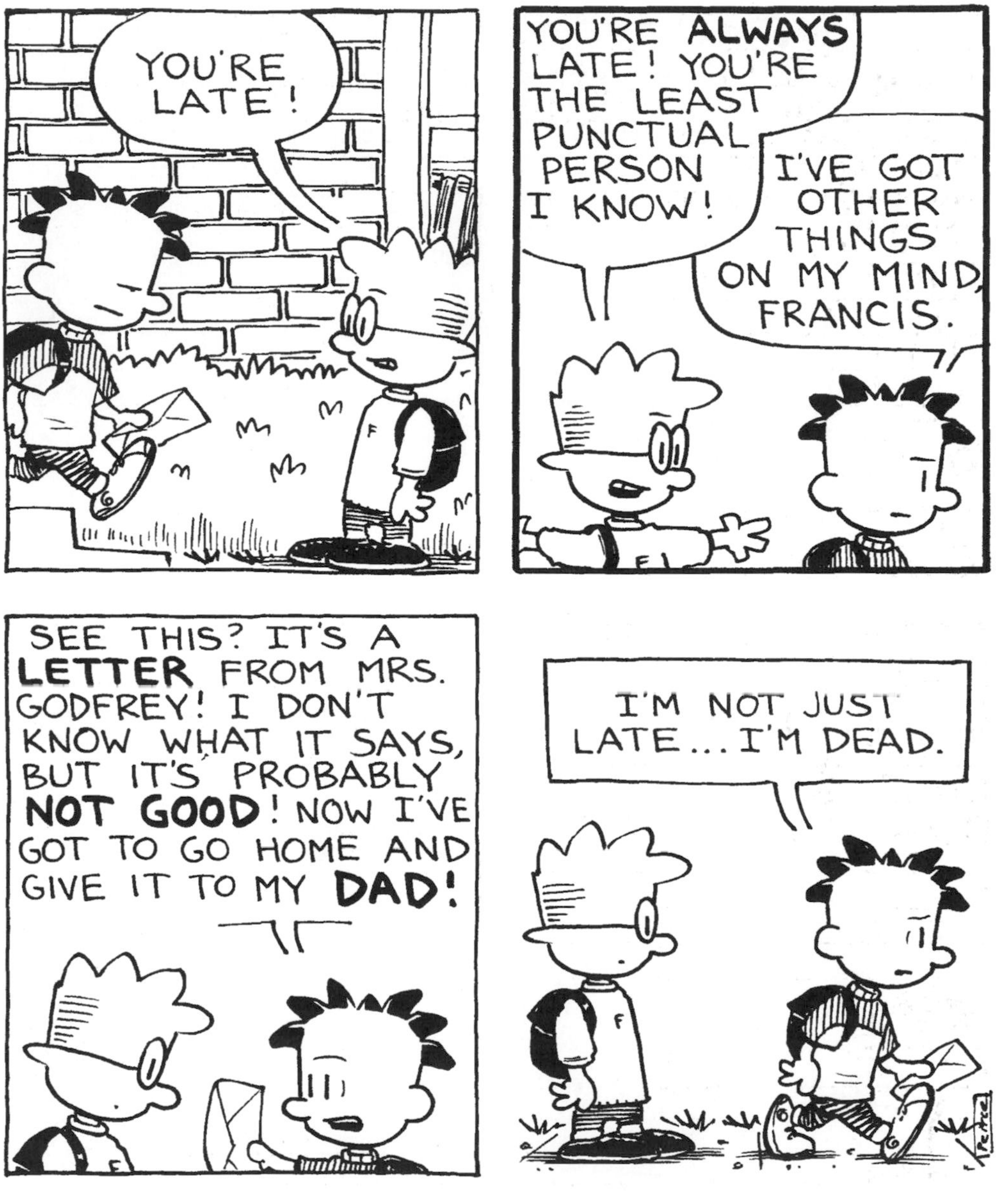
YOU'RE LATE!
YOU'RE ALWAYS LATE! YOU'RE THE LEAST PUNCTUAL PERSON I KNOW!
I'VE GOT OTHER THINGS ON MY MIND, FRANCIS.
SEE THIS? IT'S A LETTER FROM MRS. GODFREY! I DON'T KNOW WHAT IT SAYS, BUT IT'S PROBABLY NOT GOOD! NOW I'VE GOT TO GO HOME AND GIVE IT TO MY DAD!
I'M NOT JUST LATE... I'M DEAD.
Peirce

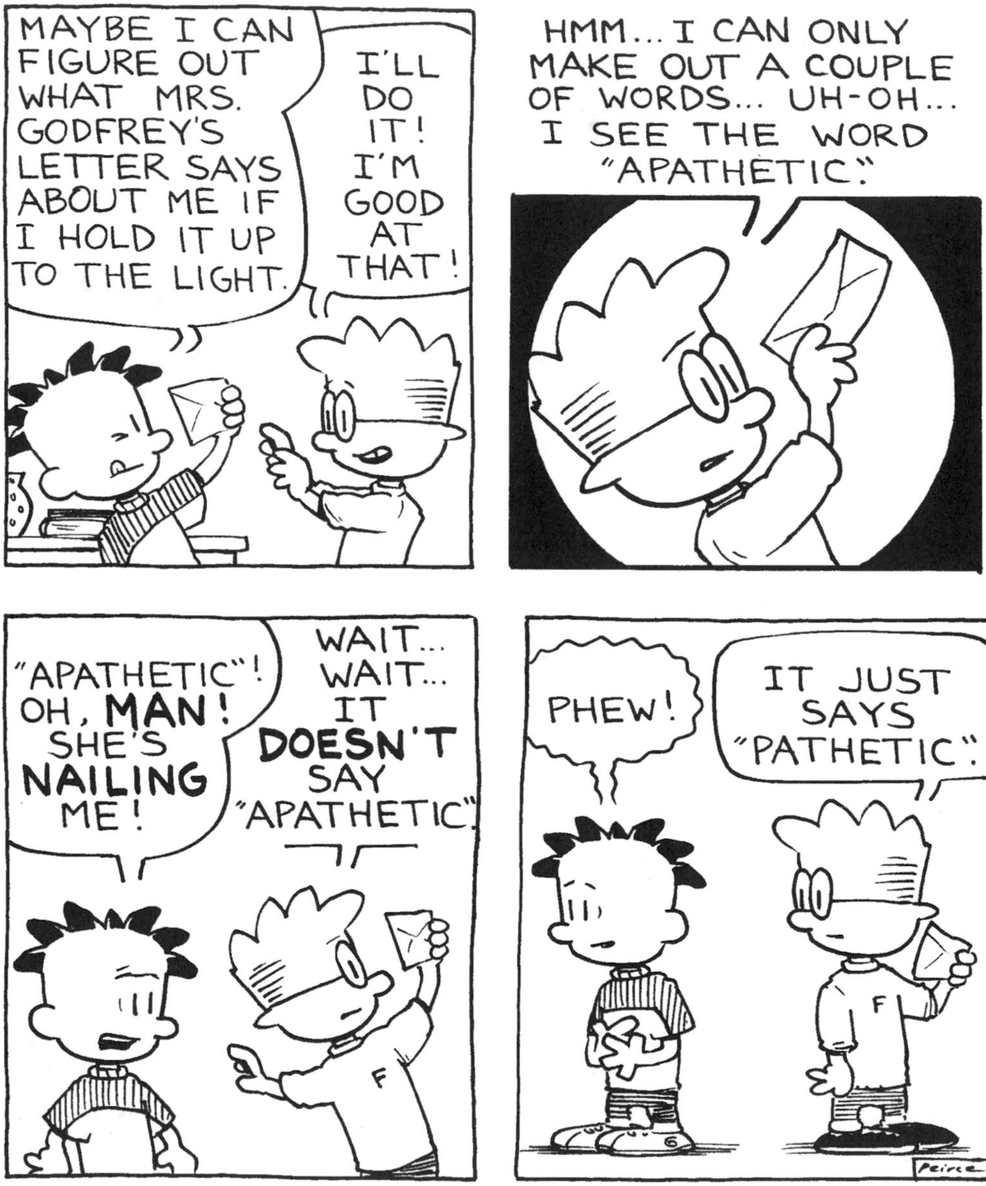
MAYBE I CAN FIGURE OUT WHAT MRS. GODFREY'S LETTER SAYS ABOUT ME IF I HOLD IT UP TO THE LIGHT.
I'LL DO IT! I'M GOOD AT THAT!
HMM... I CAN ONLY MAKE OUT A COUPLE OF WORDS... UH-OH... I SEE THE WORD "APATHETIC."
"APATHETIC"! OH, MAN! SHE'S NAILING ME!
WAIT... WAIT... IT DOESN'T SAY "APATHETIC."
PHEW!
IT JUST SAYS "PATHETIC."
Peirce

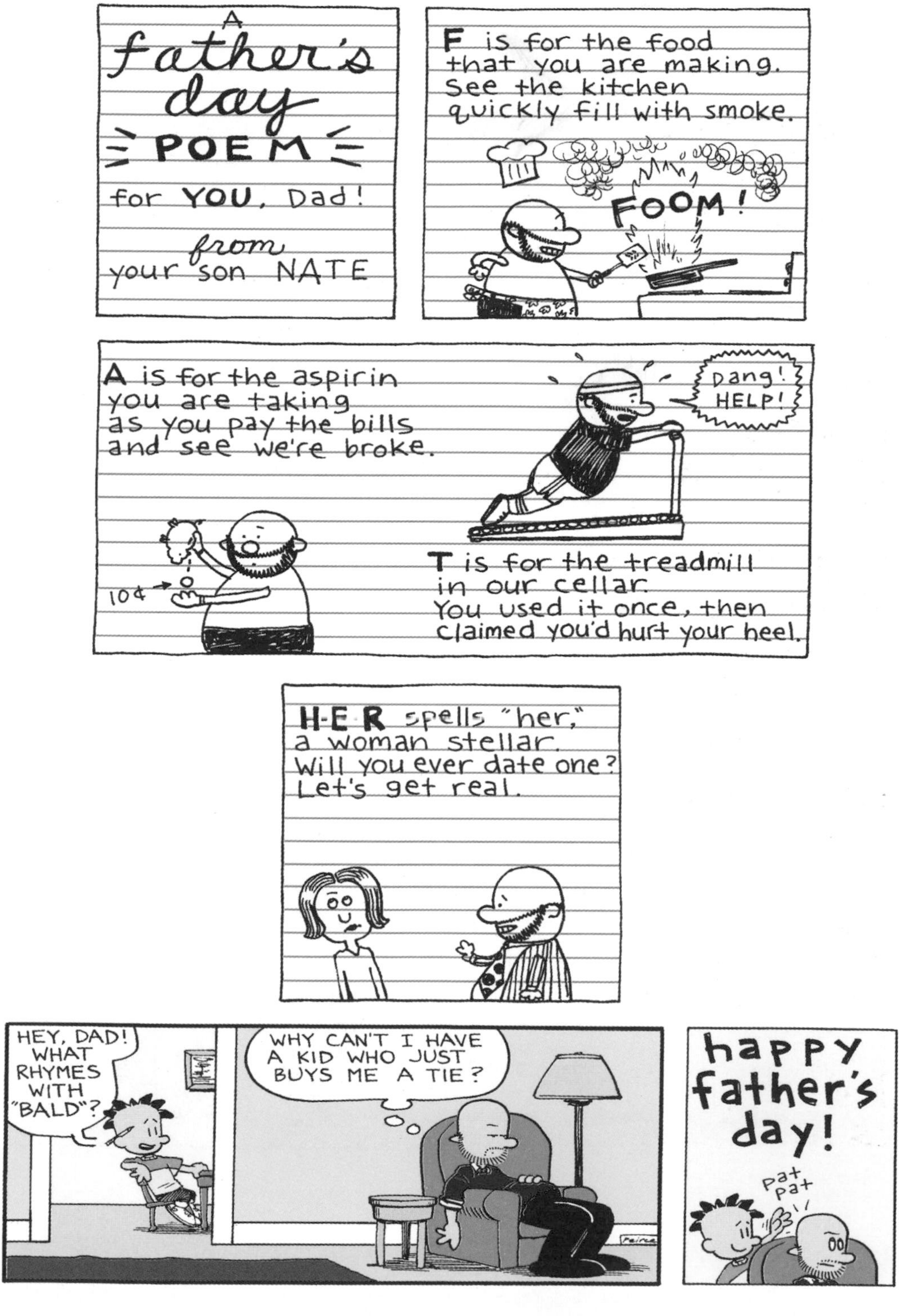
A father's day POEM
for YOU, Dad!
from your son NATE
F is for the food that you are making. See the kitchen quickly fill with smoke.
FOOM!
A is for the aspirin you are taking as you pay the bills and see we're broke.
104
Dang! HELP!
T is for the treadmill in our cellar. You used it once, then claimed you'd hurt your heel.
H-E-R spells "her," a woman stellar. Will you ever date one? Let's get real.
HEY, DAD! WHAT RHYMES WITH "BALD"?
WHY CAN'T I HAVE A KID WHO JUST BUYS ME A TIE?
happy father's day!
Pat Pat

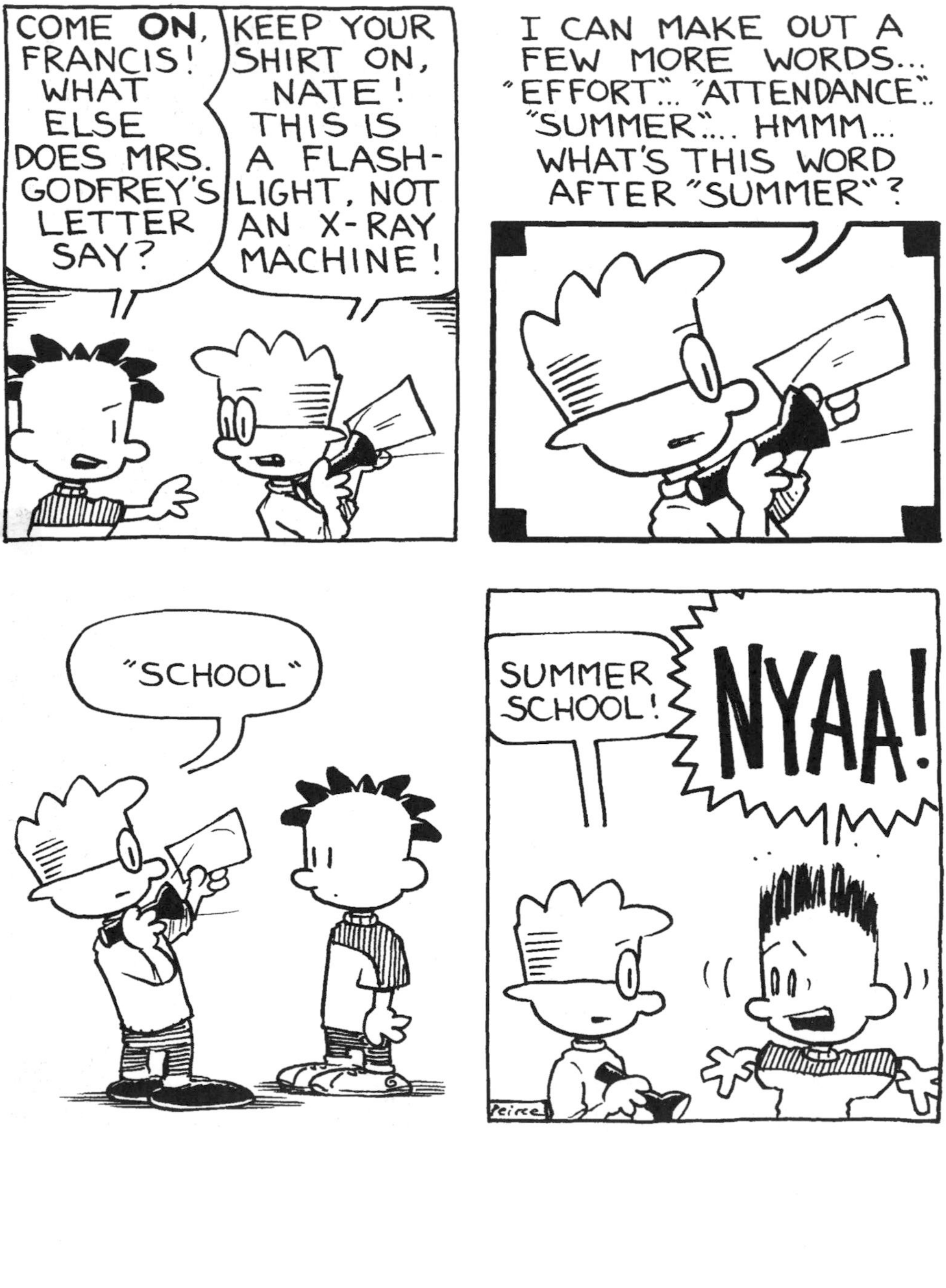
COME ON, FRANCIS! WHAT ELSE DOES MRS. GODFREY'S LETTER SAY?
KEEP YOUR SHIRT ON, NATE! THIS IS A FLASH-LIGHT, NOT AN X-RAY MACHINE!
I CAN MAKE OUT A FEW MORE WORDS... "EFFORT"... "ATTENDANCE"... "SUMMER"... HMMM... WHAT'S THIS WORD AFTER "SUMMER"?
"SCHOOL"
SUMMER SCHOOL!
NYAA!
Peirce

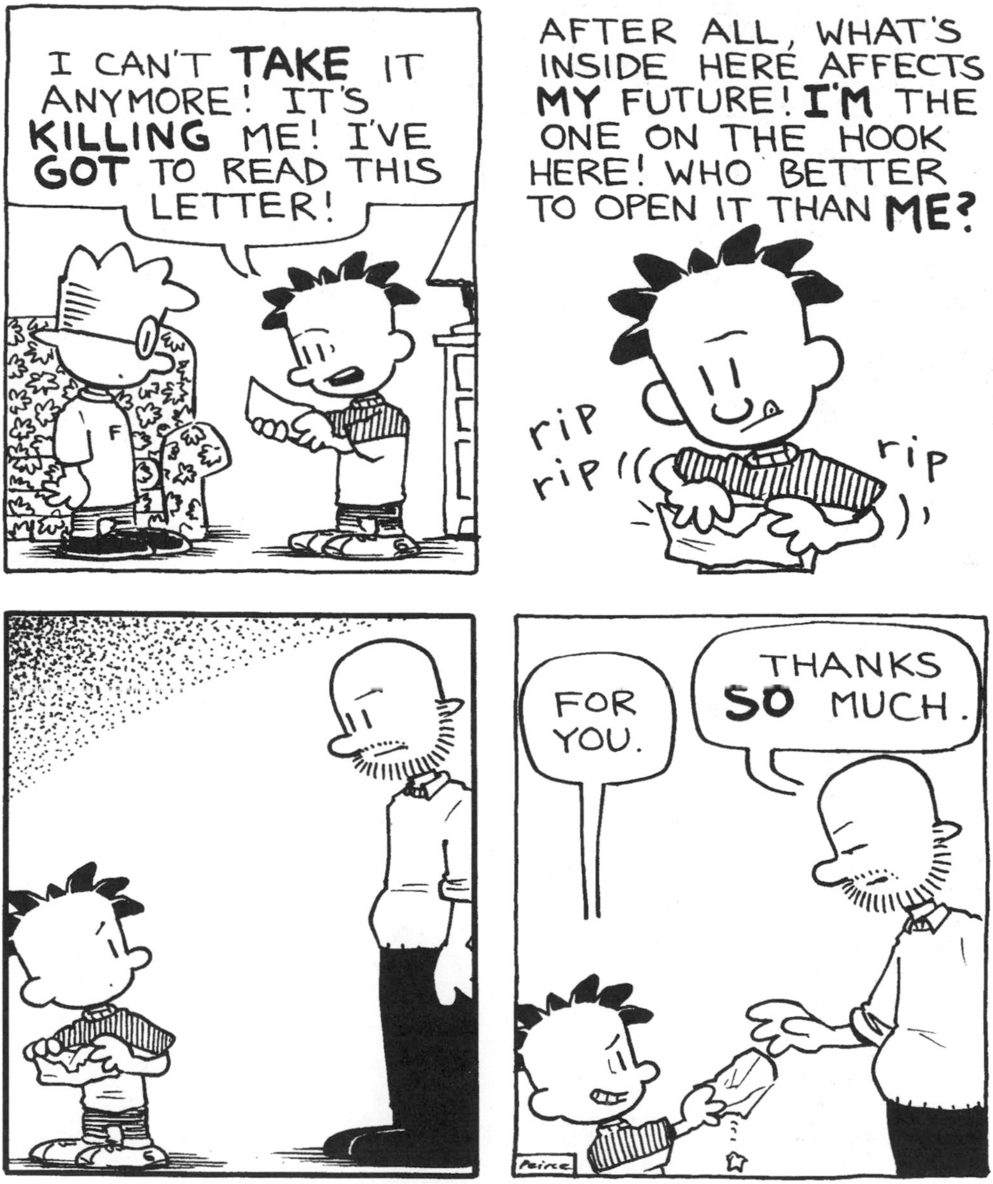
I CAN'T TAKE IT ANYMORE! IT'S KILLING ME! I'VE GOT TO READ THIS LETTER!
AFTER ALL, WHAT'S INSIDE HERE AFFECTS MY FUTURE! I'M THE ONE ON THE HOOK HERE! WHO BETTER TO OPEN IT THAN ME?
rip rip
rip
FOR YOU.
THANKS SO MUCH.
Peirce

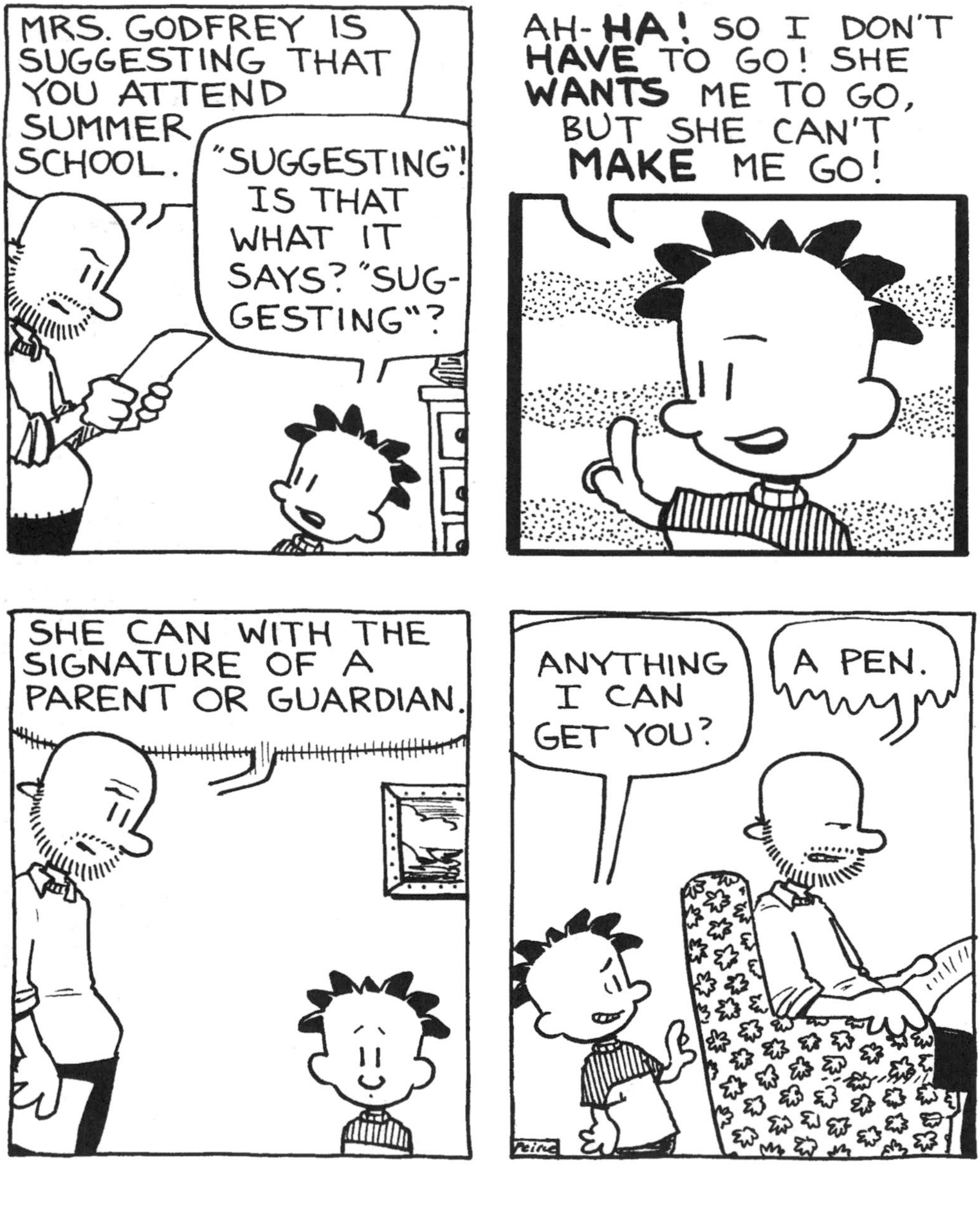
MRS. GODFREY IS SUGGESTING THAT YOU ATTEND SUMMER SCHOOL.
"SUGGESTING"! IS THAT WHAT IT SAYS? "SUG-GESTING"?
AH-**HA!** SO I DON'T **HAVE** TO GO! SHE **WANTS** ME TO GO, BUT SHE CAN'T **MAKE** ME GO!
SHE CAN WITH THE SIGNATURE OF A PARENT OR GUARDIAN.
ANYTHING I CAN GET YOU?
A PEN.

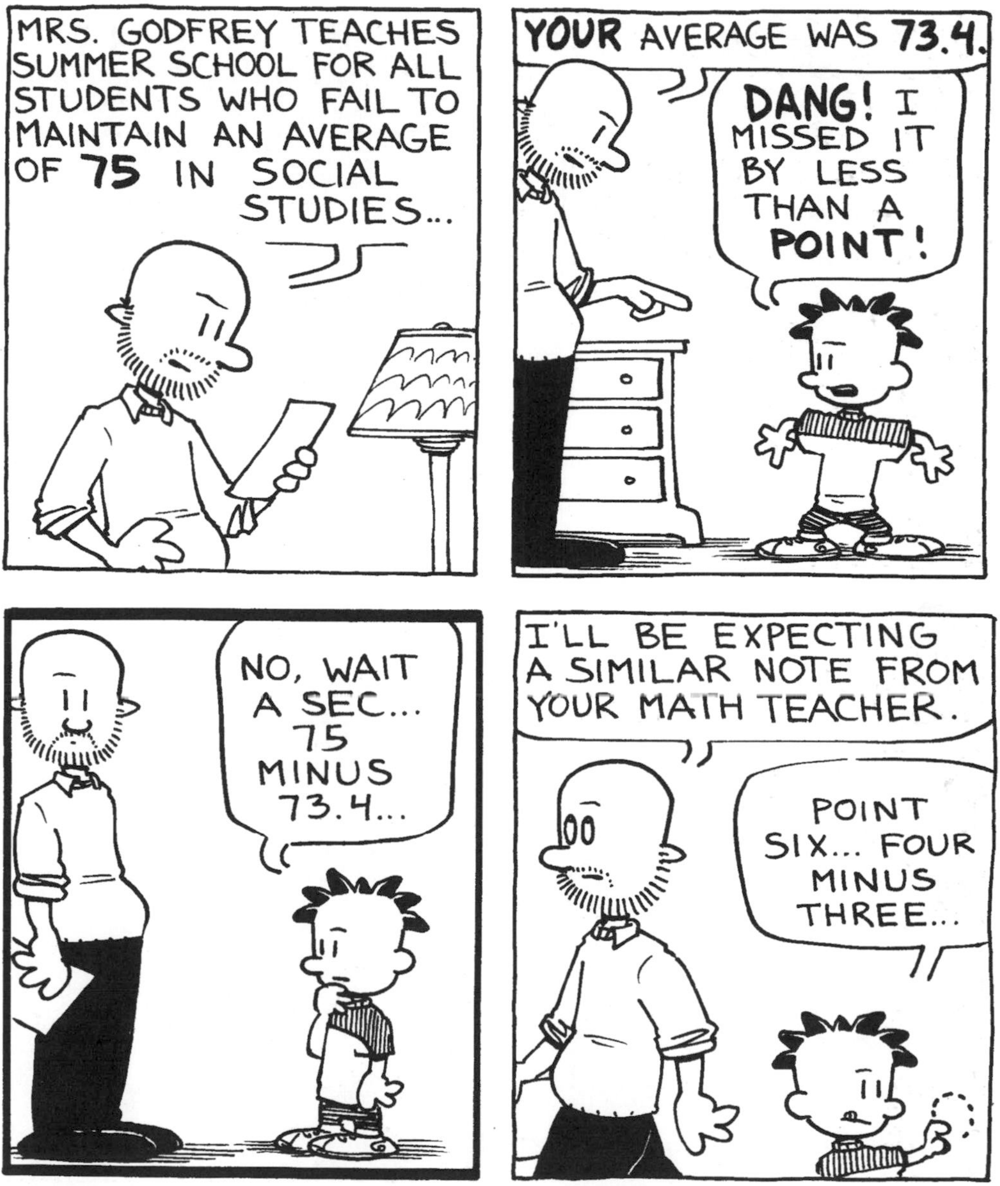
MRS. GODFREY TEACHES SUMMER SCHOOL FOR ALL STUDENTS WHO FAIL TO MAINTAIN AN AVERAGE OF 75 IN SOCIAL STUDIES...
YOUR AVERAGE WAS 73.4.
DANG! I MISSED IT BY LESS THAN A POINT!
NO, WAIT A SEC... 75 MINUS 73.4...
I'LL BE EXPECTING A SIMILAR NOTE FROM YOUR MATH TEACHER.
POINT SIX... FOUR MINUS THREE...

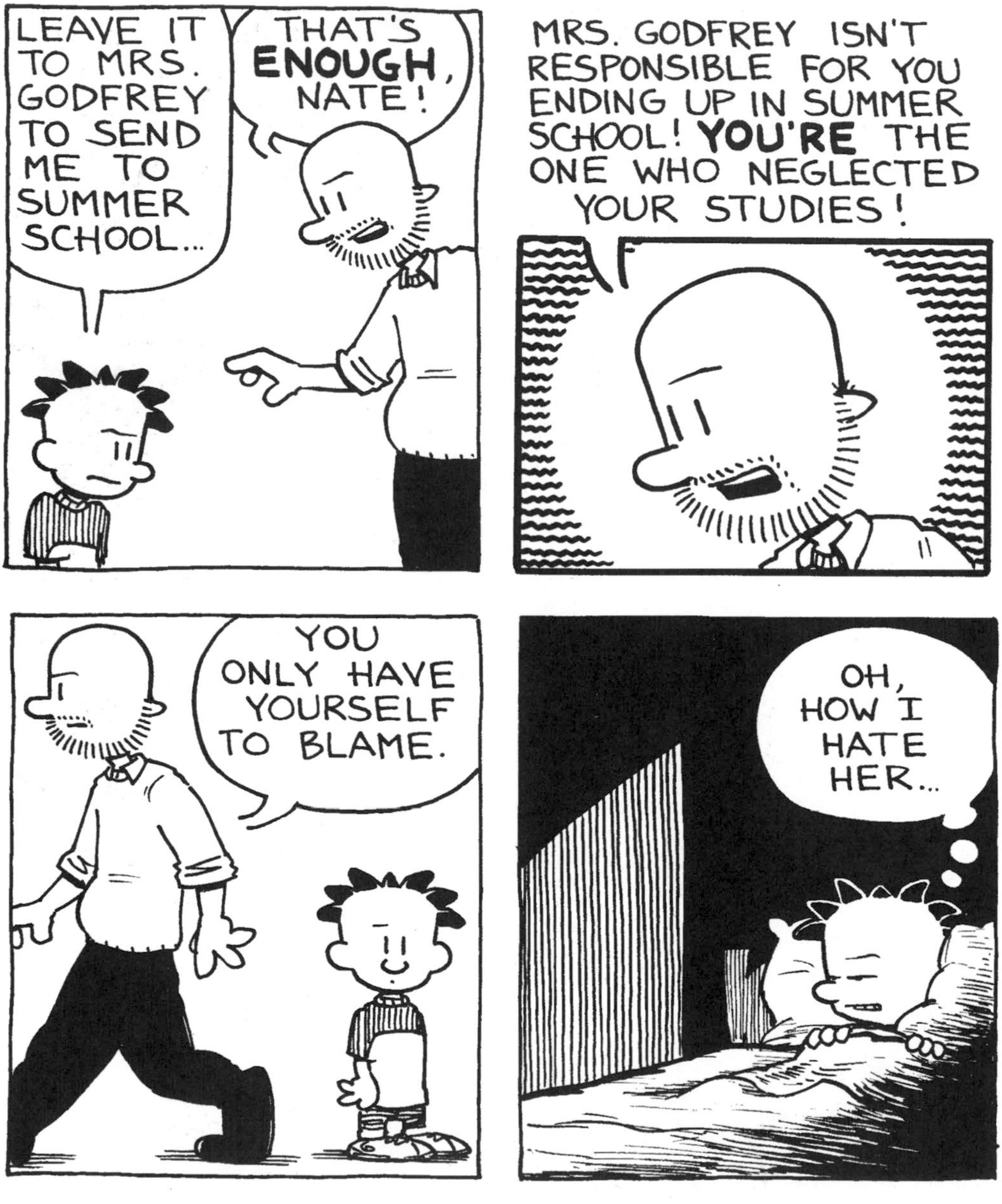
LEAVE IT TO MRS. GODFREY TO SEND ME TO SUMMER SCHOOL...
THAT'S **ENOUGH**, NATE!
MRS. GODFREY ISN'T RESPONSIBLE FOR YOU ENDING UP IN SUMMER SCHOOL! **YOU'RE** THE ONE WHO NEGLECTED YOUR STUDIES!
YOU ONLY HAVE YOURSELF TO BLAME.
OH, HOW I HATE HER...

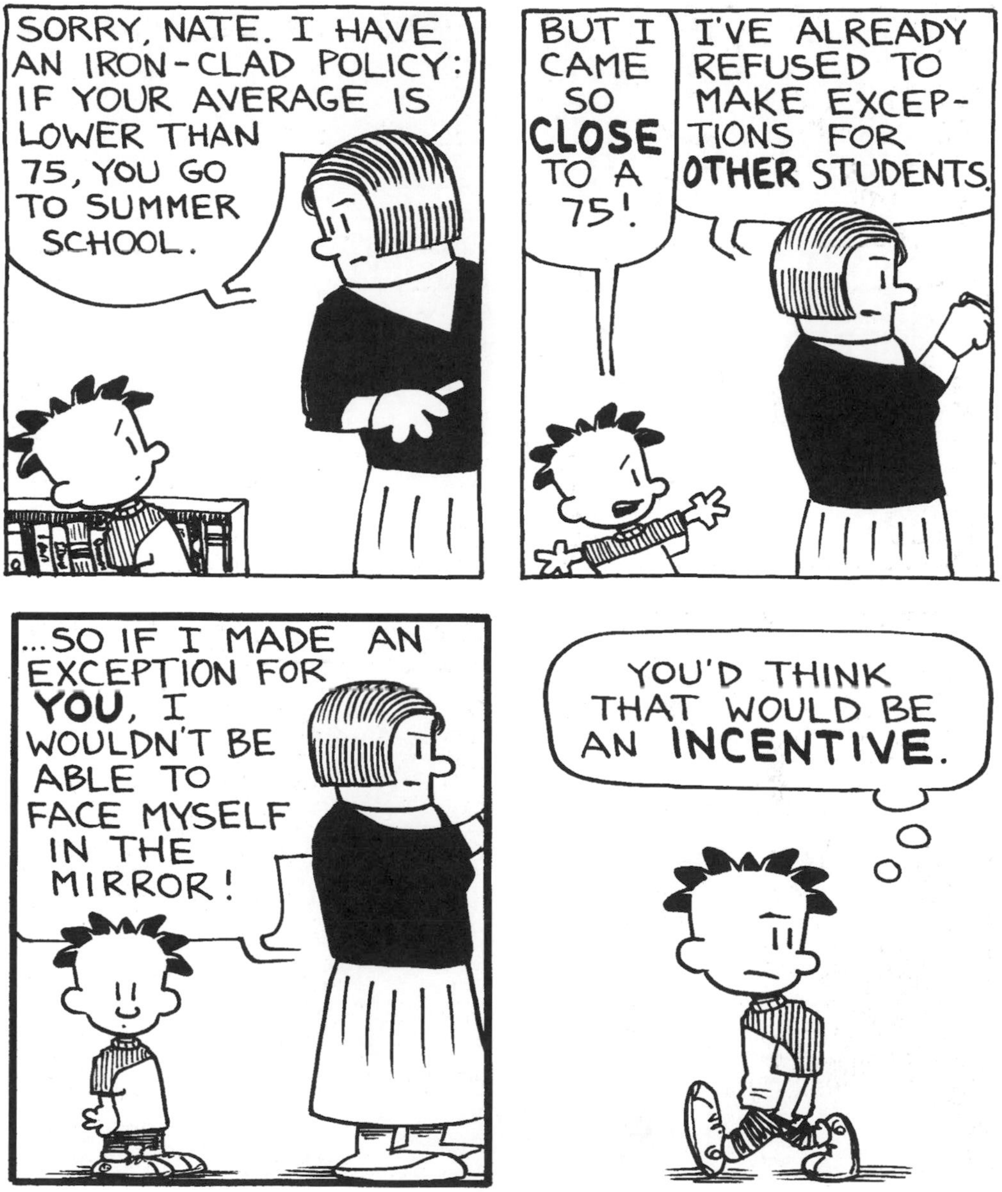
SORRY, NATE. I HAVE AN IRON-CLAD POLICY: IF YOUR AVERAGE IS LOWER THAN 75, YOU GO TO SUMMER SCHOOL.
BUT I CAME SO **CLOSE** TO A 75!
I'VE ALREADY REFUSED TO MAKE EXCEPTIONS FOR **OTHER** STUDENTS.
...SO IF I MADE AN EXCEPTION FOR **YOU**, I WOULDN'T BE ABLE TO FACE MYSELF IN THE MIRROR!
YOU'D THINK THAT WOULD BE AN **INCENTIVE**.

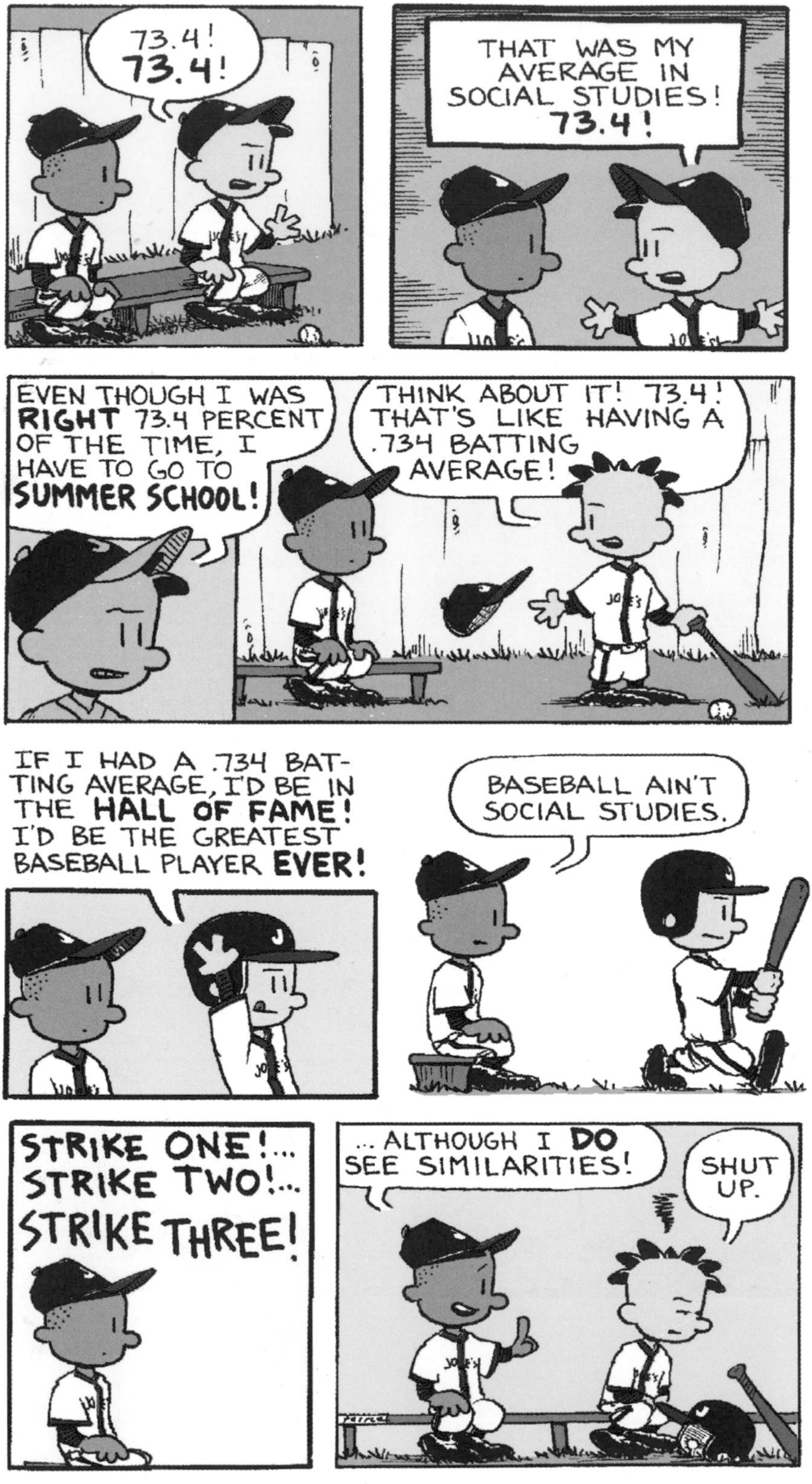
73.4! 73.4!
THAT WAS MY AVERAGE IN SOCIAL STUDIES! 73.4!
EVEN THOUGH I WAS RIGHT 73.4 PERCENT OF THE TIME, I HAVE TO GO TO SUMMER SCHOOL!
THINK ABOUT IT! 73.4! THAT'S LIKE HAVING A .734 BATTING AVERAGE!
IF I HAD A .734 BATTING AVERAGE, I'D BE IN THE HALL OF FAME! I'D BE THE GREATEST BASEBALL PLAYER EVER!
BASEBALL AIN'T SOCIAL STUDIES.
STRIKE ONE!... STRIKE TWO!... STRIKE THREE!
... ALTHOUGH I DO SEE SIMILARITIES!
SHUT UP.

I'M BEING FORCED TO ATTEND SUMMER SCHOOL AGAINST MY WILL, AND YOU GUYS DON'T EVEN **CARE**!
YOU'LL BE HAVING FUN WHILE **I'M** CHAINED TO A DESK! IS THERE NO PITY? **IS THERE NO PITY??**
GUESS NOT. IS THERE NO KETCHUP?
HEE HEE
HEH HEH HA
HA
IS THERE NO RELISH?
HA HA
ARE THERE NO ONIONS?
HA HEE HEE HA

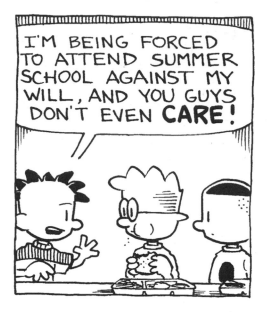

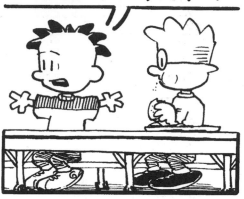

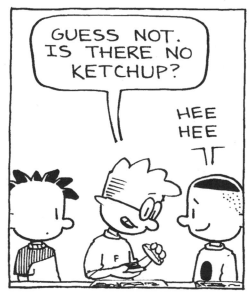

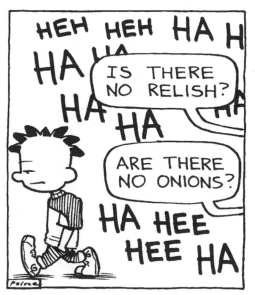

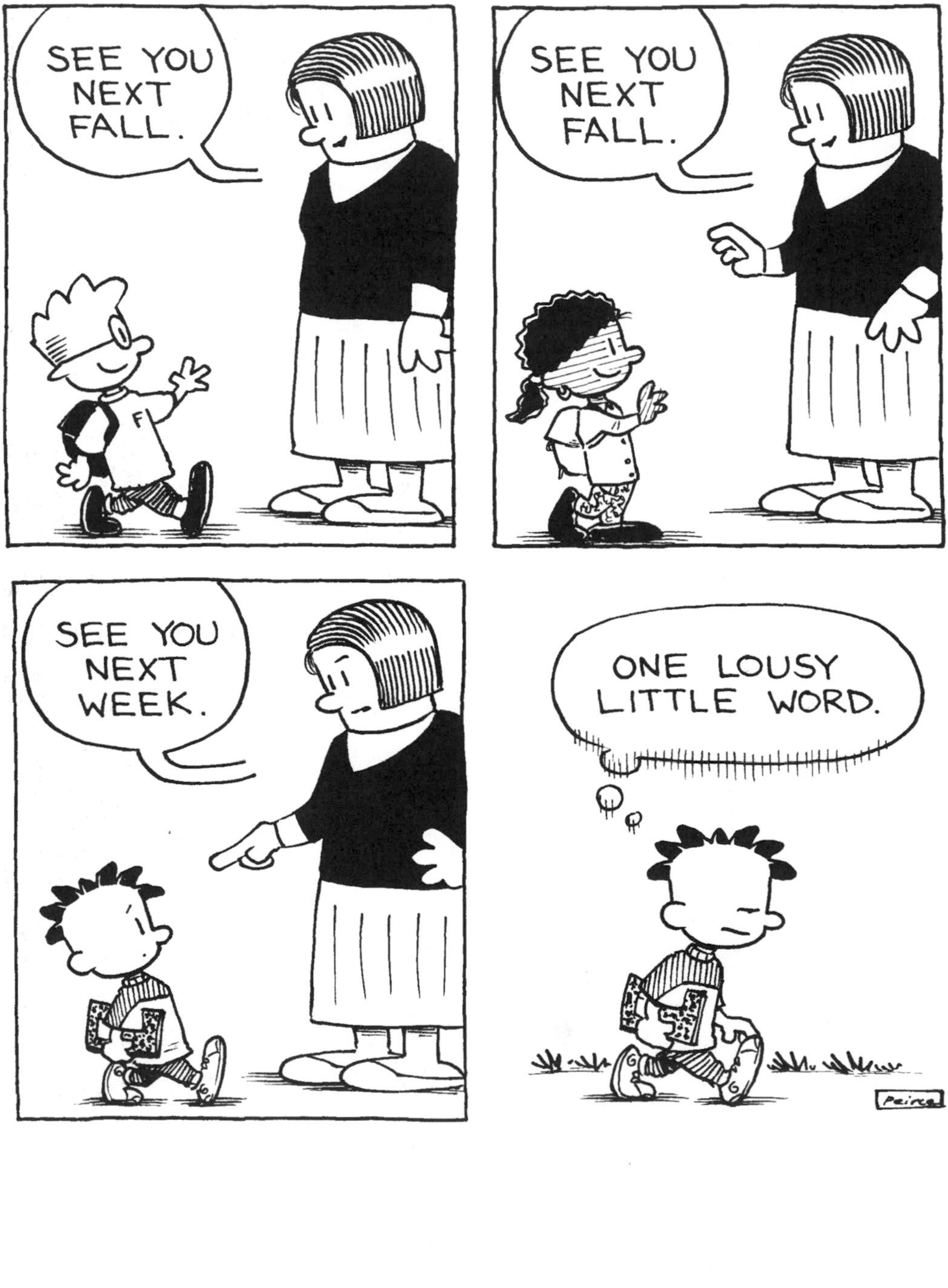
SEE YOU NEXT FALL.
SEE YOU NEXT FALL.
SEE YOU NEXT WEEK.
ONE LOUSY LITTLE WORD.
Peirce

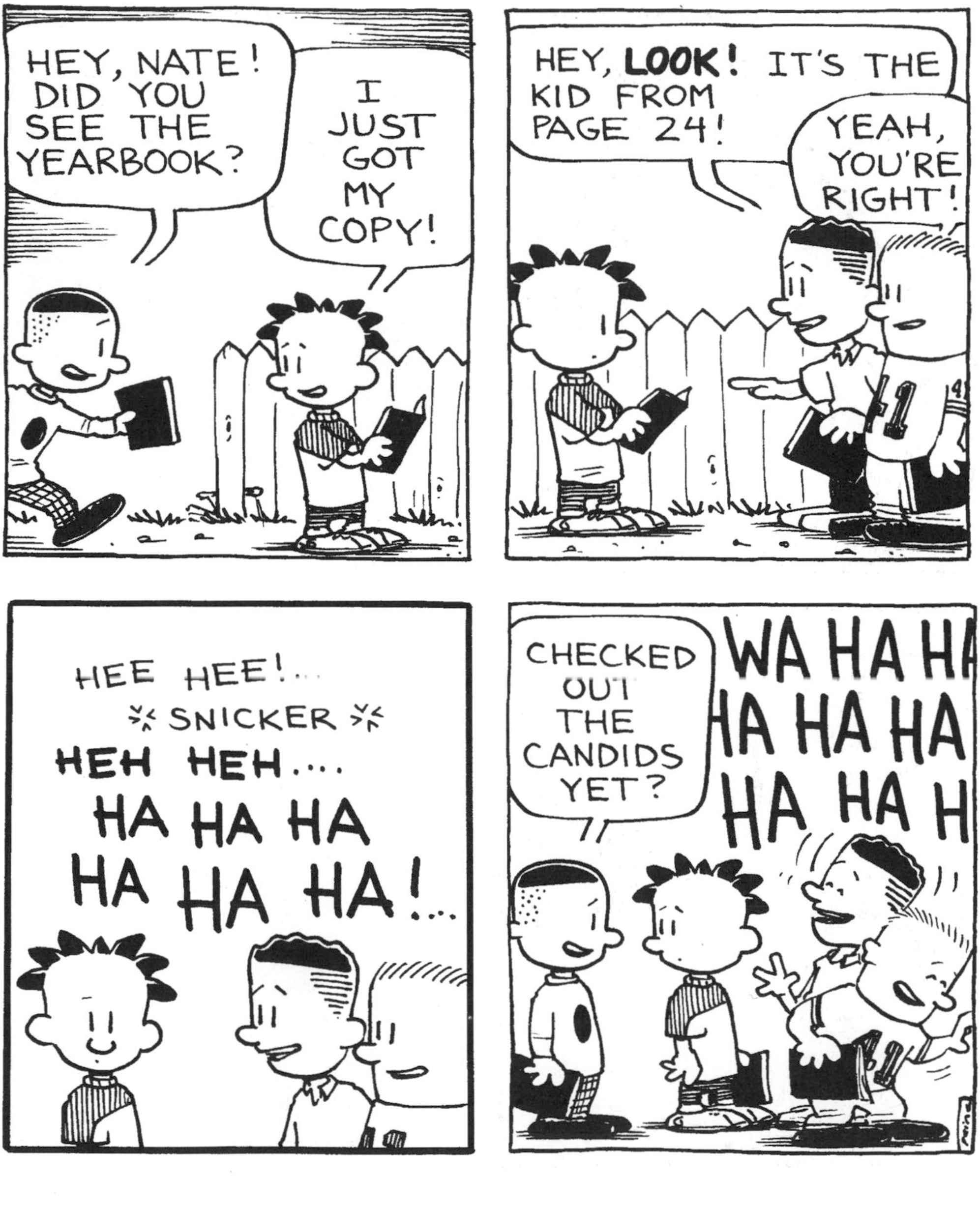
HEY, NATE! DID YOU SEE THE YEARBOOK?
I JUST GOT MY COPY!
HEY, **LOOK!** IT'S THE KID FROM PAGE 24!
YEAH, YOU'RE RIGHT!
HEE HEE!...
SNICKER
HEH HEH....
HA HA HA
HA HA HA!...
CHECKED OUT THE CANDIDS YET?
WA HA HA
HA HA HA
HA HA H

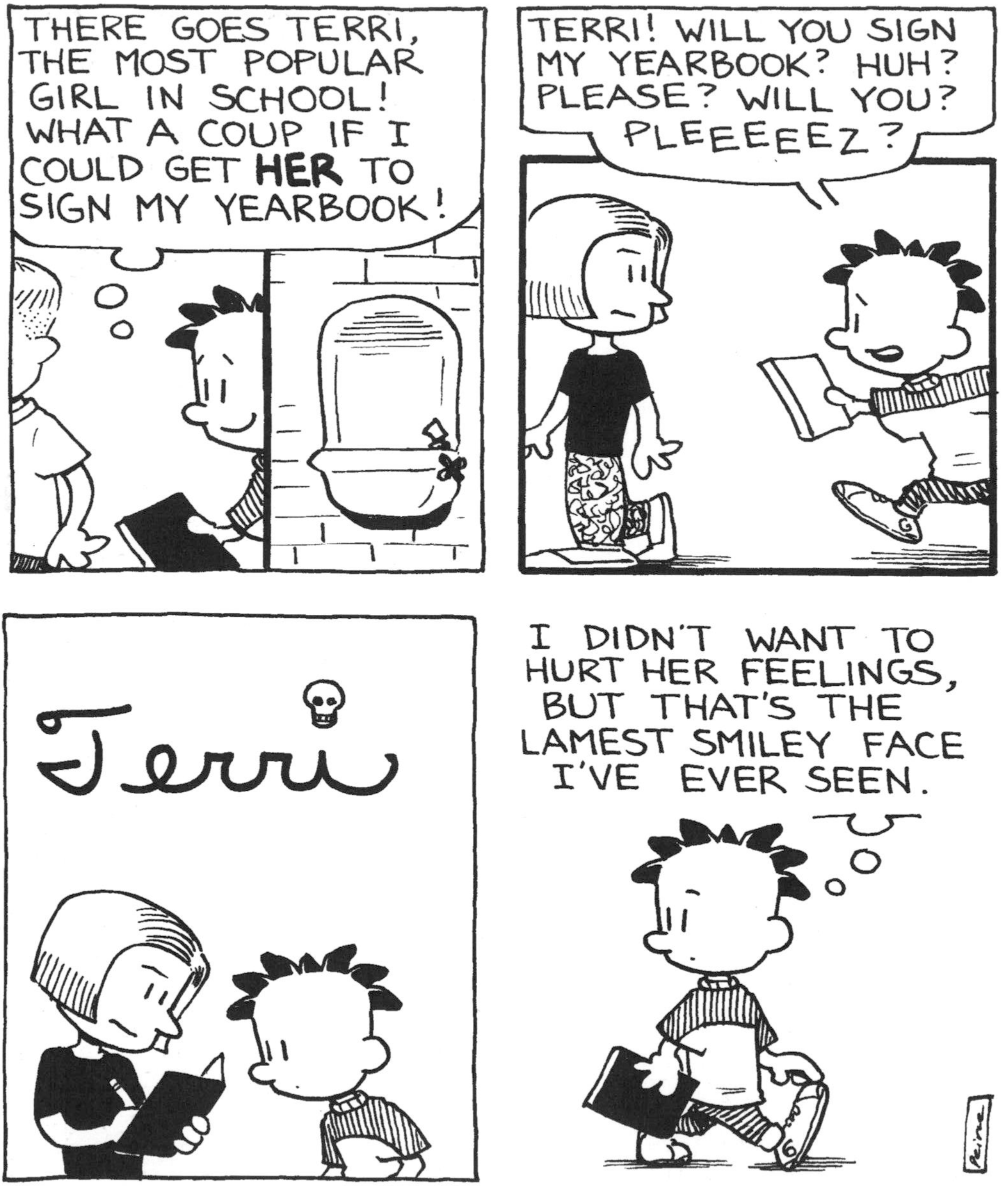
THERE GOES TERRI, THE MOST POPULAR GIRL IN SCHOOL! WHAT A COUP IF I COULD GET **HER** TO SIGN MY YEARBOOK!
TERRI! WILL YOU SIGN MY YEARBOOK? HUH? PLEASE? WILL YOU? PLEEEEEEZ?
Terri
I DIDN'T WANT TO HURT HER FEELINGS, BUT THAT'S THE LAMEST SMILEY FACE I'VE EVER SEEN.

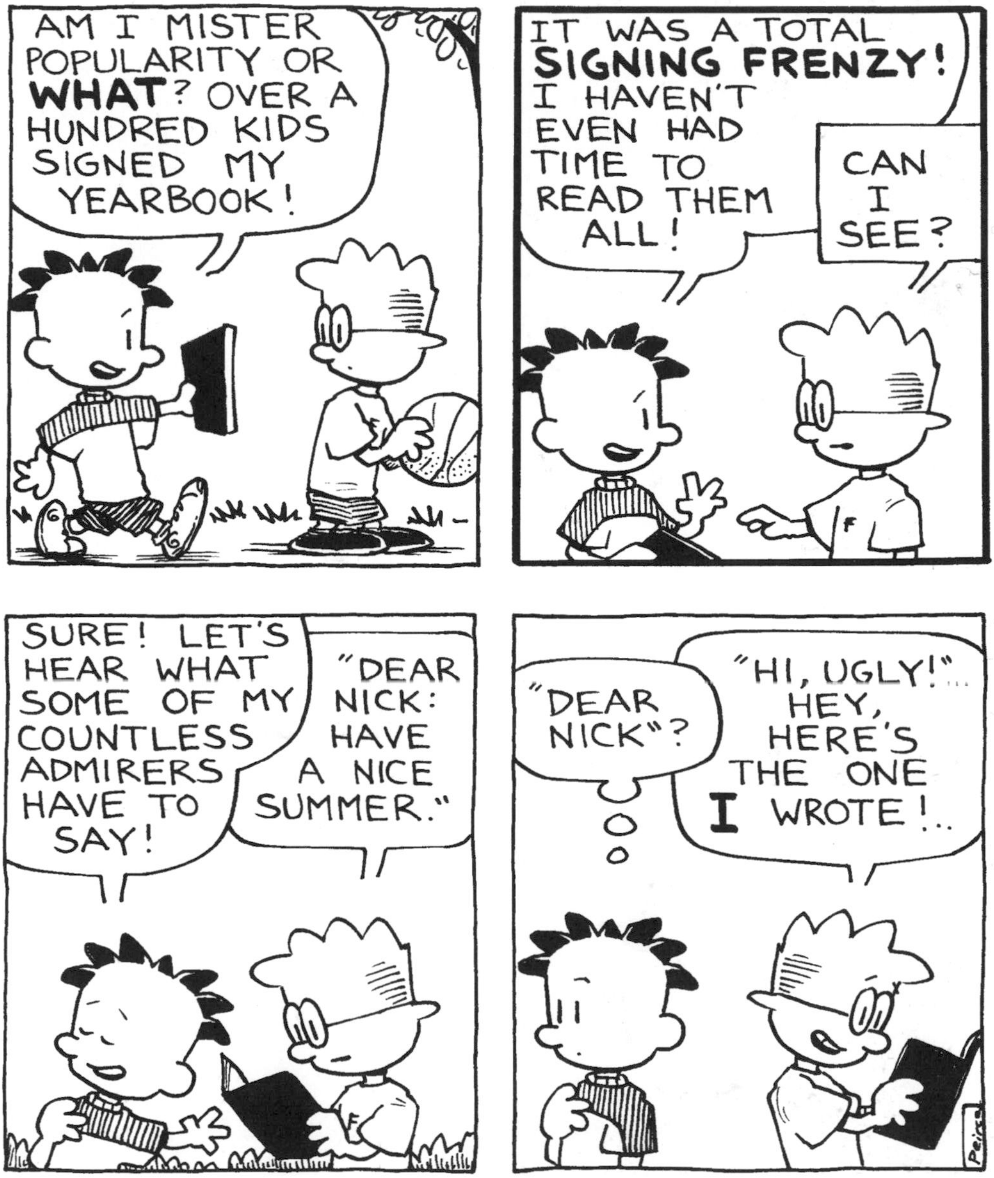
AM I MISTER POPULARITY OR WHAT? OVER A HUNDRED KIDS SIGNED MY YEARBOOK!
IT WAS A TOTAL SIGNING FRENZY! I HAVEN'T EVEN HAD TIME TO READ THEM ALL!
CAN I SEE?
SURE! LET'S HEAR WHAT SOME OF MY COUNTLESS ADMIRERS HAVE TO SAY!
"DEAR NICK: HAVE A NICE SUMMER."
"DEAR NICK"?
"HI, UGLY!"... HEY, HERE'S THE ONE I WROTE!..
Peirce

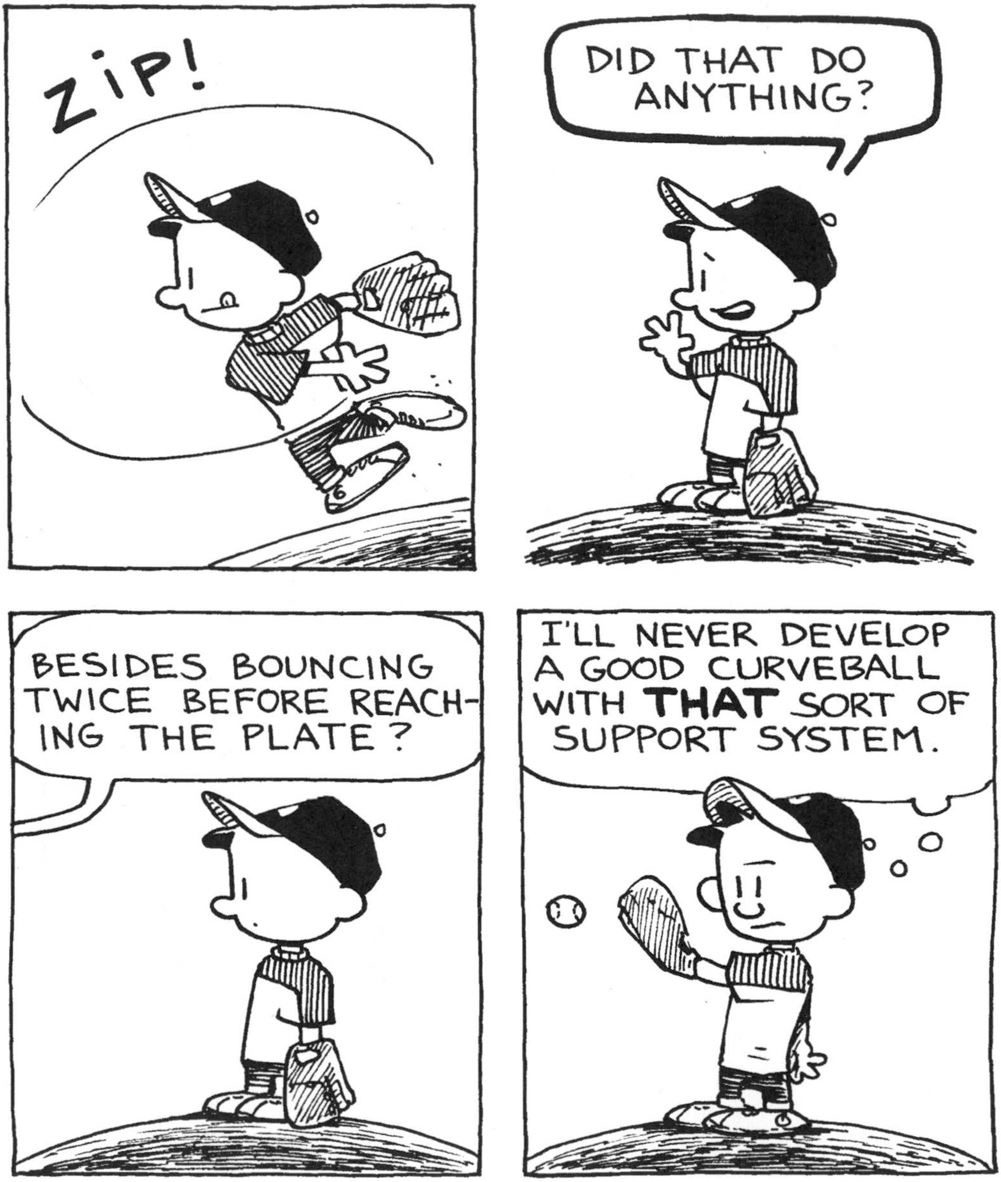
ZIP!
DID THAT DO ANYTHING?
BESIDES BOUNCING TWICE BEFORE REACHING THE PLATE?
I'LL NEVER DEVELOP A GOOD CURVEBALL WITH THAT SORT OF SUPPORT SYSTEM.

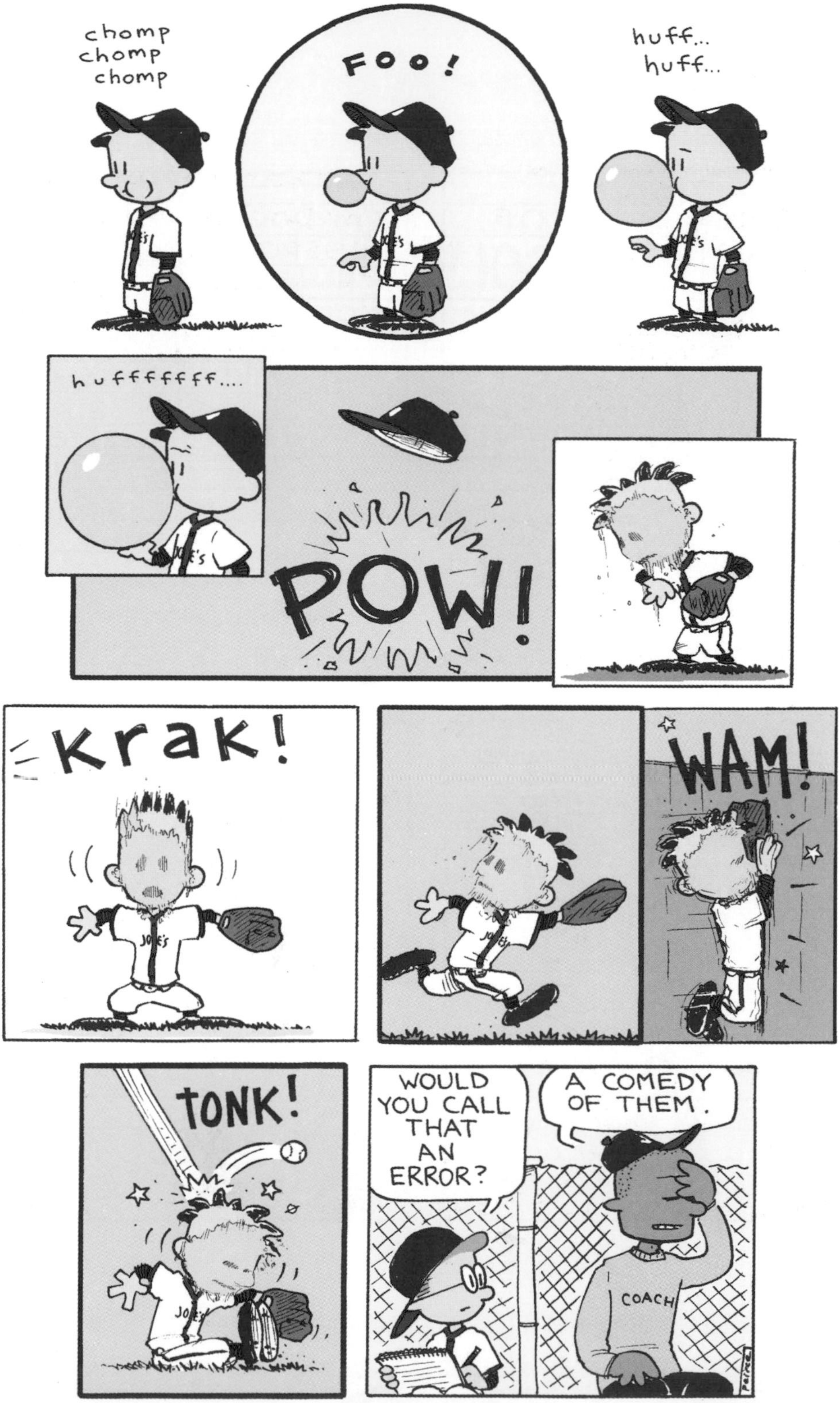
chomp
chomp
chomp
FOO!
huff...
huff...
hufffffff....
POW!
krak!
WAM!
TONK!
WOULD YOU CALL THAT AN ERROR?
A COMEDY OF THEM.
COACH

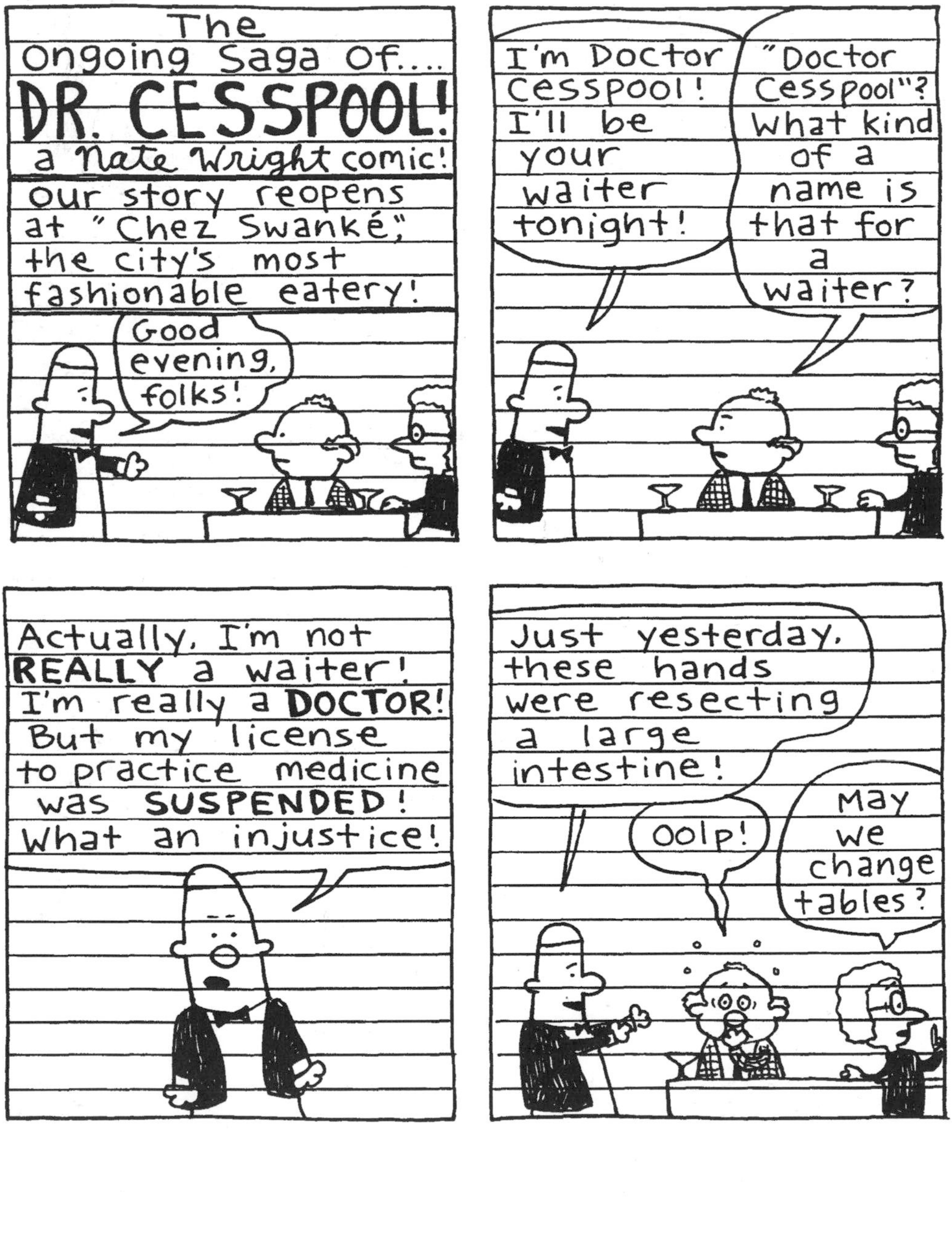
The Ongoing Saga of....
DR. CESSPOOL!
a Nate Wright comic!
Our story reopens at "Chez Swanké," the city's most fashionable eatery!
Good evening, folks!
I'm Doctor Cesspool! I'll be your waiter tonight!
"Doctor Cesspool"? What kind of a name is that for a waiter?
Actually, I'm not REALLY a waiter! I'm really a DOCTOR! But my license to practice medicine was SUSPENDED! What an injustice!
Just yesterday, these hands were resecting a large intestine!
Oolp!
May we change tables?

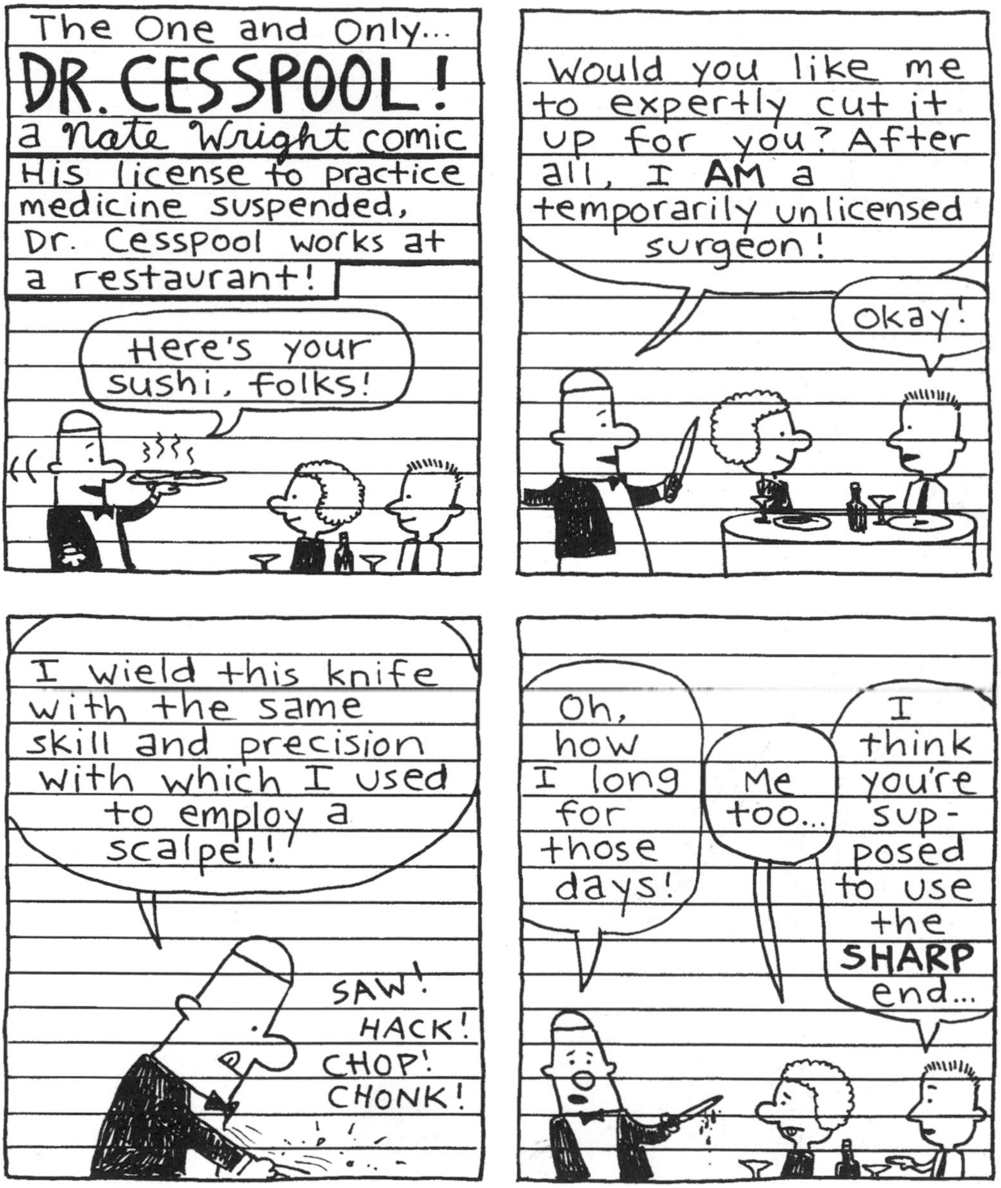
The One and Only...
DR. CESSPOOL!
a Nate Wright comic
His license to practice medicine suspended, Dr. Cesspool works at a restaurant!
Here's your sushi, folks!
Would you like me to expertly cut it up for you? After all, I **AM** a temporarily unlicensed surgeon!
Okay!
I wield this knife with the same skill and precision with which I used to employ a scalpel!
SAW! HACK! CHOP! CHONK!
Oh, how I long for those days!
Me too...
I think you're sup-posed to use the **SHARP** end...

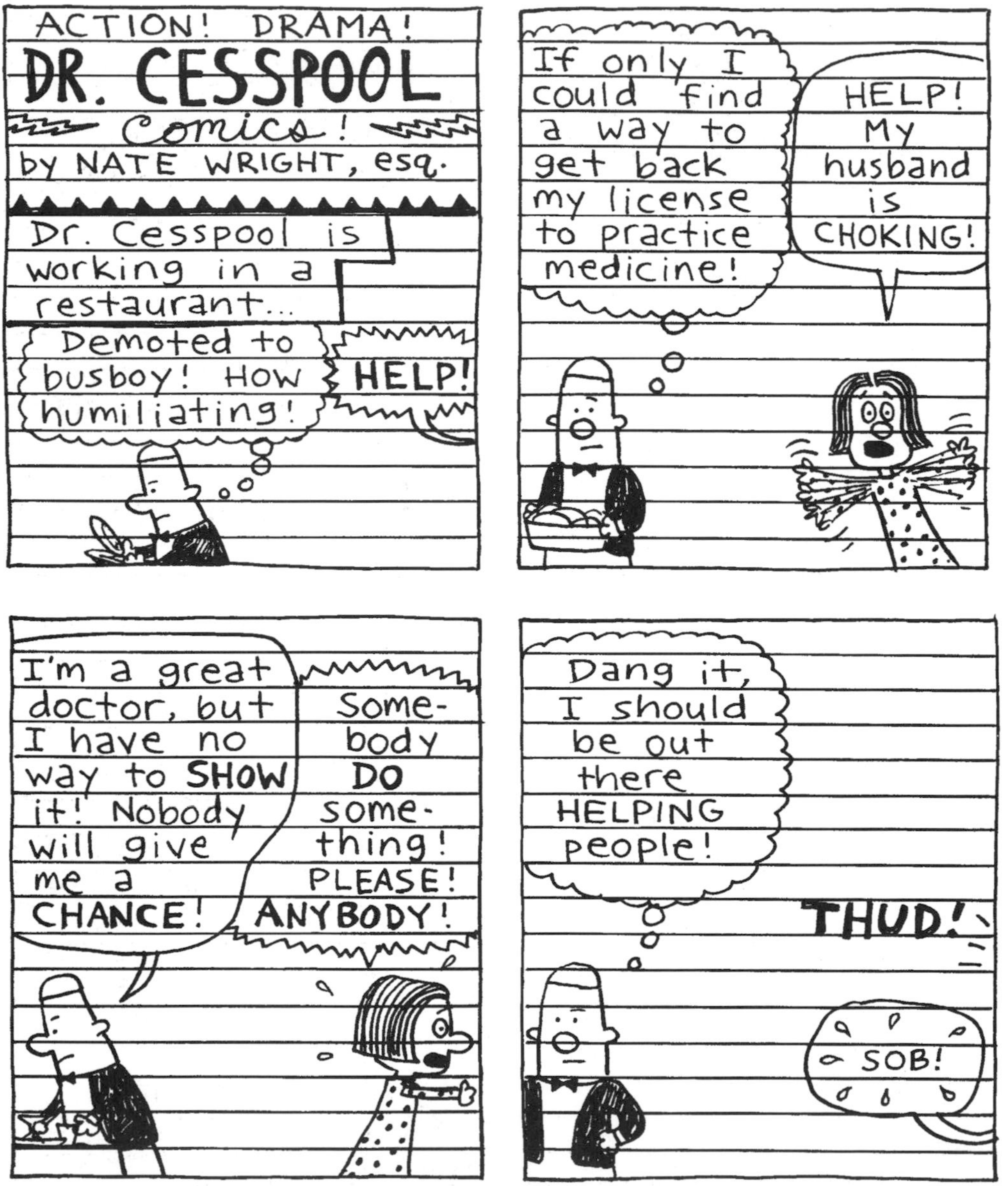

ACTION! DRAMA!
DR. CESSPOOL
Comics!
by NATE WRIGHT, esq.
Dr. Cesspool is working in a restaurant...
Demoted to busboy! How humiliating!
HELP!
If only I could find a way to get back my license to practice medicine!
HELP! My husband is CHOKING!
I'm a great doctor, but I have no way to SHOW it! Nobody will give me a CHANCE!
Some-body DO some-thing! PLEASE! ANYBODY!
Dang it, I should be out there HELPING people!
THUD!
SOB!

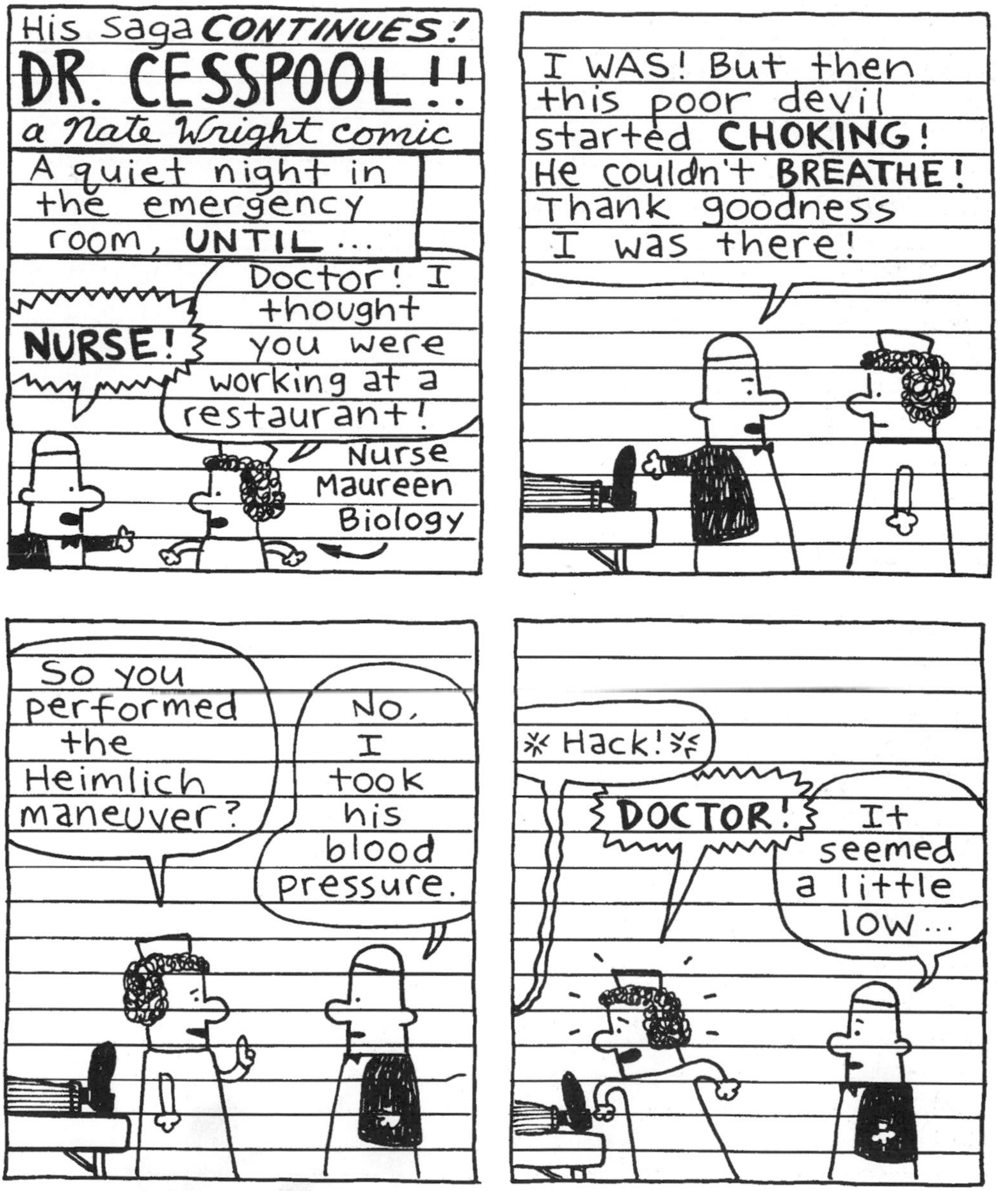

His saga CONTINUES!
DR. CESSPOOL!!
a Nate Wright comic
A quiet night in the emergency room, UNTIL...
NURSE!
Doctor! I thought you were working at a restaurant!
Nurse Maureen Biology
I WAS! But then this poor devil started CHOKING! He couldn't BREATHE! Thank goodness I was there!
So you performed the Heimlich maneuver?
No, I took his blood pressure.
Hack!
DOCTOR!
It seemed a little low...

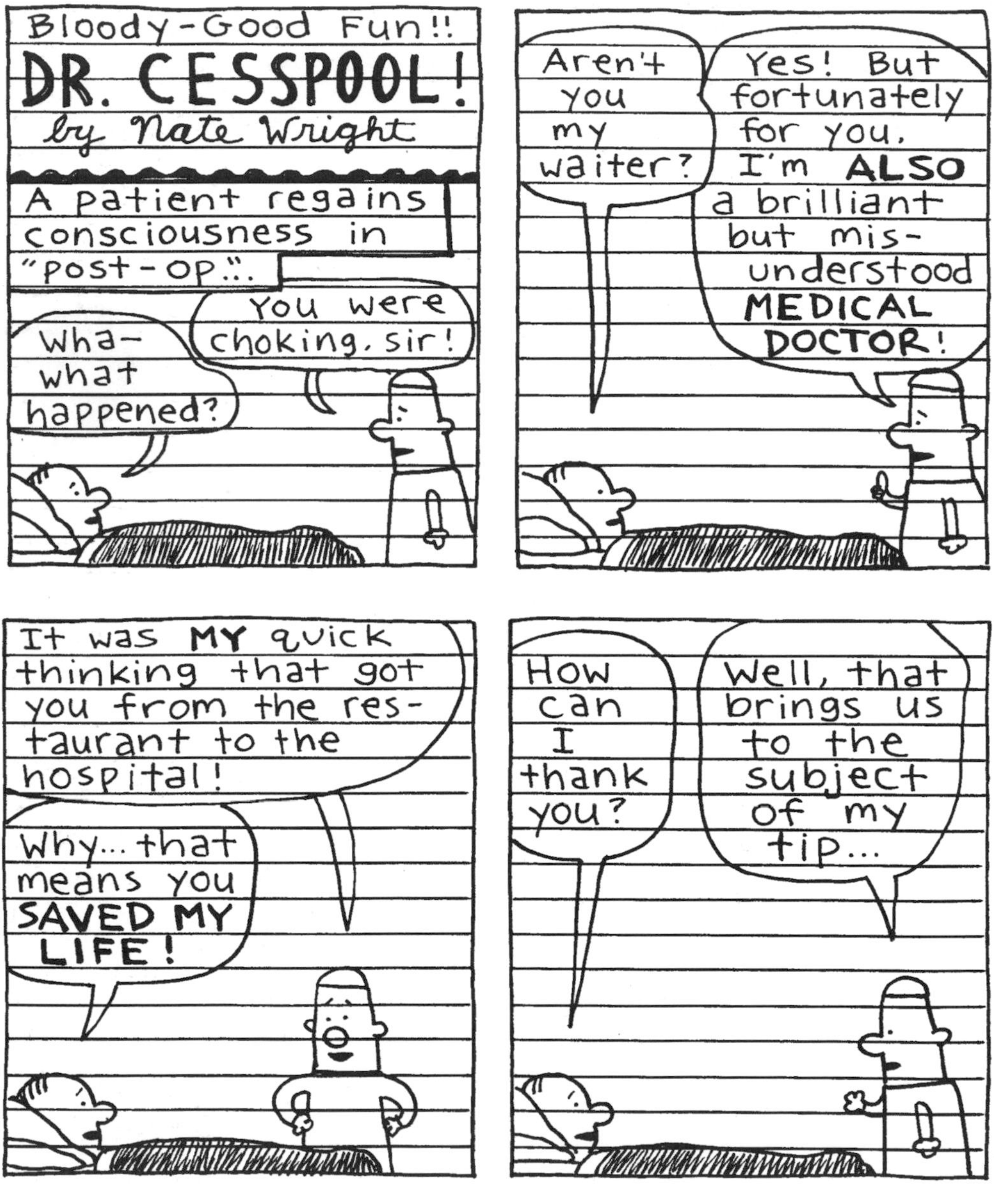

Bloody-Good Fun!!
DR. CESSPOOL!
by Nate Wright
A patient regains consciousness in "post-op."
Wha-what happened?
You were choking, sir!
Aren't you my waiter?
Yes! But fortunately for you, I'm ALSO a brilliant but misunderstood MEDICAL DOCTOR!
It was MY quick thinking that got you from the restaurant to the hospital!
Why... that means you SAVED MY LIFE!
How can I thank you?
Well, that brings us to the subject of my tip...

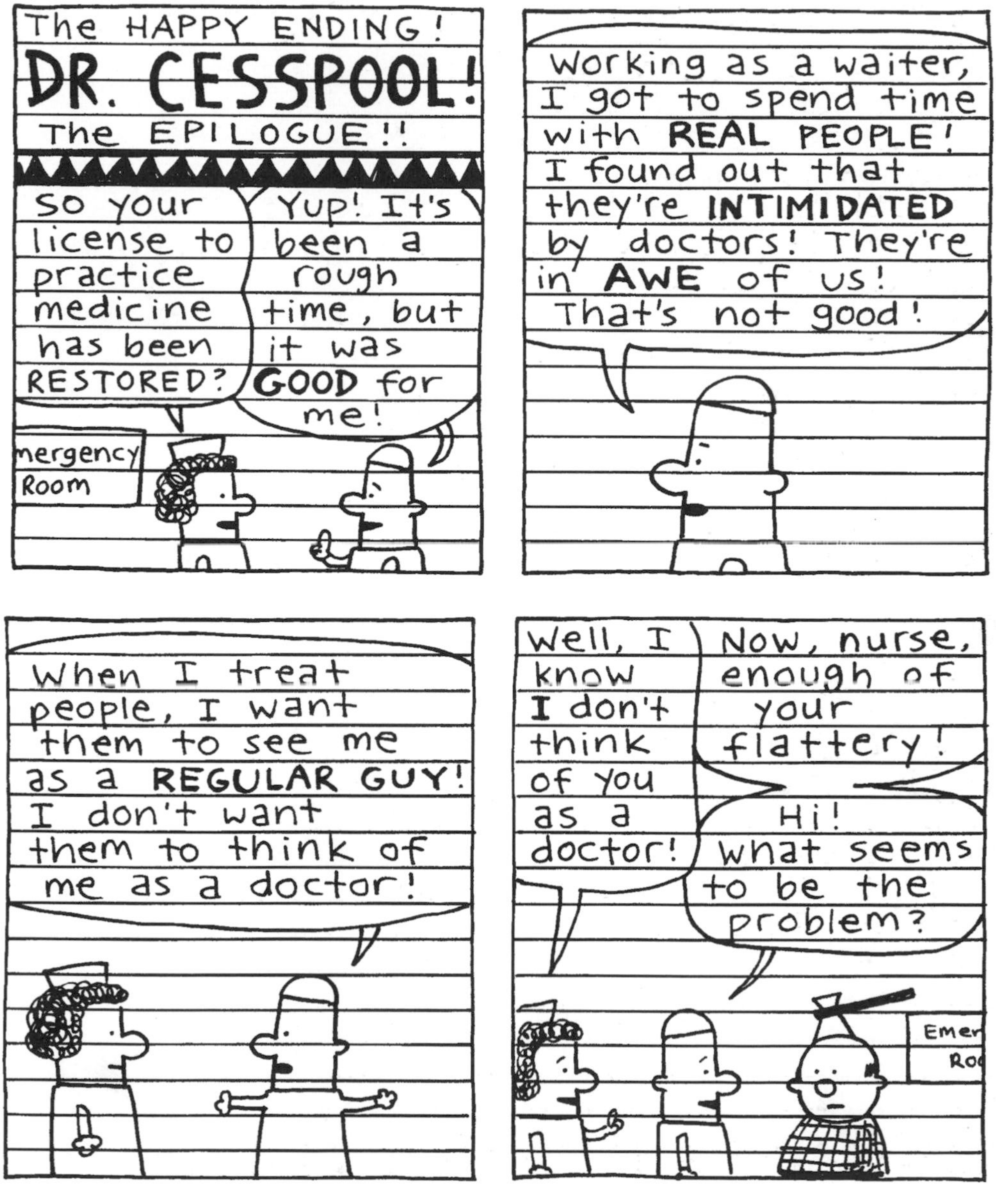
The HAPPY ENDING!
DR. CESSPOOL!
The EPILOGUE!!
So your license to practice medicine has been RESTORED?
Yup! It's been a rough time, but it was GOOD for me!
mergency Room
Working as a waiter, I got to spend time with REAL PEOPLE! I found out that they're INTIMIDATED by doctors! They're in AWE of us! That's not good!
When I treat people, I want them to see me as a REGULAR GUY! I don't want them to think of me as a doctor!
Well, I know I don't think of you as a doctor!
Now, nurse, enough of your flattery!
Hi! What seems to be the problem?
Emer
Ro

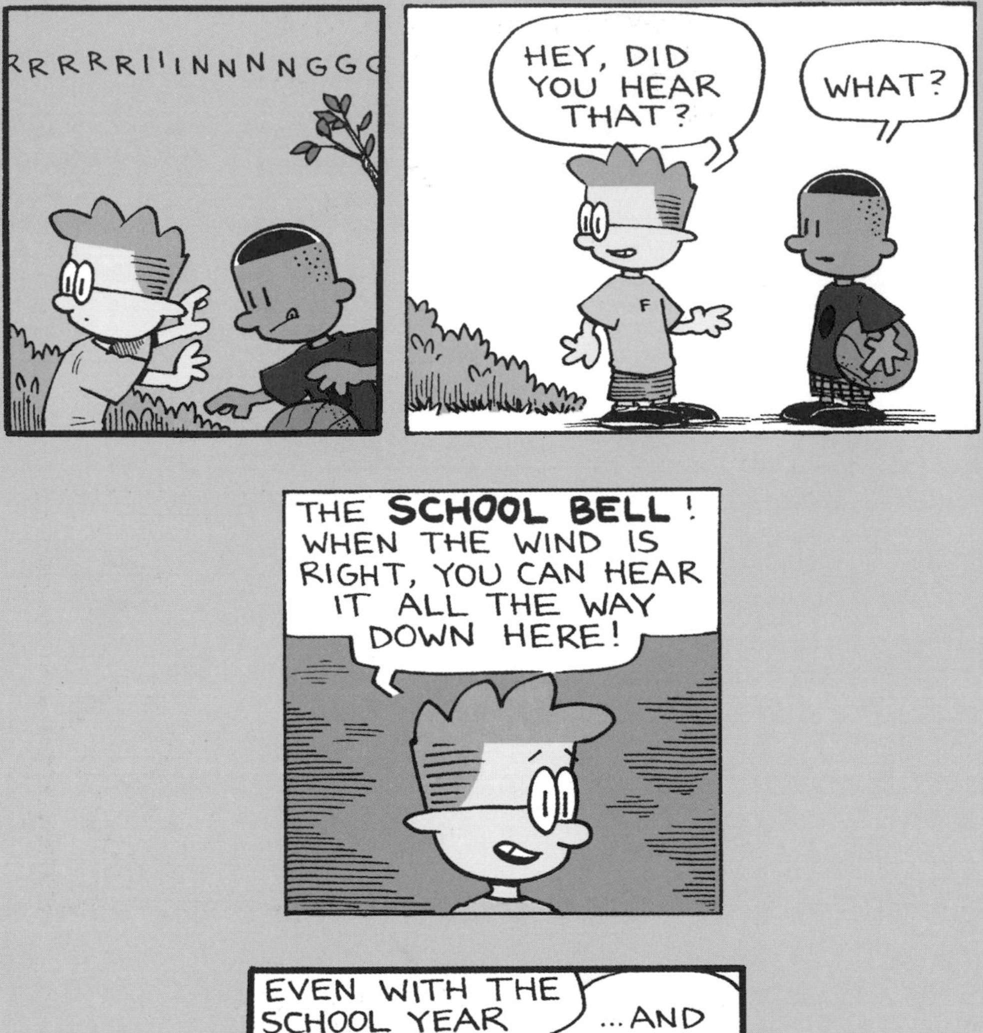
RRRRRIIINNNNGGG
HEY, DID YOU HEAR THAT?
WHAT?
THE **SCHOOL BELL**! WHEN THE WIND IS RIGHT, YOU CAN HEAR IT ALL THE WAY DOWN HERE!
EVEN WITH THE SCHOOL YEAR OVER, IT KEEPS RINGING ALL SUMMER!
...AND WE CAN **IGNORE** IT!

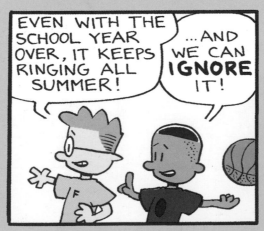

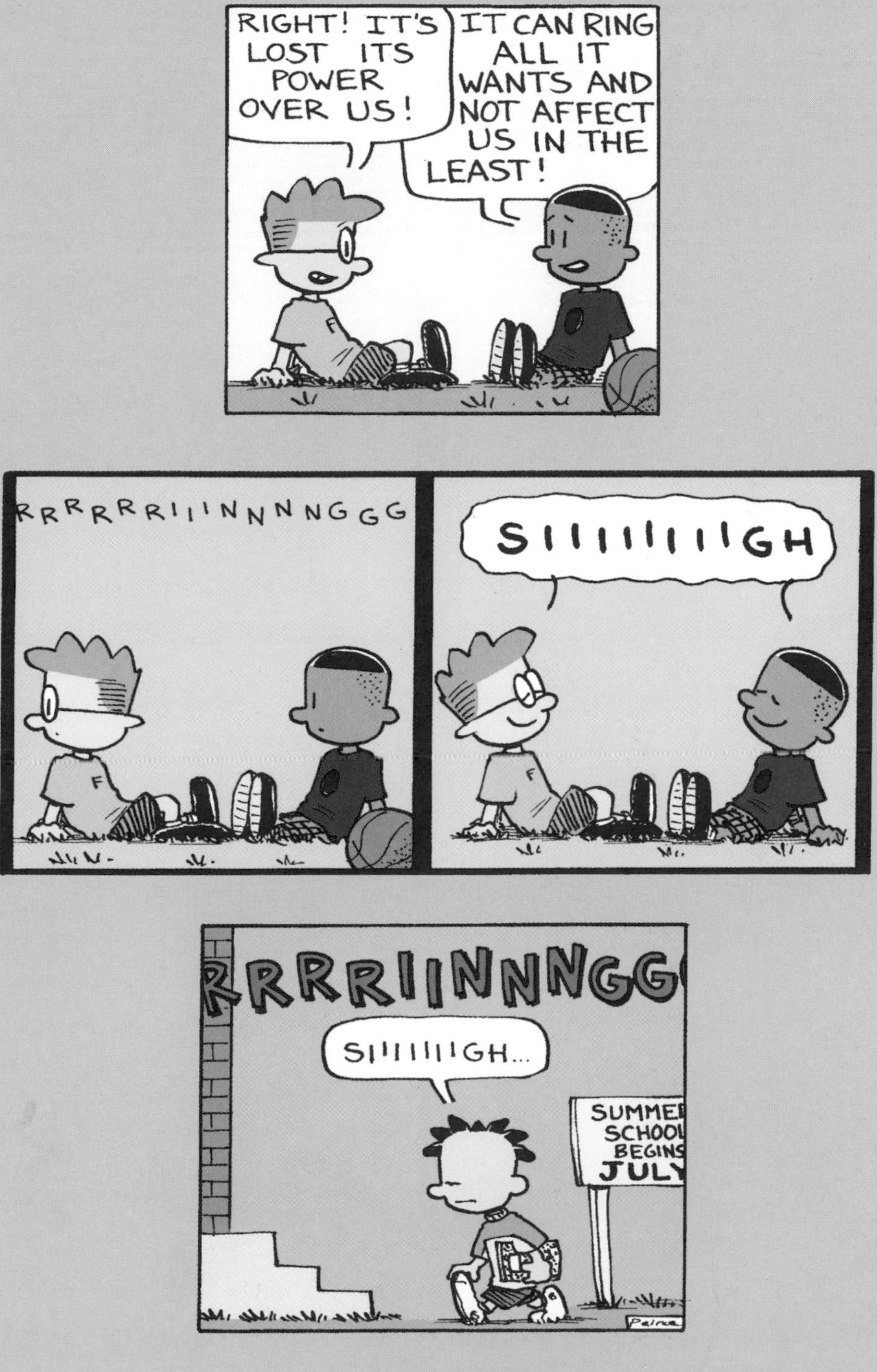

RIGHT! IT'S LOST ITS POWER OVER US!
IT CAN RING ALL IT WANTS AND NOT AFFECT US IN THE LEAST!
RRRRRRIIINNNNGGG
SIIIIIIIIGH
RRRRIINNNGG
SIIIIIIGH...
SUMME
SCHOOL
BEGINS
JULY
Peirce

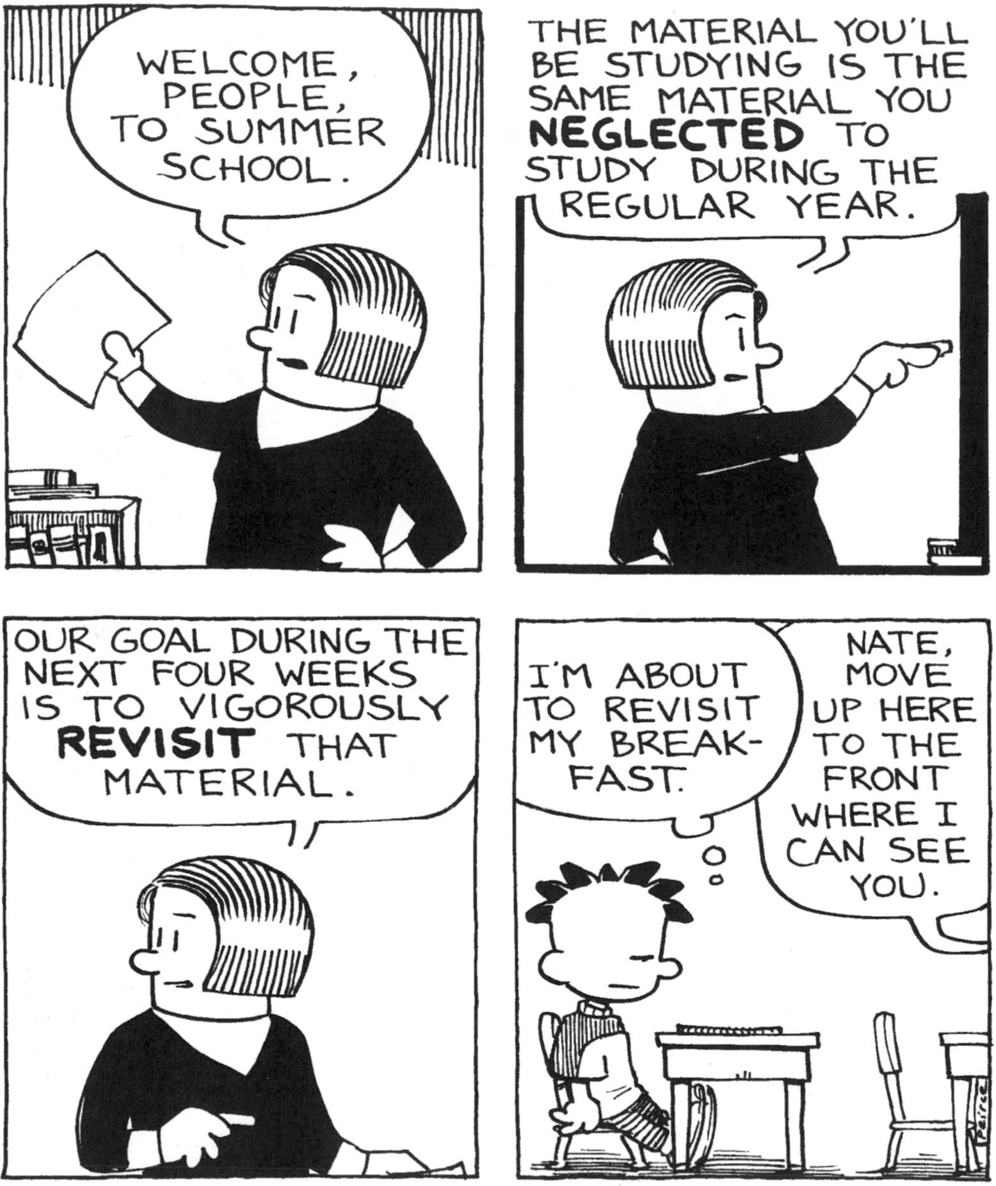
WELCOME, PEOPLE, TO SUMMER SCHOOL.
THE MATERIAL YOU'LL BE STUDYING IS THE SAME MATERIAL YOU **NEGLECTED** TO STUDY DURING THE REGULAR YEAR.
OUR GOAL DURING THE NEXT FOUR WEEKS IS TO VIGOROUSLY **REVISIT** THAT MATERIAL.
NATE, MOVE UP HERE TO THE FRONT WHERE I CAN SEE YOU.
I'M ABOUT TO REVISIT MY BREAK-FAST.
PEIRCE

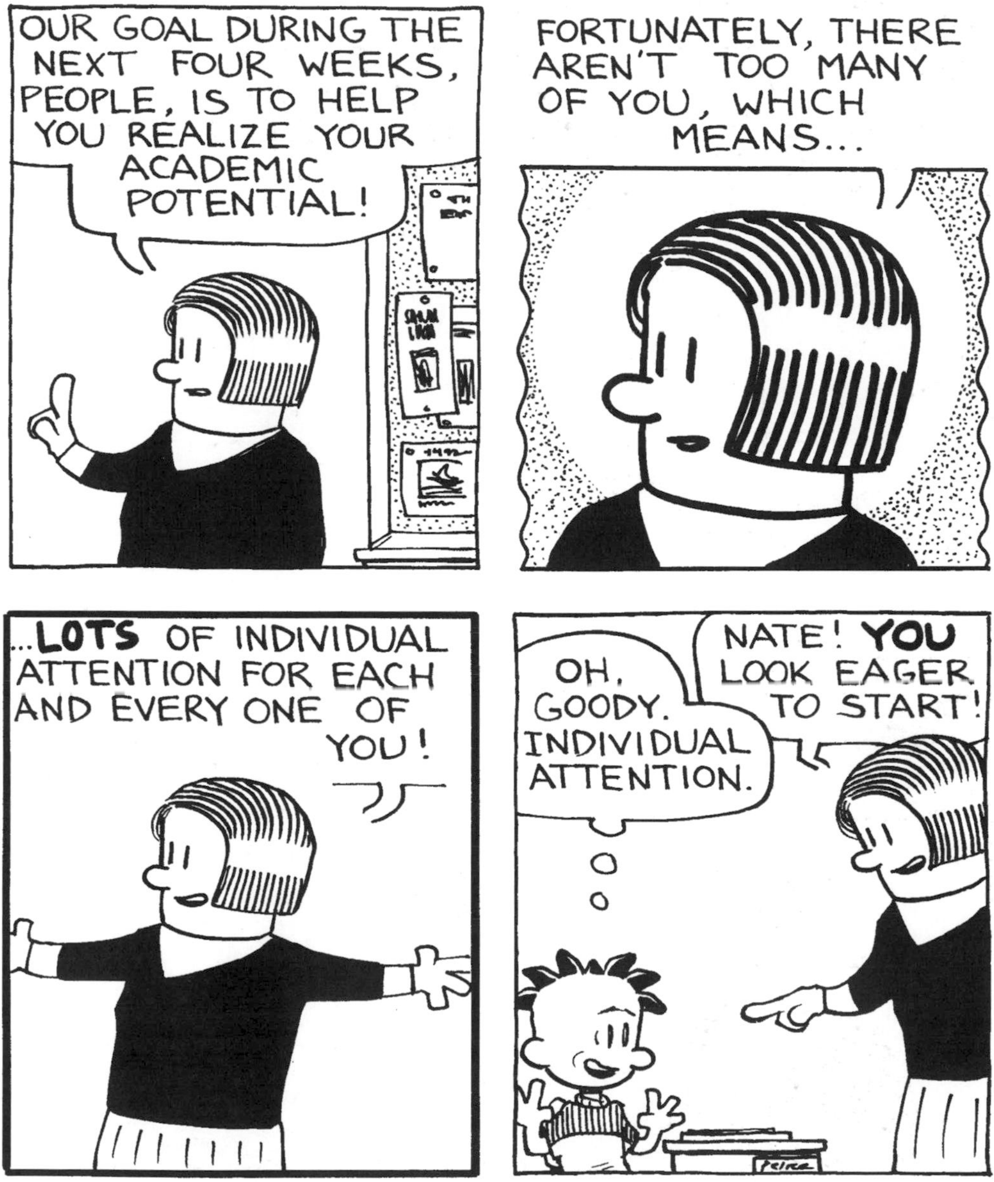
OUR GOAL DURING THE NEXT FOUR WEEKS, PEOPLE, IS TO HELP YOU REALIZE YOUR ACADEMIC POTENTIAL!
FORTUNATELY, THERE AREN'T TOO MANY OF YOU, WHICH MEANS...
...LOTS OF INDIVIDUAL ATTENTION FOR EACH AND EVERY ONE OF YOU!
OH, GOODY. INDIVIDUAL ATTENTION.
NATE! YOU LOOK EAGER TO START!
Peirce

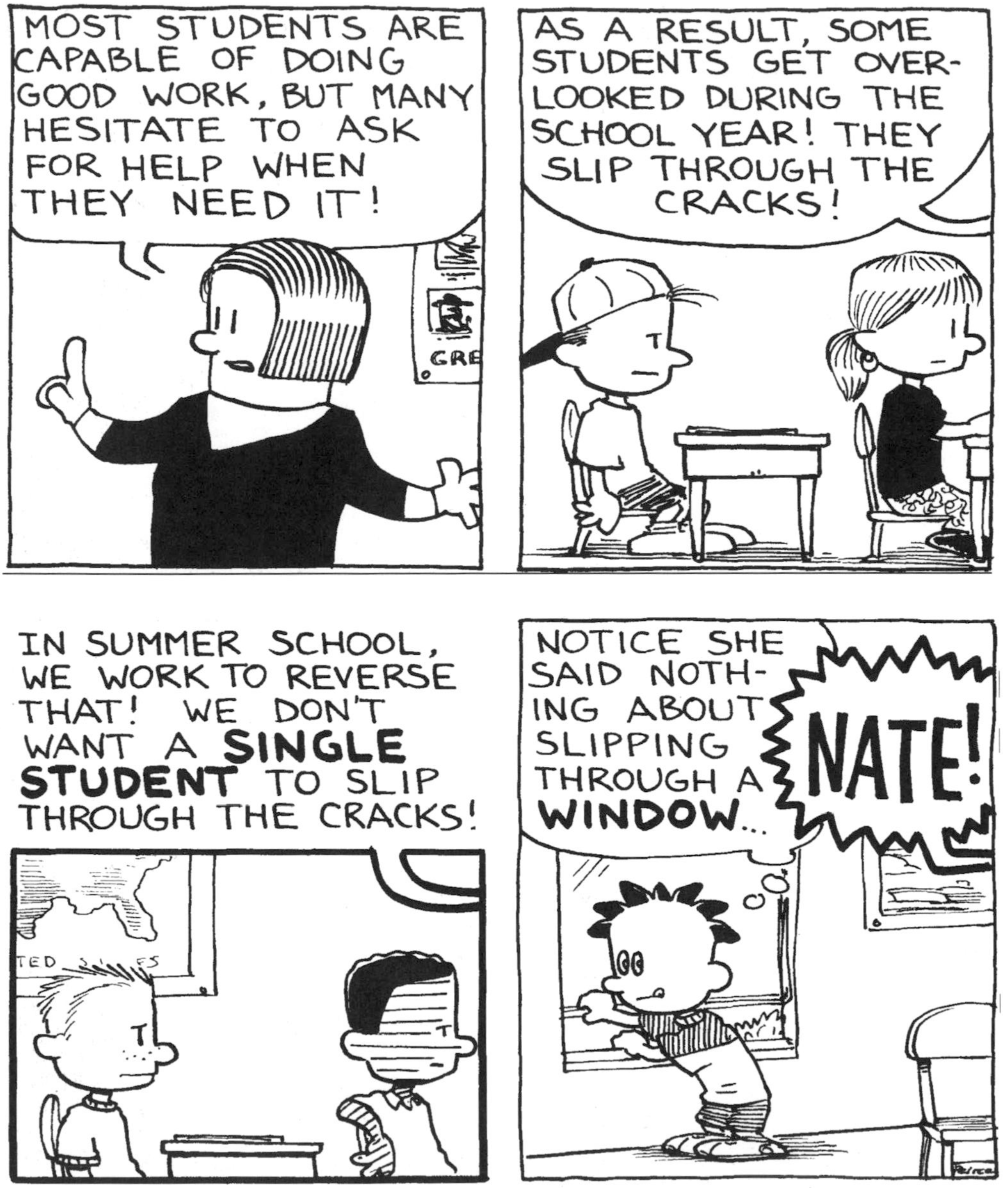
MOST STUDENTS ARE CAPABLE OF DOING GOOD WORK, BUT MANY HESITATE TO ASK FOR HELP WHEN THEY NEED IT!
AS A RESULT, SOME STUDENTS GET OVER-LOOKED DURING THE SCHOOL YEAR! THEY SLIP THROUGH THE CRACKS!
IN SUMMER SCHOOL, WE WORK TO REVERSE THAT! WE DON'T WANT A **SINGLE STUDENT** TO SLIP THROUGH THE CRACKS!
NOTICE SHE SAID NOTH-ING ABOUT SLIPPING THROUGH A **WINDOW**...
NATE!

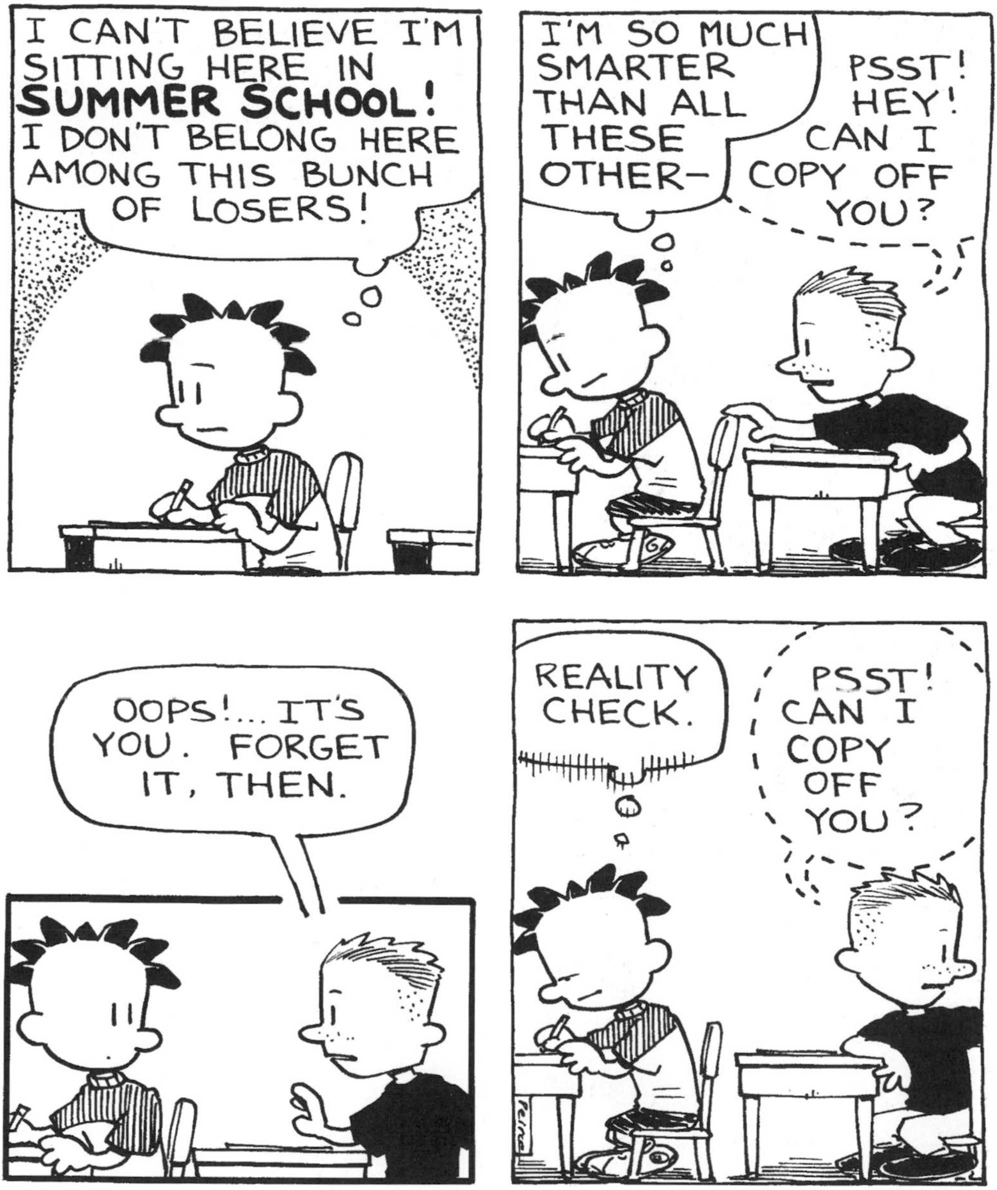
I CAN'T BELIEVE I'M SITTING HERE IN **SUMMER SCHOOL**! I DON'T BELONG HERE AMONG THIS BUNCH OF LOSERS!
I'M SO MUCH SMARTER THAN ALL THESE OTHER–
PSST! HEY! CAN I COPY OFF YOU?
OOPS!... IT'S YOU. FORGET IT, THEN.
REALITY CHECK.
PSST! CAN I COPY OFF YOU?
Peirce

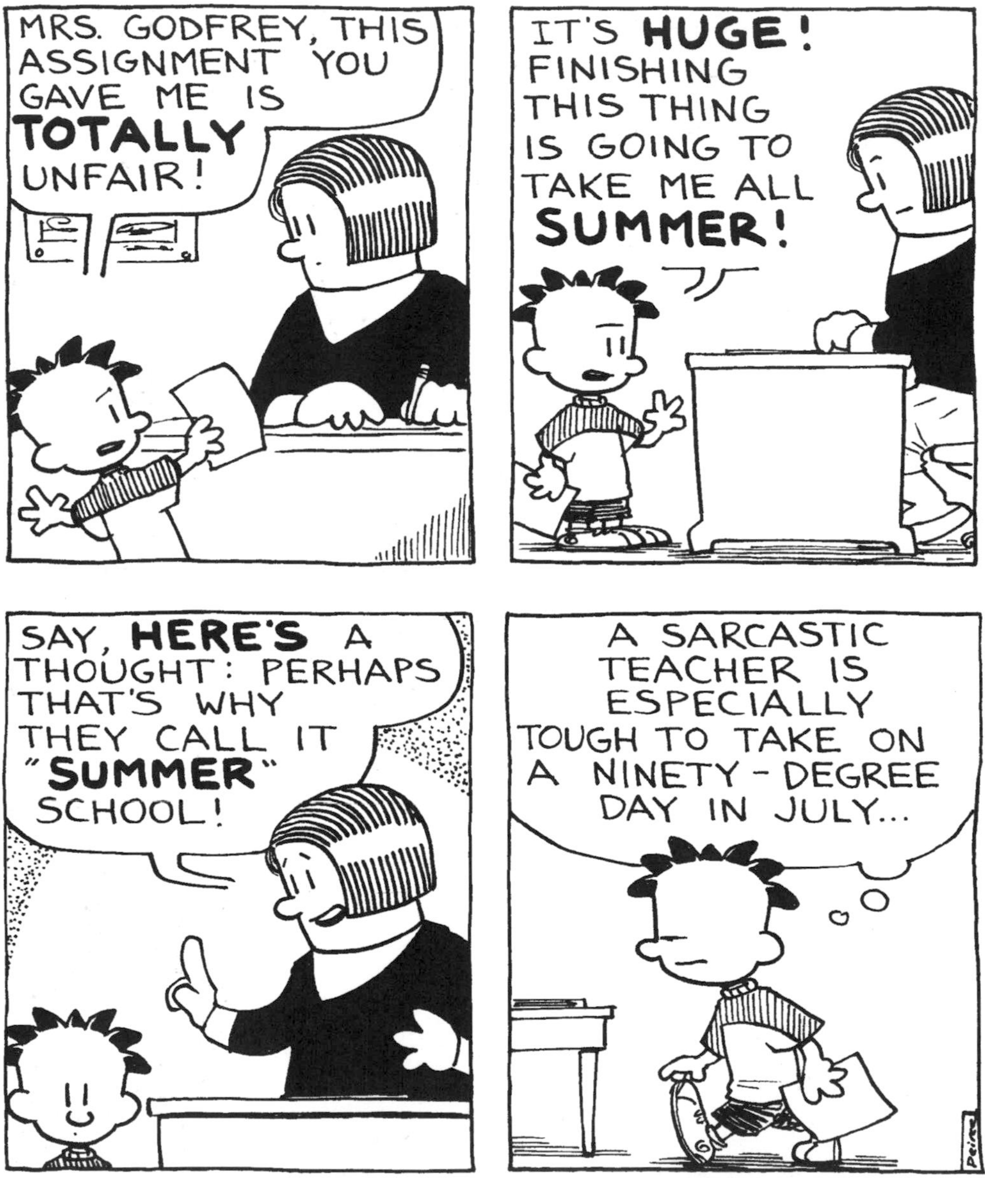
MRS. GODFREY, THIS ASSIGNMENT YOU GAVE ME IS **TOTALLY** UNFAIR!
IT'S **HUGE**! FINISHING THIS THING IS GOING TO TAKE ME ALL **SUMMER**!
SAY, **HERE'S** A THOUGHT: PERHAPS THAT'S WHY THEY CALL IT "**SUMMER**" SCHOOL!
A SARCASTIC TEACHER IS ESPECIALLY TOUGH TO TAKE ON A NINETY-DEGREE DAY IN JULY...

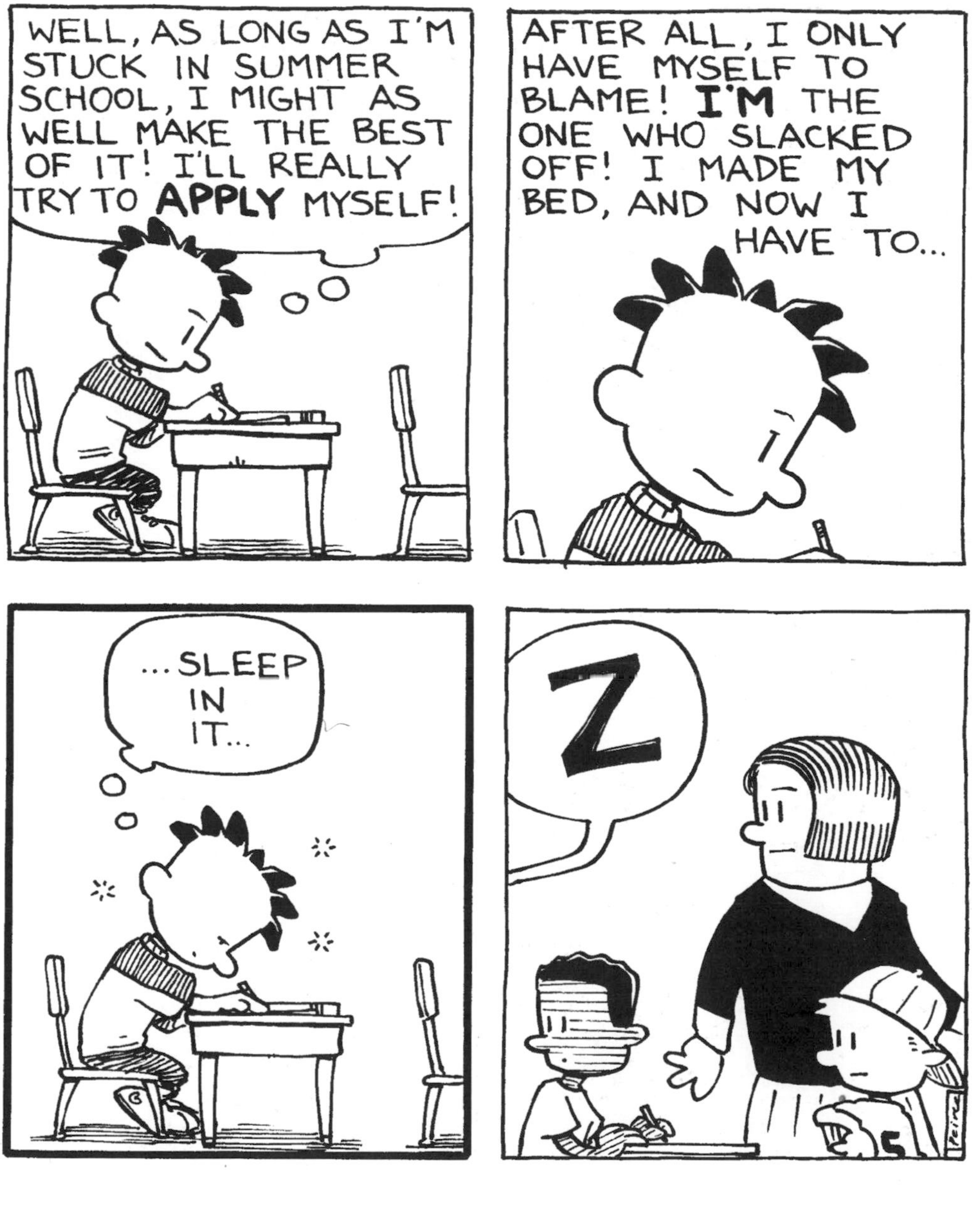
WELL, AS LONG AS I'M STUCK IN SUMMER SCHOOL, I MIGHT AS WELL MAKE THE BEST OF IT! I'LL REALLY TRY TO **APPLY** MYSELF!
AFTER ALL, I ONLY HAVE MYSELF TO BLAME! **I'M** THE ONE WHO SLACKED OFF! I MADE MY BED, AND NOW I HAVE TO...
...SLEEP IN IT...
Z

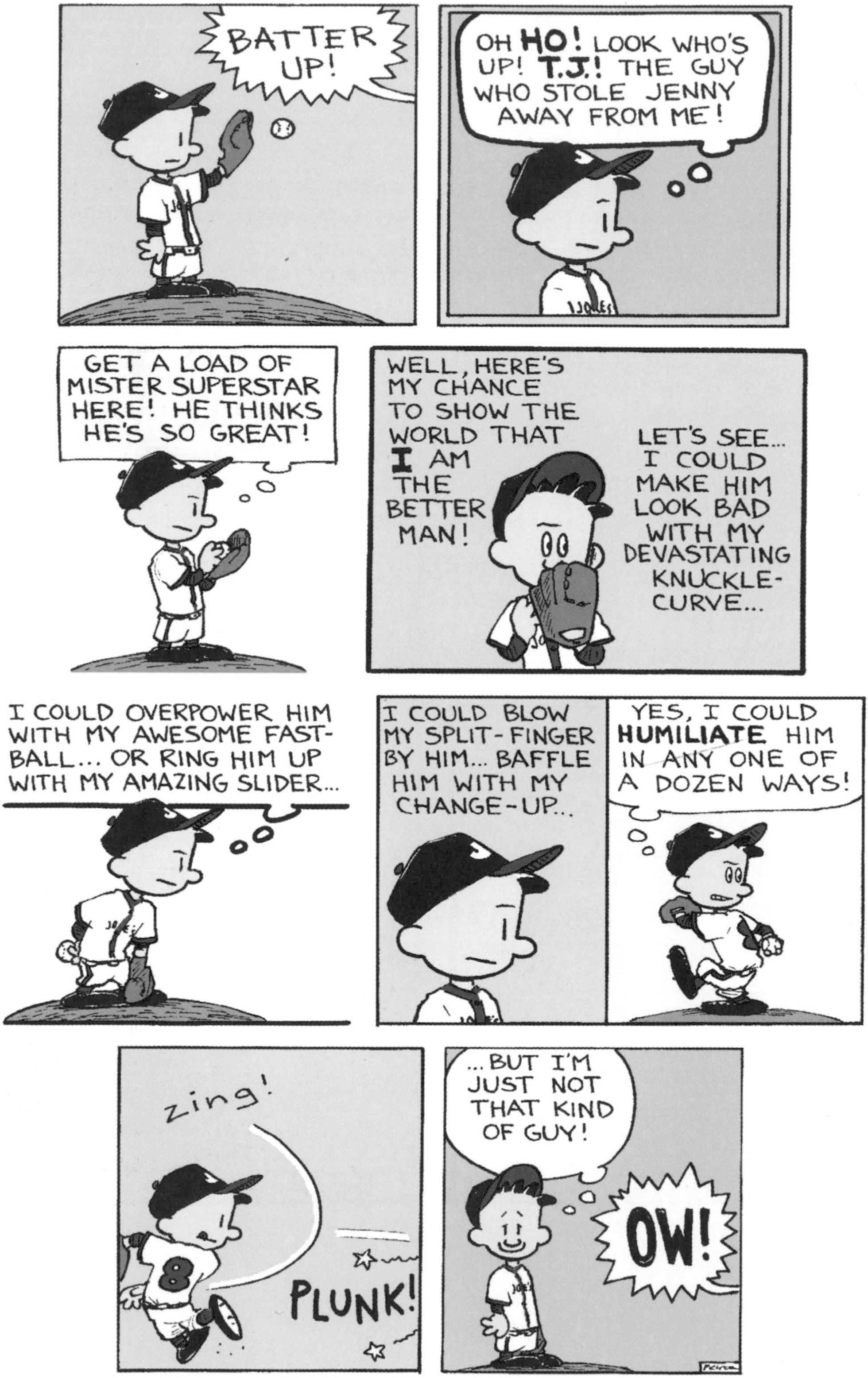
BATTER UP!
OH HO! LOOK WHO'S UP! T.J.! THE GUY WHO STOLE JENNY AWAY FROM ME!
GET A LOAD OF MISTER SUPERSTAR HERE! HE THINKS HE'S SO GREAT!
WELL, HERE'S MY CHANCE TO SHOW THE WORLD THAT I AM THE BETTER MAN!
LET'S SEE... I COULD MAKE HIM LOOK BAD WITH MY DEVASTATING KNUCKLE-CURVE...
I COULD OVERPOWER HIM WITH MY AWESOME FAST-BALL... OR RING HIM UP WITH MY AMAZING SLIDER...
I COULD BLOW MY SPLIT-FINGER BY HIM... BAFFLE HIM WITH MY CHANGE-UP...
YES, I COULD HUMILIATE HIM IN ANY ONE OF A DOZEN WAYS!
zing!
PLUNK!
...BUT I'M JUST NOT THAT KIND OF GUY!
OW!

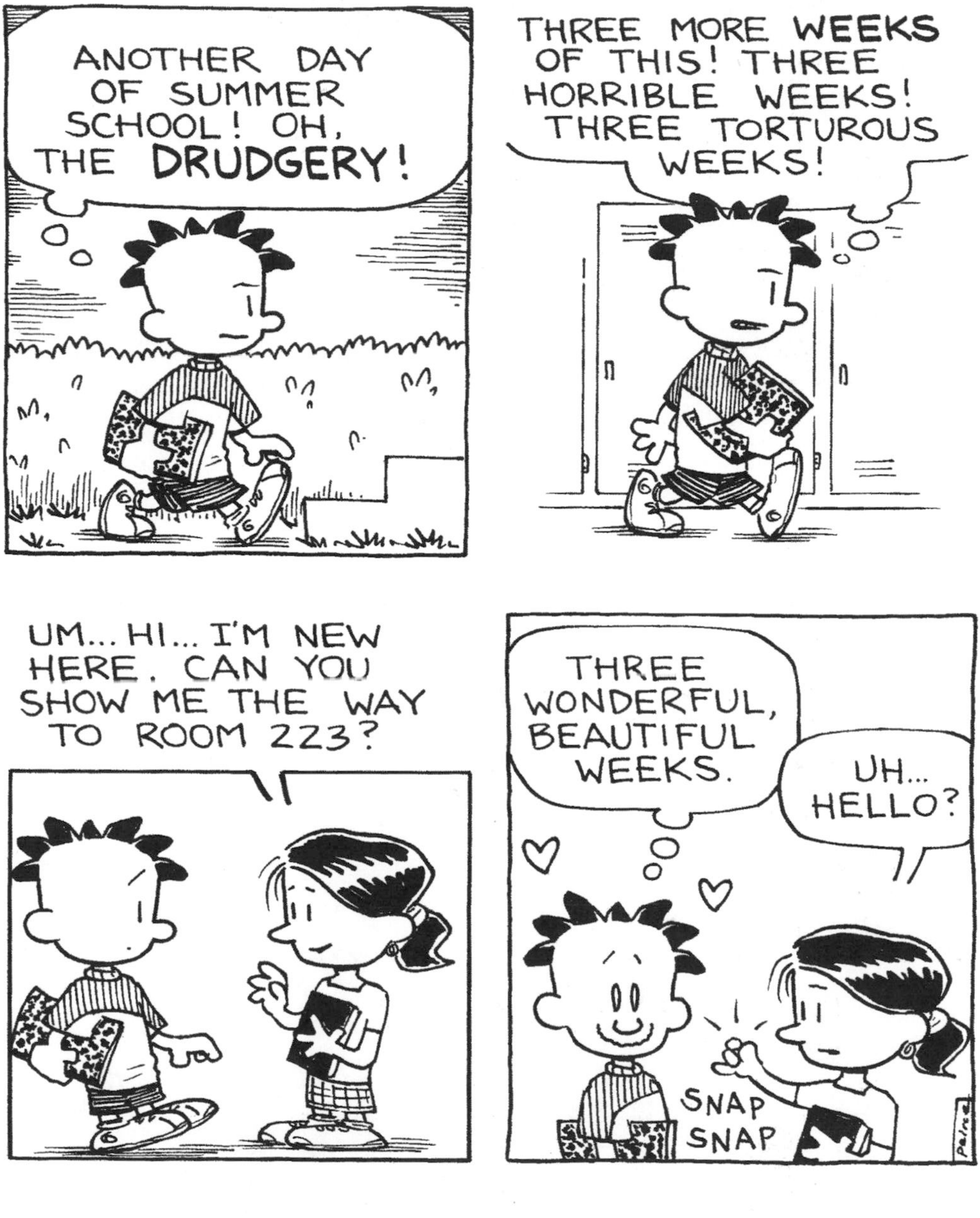
ANOTHER DAY OF SUMMER SCHOOL! OH, THE DRUDGERY!
THREE MORE WEEKS OF THIS! THREE HORRIBLE WEEKS! THREE TORTUROUS WEEKS!
UM... HI... I'M NEW HERE. CAN YOU SHOW ME THE WAY TO ROOM 223?
THREE WONDERFUL, BEAUTIFUL WEEKS.
UH... HELLO?
SNAP SNAP
Peirce

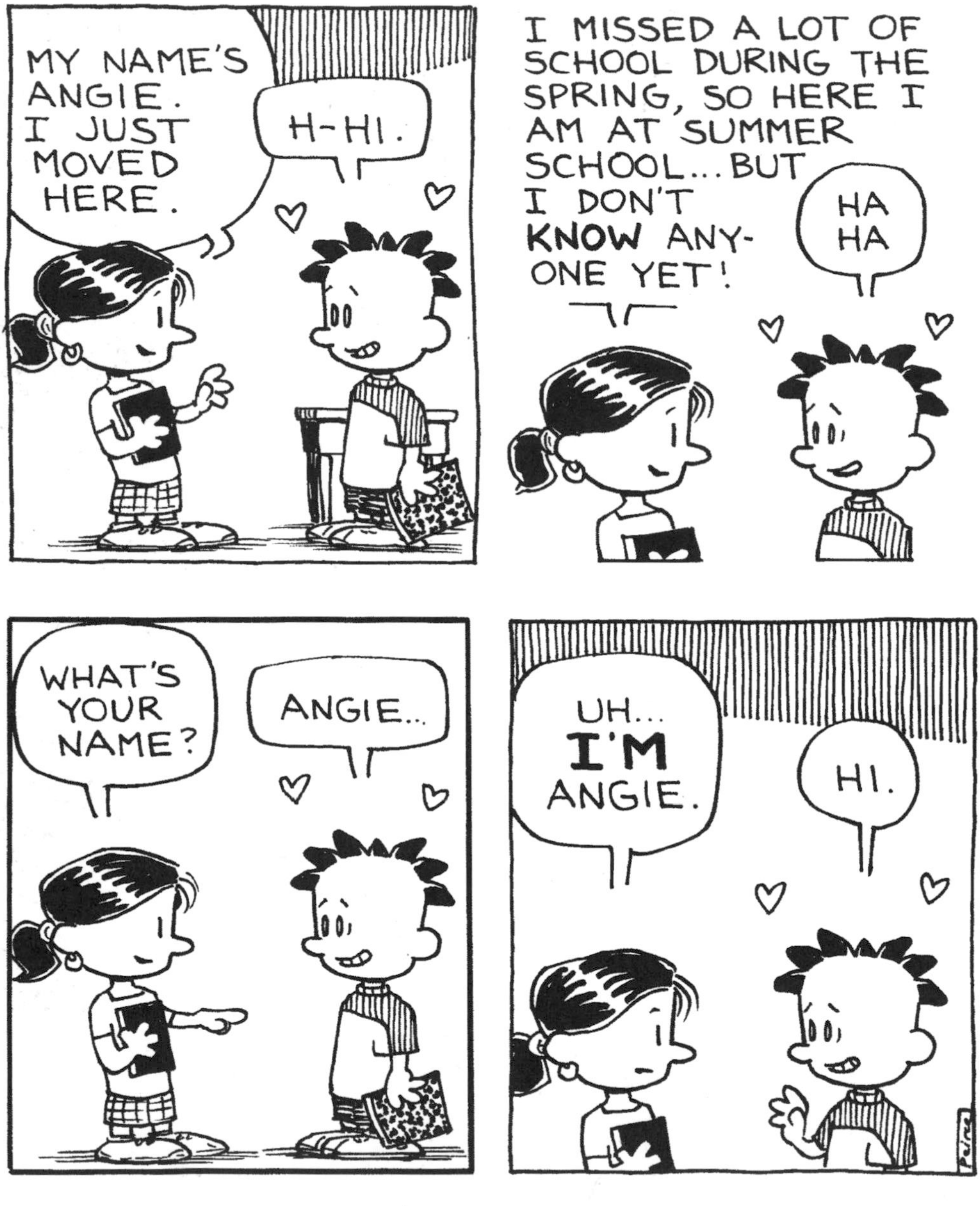
MY NAME'S ANGIE. I JUST MOVED HERE.
H-HI.
I MISSED A LOT OF SCHOOL DURING THE SPRING, SO HERE I AM AT SUMMER SCHOOL... BUT I DON'T **KNOW** ANY-ONE YET!
HA HA
WHAT'S YOUR NAME?
ANGIE...
UH... **I'M** ANGIE.
HI.
Peirce

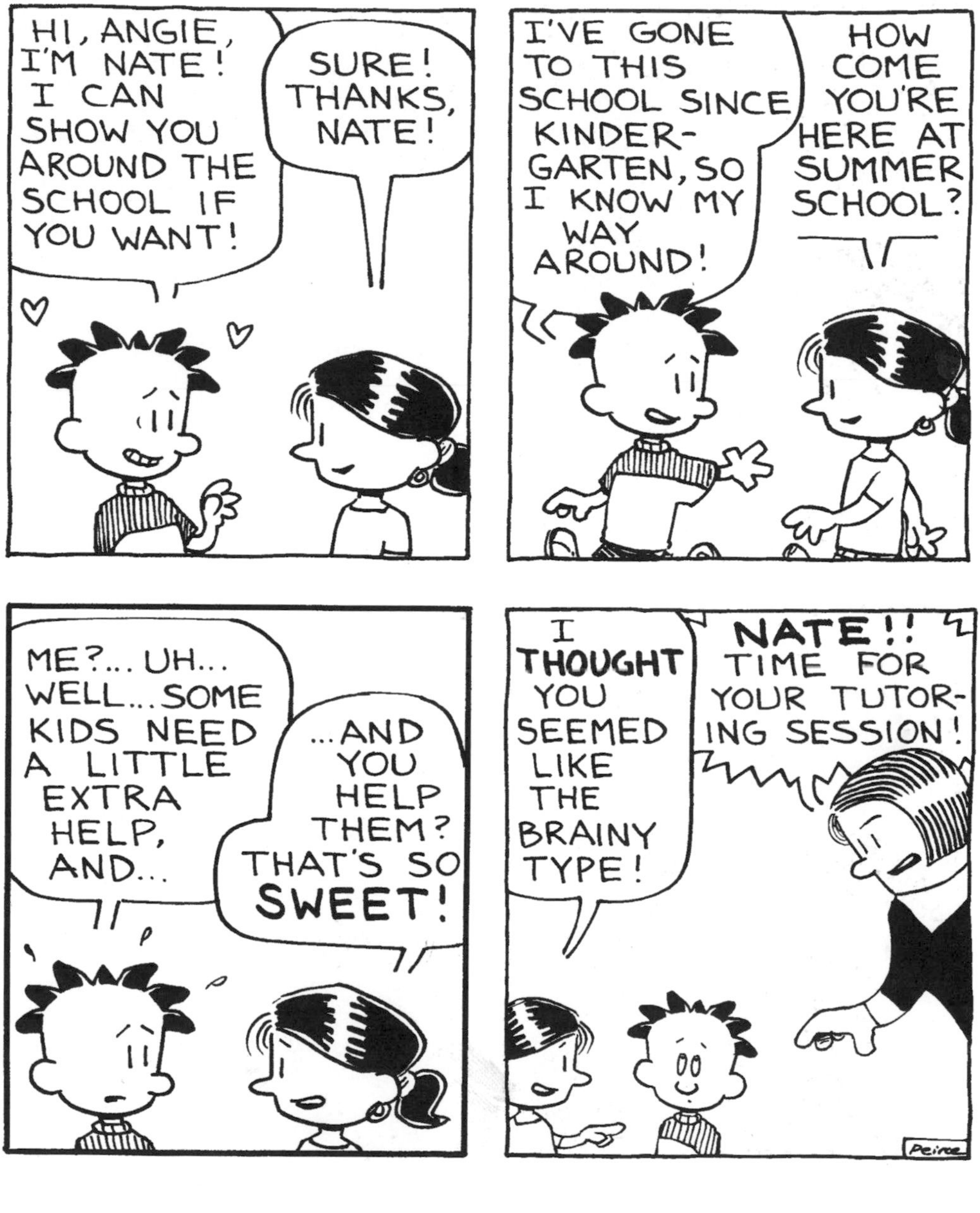
HI, ANGIE, I'M NATE! I CAN SHOW YOU AROUND THE SCHOOL IF YOU WANT!
SURE! THANKS, NATE!
I'VE GONE TO THIS SCHOOL SINCE KINDER-GARTEN, SO I KNOW MY WAY AROUND!
HOW COME YOU'RE HERE AT SUMMER SCHOOL?
ME?... UH... WELL... SOME KIDS NEED A LITTLE EXTRA HELP, AND...
...AND YOU HELP THEM? THAT'S SO **SWEET**!
I **THOUGHT** YOU SEEMED LIKE THE BRAINY TYPE!
NATE!! TIME FOR YOUR TUTOR-ING SESSION!
Peirce

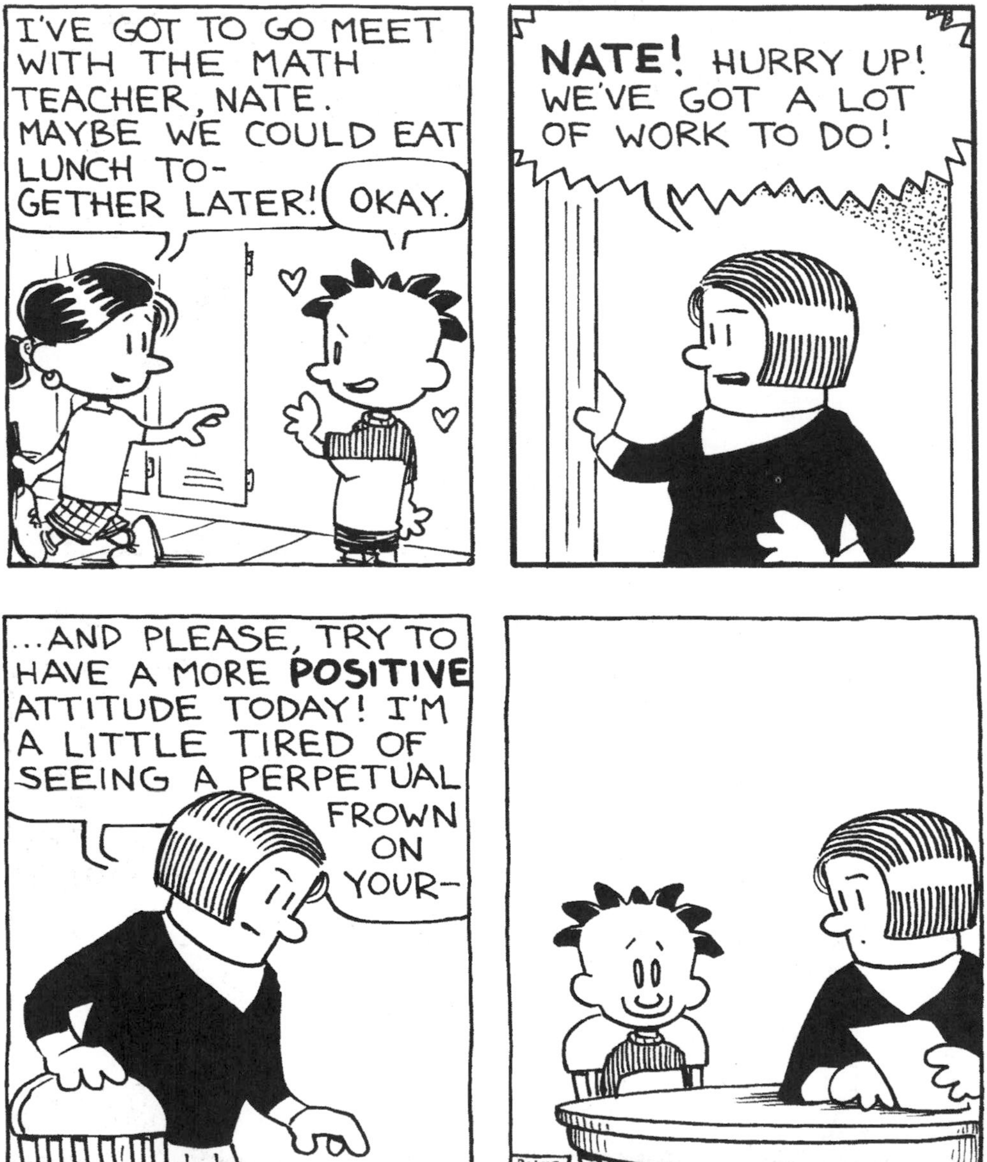
I'VE GOT TO GO MEET WITH THE MATH TEACHER, NATE. MAYBE WE COULD EAT LUNCH TOGETHER LATER!
OKAY.
NATE! HURRY UP! WE'VE GOT A LOT OF WORK TO DO!
...AND PLEASE, TRY TO HAVE A MORE POSITIVE ATTITUDE TODAY! I'M A LITTLE TIRED OF SEEING A PERPETUAL FROWN ON YOUR–
Peirce

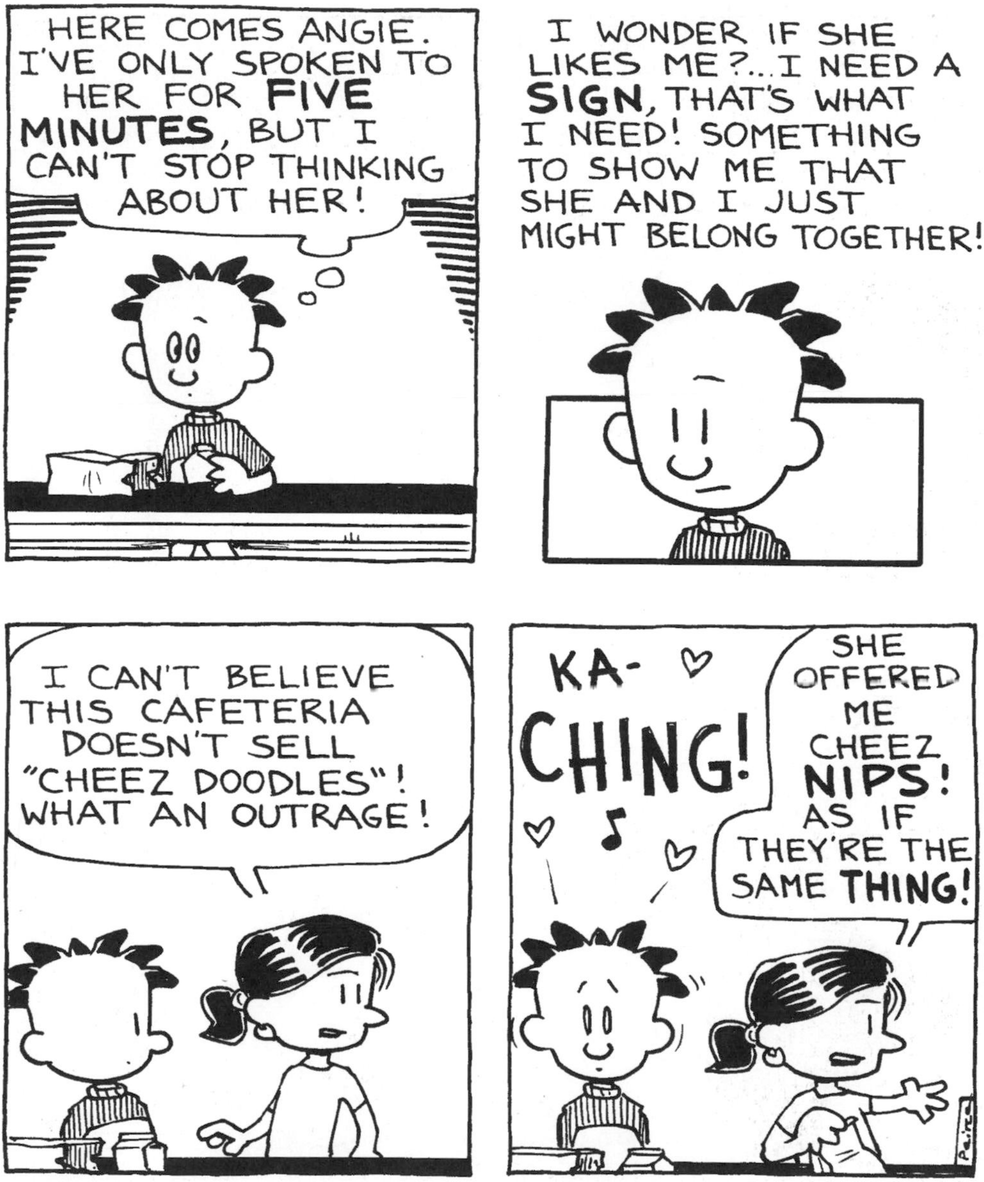
HERE COMES ANGIE. I'VE ONLY SPOKEN TO HER FOR **FIVE MINUTES**, BUT I CAN'T STOP THINKING ABOUT HER!
I WONDER IF SHE LIKES ME?...I NEED A **SIGN**, THAT'S WHAT I NEED! SOMETHING TO SHOW ME THAT SHE AND I JUST MIGHT BELONG TOGETHER!
I CAN'T BELIEVE THIS CAFETERIA DOESN'T SELL "CHEEZ DOODLES"! WHAT AN OUTRAGE!
KA-
CHING!
SHE OFFERED ME CHEEZ **NIPS**! AS IF THEY'RE THE SAME **THING**!
Peirce

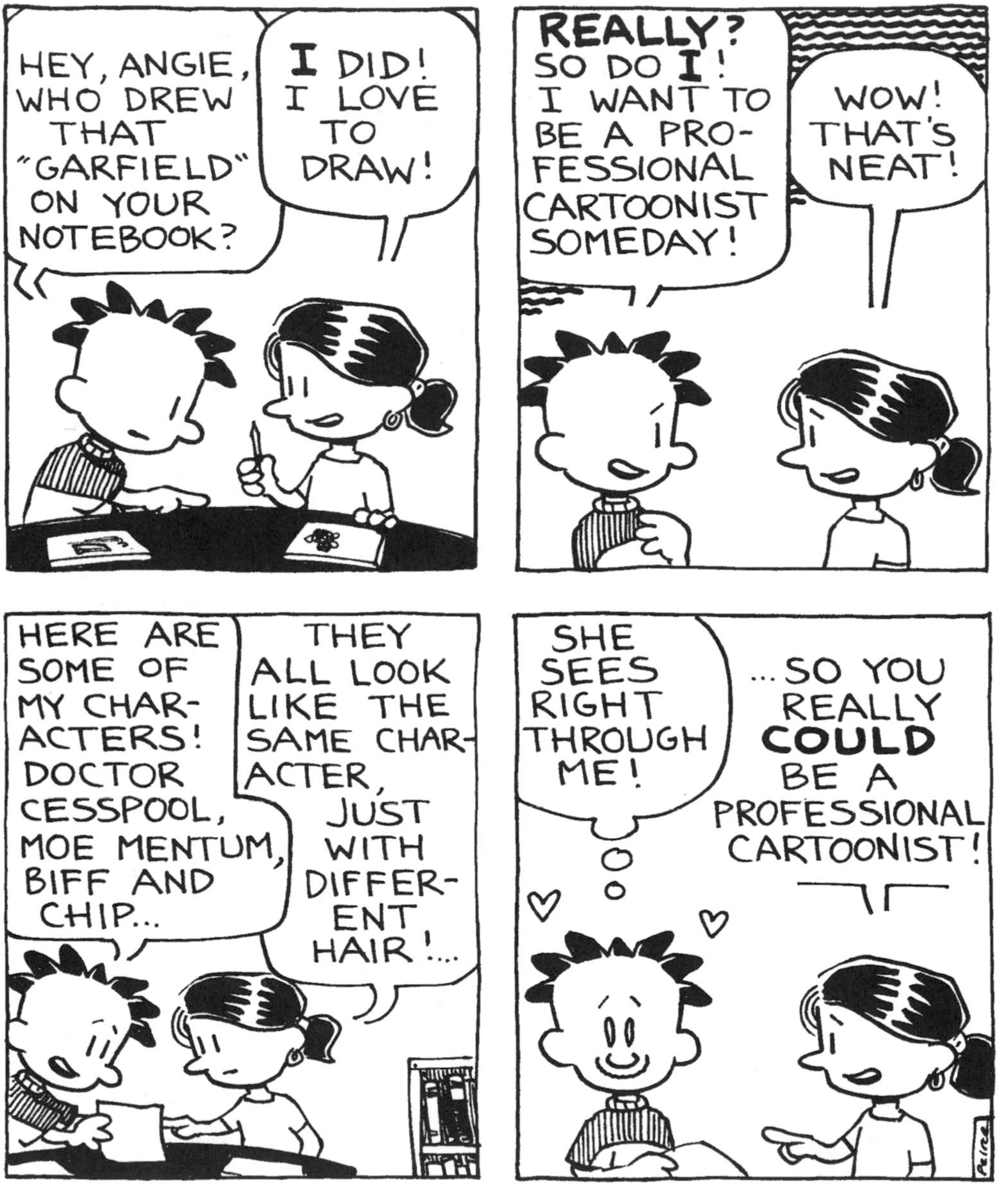
HEY, ANGIE, WHO DREW THAT "GARFIELD" ON YOUR NOTEBOOK?
I DID! I LOVE TO DRAW!
REALLY? SO DO I! I WANT TO BE A PRO-FESSIONAL CARTOONIST SOMEDAY!
WOW! THAT'S NEAT!
HERE ARE SOME OF MY CHAR-ACTERS! DOCTOR CESSPOOL, MOE MENTUM, BIFF AND CHIP...
THEY ALL LOOK LIKE THE SAME CHAR-ACTER, JUST WITH DIFFER-ENT HAIR!...
SHE SEES RIGHT THROUGH ME!
...SO YOU REALLY COULD BE A PROFESSIONAL CARTOONIST!

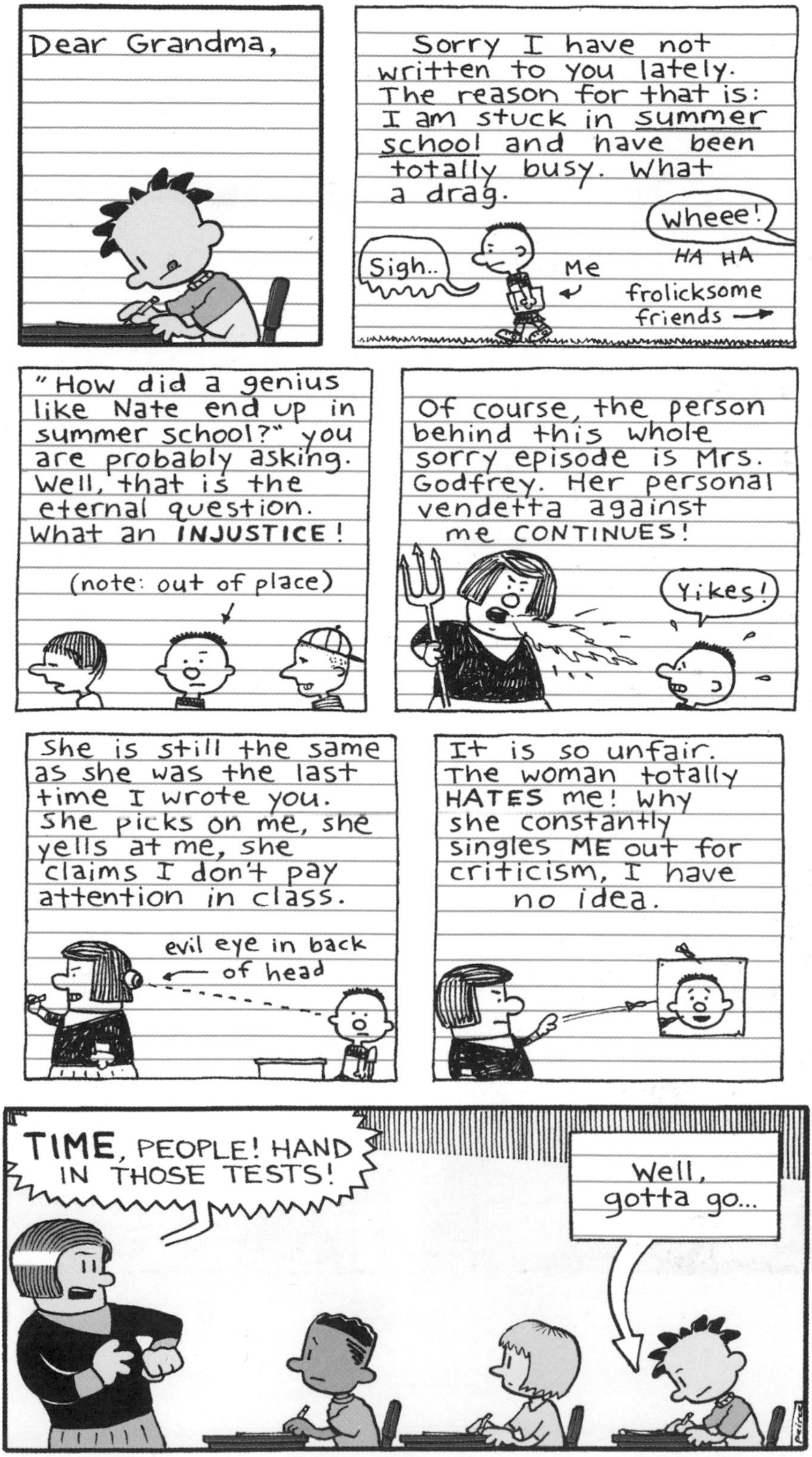
Dear Grandma,
Sorry I have not written to you lately. The reason for that is: I am stuck in summer school and have been totally busy. What a drag.
Wheee!
HA HA
Sigh..
Me
frolicksome friends
"How did a genius like Nate end up in summer school?" you are probably asking. Well, that is the eternal question. What an INJUSTICE!
(note: out of place)
Of course, the person behind this whole sorry episode is Mrs. Godfrey. Her personal vendetta against me CONTINUES!
Yikes!
She is still the same as she was the last time I wrote you. She picks on me, she yells at me, she claims I don't pay attention in class.
evil eye in back of head
It is so unfair. The woman totally HATES me! Why she constantly singles ME out for criticism, I have no idea.
TIME, PEOPLE! HAND IN THOSE TESTS!
Well, gotta go...

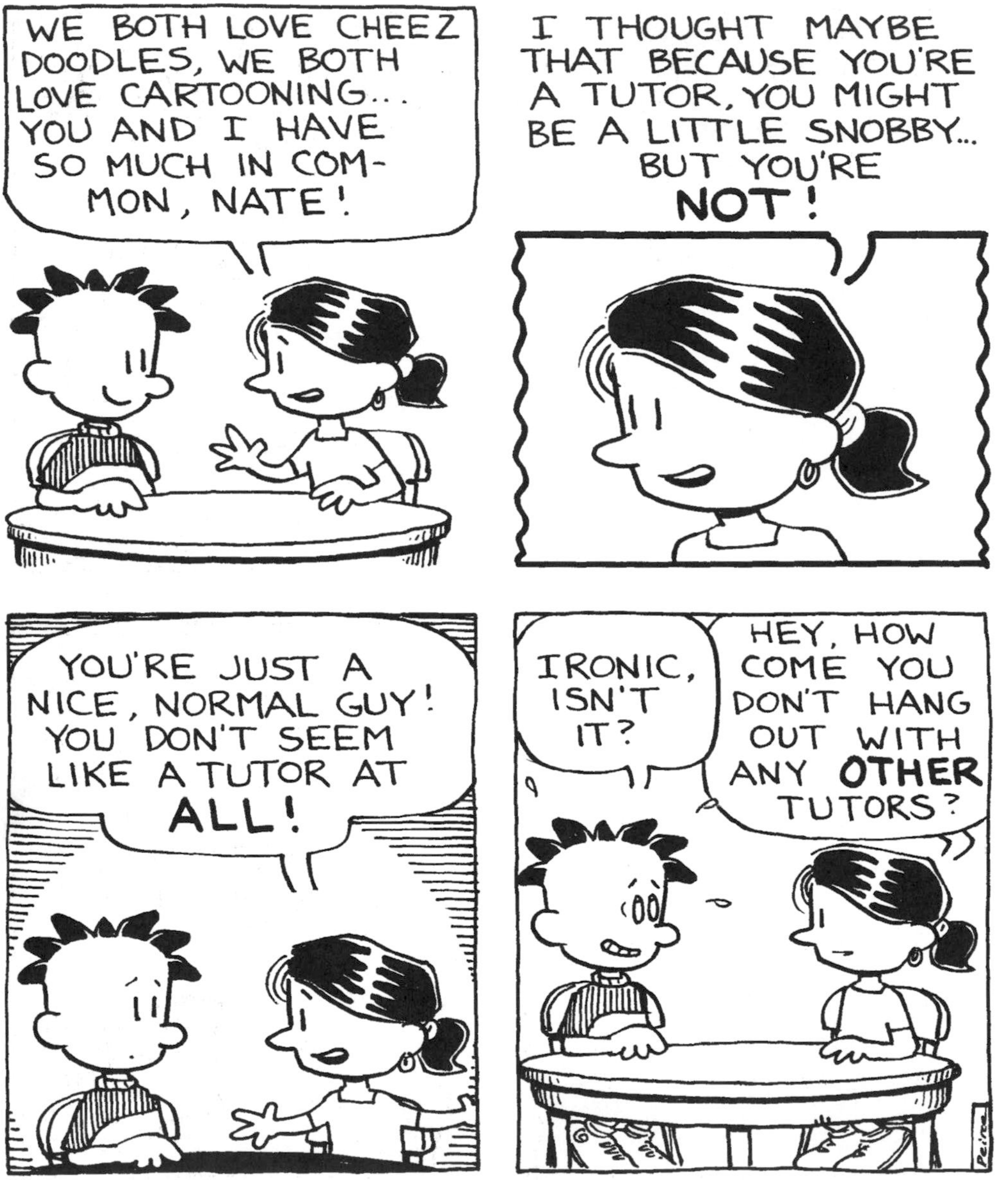
WE BOTH LOVE CHEEZ DOODLES, WE BOTH LOVE CARTOONING... YOU AND I HAVE SO MUCH IN COMMON, NATE!
I THOUGHT MAYBE THAT BECAUSE YOU'RE A TUTOR, YOU MIGHT BE A LITTLE SNOBBY... BUT YOU'RE **NOT**!
YOU'RE JUST A NICE, NORMAL GUY! YOU DON'T SEEM LIKE A TUTOR AT **ALL**!
IRONIC, ISN'T IT?
HEY, HOW COME YOU DON'T HANG OUT WITH ANY **OTHER** TUTORS?
Peirce

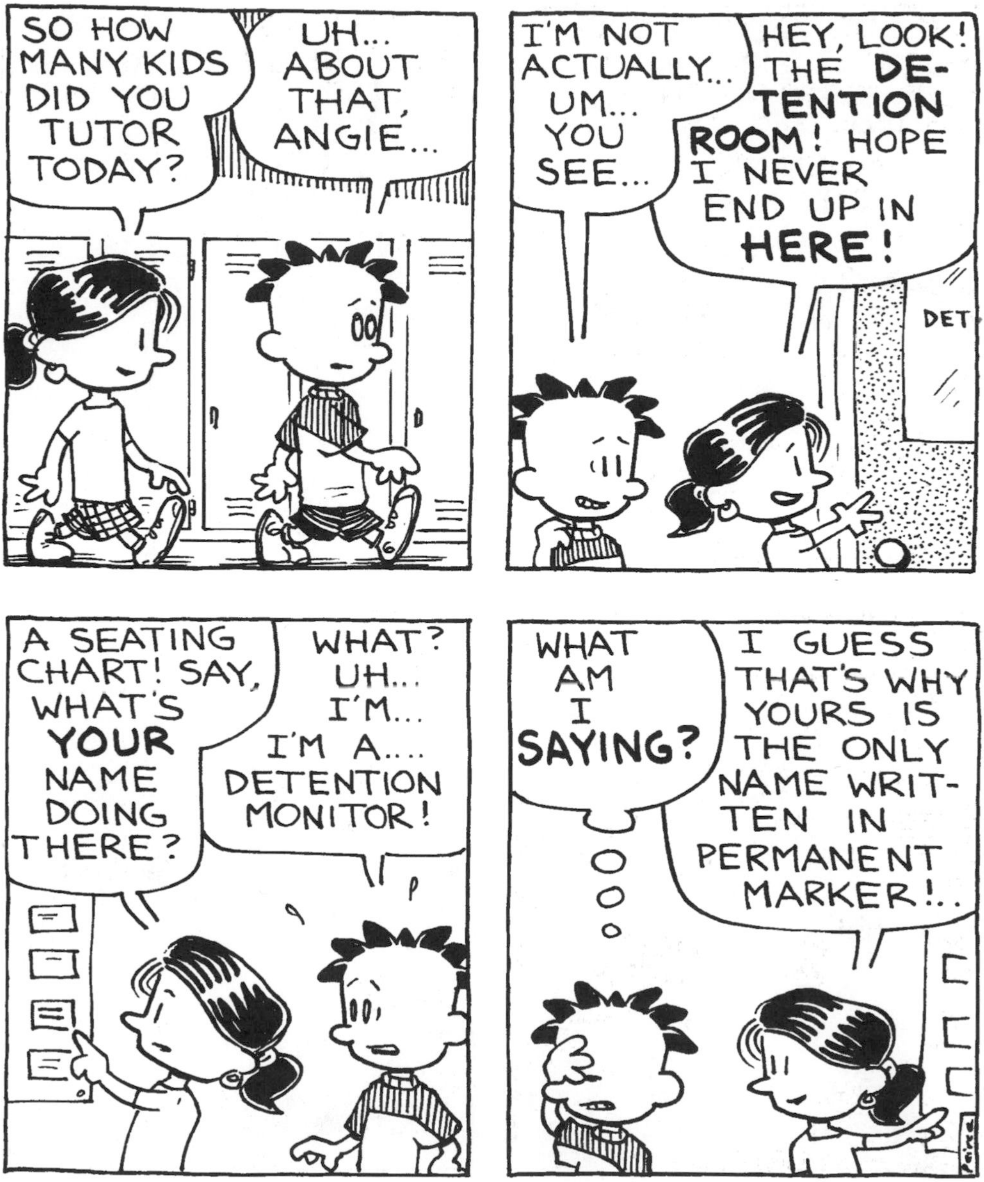
SO HOW MANY KIDS DID YOU TUTOR TODAY?
UH... ABOUT THAT, ANGIE...
I'M NOT ACTUALLY... UM... YOU SEE...
HEY, LOOK! THE DETENTION ROOM! HOPE I NEVER END UP IN HERE!
DET
A SEATING CHART! SAY, WHAT'S YOUR NAME DOING THERE?
WHAT? UH... I'M... I'M A.... DETENTION MONITOR!
WHAT AM I SAYING?
I GUESS THAT'S WHY YOURS IS THE ONLY NAME WRITTEN IN PERMANENT MARKER!..

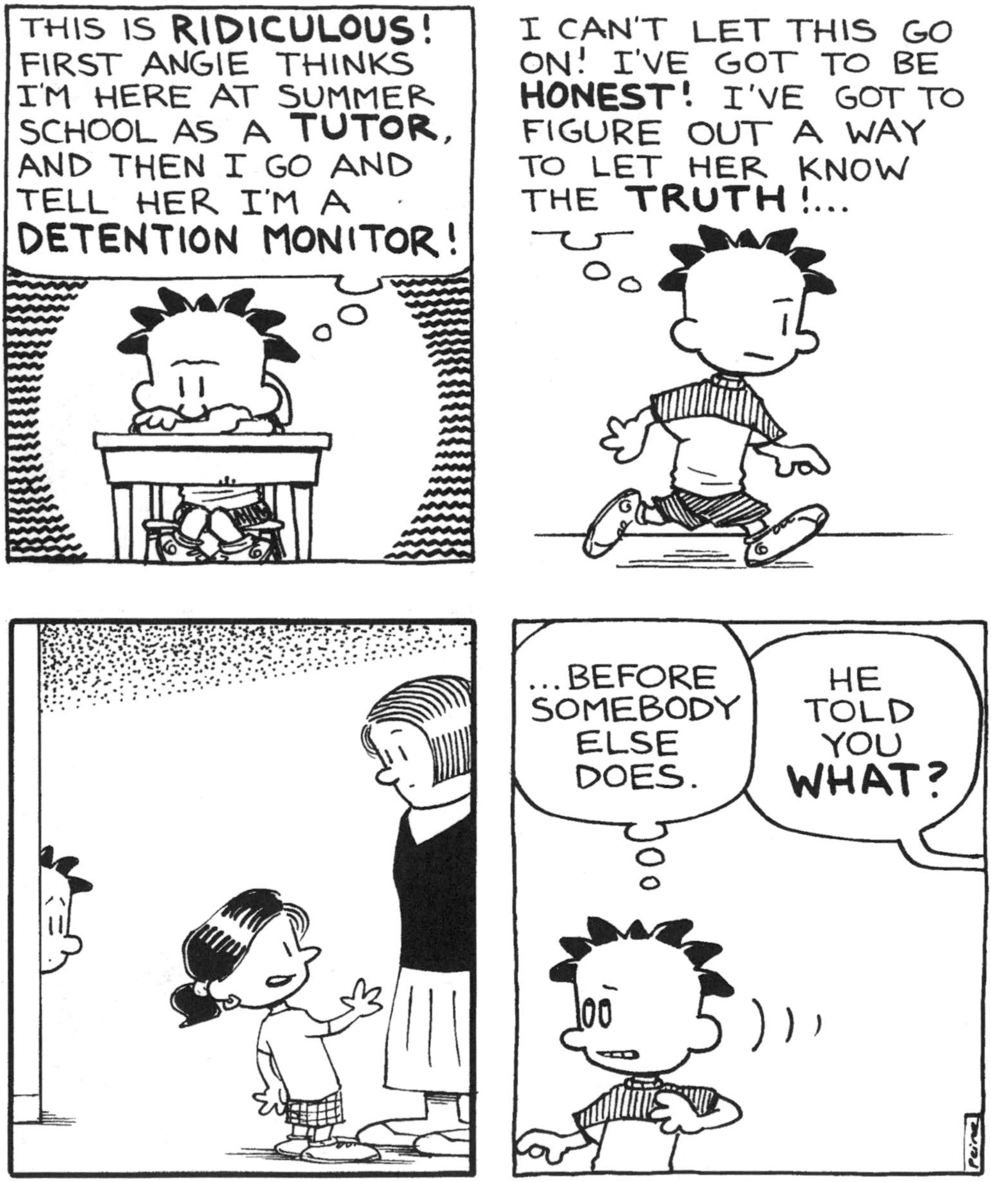
THIS IS RIDICULOUS! FIRST ANGIE THINKS I'M HERE AT SUMMER SCHOOL AS A TUTOR, AND THEN I GO AND TELL HER I'M A DETENTION MONITOR!
I CAN'T LET THIS GO ON! I'VE GOT TO BE HONEST! I'VE GOT TO FIGURE OUT A WAY TO LET HER KNOW THE TRUTH!...
...BEFORE SOMEBODY ELSE DOES.
HE TOLD YOU WHAT?

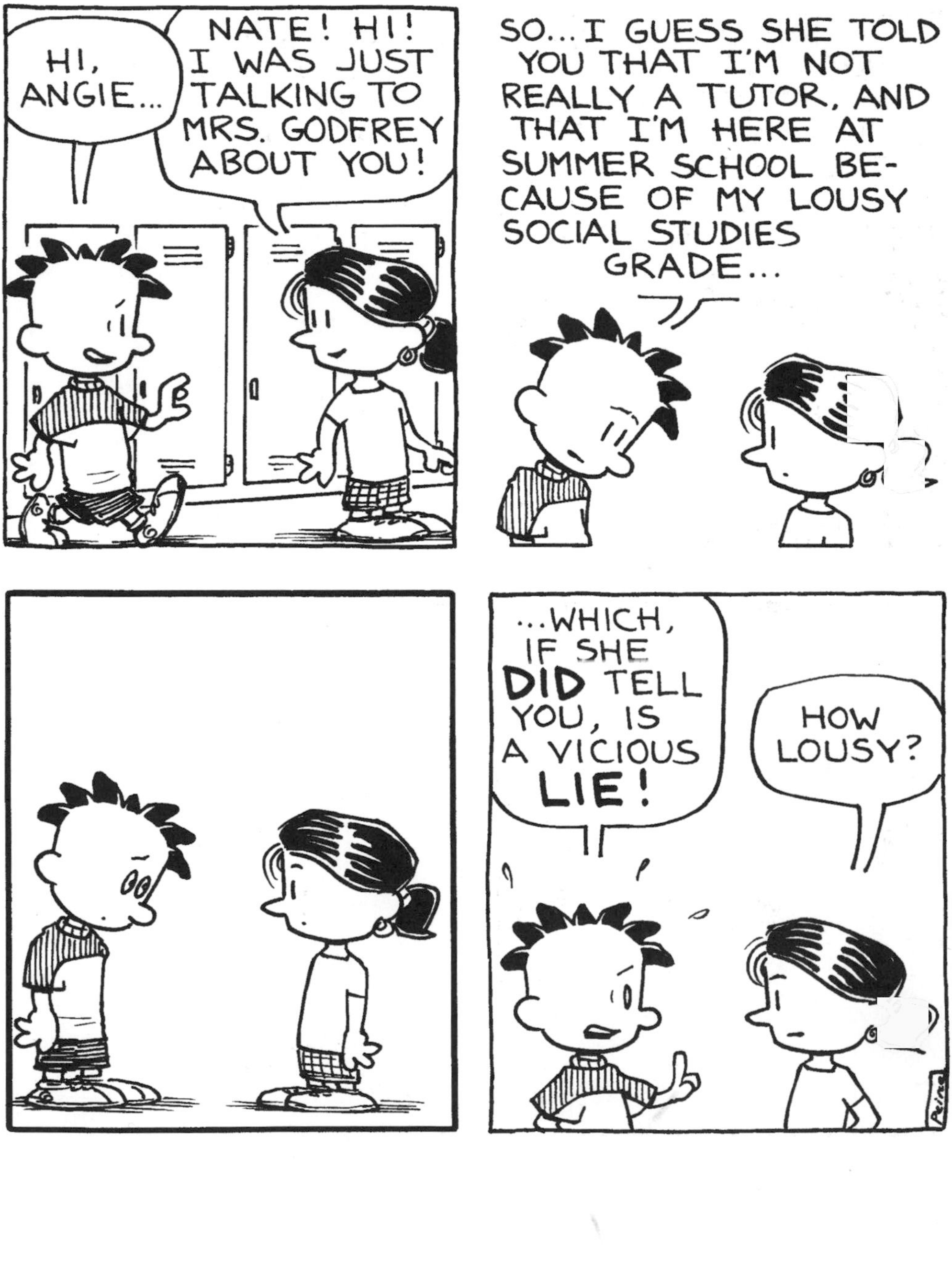
HI, ANGIE...
NATE! HI! I WAS JUST TALKING TO MRS. GODFREY ABOUT YOU!
SO... I GUESS SHE TOLD YOU THAT I'M NOT REALLY A TUTOR, AND THAT I'M HERE AT SUMMER SCHOOL BECAUSE OF MY LOUSY SOCIAL STUDIES GRADE...
...WHICH, IF SHE **DID** TELL YOU, IS A VICIOUS **LIE**!
HOW LOUSY?
Peirce

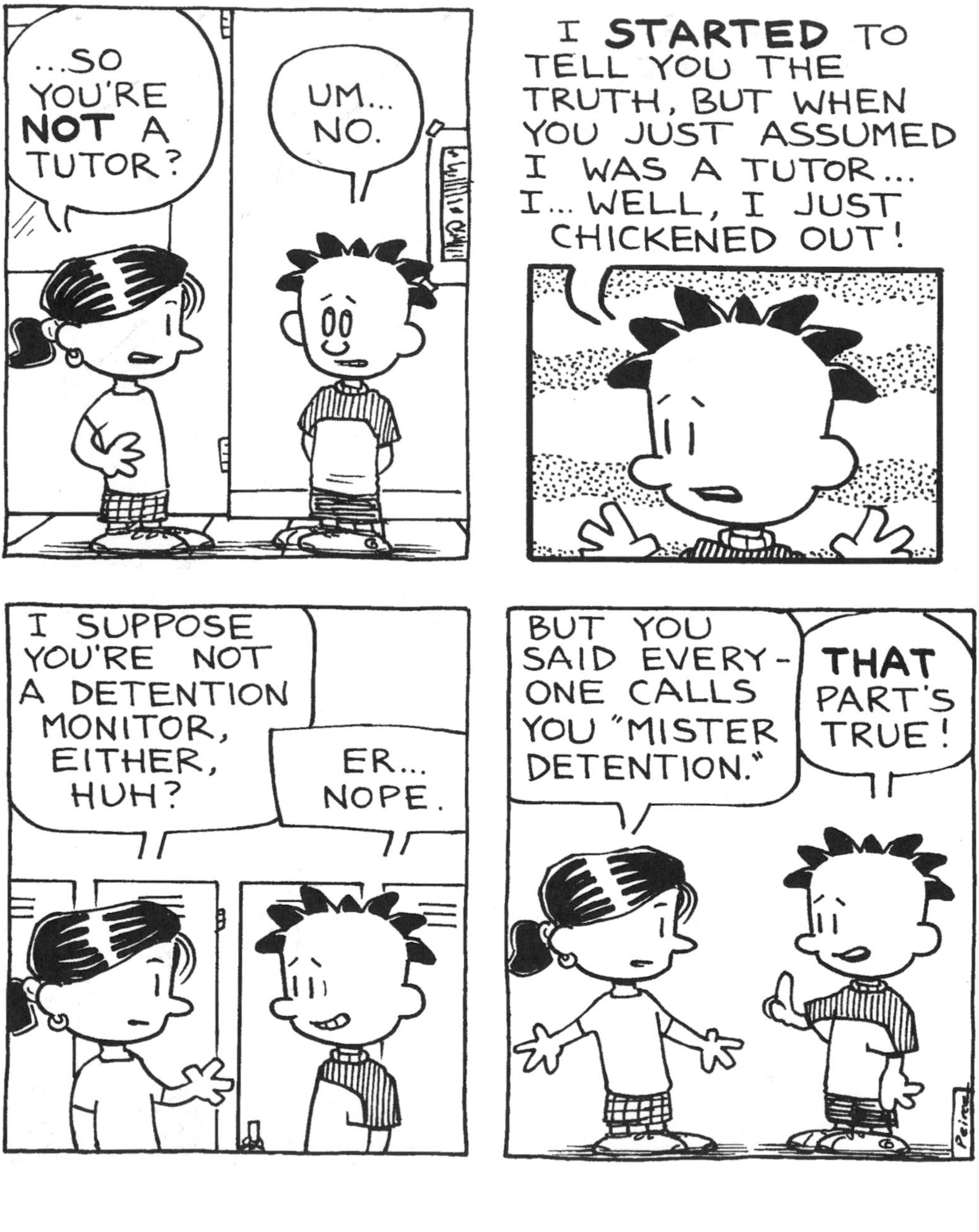
...SO YOU'RE **NOT** A TUTOR?
UM... NO.
I **STARTED** TO TELL YOU THE TRUTH, BUT WHEN YOU JUST ASSUMED I WAS A TUTOR... I... WELL, I JUST CHICKENED OUT!
I SUPPOSE YOU'RE NOT A DETENTION MONITOR, EITHER, HUH?
ER... NOPE.
BUT YOU SAID EVERY-ONE CALLS YOU "MISTER DETENTION."
THAT PART'S TRUE!
Peirce

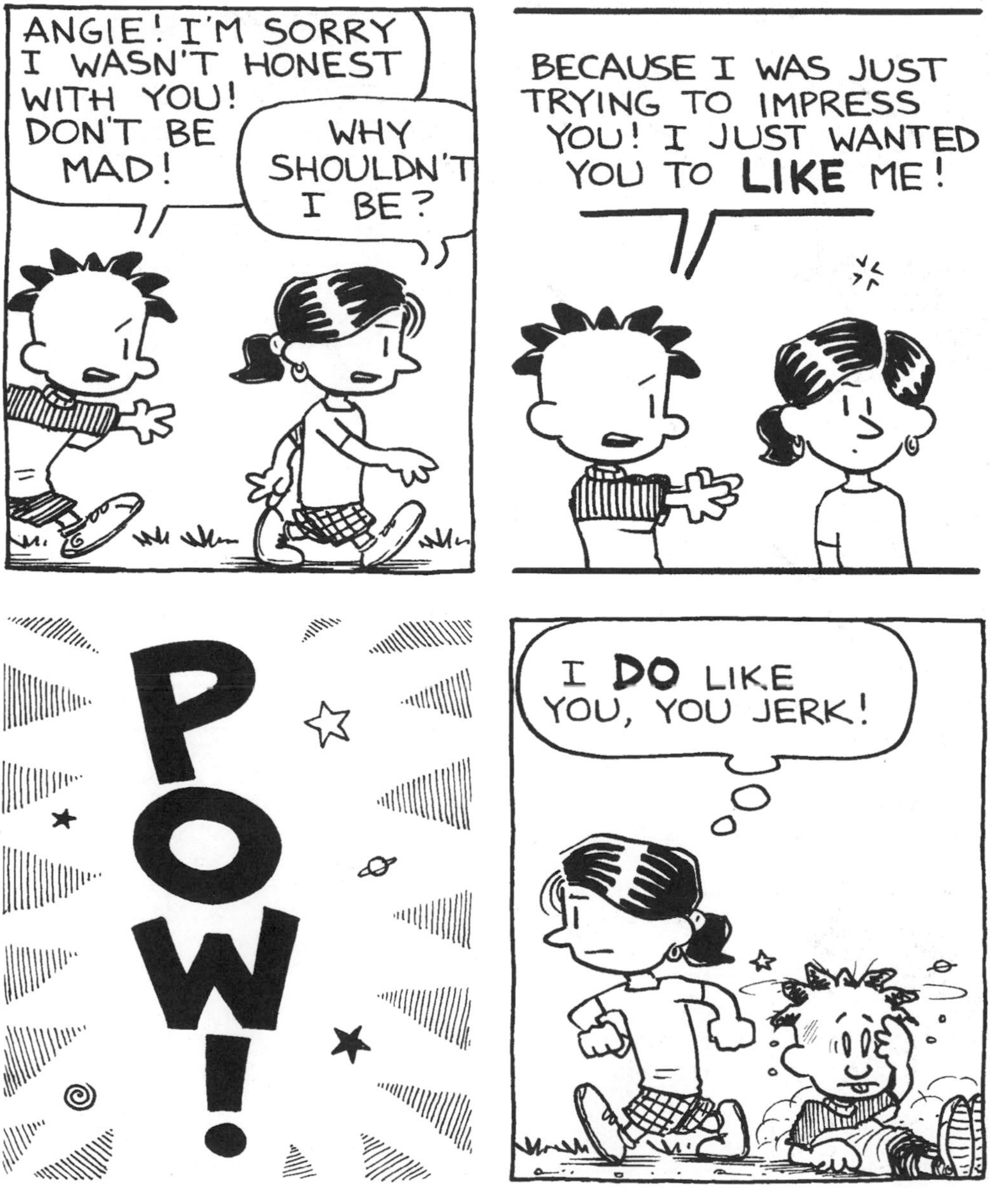
ANGIE! I'M SORRY I WASN'T HONEST WITH YOU! DON'T BE MAD!
WHY SHOULDN'T I BE?
BECAUSE I WAS JUST TRYING TO IMPRESS YOU! I JUST WANTED YOU TO LIKE ME!
POW!
I DO LIKE YOU, YOU JERK!

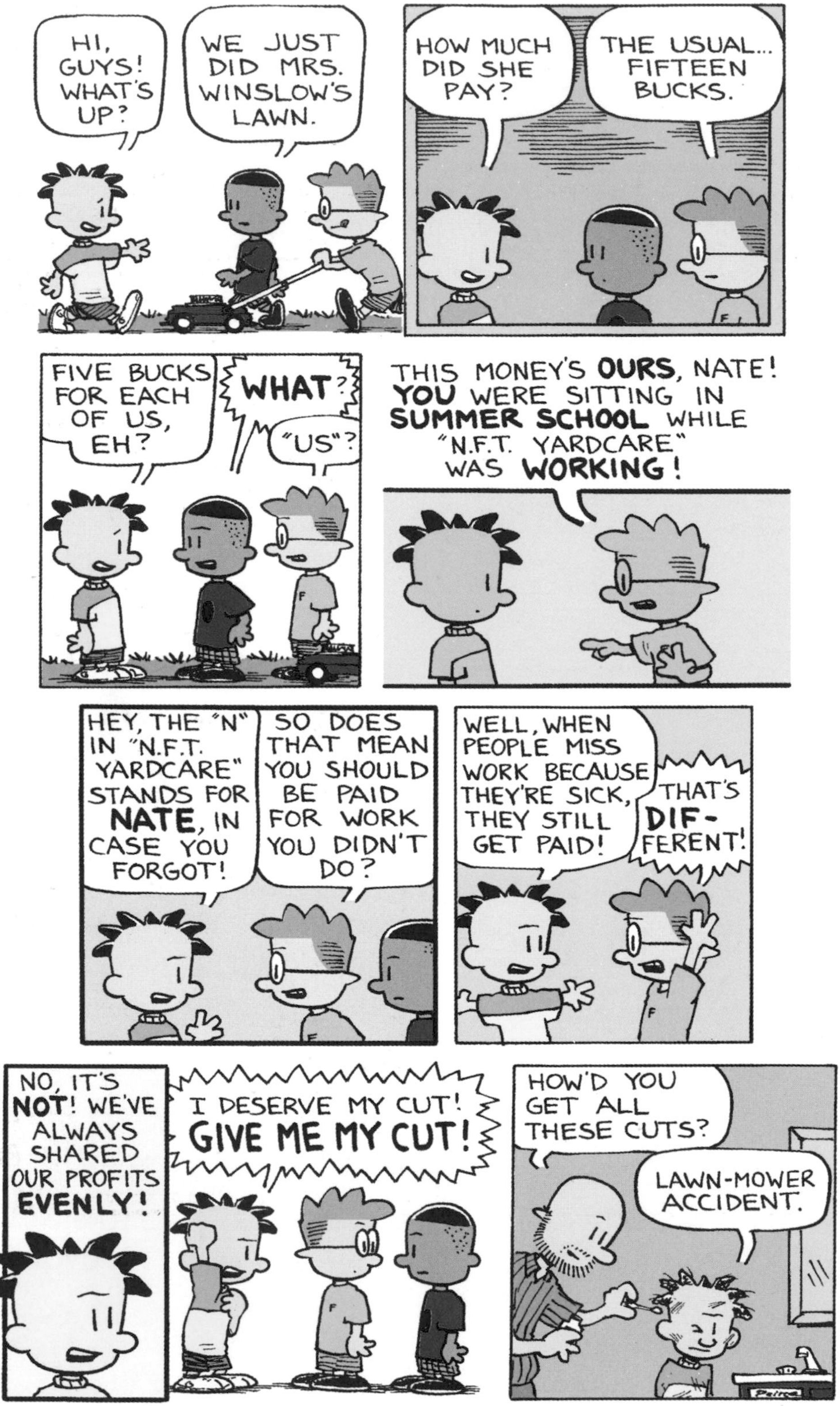
HI, GUYS! WHAT'S UP?
WE JUST DID MRS. WINSLOW'S LAWN.
HOW MUCH DID SHE PAY?
THE USUAL... FIFTEEN BUCKS.
FIVE BUCKS FOR EACH OF US, EH?
WHAT?
"US"?
THIS MONEY'S OURS, NATE! YOU WERE SITTING IN SUMMER SCHOOL WHILE "N.F.T. YARDCARE" WAS WORKING!
HEY, THE "N" IN "N.F.T. YARDCARE" STANDS FOR NATE, IN CASE YOU FORGOT!
SO DOES THAT MEAN YOU SHOULD BE PAID FOR WORK YOU DIDN'T DO?
WELL, WHEN PEOPLE MISS WORK BECAUSE THEY'RE SICK, THEY STILL GET PAID!
THAT'S DIF-FERENT!
NO, IT'S NOT! WE'VE ALWAYS SHARED OUR PROFITS EVENLY!
I DESERVE MY CUT! GIVE ME MY CUT!
HOW'D YOU GET ALL THESE CUTS?
LAWN-MOWER ACCIDENT.

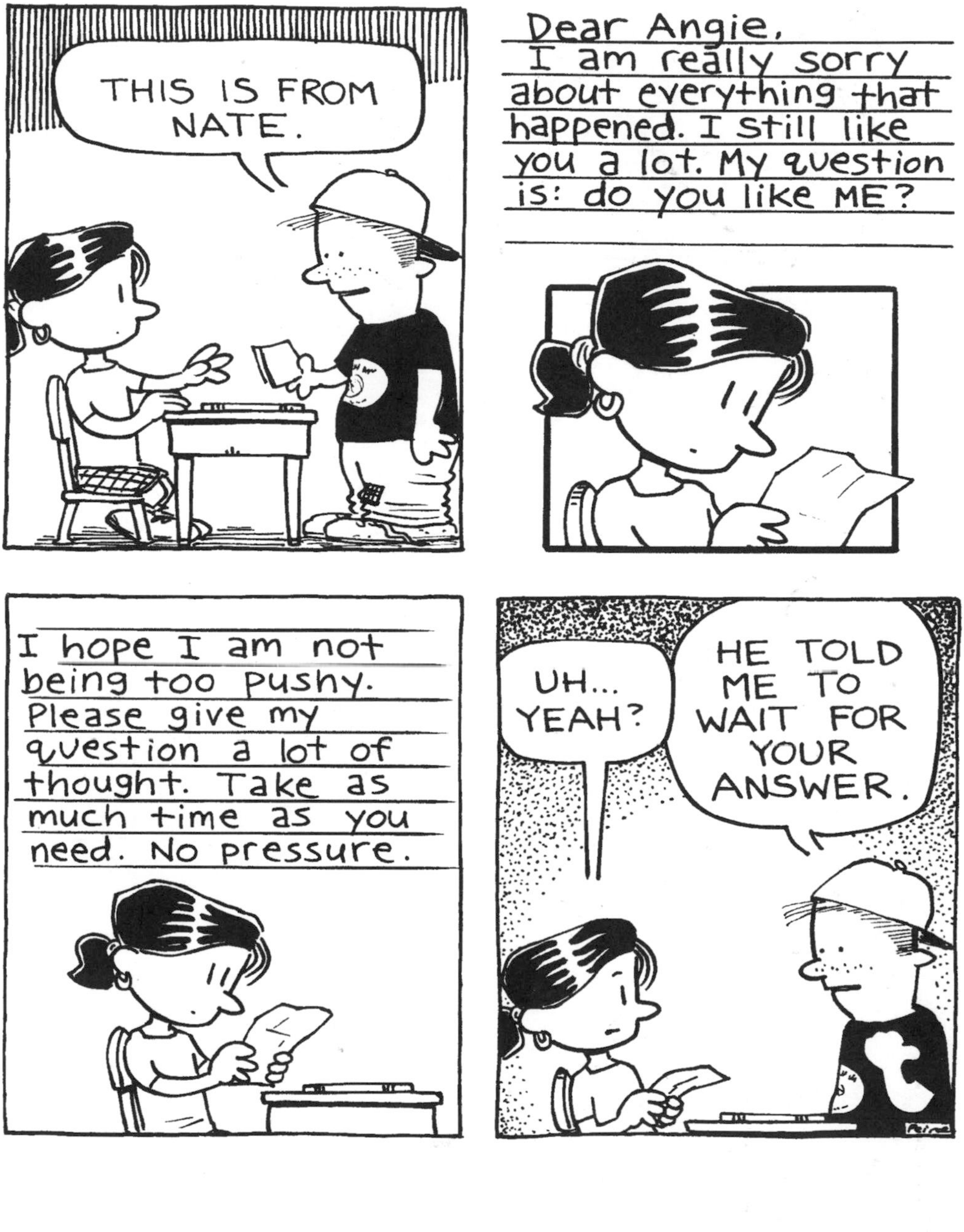
THIS IS FROM NATE.
Dear Angie,
I am really sorry about everything that happened. I still like you a lot. My question is: do you like ME?
I hope I am not being too pushy. Please give my question a lot of thought. Take as much time as you need. No pressure.
UH... YEAH?
HE TOLD ME TO WAIT FOR YOUR ANSWER.

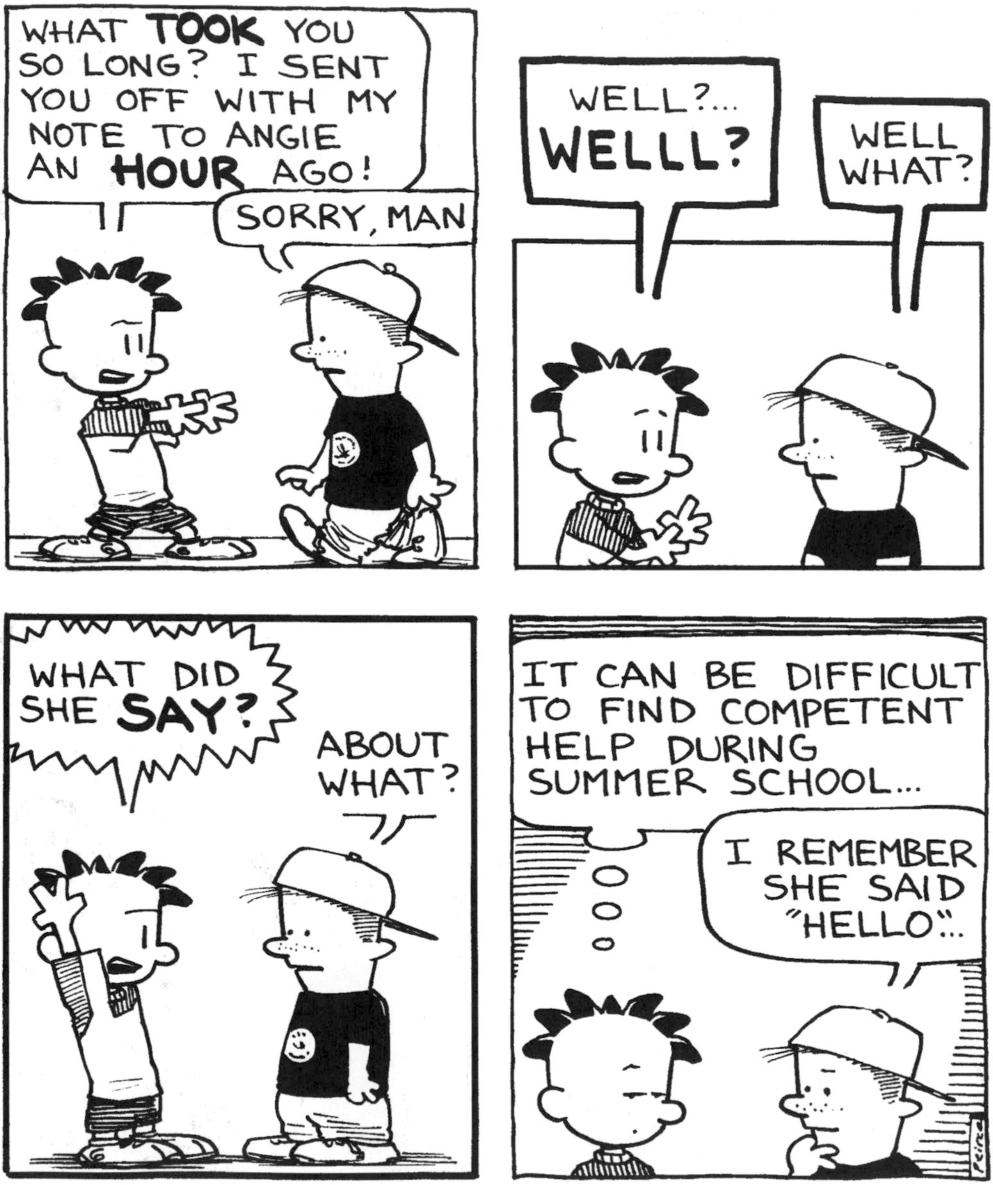
WHAT TOOK YOU SO LONG? I SENT YOU OFF WITH MY NOTE TO ANGIE AN HOUR AGO!
SORRY, MAN
WELL?... WELLL?
WELL WHAT?
WHAT DID SHE SAY?
ABOUT WHAT?
IT CAN BE DIFFICULT TO FIND COMPETENT HELP DURING SUMMER SCHOOL...
I REMEMBER SHE SAID "HELLO"...
Peirce

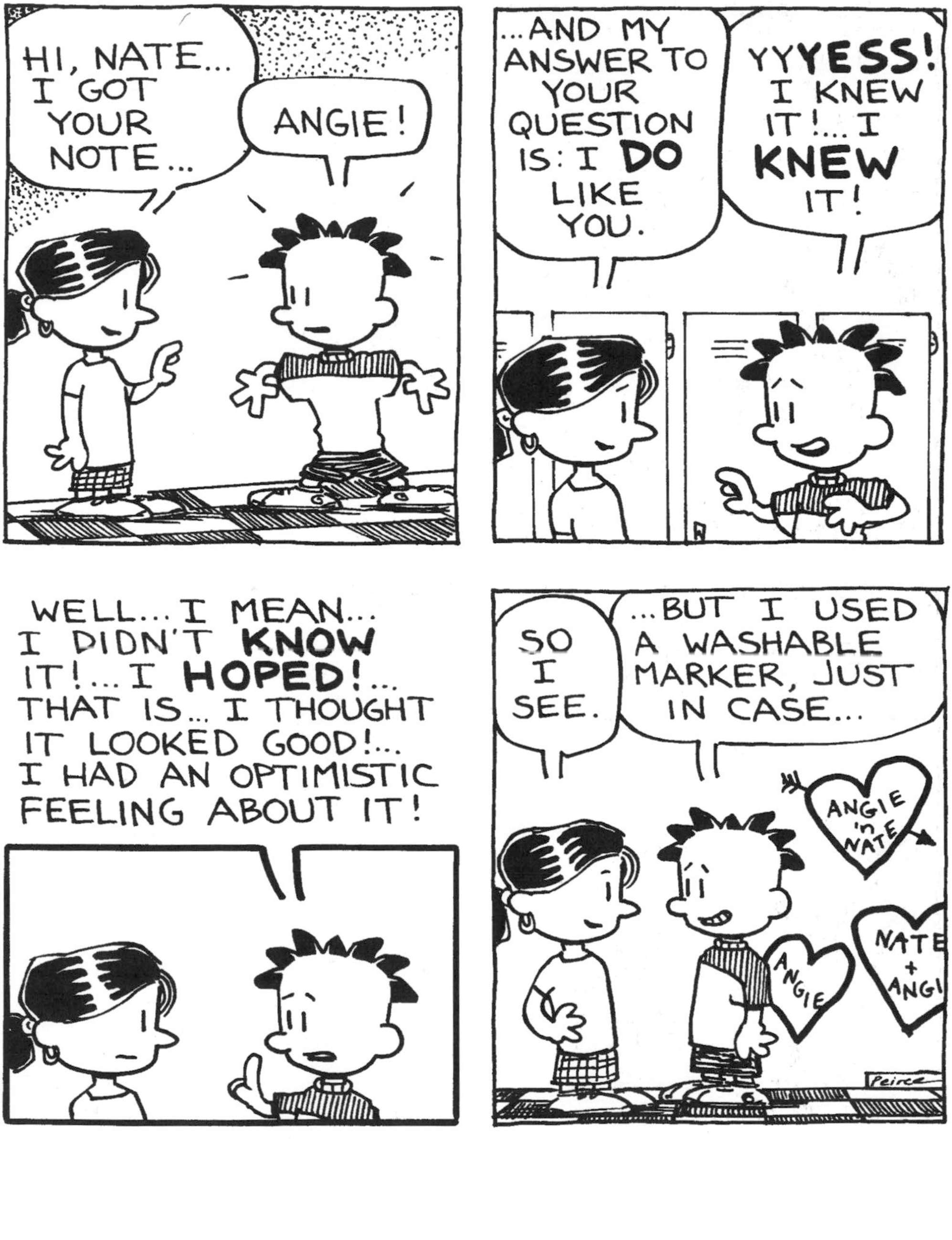
HI, NATE... I GOT YOUR NOTE...
ANGIE!
...AND MY ANSWER TO YOUR QUESTION IS: I **DO** LIKE YOU.
YY**YESS!** I KNEW IT!... I **KNEW** IT!
WELL... I MEAN... I DIDN'T **KNOW** IT!... I **HOPED!**... THAT IS... I THOUGHT IT LOOKED GOOD!... I HAD AN OPTIMISTIC FEELING ABOUT IT!
SO I SEE.
...BUT I USED A WASHABLE MARKER, JUST IN CASE...
ANGIE in NATE
NATE + ANGI
ANGIE
Peirce

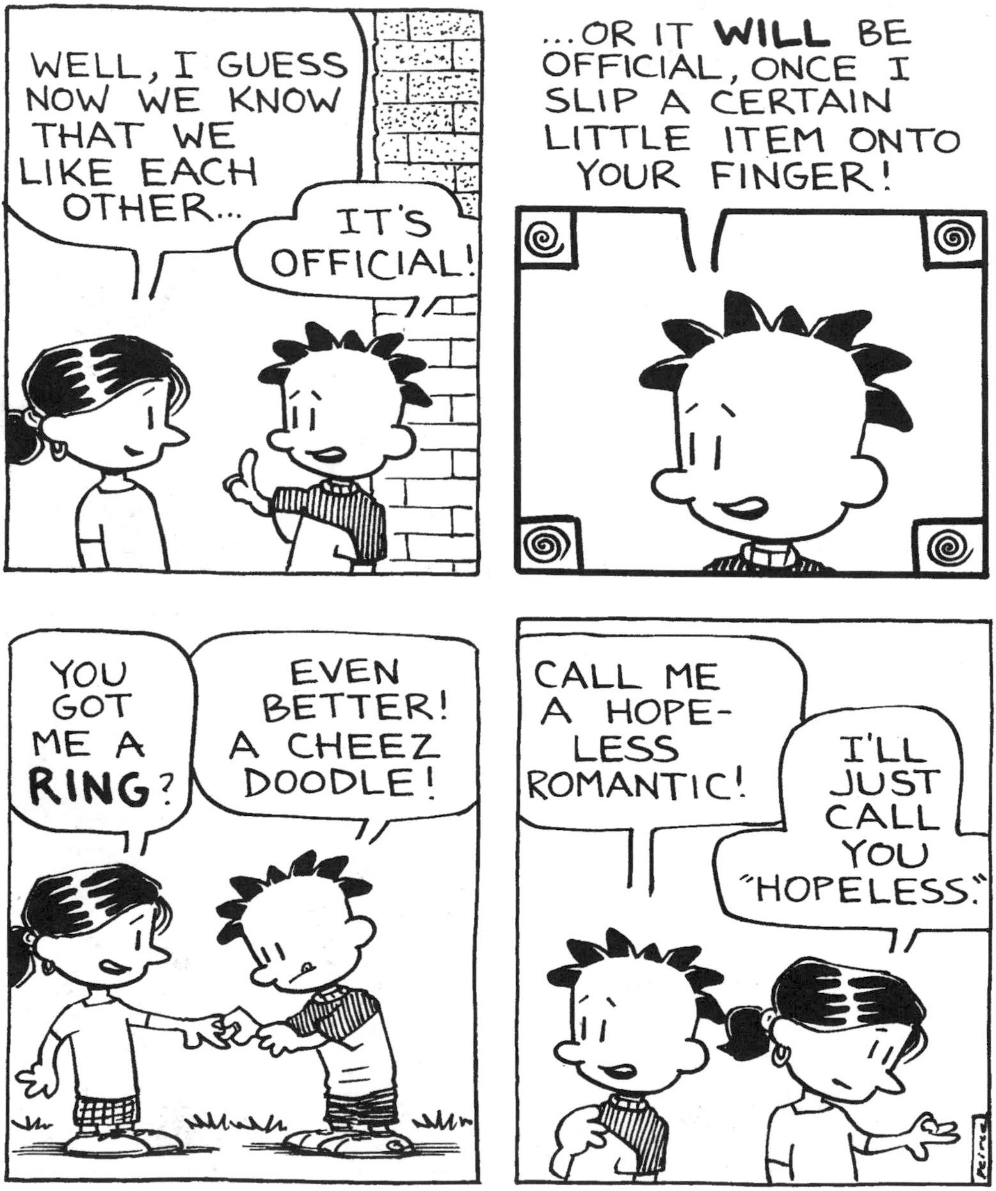
WELL, I GUESS NOW WE KNOW THAT WE LIKE EACH OTHER...
IT'S OFFICIAL!
...OR IT **WILL** BE OFFICIAL, ONCE I SLIP A CERTAIN LITTLE ITEM ONTO YOUR FINGER!
YOU GOT ME A **RING**?
EVEN BETTER! A CHEEZ DOODLE!
CALL ME A HOPE-LESS ROMANTIC!
I'LL JUST CALL YOU "HOPELESS."

WELL... SEE YOU TOMORROW, ANGIE...
OH, WAIT! I'VE GOT SOME-THING FOR YOU!
WHAT IS IT? A NOTE?
NO, I'M NOT REALLY A "NOTE" PERSON...
SMAK!
READ ME?
LOUD AND CLEAR...
Peirce

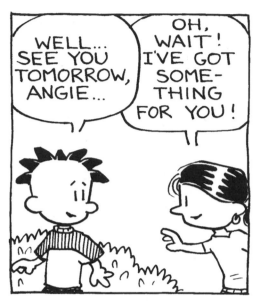

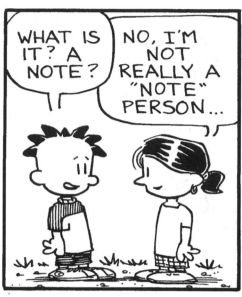

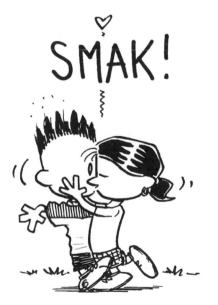

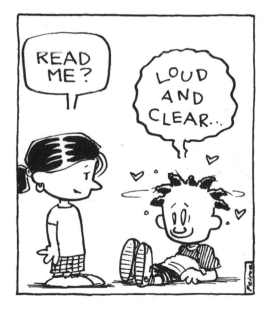

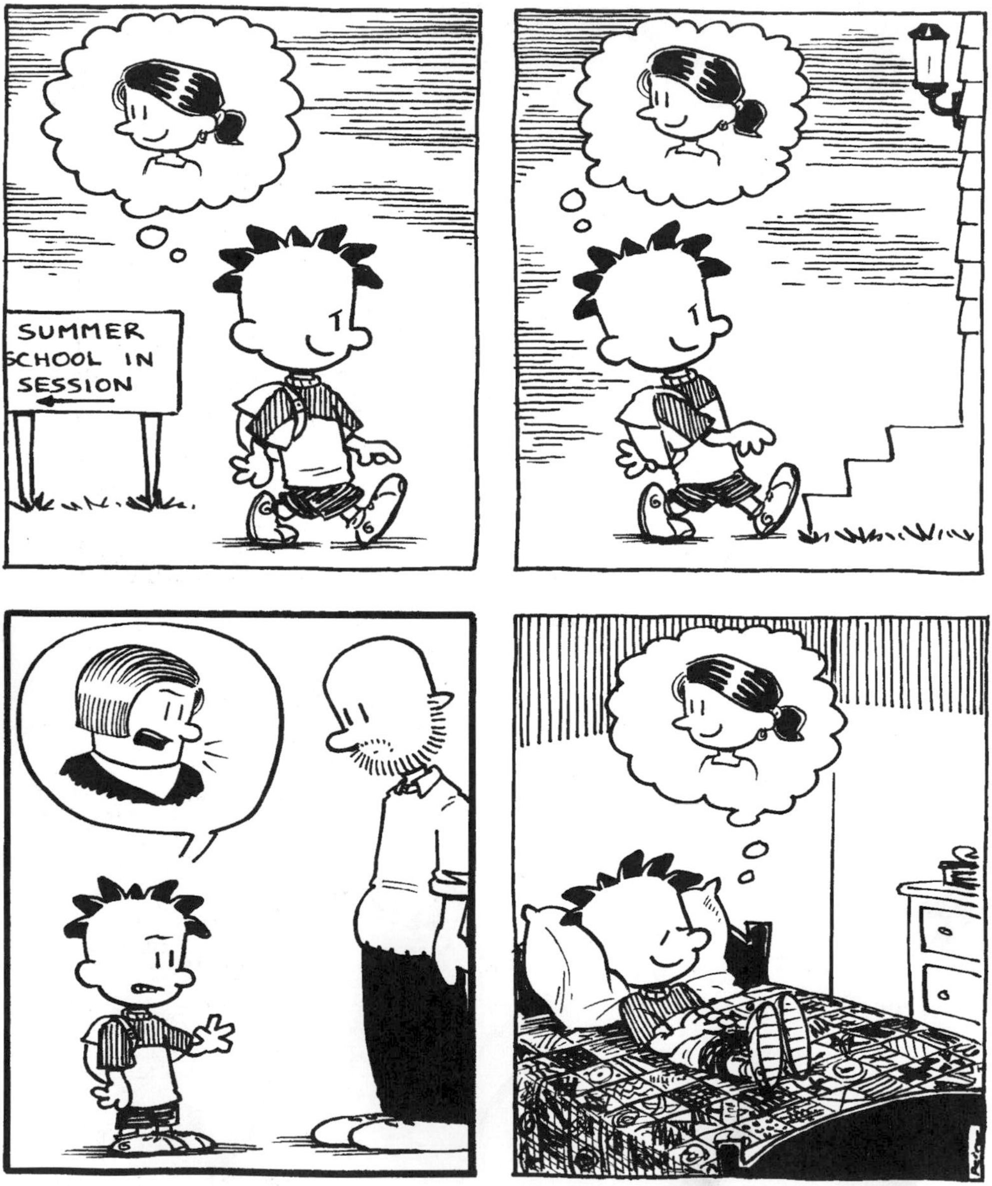
SUMMER
SCHOOL IN
SESSION

BASEBALL IS A GAME OF **DECISIONS**!

EACH GAME, EACH INNING CONSISTS OF **DOZENS** OF DECISION-MAKING SITUATIONS!

THE CHALLENGE IS TO MAKE THE **RIGHT** DECISION!

MENTAL PREPARATION! THAT'S **KEY**! YOU'VE GOT TO CONSTANTLY ASK YOURSELF: "WHAT WILL I DO IF THE BALL IS HIT TO **ME**?"

THEN IT BECOMES SECOND NATURE TO MAKE THE RIGHT DECISION IN A **SPLIT SECOND**!

CRAK!

TRIP!

SELECT ONE:

A.) PICK SELF UP, DUST SELF OFF.
B.) ADMIT MISTAKE, MOVE ON.

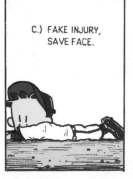

C.) FAKE INJURY, SAVE FACE.

OOOOOH..

YOU OKAY, MAN?

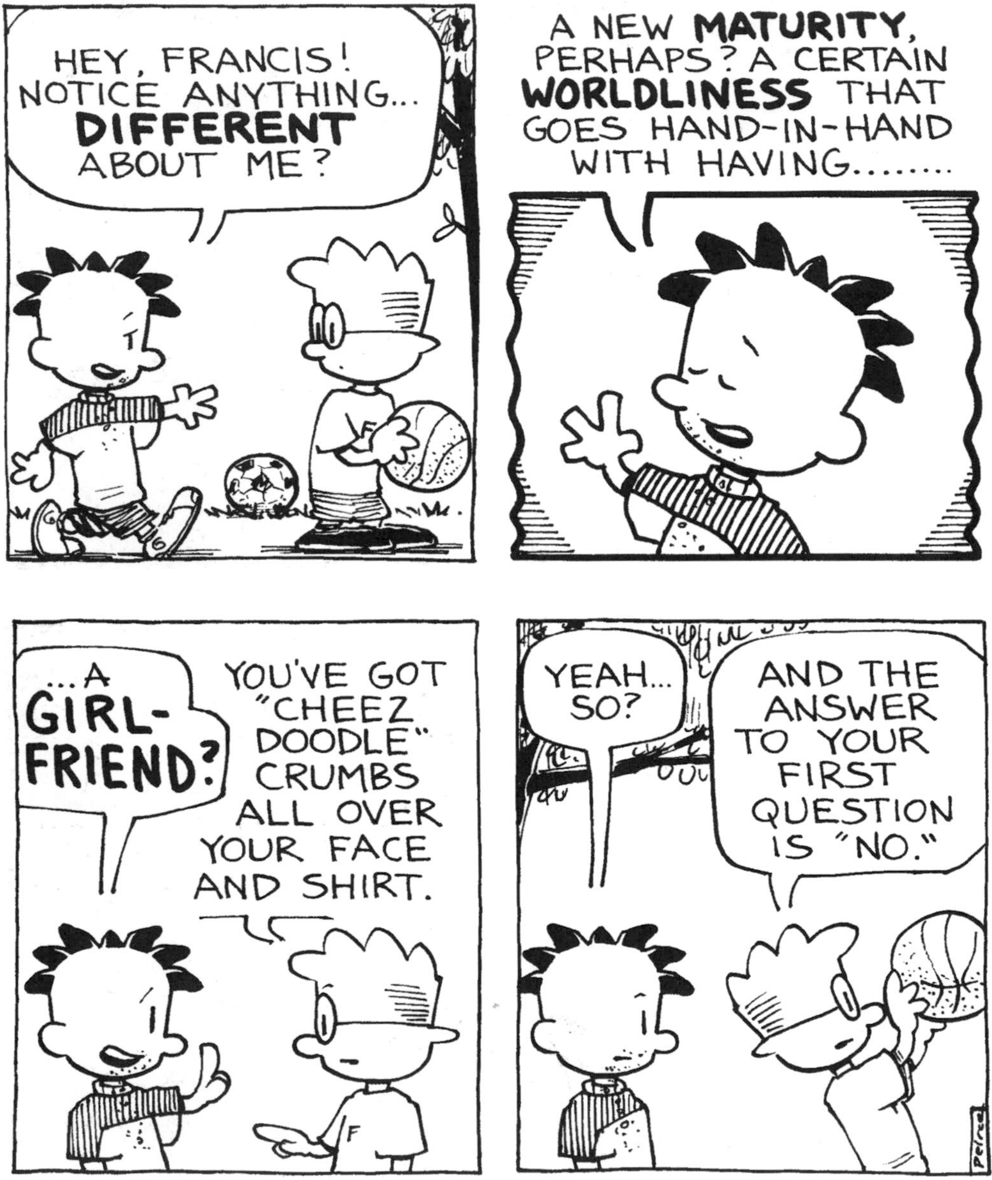
HEY, FRANCIS! NOTICE ANYTHING... DIFFERENT ABOUT ME?
A NEW MATURITY, PERHAPS? A CERTAIN WORLDLINESS THAT GOES HAND-IN-HAND WITH HAVING........
...A GIRL-FRIEND?
YOU'VE GOT "CHEEZ DOODLE" CRUMBS ALL OVER YOUR FACE AND SHIRT.
YEAH... SO?
AND THE ANSWER TO YOUR FIRST QUESTION IS "NO."
Peirce

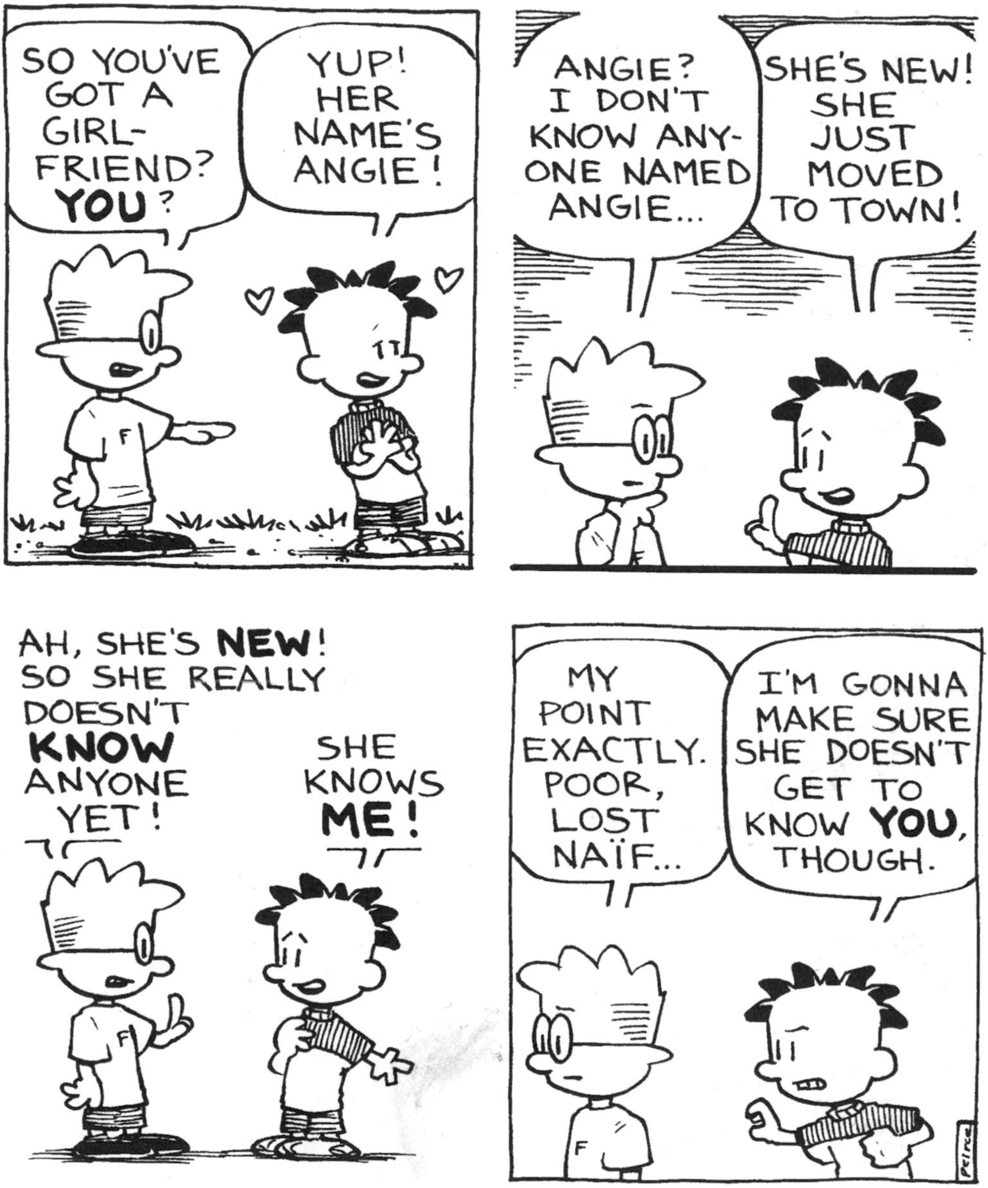
SO YOU'VE GOT A GIRL-FRIEND? YOU?
YUP! HER NAME'S ANGIE!
ANGIE? I DON'T KNOW ANY-ONE NAMED ANGIE...
SHE'S NEW! SHE JUST MOVED TO TOWN!
AH, SHE'S NEW! SO SHE REALLY DOESN'T KNOW ANYONE YET!
SHE KNOWS ME!
MY POINT EXACTLY. POOR, LOST NAÏF...
I'M GONNA MAKE SURE SHE DOESN'T GET TO KNOW YOU, THOUGH.
PEIRCE

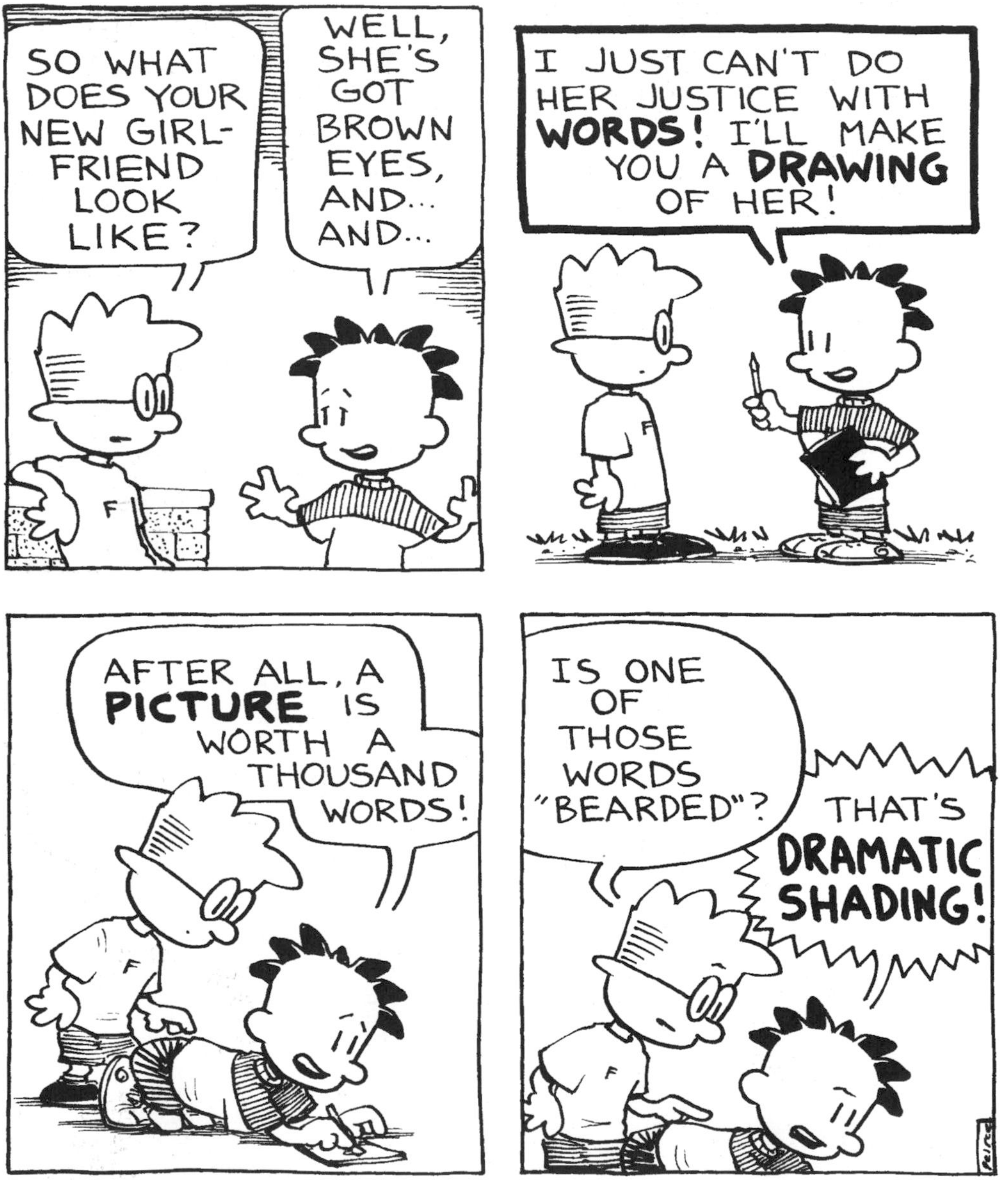
SO WHAT DOES YOUR NEW GIRL-FRIEND LOOK LIKE?
WELL, SHE'S GOT BROWN EYES, AND... AND...
I JUST CAN'T DO HER JUSTICE WITH WORDS! I'LL MAKE YOU A DRAWING OF HER!
AFTER ALL, A PICTURE IS WORTH A THOUSAND WORDS!
IS ONE OF THOSE WORDS "BEARDED"?
THAT'S DRAMATIC SHADING!
PEIRCE

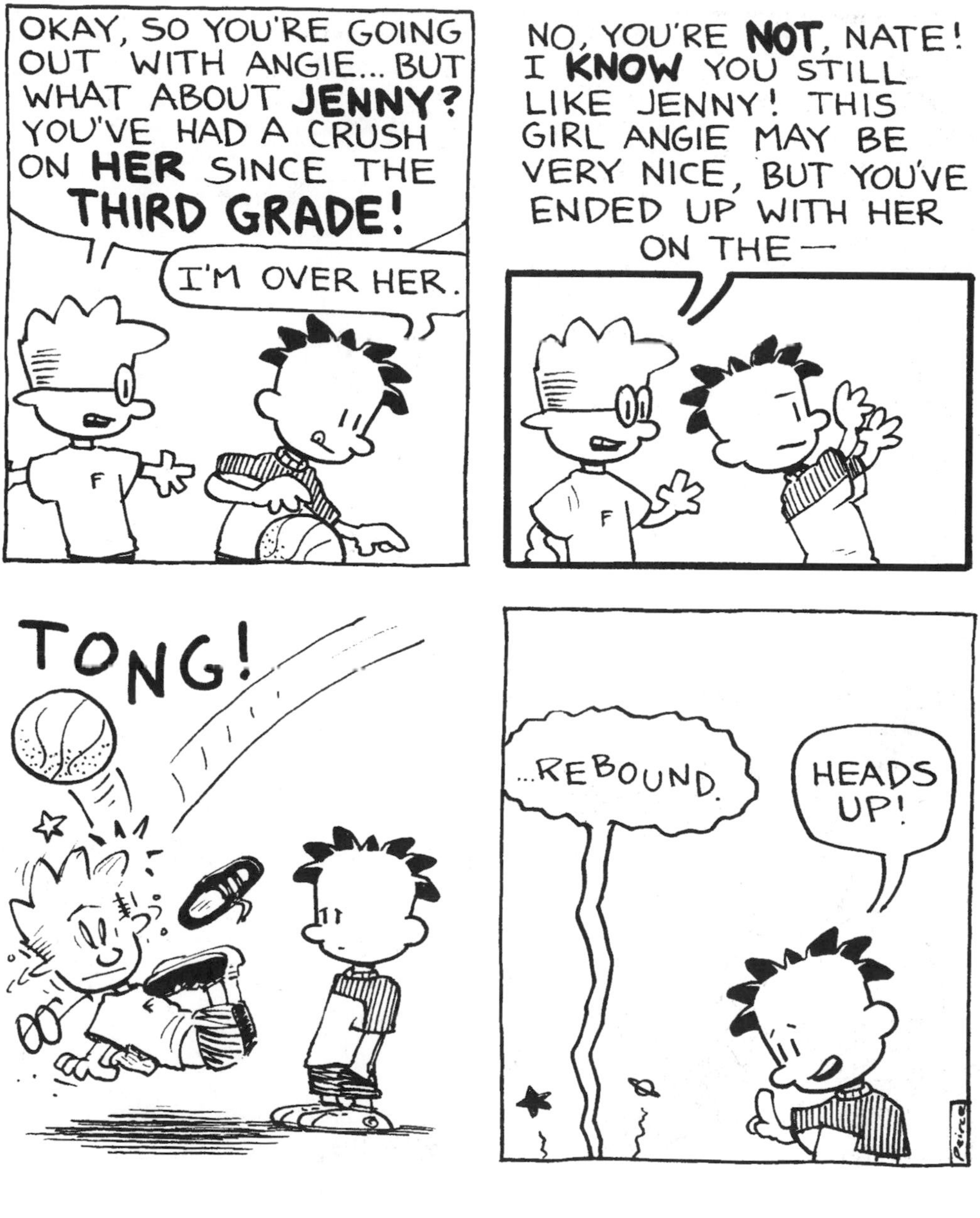

OKAY, SO YOU'RE GOING OUT WITH ANGIE... BUT WHAT ABOUT JENNY? YOU'VE HAD A CRUSH ON HER SINCE THE THIRD GRADE!
I'M OVER HER.
NO, YOU'RE NOT, NATE! I KNOW YOU STILL LIKE JENNY! THIS GIRL ANGIE MAY BE VERY NICE, BUT YOU'VE ENDED UP WITH HER ON THE—
TONG!
...REBOUND.
HEADS UP!
Peirce

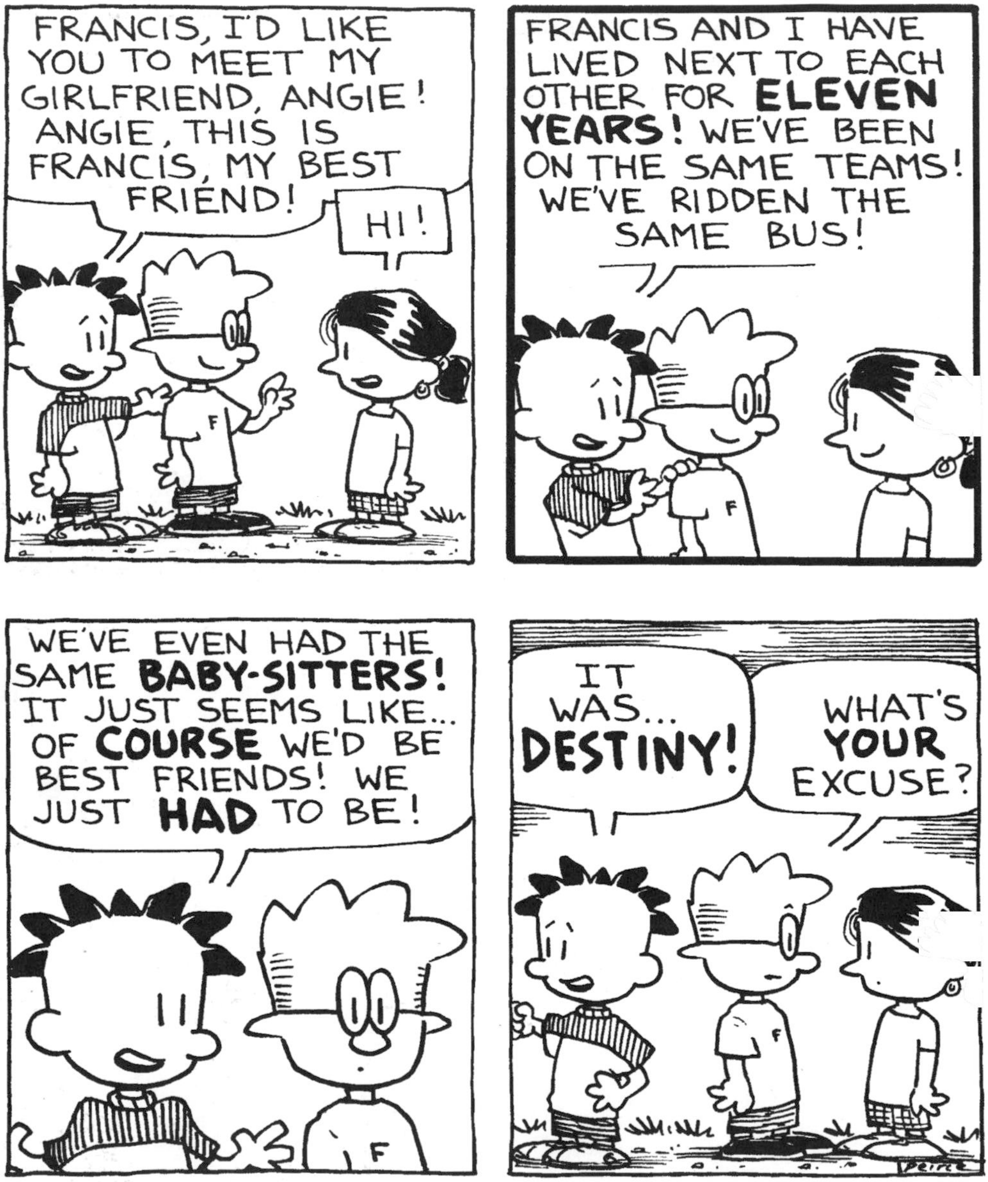
FRANCIS, I'D LIKE YOU TO MEET MY GIRLFRIEND, ANGIE! ANGIE, THIS IS FRANCIS, MY BEST FRIEND!
HI!
FRANCIS AND I HAVE LIVED NEXT TO EACH OTHER FOR **ELEVEN YEARS!** WE'VE BEEN ON THE SAME TEAMS! WE'VE RIDDEN THE SAME BUS!
WE'VE EVEN HAD THE SAME **BABY-SITTERS!** IT JUST SEEMS LIKE... OF **COURSE** WE'D BE BEST FRIENDS! WE JUST **HAD** TO BE!
IT WAS... **DESTINY!**
WHAT'S **YOUR** EXCUSE?
PEIRCE

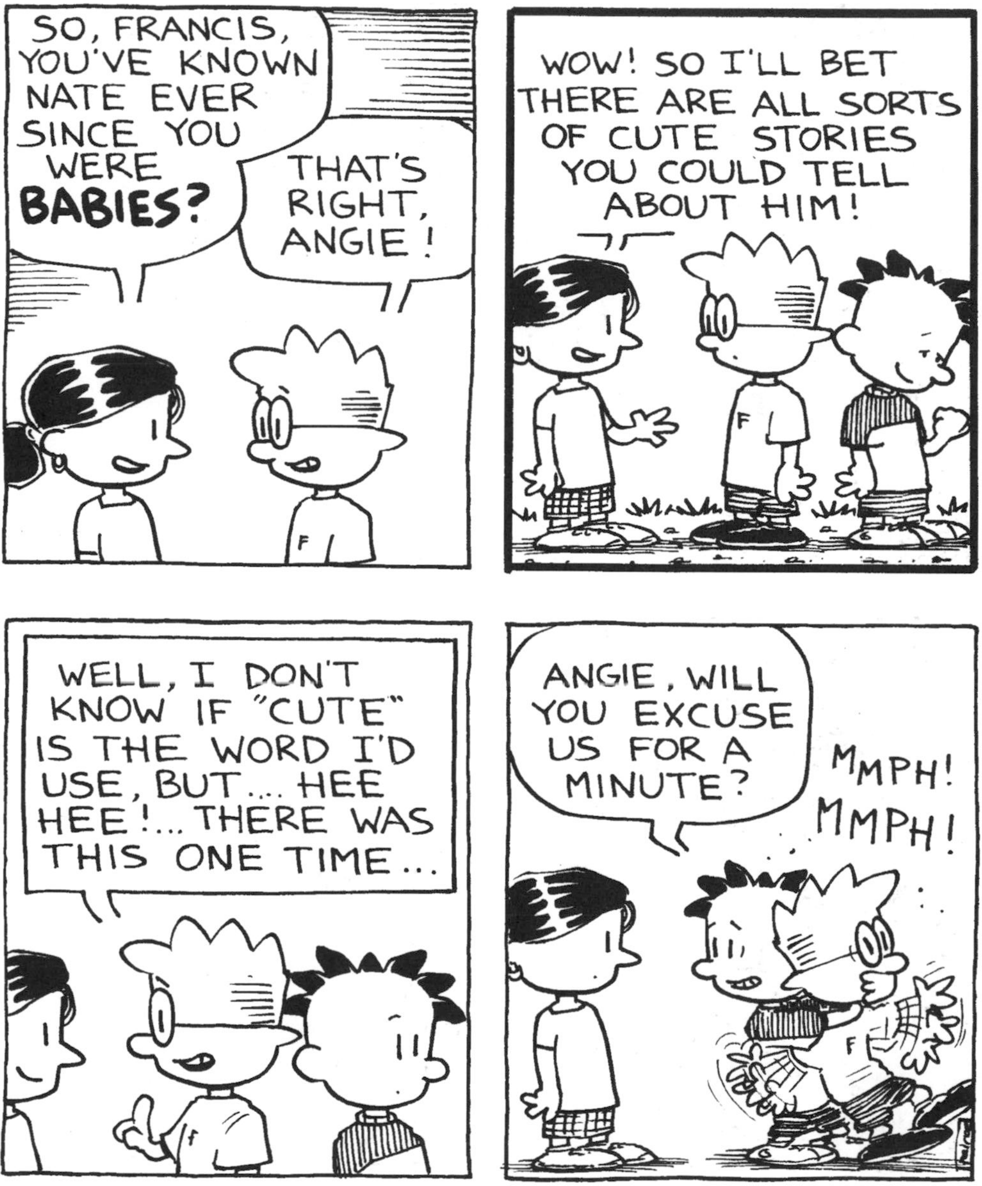
SO, FRANCIS, YOU'VE KNOWN NATE EVER SINCE YOU WERE **BABIES?**
THAT'S RIGHT, ANGIE!
WOW! SO I'LL BET THERE ARE ALL SORTS OF CUTE STORIES YOU COULD TELL ABOUT HIM!
WELL, I DON'T KNOW IF "CUTE" IS THE WORD I'D USE, BUT... HEE HEE!... THERE WAS THIS ONE TIME...
ANGIE, WILL YOU EXCUSE US FOR A MINUTE?
MMPH! MMPH!

"FEELINGS"

with your host:

Dr. Warren Fuzzy

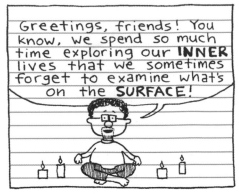

Greetings, friends! You know, we spend so much time exploring our **INNER** lives that we sometimes forget to examine what's on the **SURFACE!**

Yes, the way we **LOOK** can often hold the key to how we **FEEL** about ourselves!

Specifically, an outrageous appearance sometimes masks an emotional life in **TURMOIL!**

Dennis Rodman →

That's right! Crazy clothes and over-the-top outfits are much **MORE** than a simple fashion statement!...

They're a **CRY FOR HELP!** These poor souls need our compassion! Our understanding! Our companionship!

BEACH?

YOU'RE ON YOUR OWN.

230

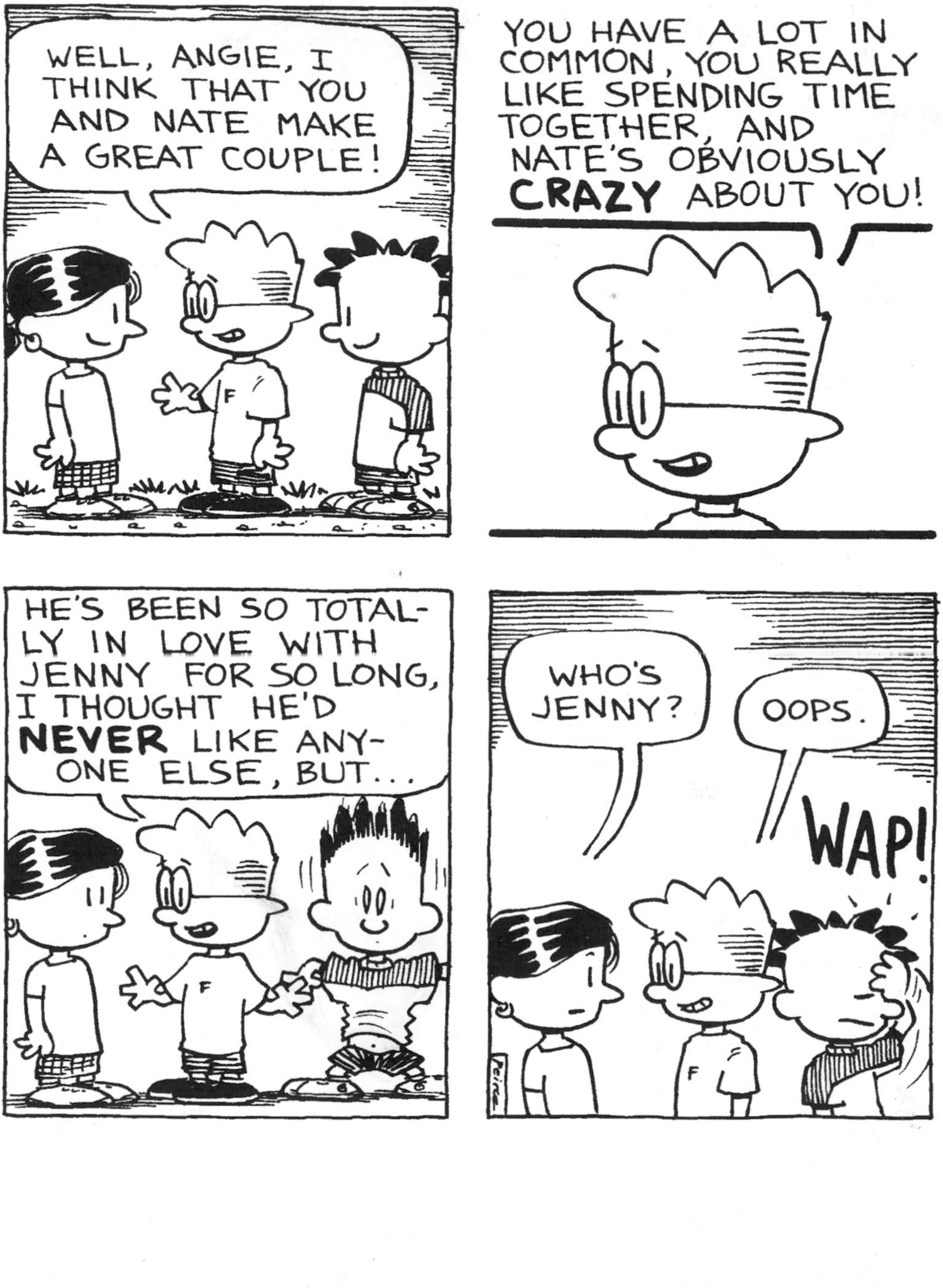
WELL, ANGIE, I THINK THAT YOU AND NATE MAKE A GREAT COUPLE!
YOU HAVE A LOT IN COMMON, YOU REALLY LIKE SPENDING TIME TOGETHER, AND NATE'S OBVIOUSLY **CRAZY** ABOUT YOU!
HE'S BEEN SO TOTALLY IN LOVE WITH JENNY FOR SO LONG, I THOUGHT HE'D **NEVER** LIKE ANYONE ELSE, BUT...
WHO'S JENNY?
OOPS.
WAP!
PEIRCE

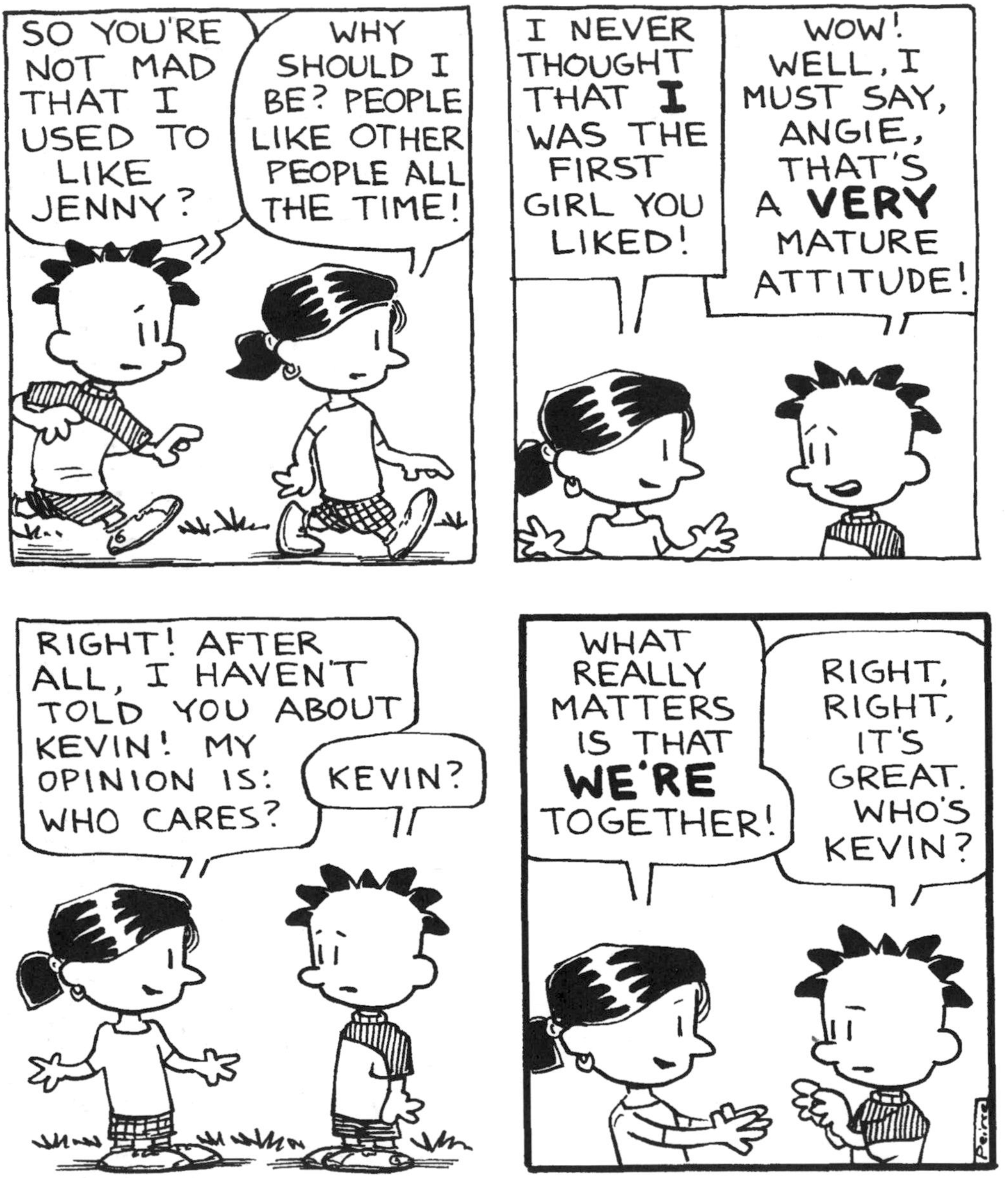
SO YOU'RE NOT MAD THAT I USED TO LIKE JENNY?
WHY SHOULD I BE? PEOPLE LIKE OTHER PEOPLE ALL THE TIME!
I NEVER THOUGHT THAT I WAS THE FIRST GIRL YOU LIKED!
WOW! WELL, I MUST SAY, ANGIE, THAT'S A VERY MATURE ATTITUDE!
RIGHT! AFTER ALL, I HAVEN'T TOLD YOU ABOUT KEVIN! MY OPINION IS: WHO CARES?
KEVIN?
WHAT REALLY MATTERS IS THAT WE'RE TOGETHER!
RIGHT, RIGHT, IT'S GREAT. WHO'S KEVIN?
Peirce

★☆★☆★☆★☆★☆

everlovin' ELLEN!

the "life" and loves of a clueless high school sophomore!

One day at "Dilly Burger"...

ELLEN! You left the onion-ring machine on!

That's a **VERY** serious mistake! I'm afraid I'll have to put this incident in your record as a "blemish"!

I'm sorry, boss!

Well, at least I've only got **ONE** blemish!

Um... checked a mirror lately?

WHEN I ASKED ABOUT YOUR SIS- TER, I THOUGHT MAYBE YOU'D INTRO- **DUCE** US.

WHY BOTHER? THIS SHOWS YOU WHAT SHE'S **REALLY** LIKE!

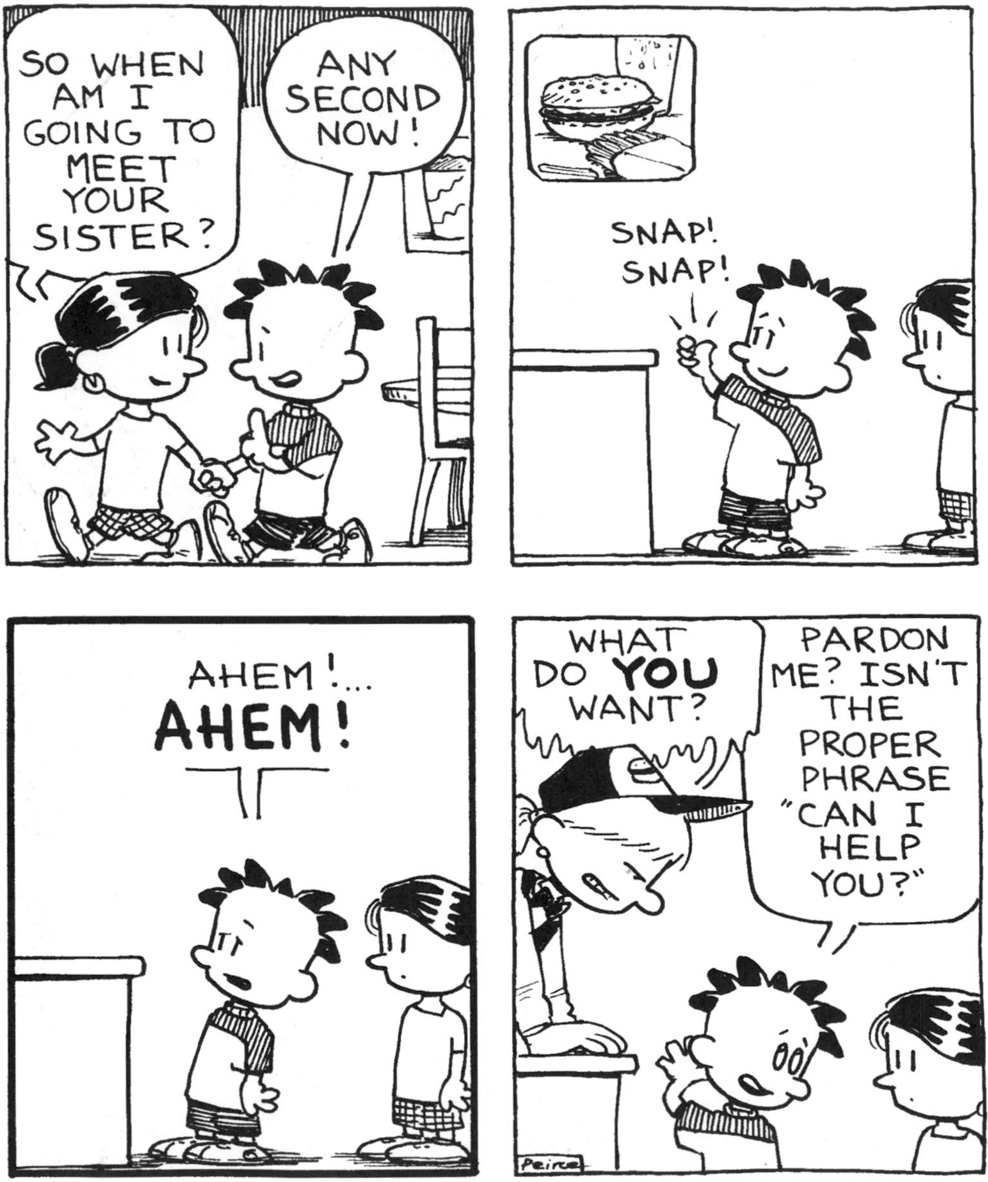
SO WHEN AM I GOING TO MEET YOUR SISTER?
ANY SECOND NOW!
SNAP! SNAP!
AHEM!... AHEM!
WHAT DO YOU WANT?
PARDON ME? ISN'T THE PROPER PHRASE "CAN I HELP YOU?"
Peirce

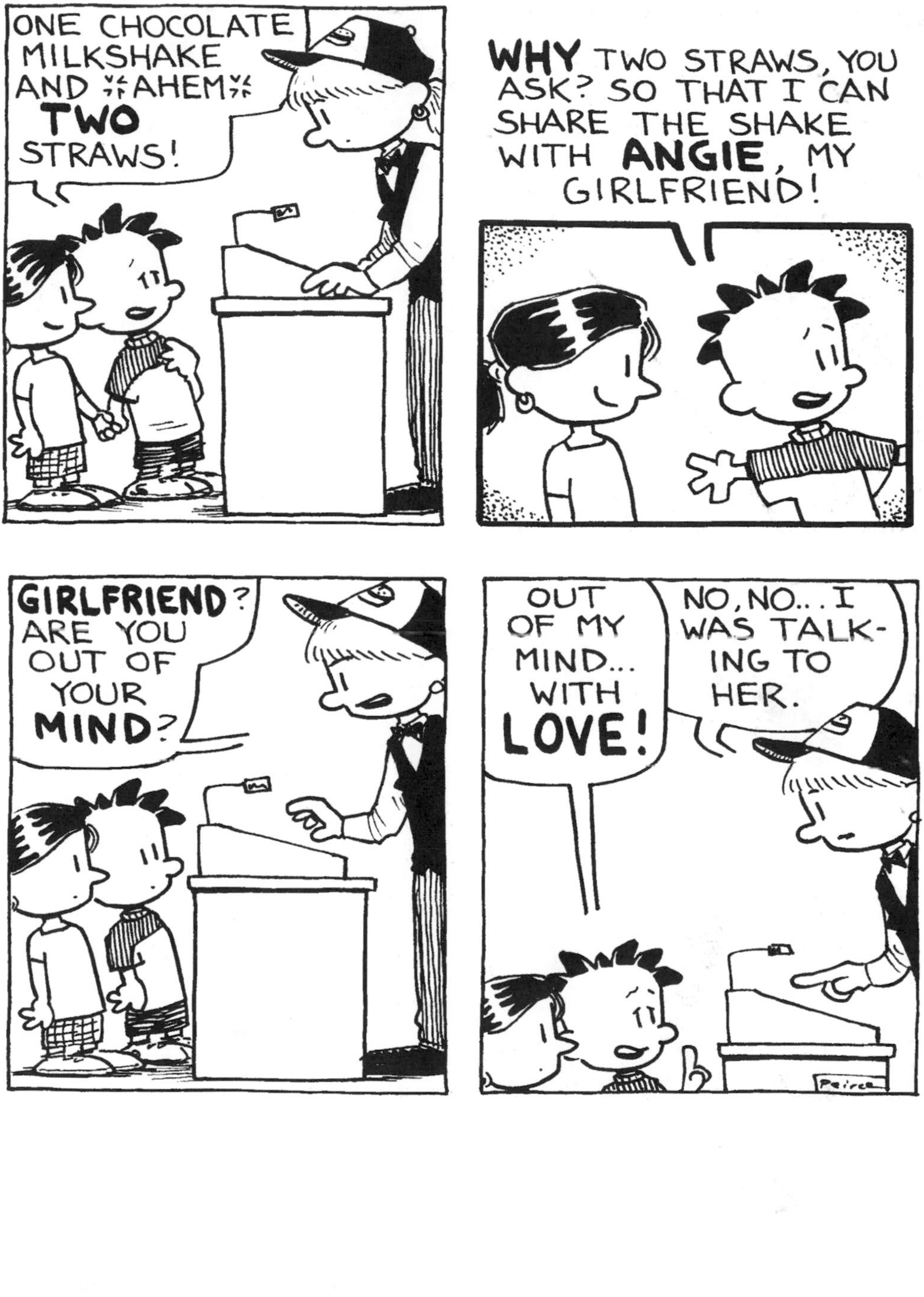

ONE CHOCOLATE MILKSHAKE AND ✳AHEM✳ TWO STRAWS!
WHY TWO STRAWS, YOU ASK? SO THAT I CAN SHARE THE SHAKE WITH ANGIE, MY GIRLFRIEND!
GIRLFRIEND? ARE YOU OUT OF YOUR MIND?
OUT OF MY MIND... WITH LOVE!
NO, NO.. . I WAS TALKING TO HER.
Peirce

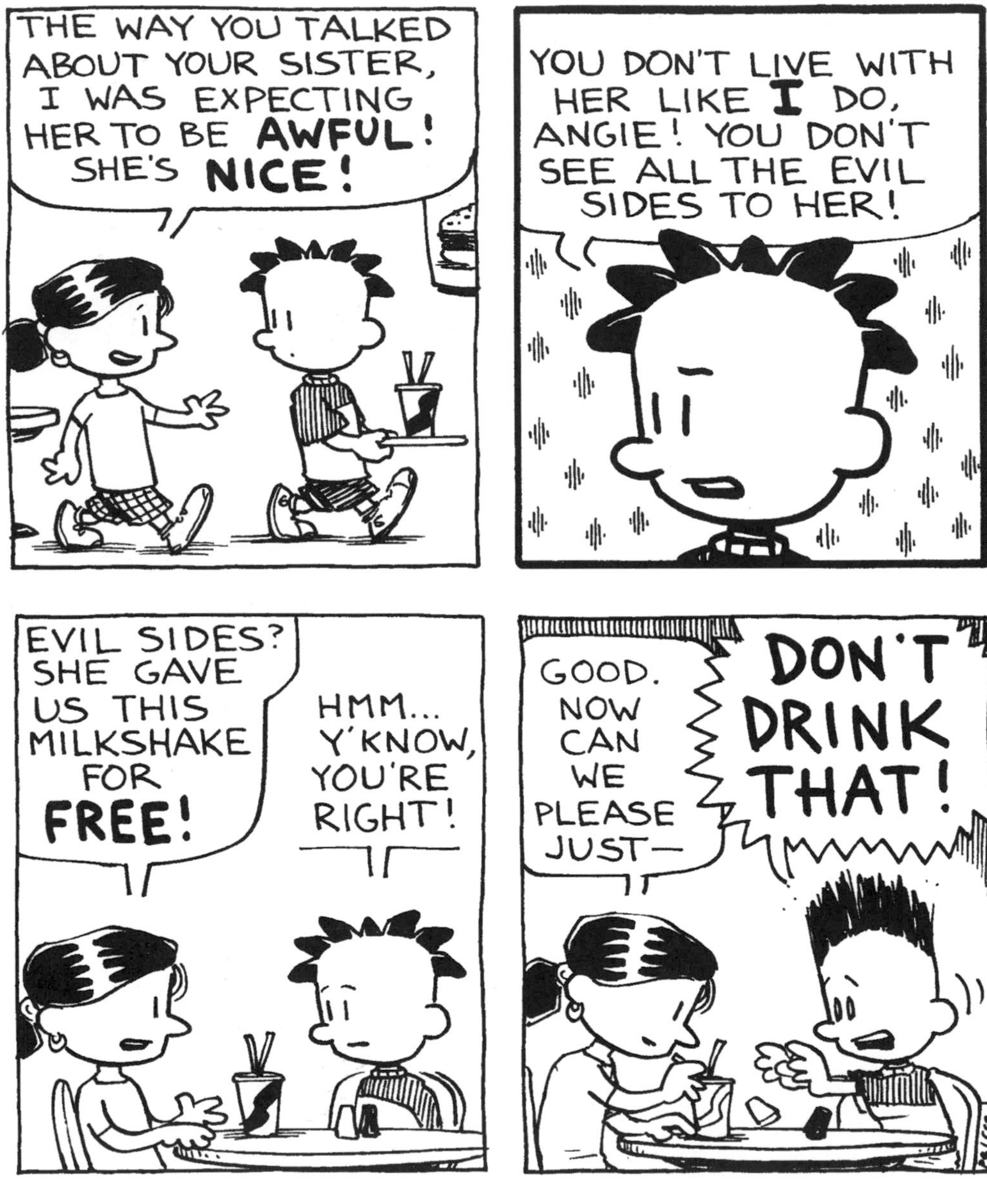
THE WAY YOU TALKED ABOUT YOUR SISTER, I WAS EXPECTING HER TO BE AWFUL! SHE'S NICE!
YOU DON'T LIVE WITH HER LIKE I DO, ANGIE! YOU DON'T SEE ALL THE EVIL SIDES TO HER!
EVIL SIDES? SHE GAVE US THIS MILKSHAKE FOR FREE!
HMM... Y'KNOW, YOU'RE RIGHT!
GOOD. NOW CAN WE PLEASE JUST—
DON'T DRINK THAT!

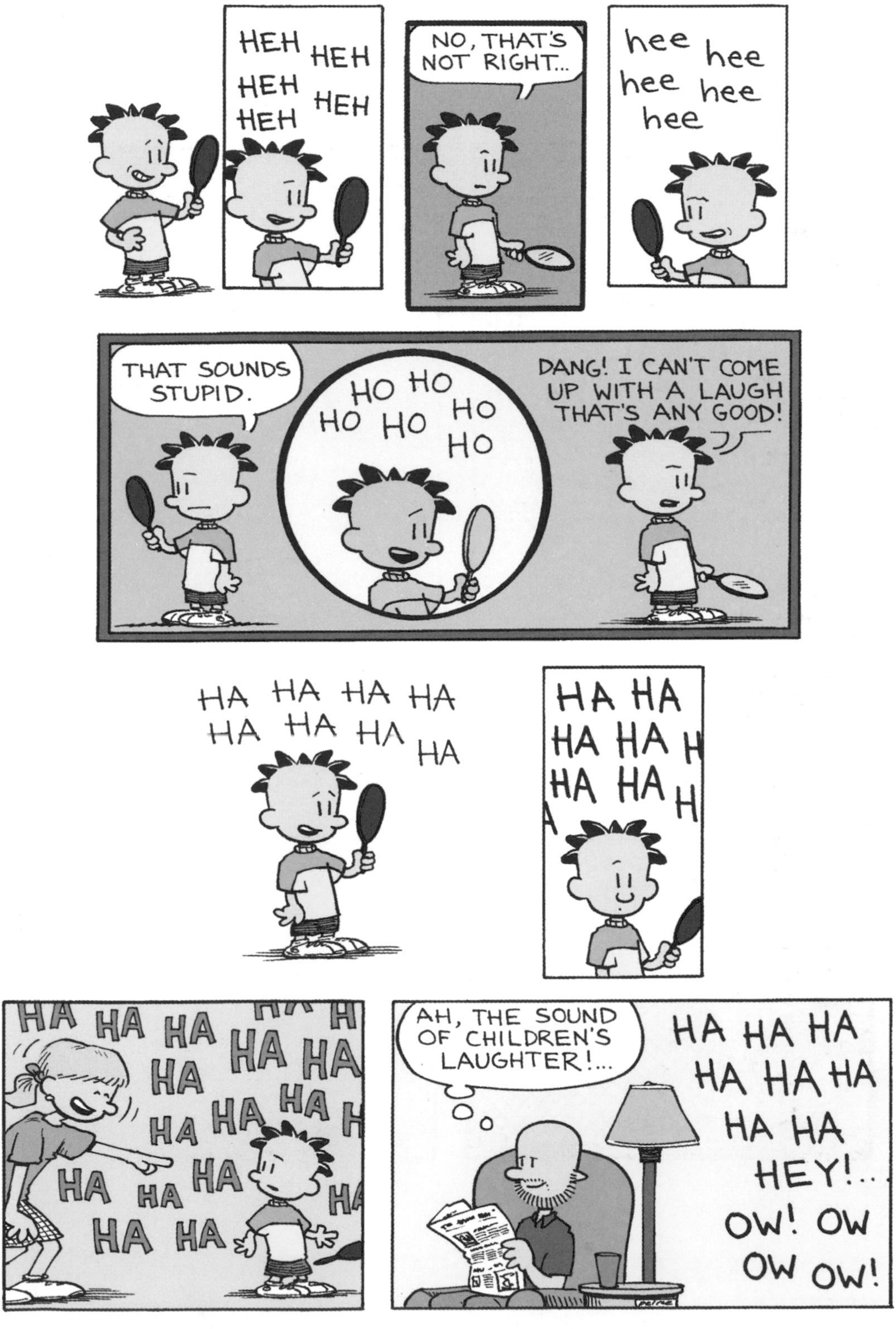
HEH HEH
HEH HEH
HEH HEH
NO, THAT'S NOT RIGHT...
hee hee
hee hee
hee
THAT SOUNDS STUPID.
HO HO
HO HO HO
HO
DANG! I CAN'T COME UP WITH A LAUGH THAT'S ANY GOOD!
HA HA HA HA
HA HA HA HA
HA HA
HA HA
HA HA
HA HA HA HA HA HA HA HA HA HA HA HA HA HA HA HA
AH, THE SOUND OF CHILDREN'S LAUGHTER!...
HA HA HA
HA HA HA
HA HA
HEY!...
OW! OW
OW OW!

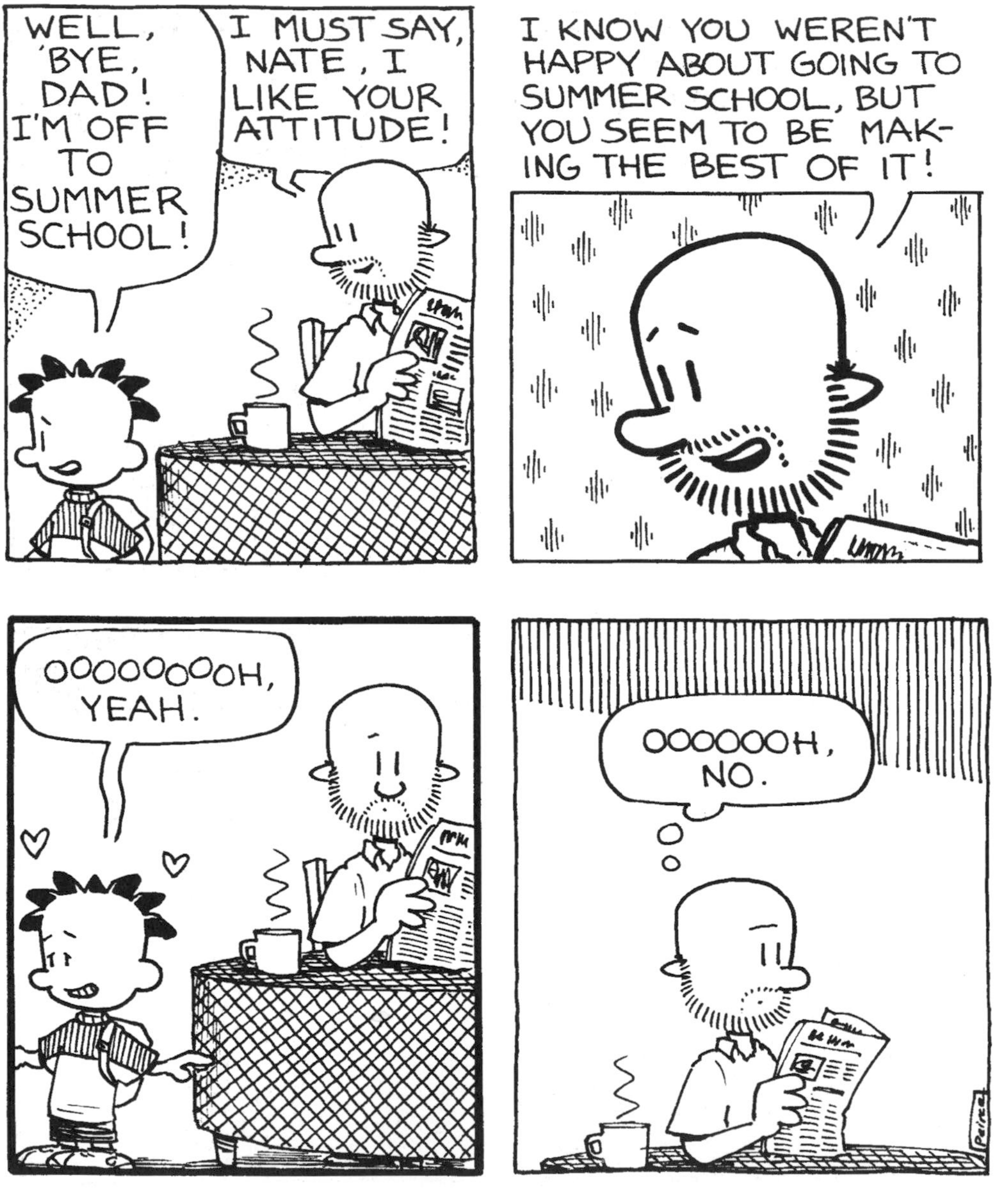
WELL, 'BYE, DAD! I'M OFF TO SUMMER SCHOOL!
I MUST SAY, NATE, I LIKE YOUR ATTITUDE!
I KNOW YOU WEREN'T HAPPY ABOUT GOING TO SUMMER SCHOOL, BUT YOU SEEM TO BE MAK-ING THE BEST OF IT!
OOOOOOOOH, YEAH.
OOOOOOH, NO.

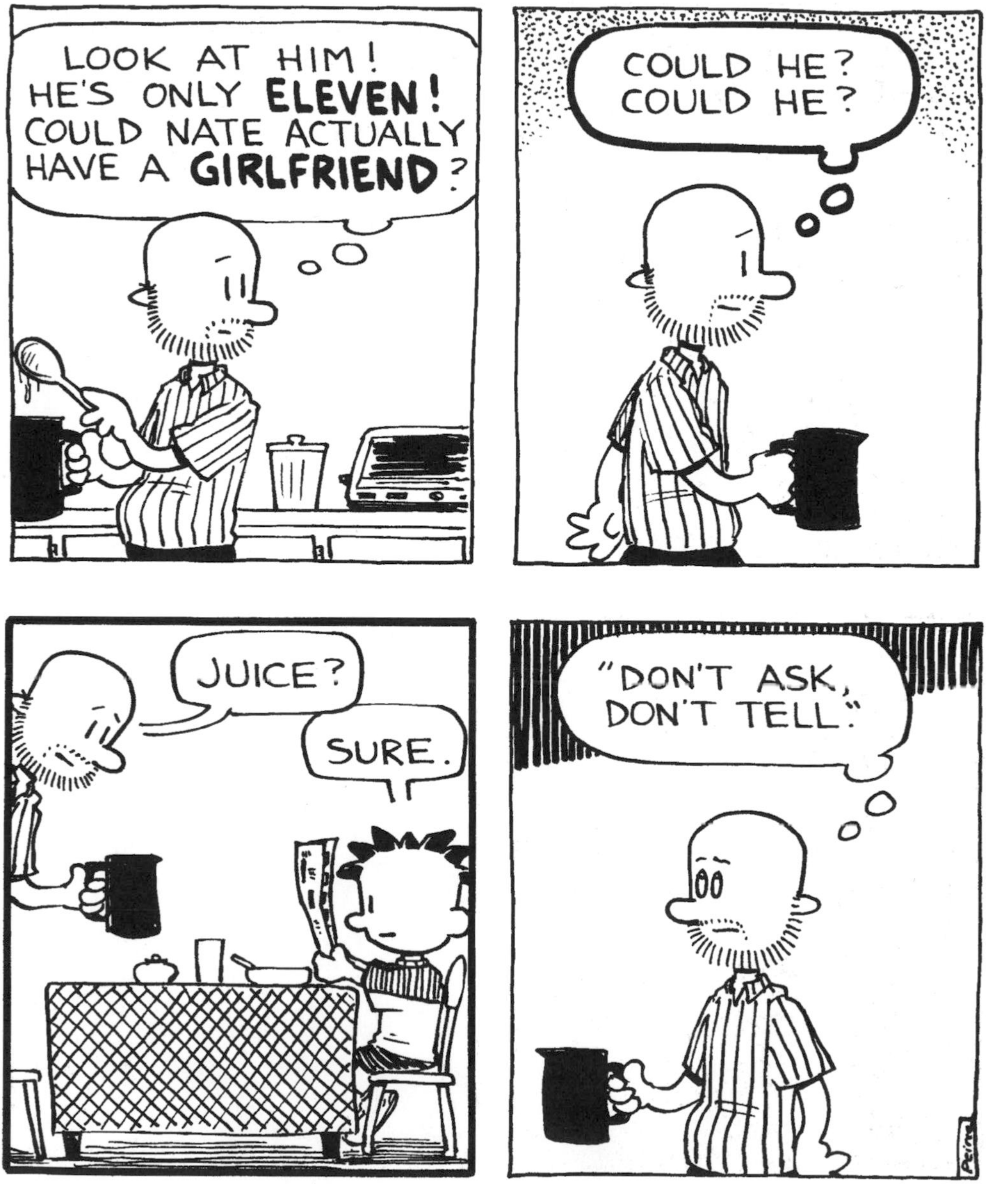
LOOK AT HIM! HE'S ONLY ELEVEN! COULD NATE ACTUALLY HAVE A GIRLFRIEND?
COULD HE? COULD HE?
JUICE?
SURE.
"DON'T ASK, DON'T TELL."
Peirce

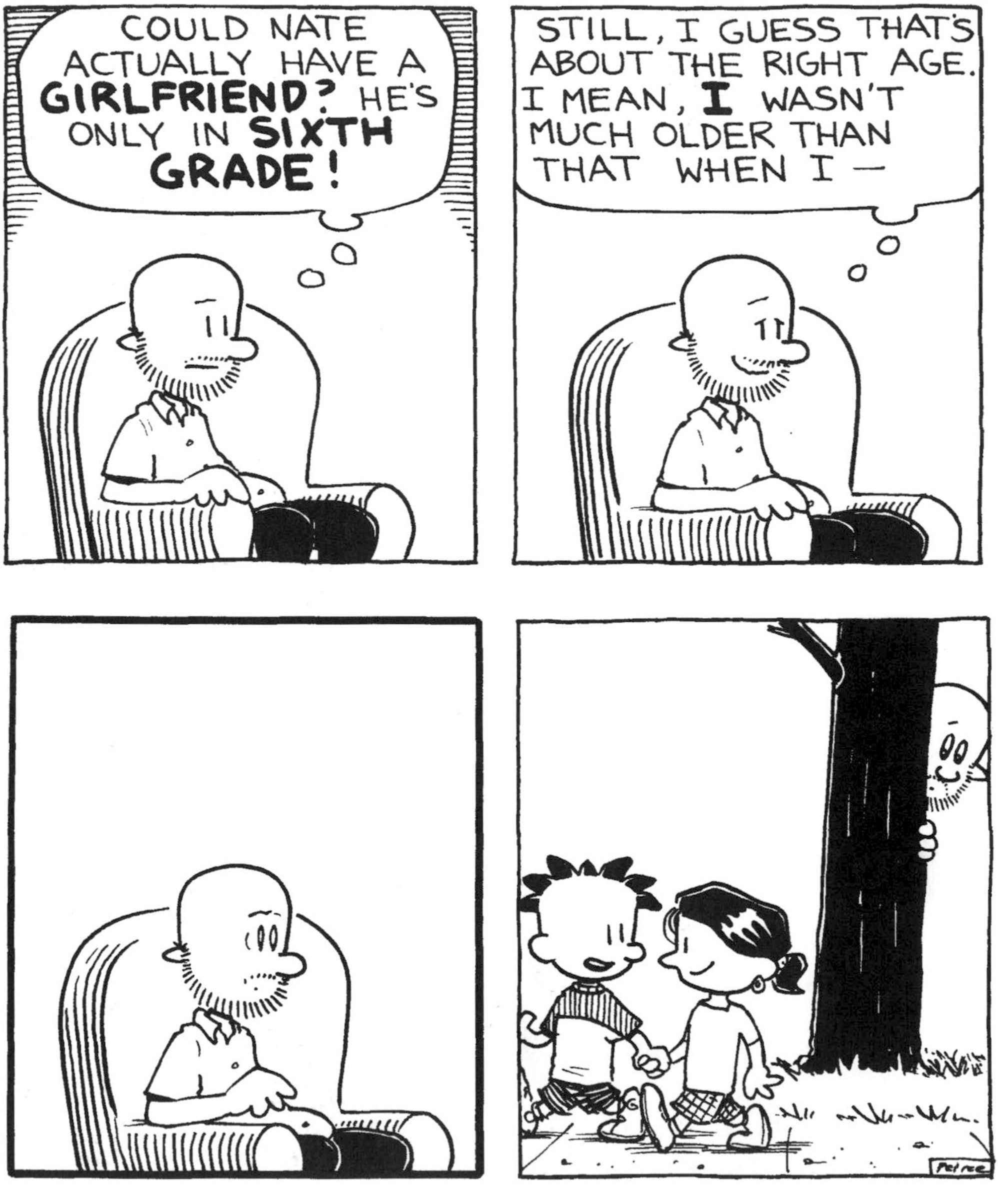
COULD NATE ACTUALLY HAVE A **GIRLFRIEND?** HE'S ONLY IN **SIXTH GRADE**!
STILL, I GUESS THAT'S ABOUT THE RIGHT AGE. I MEAN, **I** WASN'T MUCH OLDER THAN THAT WHEN I —
Peirce

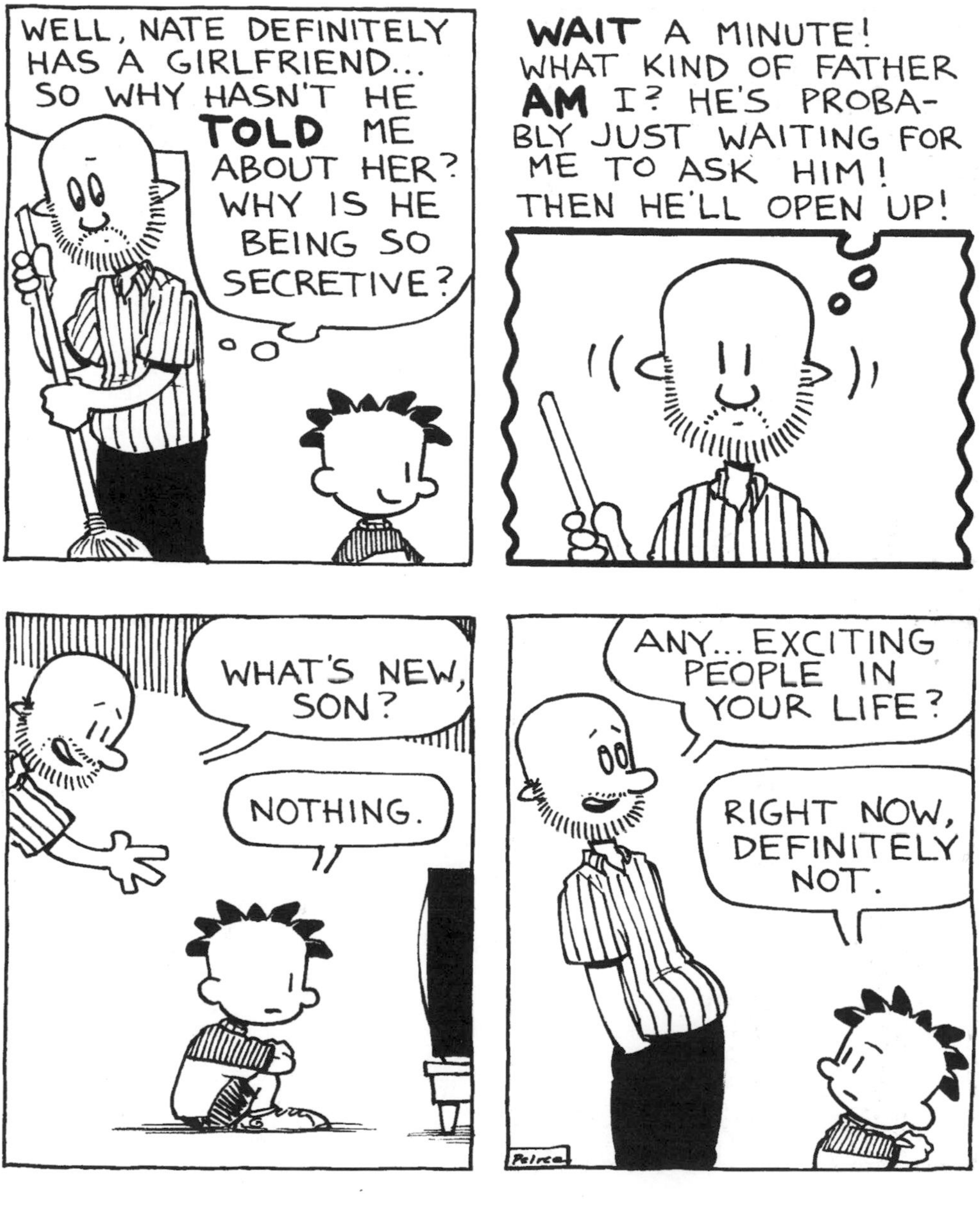
WELL, NATE DEFINITELY HAS A GIRLFRIEND... SO WHY HASN'T HE **TOLD** ME ABOUT HER? WHY IS HE BEING SO SECRETIVE?
WAIT A MINUTE! WHAT KIND OF FATHER **AM** I? HE'S PROBABLY JUST WAITING FOR ME TO ASK HIM! THEN HE'LL OPEN UP!
WHAT'S NEW, SON?
NOTHING.
ANY... EXCITING PEOPLE IN YOUR LIFE?
RIGHT NOW, DEFINITELY NOT.
Peirce

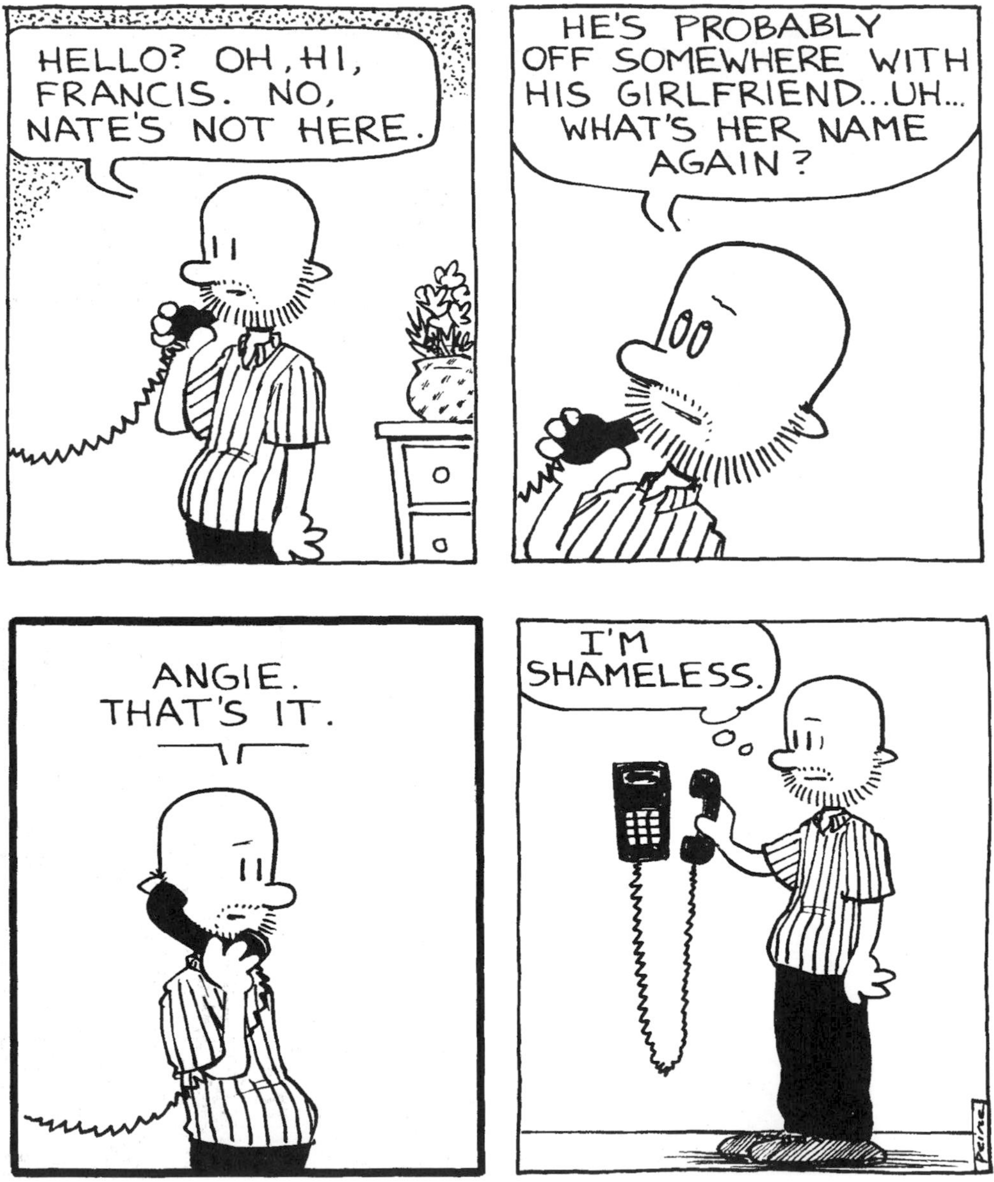
HELLO? OH, HI, FRANCIS. NO, NATE'S NOT HERE.
HE'S PROBABLY OFF SOMEWHERE WITH HIS GIRLFRIEND...UH... WHAT'S HER NAME AGAIN?
ANGIE. THAT'S IT.
I'M SHAMELESS.

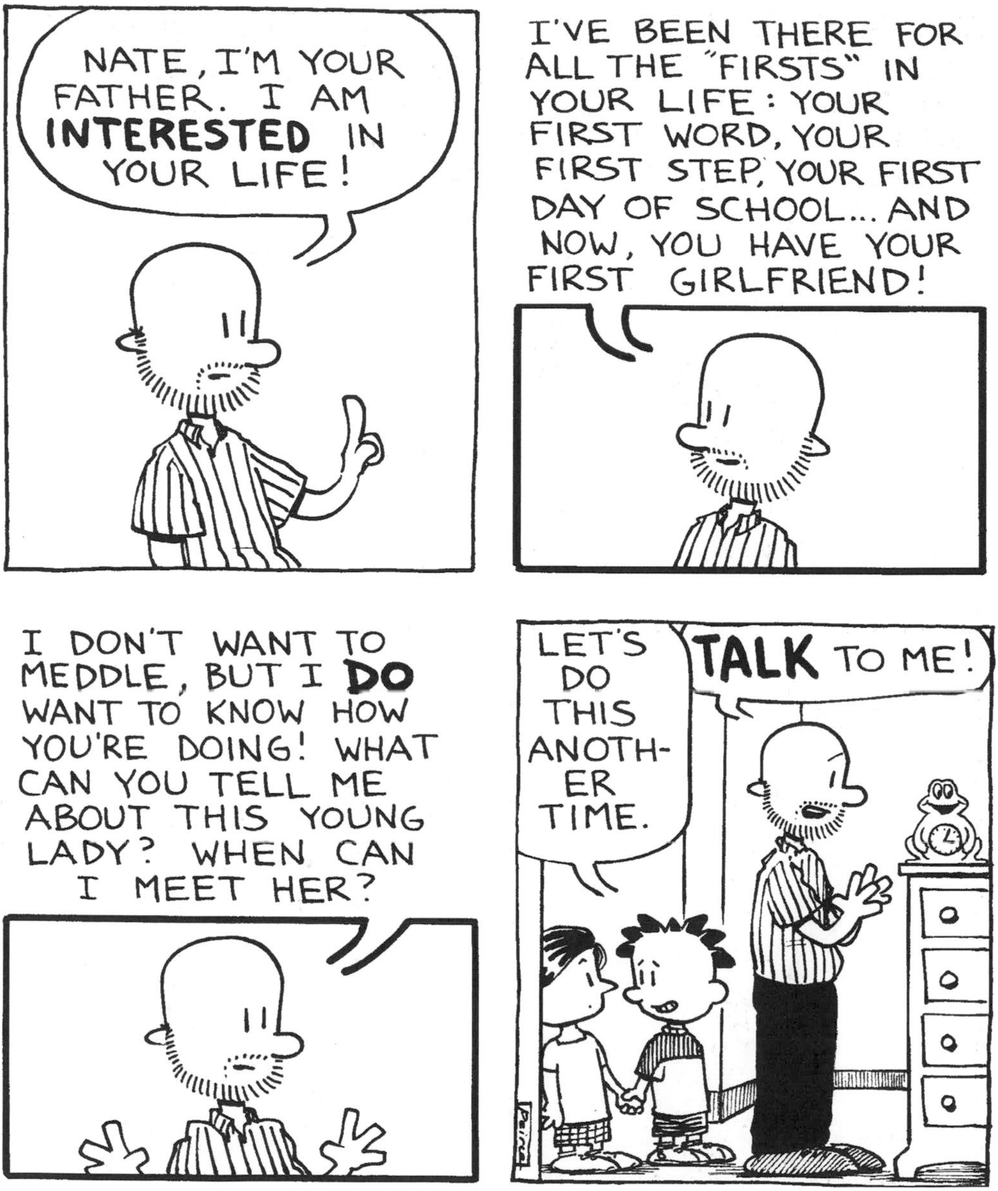
NATE, I'M YOUR FATHER. I AM **INTERESTED** IN YOUR LIFE!
I'VE BEEN THERE FOR ALL THE "FIRSTS" IN YOUR LIFE: YOUR FIRST WORD, YOUR FIRST STEP, YOUR FIRST DAY OF SCHOOL... AND NOW, YOU HAVE YOUR FIRST GIRLFRIEND!
I DON'T WANT TO MEDDLE, BUT I **DO** WANT TO KNOW HOW YOU'RE DOING! WHAT CAN YOU TELL ME ABOUT THIS YOUNG LADY? WHEN CAN I MEET HER?
LET'S DO THIS ANOTH- ER TIME.
TALK TO ME!
PEIRCE

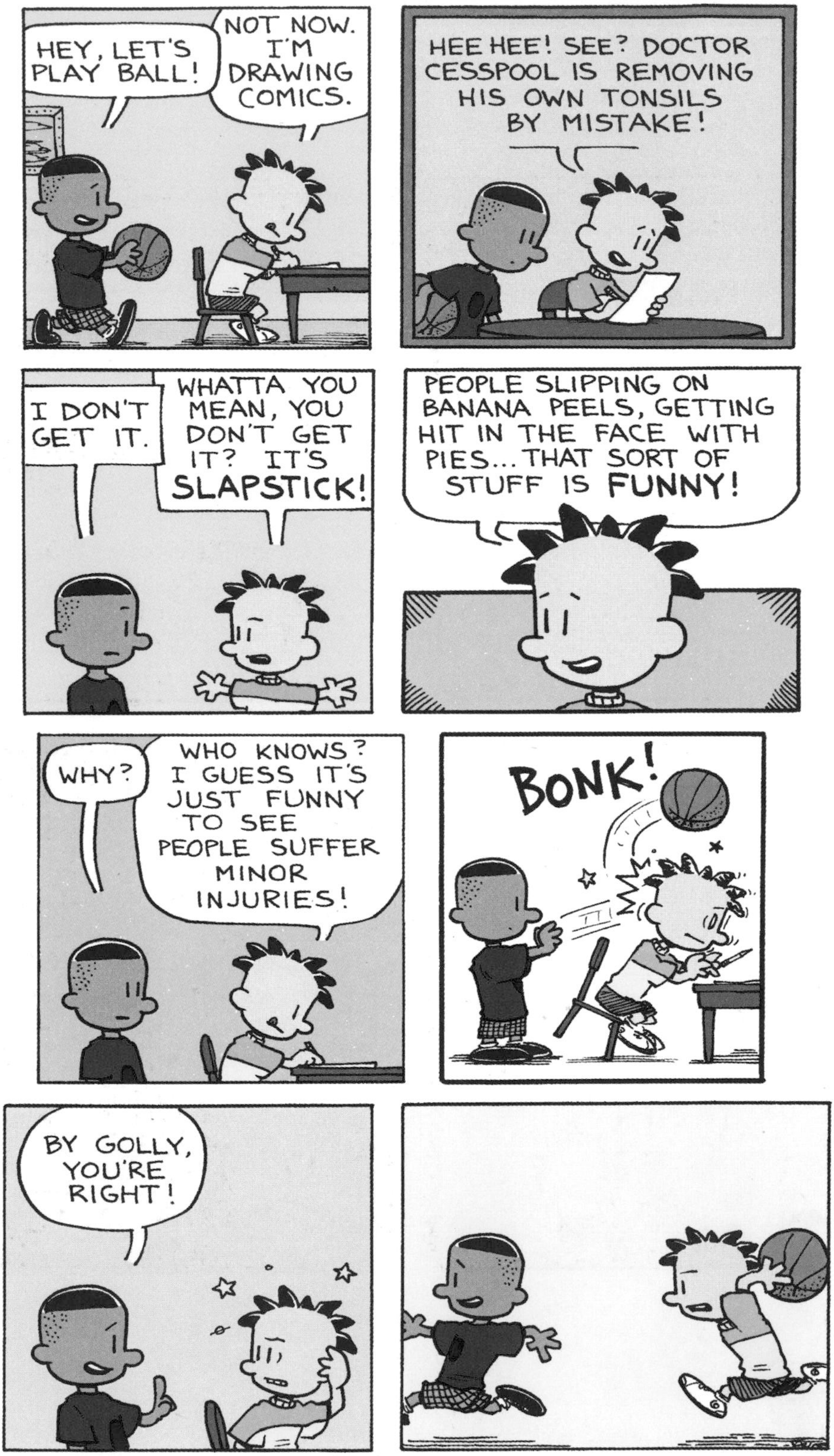
HEY, LET'S PLAY BALL!
NOT NOW. I'M DRAWING COMICS.
HEE HEE! SEE? DOCTOR CESSPOOL IS REMOVING HIS OWN TONSILS BY MISTAKE!
I DON'T GET IT.
WHATTA YOU MEAN, YOU DON'T GET IT? IT'S SLAPSTICK!
PEOPLE SLIPPING ON BANANA PEELS, GETTING HIT IN THE FACE WITH PIES... THAT SORT OF STUFF IS FUNNY!
WHY?
WHO KNOWS? I GUESS IT'S JUST FUNNY TO SEE PEOPLE SUFFER MINOR INJURIES!
BONK!
BY GOLLY, YOU'RE RIGHT!

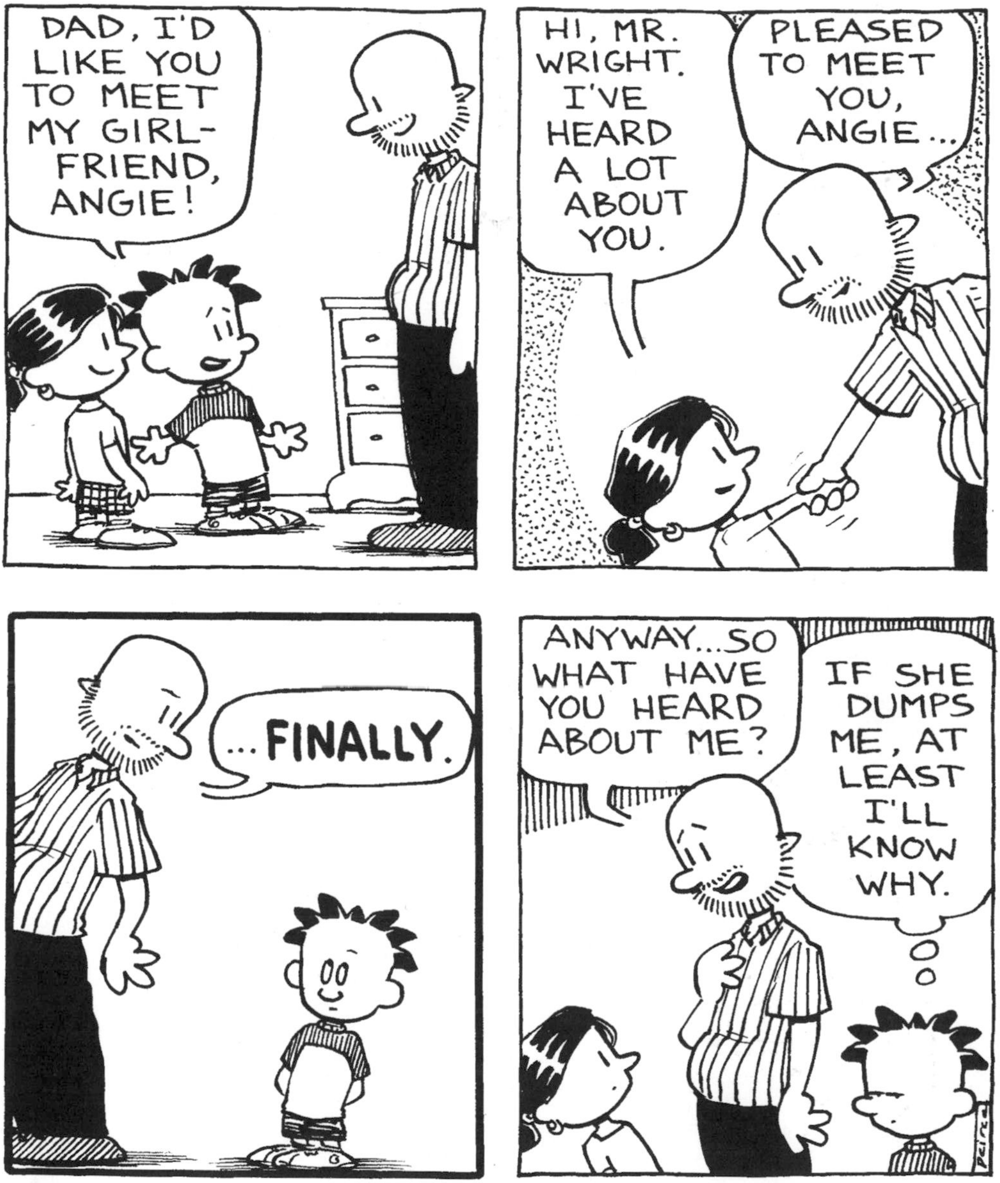
DAD, I'D LIKE YOU TO MEET MY GIRL-FRIEND, ANGIE!
HI, MR. WRIGHT. I'VE HEARD A LOT ABOUT YOU.
PLEASED TO MEET YOU, ANGIE...
...FINALLY.
ANYWAY...SO WHAT HAVE YOU HEARD ABOUT ME?
IF SHE DUMPS ME, AT LEAST I'LL KNOW WHY.

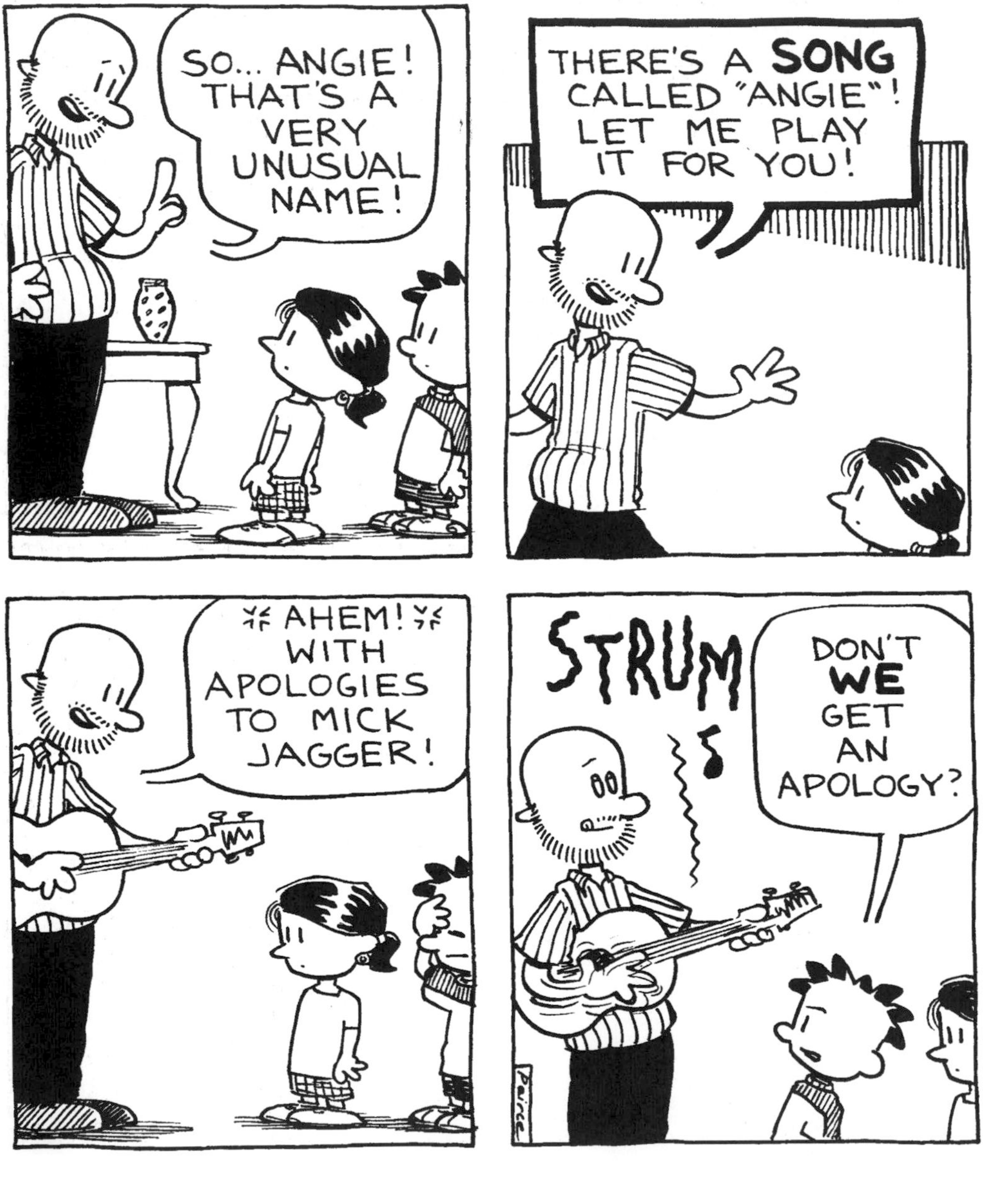
SO... ANGIE! THAT'S A VERY UNUSUAL NAME!
THERE'S A **SONG** CALLED "ANGIE"! LET ME PLAY IT FOR YOU!
AHEM! WITH APOLOGIES TO MICK JAGGER!
STRUM
DON'T **WE** GET AN APOLOGY?
PEIRCE

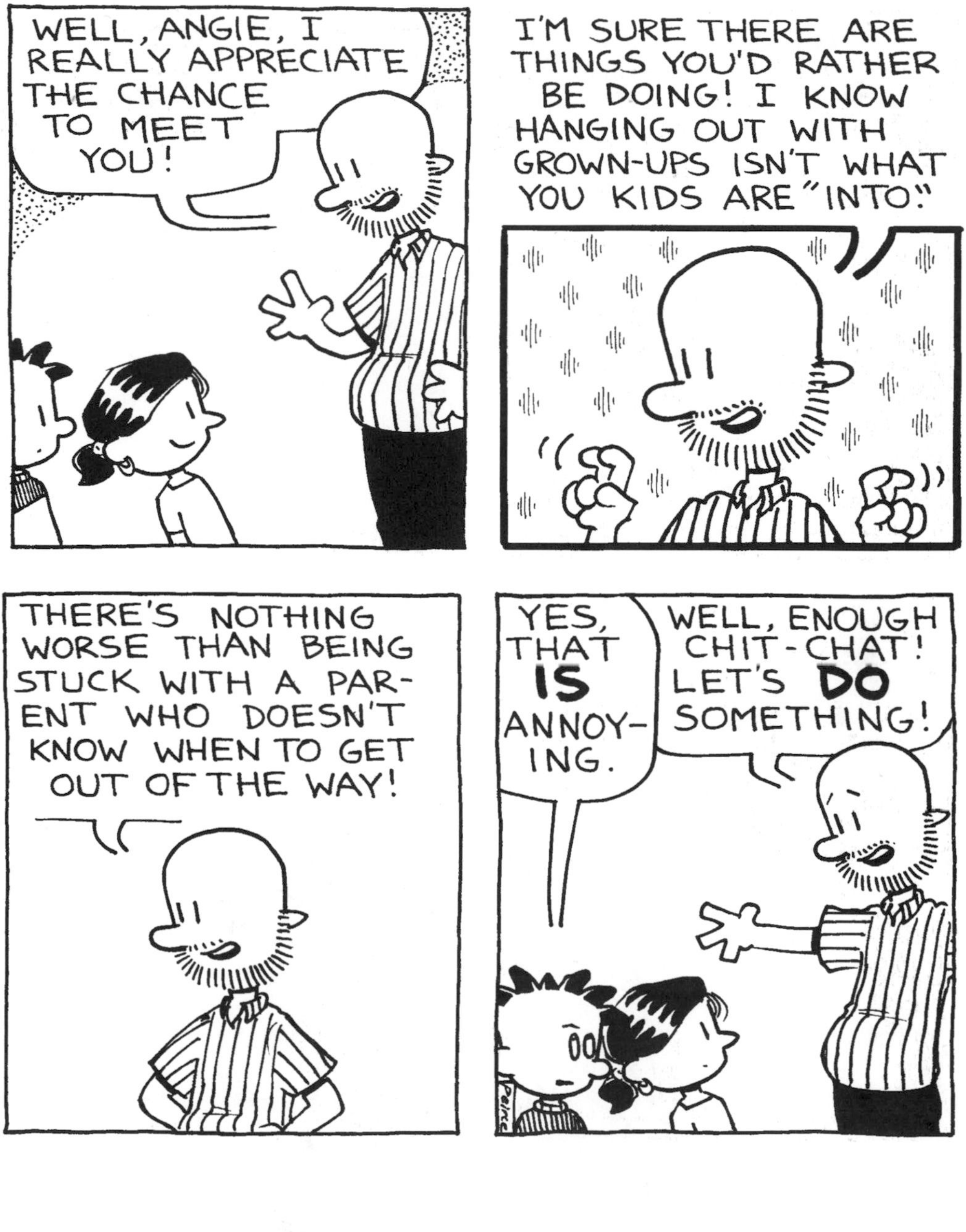
WELL, ANGIE, I REALLY APPRECIATE THE CHANCE TO MEET YOU!
I'M SURE THERE ARE THINGS YOU'D RATHER BE DOING! I KNOW HANGING OUT WITH GROWN-UPS ISN'T WHAT YOU KIDS ARE "INTO."
THERE'S NOTHING WORSE THAN BEING STUCK WITH A PAR-ENT WHO DOESN'T KNOW WHEN TO GET OUT OF THE WAY!
YES, THAT **IS** ANNOY-ING.
WELL, ENOUGH CHIT-CHAT! LET'S **DO** SOMETHING!
PEIRCE

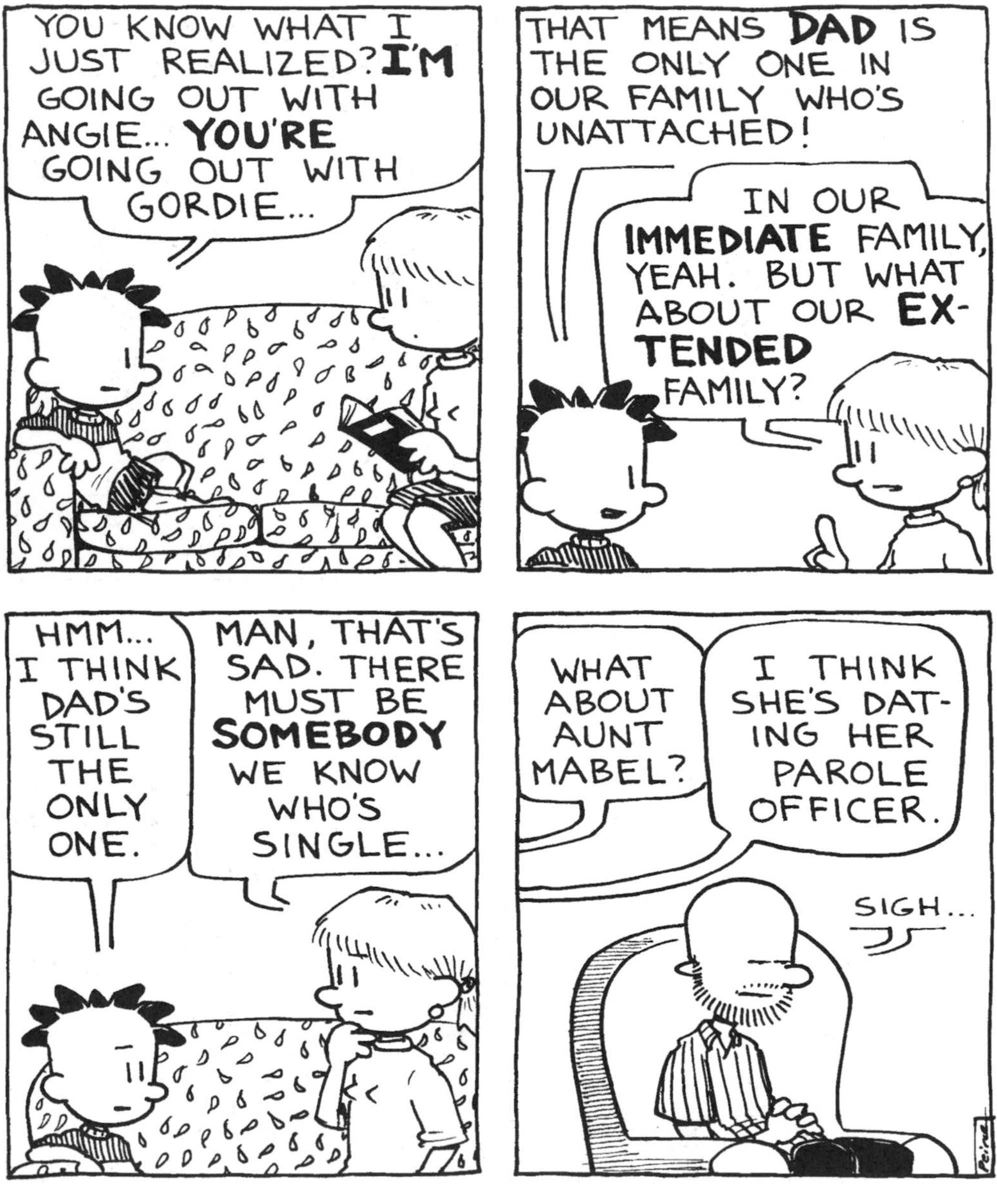
YOU KNOW WHAT I JUST REALIZED? I'M GOING OUT WITH ANGIE... YOU'RE GOING OUT WITH GORDIE...
THAT MEANS DAD IS THE ONLY ONE IN OUR FAMILY WHO'S UNATTACHED!
IN OUR IMMEDIATE FAMILY, YEAH. BUT WHAT ABOUT OUR EXTENDED FAMILY?
HMM... I THINK DAD'S STILL THE ONLY ONE.
MAN, THAT'S SAD. THERE MUST BE SOMEBODY WE KNOW WHO'S SINGLE...
WHAT ABOUT AUNT MABEL?
I THINK SHE'S DATING HER PAROLE OFFICER.
SIGH...

TIME OUT.
I NEED TO
TALK TO THE
PITCHER.

LISTEN, BUDDY... MY
NEW GIRLFRIEND'S HERE
AT THE GAME, AND I
WANT TO IMPRESS
HER, IF YOU GET MY
DRIFT...

I'LL GO GET READY,
AND YOU MAKE ME
LOOK GOOD, OKAY?
GIVE ME A NICE FAT
ONE, RIGHT DOWN
THE PIKE! OKAY?
THANKS, MAN!

doof!

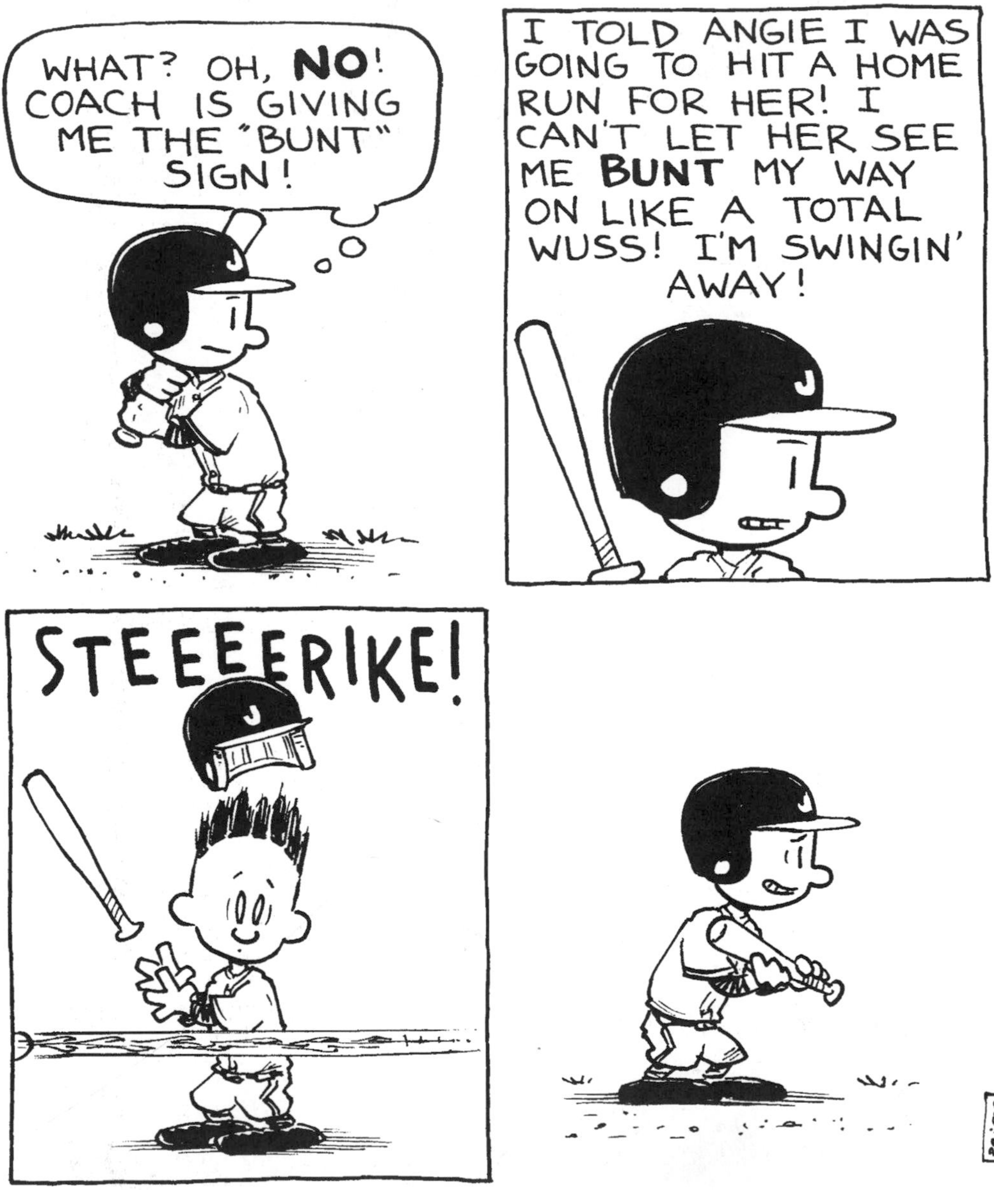
WHAT? OH, **NO**! COACH IS GIVING ME THE "BUNT" SIGN!
I TOLD ANGIE I WAS GOING TO HIT A HOME RUN FOR HER! I CAN'T LET HER SEE ME **BUNT** MY WAY ON LIKE A TOTAL WUSS! I'M SWINGIN' AWAY!
STEEEERIKE!
Peirce

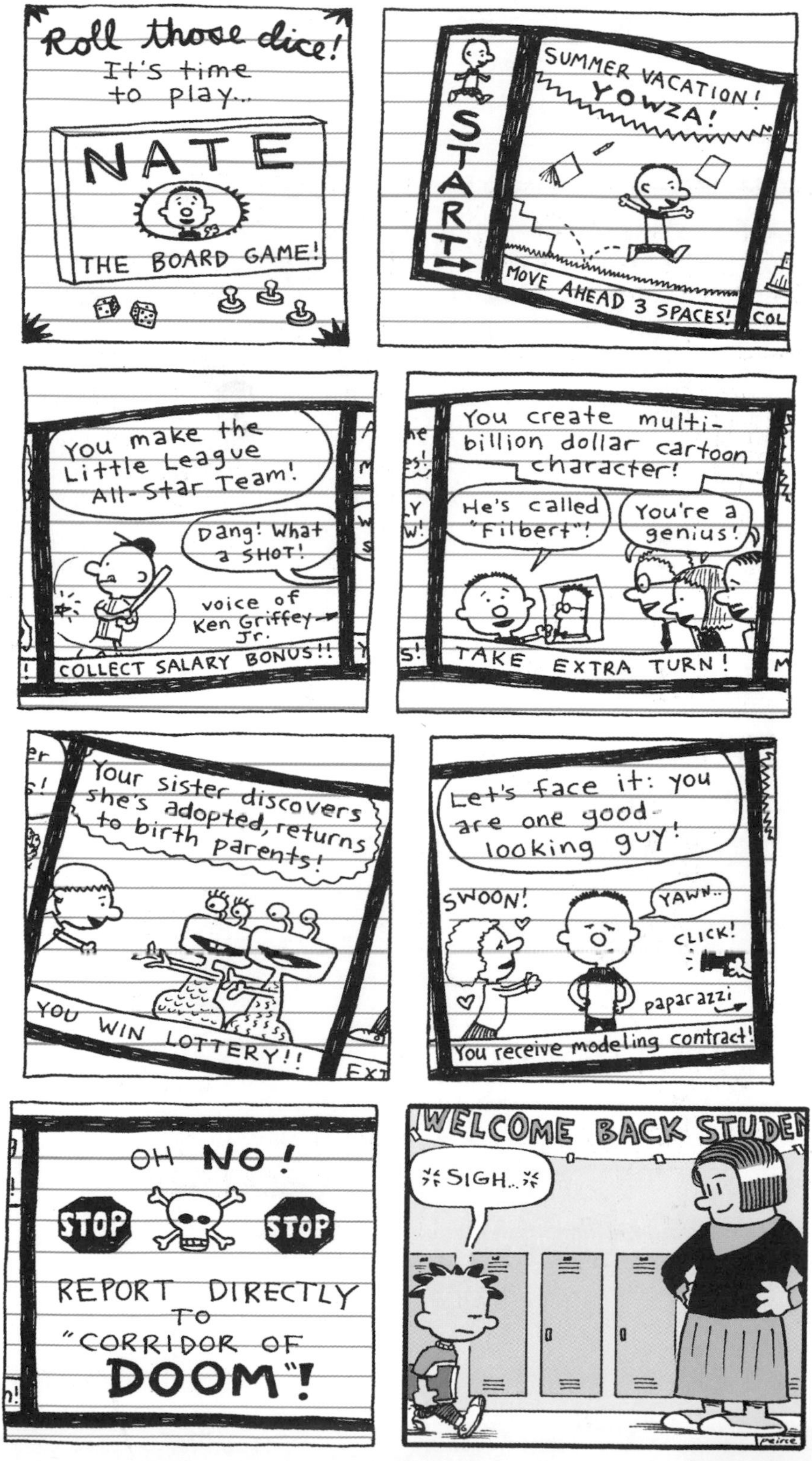
Roll those dice! It's time to play...
NATE
THE BOARD GAME!
START
SUMMER VACATION! YOWZA!
MOVE AHEAD 3 SPACES!
You make the Little League All-Star Team!
Dang! What a SHOT!
voice of Ken Griffey Jr.
COLLECT SALARY BONUS!!
You create multi-billion dollar cartoon character!
He's called "Filbert"!
You're a genius!
TAKE EXTRA TURN!
Your sister discovers she's adopted, returns to birth parents!
YOU WIN LOTTERY!!
Let's face it: you are one good-looking guy!
SWOON!
YAWN..
CLICK!
paparazzi
You receive modeling contract!
OH NO!
STOP
STOP
REPORT DIRECTLY TO "CORRIDOR OF DOOM"!
WELCOME BACK STUDEN
SIGH..
peirce

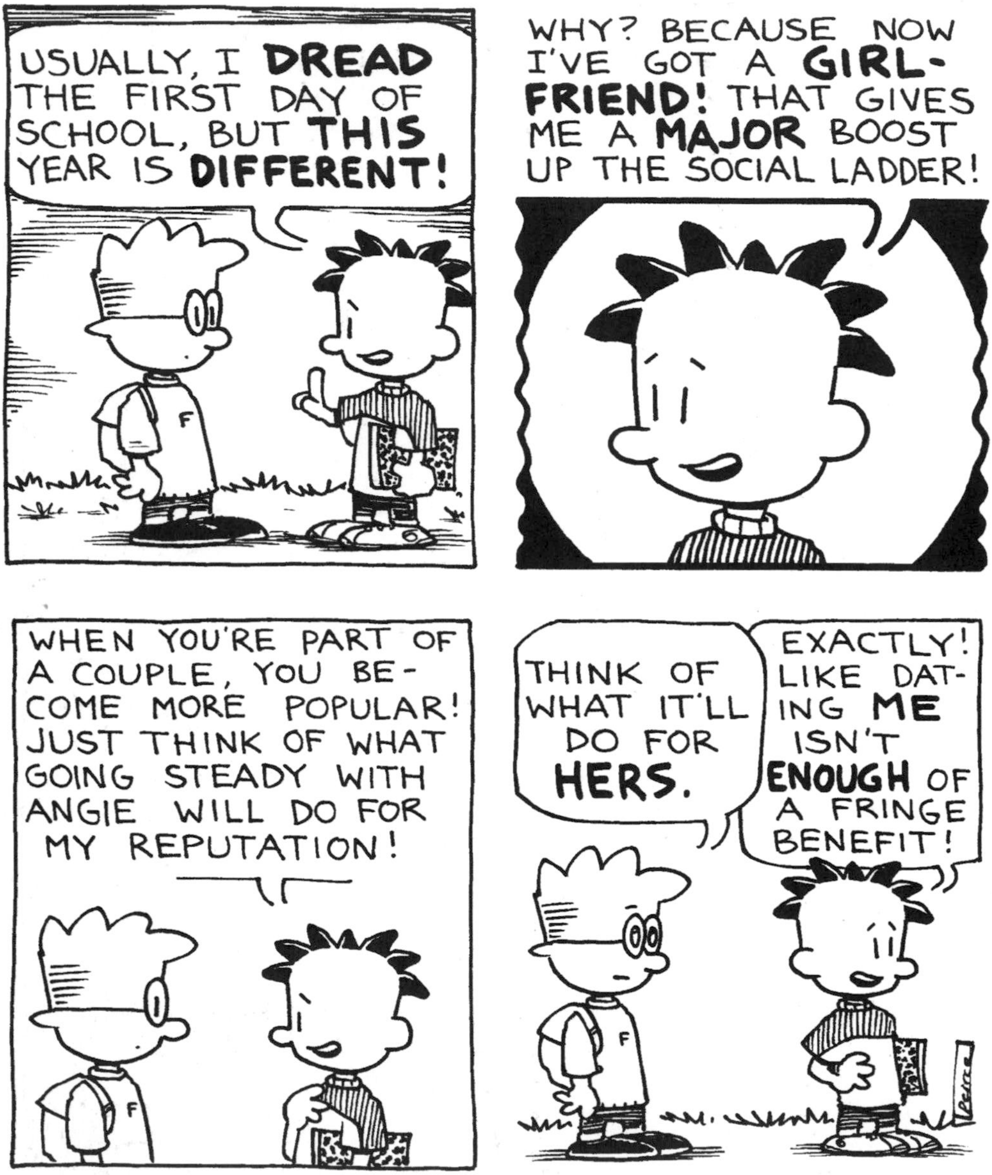
USUALLY, I DREAD THE FIRST DAY OF SCHOOL, BUT THIS YEAR IS DIFFERENT!
WHY? BECAUSE NOW I'VE GOT A GIRL-FRIEND! THAT GIVES ME A MAJOR BOOST UP THE SOCIAL LADDER!
WHEN YOU'RE PART OF A COUPLE, YOU BE-COME MORE POPULAR! JUST THINK OF WHAT GOING STEADY WITH ANGIE WILL DO FOR MY REPUTATION!
THINK OF WHAT IT'LL DO FOR HERS.
EXACTLY! LIKE DAT-ING ME ISN'T ENOUGH OF A FRINGE BENEFIT!

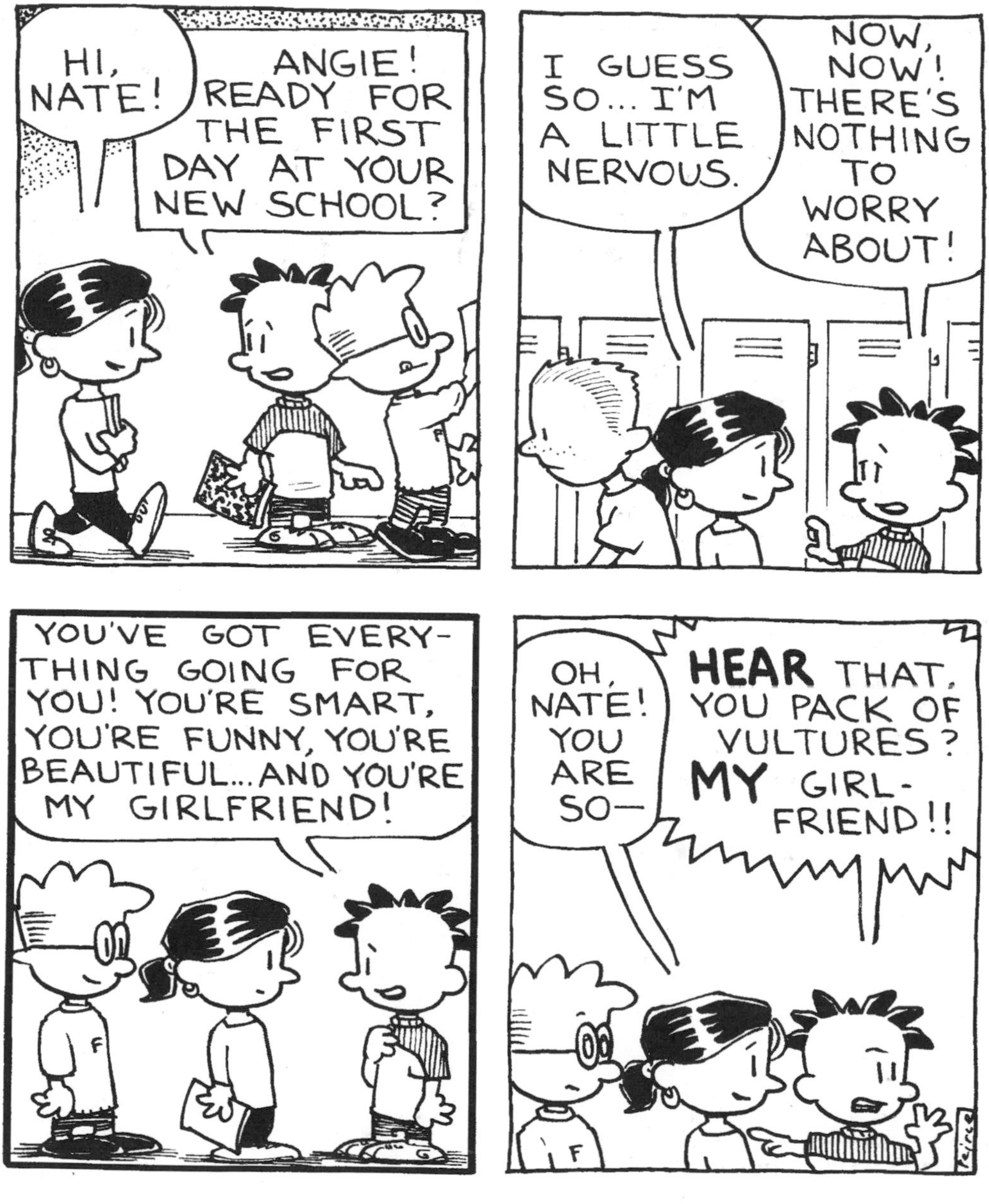
HI, NATE!
ANGIE! READY FOR THE FIRST DAY AT YOUR NEW SCHOOL?
I GUESS SO... I'M A LITTLE NERVOUS.
NOW, NOW! THERE'S NOTHING TO WORRY ABOUT!
YOU'VE GOT EVERYTHING GOING FOR YOU! YOU'RE SMART, YOU'RE FUNNY, YOU'RE BEAUTIFUL... AND YOU'RE MY GIRLFRIEND!
OH, NATE! YOU ARE SO—
HEAR THAT, YOU PACK OF VULTURES? MY GIRLFRIEND!!

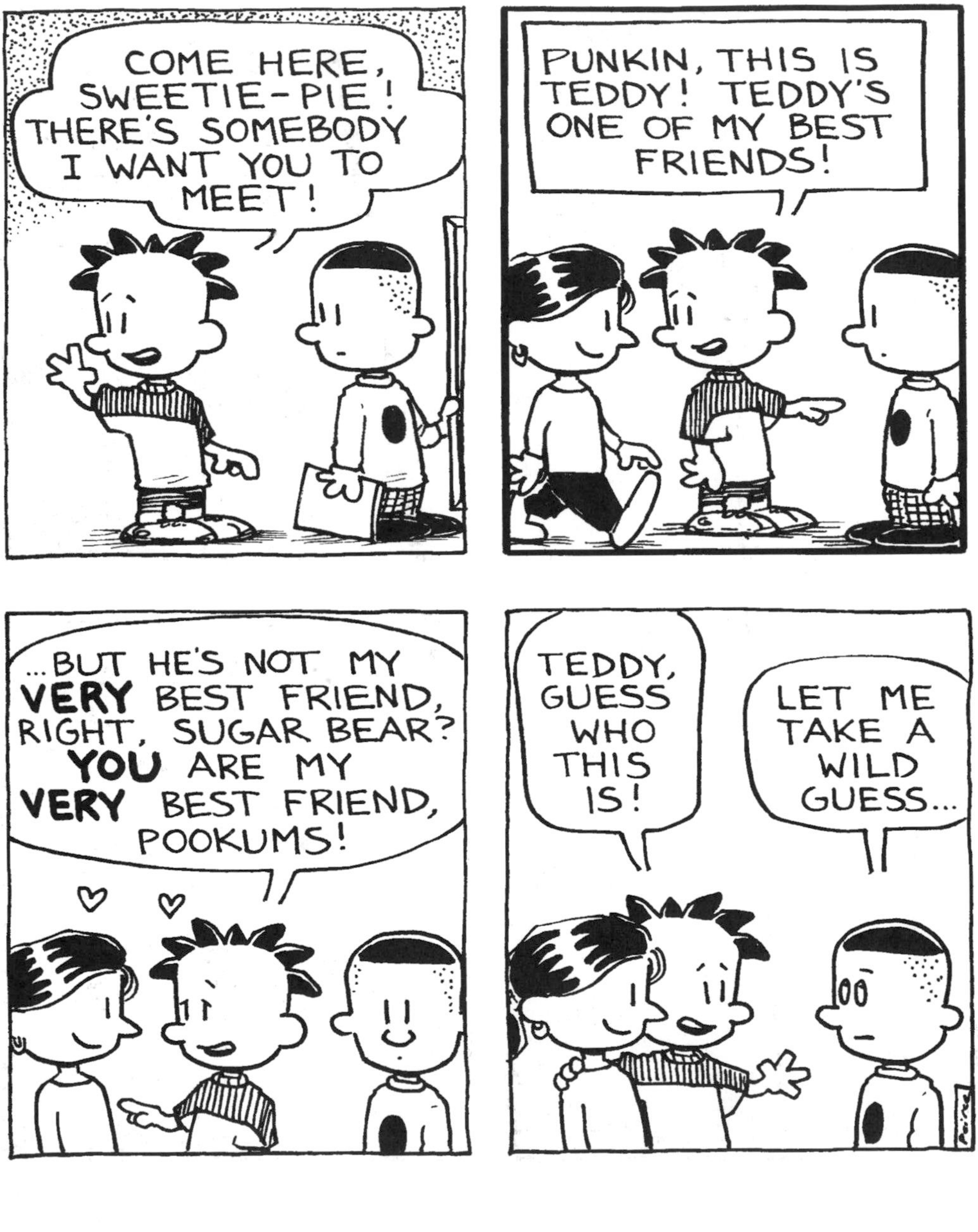
COME HERE, SWEETIE-PIE! THERE'S SOMEBODY I WANT YOU TO MEET!
PUNKIN, THIS IS TEDDY! TEDDY'S ONE OF MY BEST FRIENDS!
...BUT HE'S NOT MY **VERY** BEST FRIEND, RIGHT, SUGAR BEAR? **YOU** ARE MY **VERY** BEST FRIEND, POOKUMS!
TEDDY, GUESS WHO THIS IS!
LET ME TAKE A WILD GUESS...

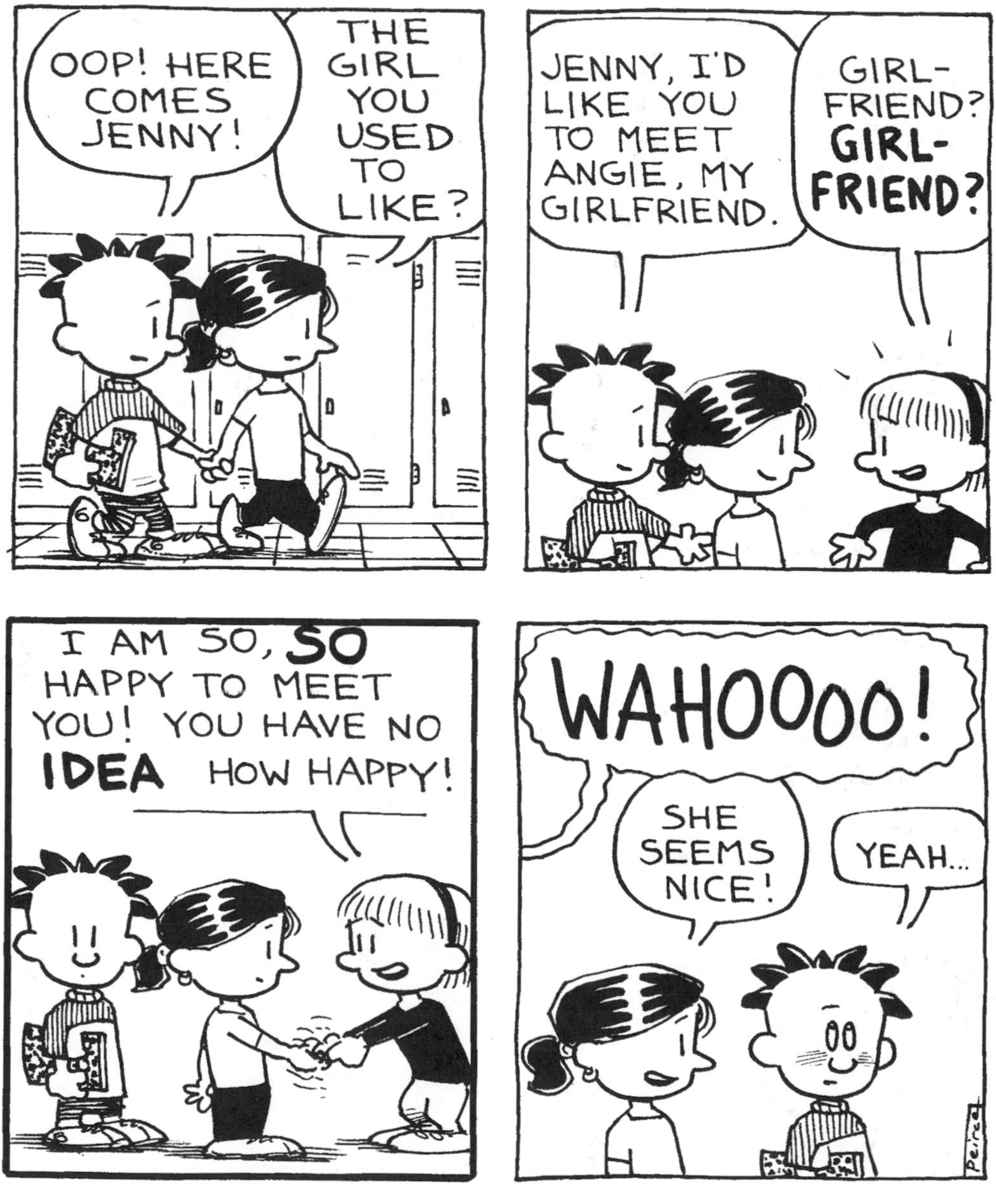
OOP! HERE COMES JENNY!
THE GIRL YOU USED TO LIKE?
JENNY, I'D LIKE YOU TO MEET ANGIE, MY GIRLFRIEND.
GIRL-FRIEND? GIRL-FRIEND?
I AM SO, SO HAPPY TO MEET YOU! YOU HAVE NO IDEA HOW HAPPY!
WAHOOOO!
SHE SEEMS NICE!
YEAH...
Peirce

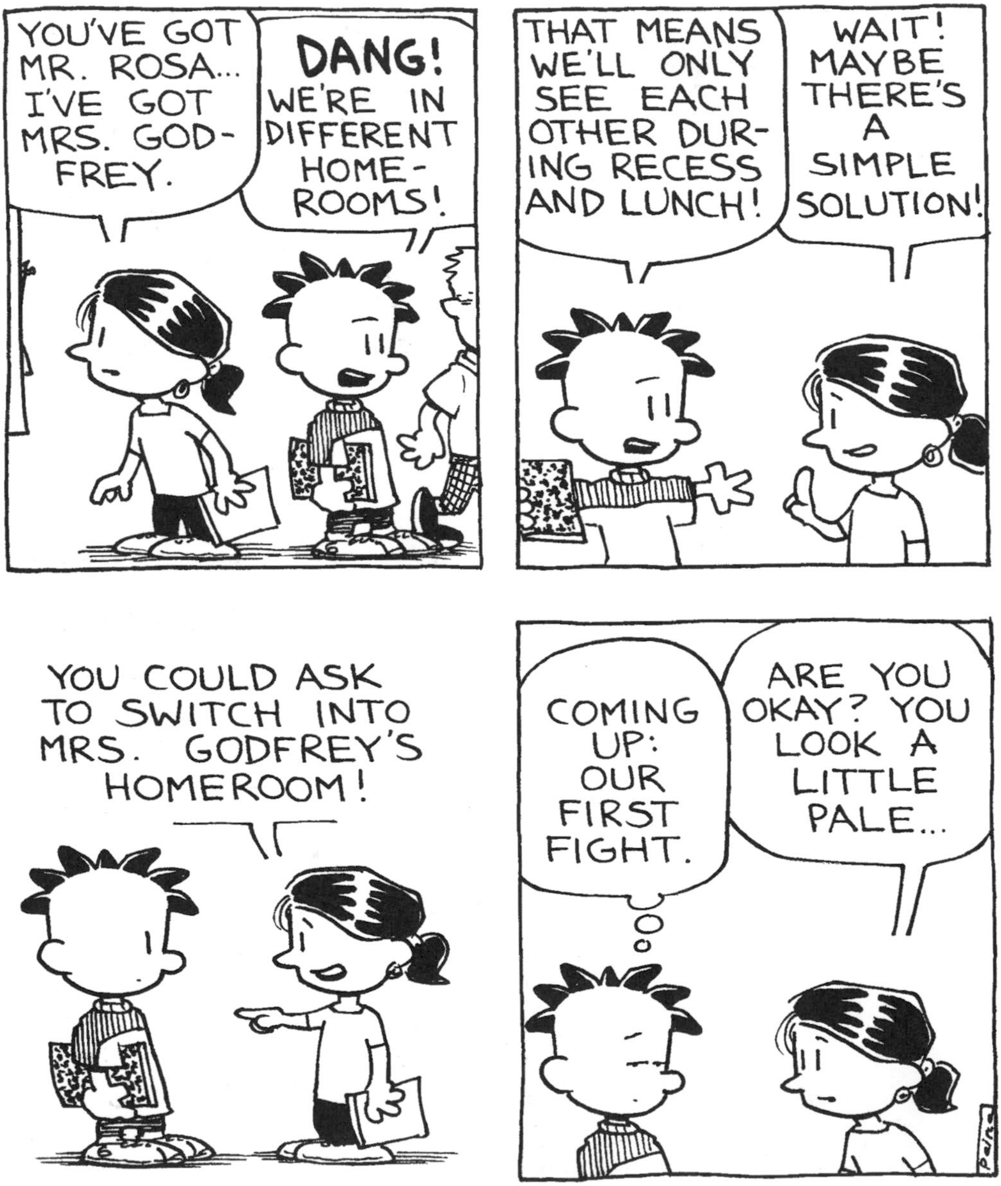

YOU'VE GOT MR. ROSA... I'VE GOT MRS. GOD-FREY.
DANG! WE'RE IN DIFFERENT HOME-ROOMS!
THAT MEANS WE'LL ONLY SEE EACH OTHER DUR-ING RECESS AND LUNCH!
WAIT! MAYBE THERE'S A SIMPLE SOLUTION!
YOU COULD ASK TO SWITCH INTO MRS. GODFREY'S HOMEROOM!
COMING UP: OUR FIRST FIGHT.
ARE YOU OKAY? YOU LOOK A LITTLE PALE...

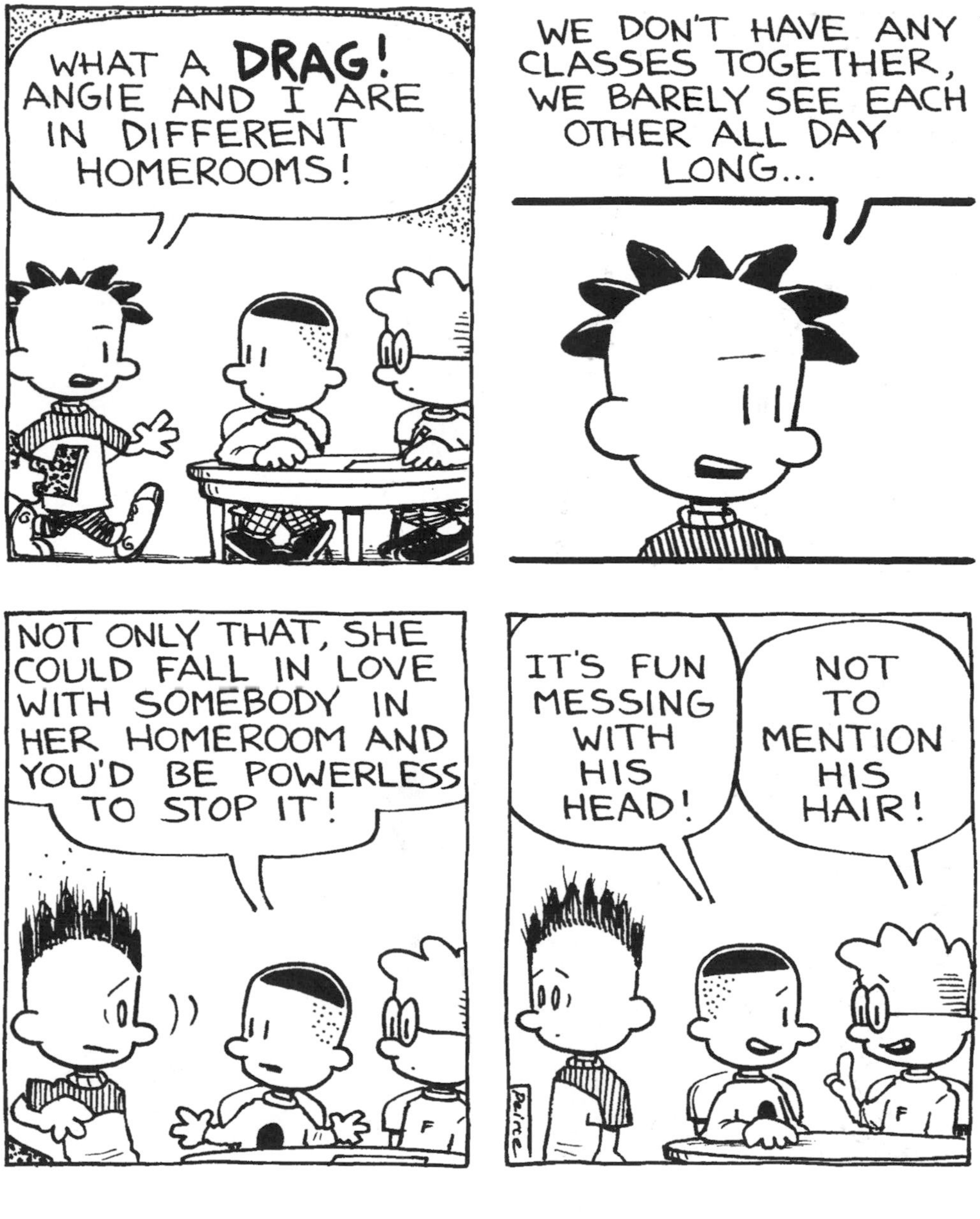
WHAT A DRAG! ANGIE AND I ARE IN DIFFERENT HOMEROOMS!
WE DON'T HAVE ANY CLASSES TOGETHER, WE BARELY SEE EACH OTHER ALL DAY LONG...
NOT ONLY THAT, SHE COULD FALL IN LOVE WITH SOMEBODY IN HER HOMEROOM AND YOU'D BE POWERLESS TO STOP IT!
IT'S FUN MESSING WITH HIS HEAD!
NOT TO MENTION HIS HAIR!
PEIRCE

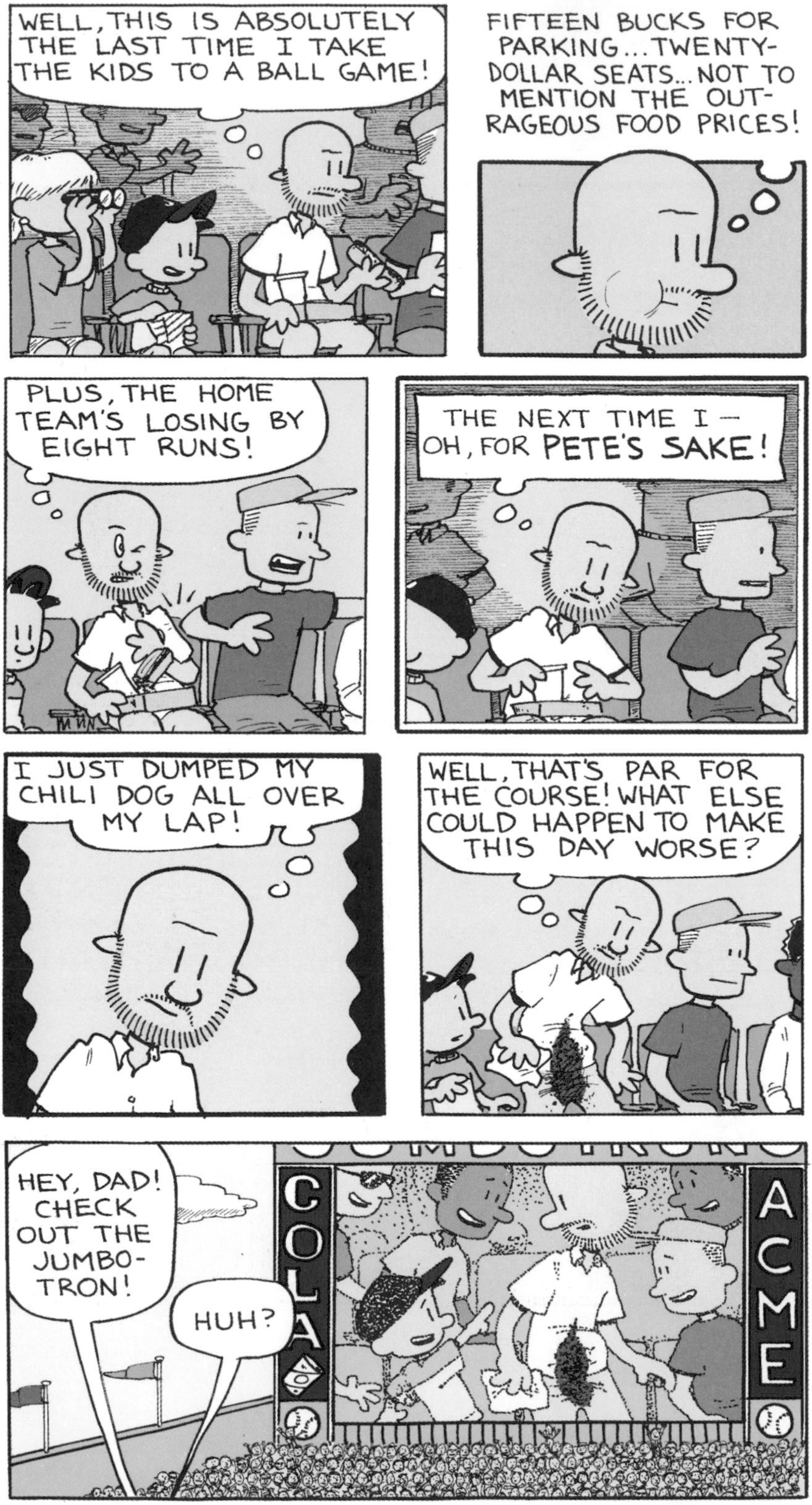
WELL, THIS IS ABSOLUTELY THE LAST TIME I TAKE THE KIDS TO A BALL GAME!
FIFTEEN BUCKS FOR PARKING... TWENTY-DOLLAR SEATS... NOT TO MENTION THE OUT-RAGEOUS FOOD PRICES!
PLUS, THE HOME TEAM'S LOSING BY EIGHT RUNS!
THE NEXT TIME I — OH, FOR PETE'S SAKE!
I JUST DUMPED MY CHILI DOG ALL OVER MY LAP!
WELL, THAT'S PAR FOR THE COURSE! WHAT ELSE COULD HAPPEN TO MAKE THIS DAY WORSE?
HEY, DAD! CHECK OUT THE JUMBO-TRON!
HUH?
COLA
ACME

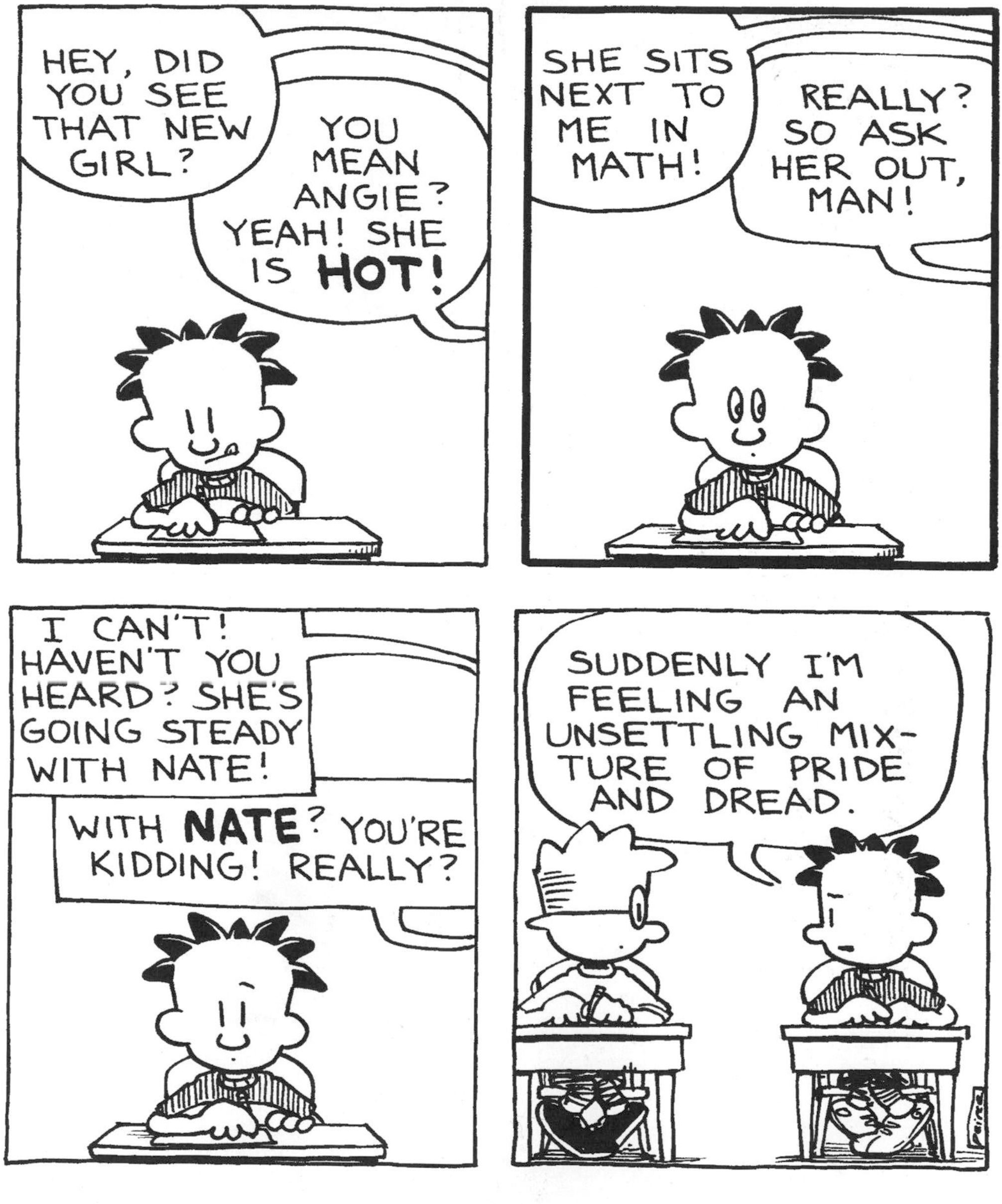
HEY, DID YOU SEE THAT NEW GIRL?
YOU MEAN ANGIE? YEAH! SHE IS **HOT**!
SHE SITS NEXT TO ME IN MATH!
REALLY? SO ASK HER OUT, MAN!
I CAN'T! HAVEN'T YOU HEARD? SHE'S GOING STEADY WITH NATE!
WITH **NATE**? YOU'RE KIDDING! REALLY?
SUDDENLY I'M FEELING AN UNSETTLING MIX-TURE OF PRIDE AND DREAD.

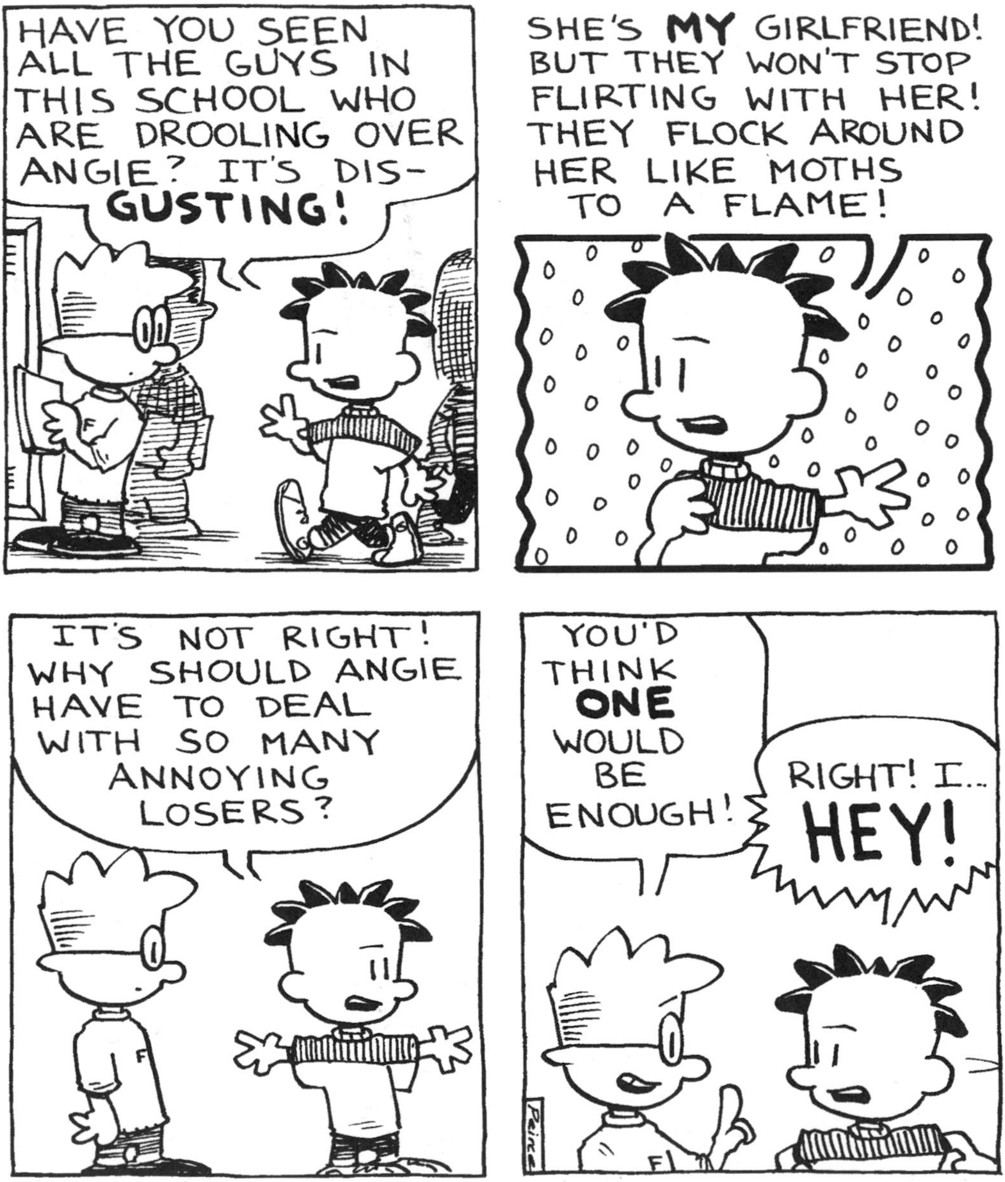
HAVE YOU SEEN ALL THE GUYS IN THIS SCHOOL WHO ARE DROOLING OVER ANGIE? IT'S DIS-**GUSTING!**
SHE'S **MY** GIRLFRIEND! BUT THEY WON'T STOP FLIRTING WITH HER! THEY FLOCK AROUND HER LIKE MOTHS TO A FLAME!
IT'S NOT RIGHT! WHY SHOULD ANGIE HAVE TO DEAL WITH SO MANY ANNOYING LOSERS?
YOU'D THINK **ONE** WOULD BE ENOUGH!
RIGHT! I... HEY!

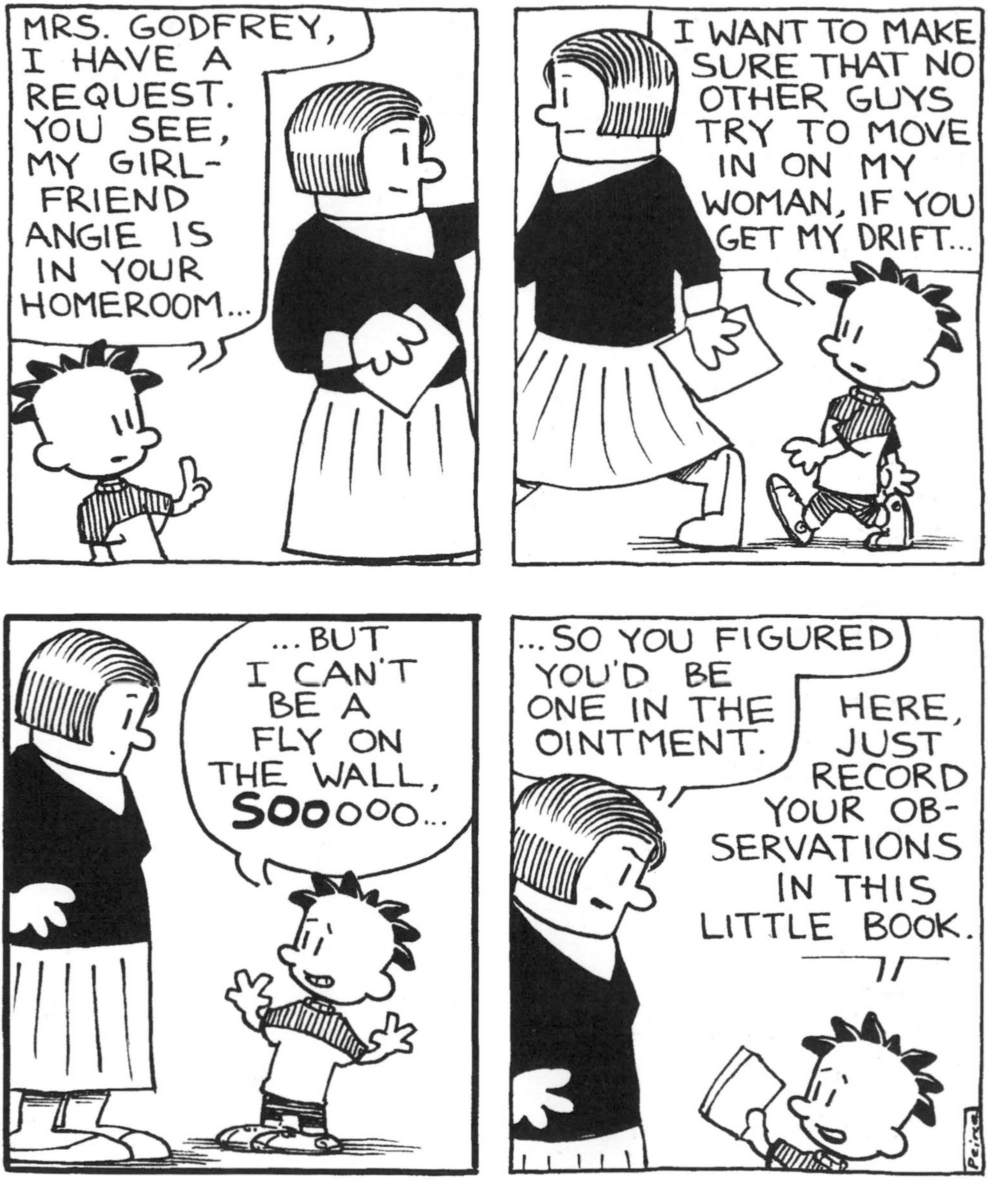
MRS. GODFREY, I HAVE A REQUEST. YOU SEE, MY GIRL-FRIEND ANGIE IS IN YOUR HOMEROOM...
I WANT TO MAKE SURE THAT NO OTHER GUYS TRY TO MOVE IN ON MY WOMAN, IF YOU GET MY DRIFT...
...BUT I CAN'T BE A FLY ON THE WALL, SOOOOO...
...SO YOU FIGURED YOU'D BE ONE IN THE OINTMENT.
HERE, JUST RECORD YOUR OBSERVATIONS IN THIS LITTLE BOOK.
Peirce

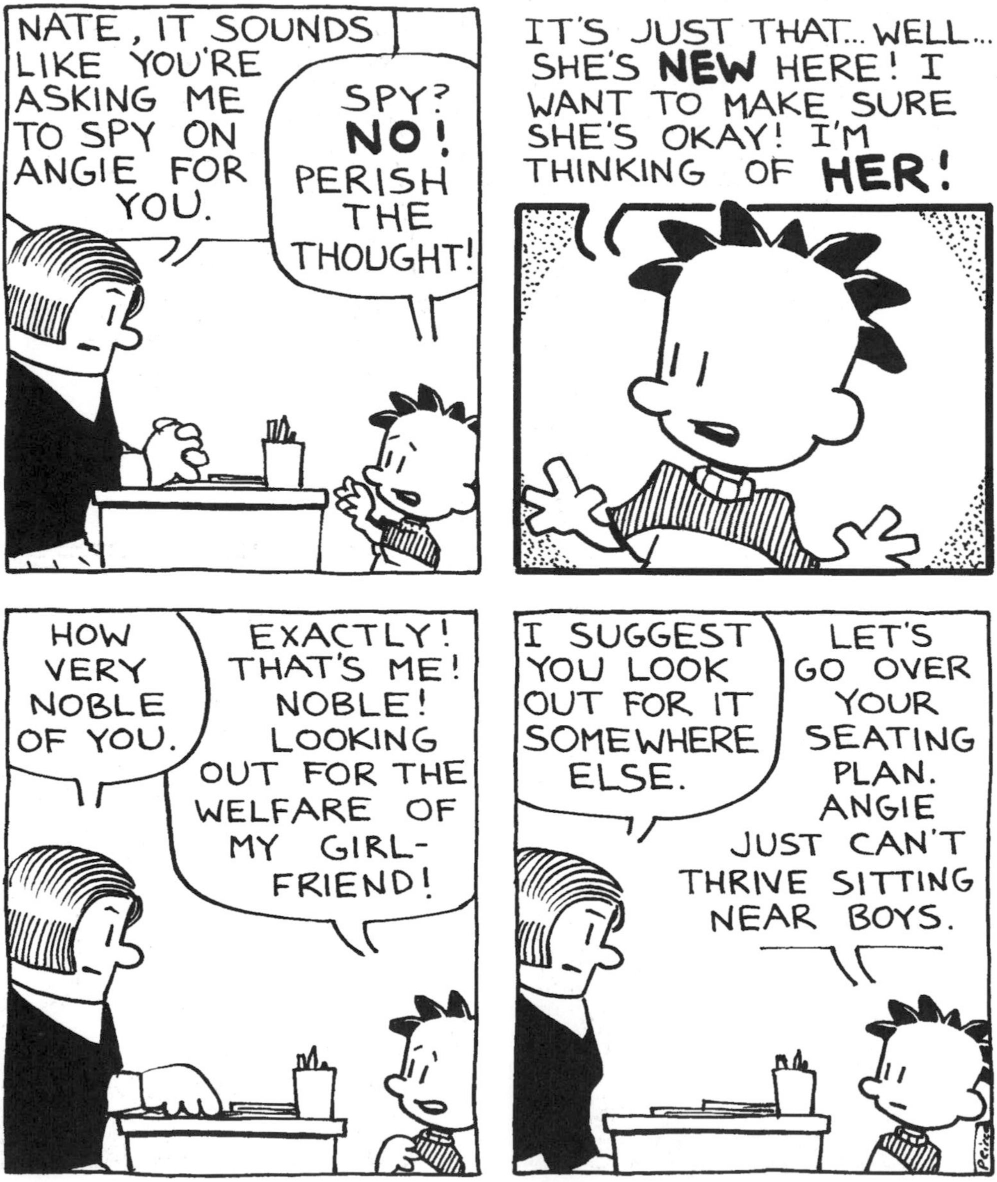

NATE, IT SOUNDS LIKE YOU'RE ASKING ME TO SPY ON ANGIE FOR YOU.
SPY? NO! PERISH THE THOUGHT!
IT'S JUST THAT... WELL... SHE'S NEW HERE! I WANT TO MAKE SURE SHE'S OKAY! I'M THINKING OF HER!
HOW VERY NOBLE OF YOU.
EXACTLY! THAT'S ME! NOBLE! LOOKING OUT FOR THE WELFARE OF MY GIRL-FRIEND!
I SUGGEST YOU LOOK OUT FOR IT SOMEWHERE ELSE.
LET'S GO OVER YOUR SEATING PLAN. ANGIE JUST CAN'T THRIVE SITTING NEAR BOYS.

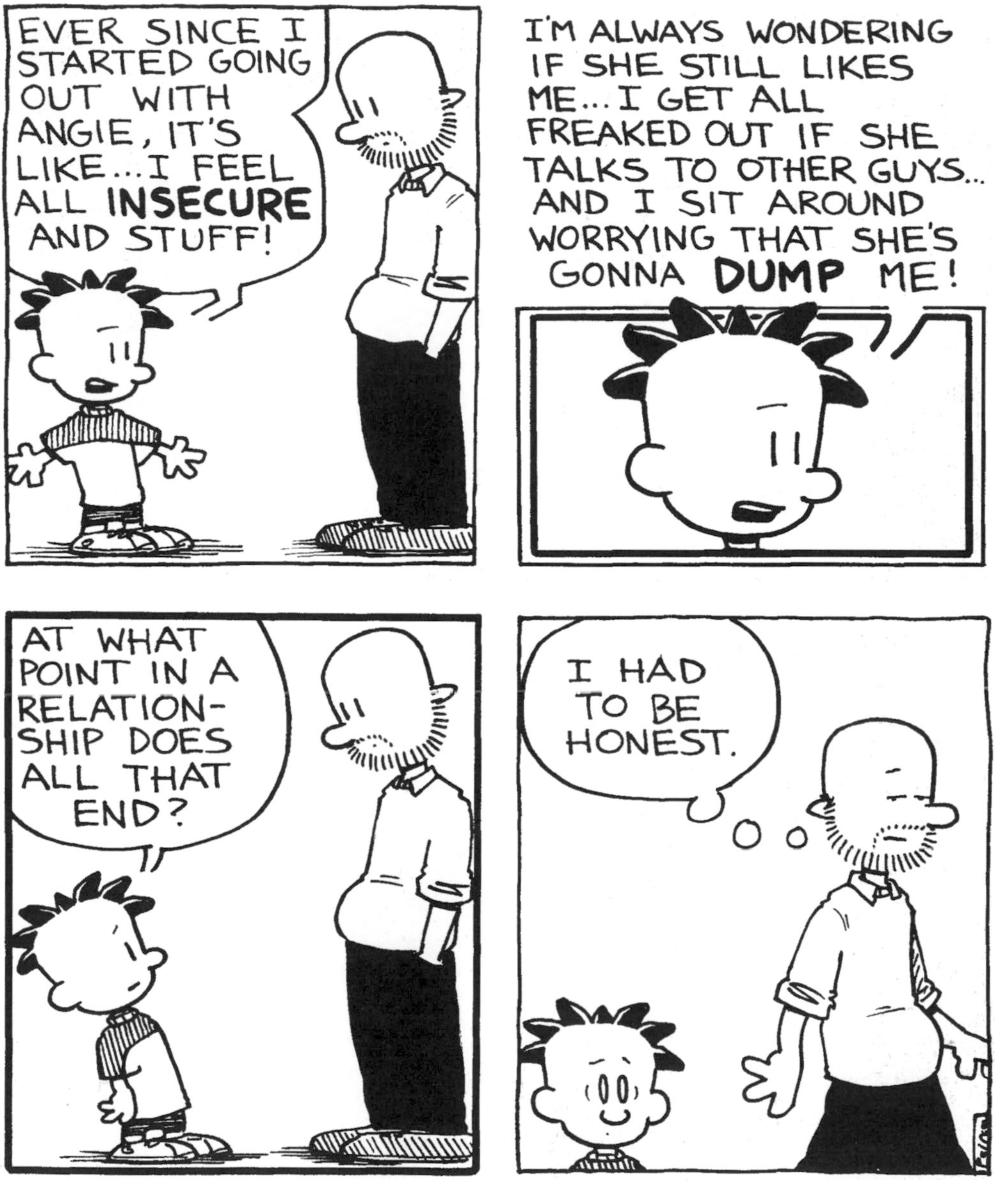
EVER SINCE I STARTED GOING OUT WITH ANGIE, IT'S LIKE... I FEEL ALL **INSECURE** AND STUFF!
I'M ALWAYS WONDERING IF SHE STILL LIKES ME... I GET ALL FREAKED OUT IF SHE TALKS TO OTHER GUYS... AND I SIT AROUND WORRYING THAT SHE'S GONNA **DUMP** ME!
AT WHAT POINT IN A RELATION-SHIP DOES ALL THAT END?
I HAD TO BE HONEST.

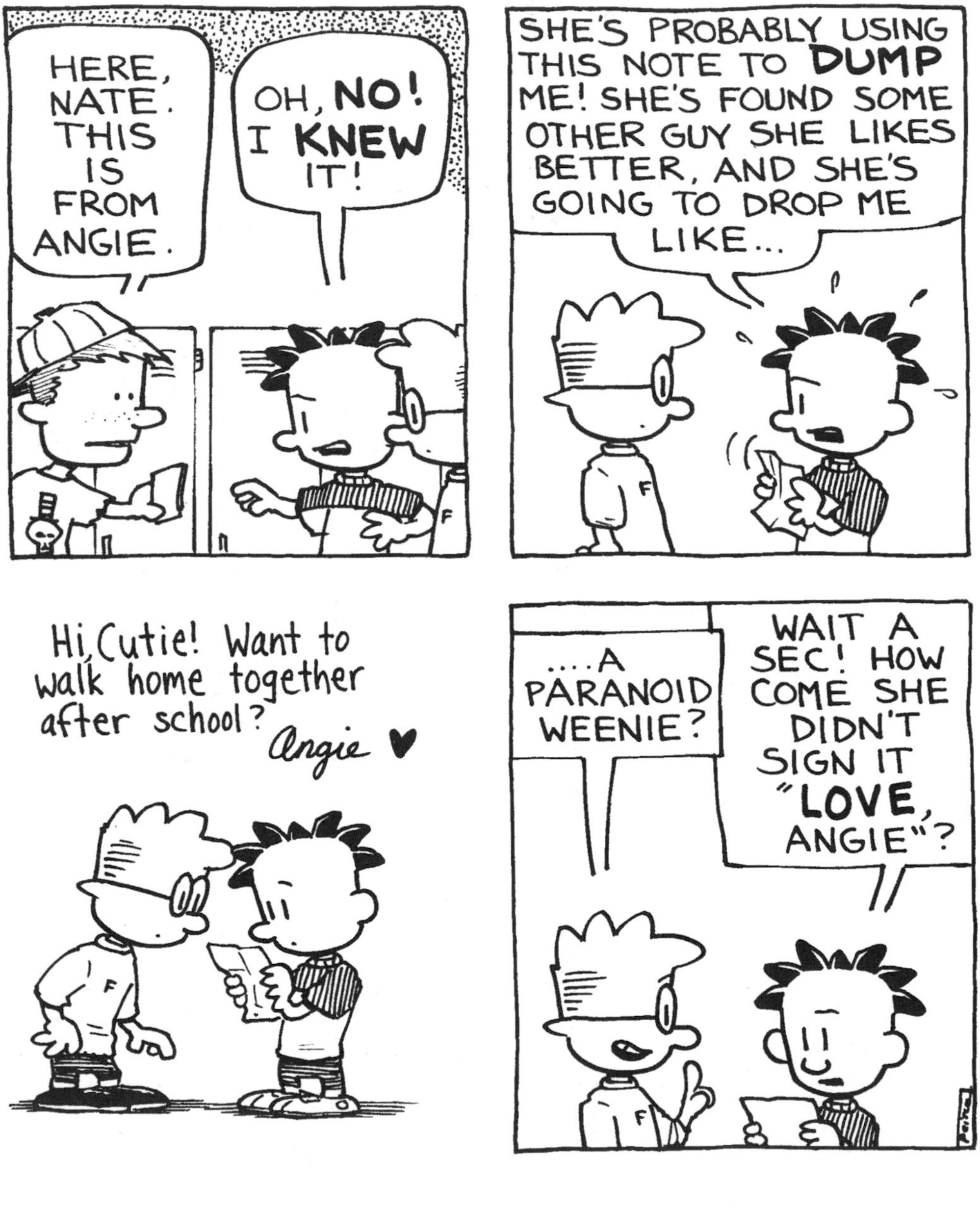

HERE, NATE. THIS IS FROM ANGIE.
OH, **NO**! I **KNEW** IT!
SHE'S PROBABLY USING THIS NOTE TO **DUMP** ME! SHE'S FOUND SOME OTHER GUY SHE LIKES BETTER, AND SHE'S GOING TO DROP ME LIKE...
Hi, Cutie! Want to walk home together after school? Angie ♥
....A PARANOID WEENIE?
WAIT A SEC! HOW COME SHE DIDN'T SIGN IT "**LOVE**, ANGIE"?

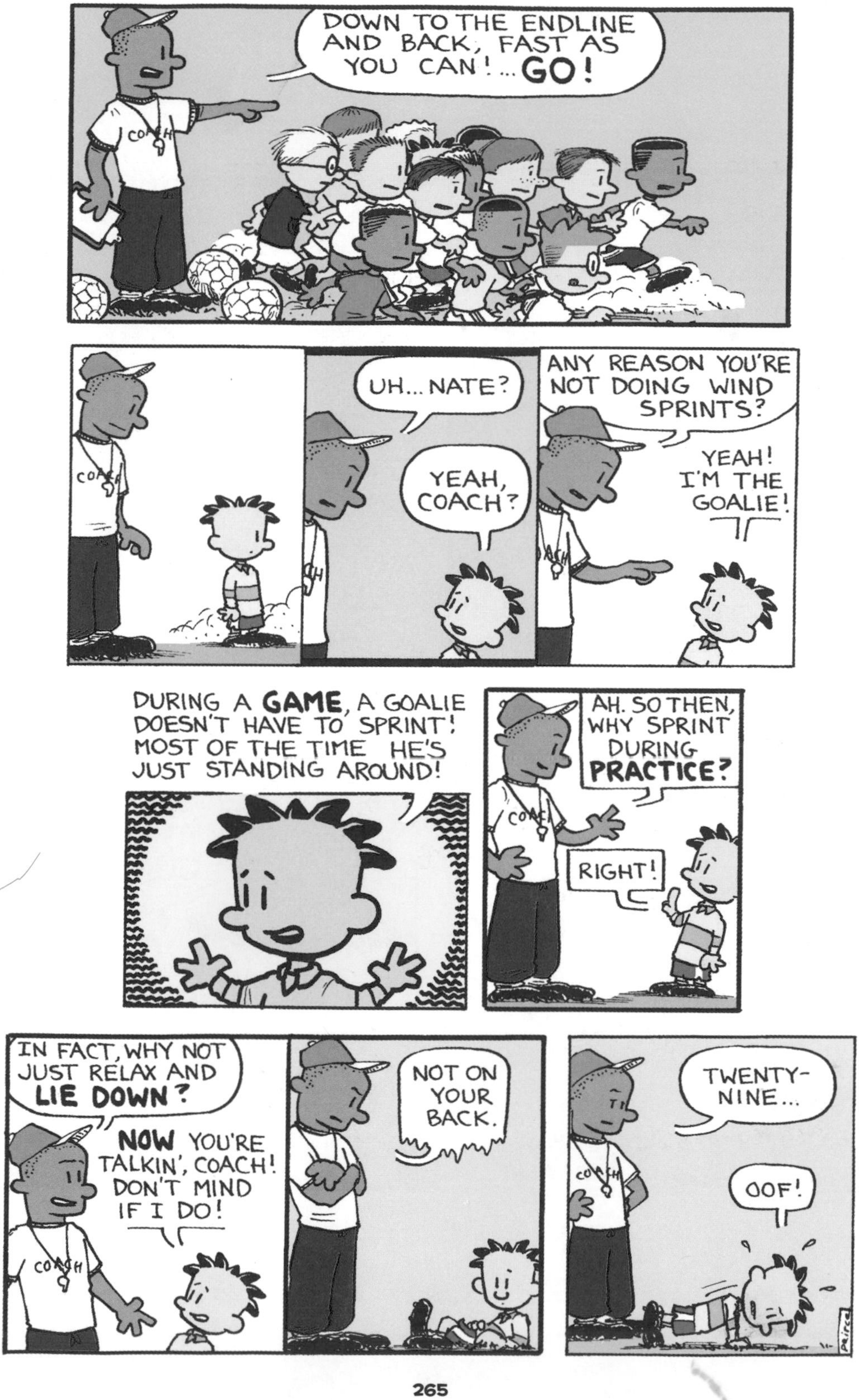

DOWN TO THE ENDLINE AND BACK, FAST AS YOU CAN!... GO!
COACH
COACH
UH... NATE?
YEAH, COACH?
ANY REASON YOU'RE NOT DOING WIND SPRINTS?
YEAH! I'M THE GOALIE!
DURING A GAME, A GOALIE DOESN'T HAVE TO SPRINT! MOST OF THE TIME HE'S JUST STANDING AROUND!
AH. SO THEN, WHY SPRINT DURING PRACTICE?
COACH
RIGHT!
IN FACT, WHY NOT JUST RELAX AND LIE DOWN?
NOW YOU'RE TALKIN', COACH! DON'T MIND IF I DO!
COACH
NOT ON YOUR BACK.
TWENTY-NINE...
COACH
OOF!
PEIRCE

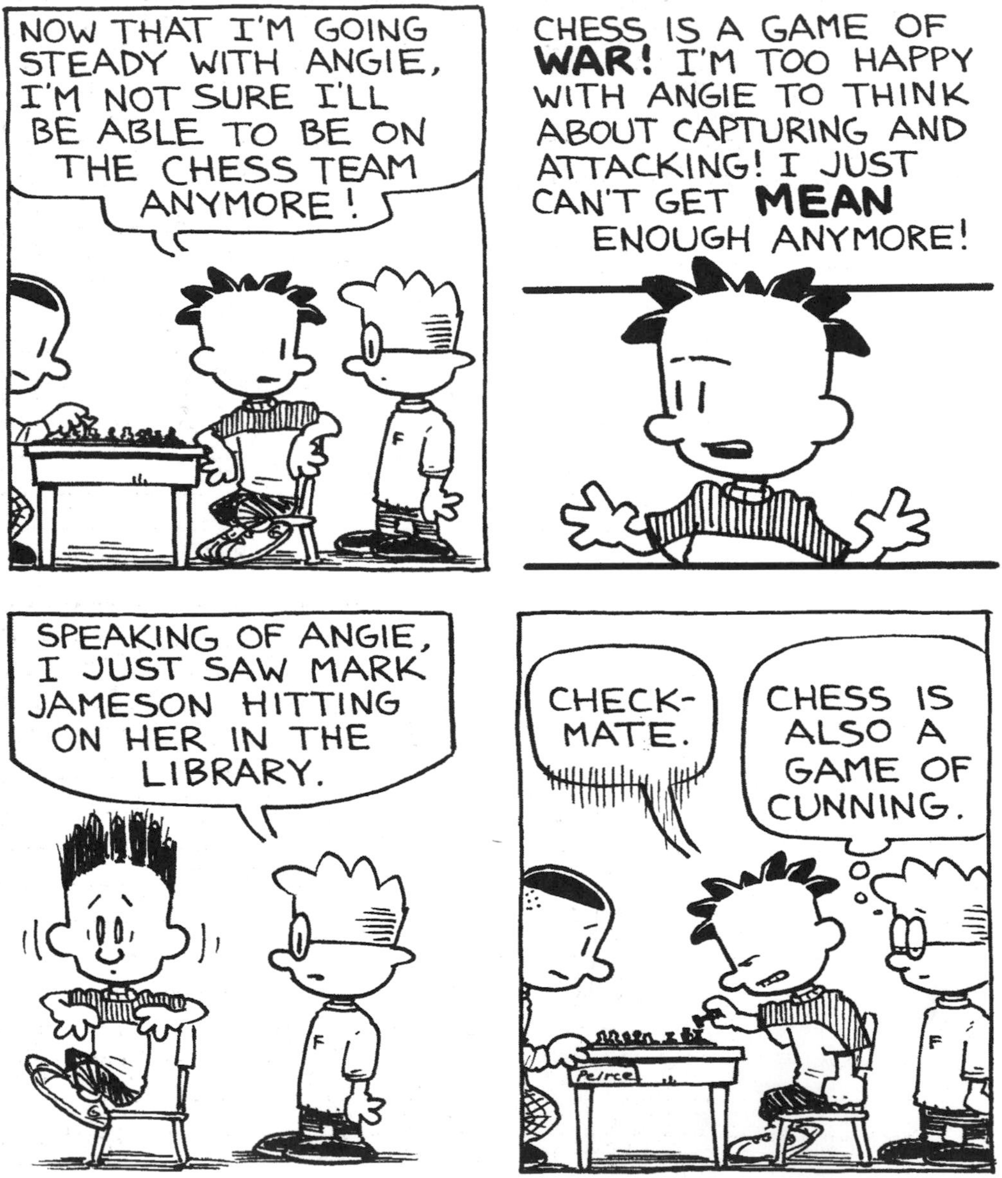
NOW THAT I'M GOING STEADY WITH ANGIE, I'M NOT SURE I'LL BE ABLE TO BE ON THE CHESS TEAM ANYMORE!
CHESS IS A GAME OF **WAR!** I'M TOO HAPPY WITH ANGIE TO THINK ABOUT CAPTURING AND ATTACKING! I JUST CAN'T GET **MEAN** ENOUGH ANYMORE!
SPEAKING OF ANGIE, I JUST SAW MARK JAMESON HITTING ON HER IN THE LIBRARY.
CHECK-MATE.
CHESS IS ALSO A GAME OF CUNNING.
Peirce

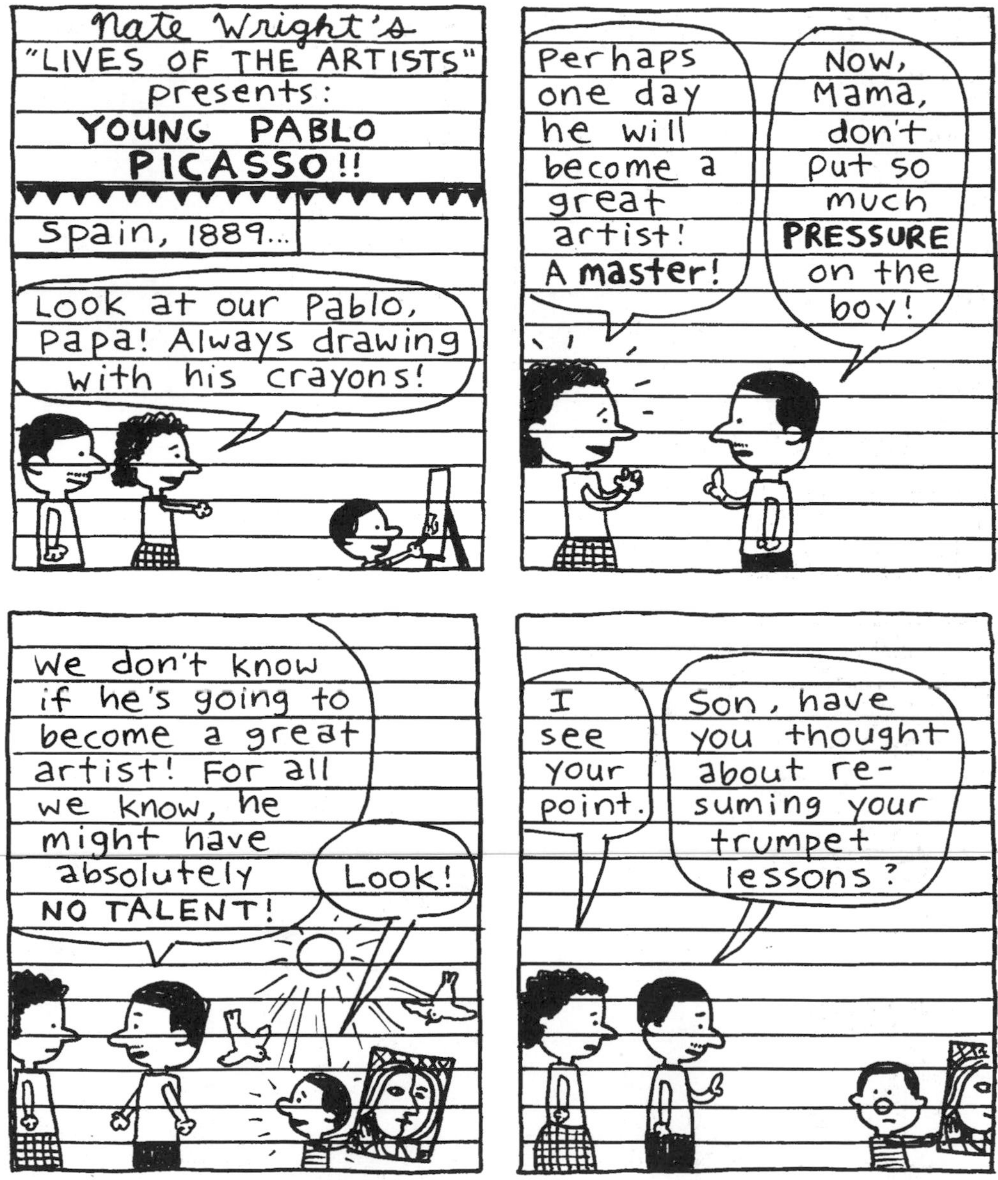
Nate Wright's
"LIVES OF THE ARTISTS"
presents:
YOUNG PABLO PICASSO!!
Spain, 1889...
Look at our Pablo, Papa! Always drawing with his crayons!
Perhaps one day he will become a great artist! A master!
Now, Mama, don't put so much PRESSURE on the boy!
We don't know if he's going to become a great artist! For all we know, he might have absolutely NO TALENT!
Look!
I see your point.
Son, have you thought about re-suming your trumpet lessons?

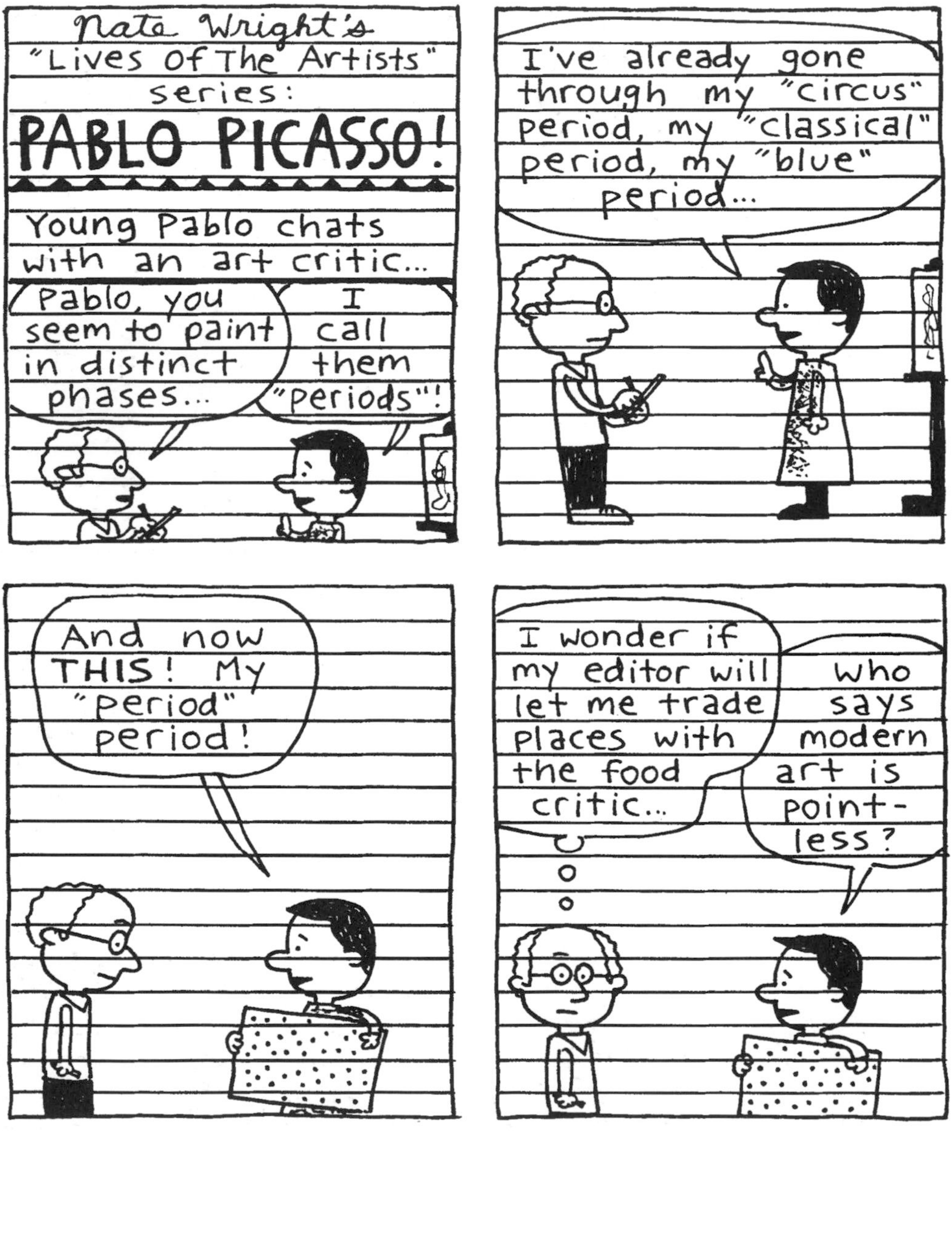
Nate Wright's
"Lives of The Artists" series:
PABLO PICASSO!
Young Pablo chats with an art critic...
Pablo, you seem to paint in distinct phases...
I call them "periods"!
I've already gone through my "circus" period, my "classical" period, my "blue" period...
And now THIS! My "period" period!
I wonder if my editor will let me trade places with the food critic...
Who says modern art is point-less?

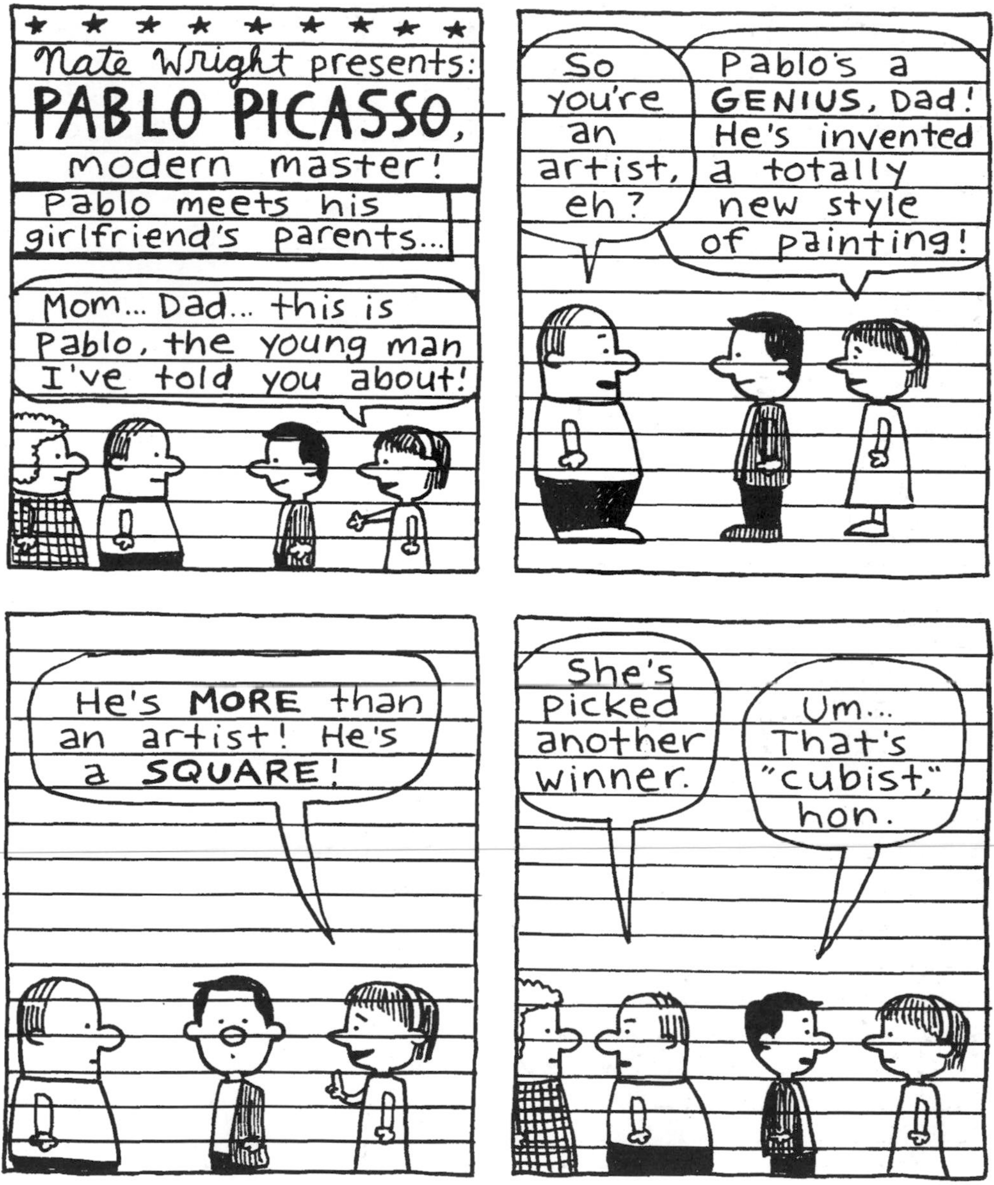
Nate Wright presents:
PABLO PICASSO, modern master!
Pablo meets his girlfriend's parents...
Mom... Dad... this is Pablo, the young man I've told you about!
So you're an artist, eh?
Pablo's a GENIUS, Dad! He's invented a totally new style of painting!
He's MORE than an artist! He's a SQUARE!
She's picked another winner.
Um... That's "cubist," hon.

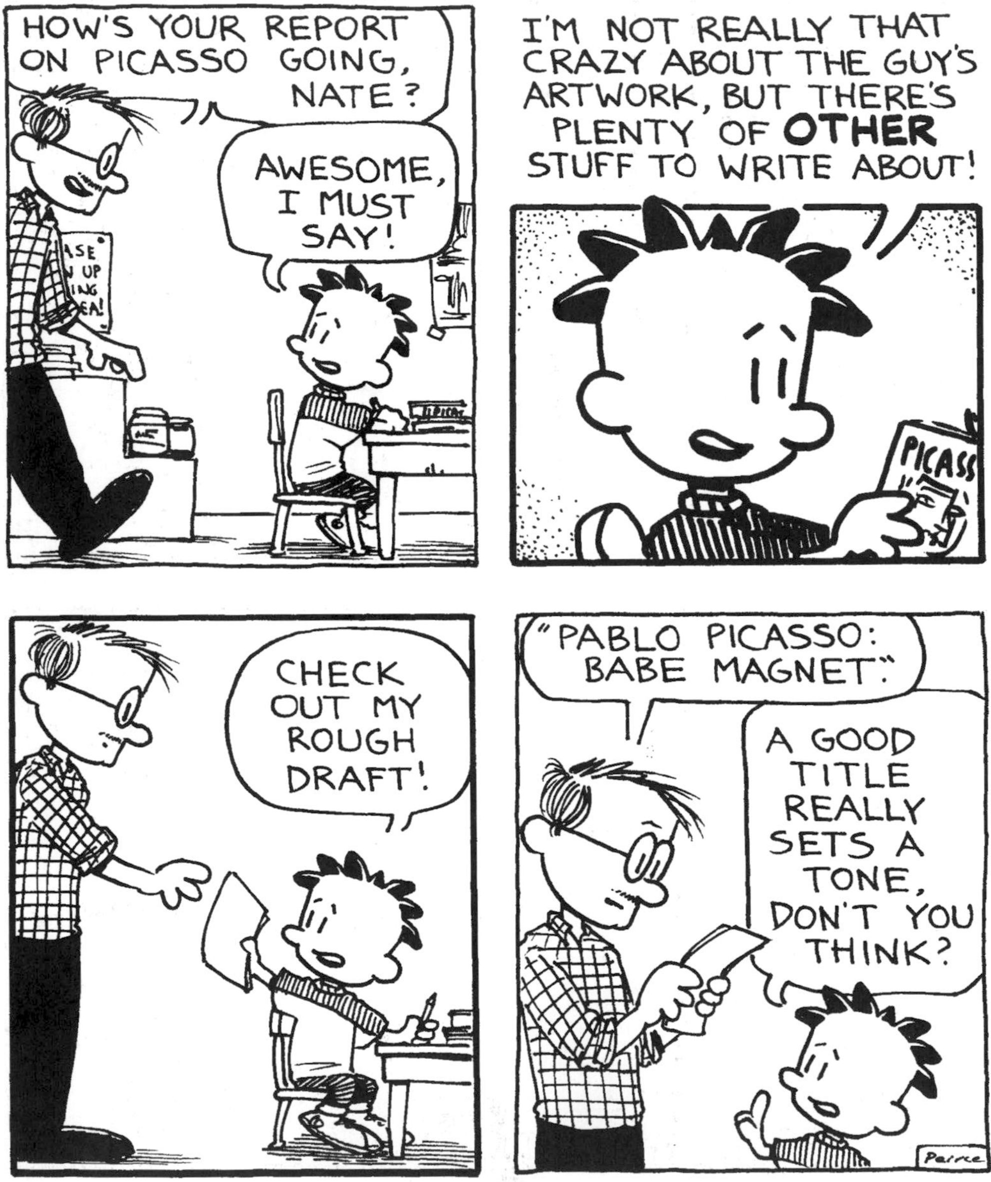
HOW'S YOUR REPORT ON PICASSO GOING, NATE?
AWESOME, I MUST SAY!
I'M NOT REALLY THAT CRAZY ABOUT THE GUY'S ARTWORK, BUT THERE'S PLENTY OF **OTHER** STUFF TO WRITE ABOUT!
PICASS
CHECK OUT MY ROUGH DRAFT!
"PABLO PICASSO: BABE MAGNET."
A GOOD TITLE REALLY SETS A TONE, DON'T YOU THINK?
Peirce

DOING THIS REPORT HAS INSPIRED ME TO PATTERN MY ART CAREER AFTER PICASSO'S! I'M GOING TO DO JUST WHAT HE DID!
IT'LL BE A LIFETIME OF HARD WORK,
BUT SOMEDAY I, TOO, WILL BE ABLE TO DRAW LIKE THIS!
IT SAYS HE DID THIS WHEN HE WAS TWELVE.
TWELVE?
WHEN'S YOUR BIRTH-DAY?
FORGET IT.
Peirce

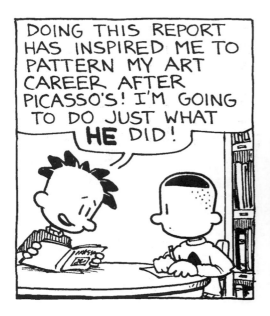

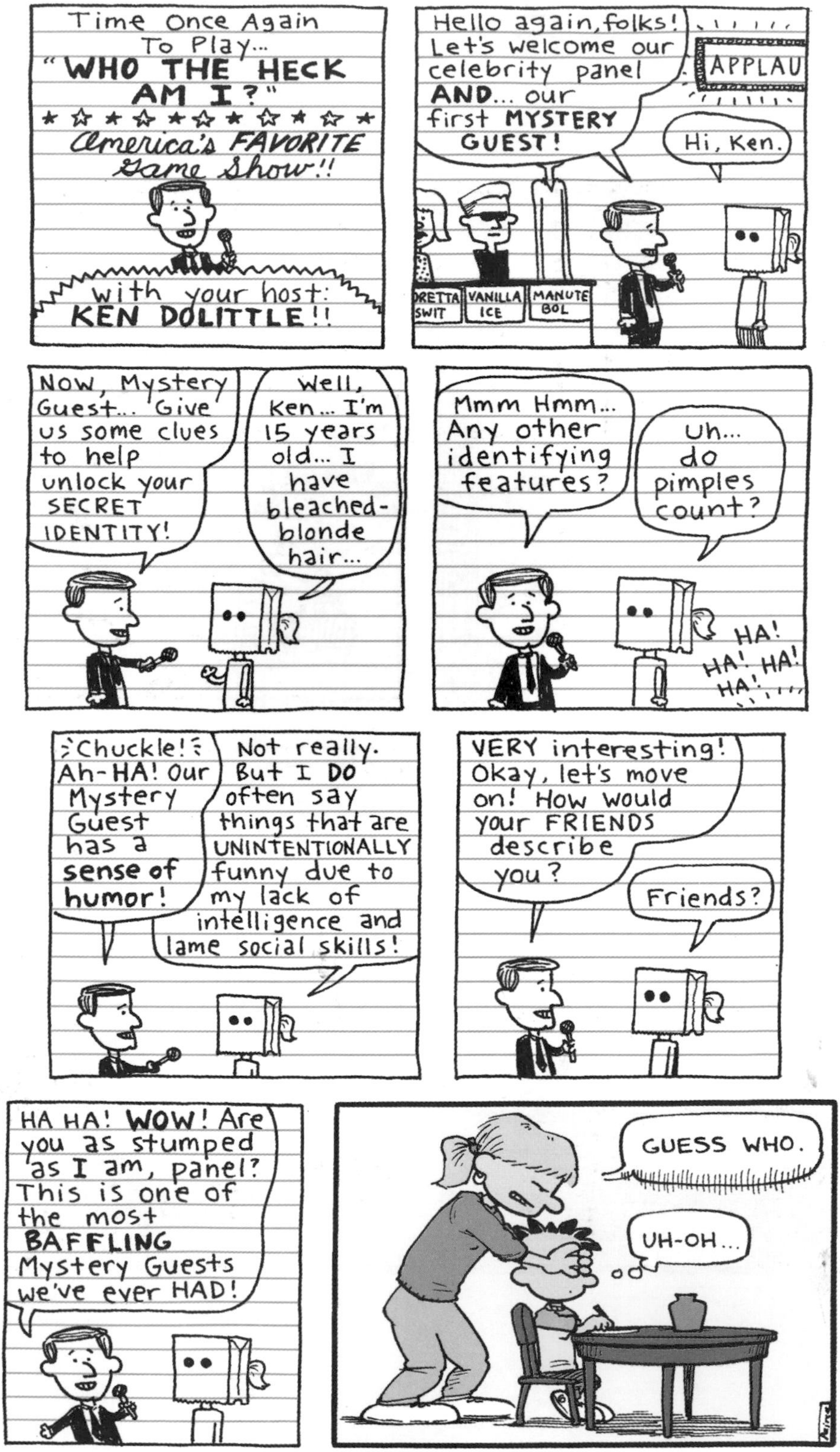
Time Once Again To Play... "WHO THE HECK AM I?"
America's FAVORITE Game Show!!
with your host: KEN DOLITTLE!!
Hello again, folks! Let's welcome our celebrity panel AND... our first MYSTERY GUEST!
APPLAU
Hi, Ken.
RETTA SWIT
VANILLA ICE
MANUTE BOL
Now, Mystery Guest... Give us some clues to help unlock your SECRET IDENTITY!
Well, Ken... I'm 15 years old... I have bleached-blonde hair...
Mmm Hmm... Any other identifying features?
Uh... do pimples count?
HA! HA! HA! HA!
Chuckle! Ah-HA! Our Mystery Guest has a sense of humor!
Not really. But I DO often say things that are UNINTENTIONALLY funny due to my lack of intelligence and lame social skills!
VERY interesting! Okay, let's move on! How would your FRIENDS describe you?
Friends?
HA HA! WOW! Are you as stumped as I am, panel? This is one of the most BAFFLING Mystery Guests we've ever HAD!
GUESS WHO.
UH-OH...

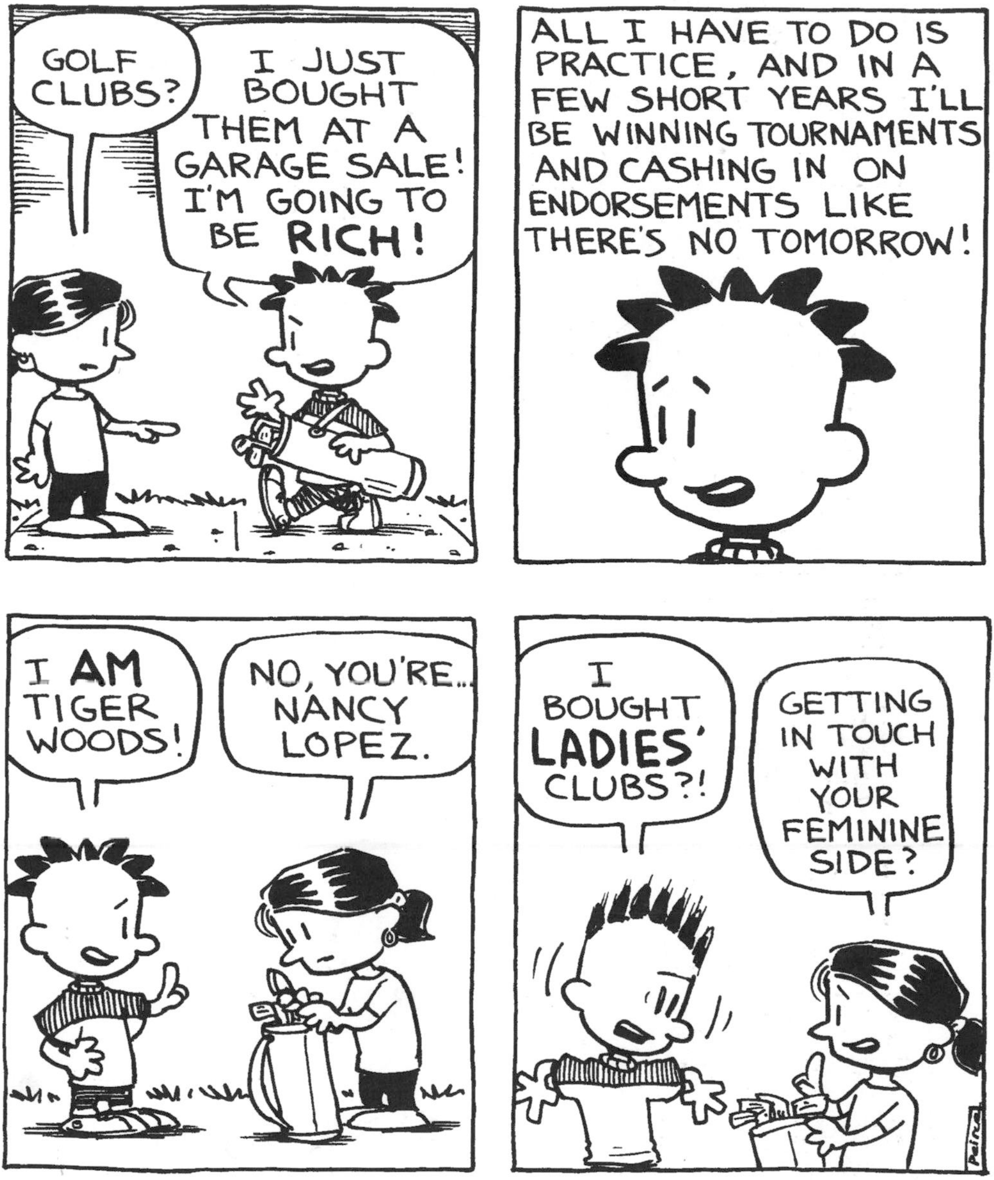
GOLF CLUBS?
I JUST BOUGHT THEM AT A GARAGE SALE! I'M GOING TO BE **RICH**!
ALL I HAVE TO DO IS PRACTICE, AND IN A FEW SHORT YEARS I'LL BE WINNING TOURNAMENTS AND CASHING IN ON ENDORSEMENTS LIKE THERE'S NO TOMORROW!
I **AM** TIGER WOODS!
NO, YOU'RE... NANCY LOPEZ.
I BOUGHT **LADIES'** CLUBS?!
GETTING IN TOUCH WITH YOUR FEMININE SIDE?
Peirce

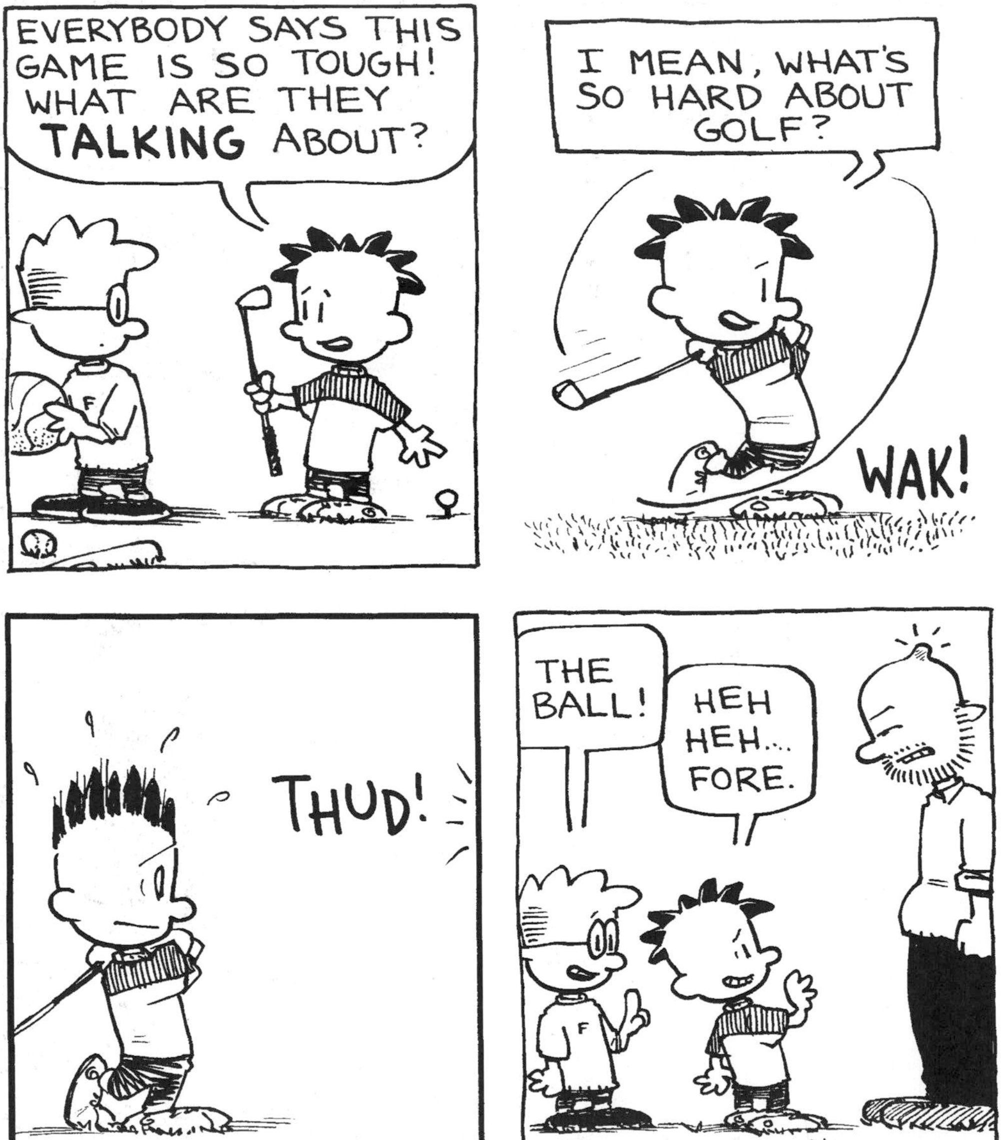
EVERYBODY SAYS THIS GAME IS SO TOUGH! WHAT ARE THEY **TALKING** ABOUT?
I MEAN, WHAT'S SO HARD ABOUT GOLF?
WAK!
THUD!
THE BALL!
HEH HEH... FORE.
Peirce

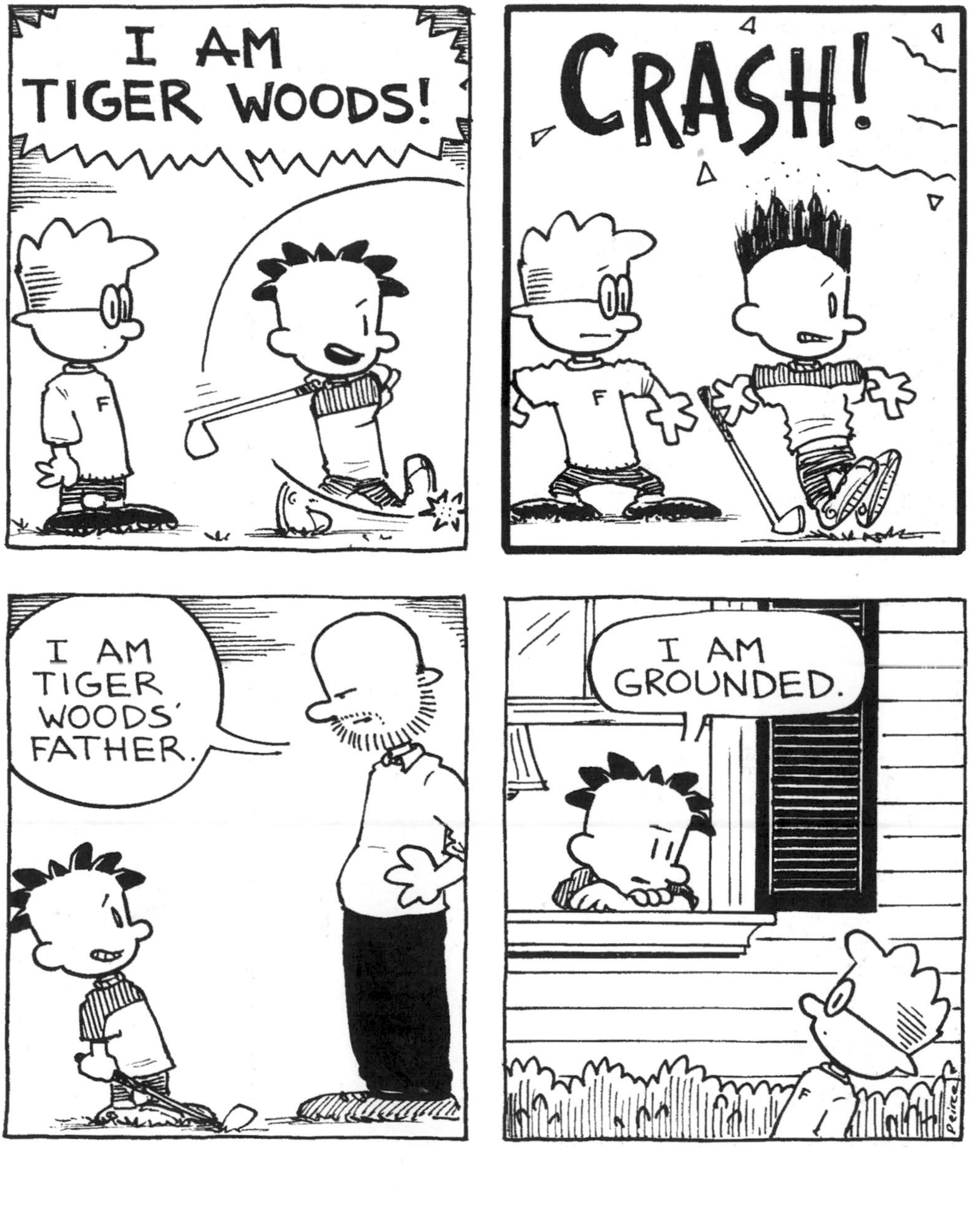
I AM TIGER WOODS!
CRASH!
I AM TIGER WOODS' FATHER.
I AM GROUNDED.
Peirce

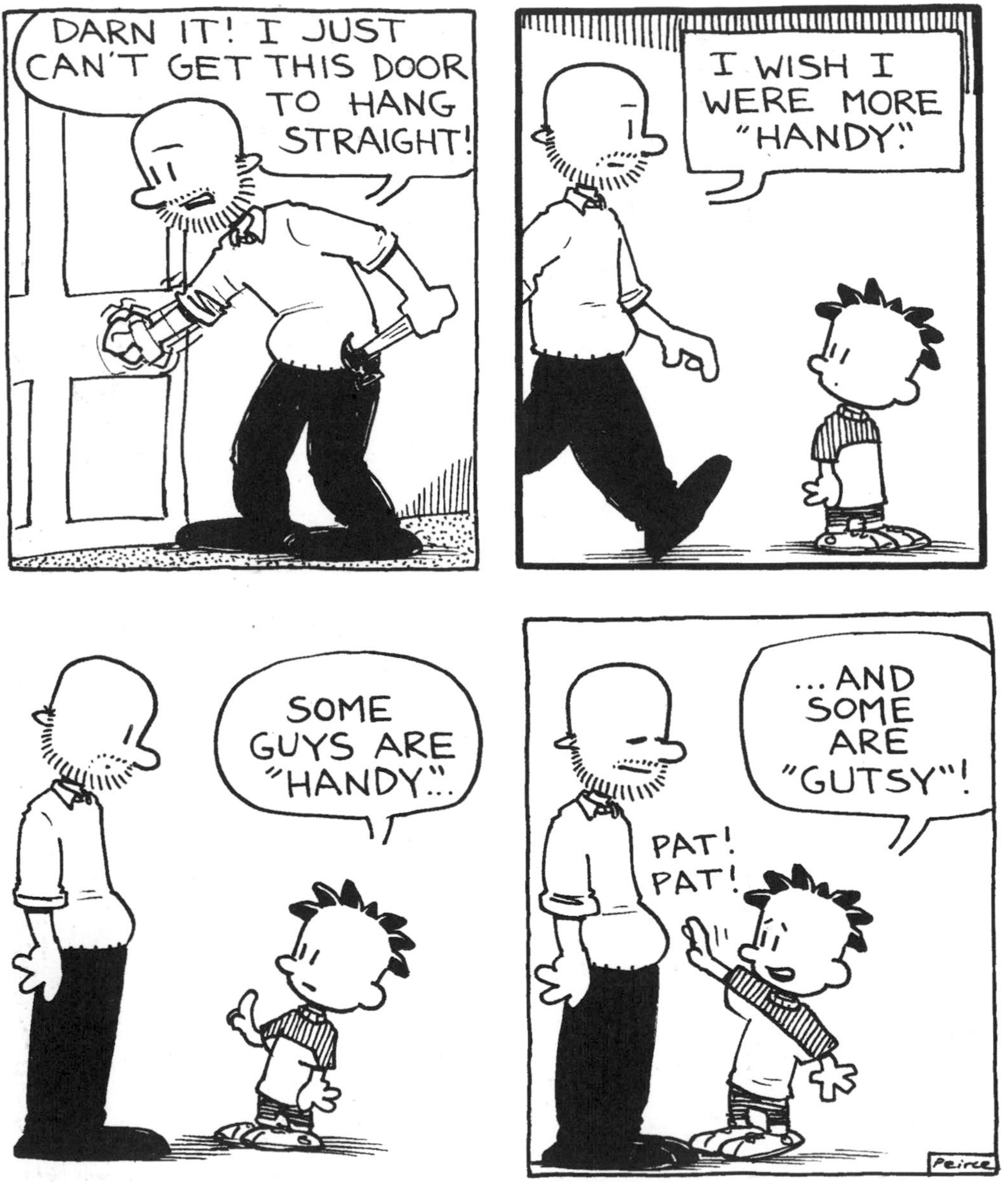
DARN IT! I JUST CAN'T GET THIS DOOR TO HANG STRAIGHT!
I WISH I WERE MORE "HANDY."
SOME GUYS ARE "HANDY"...
PAT! PAT!
...AND SOME ARE "GUTSY"!
Peirce

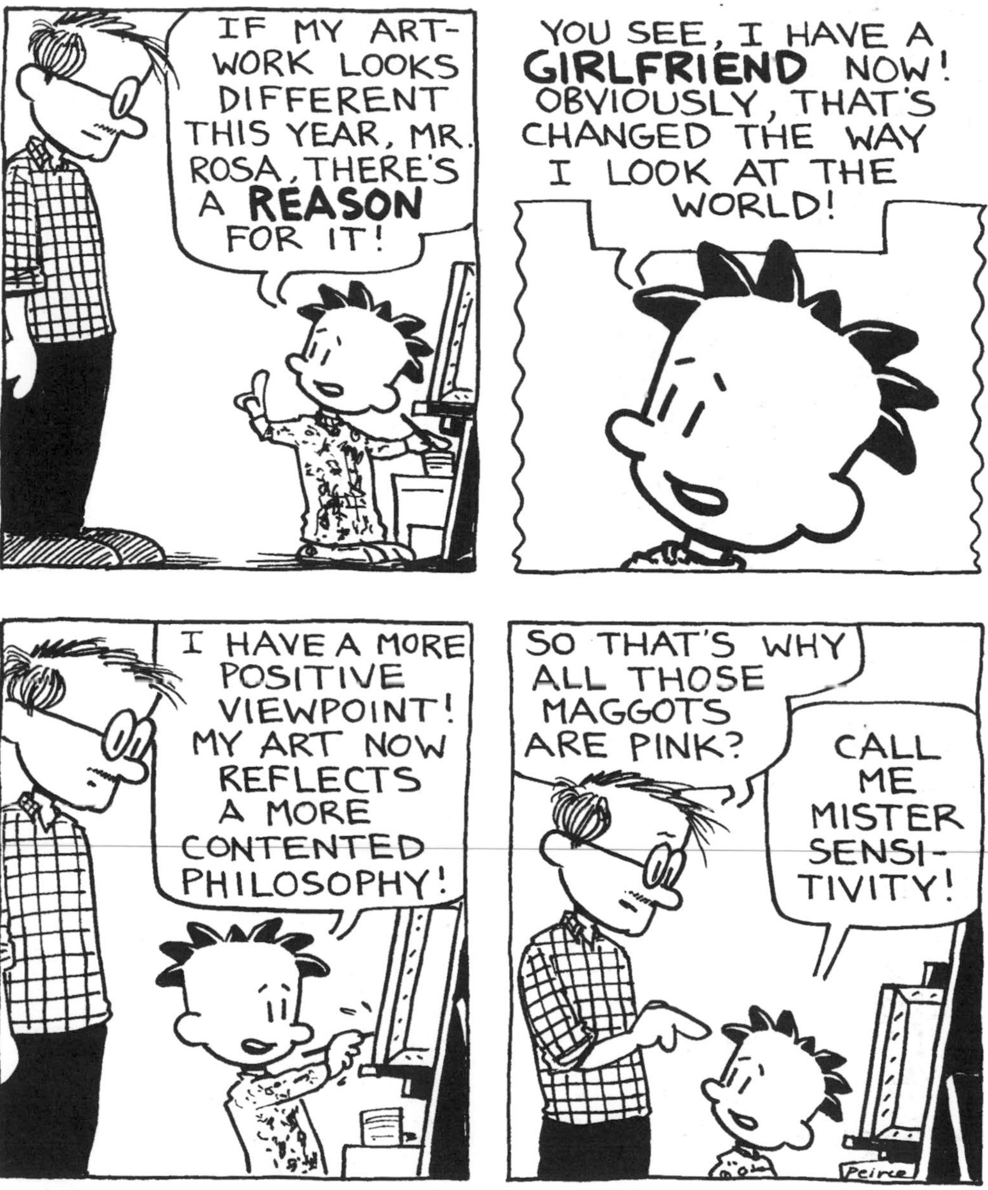
IF MY ART-WORK LOOKS DIFFERENT THIS YEAR, MR. ROSA, THERE'S A **REASON** FOR IT!
YOU SEE, I HAVE A **GIRLFRIEND** NOW! OBVIOUSLY, THAT'S CHANGED THE WAY I LOOK AT THE WORLD!
I HAVE A MORE POSITIVE VIEWPOINT! MY ART NOW REFLECTS A MORE CONTENTED PHILOSOPHY!
SO THAT'S WHY ALL THOSE MAGGOTS ARE PINK?
CALL ME MISTER SENSI-TIVITY!
Peirce

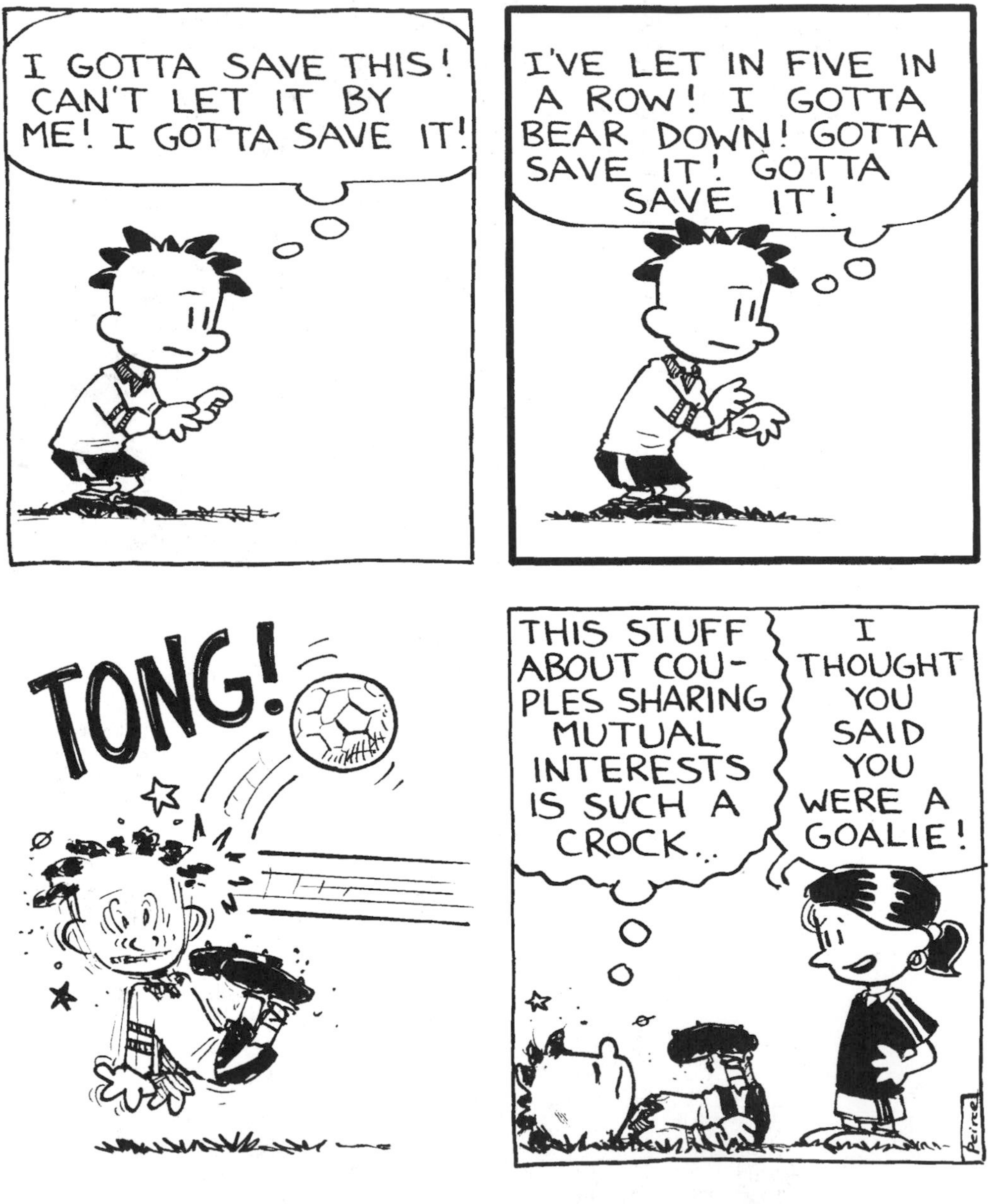
I GOTTA SAVE THIS! CAN'T LET IT BY ME! I GOTTA SAVE IT!
I'VE LET IN FIVE IN A ROW! I GOTTA BEAR DOWN! GOTTA SAVE IT! GOTTA SAVE IT!
TONG!
THIS STUFF ABOUT COUPLES SHARING MUTUAL INTERESTS IS SUCH A CROCK...
I THOUGHT YOU SAID YOU WERE A GOALIE!
Peirce

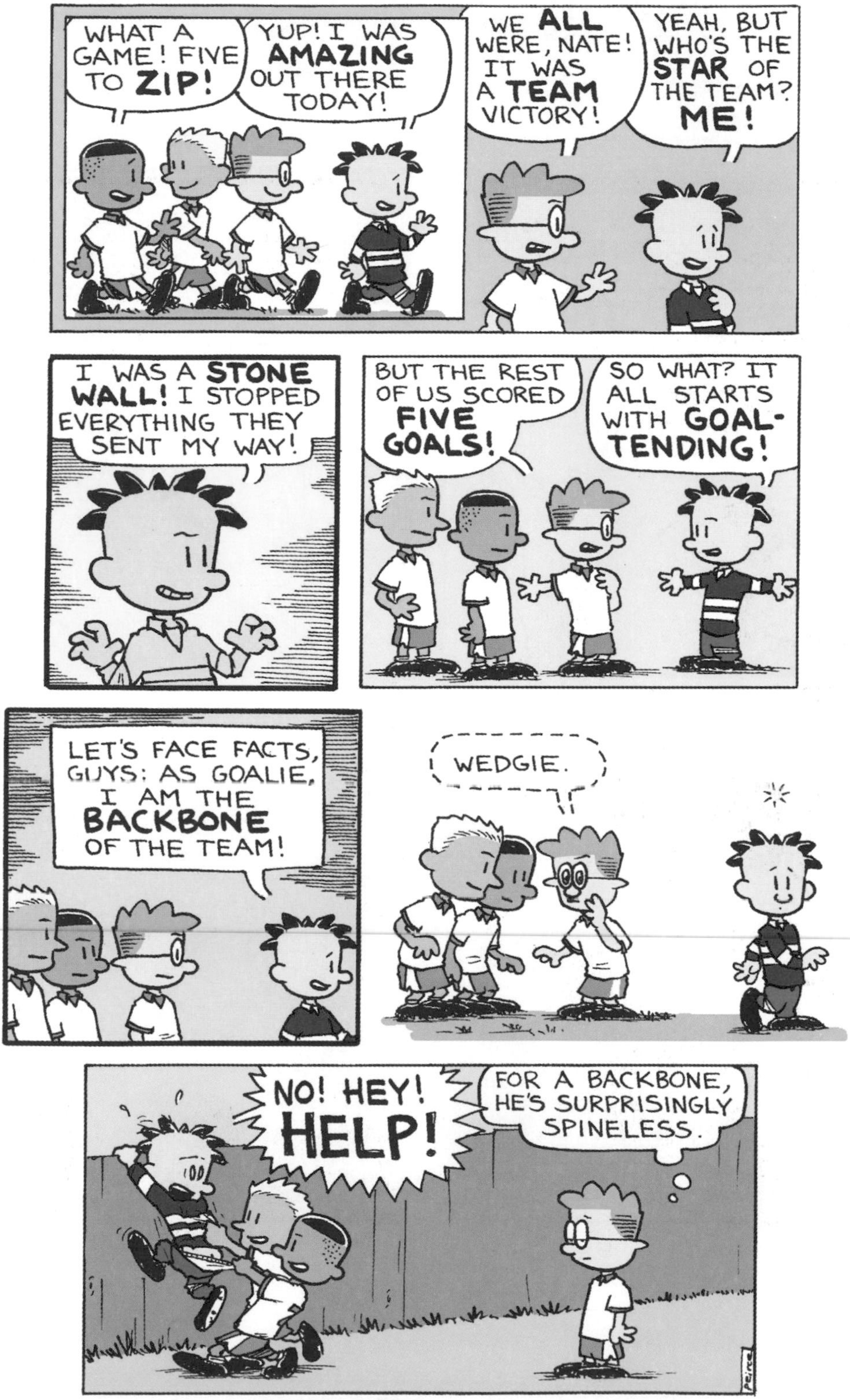
WHAT A GAME! FIVE TO ZIP!
YUP! I WAS AMAZING OUT THERE TODAY!
WE ALL WERE, NATE! IT WAS A TEAM VICTORY!
YEAH, BUT WHO'S THE STAR OF THE TEAM? ME!
I WAS A STONE WALL! I STOPPED EVERYTHING THEY SENT MY WAY!
BUT THE REST OF US SCORED FIVE GOALS!
SO WHAT? IT ALL STARTS WITH GOAL-TENDING!
LET'S FACE FACTS, GUYS: AS GOALIE, I AM THE BACKBONE OF THE TEAM!
WEDGIE.
NO! HEY! HELP!
FOR A BACKBONE, HE'S SURPRISINGLY SPINELESS.
PEIRCE

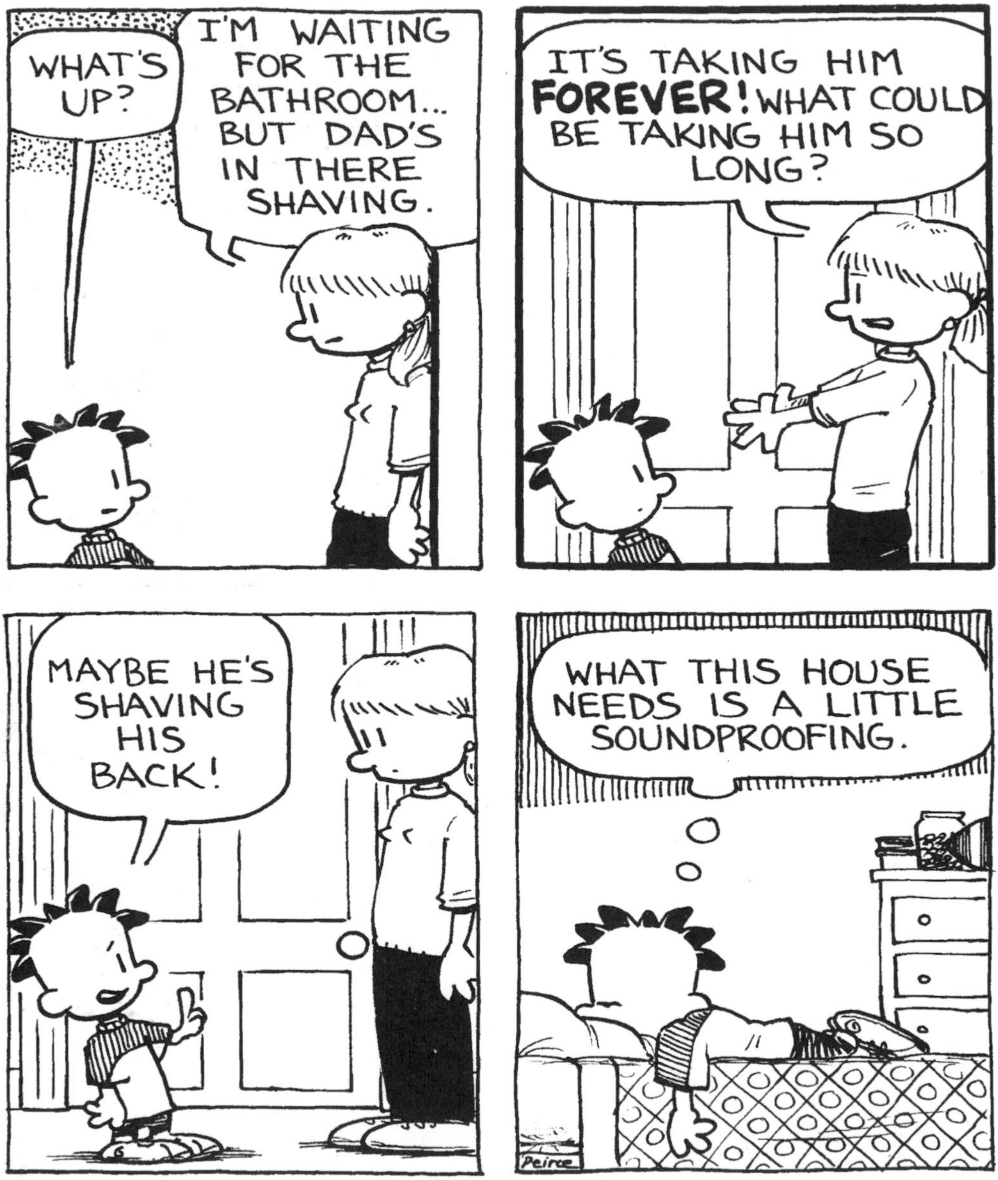
WHAT'S UP?
I'M WAITING FOR THE BATHROOM... BUT DAD'S IN THERE SHAVING.
IT'S TAKING HIM **FOREVER!** WHAT COULD BE TAKING HIM SO LONG?
MAYBE HE'S SHAVING HIS BACK!
WHAT THIS HOUSE NEEDS IS A LITTLE SOUNDPROOFING.
Peirce

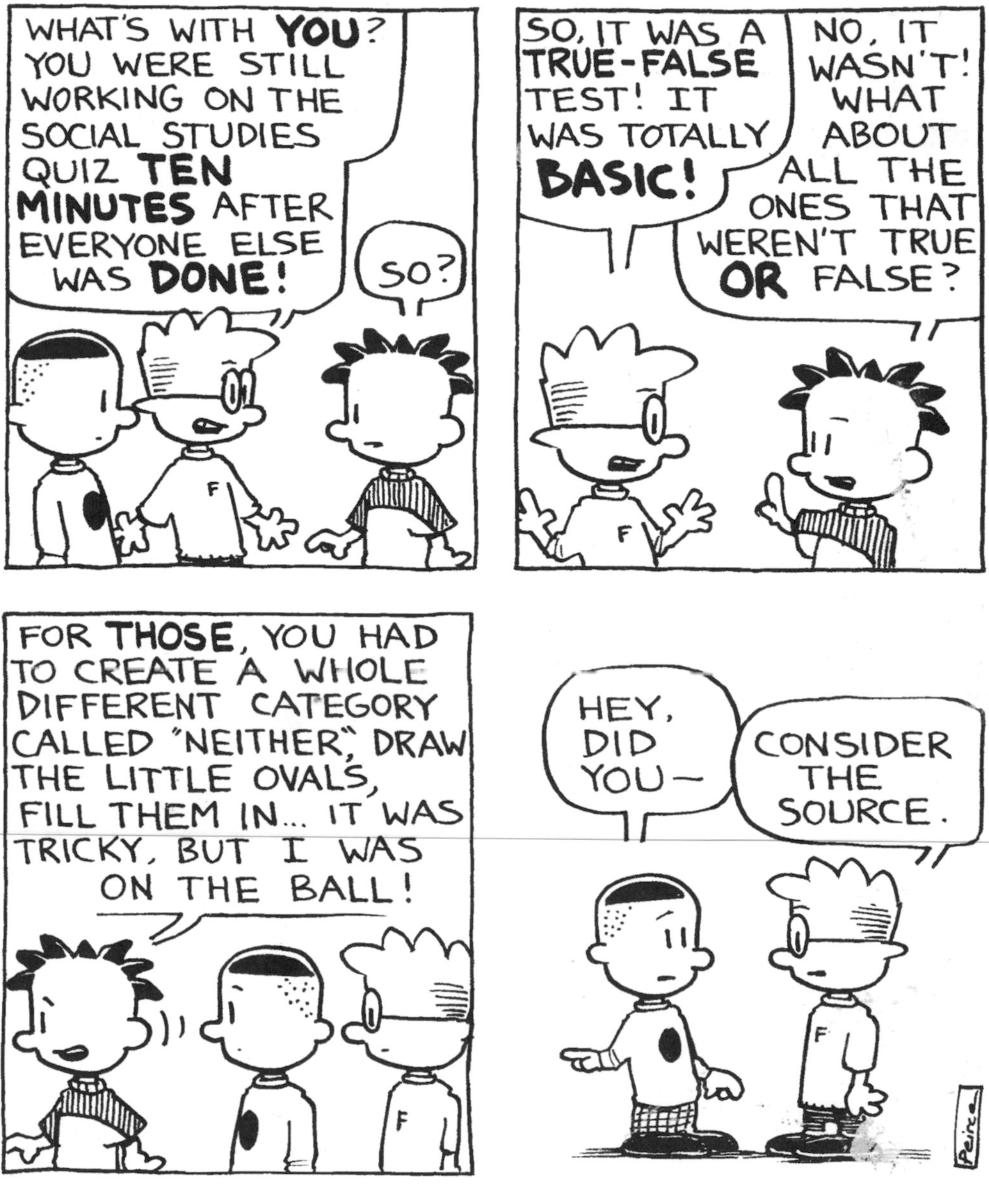
WHAT'S WITH YOU? YOU WERE STILL WORKING ON THE SOCIAL STUDIES QUIZ TEN MINUTES AFTER EVERYONE ELSE WAS DONE!
SO?
SO, IT WAS A TRUE-FALSE TEST! IT WAS TOTALLY BASIC!
NO, IT WASN'T! WHAT ABOUT ALL THE ONES THAT WEREN'T TRUE OR FALSE?
FOR THOSE, YOU HAD TO CREATE A WHOLE DIFFERENT CATEGORY CALLED "NEITHER," DRAW THE LITTLE OVALS, FILL THEM IN... IT WAS TRICKY, BUT I WAS ON THE BALL!
HEY, DID YOU—
CONSIDER THE SOURCE.
Peirce

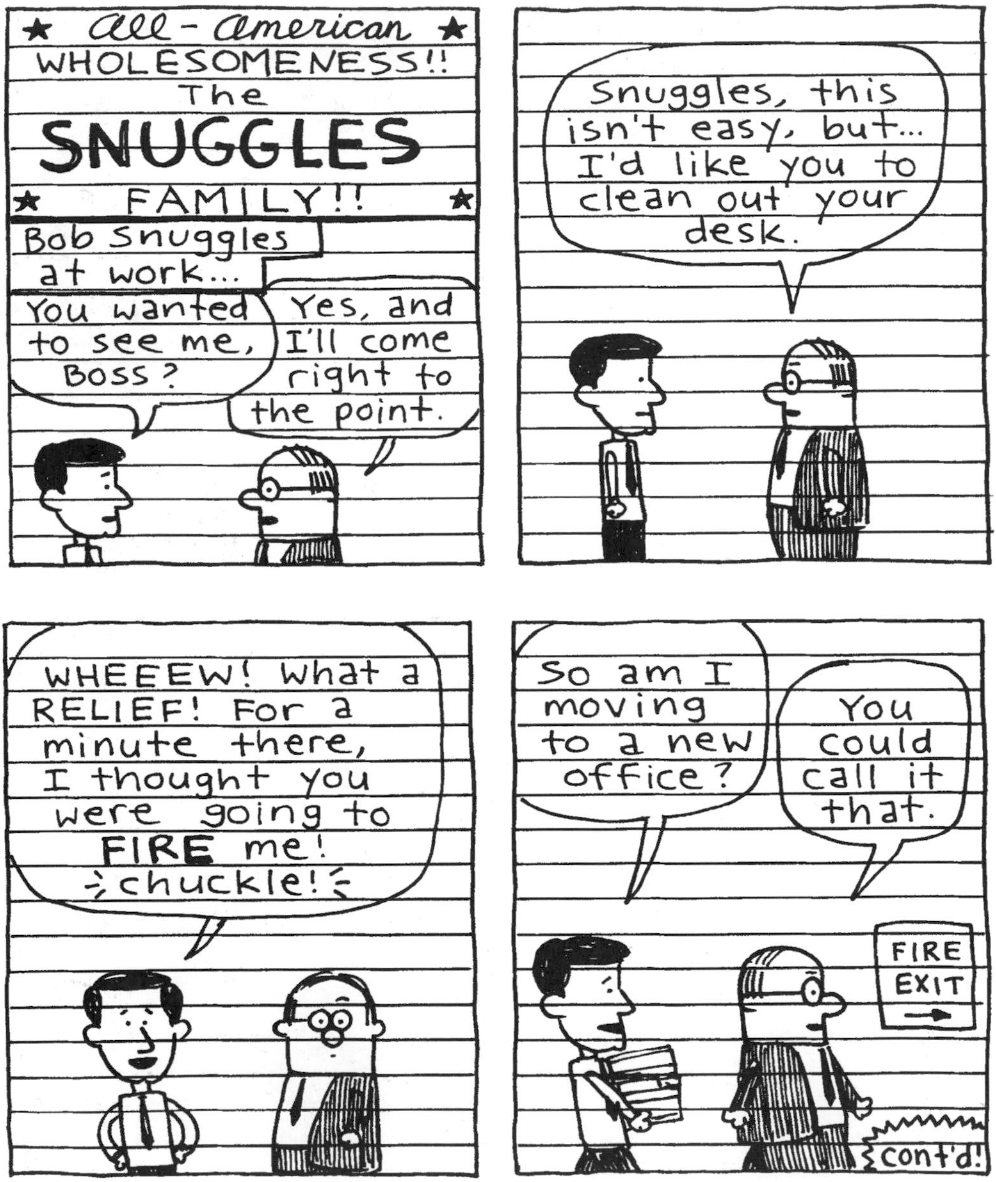
★ All-American ★
WHOLESOMENESS!!
The
SNUGGLES
★ FAMILY!! ★
Bob Snuggles at work...
You wanted to see me, Boss?
Yes, and I'll come right to the point.
Snuggles, this isn't easy, but... I'd like you to clean out your desk.
WHEEEW! What a RELIEF! For a minute there, I thought you were going to FIRE me! chuckle!
So am I moving to a new office?
You could call it that.
FIRE EXIT
cont'd!

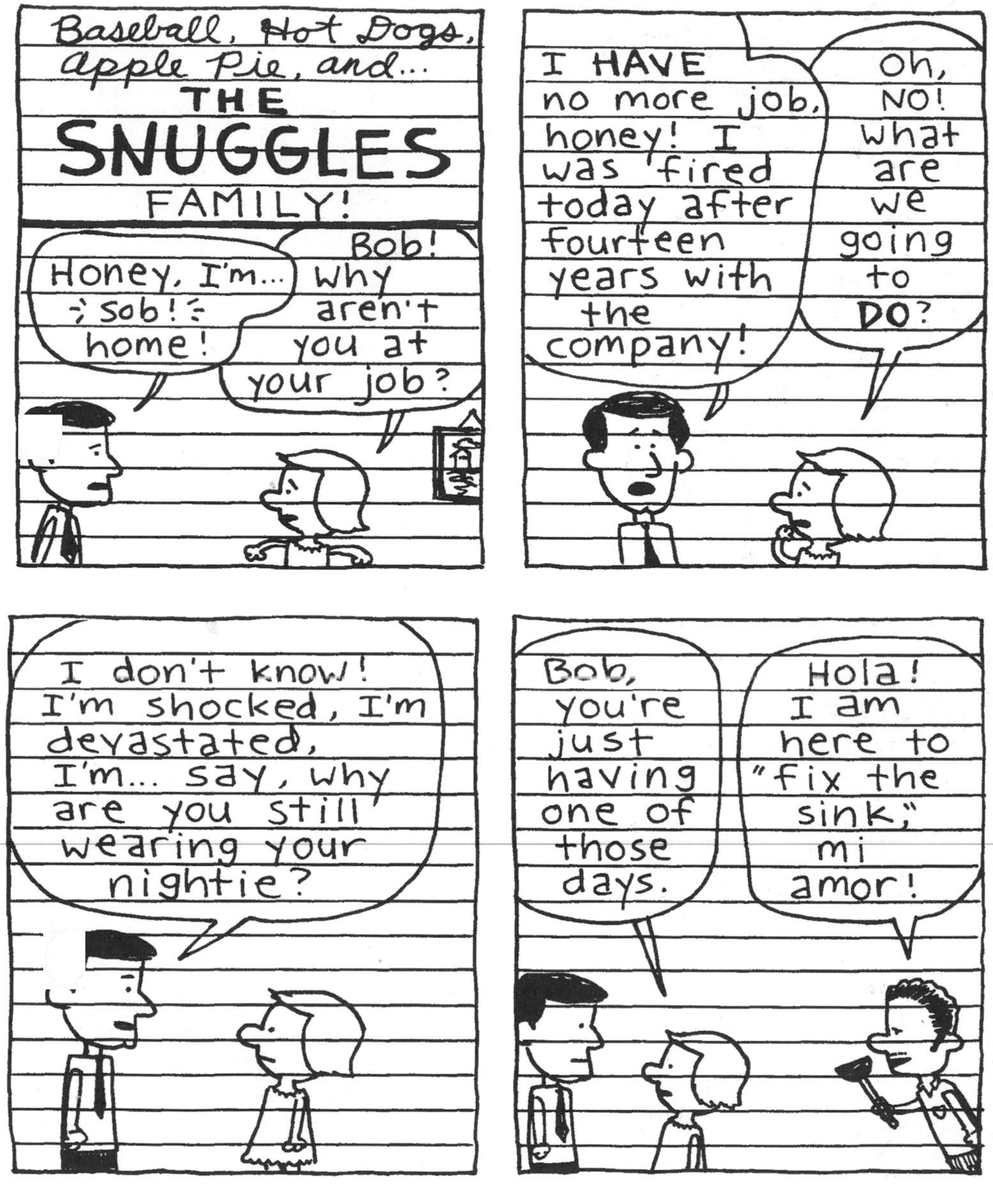
Baseball, Hot Dogs, Apple Pie, and...
THE SNUGGLES FAMILY!
Honey, I'm... sob! home!
Bob! Why aren't you at your job?
I HAVE no more job, honey! I was fired today after fourteen years with the company!
Oh, NO! What are we going to DO?
I don't know! I'm shocked, I'm devastated, I'm... say, why are you still wearing your nightie?
Bob, you're just having one of those days.
Hola! I am here to "fix the sink," mi amor!

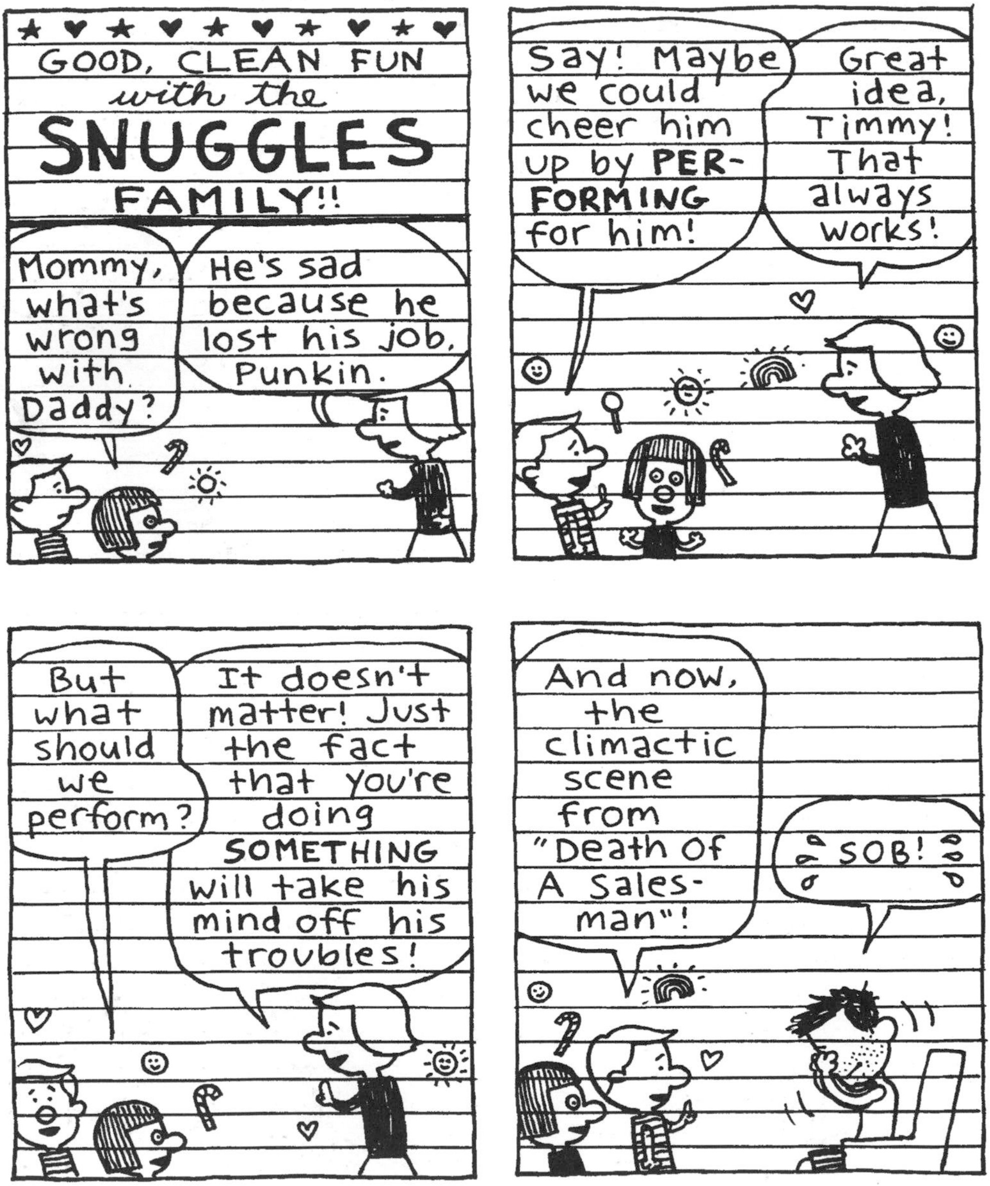
GOOD, CLEAN FUN with the SNUGGLES FAMILY!!
Mommy, what's wrong with Daddy?
He's sad because he lost his job, Punkin.
Say! Maybe we could cheer him up by PERFORMING for him!
Great idea, Timmy! That always works!
But what should we perform?
It doesn't matter! Just the fact that you're doing SOMETHING will take his mind off his troubles!
And now, the climactic scene from "Death of A Salesman"!
SOB!

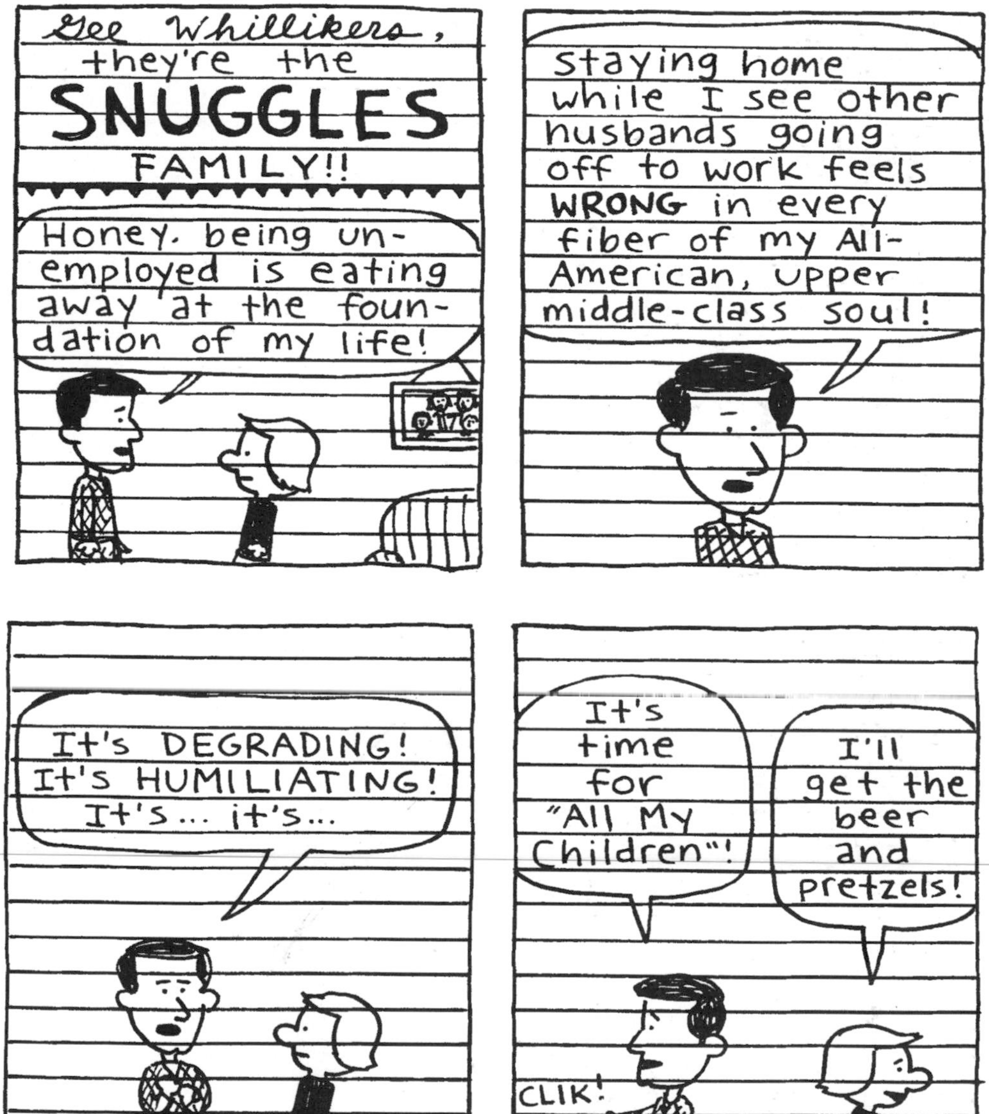
Gee Whillikers, they're the SNUGGLES FAMILY!!
Honey. being unemployed is eating away at the foundation of my life!
staying home while I see other husbands going off to work feels WRONG in every fiber of my All-American, upper middle-class soul!
It's DEGRADING! It's HUMILIATING! It's... it's...
It's time for "All My Children"!
I'll get the beer and pretzels!
CLIK!

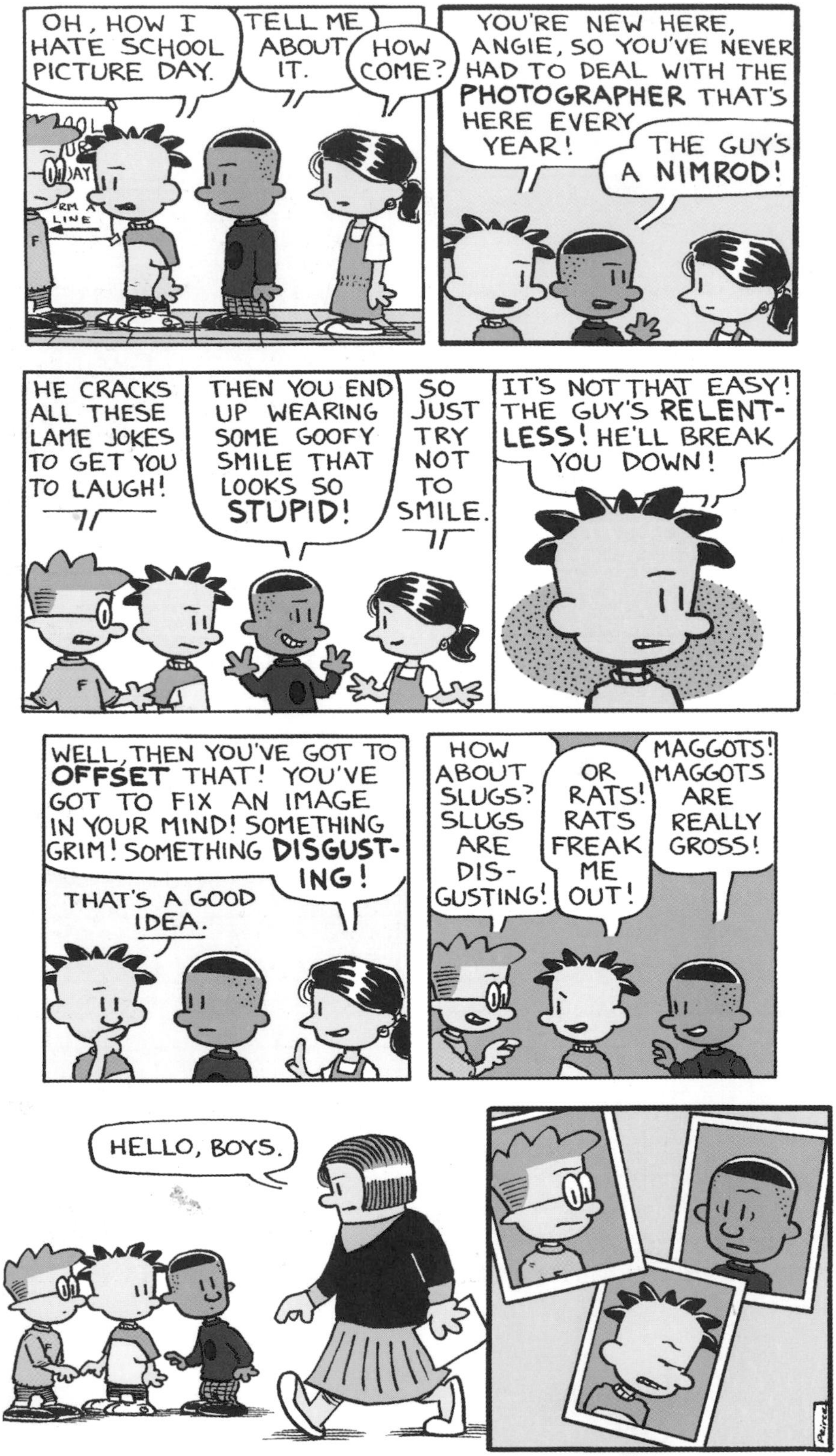
OH, HOW I HATE SCHOOL PICTURE DAY.
TELL ME ABOUT IT.
HOW COME?
YOU'RE NEW HERE, ANGIE, SO YOU'VE NEVER HAD TO DEAL WITH THE PHOTOGRAPHER THAT'S HERE EVERY YEAR!
THE GUY'S A NIMROD!
HE CRACKS ALL THESE LAME JOKES TO GET YOU TO LAUGH!
THEN YOU END UP WEARING SOME GOOFY SMILE THAT LOOKS SO STUPID!
SO JUST TRY NOT TO SMILE.
IT'S NOT THAT EASY! THE GUY'S RELENTLESS! HE'LL BREAK YOU DOWN!
WELL, THEN YOU'VE GOT TO OFFSET THAT! YOU'VE GOT TO FIX AN IMAGE IN YOUR MIND! SOMETHING GRIM! SOMETHING DISGUSTING!
THAT'S A GOOD IDEA.
HOW ABOUT SLUGS? SLUGS ARE DISGUSTING!
OR RATS! RATS FREAK ME OUT!
MAGGOTS! MAGGOTS ARE REALLY GROSS!
HELLO, BOYS.

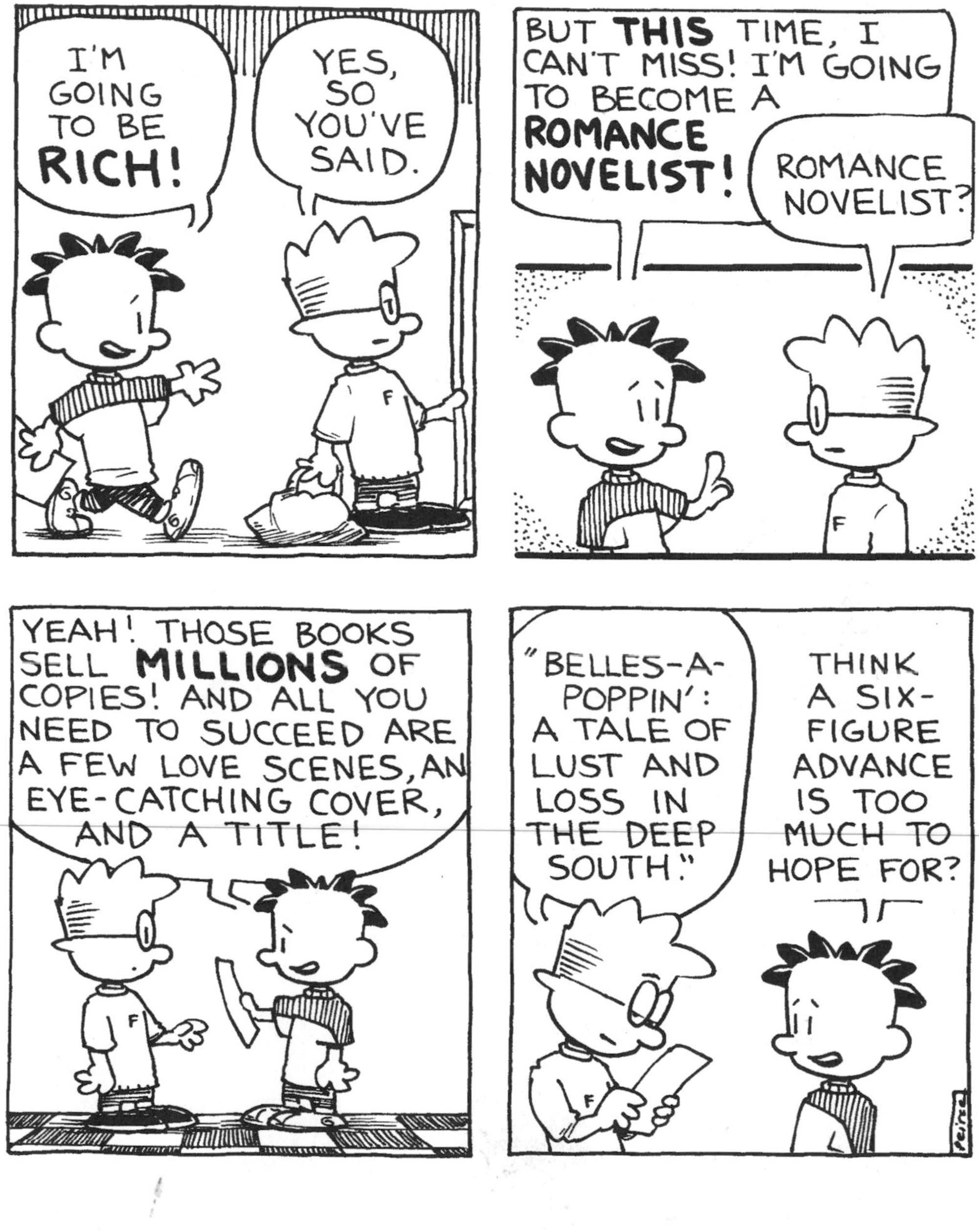
I'M GOING TO BE RICH!
YES, SO YOU'VE SAID.
BUT THIS TIME, I CAN'T MISS! I'M GOING TO BECOME A ROMANCE NOVELIST!
ROMANCE NOVELIST?
YEAH! THOSE BOOKS SELL MILLIONS OF COPIES! AND ALL YOU NEED TO SUCCEED ARE A FEW LOVE SCENES, AN EYE-CATCHING COVER, AND A TITLE!
"BELLES-A-POPPIN': A TALE OF LUST AND LOSS IN THE DEEP SOUTH."
THINK A SIX-FIGURE ADVANCE IS TOO MUCH TO HOPE FOR?
Peirce

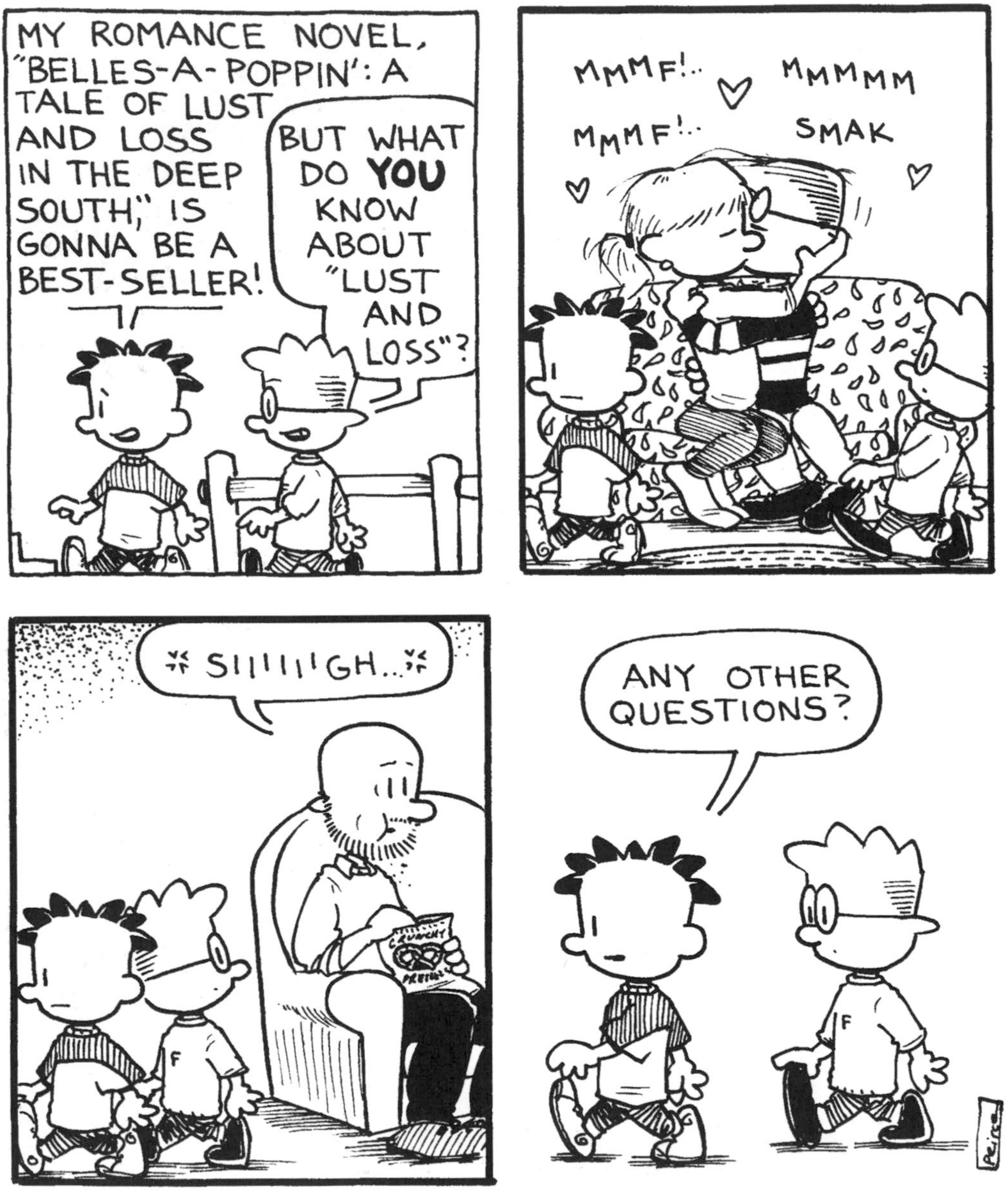
MY ROMANCE NOVEL, "BELLES-A-POPPIN': A TALE OF LUST AND LOSS IN THE DEEP SOUTH," IS GONNA BE A BEST-SELLER!
BUT WHAT DO **YOU** KNOW ABOUT "LUST AND LOSS"?
MMMF!..
MMMMMM
MMMF!..
SMAK
SIIIIIGH...
CRUNCHY PRETZELS
ANY OTHER QUESTIONS?
Peirce

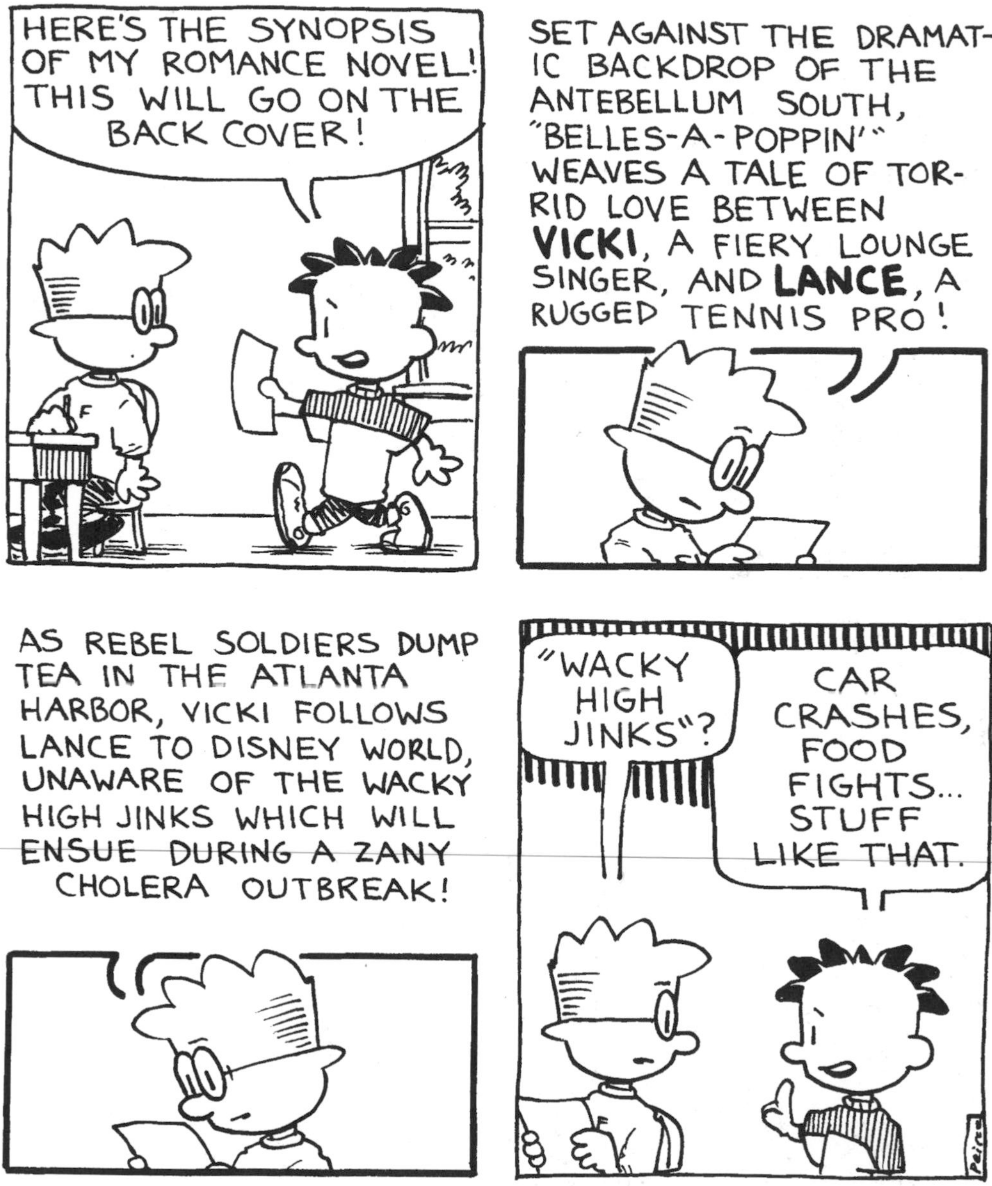
HERE'S THE SYNOPSIS OF MY ROMANCE NOVEL! THIS WILL GO ON THE BACK COVER!
SET AGAINST THE DRAMATIC BACKDROP OF THE ANTEBELLUM SOUTH, "BELLES-A-POPPIN'" WEAVES A TALE OF TORRID LOVE BETWEEN **VICKI**, A FIERY LOUNGE SINGER, AND **LANCE**, A RUGGED TENNIS PRO!
AS REBEL SOLDIERS DUMP TEA IN THE ATLANTA HARBOR, VICKI FOLLOWS LANCE TO DISNEY WORLD, UNAWARE OF THE WACKY HIGH JINKS WHICH WILL ENSUE DURING A ZANY CHOLERA OUTBREAK!
"WACKY HIGH JINKS"?
CAR CRASHES, FOOD FIGHTS... STUFF LIKE THAT.
Peirce

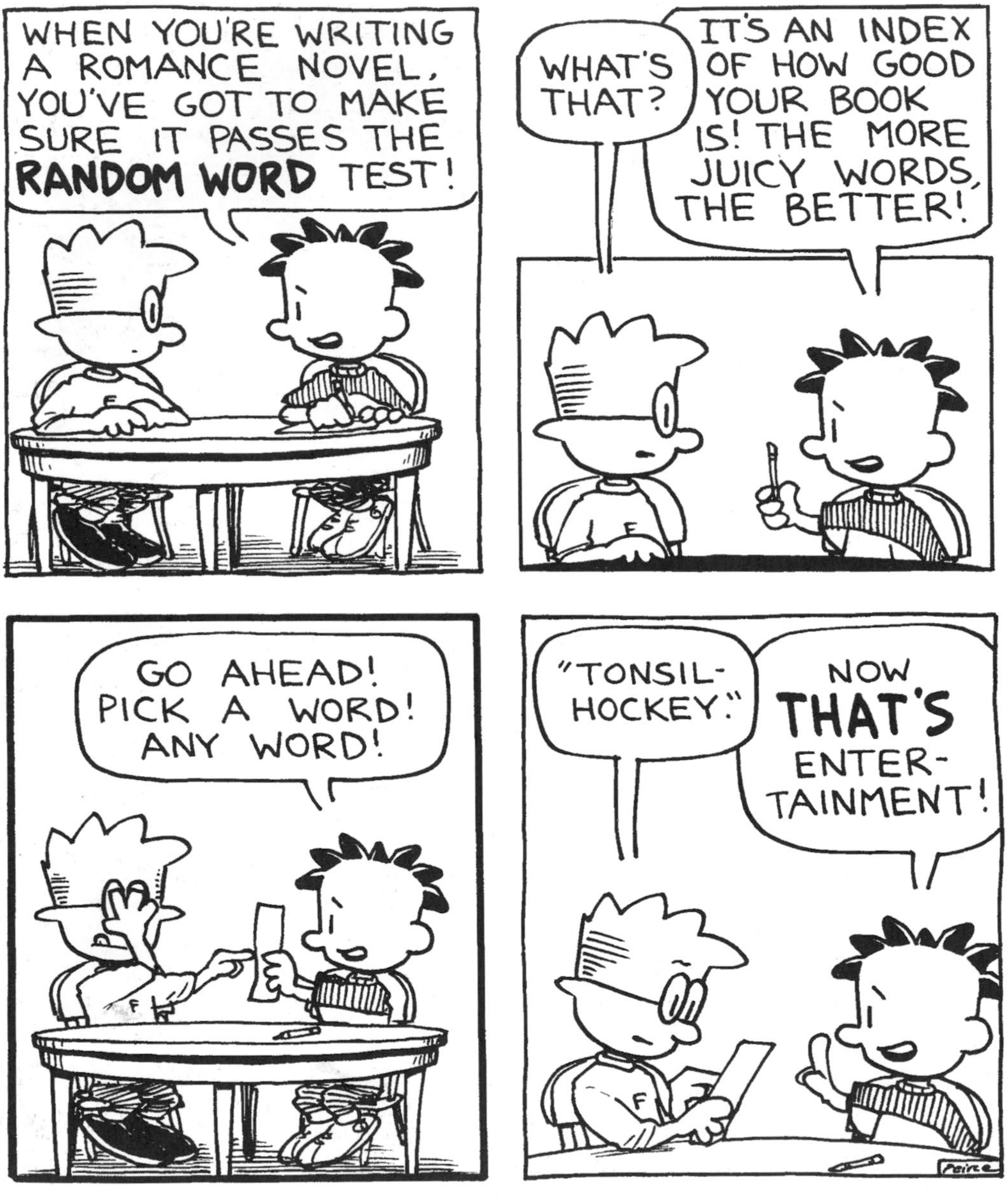
WHEN YOU'RE WRITING A ROMANCE NOVEL, YOU'VE GOT TO MAKE SURE IT PASSES THE RANDOM WORD TEST!
WHAT'S THAT?
IT'S AN INDEX OF HOW GOOD YOUR BOOK IS! THE MORE JUICY WORDS, THE BETTER!
GO AHEAD! PICK A WORD! ANY WORD!
"TONSIL-HOCKEY."
NOW THAT'S ENTER-TAINMENT!
Peirce

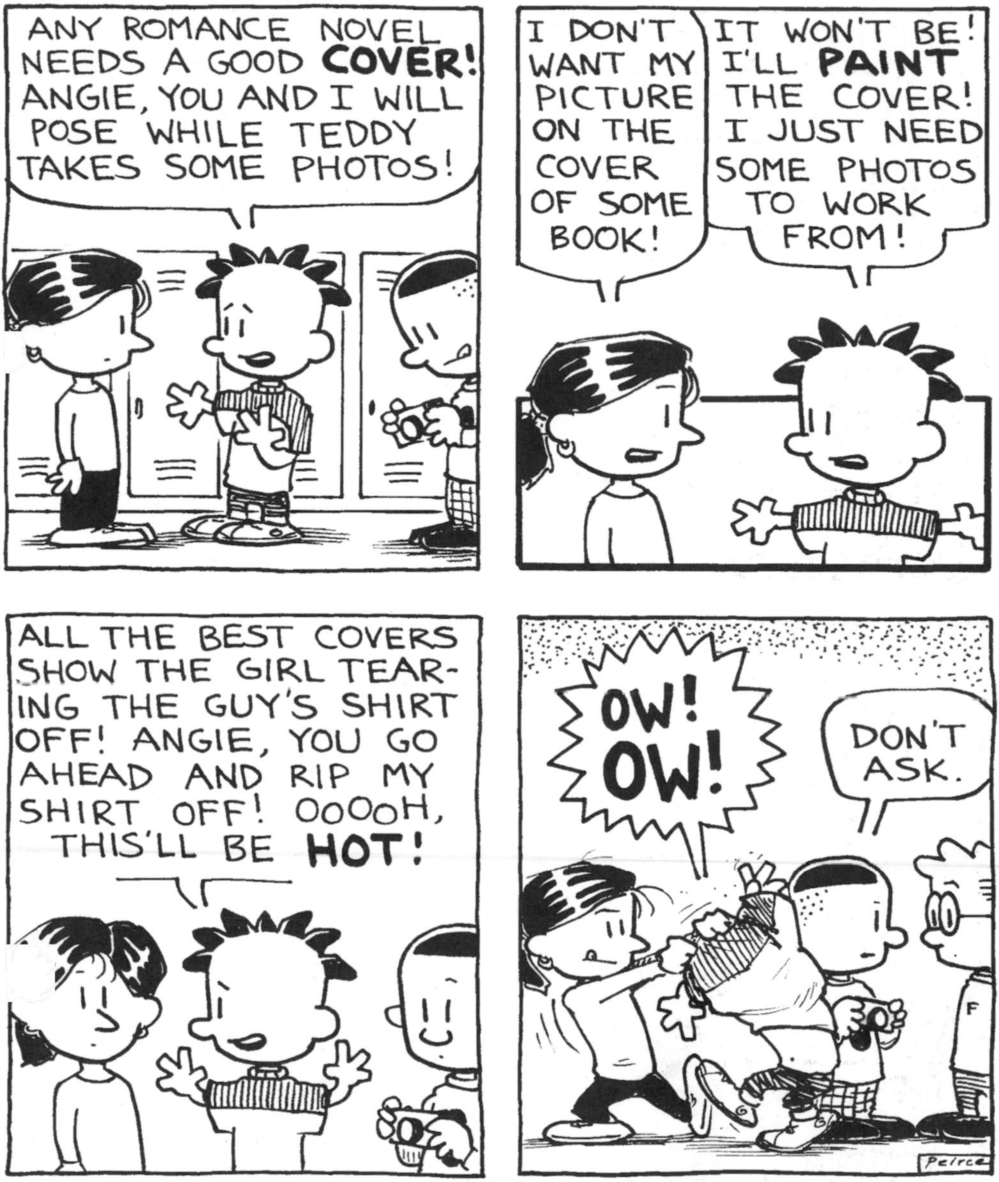
ANY ROMANCE NOVEL NEEDS A GOOD **COVER**! ANGIE, YOU AND I WILL POSE WHILE TEDDY TAKES SOME PHOTOS!
I DON'T WANT MY PICTURE ON THE COVER OF SOME BOOK!
IT WON'T BE! I'LL **PAINT** THE COVER! I JUST NEED SOME PHOTOS TO WORK FROM!
ALL THE BEST COVERS SHOW THE GIRL TEARING THE GUY'S SHIRT OFF! ANGIE, YOU GO AHEAD AND RIP MY SHIRT OFF! OOOOH, THIS'LL BE **HOT**!
OW! OW!
DON'T ASK.
F
Peirce

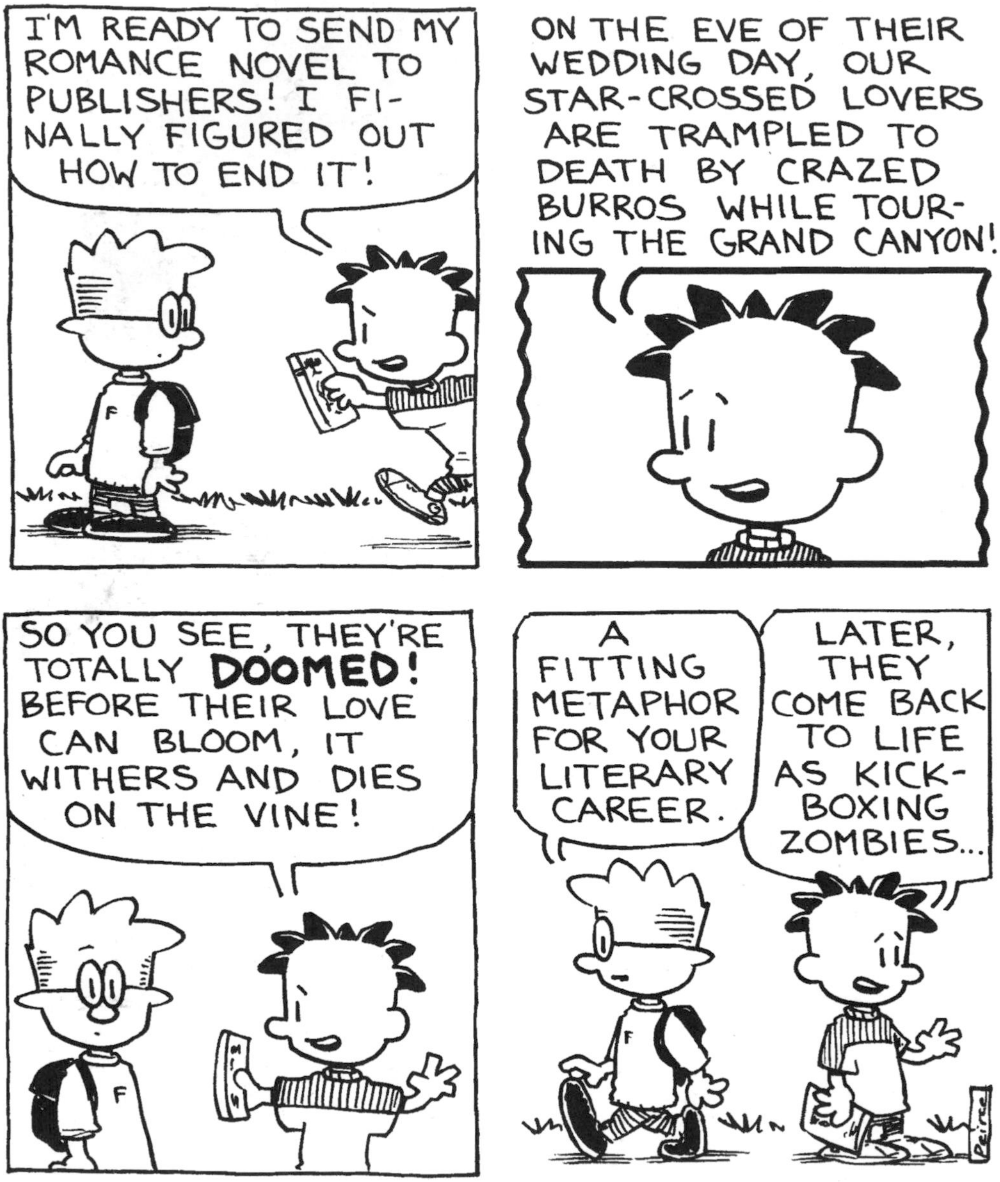
I'M READY TO SEND MY ROMANCE NOVEL TO PUBLISHERS! I FINALLY FIGURED OUT HOW TO END IT!
ON THE EVE OF THEIR WEDDING DAY, OUR STAR-CROSSED LOVERS ARE TRAMPLED TO DEATH BY CRAZED BURROS WHILE TOURING THE GRAND CANYON!
SO YOU SEE, THEY'RE TOTALLY DOOMED! BEFORE THEIR LOVE CAN BLOOM, IT WITHERS AND DIES ON THE VINE!
A FITTING METAPHOR FOR YOUR LITERARY CAREER.
LATER, THEY COME BACK TO LIFE AS KICK-BOXING ZOMBIES...
Peirce

Nate Wright's O-FFICIAL 1997 6th grade HOT and COLD Guide! "★★★★"
HOT: Mr. Galvin!
Let's turn to page... ZZZ..
He fell asleep again!
High-five me!
COLD: Duh.
I summon thee, demons of darkness!
Dang!
She's goin' postal!
HOT: Slides (recess)
WA-HOO!
COLD: Slides (biology)
Here's another example of cell division...
Sigh...
HOT: Hangin' out by your locker!
What's happenin', ladies?
♡ Hiiiiiii
COLD: Hangin' out WITH your locker!
You are my only friend! SOB!
HOT: Bringing your own lunch from home!
Hey, HEY! Pizza and chips again!
HOW'S THE MEAT-LOAF?
COLD.
WHY DON'T YOU JUST BRING YOUR OWN LUNCH?

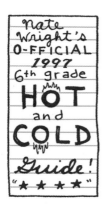

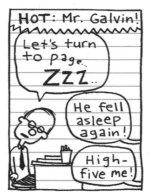

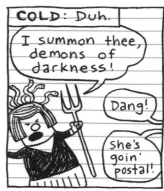

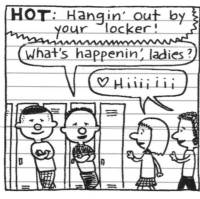

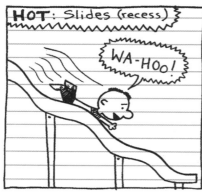

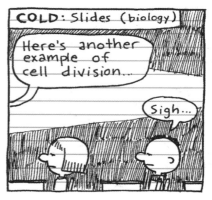

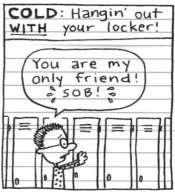

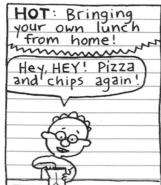

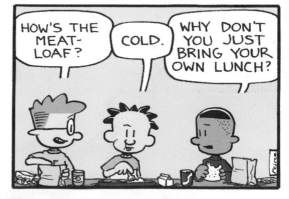

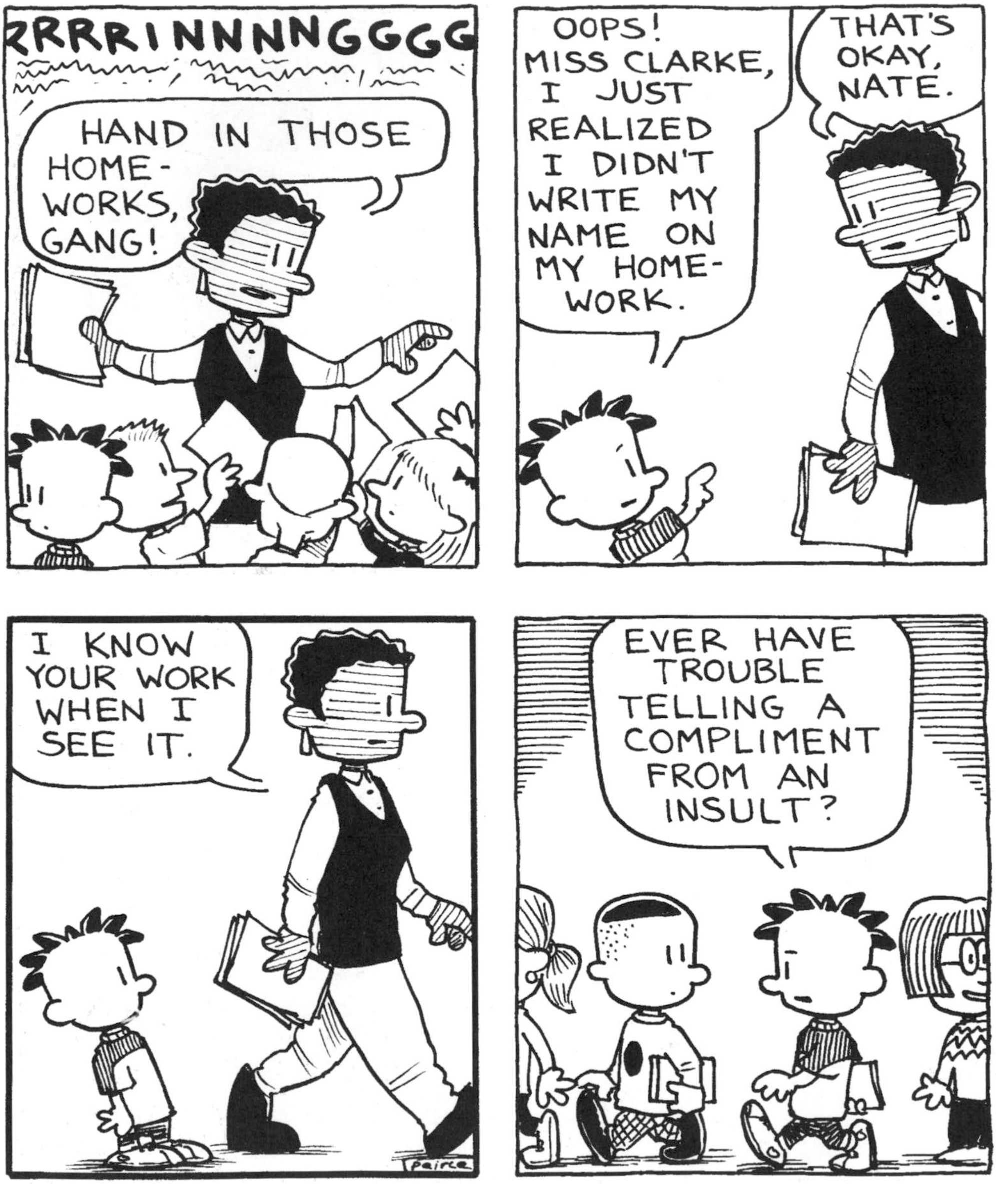
RRRRINNNNGGGG
HAND IN THOSE HOME-WORKS, GANG!
OOPS! MISS CLARKE, I JUST REALIZED I DIDN'T WRITE MY NAME ON MY HOME-WORK.
THAT'S OKAY, NATE.
I KNOW YOUR WORK WHEN I SEE IT.
EVER HAVE TROUBLE TELLING A COMPLIMENT FROM AN INSULT?
Peirce

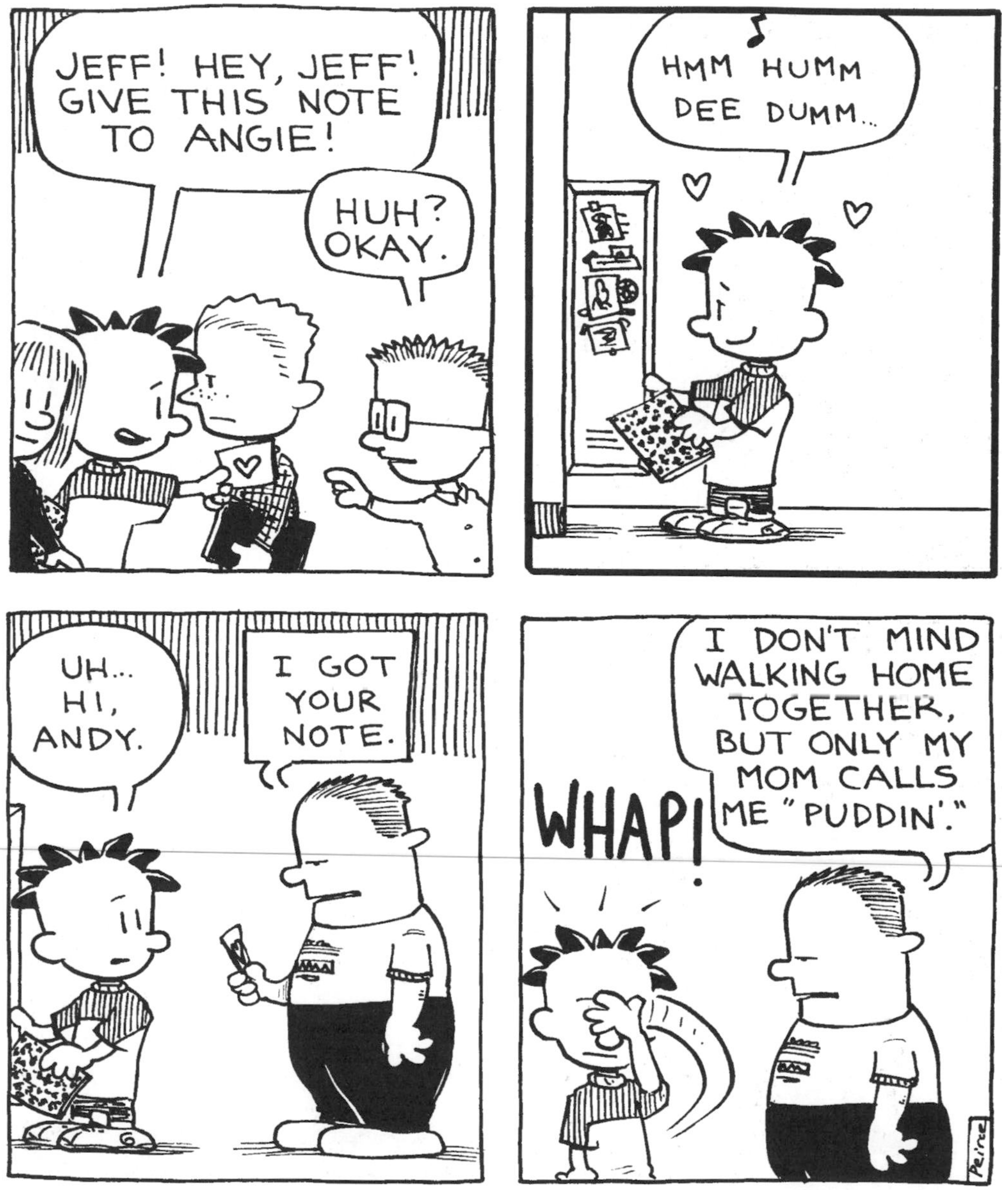
JEFF! HEY, JEFF! GIVE THIS NOTE TO ANGIE!
HUH? OKAY.
HMM HUMM DEE DUMM...
UH... HI, ANDY.
I GOT YOUR NOTE.
I DON'T MIND WALKING HOME TOGETHER, BUT ONLY MY MOM CALLS ME "PUDDIN'."
WHAP!
Peirce

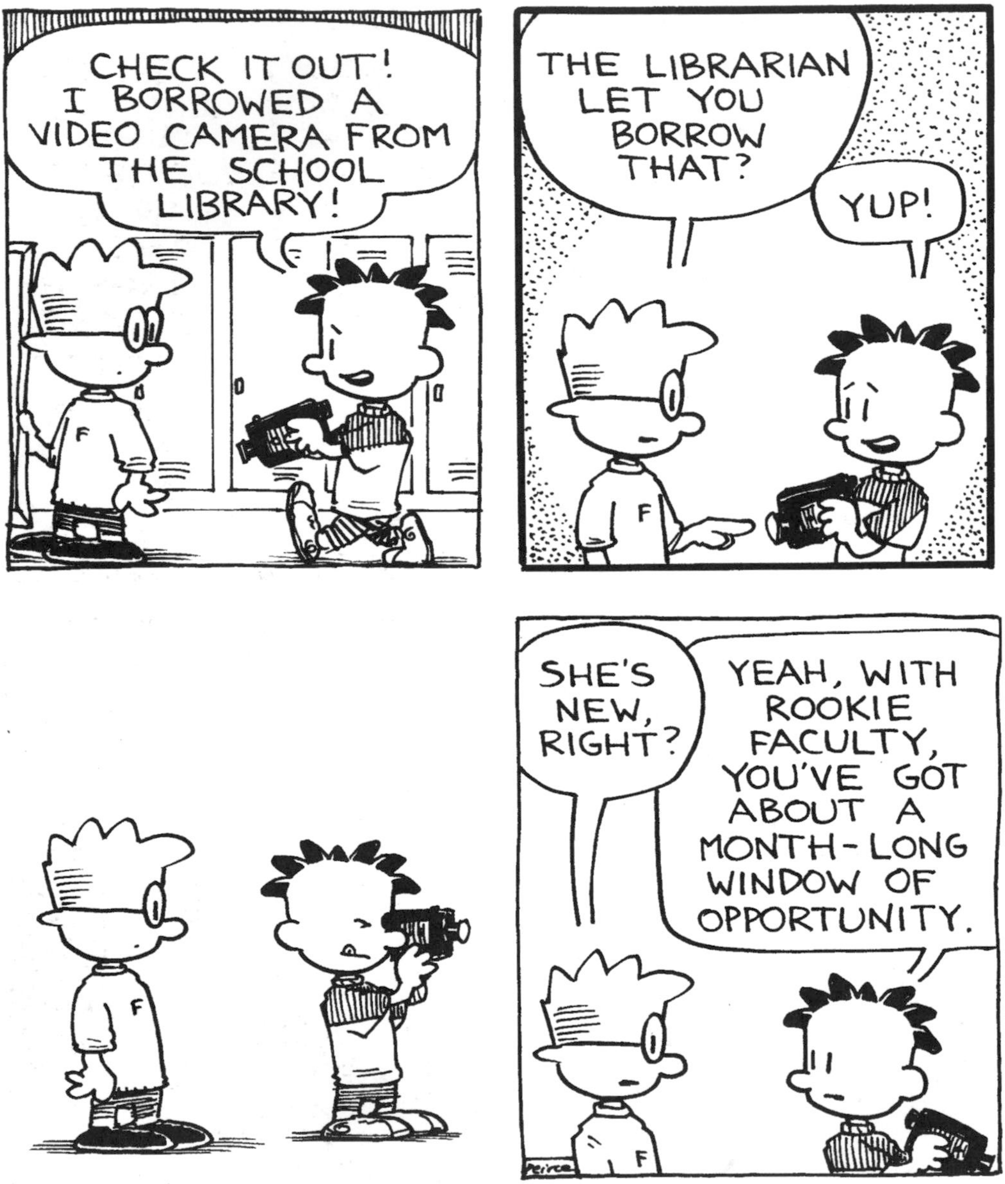
CHECK IT OUT! I BORROWED A VIDEO CAMERA FROM THE SCHOOL LIBRARY!
THE LIBRARIAN LET YOU BORROW THAT?
YUP!
SHE'S NEW, RIGHT?
YEAH, WITH ROOKIE FACULTY, YOU'VE GOT ABOUT A MONTH-LONG WINDOW OF OPPORTUNITY.
Peirce

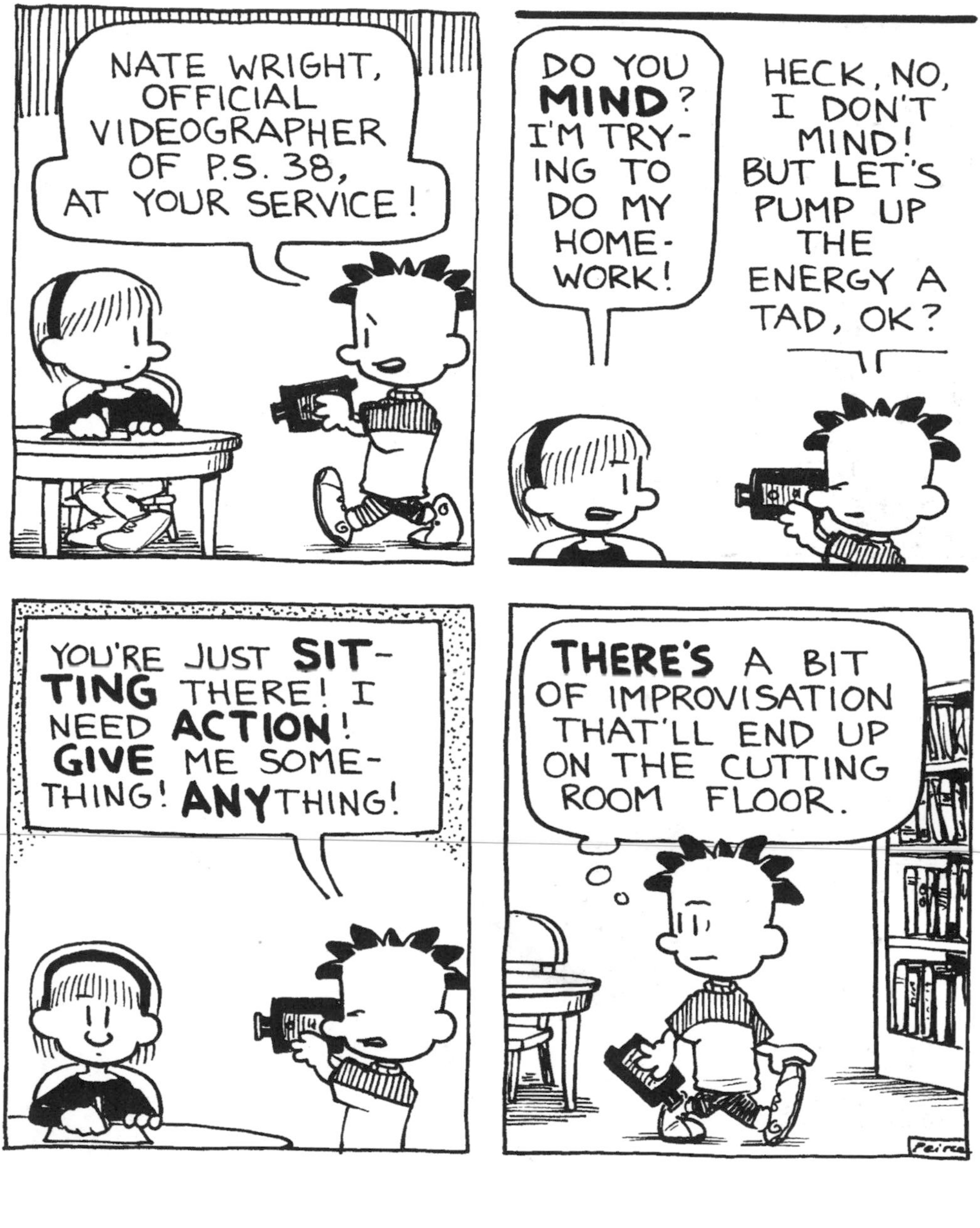
NATE WRIGHT, OFFICIAL VIDEOGRAPHER OF P.S. 38, AT YOUR SERVICE!
DO YOU **MIND**? I'M TRYING TO DO MY HOMEWORK!
HECK, NO, I DON'T MIND! BUT LET'S PUMP UP THE ENERGY A TAD, OK?
YOU'RE JUST **SITTING** THERE! I NEED **ACTION**! **GIVE** ME SOMETHING! **ANY**THING!
THERE'S A BIT OF IMPROVISATION THAT'LL END UP ON THE CUTTING ROOM FLOOR.
Peirce

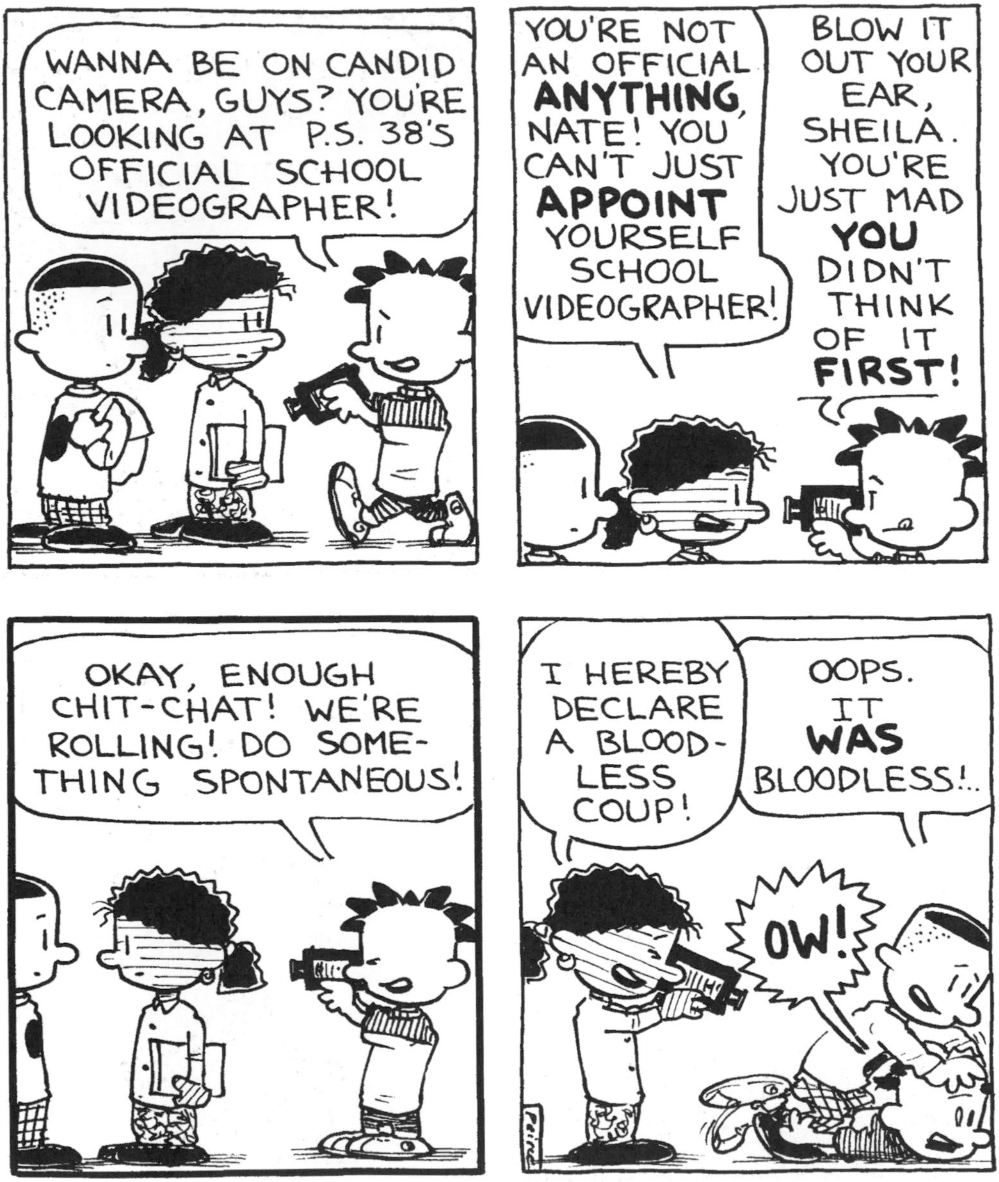
WANNA BE ON CANDID CAMERA, GUYS? YOU'RE LOOKING AT P.S. 38'S OFFICIAL SCHOOL VIDEOGRAPHER!
YOU'RE NOT AN OFFICIAL **ANYTHING**, NATE! YOU CAN'T JUST **APPOINT** YOURSELF SCHOOL VIDEOGRAPHER!
BLOW IT OUT YOUR EAR, SHEILA. YOU'RE JUST MAD **YOU** DIDN'T THINK OF IT **FIRST**!
OKAY, ENOUGH CHIT-CHAT! WE'RE ROLLING! DO SOMETHING SPONTANEOUS!
I HEREBY DECLARE A BLOODLESS COUP!
OOPS. IT **WAS** BLOODLESS!..
OW!
Peirce

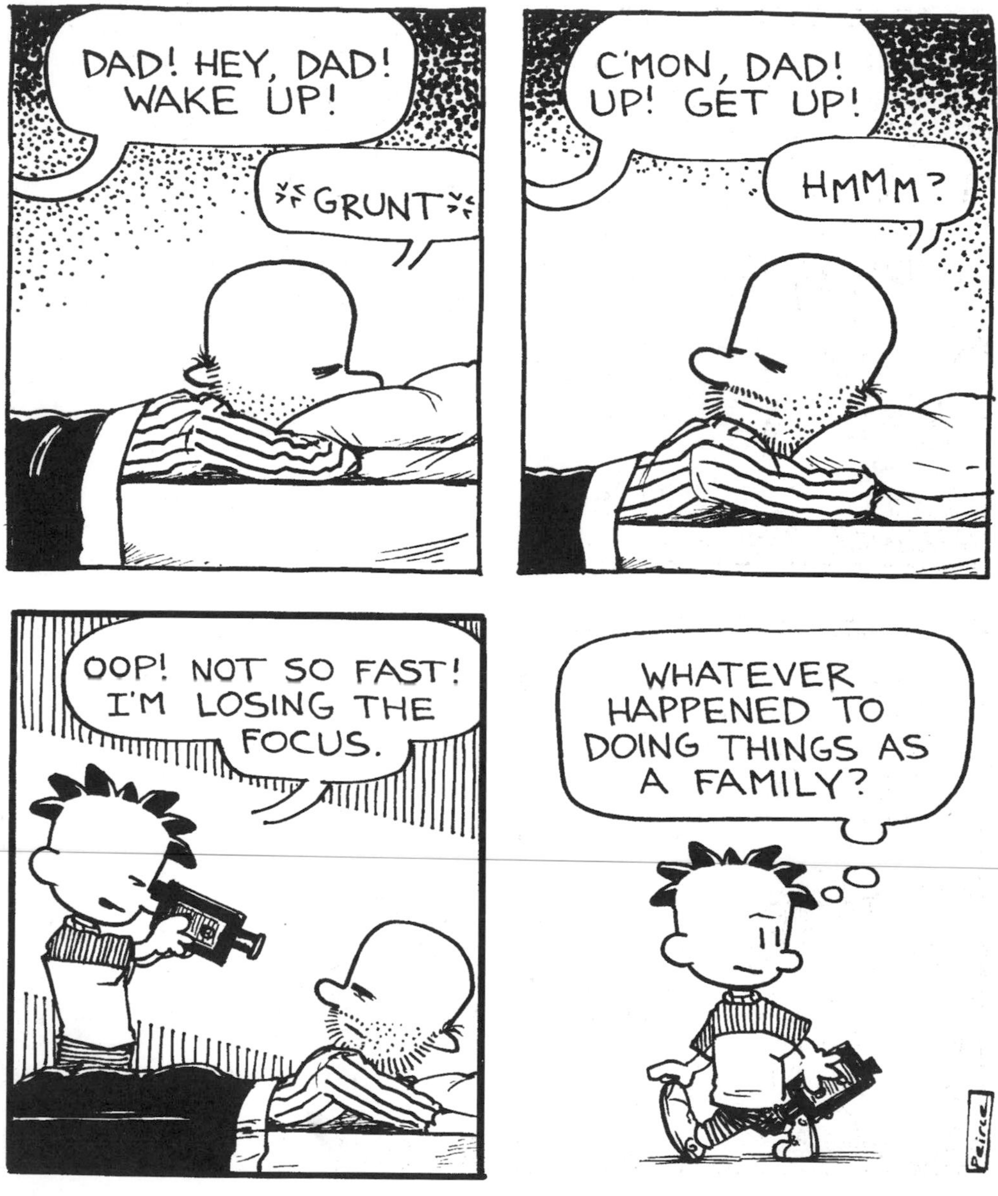
DAD! HEY, DAD! WAKE UP!
GRUNT
C'MON, DAD! UP! GET UP!
HMMM?
OOP! NOT SO FAST! I'M LOSING THE FOCUS.
WHATEVER HAPPENED TO DOING THINGS AS A FAMILY?
Peirce

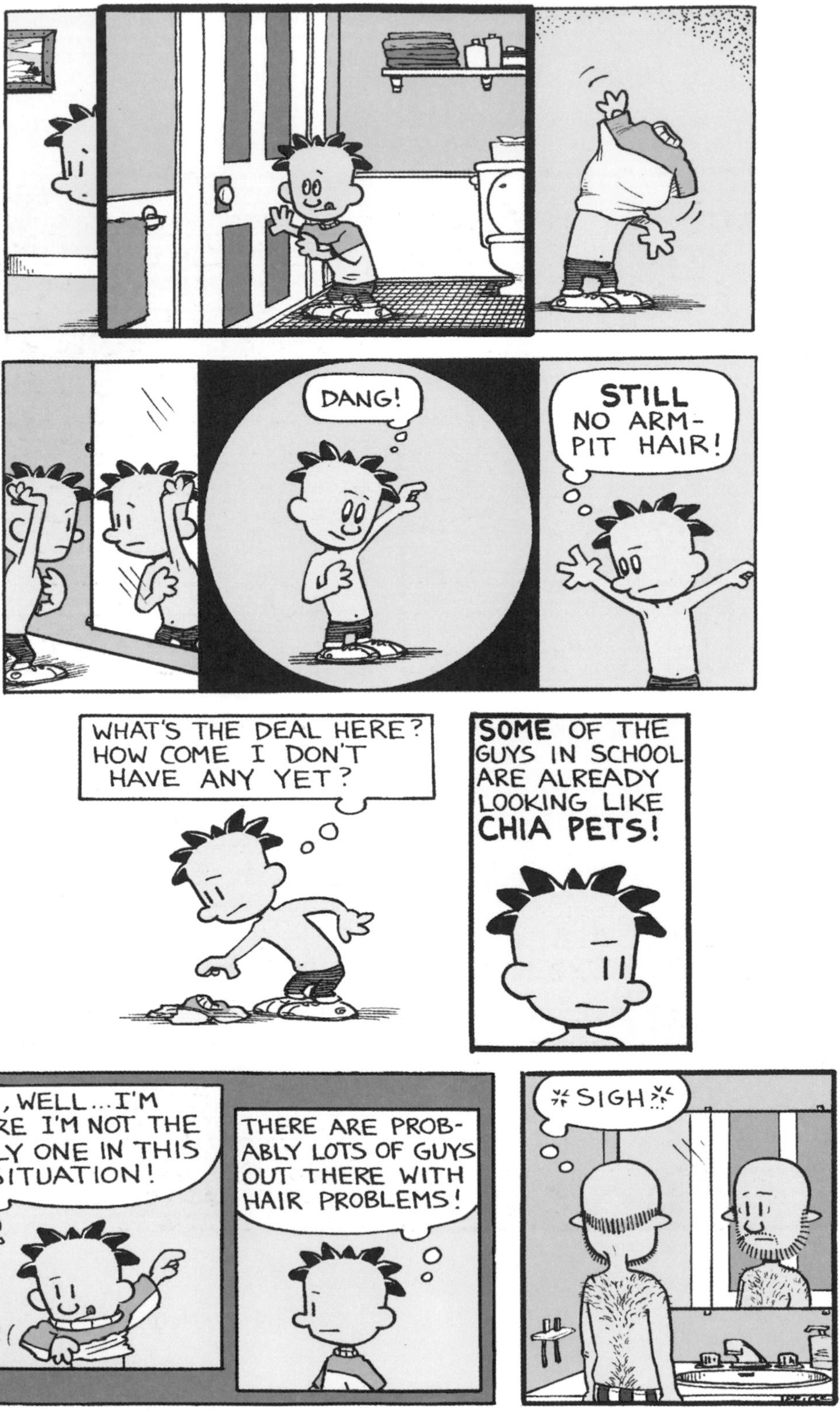
DANG!
STILL NO ARM-PIT HAIR!
WHAT'S THE DEAL HERE? HOW COME I DON'T HAVE ANY YET?
SOME OF THE GUYS IN SCHOOL ARE ALREADY LOOKING LIKE CHIA PETS!
OH, WELL...I'M SURE I'M NOT THE ONLY ONE IN THIS SITUATION!
THERE ARE PROBABLY LOTS OF GUYS OUT THERE WITH HAIR PROBLEMS!
SIGH

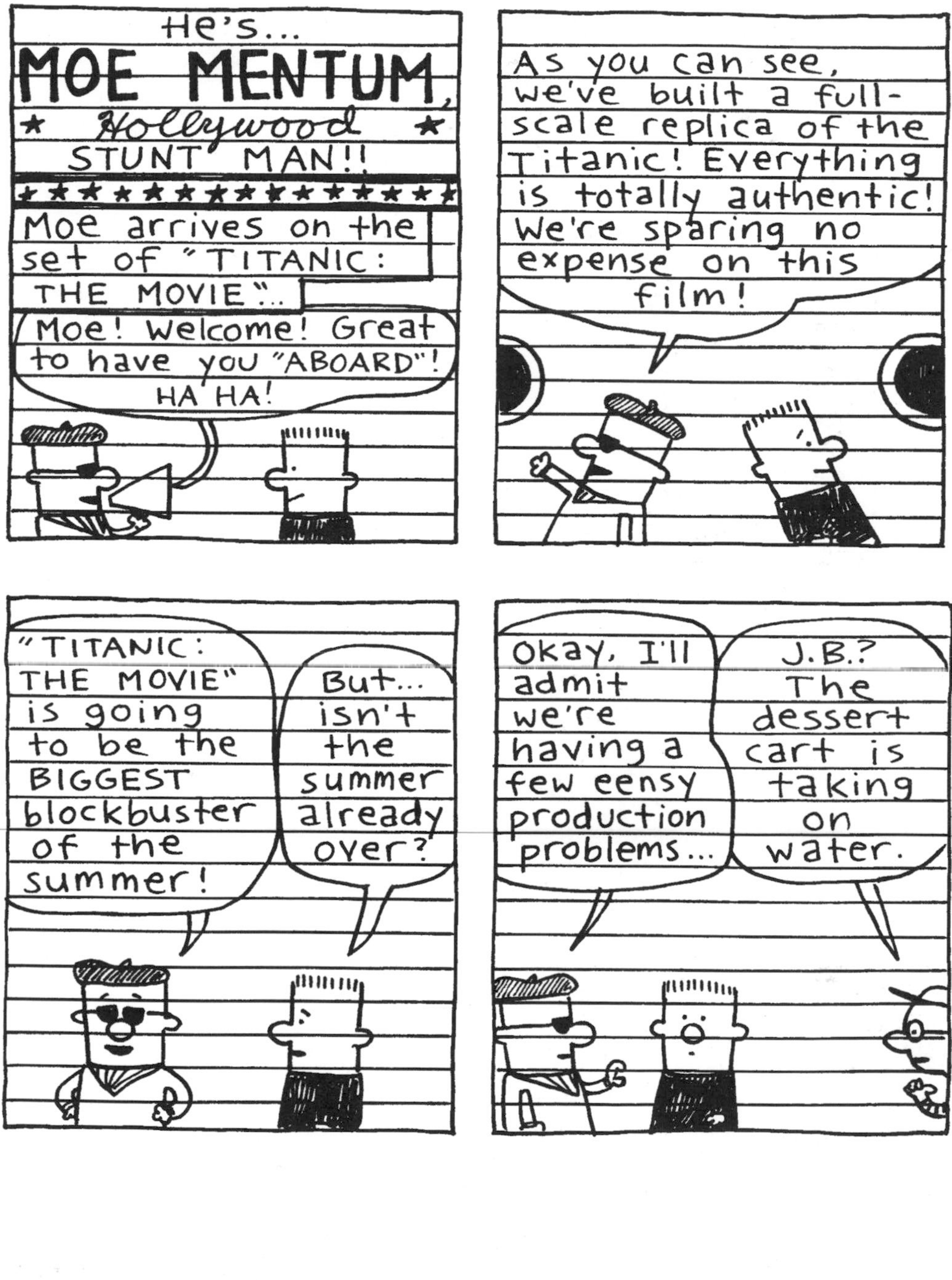
He's...
MOE MENTUM,
Hollywood
STUNT MAN!!
Moe arrives on the set of "TITANIC: THE MOVIE"...
Moe! Welcome! Great to have you "ABOARD"! HA HA!
As you can see, we've built a full-scale replica of the Titanic! Everything is totally authentic! We're sparing no expense on this film!
"TITANIC: THE MOVIE" is going to be the BIGGEST blockbuster of the summer!
But... isn't the summer already over?
Okay, I'll admit we're having a few eensy production problems...
J.B.? The dessert cart is taking on water.

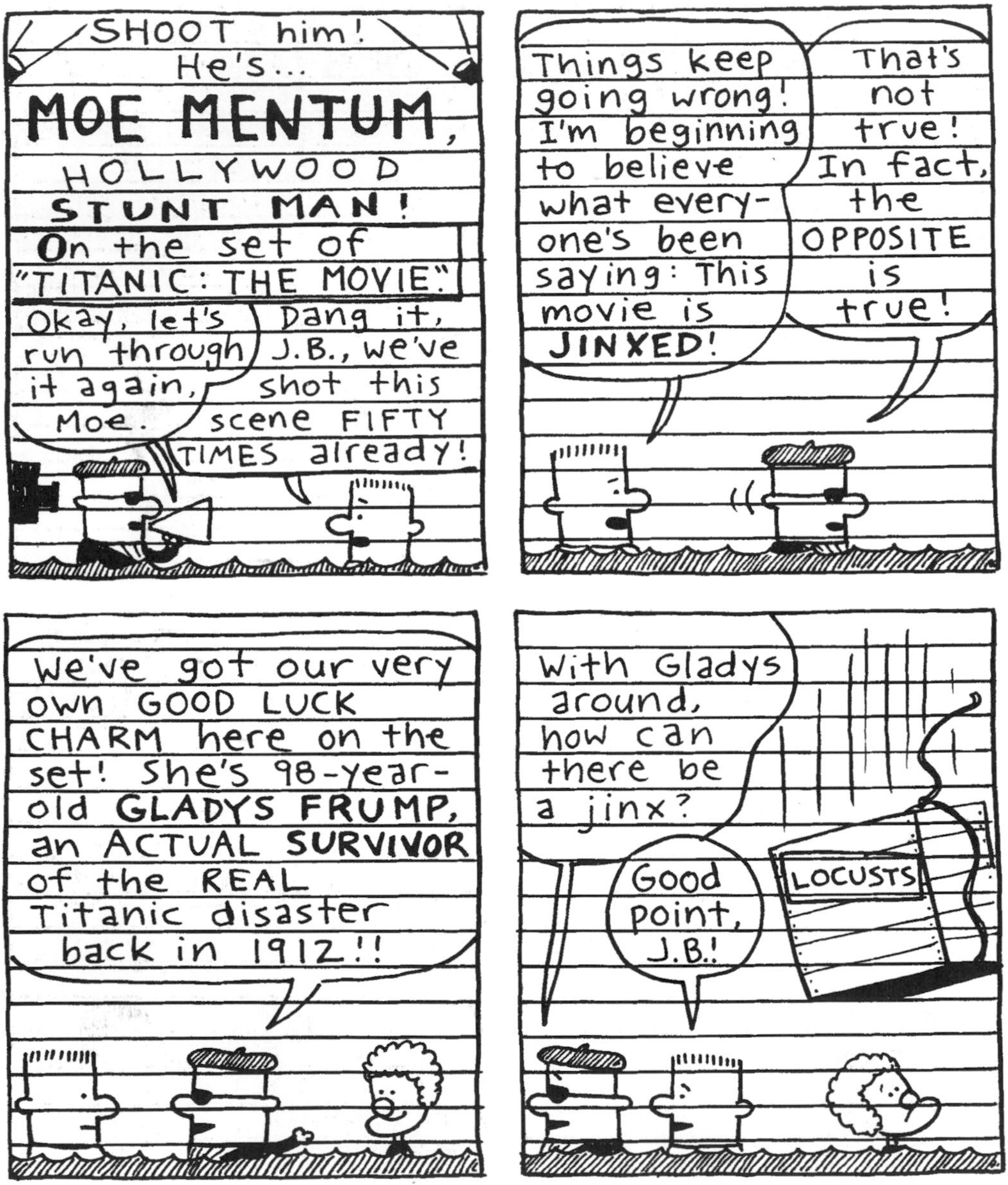
SHOOT him! He's...
MOE MENTUM, HOLLYWOOD STUNT MAN!
On the set of "TITANIC: THE MOVIE."
Okay, let's run through it again, Moe.
Dang it, J.B., we've shot this scene FIFTY TIMES already!
Things keep going wrong! I'm beginning to believe what every-one's been saying: This movie is JINXED!
That's not true! In fact, the OPPOSITE is true!
We've got our very own GOOD LUCK CHARM here on the set! She's 98-year-old GLADYS FRUMP, an ACTUAL SURVIVOR of the REAL Titanic disaster back in 1912!!
With Gladys around, how can there be a jinx?
Good point, J.B.!
LOCUSTS

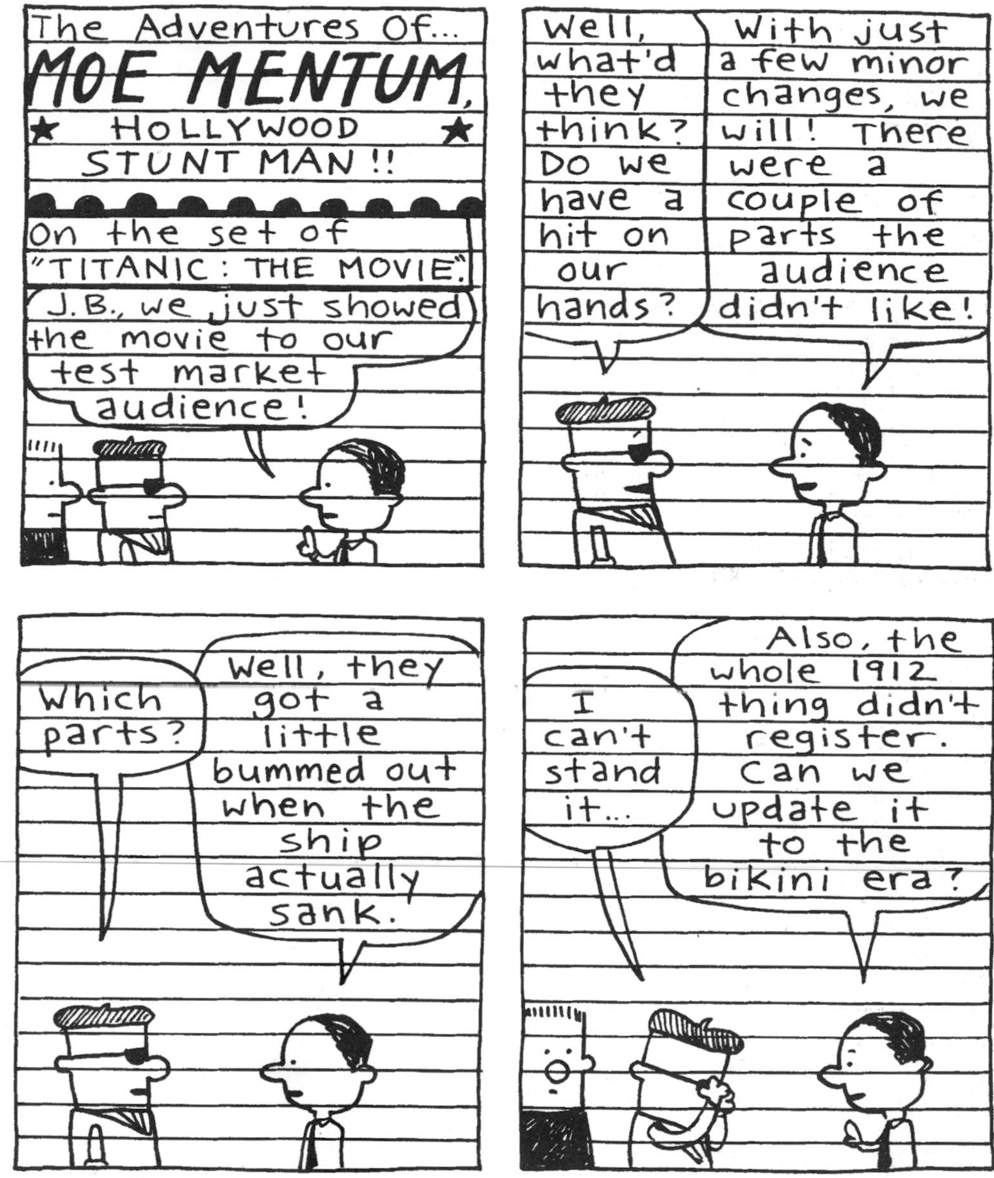
The Adventures Of...
MOE MENTUM,
★ HOLLYWOOD ★
STUNT MAN!!
On the set of "TITANIC: THE MOVIE"
J.B., we just showed the movie to our test market audience!
Well, what'd they think? Do we have a hit on our hands?
With just a few minor changes, we will! There were a couple of parts the audience didn't like!
Which parts?
Well, they got a little bummed out when the ship actually sank.
I can't stand it...
Also, the whole 1912 thing didn't register. Can we update it to the bikini era?

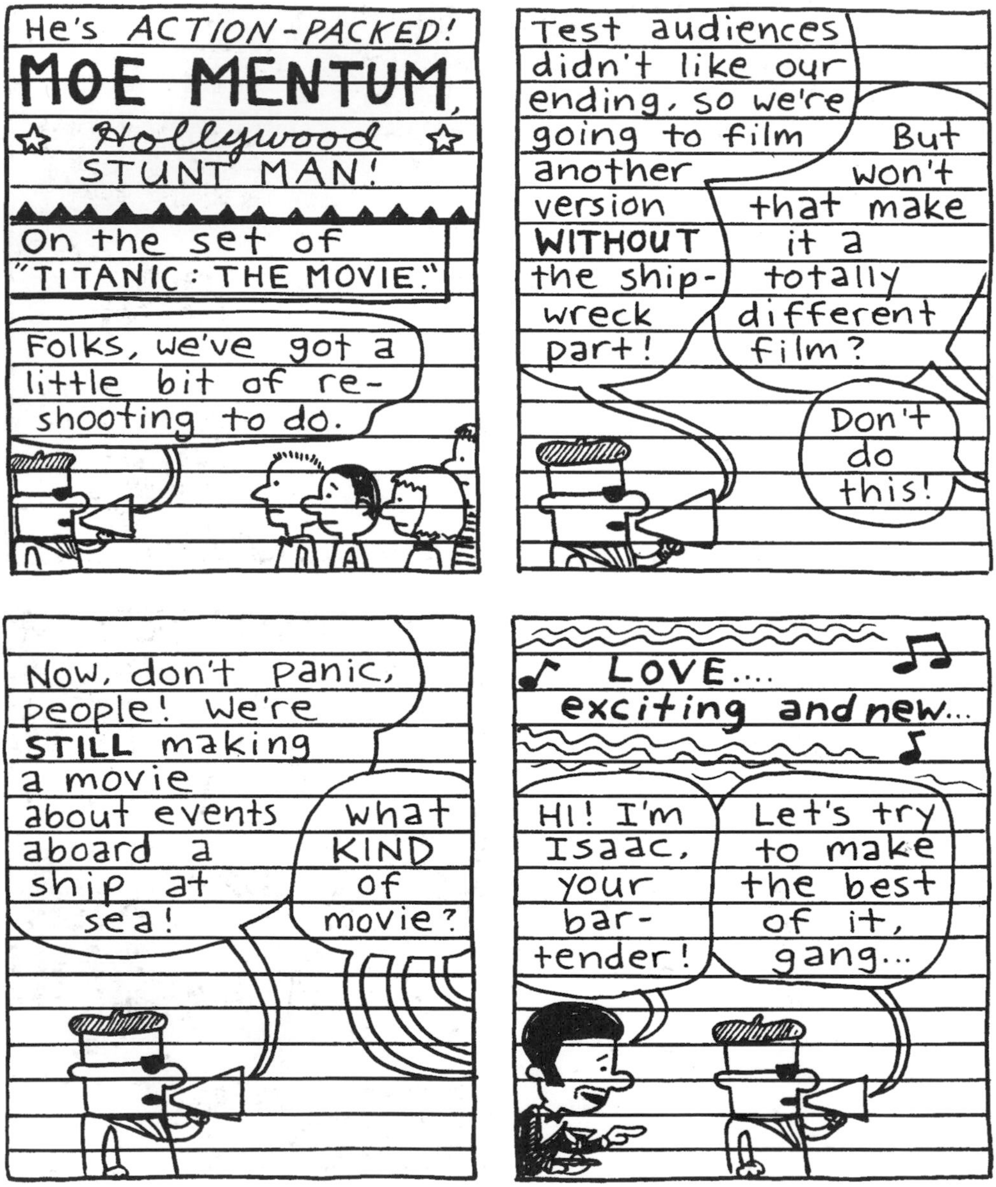
He's ACTION-PACKED!
MOE MENTUM,
Hollywood
STUNT MAN!
On the set of "TITANIC: THE MOVIE."
Folks, we've got a little bit of re-shooting to do.
Test audiences didn't like our ending, so we're going to film another version WITHOUT the ship-wreck part!
But won't that make it a totally different film?
Don't do this!
Now, don't panic, people! We're STILL making a movie about events aboard a ship at sea!
what KIND of movie?
LOVE.... exciting and new...
HI! I'm Isaac, your bar-tender!
Let's try to make the best of it, gang...

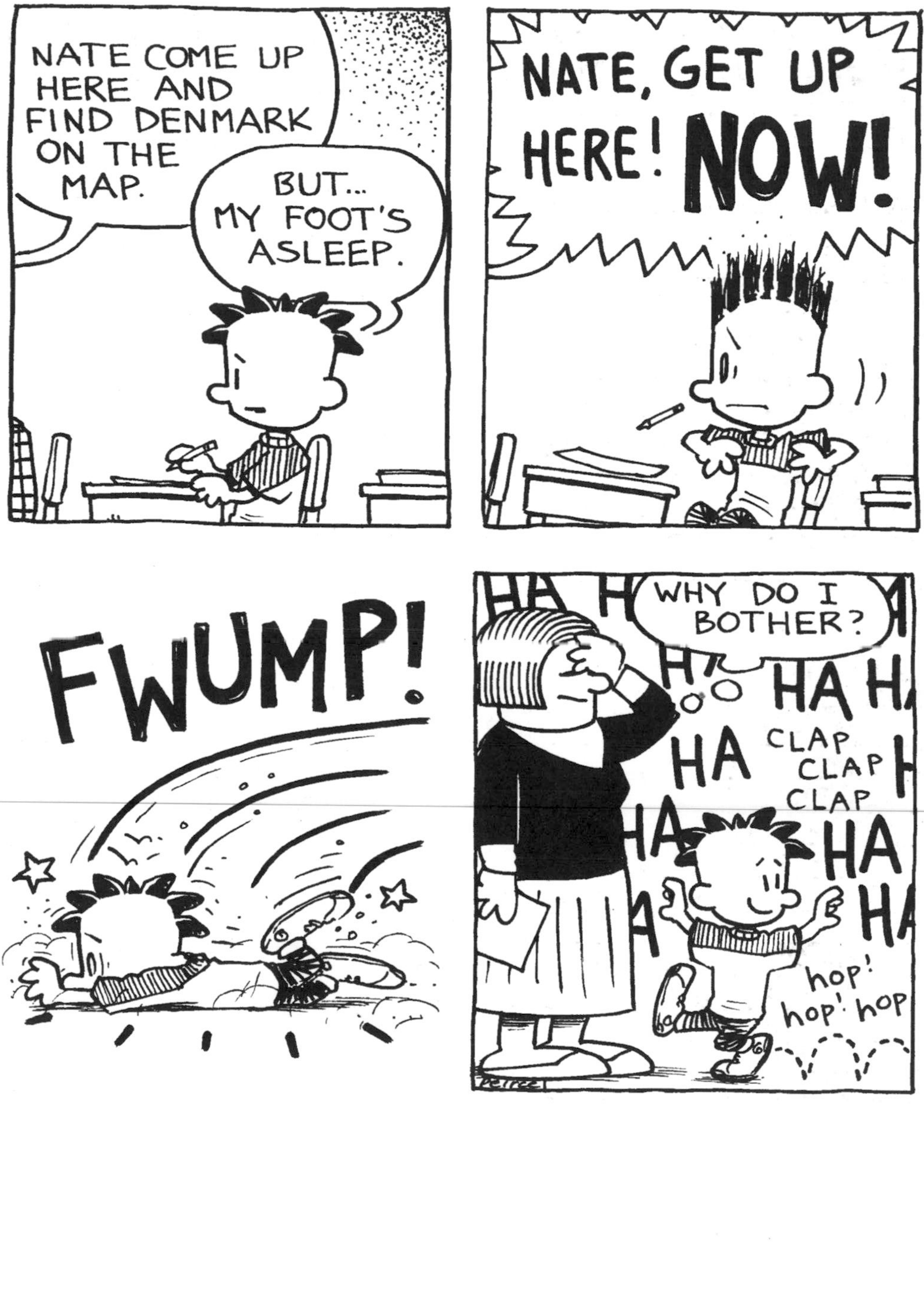
NATE COME UP HERE AND FIND DENMARK ON THE MAP.
BUT... MY FOOT'S ASLEEP.
NATE, GET UP HERE! NOW!
FWUMP!
WHY DO I BOTHER?
HA HA HA HA HA HA HA
CLAP CLAP CLAP
hop! hop! hop

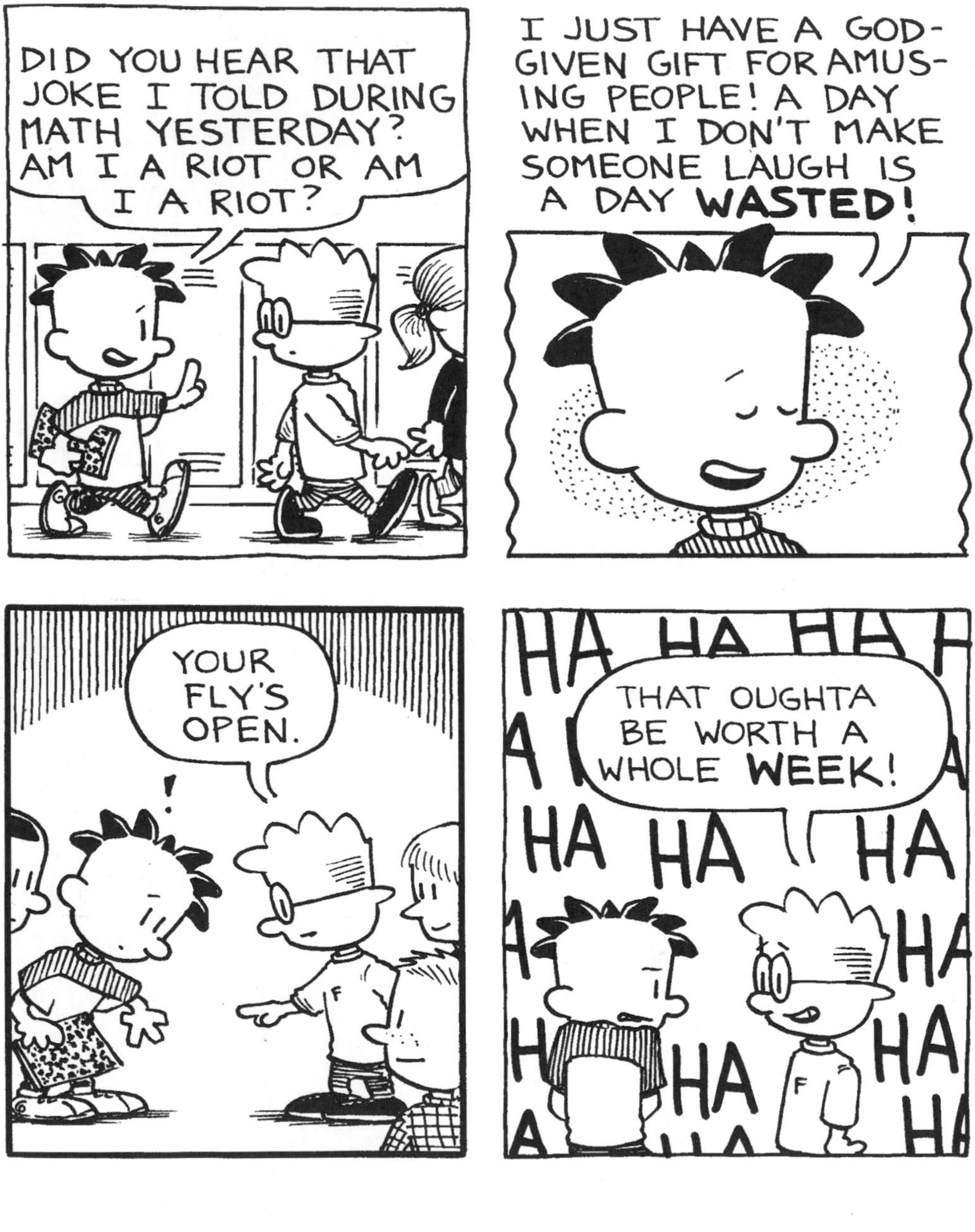
DID YOU HEAR THAT JOKE I TOLD DURING MATH YESTERDAY? AM I A RIOT OR AM I A RIOT?
I JUST HAVE A GOD-GIVEN GIFT FOR AMUSING PEOPLE! A DAY WHEN I DON'T MAKE SOMEONE LAUGH IS A DAY **WASTED**!
YOUR FLY'S OPEN.
!
HA HA HA
THAT OUGHTA BE WORTH A WHOLE **WEEK**!
HA HA HA
HA
HA
HA

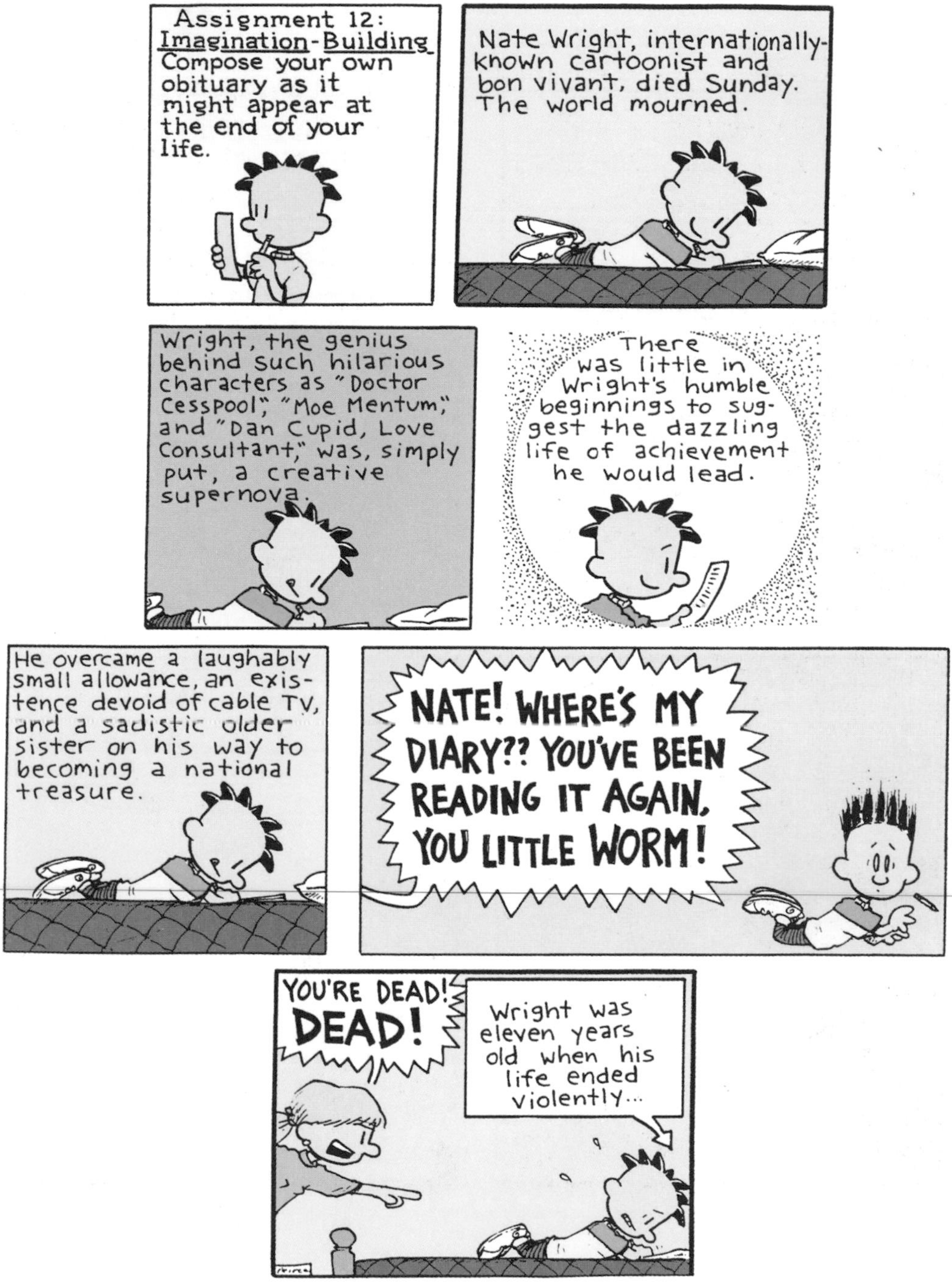

Assignment 12: Imagination-Building
Compose your own obituary as it might appear at the end of your life.
Nate Wright, internationally-known cartoonist and bon vivant, died Sunday. The world mourned.
Wright, the genius behind such hilarious characters as "Doctor Cesspool," "Moe Mentum," and "Dan Cupid, Love Consultant," was, simply put, a creative supernova.
There was little in Wright's humble beginnings to suggest the dazzling life of achievement he would lead.
He overcame a laughably small allowance, an existence devoid of cable TV, and a sadistic older sister on his way to becoming a national treasure.
NATE! WHERE'S MY DIARY?? YOU'VE BEEN READING IT AGAIN, YOU LITTLE WORM!
YOU'RE DEAD! DEAD!
Wright was eleven years old when his life ended violently...

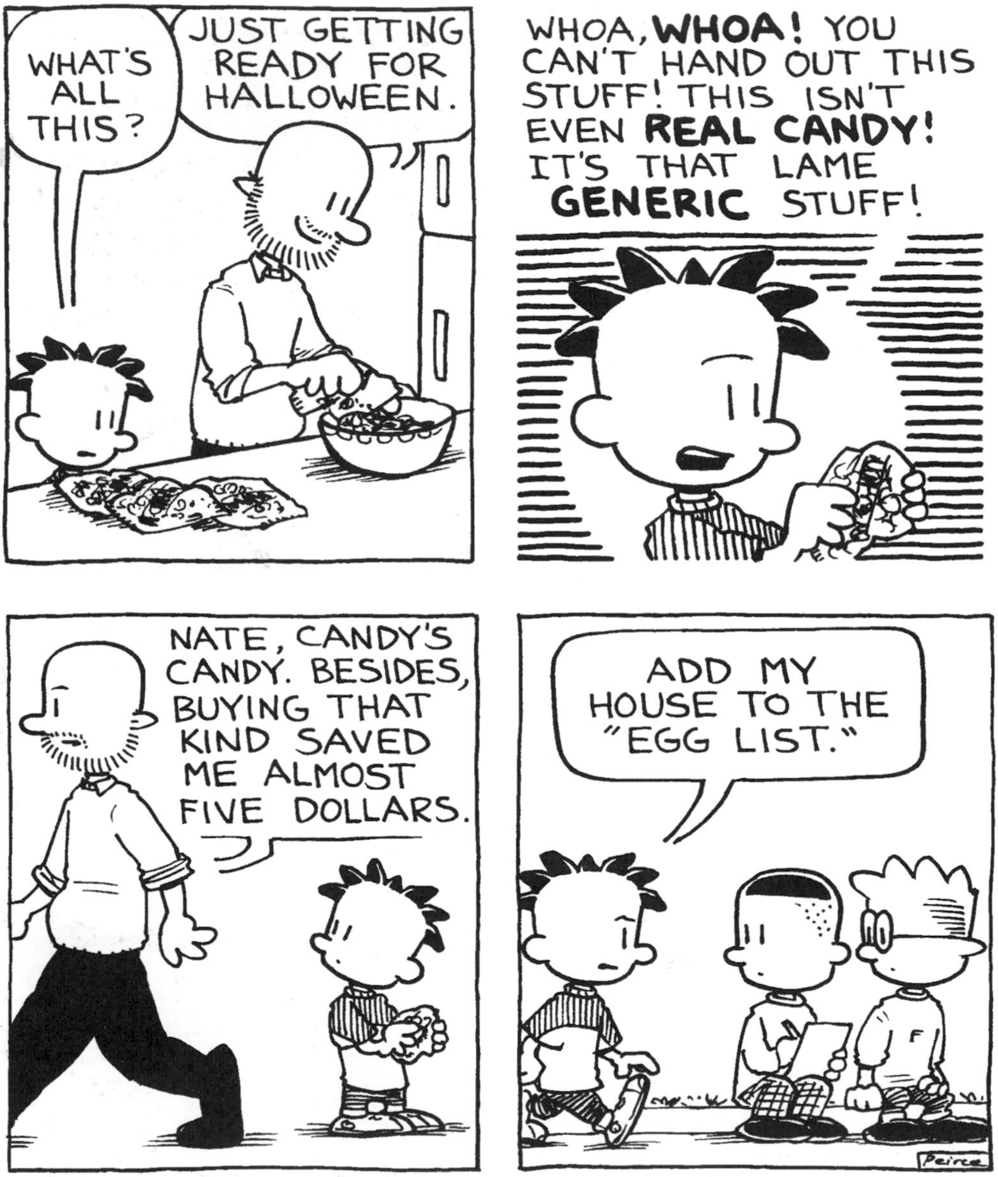
WHAT'S ALL THIS?
JUST GETTING READY FOR HALLOWEEN.
WHOA, **WHOA!** YOU CAN'T HAND OUT THIS STUFF! THIS ISN'T EVEN **REAL CANDY!** IT'S THAT LAME **GENERIC** STUFF!
NATE, CANDY'S CANDY. BESIDES, BUYING THAT KIND SAVED ME ALMOST FIVE DOLLARS.
ADD MY HOUSE TO THE "EGG LIST."
F
Peirce

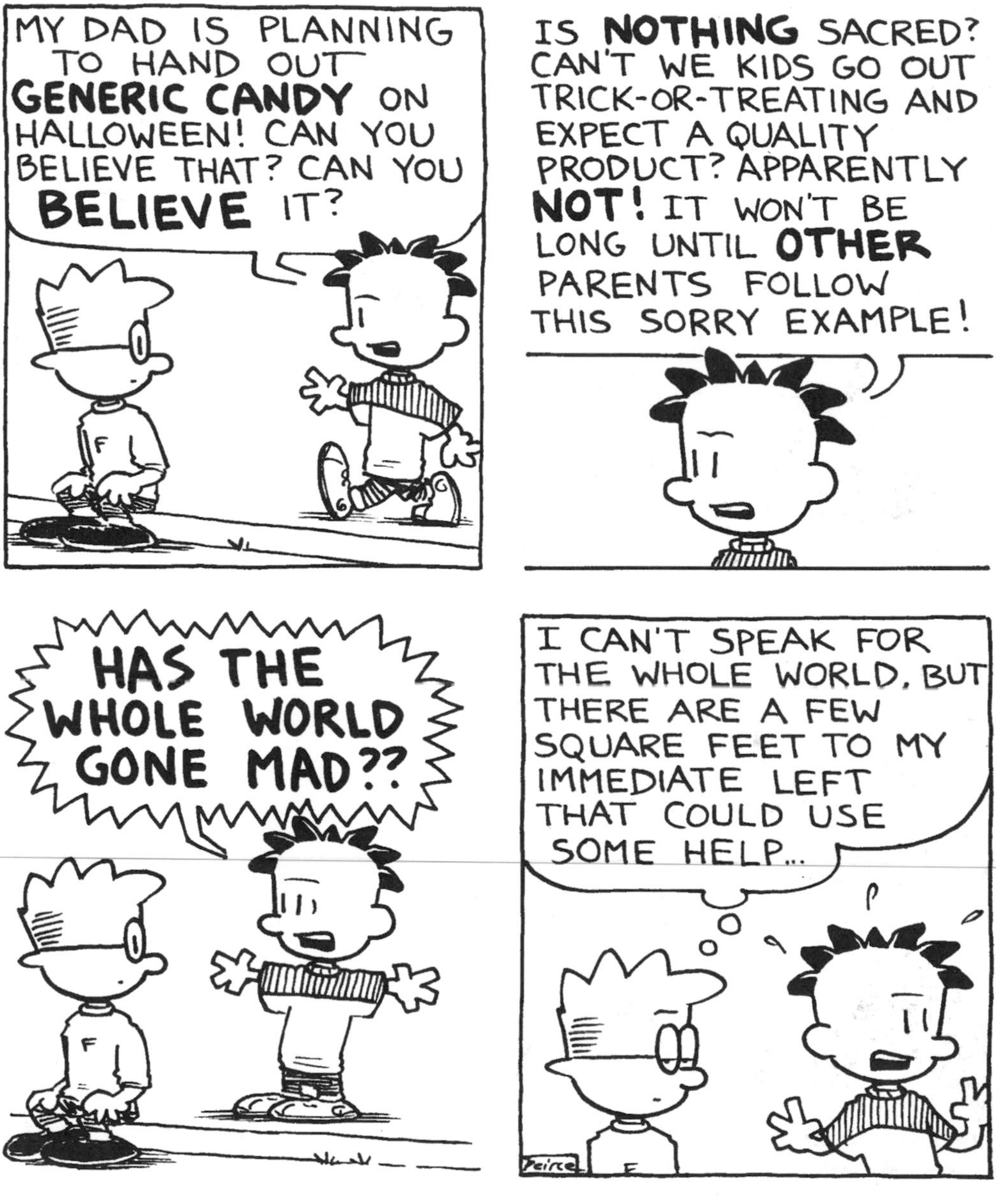
MY DAD IS PLANNING TO HAND OUT GENERIC CANDY ON HALLOWEEN! CAN YOU BELIEVE THAT? CAN YOU BELIEVE IT?
IS NOTHING SACRED? CAN'T WE KIDS GO OUT TRICK-OR-TREATING AND EXPECT A QUALITY PRODUCT? APPARENTLY NOT! IT WON'T BE LONG UNTIL OTHER PARENTS FOLLOW THIS SORRY EXAMPLE!
HAS THE WHOLE WORLD GONE MAD??
I CAN'T SPEAK FOR THE WHOLE WORLD, BUT THERE ARE A FEW SQUARE FEET TO MY IMMEDIATE LEFT THAT COULD USE SOME HELP...
Peirce

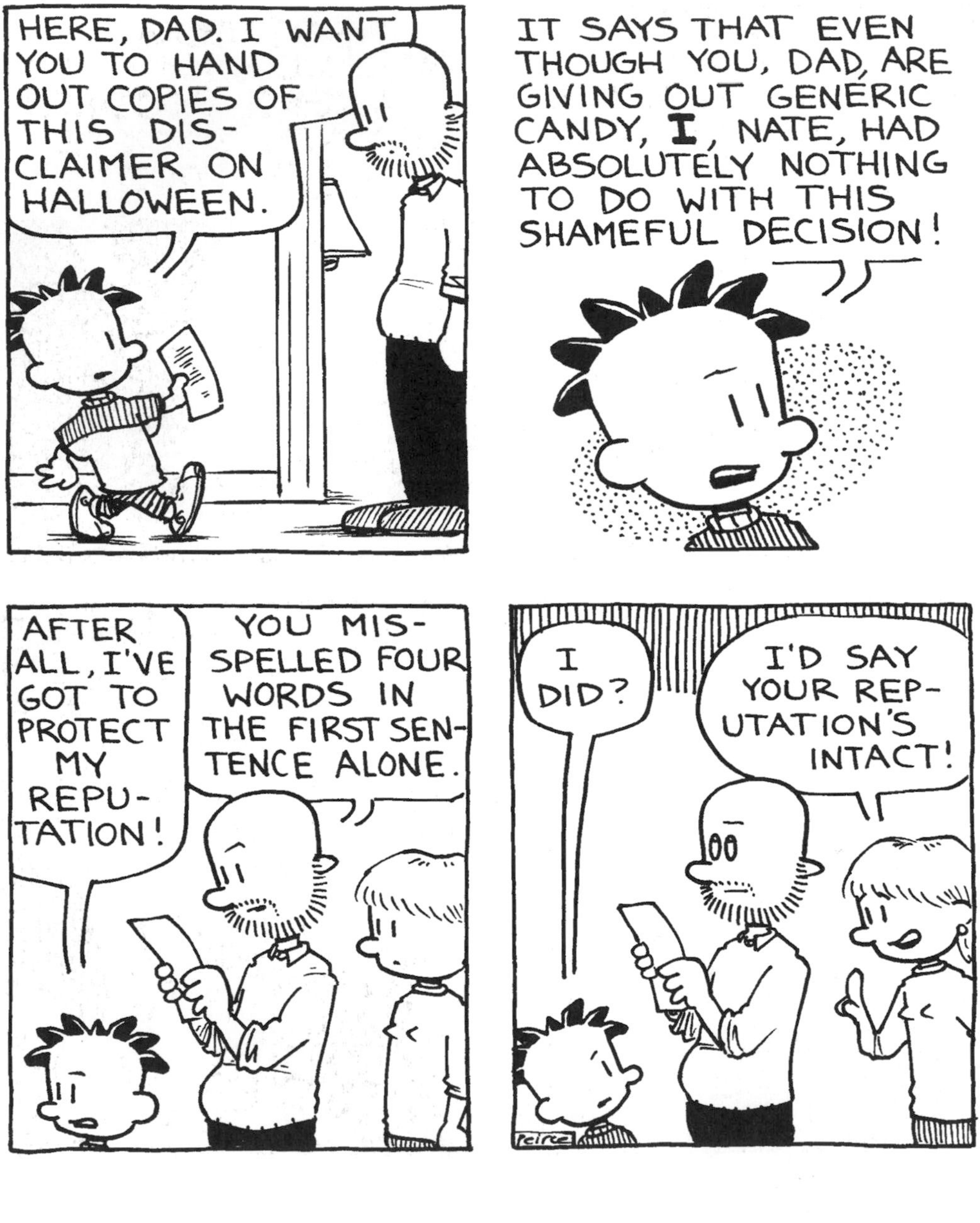
HERE, DAD. I WANT YOU TO HAND OUT COPIES OF THIS DIS-CLAIMER ON HALLOWEEN.
IT SAYS THAT EVEN THOUGH YOU, DAD, ARE GIVING OUT GENERIC CANDY, I, NATE, HAD ABSOLUTELY NOTHING TO DO WITH THIS SHAMEFUL DECISION!
AFTER ALL, I'VE GOT TO PROTECT MY REPU-TATION!
YOU MIS-SPELLED FOUR WORDS IN THE FIRST SEN-TENCE ALONE.
I DID?
I'D SAY YOUR REP-UTATION'S INTACT!
Peirce

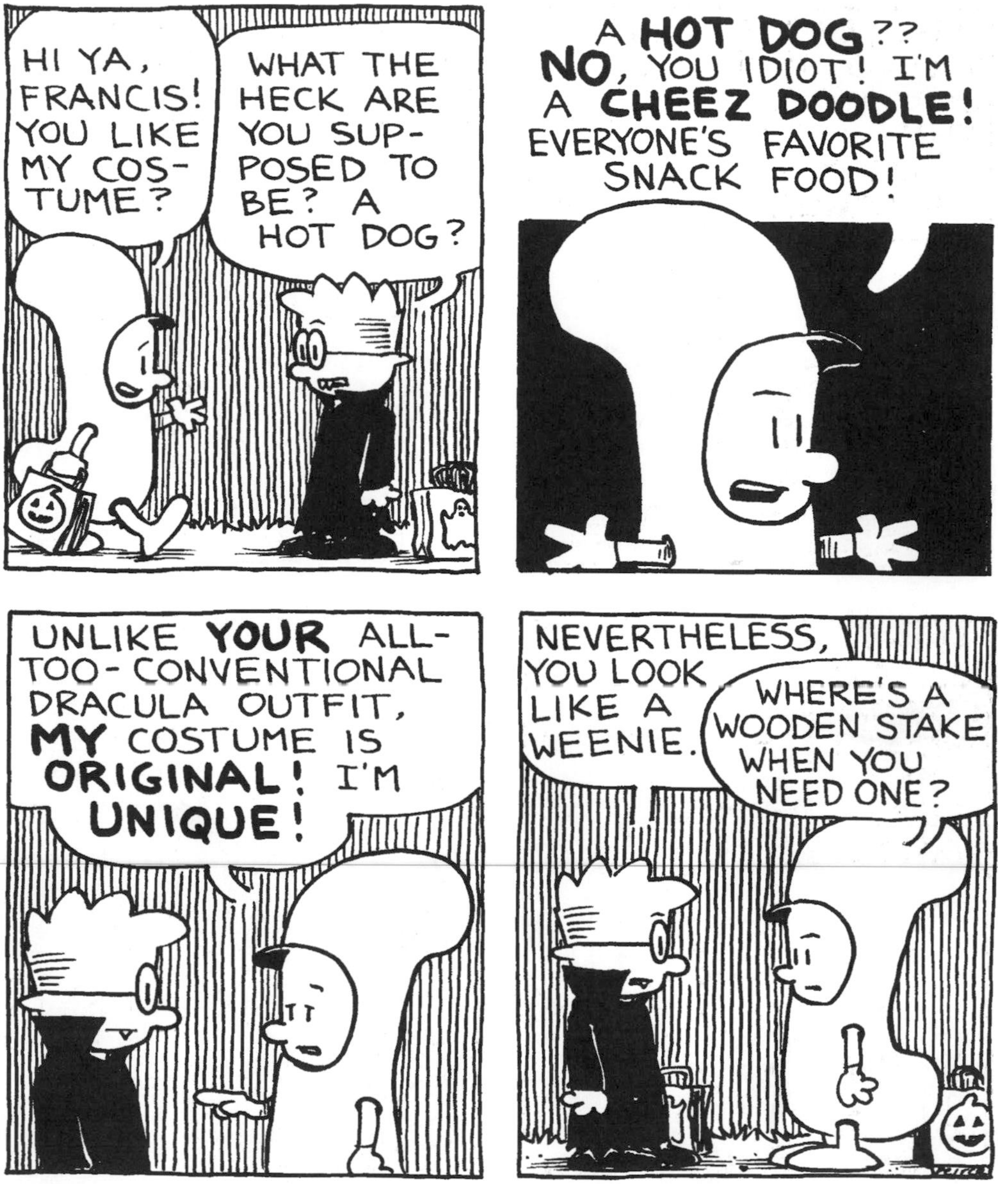
HI YA, FRANCIS! YOU LIKE MY COS-TUME?
WHAT THE HECK ARE YOU SUP-POSED TO BE? A HOT DOG?
A HOT DOG?? NO, YOU IDIOT! I'M A CHEEZ DOODLE! EVERYONE'S FAVORITE SNACK FOOD!
UNLIKE YOUR ALL-TOO-CONVENTIONAL DRACULA OUTFIT, MY COSTUME IS ORIGINAL! I'M UNIQUE!
NEVERTHELESS, YOU LOOK LIKE A WEENIE.
WHERE'S A WOODEN STAKE WHEN YOU NEED ONE?

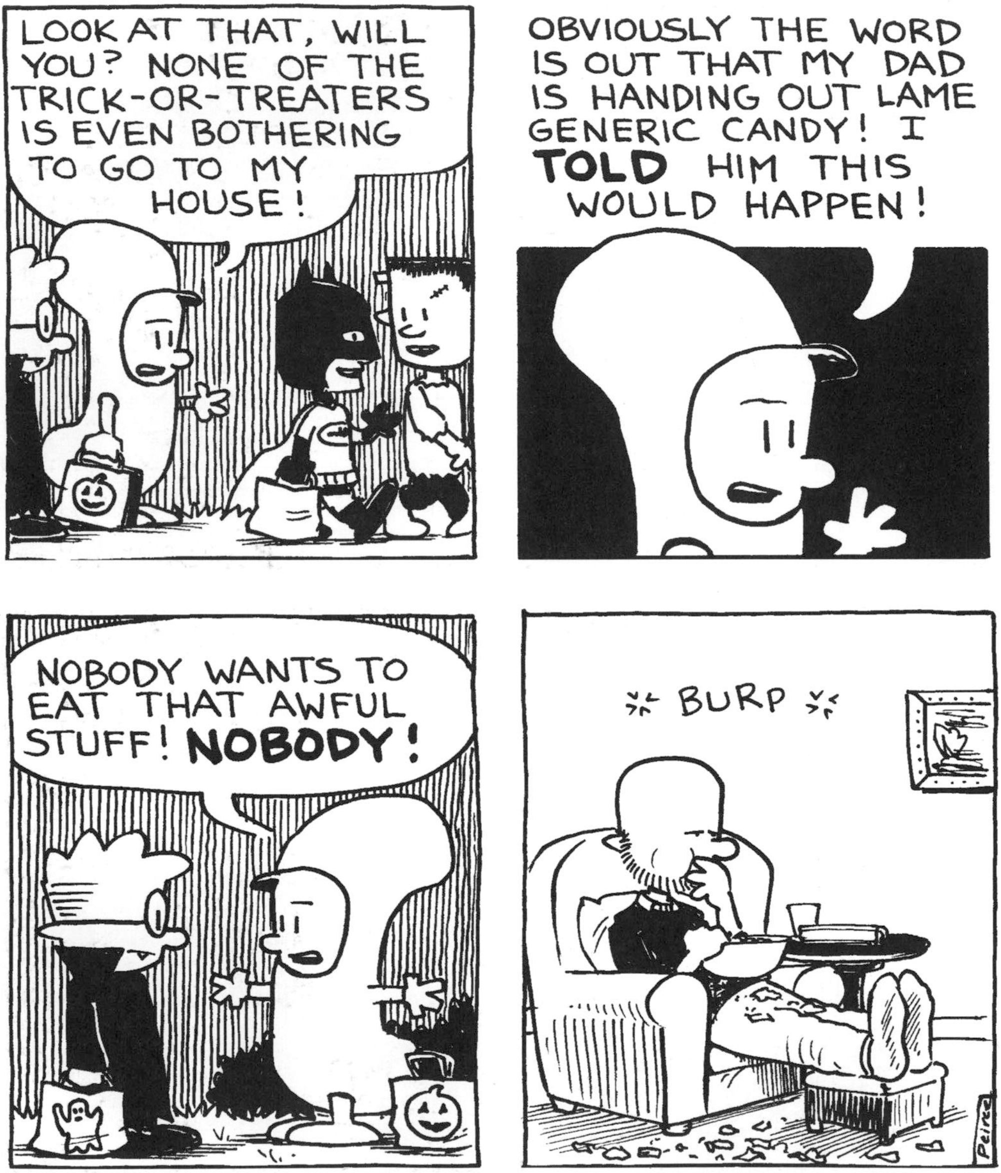
LOOK AT THAT, WILL YOU? NONE OF THE TRICK-OR-TREATERS IS EVEN BOTHERING TO GO TO MY HOUSE!
OBVIOUSLY THE WORD IS OUT THAT MY DAD IS HANDING OUT LAME GENERIC CANDY! I **TOLD** HIM THIS WOULD HAPPEN!
NOBODY WANTS TO EAT THAT AWFUL STUFF! **NOBODY**!
BURP
PEIRCE

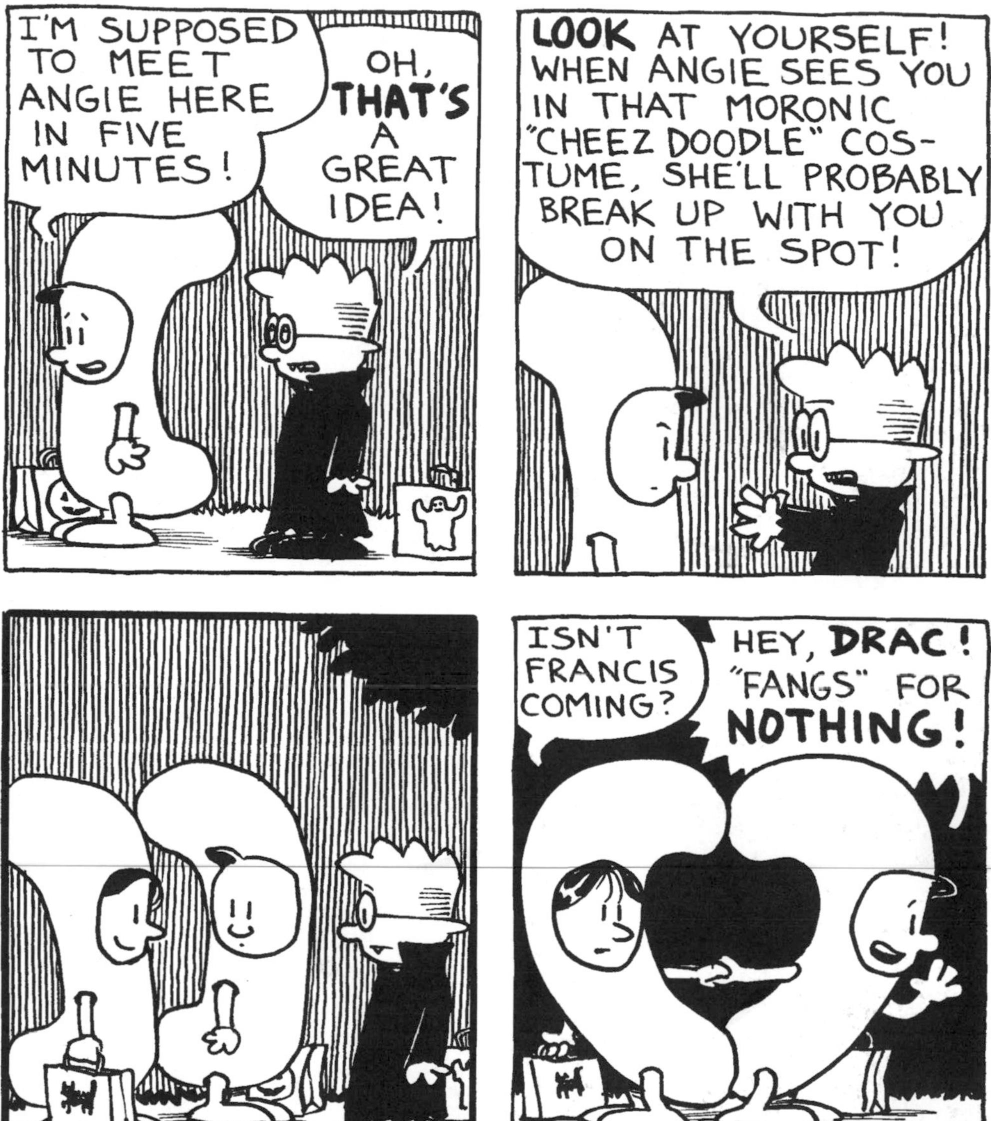
I'M SUPPOSED TO MEET ANGIE HERE IN FIVE MINUTES!
OH, **THAT'S** A GREAT IDEA!
LOOK AT YOURSELF! WHEN ANGIE SEES YOU IN THAT MORONIC "CHEEZ DOODLE" COSTUME, SHE'LL PROBABLY BREAK UP WITH YOU ON THE SPOT!
ISN'T FRANCIS COMING?
HEY, **DRAC**! "FANGS" FOR **NOTHING**!
Peirce

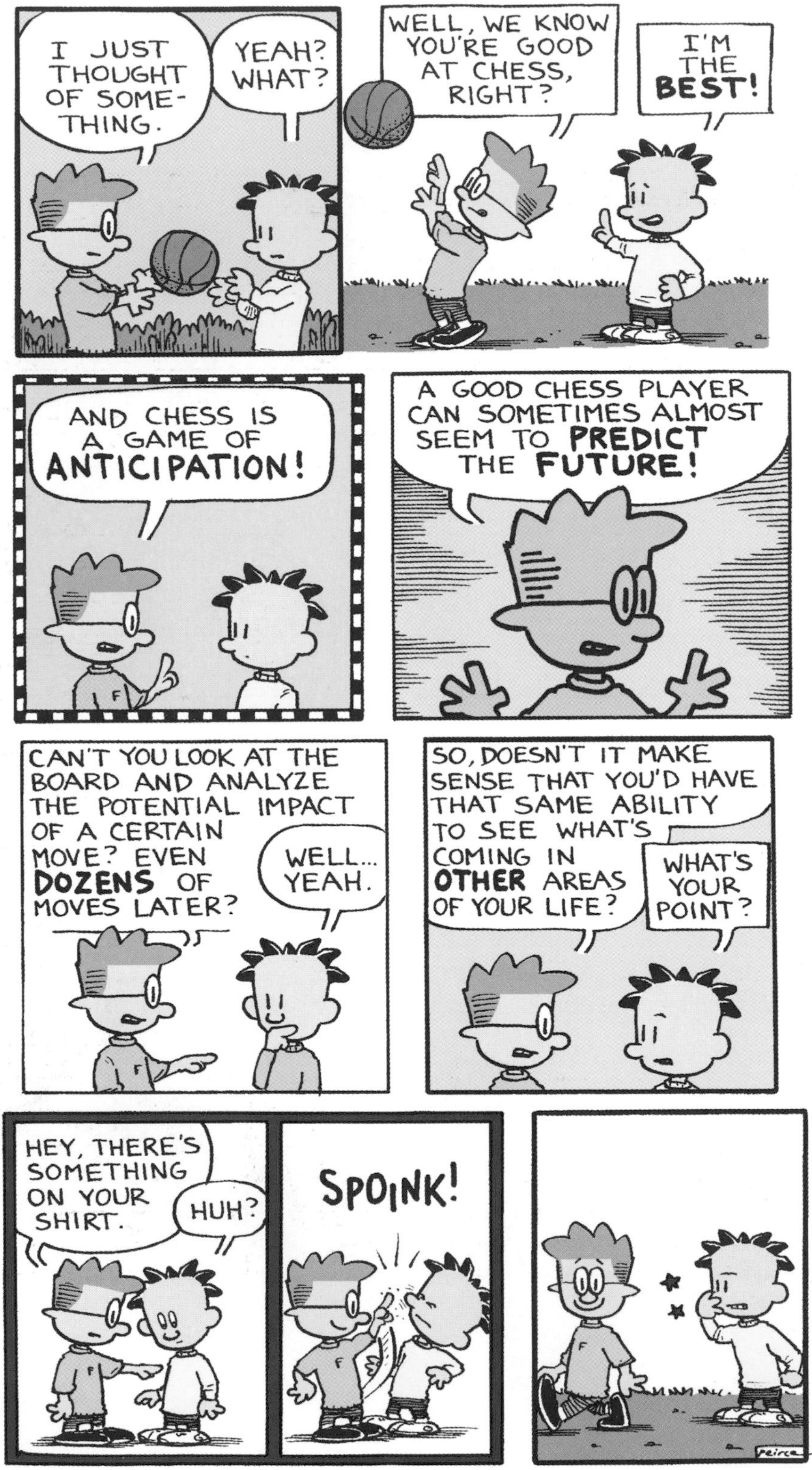
I JUST THOUGHT OF SOME-THING.
YEAH? WHAT?
WELL, WE KNOW YOU'RE GOOD AT CHESS, RIGHT?
I'M THE BEST!
AND CHESS IS A GAME OF ANTICIPATION!
A GOOD CHESS PLAYER CAN SOMETIMES ALMOST SEEM TO PREDICT THE FUTURE!
CAN'T YOU LOOK AT THE BOARD AND ANALYZE THE POTENTIAL IMPACT OF A CERTAIN MOVE? EVEN DOZENS OF MOVES LATER?
WELL... YEAH.
SO, DOESN'T IT MAKE SENSE THAT YOU'D HAVE THAT SAME ABILITY TO SEE WHAT'S COMING IN OTHER AREAS OF YOUR LIFE?
WHAT'S YOUR POINT?
HEY, THERE'S SOMETHING ON YOUR SHIRT.
HUH?
SPOINK!
peirce

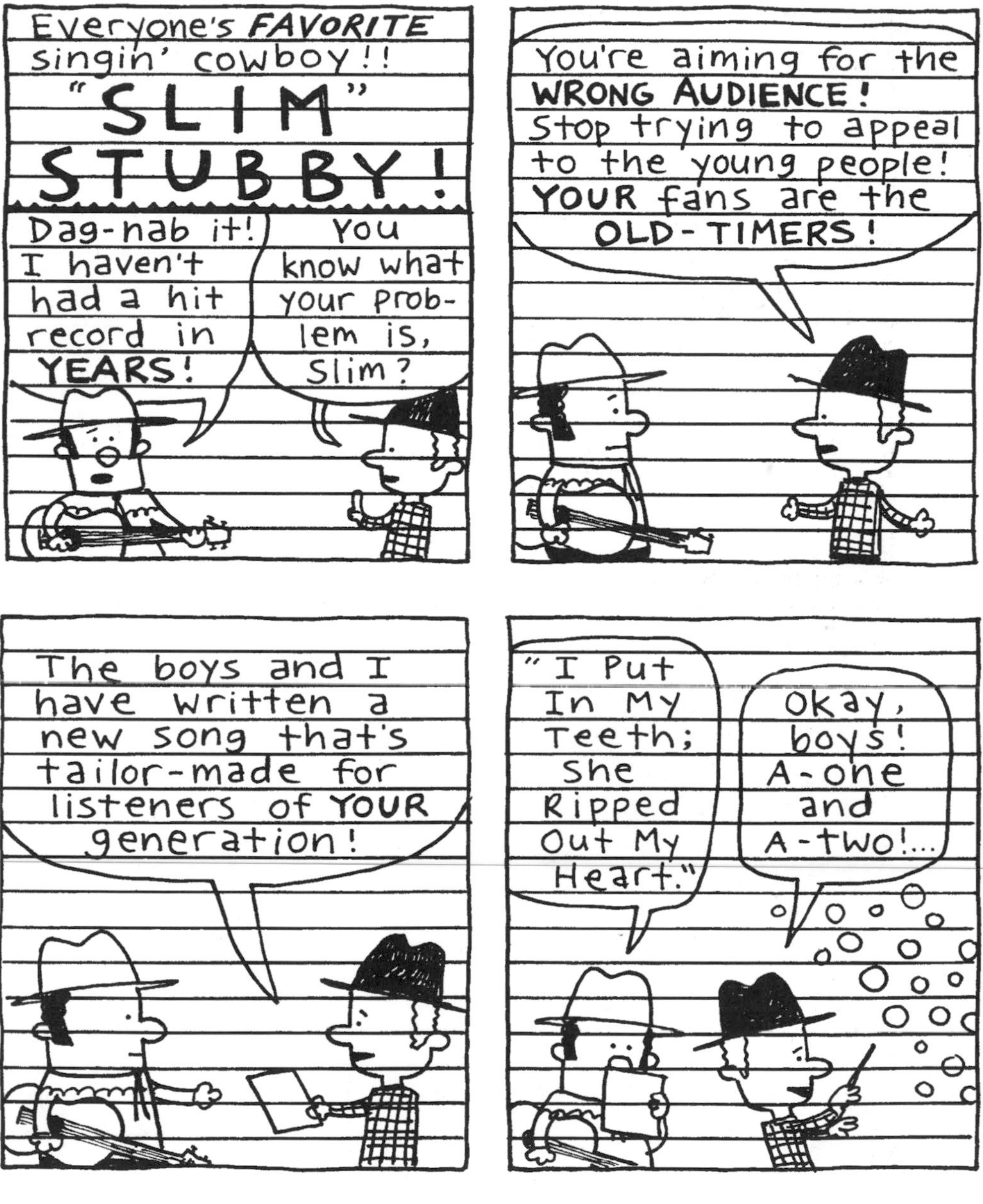
Everyone's FAVORITE singin' cowboy!! "SLIM" STUBBY!
Dag-nab it! I haven't had a hit record in YEARS!
You know what your prob-lem is, Slim?
You're aiming for the WRONG AUDIENCE! Stop trying to appeal to the young people! YOUR fans are the OLD-TIMERS!
The boys and I have written a new song that's tailor-made for listeners of YOUR generation!
"I Put In My Teeth; She Ripped Out My Heart."
Okay, boys! A-one and A-two!...

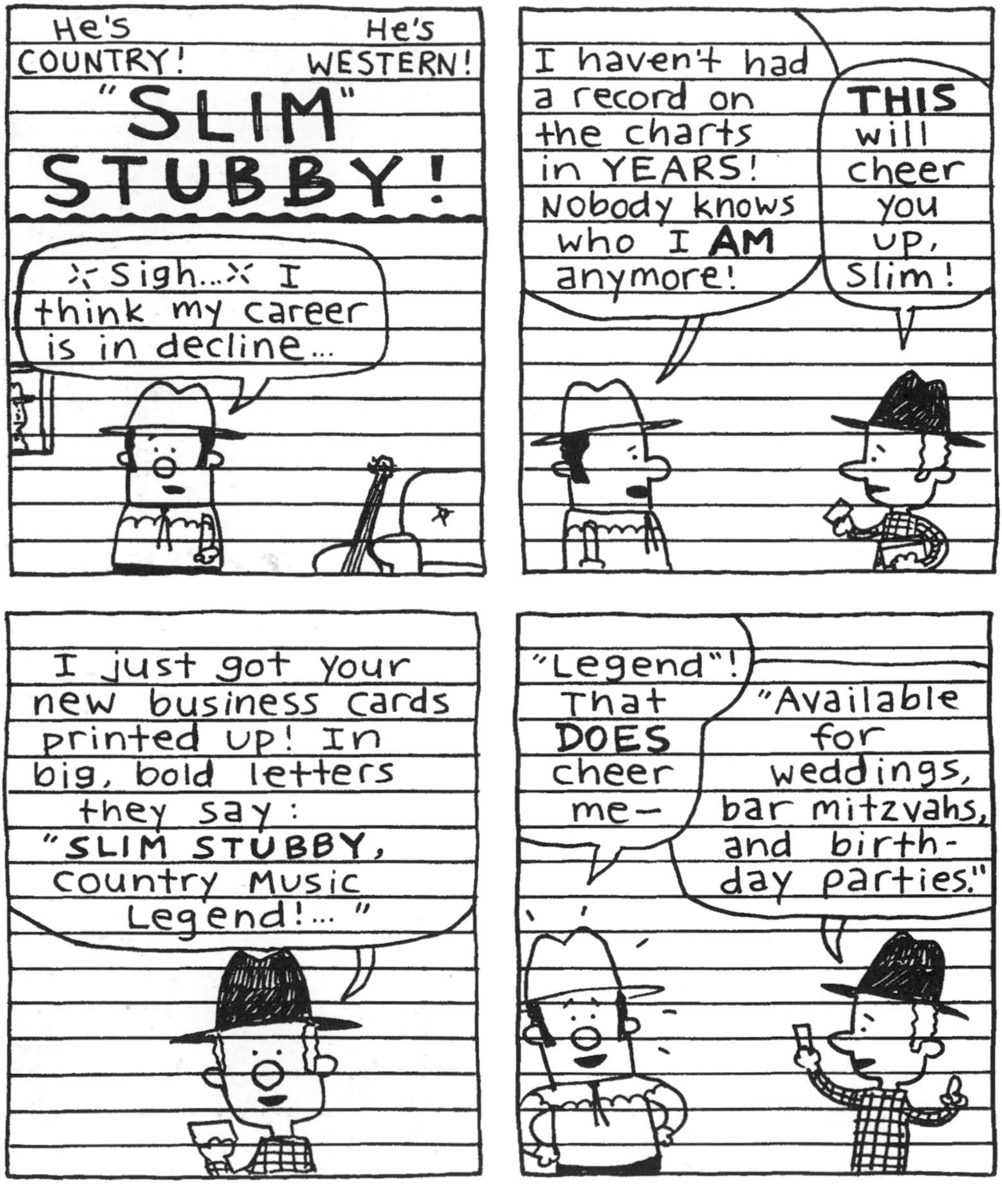
He's COUNTRY! He's WESTERN!
"SLIM" STUBBY!
Sigh... I think my career is in decline...
I haven't had a record on the charts in YEARS! Nobody knows who I AM anymore!
THIS will cheer you up, Slim!
I just got your new business cards printed up! In big, bold letters they say: "SLIM STUBBY, Country Music Legend!..."
"Legend"! That DOES cheer me—
"Available for weddings, bar mitzvahs, and birthday parties."

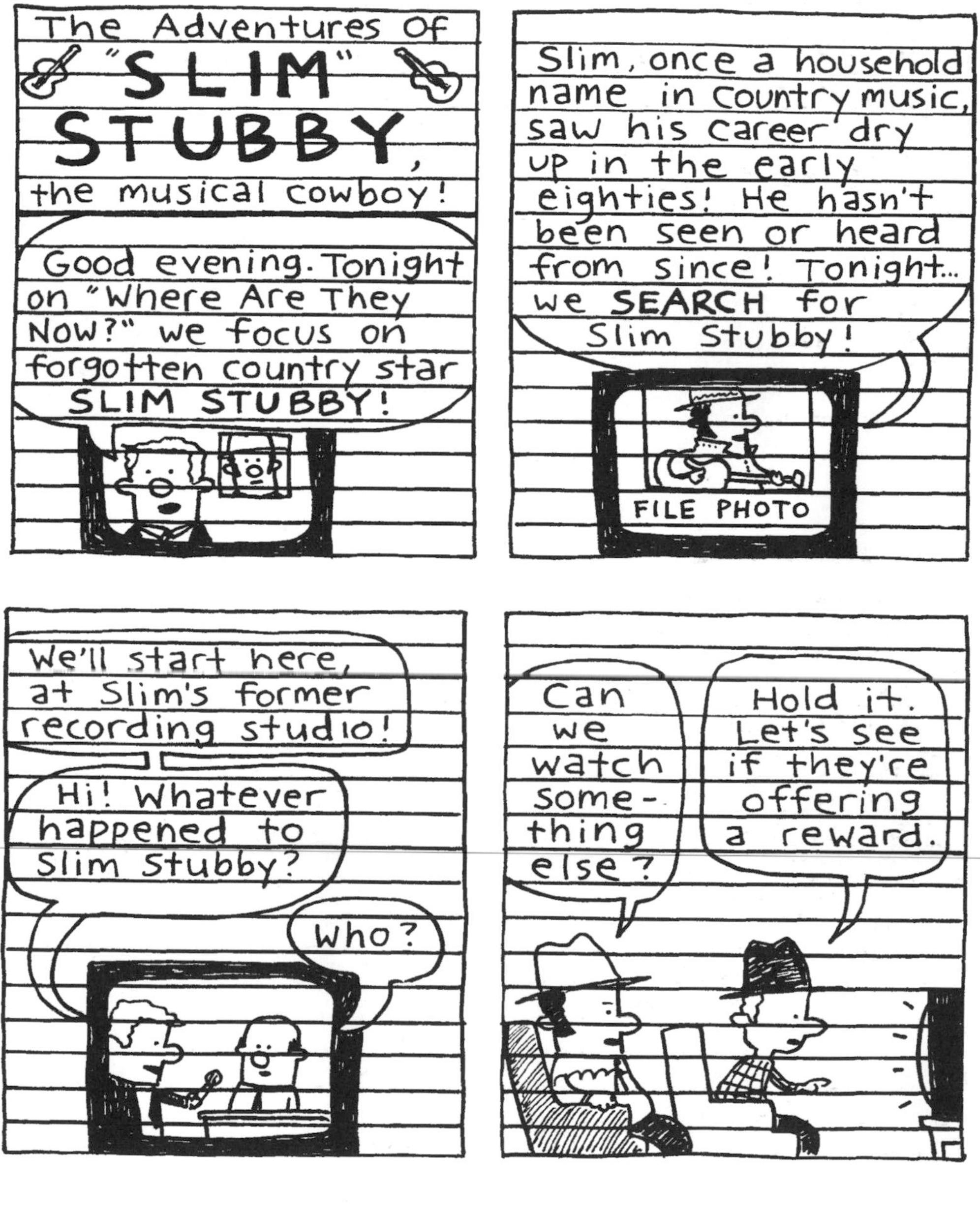
The Adventures of "SLIM" STUBBY, the musical cowboy!
Good evening. Tonight on "Where Are They Now?" we focus on forgotten country star SLIM STUBBY!
Slim, once a household name in country music, saw his career dry up in the early eighties! He hasn't been seen or heard from since! Tonight... we SEARCH for Slim Stubby!
FILE PHOTO
We'll start here, at Slim's former recording studio!
Hi! Whatever happened to Slim Stubby?
Who?
Can we watch some-thing else?
Hold it. Let's see if they're offering a reward.

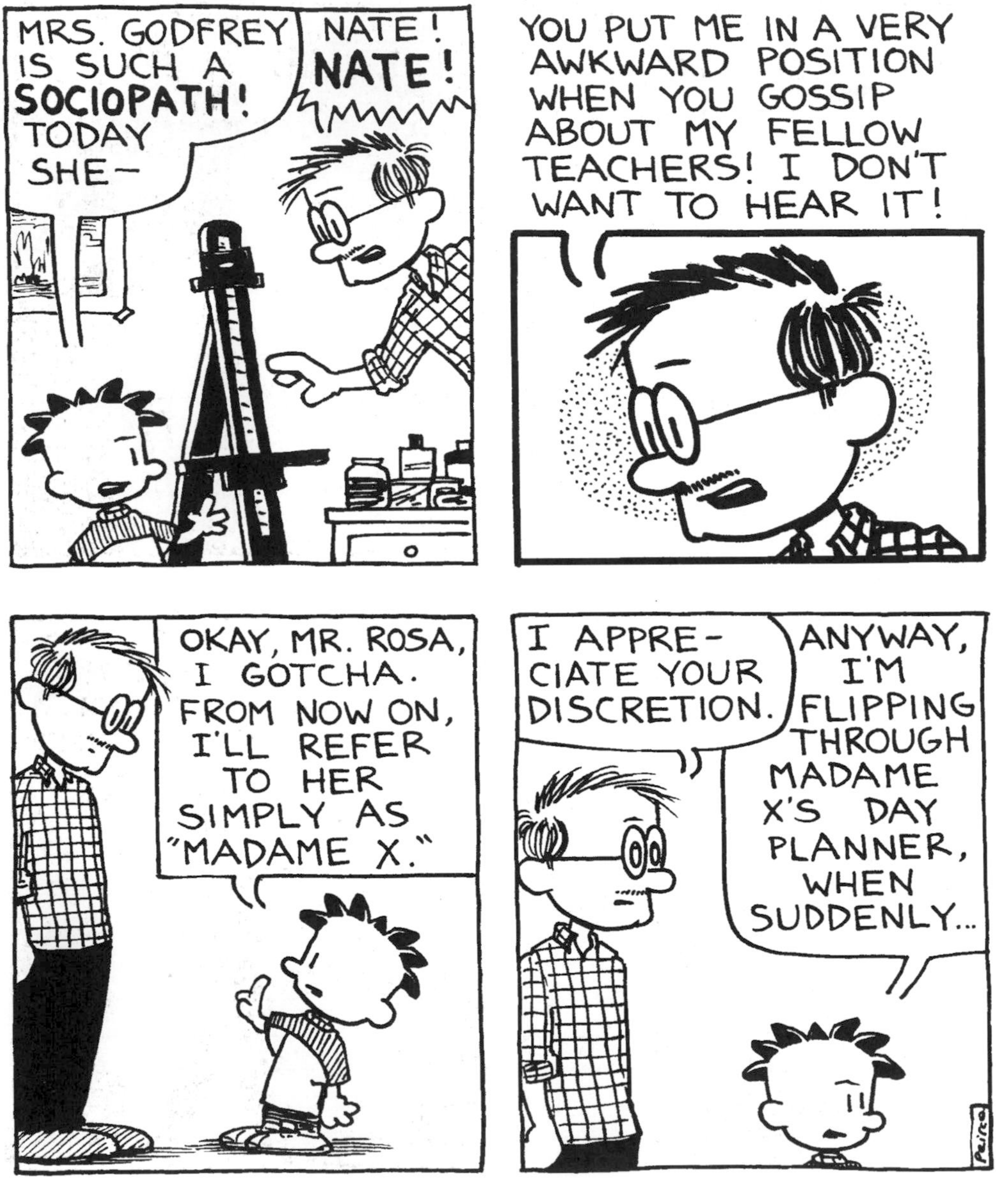
MRS. GODFREY IS SUCH A **SOCIOPATH**! TODAY SHE–
NATE! **NATE**!
YOU PUT ME IN A VERY AWKWARD POSITION WHEN YOU GOSSIP ABOUT MY FELLOW TEACHERS! I DON'T WANT TO HEAR IT!
OKAY, MR. ROSA, I GOTCHA. FROM NOW ON, I'LL REFER TO HER SIMPLY AS "MADAME X."
I APPRECIATE YOUR DISCRETION.
ANYWAY, I'M FLIPPING THROUGH MADAME X'S DAY PLANNER, WHEN SUDDENLY...
PEIRCE

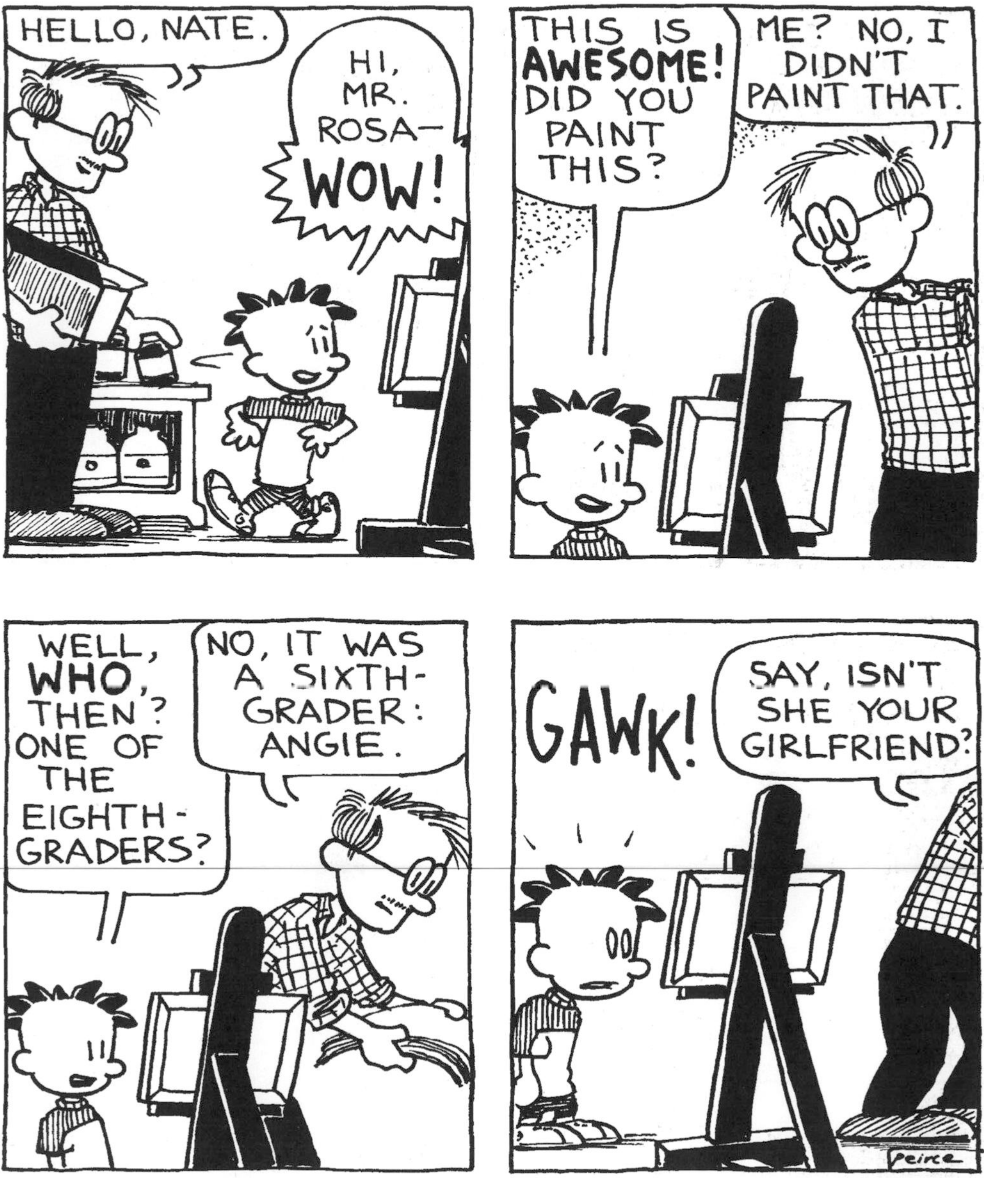
HELLO, NATE.
HI, MR. ROSA—
WOW!
THIS IS AWESOME! DID YOU PAINT THIS?
ME? NO, I DIDN'T PAINT THAT.
WELL, WHO, THEN? ONE OF THE EIGHTH-GRADERS?
NO, IT WAS A SIXTH-GRADER: ANGIE.
GAWK!
SAY, ISN'T SHE YOUR GIRLFRIEND?
Peirce

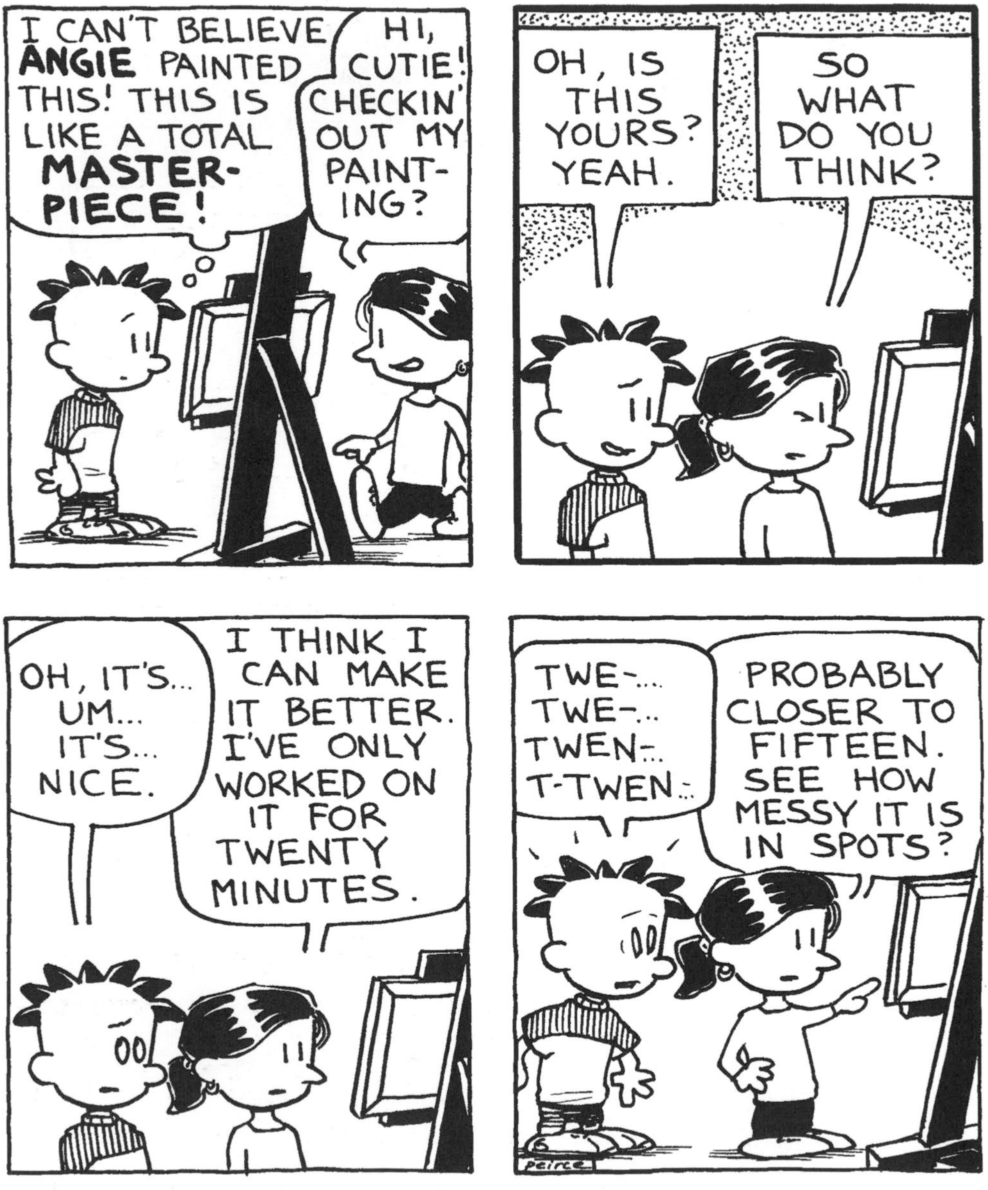
I CAN'T BELIEVE **ANGIE** PAINTED THIS! THIS IS LIKE A TOTAL **MASTER-PIECE**!
HI, CUTIE! CHECKIN' OUT MY PAINT-ING?
OH, IS THIS YOURS? YEAH.
SO WHAT DO YOU THINK?
OH, IT'S... UM... IT'S... NICE.
I THINK I CAN MAKE IT BETTER. I'VE ONLY WORKED ON IT FOR TWENTY MINUTES.
TWE-... TWE-... TWEN-.. T-TWEN-..
PROBABLY CLOSER TO FIFTEEN. SEE HOW MESSY IT IS IN SPOTS?
peirce

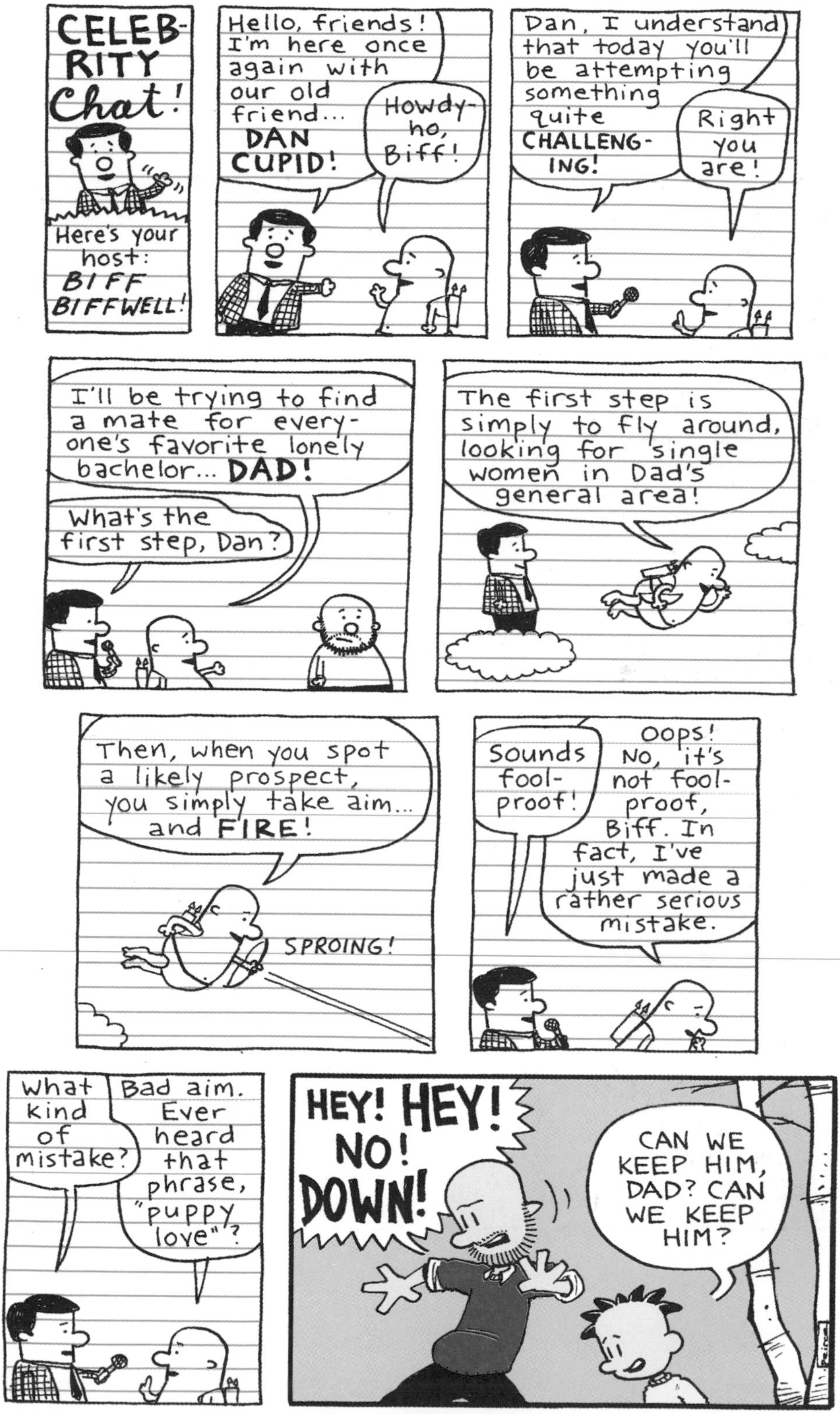
CELEBRITY Chat!
Here's your host: BIFF BIFFWELL!
Hello, friends! I'm here once again with our old friend... DAN CUPID!
Howdy-ho, Biff!
Dan, I understand that today you'll be attempting something quite CHALLENGING!
Right you are!
I'll be trying to find a mate for everyone's favorite lonely bachelor... DAD!
What's the first step, Dan?
The first step is simply to fly around, looking for single women in Dad's general area!
Then, when you spot a likely prospect, you simply take aim... and FIRE!
SPROING!
Sounds fool-proof!
Oops! No, it's not fool-proof, Biff. In fact, I've just made a rather serious mistake.
What kind of mistake?
Bad aim. Ever heard that phrase, "puppy love"?
HEY! HEY! NO! DOWN!
CAN WE KEEP HIM, DAD? CAN WE KEEP HIM?

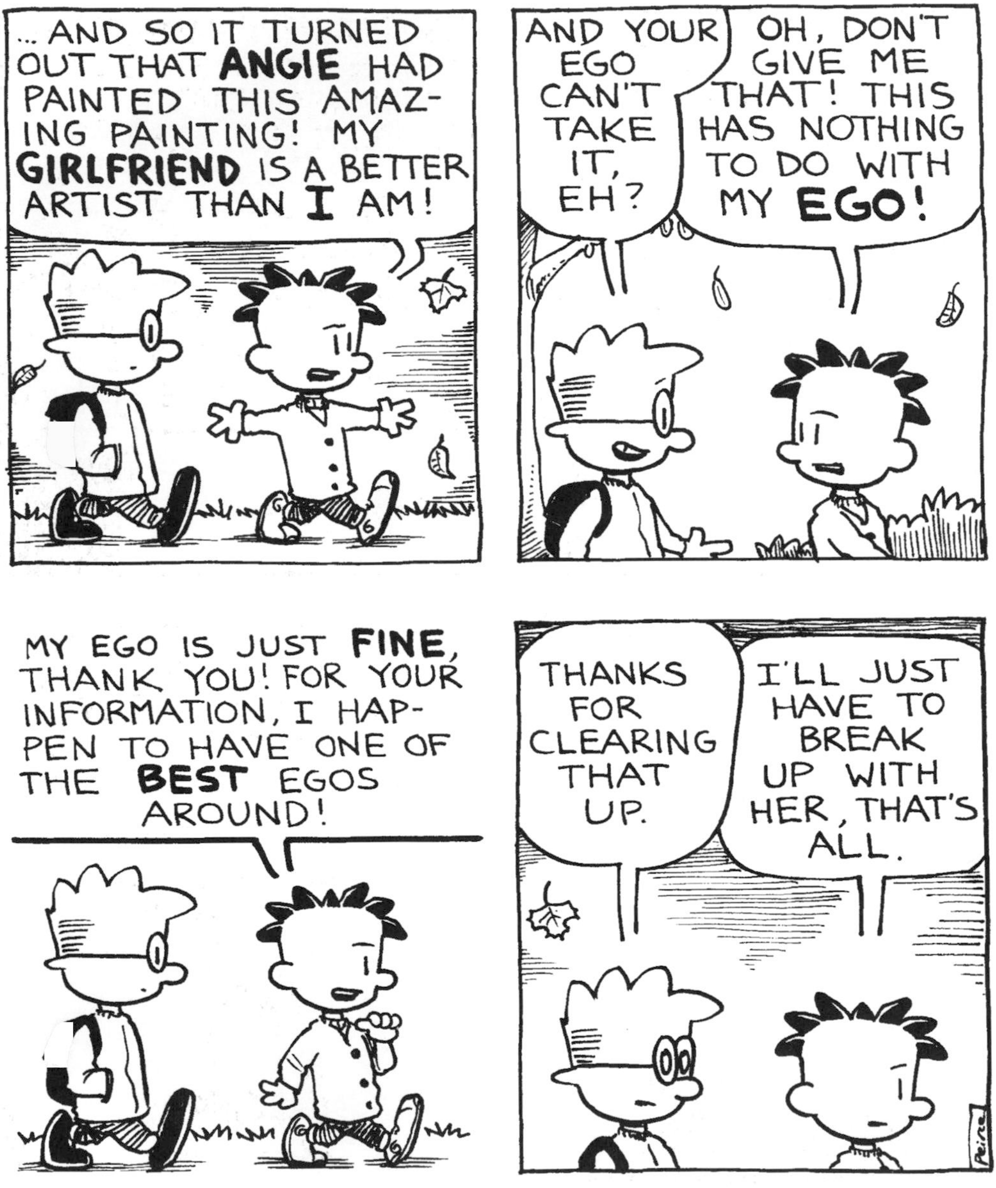
... AND SO IT TURNED OUT THAT ANGIE HAD PAINTED THIS AMAZING PAINTING! MY GIRLFRIEND IS A BETTER ARTIST THAN I AM!
AND YOUR EGO CAN'T TAKE IT, EH?
OH, DON'T GIVE ME THAT! THIS HAS NOTHING TO DO WITH MY EGO!
MY EGO IS JUST FINE, THANK YOU! FOR YOUR INFORMATION, I HAPPEN TO HAVE ONE OF THE BEST EGOS AROUND!
THANKS FOR CLEARING THAT UP.
I'LL JUST HAVE TO BREAK UP WITH HER, THAT'S ALL.
Peirce

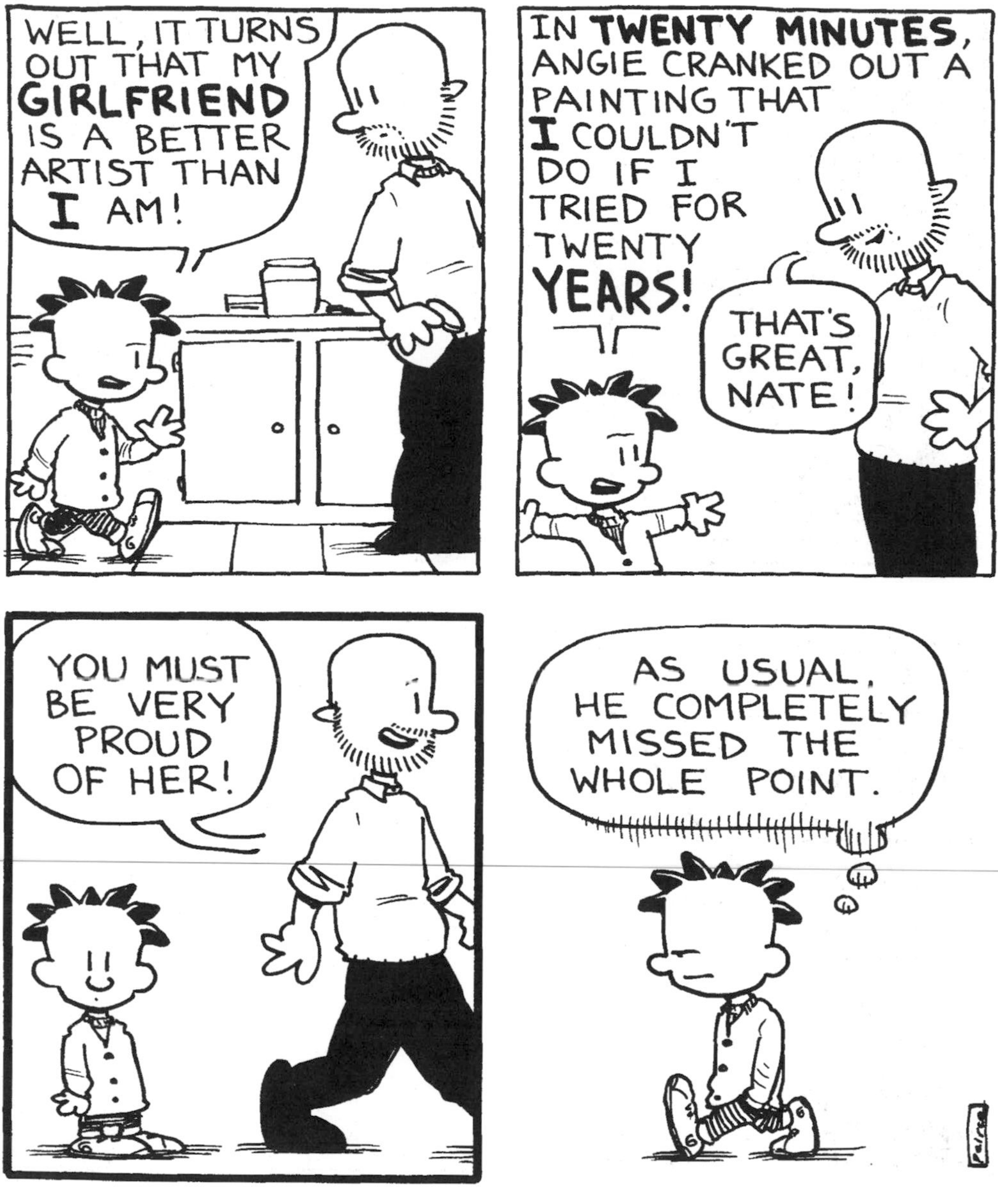
WELL, IT TURNS OUT THAT MY GIRLFRIEND IS A BETTER ARTIST THAN I AM!
IN TWENTY MINUTES, ANGIE CRANKED OUT A PAINTING THAT I COULDN'T DO IF I TRIED FOR TWENTY YEARS!
THAT'S GREAT, NATE!
YOU MUST BE VERY PROUD OF HER!
AS USUAL, HE COMPLETELY MISSED THE WHOLE POINT.
Peirce

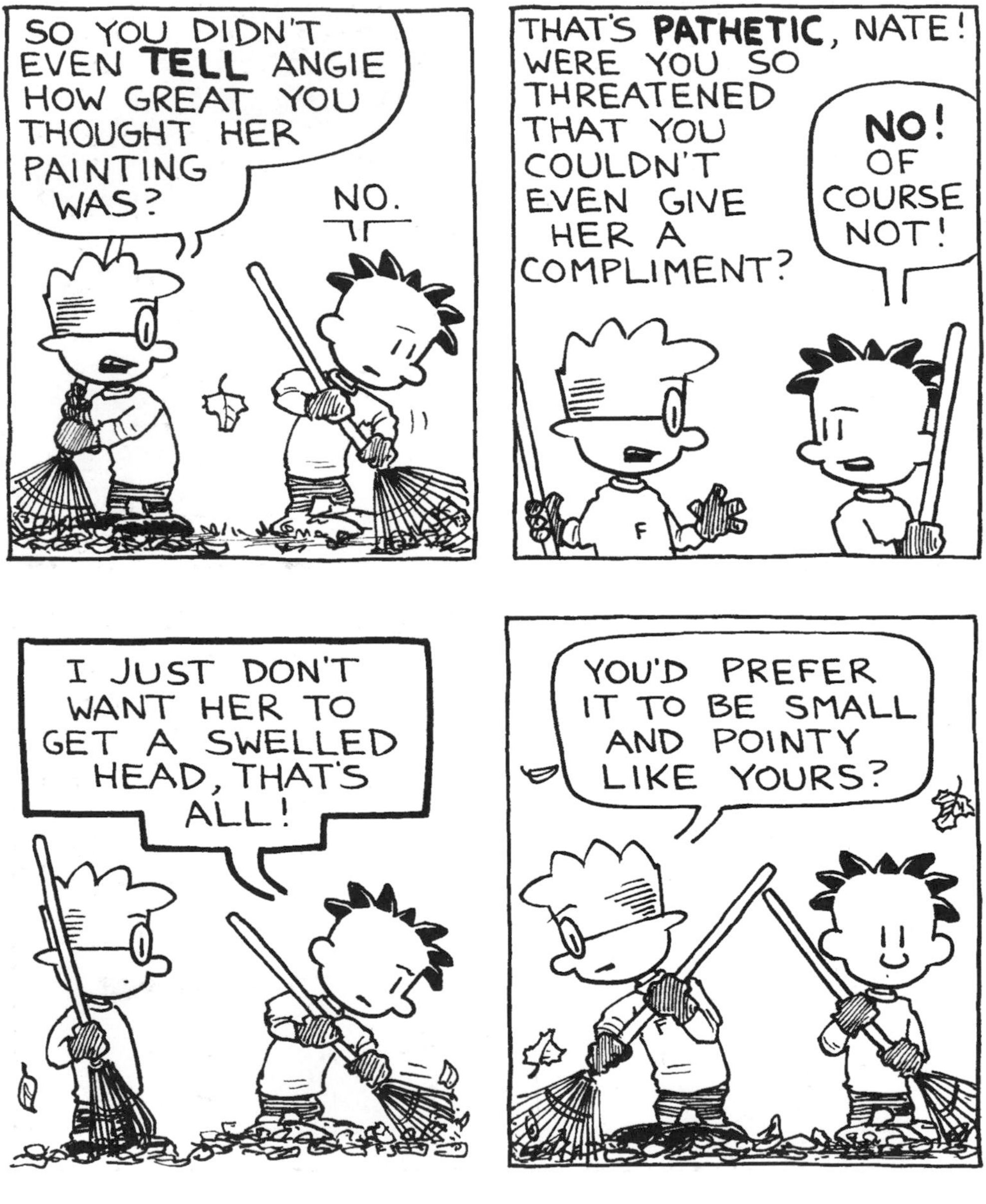
SO YOU DIDN'T EVEN **TELL** ANGIE HOW GREAT YOU THOUGHT HER PAINTING WAS?
NO.
THAT'S **PATHETIC**, NATE! WERE YOU SO THREATENED THAT YOU COULDN'T EVEN GIVE HER A COMPLIMENT?
NO! OF COURSE NOT!
I JUST DON'T WANT HER TO GET A SWELLED HEAD, THAT'S ALL!
YOU'D PREFER IT TO BE SMALL AND POINTY LIKE YOURS?

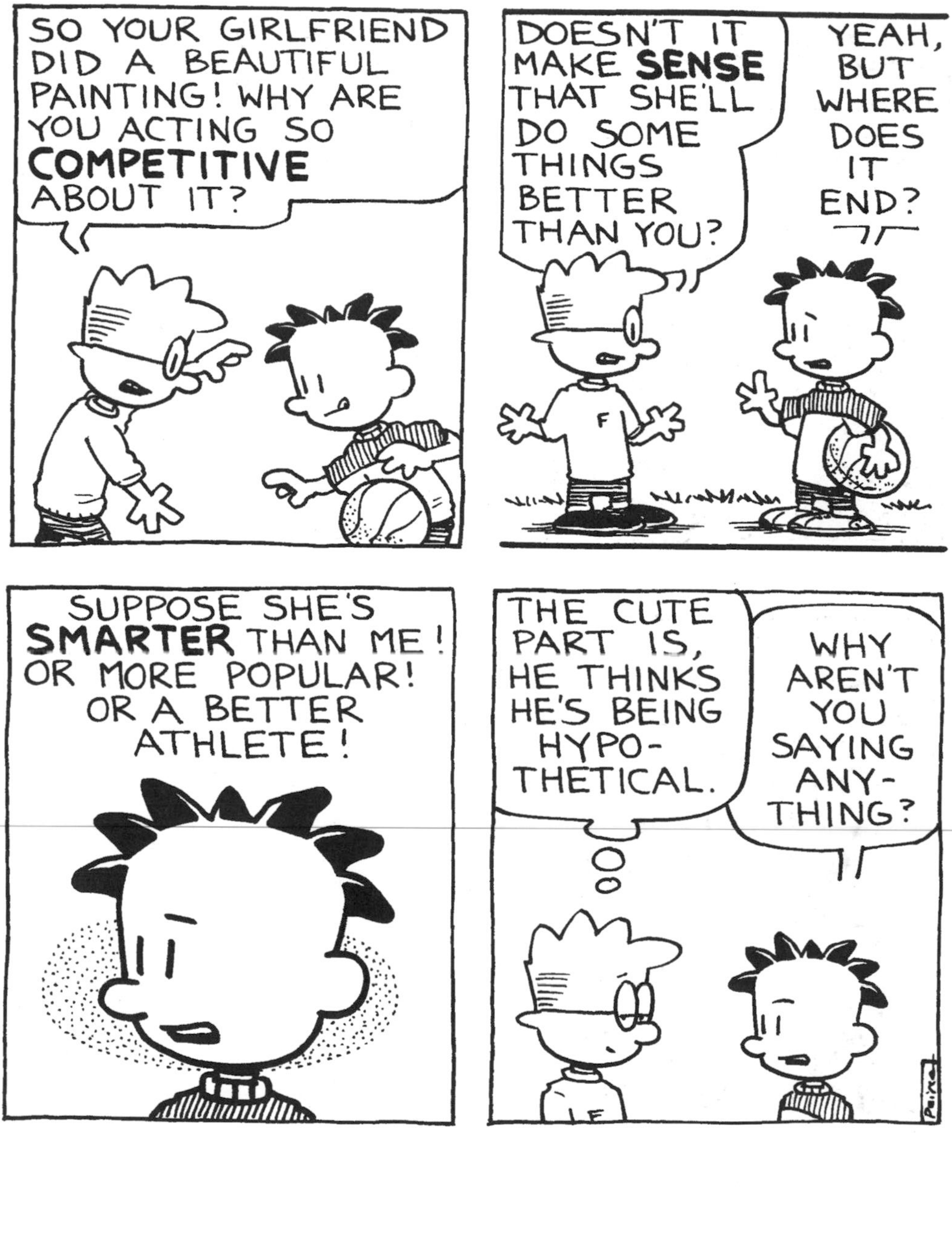
SO YOUR GIRLFRIEND DID A BEAUTIFUL PAINTING! WHY ARE YOU ACTING SO **COMPETITIVE** ABOUT IT?
DOESN'T IT MAKE **SENSE** THAT SHE'LL DO SOME THINGS BETTER THAN YOU?
YEAH, BUT WHERE DOES IT END?
SUPPOSE SHE'S **SMARTER** THAN ME! OR MORE POPULAR! OR A BETTER ATHLETE!
THE CUTE PART IS, HE THINKS HE'S BEING HYPO-THETICAL.
WHY AREN'T YOU SAYING ANY-THING?
F
F
Peirce

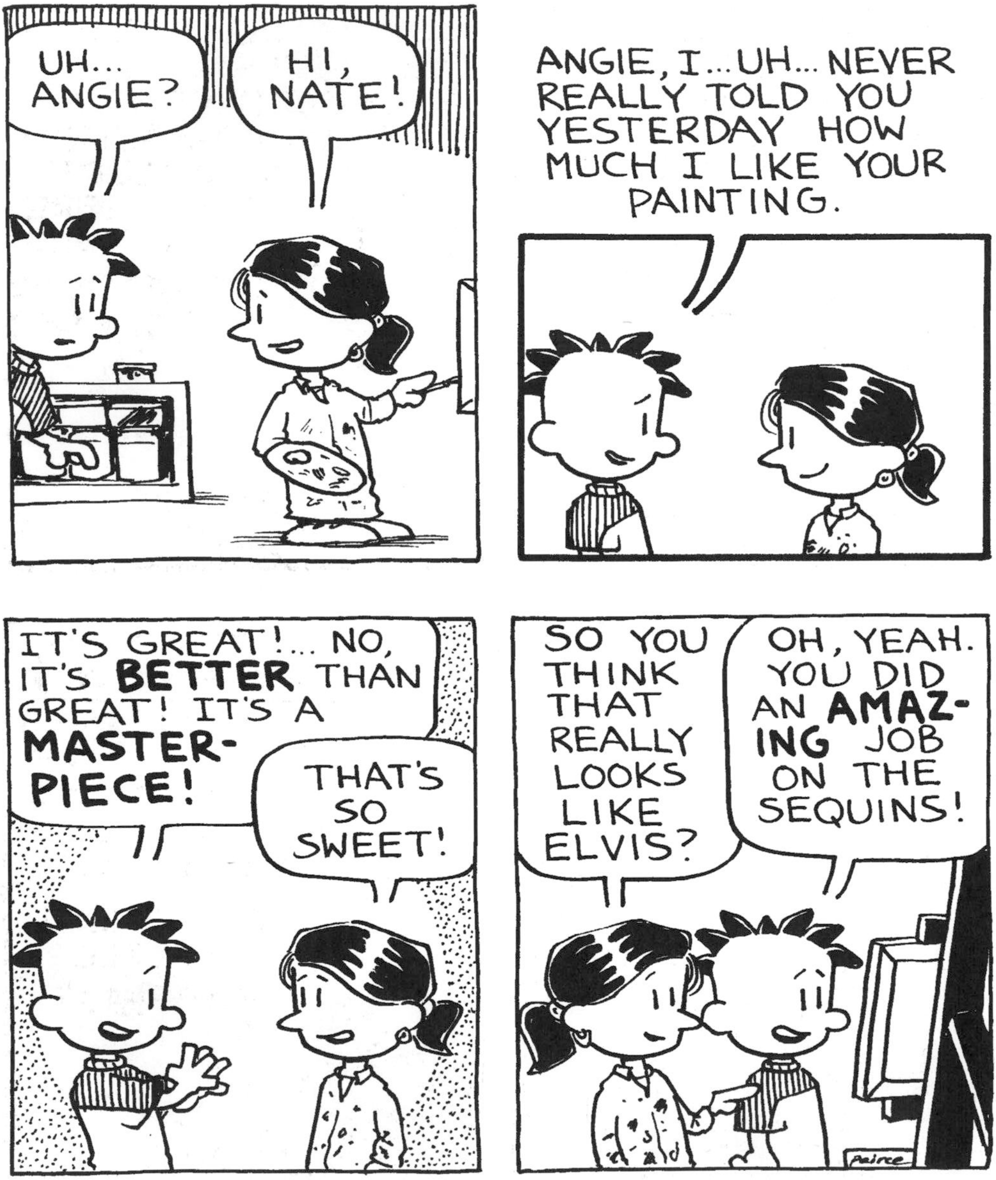
UH... ANGIE?
HI, NATE!
ANGIE, I...UH...NEVER REALLY TOLD YOU YESTERDAY HOW MUCH I LIKE YOUR PAINTING.
IT'S GREAT!... NO, IT'S **BETTER** THAN GREAT! IT'S A **MASTER-PIECE!**
THAT'S SO SWEET!
SO YOU THINK THAT REALLY LOOKS LIKE ELVIS?
OH, YEAH. YOU DID AN **AMAZ-ING** JOB ON THE SEQUINS!
Peirce

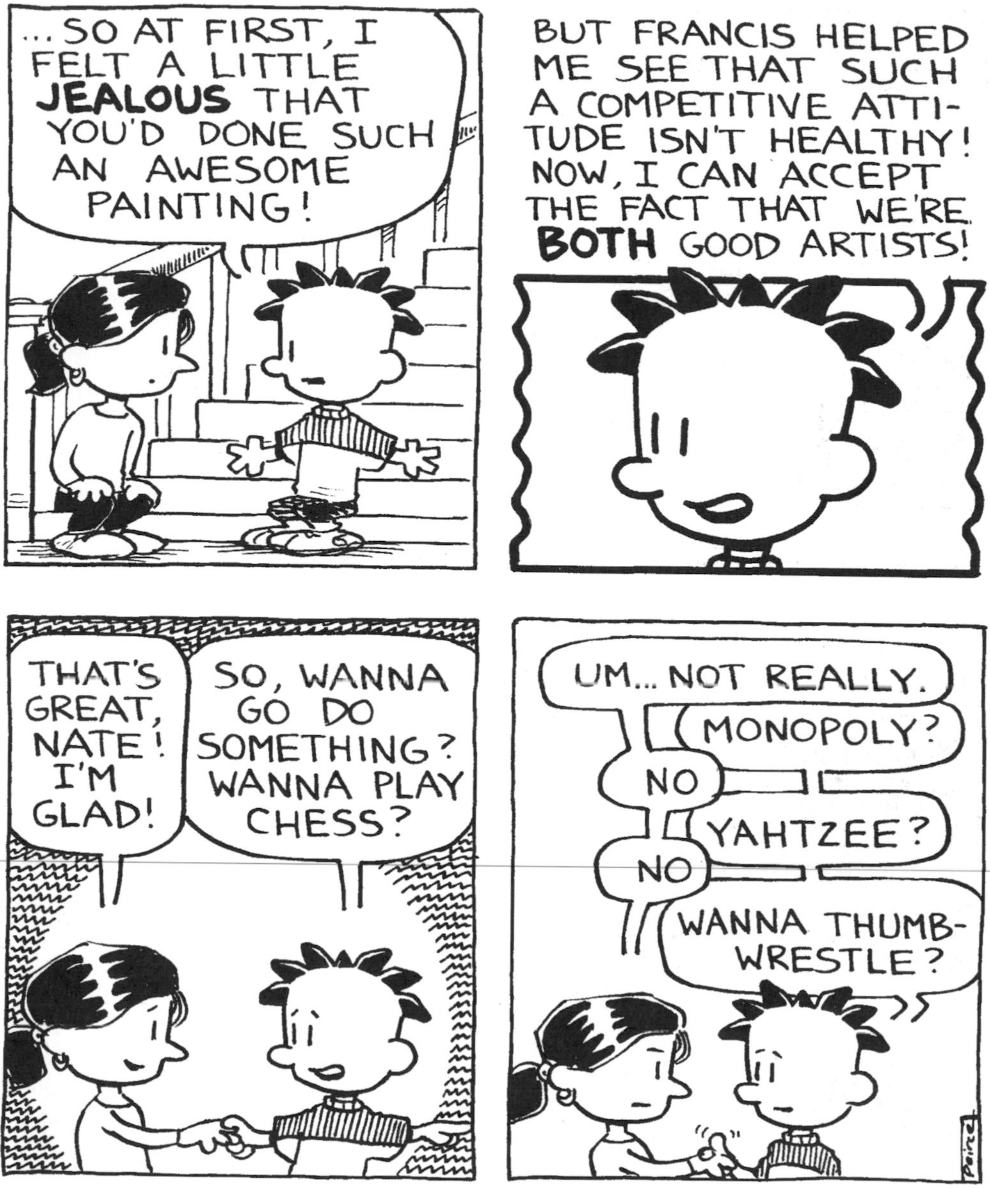
...SO AT FIRST, I FELT A LITTLE JEALOUS THAT YOU'D DONE SUCH AN AWESOME PAINTING!
BUT FRANCIS HELPED ME SEE THAT SUCH A COMPETITIVE ATTI-TUDE ISN'T HEALTHY! NOW, I CAN ACCEPT THE FACT THAT WE'RE BOTH GOOD ARTISTS!
THAT'S GREAT, NATE! I'M GLAD!
SO, WANNA GO DO SOMETHING? WANNA PLAY CHESS?
UM... NOT REALLY.
MONOPOLY?
NO
YAHTZEE?
NO
WANNA THUMB-WRESTLE?
Peirce

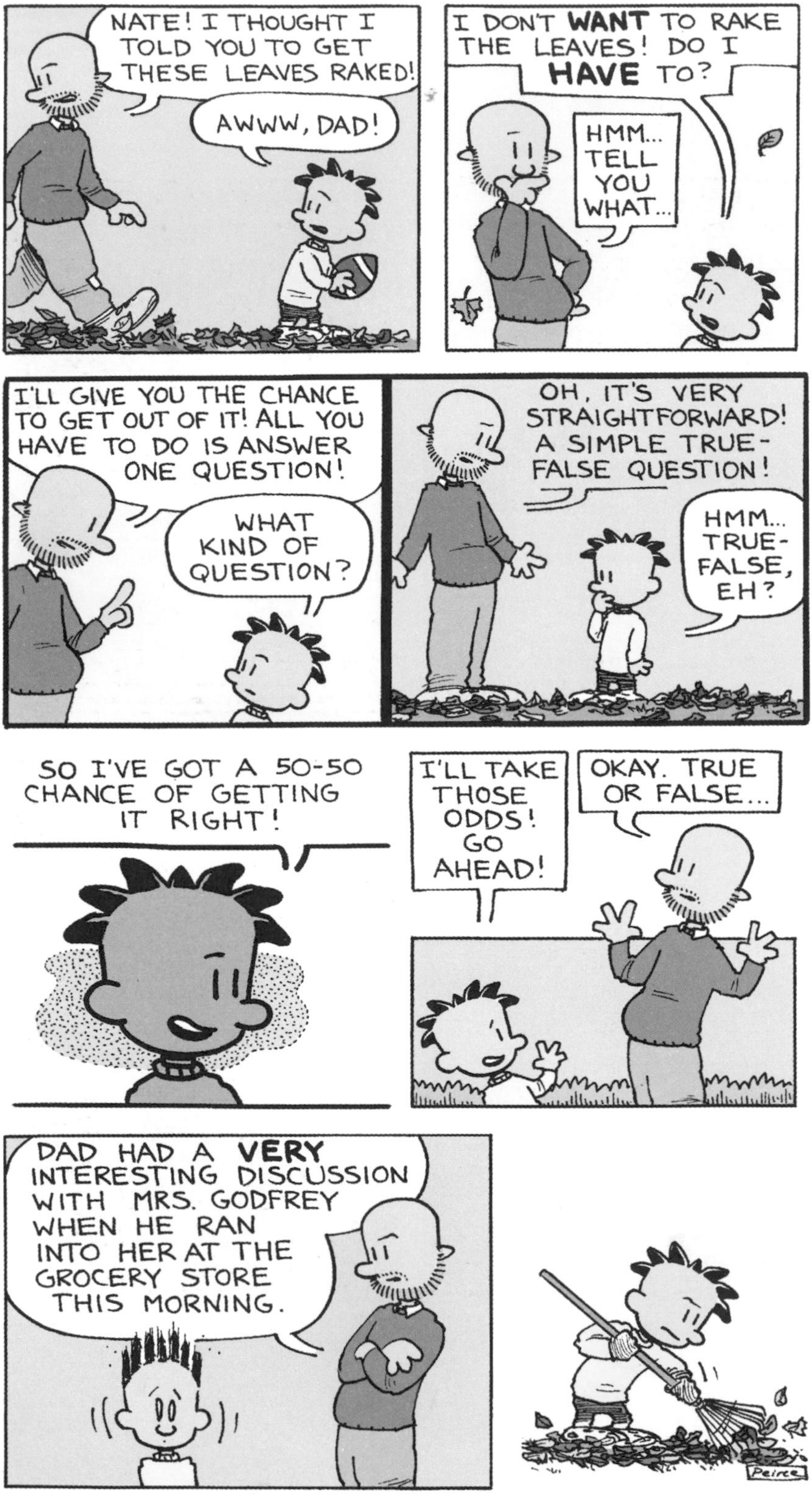
NATE! I THOUGHT I TOLD YOU TO GET THESE LEAVES RAKED!
AWWW, DAD!
I DON'T **WANT** TO RAKE THE LEAVES! DO I **HAVE** TO?
HMM... TELL YOU WHAT...
I'LL GIVE YOU THE CHANCE TO GET OUT OF IT! ALL YOU HAVE TO DO IS ANSWER ONE QUESTION!
WHAT KIND OF QUESTION?
OH, IT'S VERY STRAIGHTFORWARD! A SIMPLE TRUE-FALSE QUESTION!
HMM... TRUE-FALSE, EH?
SO I'VE GOT A 50-50 CHANCE OF GETTING IT RIGHT!
I'LL TAKE THOSE ODDS! GO AHEAD!
OKAY. TRUE OR FALSE...
DAD HAD A **VERY** INTERESTING DISCUSSION WITH MRS. GODFREY WHEN HE RAN INTO HER AT THE GROCERY STORE THIS MORNING.
Peirce

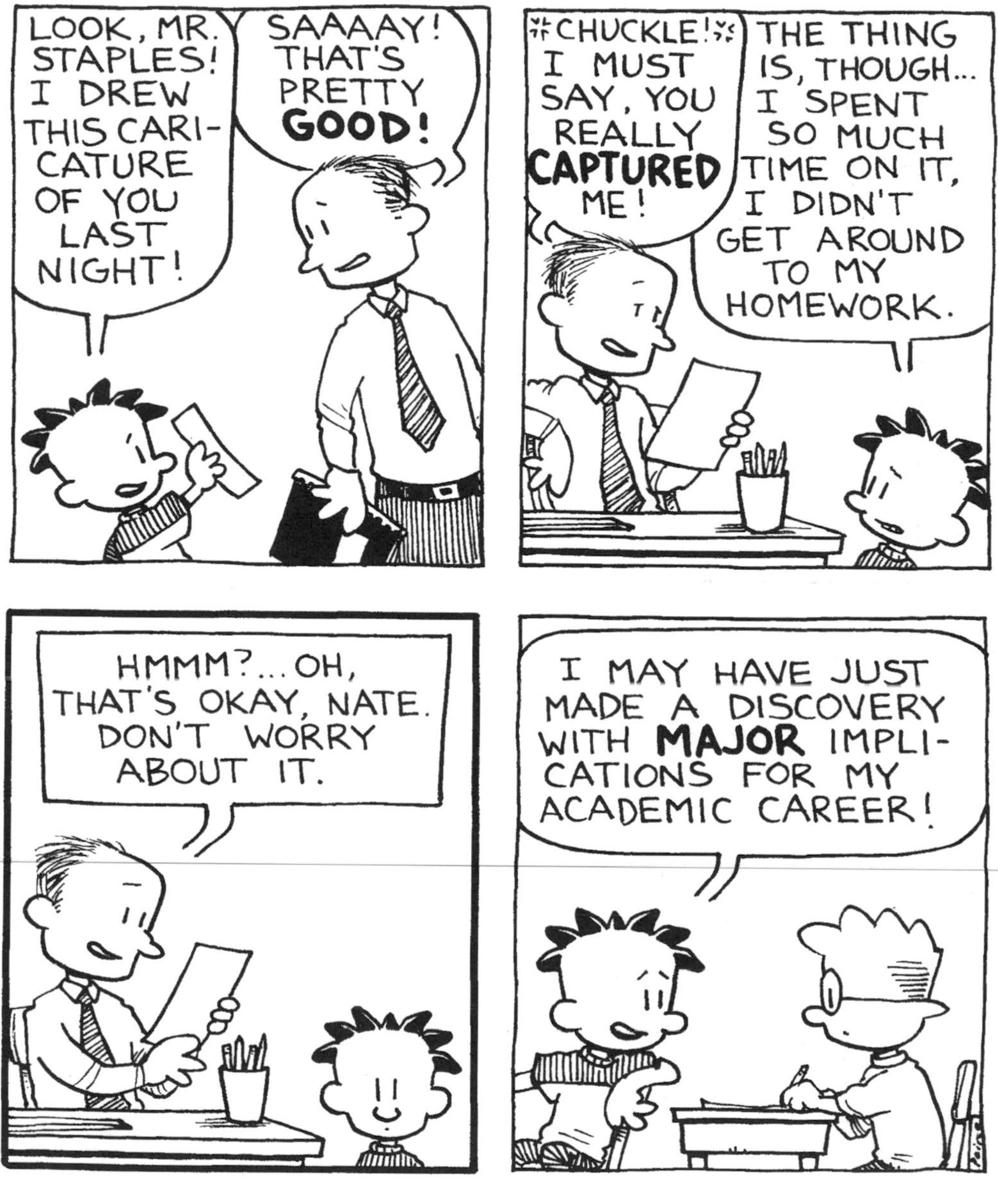
LOOK, MR. STAPLES! I DREW THIS CARICATURE OF YOU LAST NIGHT!
SAAAAY! THAT'S PRETTY GOOD!
CHUCKLE! I MUST SAY, YOU REALLY CAPTURED ME!
THE THING IS, THOUGH... I SPENT SO MUCH TIME ON IT, I DIDN'T GET AROUND TO MY HOMEWORK.
HMMM?... OH, THAT'S OKAY, NATE. DON'T WORRY ABOUT IT.
I MAY HAVE JUST MADE A DISCOVERY WITH MAJOR IMPLICATIONS FOR MY ACADEMIC CAREER!

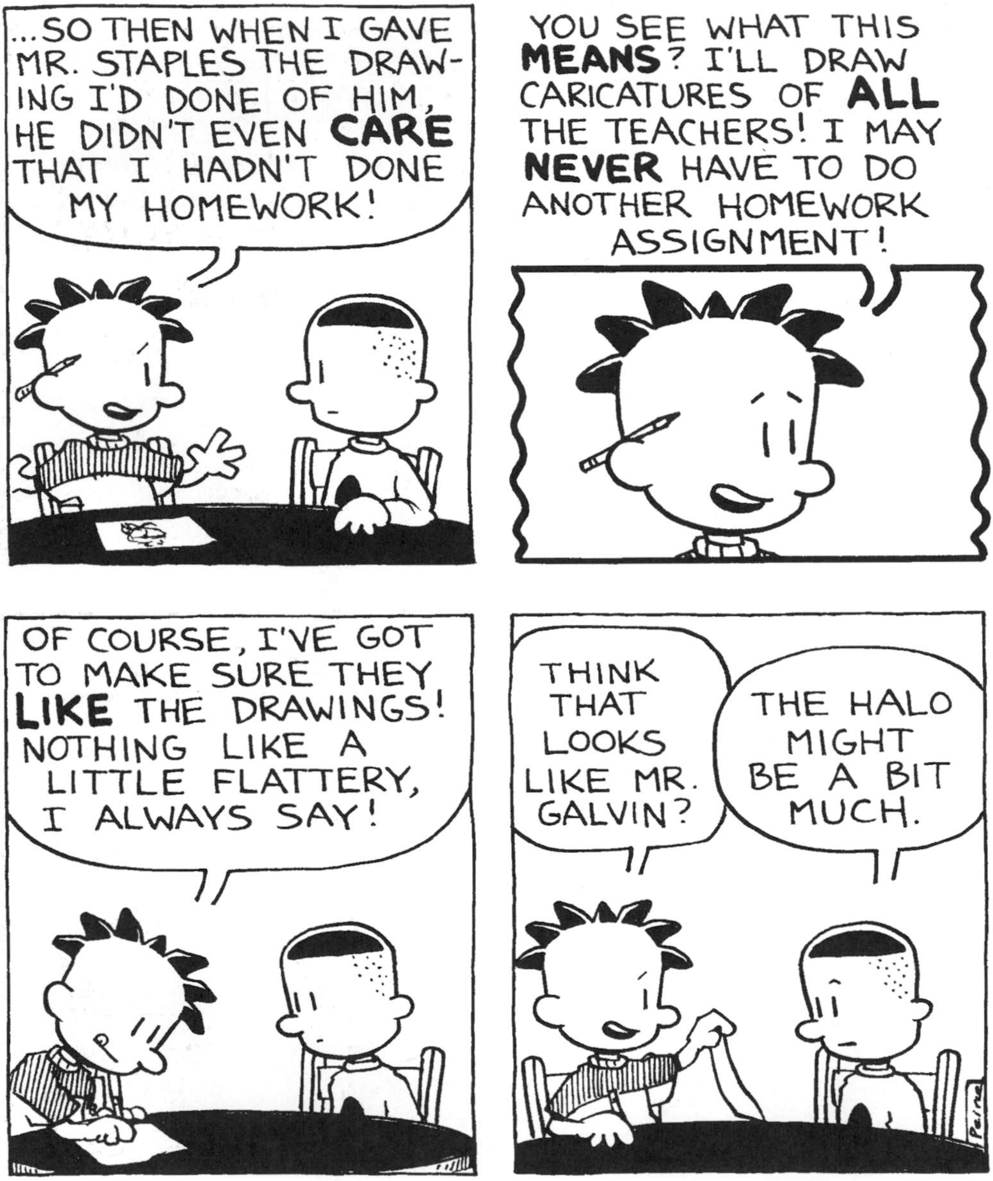
...SO THEN WHEN I GAVE MR. STAPLES THE DRAWING I'D DONE OF HIM, HE DIDN'T EVEN **CARE** THAT I HADN'T DONE MY HOMEWORK!
YOU SEE WHAT THIS **MEANS**? I'LL DRAW CARICATURES OF **ALL** THE TEACHERS! I MAY **NEVER** HAVE TO DO ANOTHER HOMEWORK ASSIGNMENT!
OF COURSE, I'VE GOT TO MAKE SURE THEY **LIKE** THE DRAWINGS! NOTHING LIKE A LITTLE FLATTERY, I ALWAYS SAY!
THINK THAT LOOKS LIKE MR. GALVIN?
THE HALO MIGHT BE A BIT MUCH.

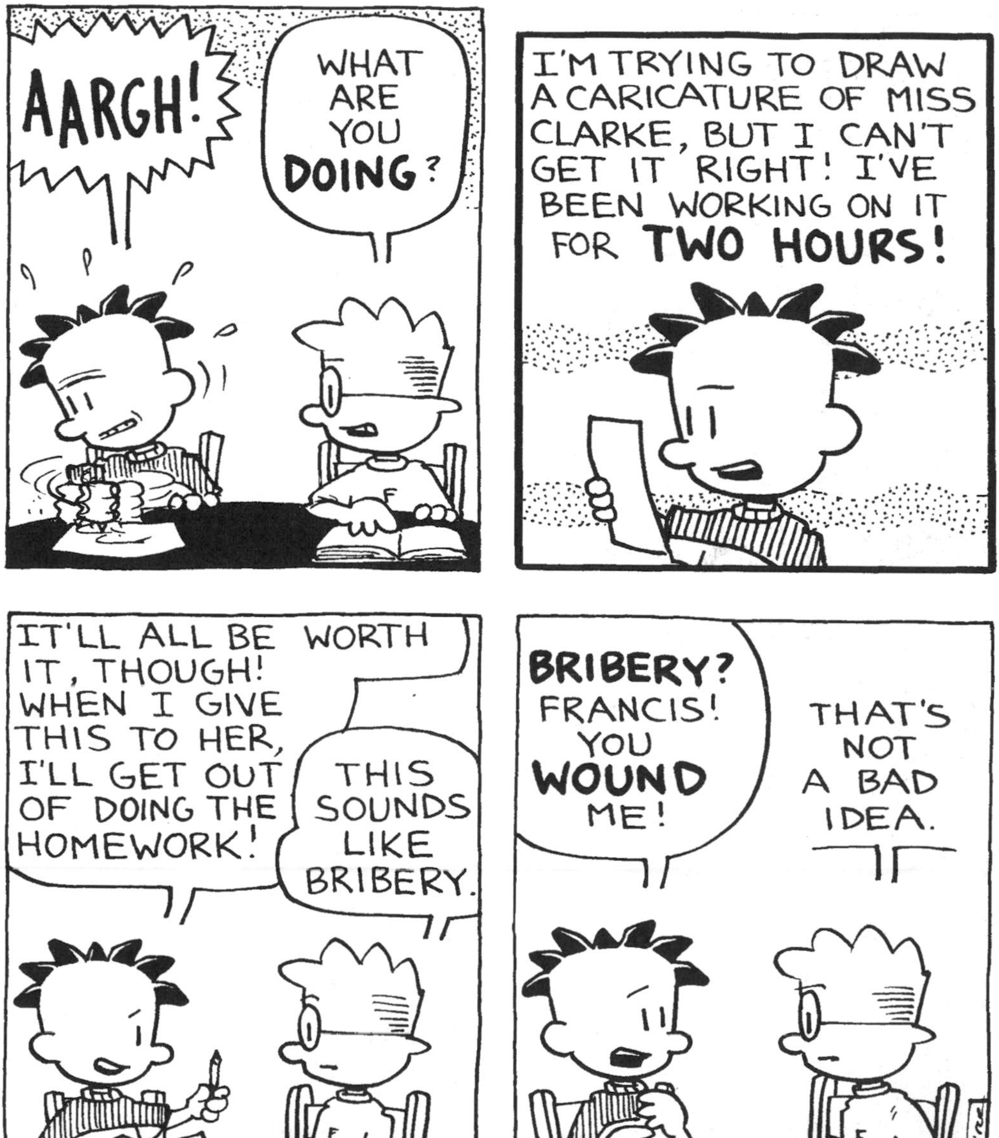
AARGH!
WHAT ARE YOU DOING?
I'M TRYING TO DRAW A CARICATURE OF MISS CLARKE, BUT I CAN'T GET IT RIGHT! I'VE BEEN WORKING ON IT FOR TWO HOURS!
IT'LL ALL BE WORTH IT, THOUGH! WHEN I GIVE THIS TO HER, I'LL GET OUT OF DOING THE HOMEWORK!
THIS SOUNDS LIKE BRIBERY.
BRIBERY? FRANCIS! YOU WOUND ME!
THAT'S NOT A BAD IDEA.
PEIRCE

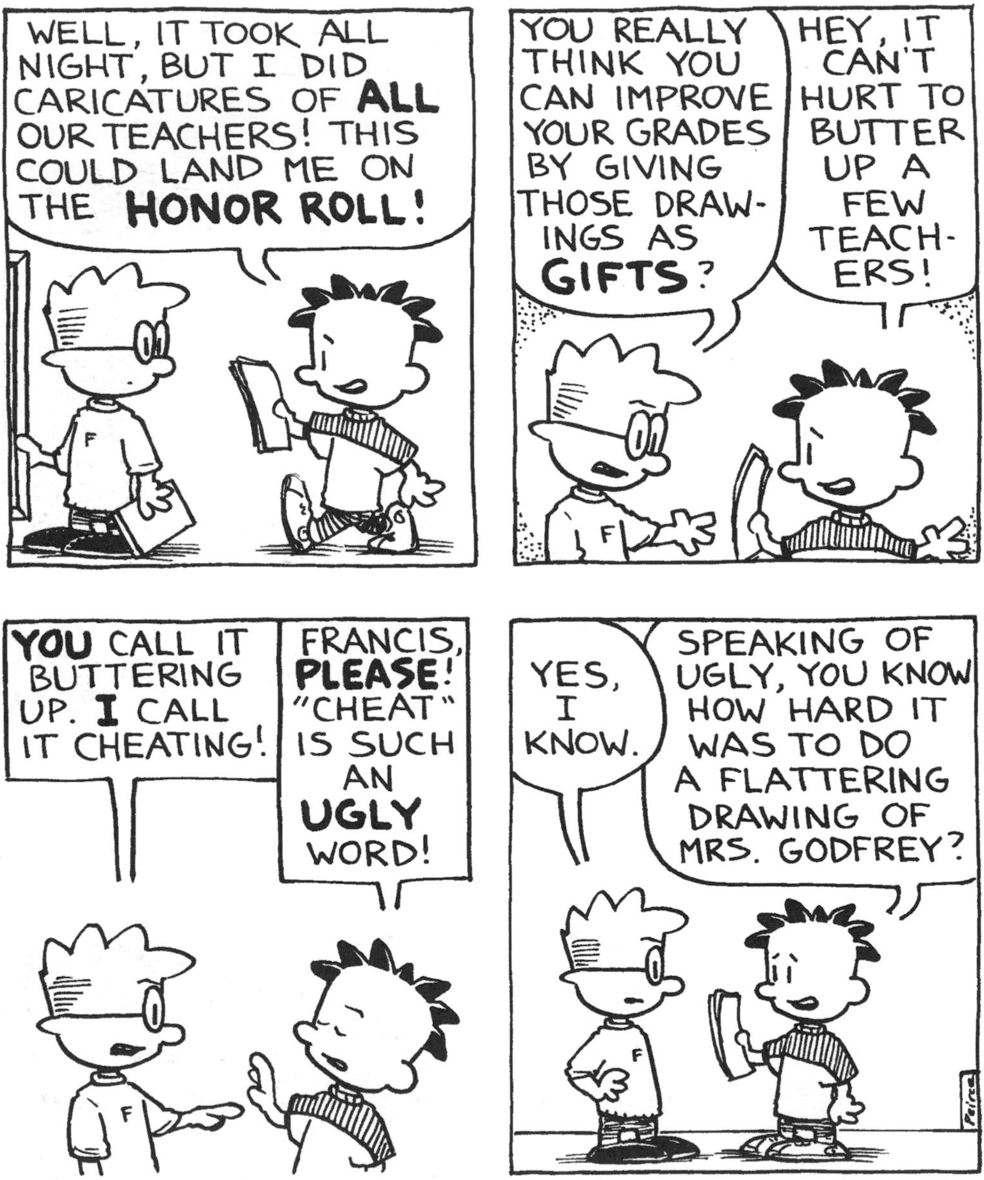
WELL, IT TOOK ALL NIGHT, BUT I DID CARICATURES OF **ALL** OUR TEACHERS! THIS COULD LAND ME ON THE **HONOR ROLL**!
YOU REALLY THINK YOU CAN IMPROVE YOUR GRADES BY GIVING THOSE DRAWINGS AS **GIFTS**?
HEY, IT CAN'T HURT TO BUTTER UP A FEW TEACHERS!
YOU CALL IT BUTTERING UP. **I** CALL IT CHEATING!
FRANCIS, **PLEASE**! "CHEAT" IS SUCH AN **UGLY** WORD!
YES, I KNOW.
SPEAKING OF UGLY, YOU KNOW HOW HARD IT WAS TO DO A FLATTERING DRAWING OF MRS. GODFREY?
Peirce

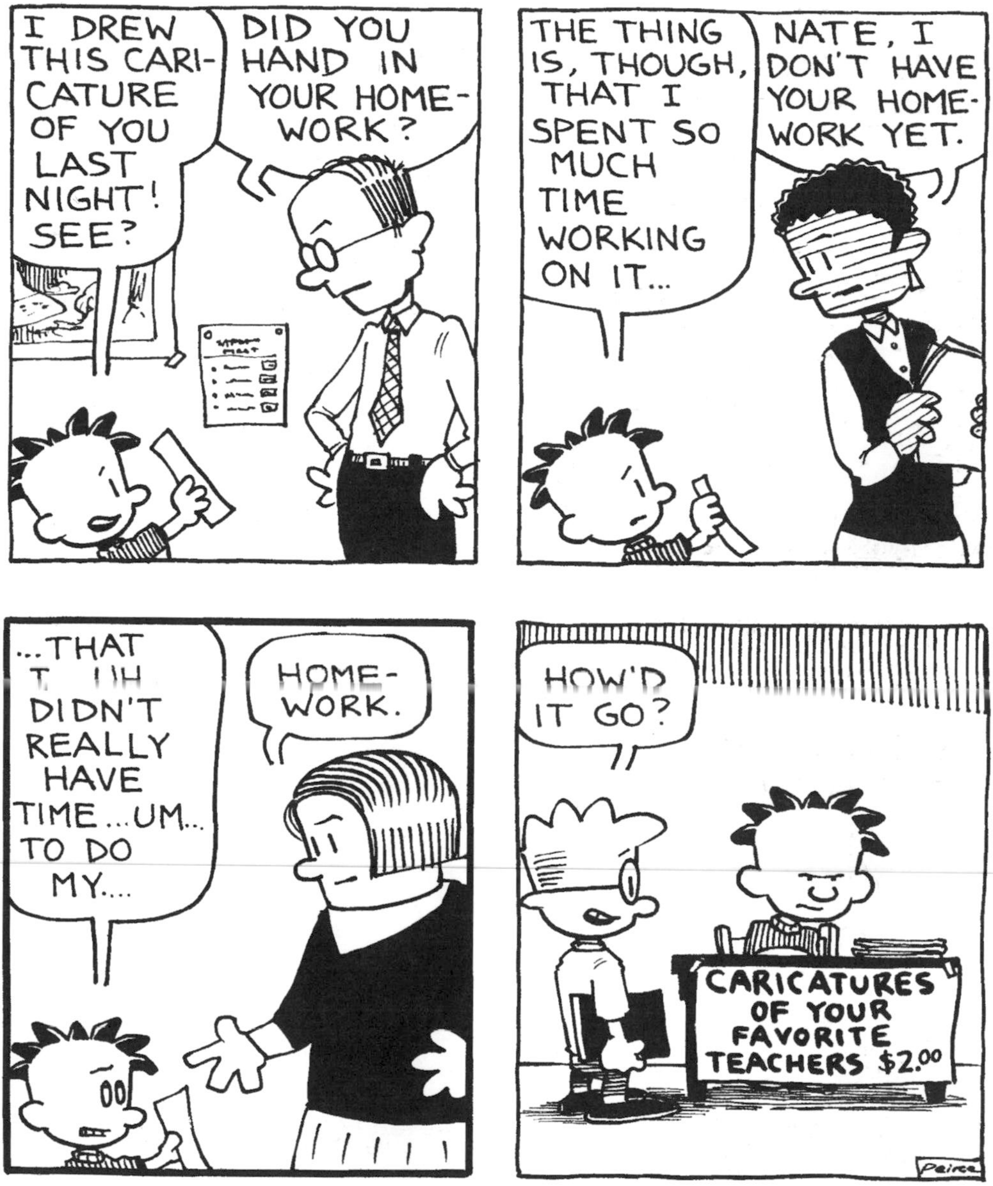
I DREW THIS CARICATURE OF YOU LAST NIGHT! SEE?
DID YOU HAND IN YOUR HOMEWORK?
THE THING IS, THOUGH, THAT I SPENT SO MUCH TIME WORKING ON IT...
NATE, I DON'T HAVE YOUR HOMEWORK YET.
...THAT I... UH DIDN'T REALLY HAVE TIME...UM... TO DO MY....
HOMEWORK.
HOW'D IT GO?
CARICATURES OF YOUR FAVORITE TEACHERS $2.00
Peirce

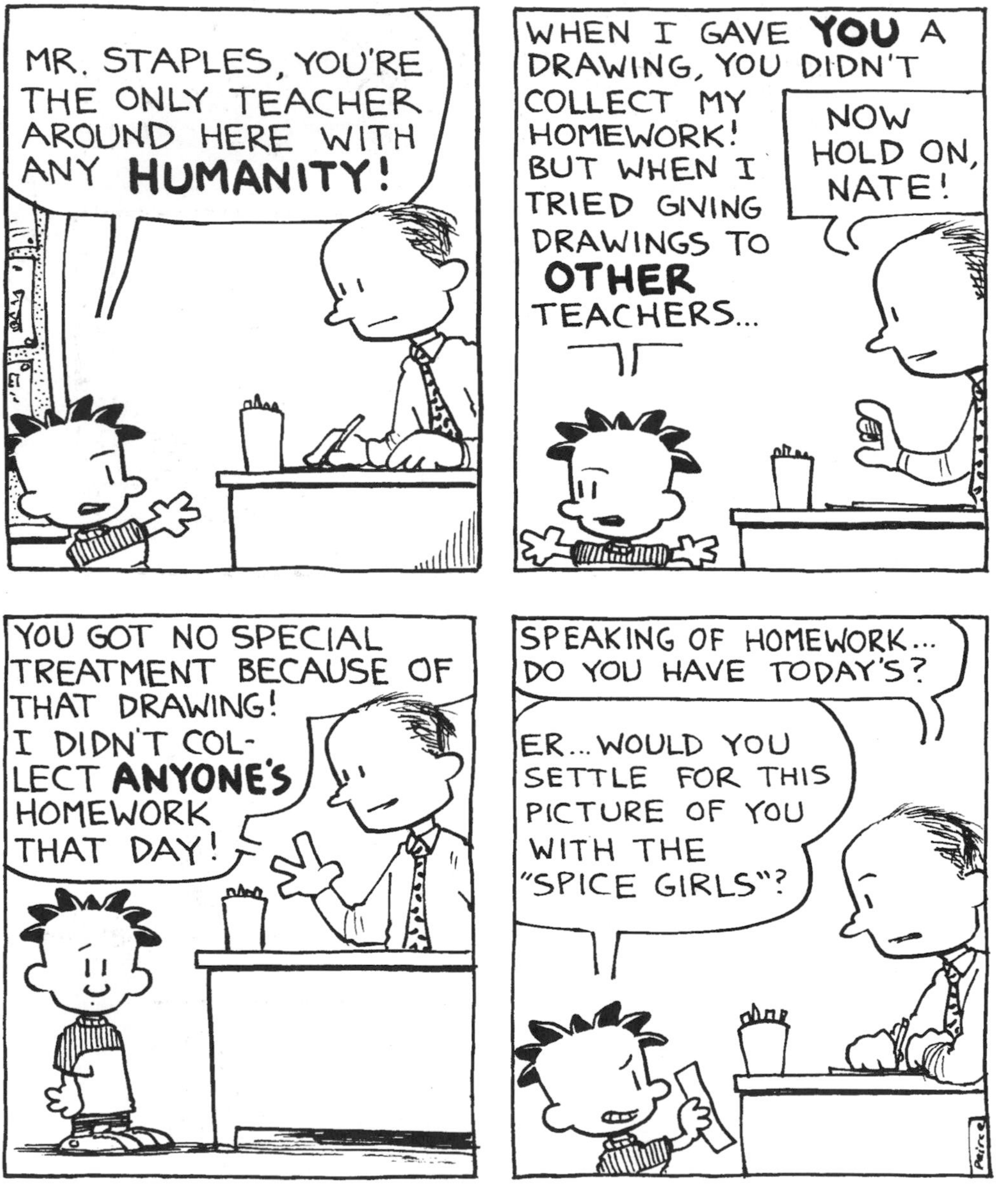
MR. STAPLES, YOU'RE THE ONLY TEACHER AROUND HERE WITH ANY HUMANITY!
WHEN I GAVE YOU A DRAWING, YOU DIDN'T COLLECT MY HOMEWORK! BUT WHEN I TRIED GIVING DRAWINGS TO OTHER TEACHERS...
NOW HOLD ON, NATE!
YOU GOT NO SPECIAL TREATMENT BECAUSE OF THAT DRAWING! I DIDN'T COL-LECT ANYONE'S HOMEWORK THAT DAY!
SPEAKING OF HOMEWORK... DO YOU HAVE TODAY'S?
ER...WOULD YOU SETTLE FOR THIS PICTURE OF YOU WITH THE "SPICE GIRLS"?
Peirce

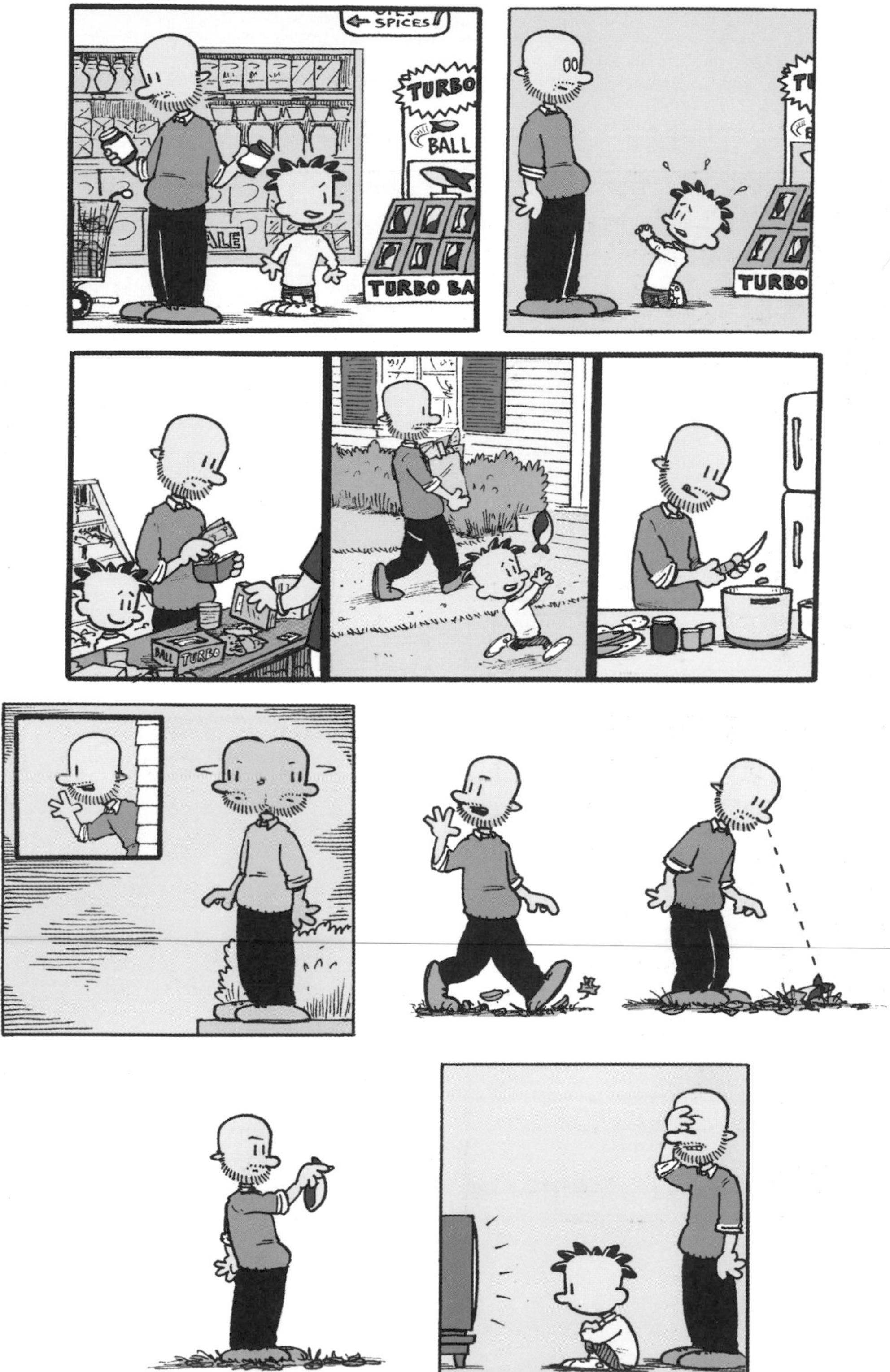
SPICES
TURBO
BALL
SALE
TURBO BA
TURBO
BALL
TURBO
Peirce

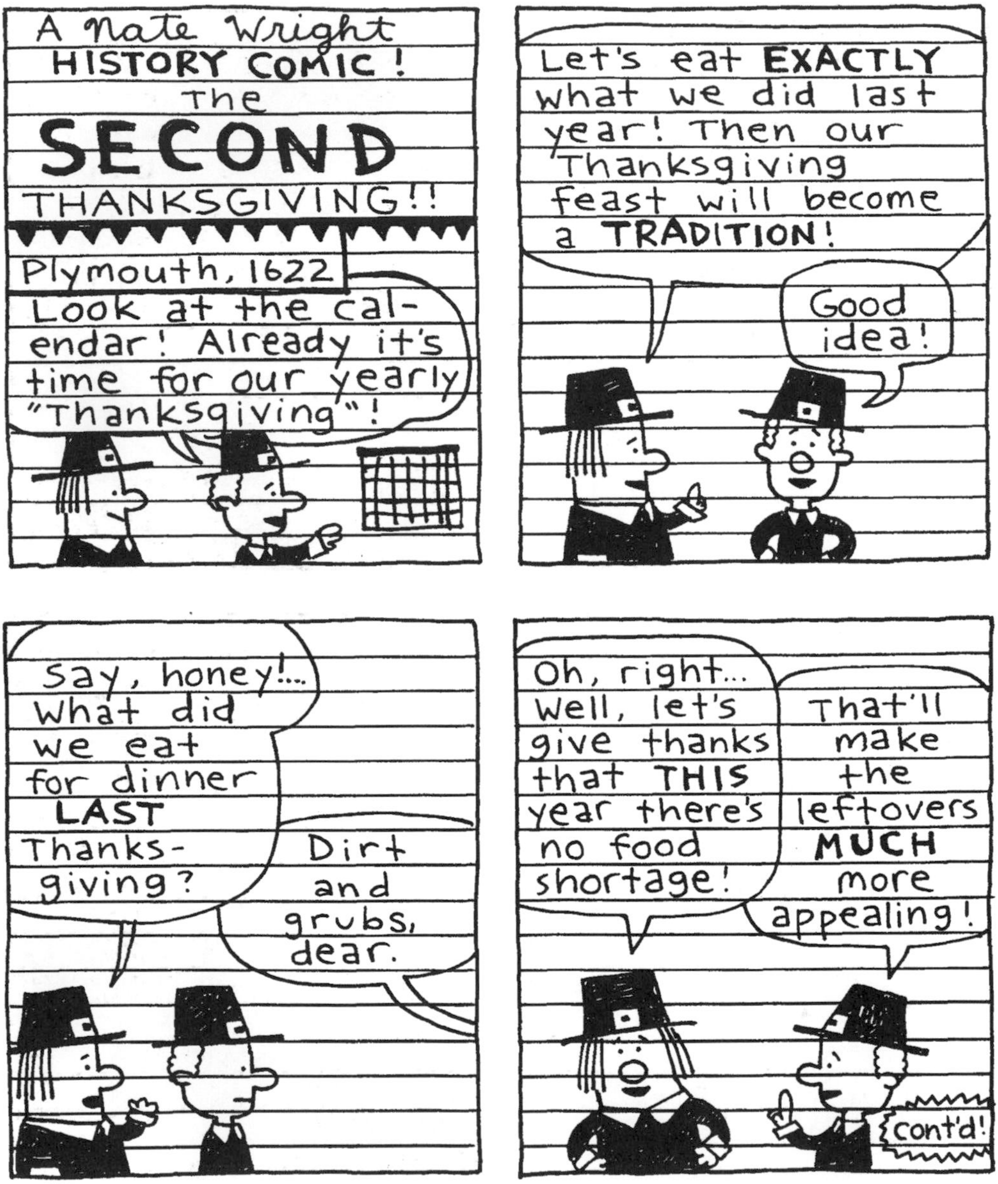
A Nate Wright
HISTORY COMIC!
The
SECOND
THANKSGIVING!!
Plymouth, 1622
Look at the calendar! Already it's time for our yearly "Thanksgiving"!
Let's eat EXACTLY what we did last year! Then our Thanksgiving feast will become a TRADITION!
Good idea!
Say, honey!... What did we eat for dinner LAST Thanksgiving?
Dirt and grubs, dear.
Oh, right... Well, let's give thanks that THIS year there's no food shortage!
That'll make the leftovers MUCH more appealing!
cont'd!

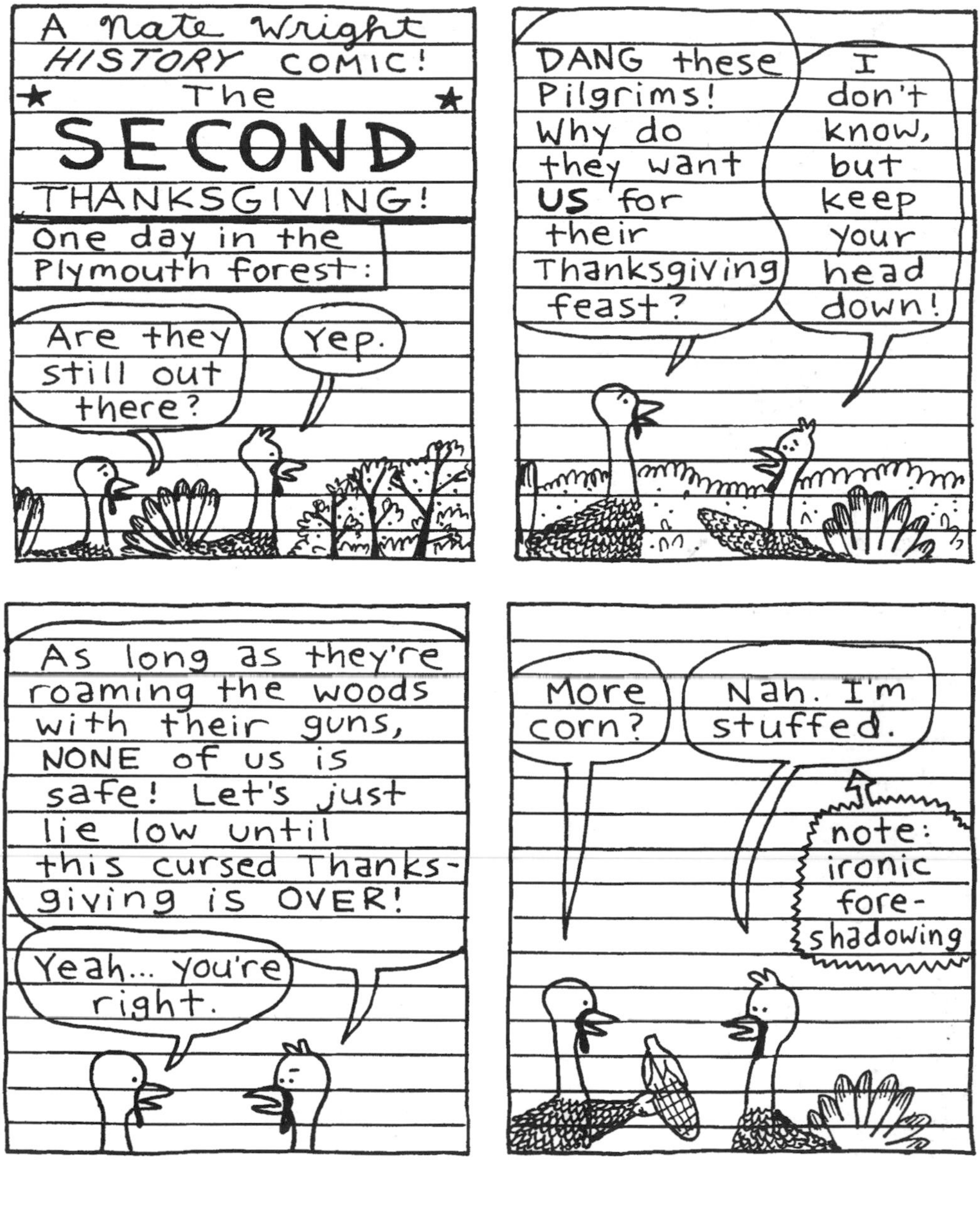
A Nate Wright HISTORY COMIC!
★ The ★ SECOND THANKSGIVING!
One day in the Plymouth forest:
Are they still out there?
Yep.
DANG these Pilgrims! Why do they want US for their Thanksgiving feast?
I don't know, but keep your head down!
As long as they're roaming the woods with their guns, NONE of us is safe! Let's just lie low until this cursed Thanks-giving is OVER!
Yeah... you're right.
More corn?
Nah. I'm stuffed.
note: ironic fore-shadowing

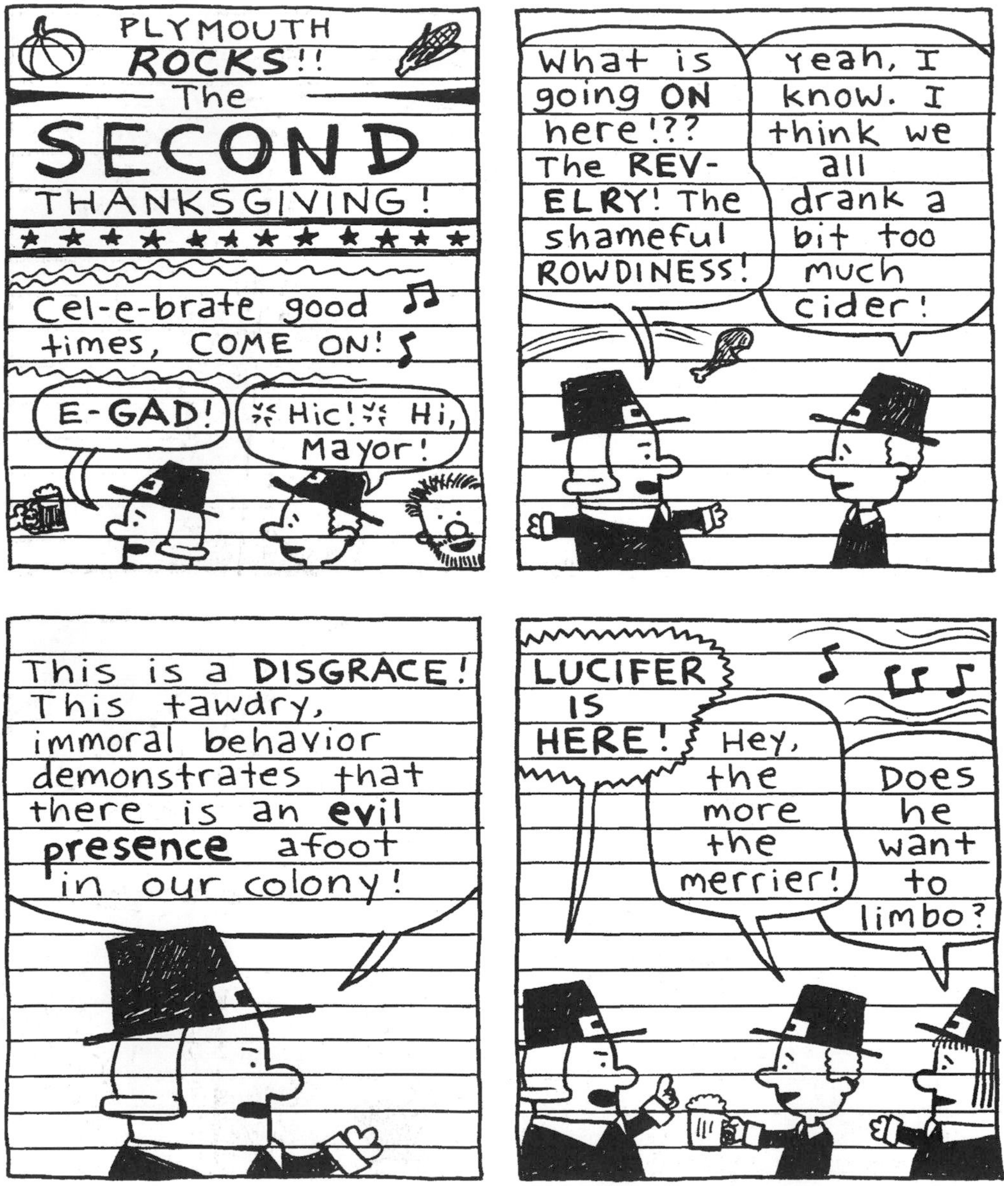
PLYMOUTH ROCKS!! The SECOND THANKSGIVING!
Cel-e-brate good times, COME ON!
E-GAD!
Hic! Hic! Hi, Mayor!
What is going ON here!?? The REV-ELRY! The shameful ROWDINESS!
Yeah, I know. I think we all drank a bit too much cider!
This is a DISGRACE! This tawdry, immoral behavior demonstrates that there is an evil presence afoot in our colony!
LUCIFER IS HERE!
Hey, the more the merrier!
Does he want to limbo?

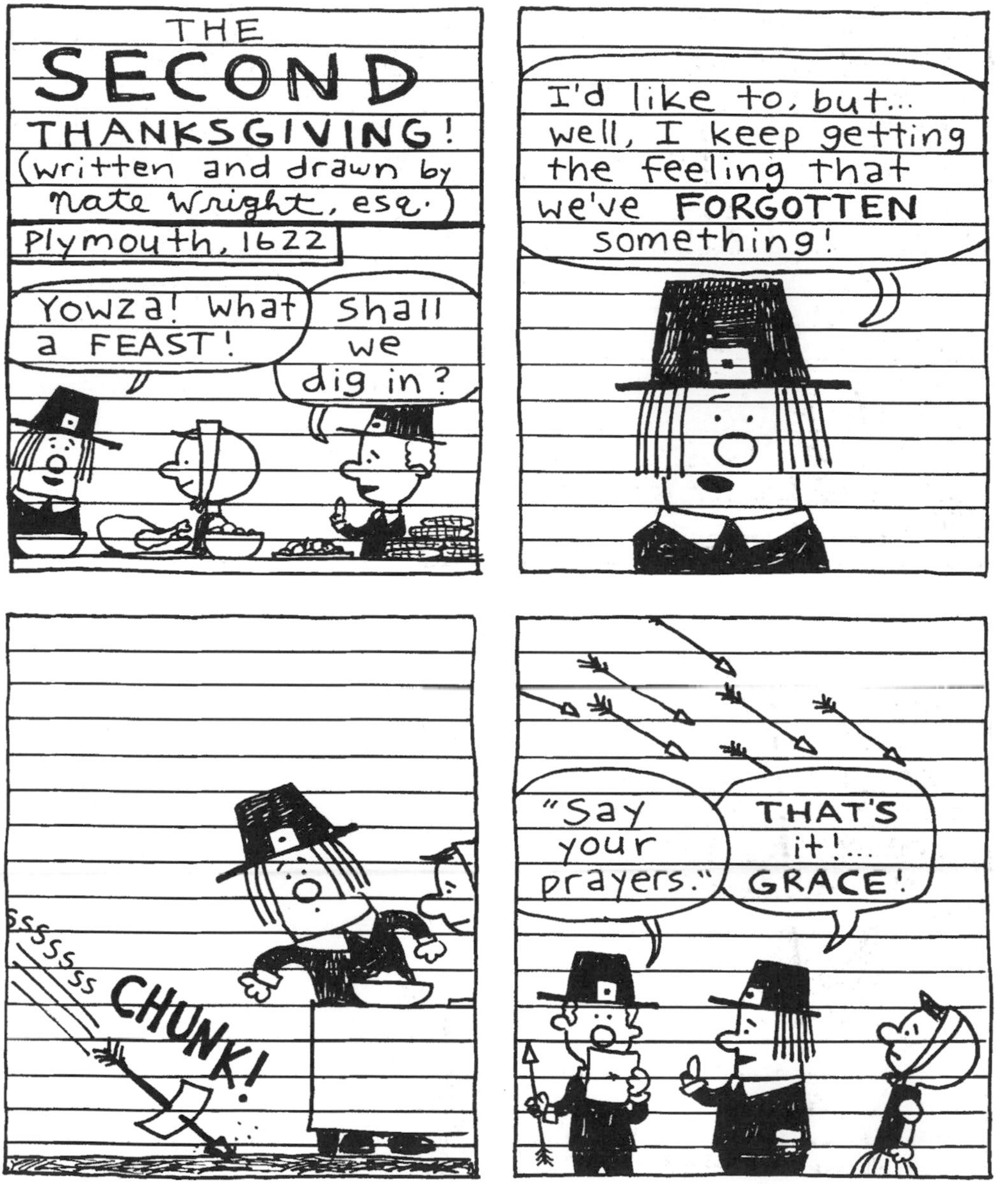
THE
SECOND
THANKSGIVING!
(written and drawn by
Nate Wright, esq.)
Plymouth, 1622
Yowza! What a FEAST!
Shall we dig in?
I'd like to, but... well, I keep getting the feeling that we've FORGOTTEN something!
SSSSSSSS
CHUNK!
"Say your prayers."
THAT'S it!... GRACE!

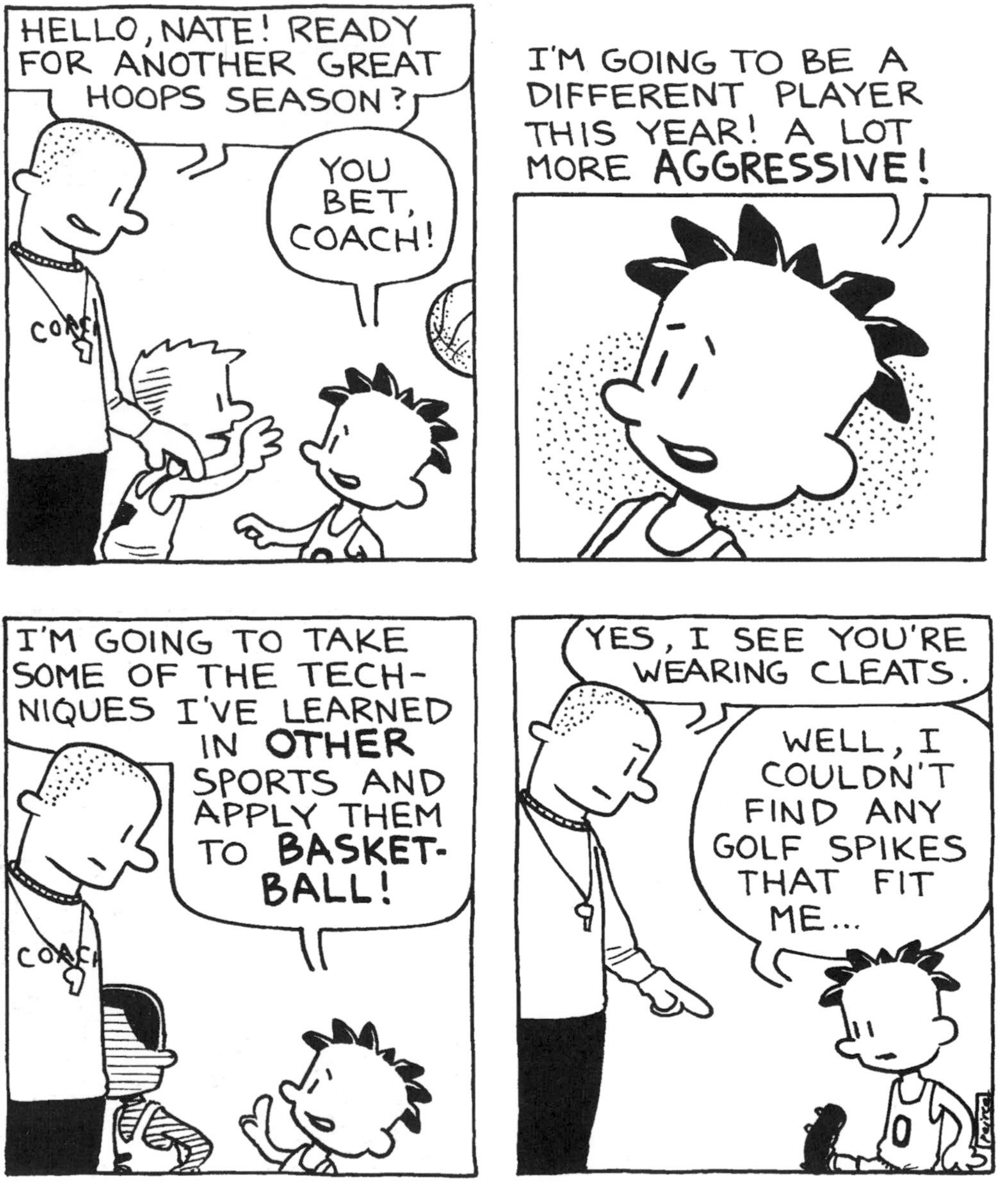
HELLO, NATE! READY FOR ANOTHER GREAT HOOPS SEASON?
YOU BET, COACH!
I'M GOING TO BE A DIFFERENT PLAYER THIS YEAR! A LOT MORE AGGRESSIVE!
I'M GOING TO TAKE SOME OF THE TECHNIQUES I'VE LEARNED IN OTHER SPORTS AND APPLY THEM TO BASKETBALL!
YES, I SEE YOU'RE WEARING CLEATS.
WELL, I COULDN'T FIND ANY GOLF SPIKES THAT FIT ME...

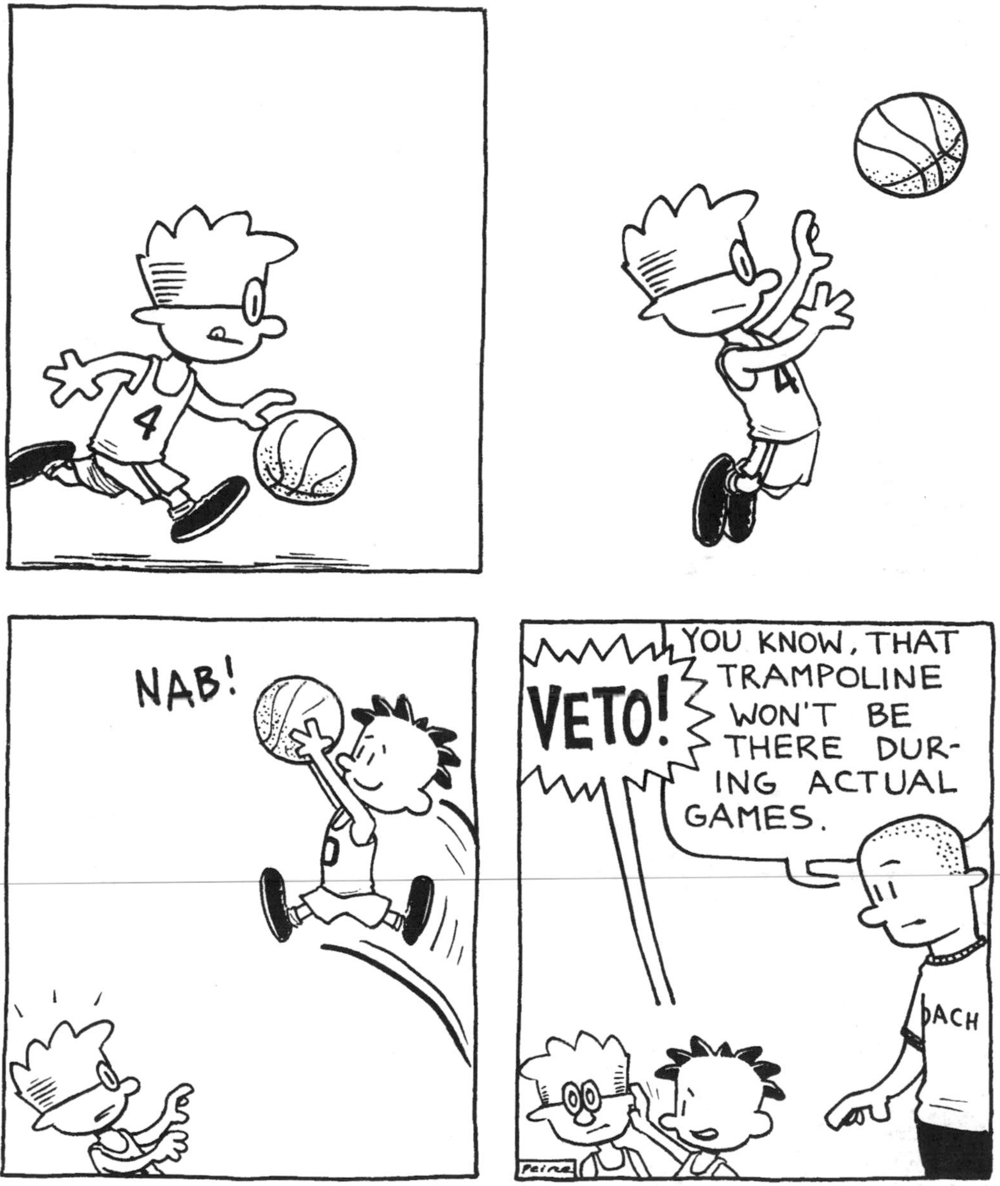
NAB!
VETO!
YOU KNOW, THAT TRAMPOLINE WON'T BE THERE DUR- ING ACTUAL GAMES.
4
4
ACH
Peirce

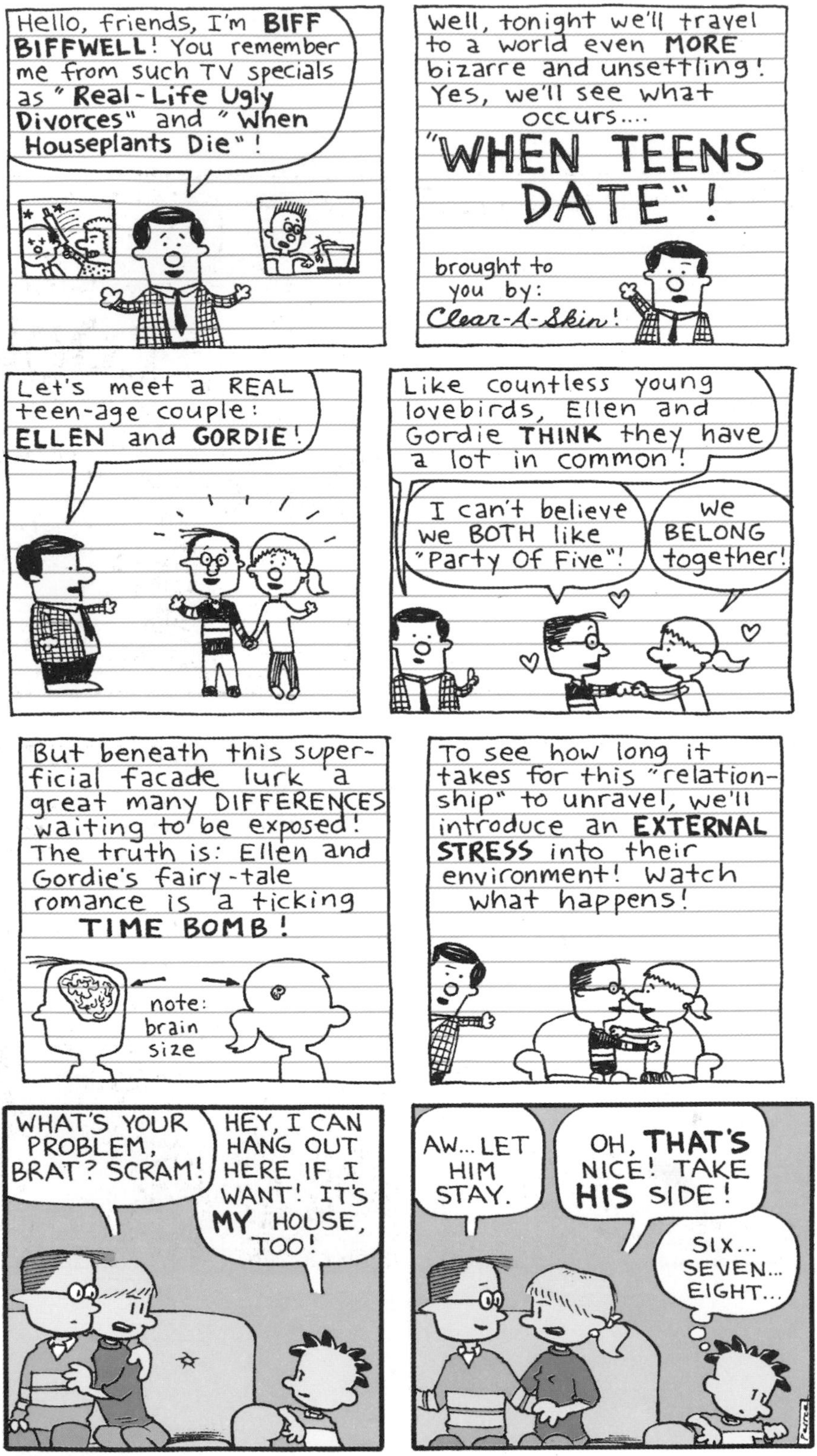
Hello, friends, I'm BIFF BIFFWELL! You remember me from such TV specials as "Real-Life Ugly Divorces" and "When Houseplants Die"!
Well, tonight we'll travel to a world even MORE bizarre and unsettling! Yes, we'll see what occurs....
"WHEN TEENS DATE"!
brought to you by: Clear-A-Skin!
Let's meet a REAL teen-age couple: ELLEN and GORDIE!
Like countless young lovebirds, Ellen and Gordie THINK they have a lot in common!
I can't believe we BOTH like "Party Of Five"!
We BELONG together!
But beneath this superficial facade lurk a great many DIFFERENCES waiting to be exposed! The truth is: Ellen and Gordie's fairy-tale romance is a ticking TIME BOMB!
note: brain size
To see how long it takes for this "relationship" to unravel, we'll introduce an EXTERNAL STRESS into their environment! Watch what happens!
WHAT'S YOUR PROBLEM, BRAT? SCRAM!
HEY, I CAN HANG OUT HERE IF I WANT! IT'S MY HOUSE, TOO!
AW... LET HIM STAY.
OH, THAT'S NICE! TAKE HIS SIDE!
SIX... SEVEN... EIGHT...

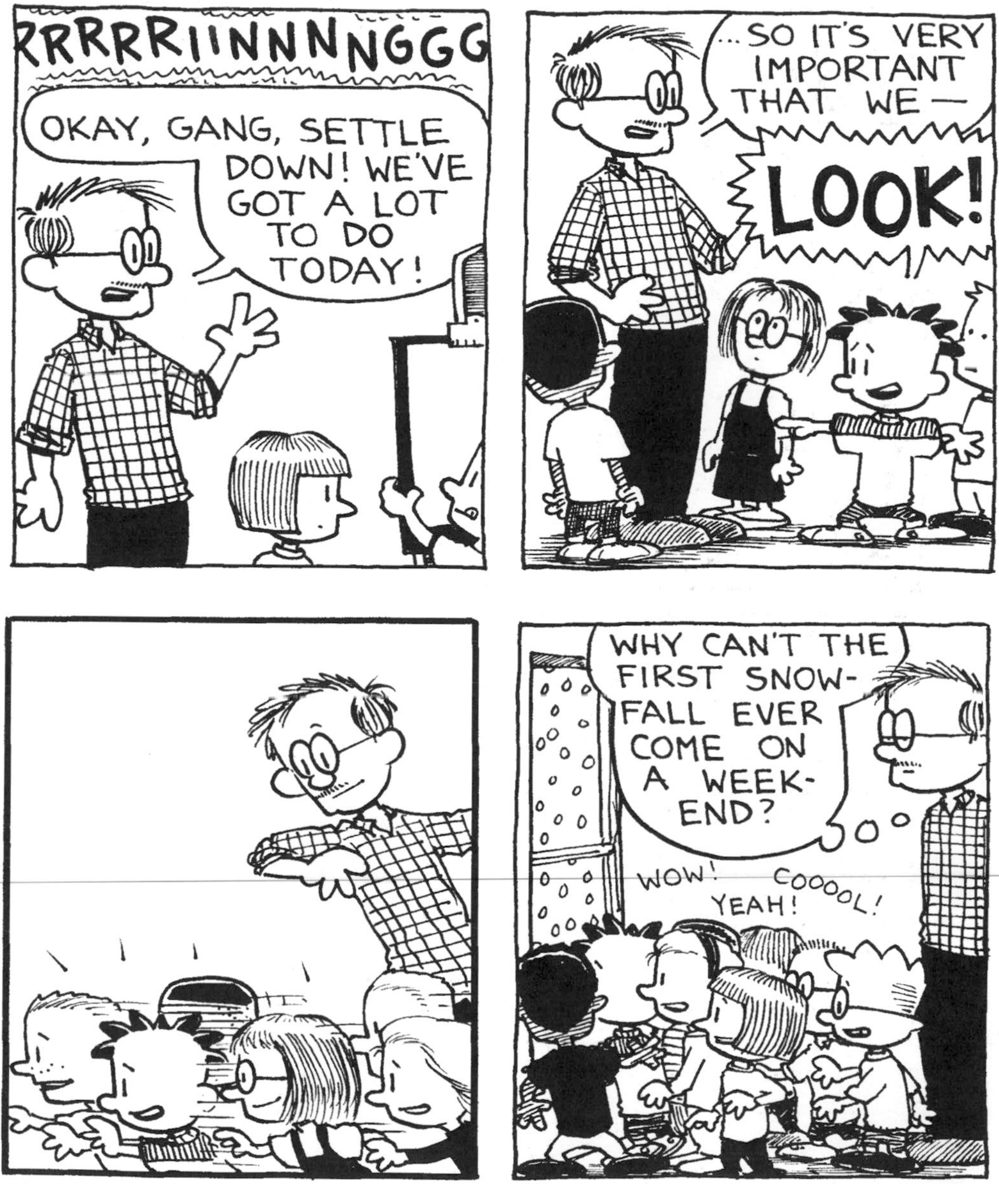

RRRRRIINNNNNGGG
OKAY, GANG, SETTLE DOWN! WE'VE GOT A LOT TO DO TODAY!
...SO IT'S VERY IMPORTANT THAT WE —
LOOK!
WHY CAN'T THE FIRST SNOW-FALL EVER COME ON A WEEK-END?
WOW!
YEAH!
COOOOL!

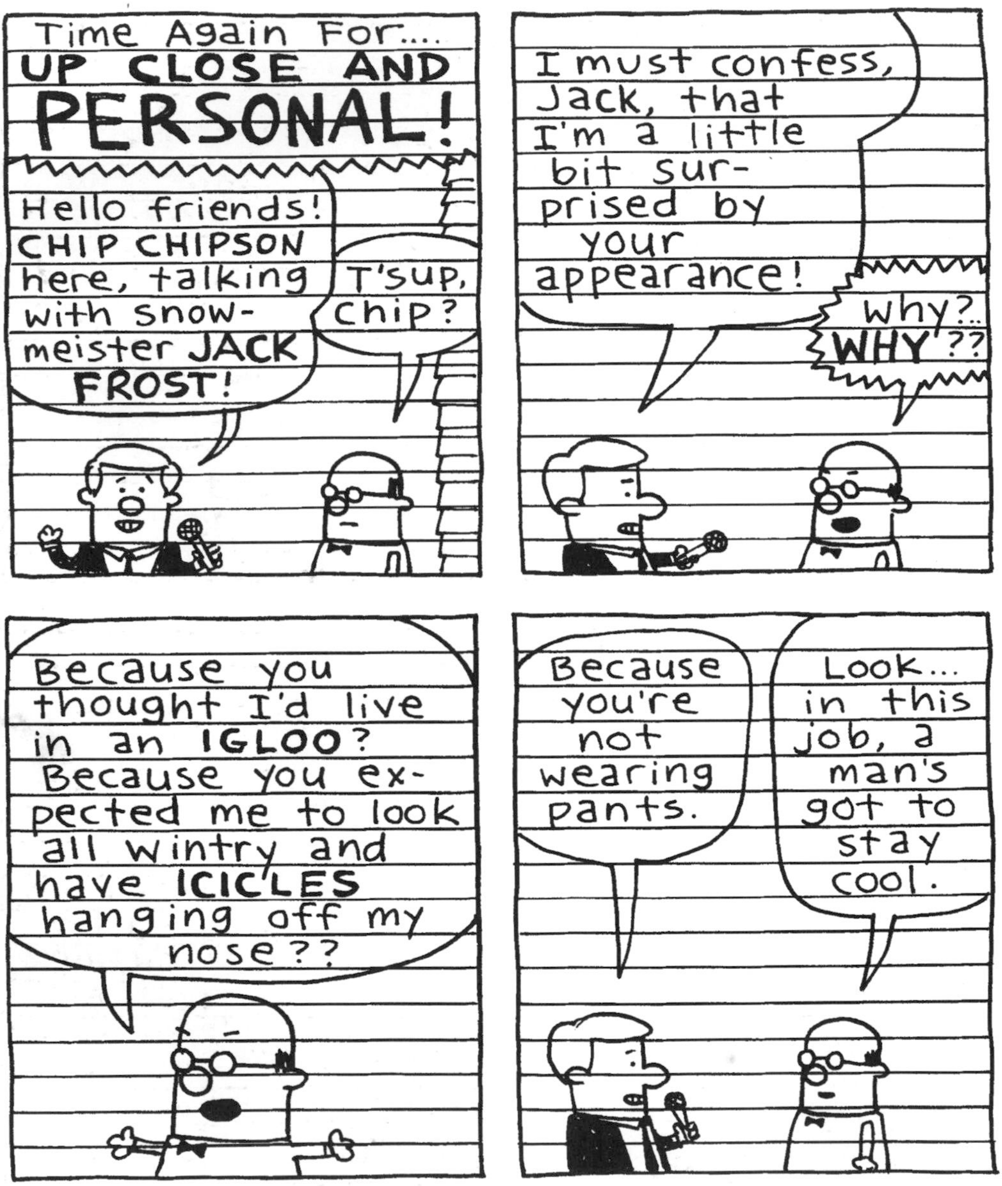
Time Again For....
UP CLOSE AND PERSONAL!
Hello friends! CHIP CHIPSON here, talking with snow-meister JACK FROST!
T'SUP, CHIP?
I must confess, Jack, that I'm a little bit sur-prised by your appearance!
Why?.. WHY??
Because you thought I'd live in an IGLOO? Because you ex-pected me to look all wintry and have ICICLES hanging off my nose??
Because you're not wearing pants.
Look... in this job, a man's got to stay cool.

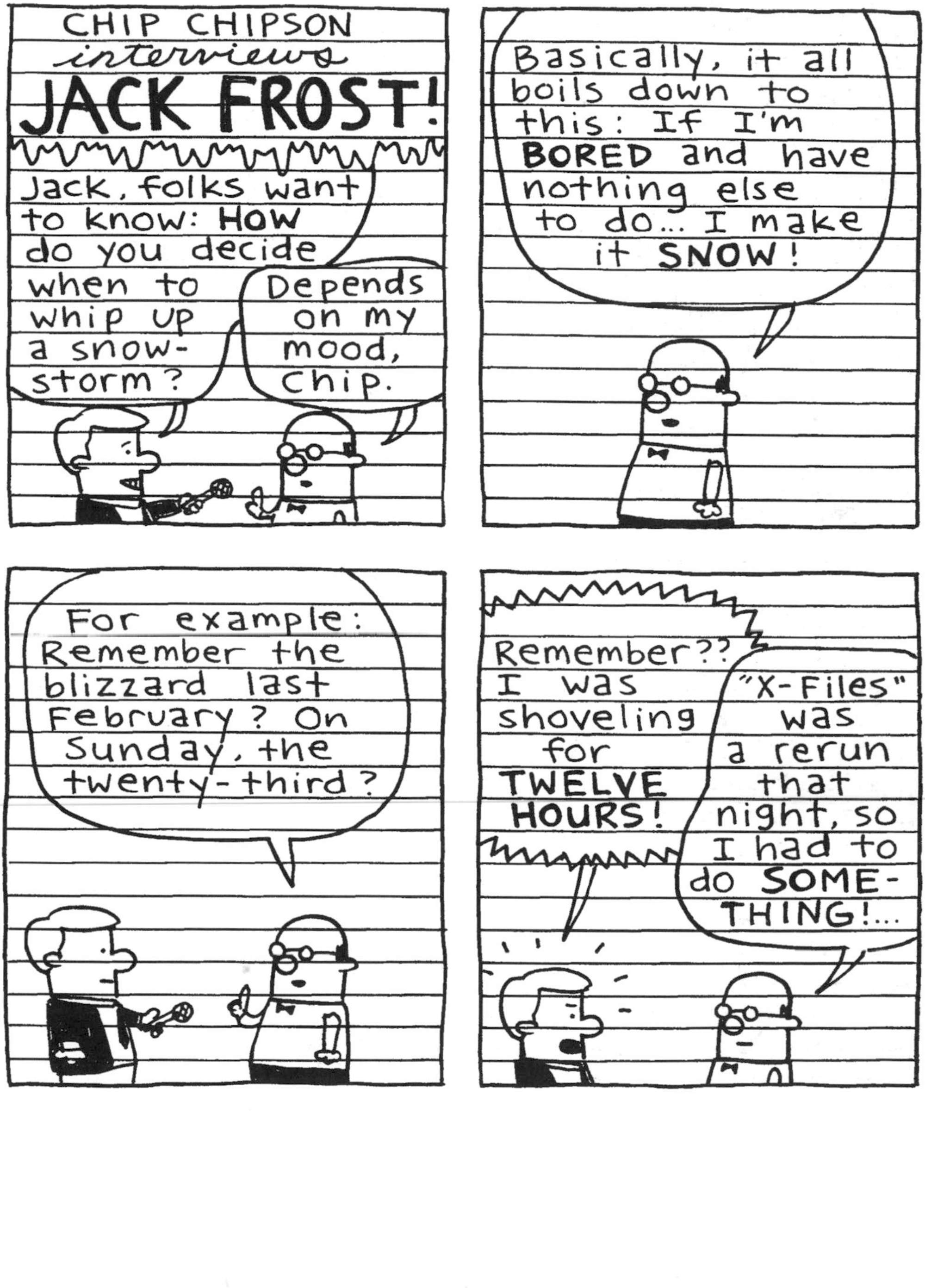
CHIP CHIPSON interviews JACK FROST!
Jack, folks want to know: HOW do you decide when to whip up a snow-storm?
Depends on my mood, Chip.
Basically, it all boils down to this: If I'm BORED and have nothing else to do... I make it SNOW!
For example: Remember the blizzard last February? On Sunday, the twenty-third?
Remember?? I was shoveling for TWELVE HOURS!
"X-Files" was a rerun that night, so I had to do SOME-THING!...

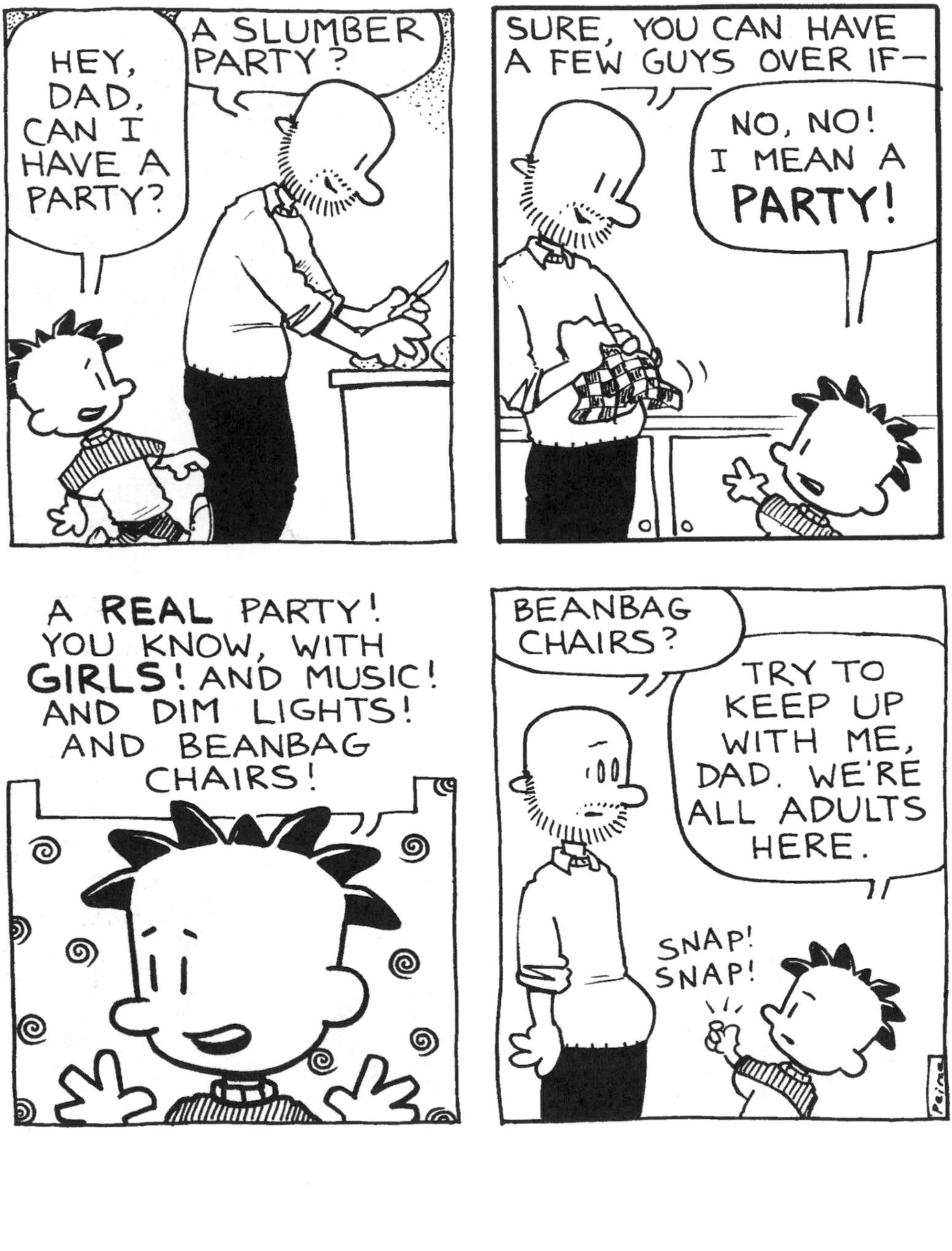
HEY, DAD, CAN I HAVE A PARTY?
A SLUMBER PARTY?
SURE, YOU CAN HAVE A FEW GUYS OVER IF—
NO, NO! I MEAN A PARTY!
A REAL PARTY! YOU KNOW, WITH GIRLS! AND MUSIC! AND DIM LIGHTS! AND BEANBAG CHAIRS!
BEANBAG CHAIRS?
TRY TO KEEP UP WITH ME, DAD. WE'RE ALL ADULTS HERE.
SNAP! SNAP!
Peirce

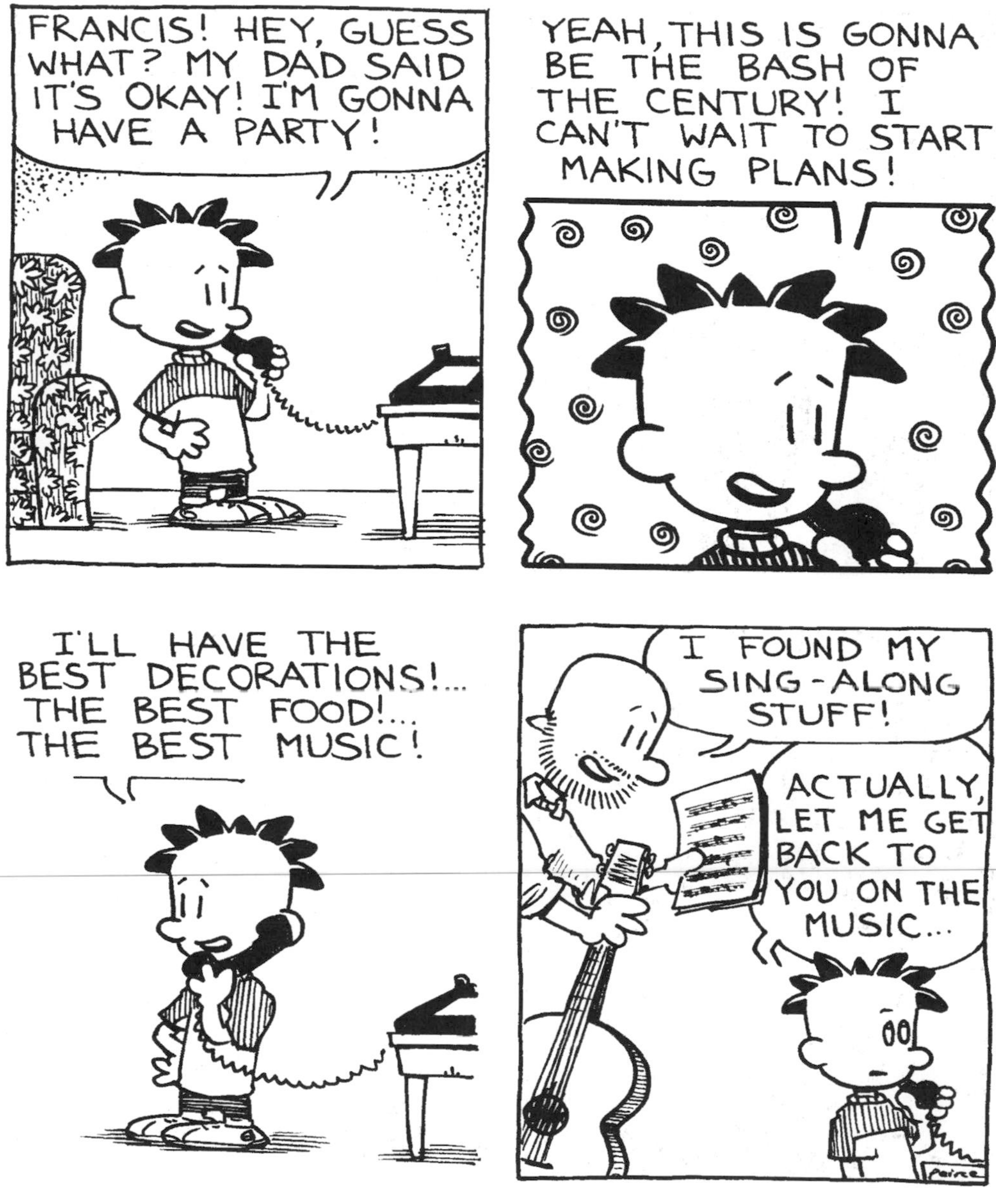
FRANCIS! HEY, GUESS WHAT? MY DAD SAID IT'S OKAY! I'M GONNA HAVE A PARTY!
YEAH, THIS IS GONNA BE THE BASH OF THE CENTURY! I CAN'T WAIT TO START MAKING PLANS!
I'LL HAVE THE BEST DECORATIONS!... THE BEST FOOD!... THE BEST MUSIC!
I FOUND MY SING-ALONG STUFF!
ACTUALLY, LET ME GET BACK TO YOU ON THE MUSIC...

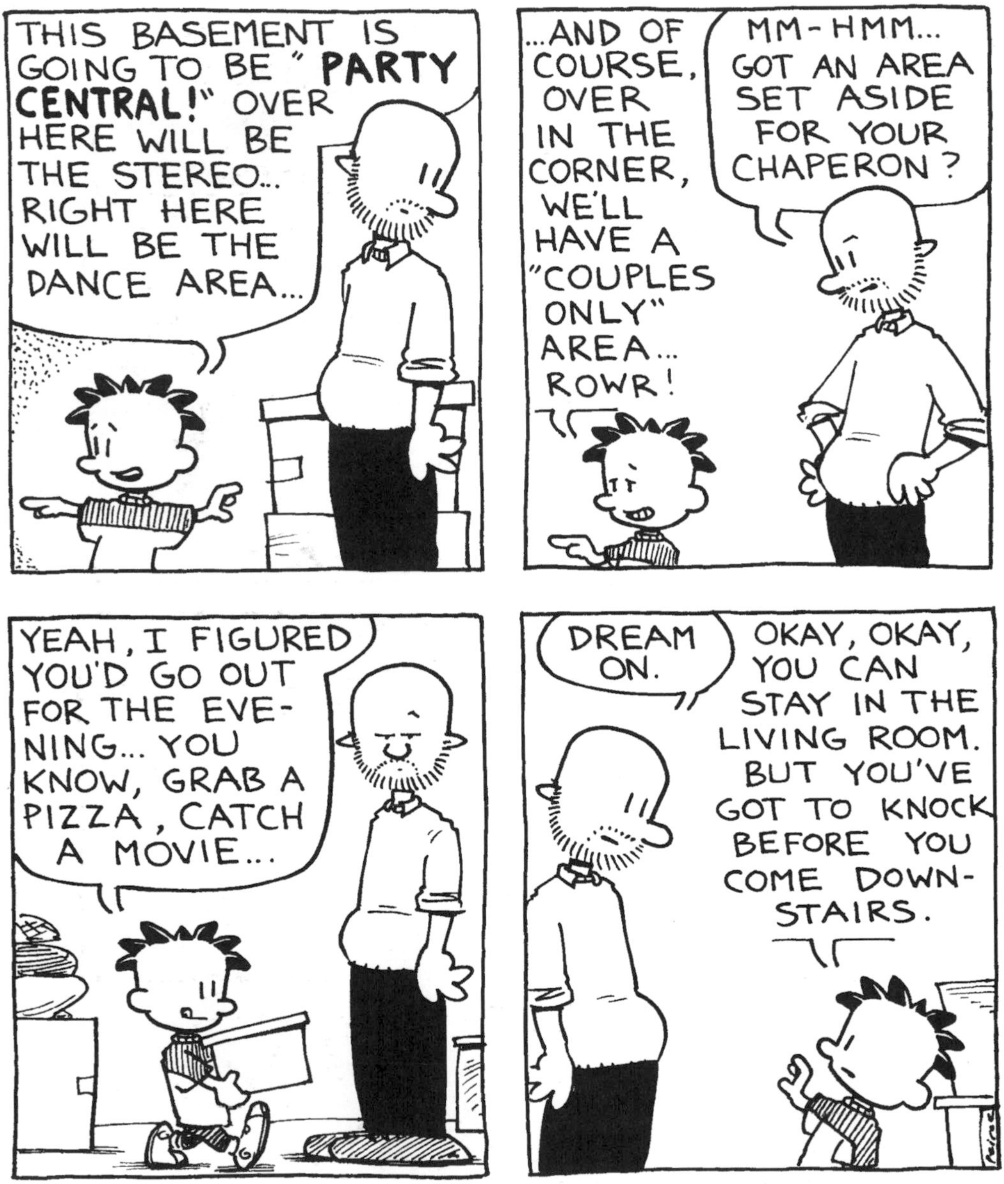
THIS BASEMENT IS GOING TO BE "PARTY CENTRAL!" OVER HERE WILL BE THE STEREO... RIGHT HERE WILL BE THE DANCE AREA...
...AND OF COURSE, OVER IN THE CORNER, WE'LL HAVE A "COUPLES ONLY" AREA... ROWR!
MM-HMM... GOT AN AREA SET ASIDE FOR YOUR CHAPERON?
YEAH, I FIGURED YOU'D GO OUT FOR THE EVE-NING... YOU KNOW, GRAB A PIZZA, CATCH A MOVIE...
DREAM ON.
OKAY, OKAY, YOU CAN STAY IN THE LIVING ROOM. BUT YOU'VE GOT TO KNOCK BEFORE YOU COME DOWN-STAIRS.

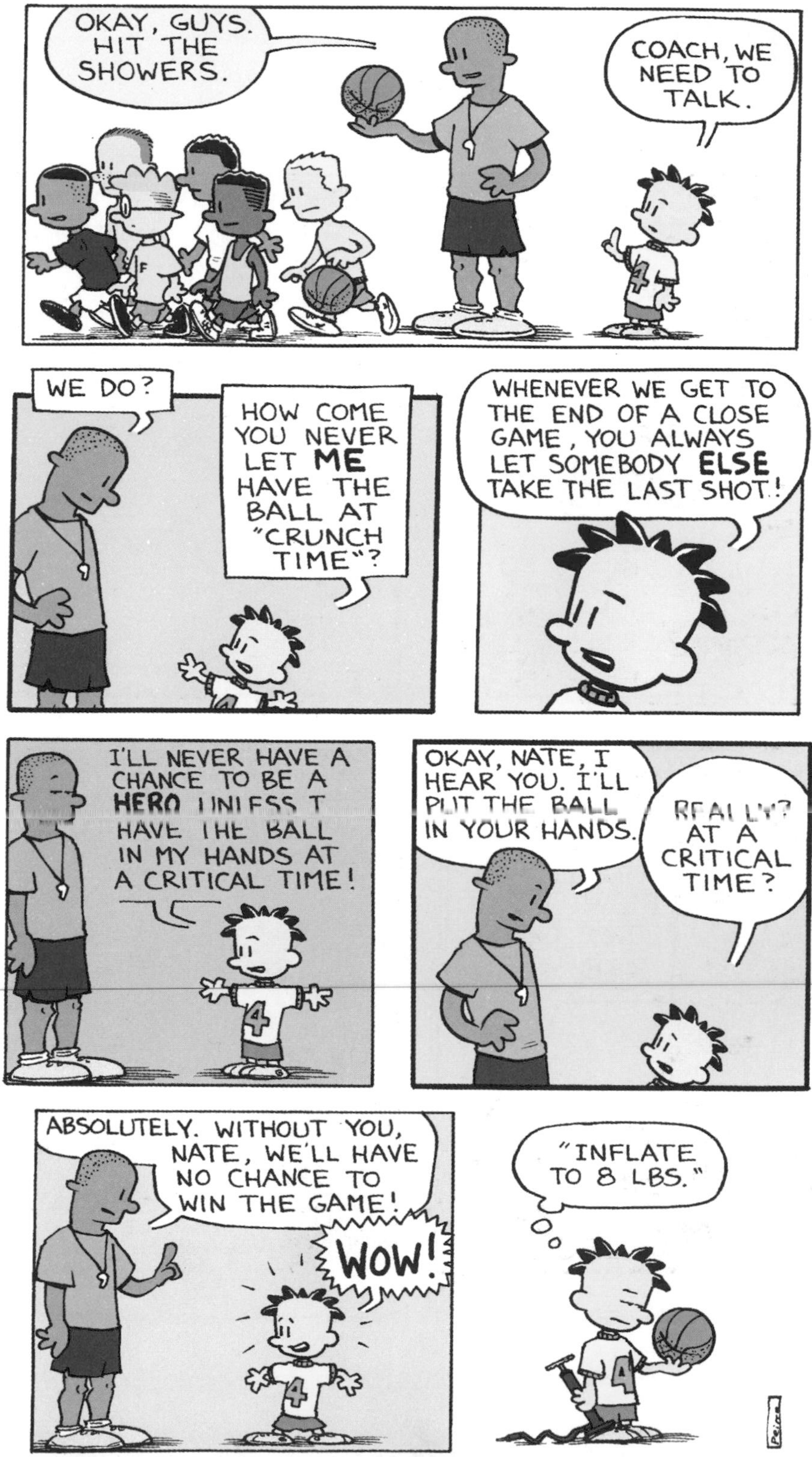

OKAY, GUYS. HIT THE SHOWERS.
COACH, WE NEED TO TALK.
WE DO?
HOW COME YOU NEVER LET ME HAVE THE BALL AT "CRUNCH TIME"?
WHENEVER WE GET TO THE END OF A CLOSE GAME, YOU ALWAYS LET SOMEBODY ELSE TAKE THE LAST SHOT!
I'LL NEVER HAVE A CHANCE TO BE A HERO UNLESS I HAVE THE BALL IN MY HANDS AT A CRITICAL TIME!
OKAY, NATE, I HEAR YOU. I'LL PUT THE BALL IN YOUR HANDS.
REALLY? AT A CRITICAL TIME?
ABSOLUTELY. WITHOUT YOU, NATE, WE'LL HAVE NO CHANCE TO WIN THE GAME!
WOW!
"INFLATE TO 8 LBS."
Peirce

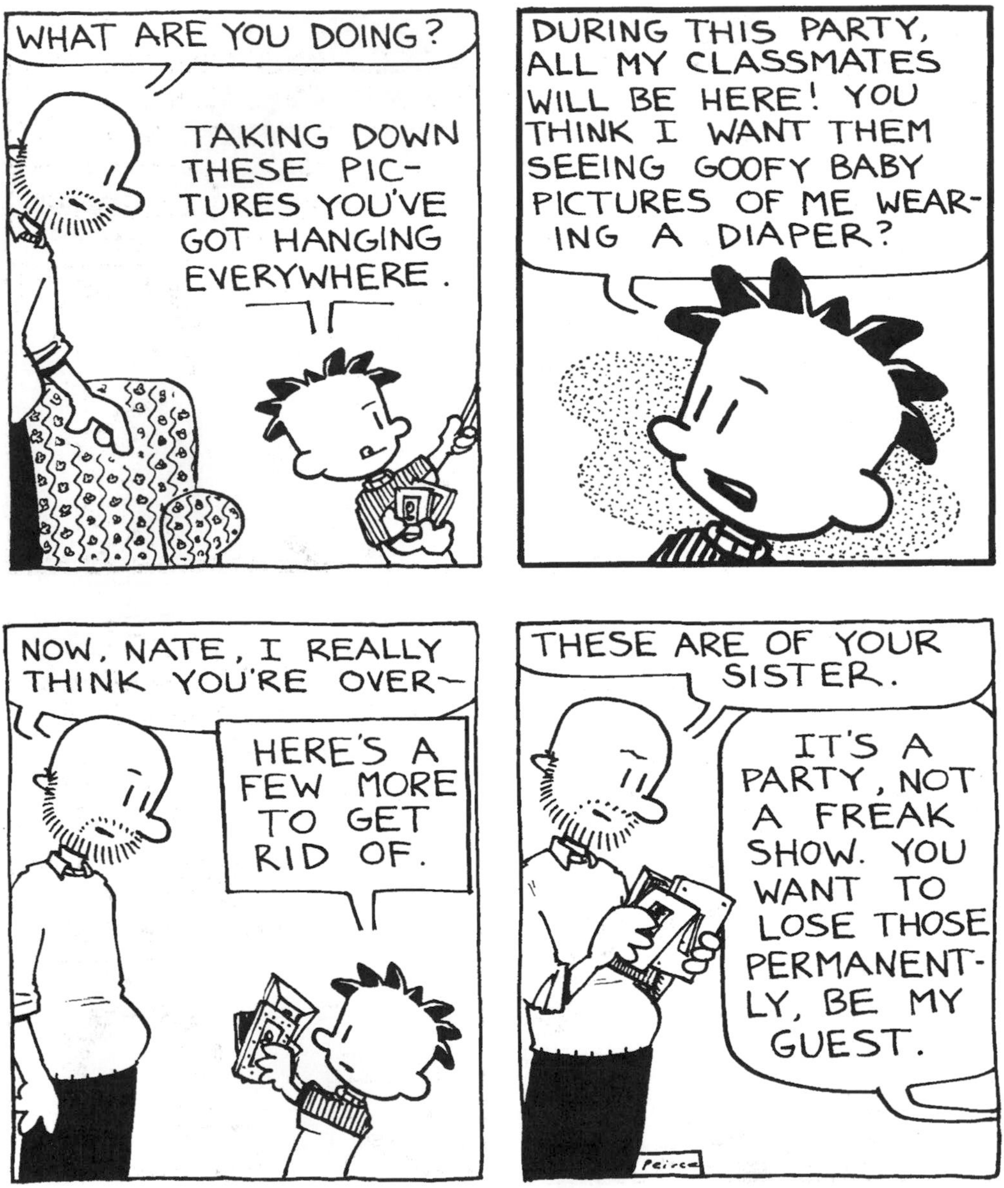
WHAT ARE YOU DOING?
TAKING DOWN THESE PICTURES YOU'VE GOT HANGING EVERYWHERE.
DURING THIS PARTY, ALL MY CLASSMATES WILL BE HERE! YOU THINK I WANT THEM SEEING GOOFY BABY PICTURES OF ME WEARING A DIAPER?
NOW, NATE, I REALLY THINK YOU'RE OVER~
HERE'S A FEW MORE TO GET RID OF.
THESE ARE OF YOUR SISTER.
IT'S A PARTY, NOT A FREAK SHOW. YOU WANT TO LOSE THOSE PERMANENTLY, BE MY GUEST.
Peirce

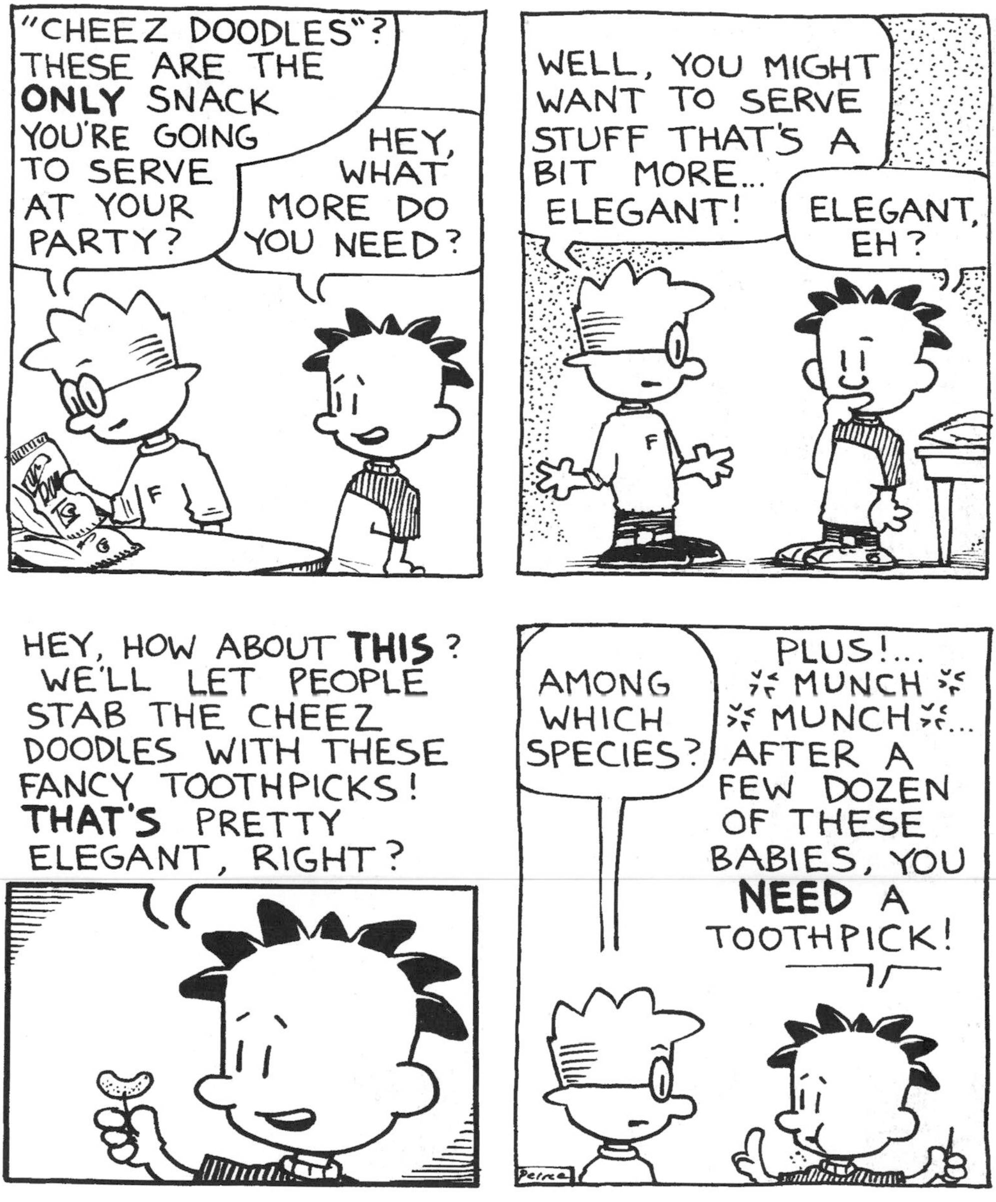
"CHEEZ DOODLES"? THESE ARE THE ONLY SNACK YOU'RE GOING TO SERVE AT YOUR PARTY?
HEY, WHAT MORE DO YOU NEED?
WELL, YOU MIGHT WANT TO SERVE STUFF THAT'S A BIT MORE... ELEGANT!
ELEGANT, EH?
HEY, HOW ABOUT THIS? WE'LL LET PEOPLE STAB THE CHEEZ DOODLES WITH THESE FANCY TOOTHPICKS! THAT'S PRETTY ELEGANT, RIGHT?
AMONG WHICH SPECIES?
PLUS!... MUNCH MUNCH... AFTER A FEW DOZEN OF THESE BABIES, YOU NEED A TOOTHPICK!
Peirce

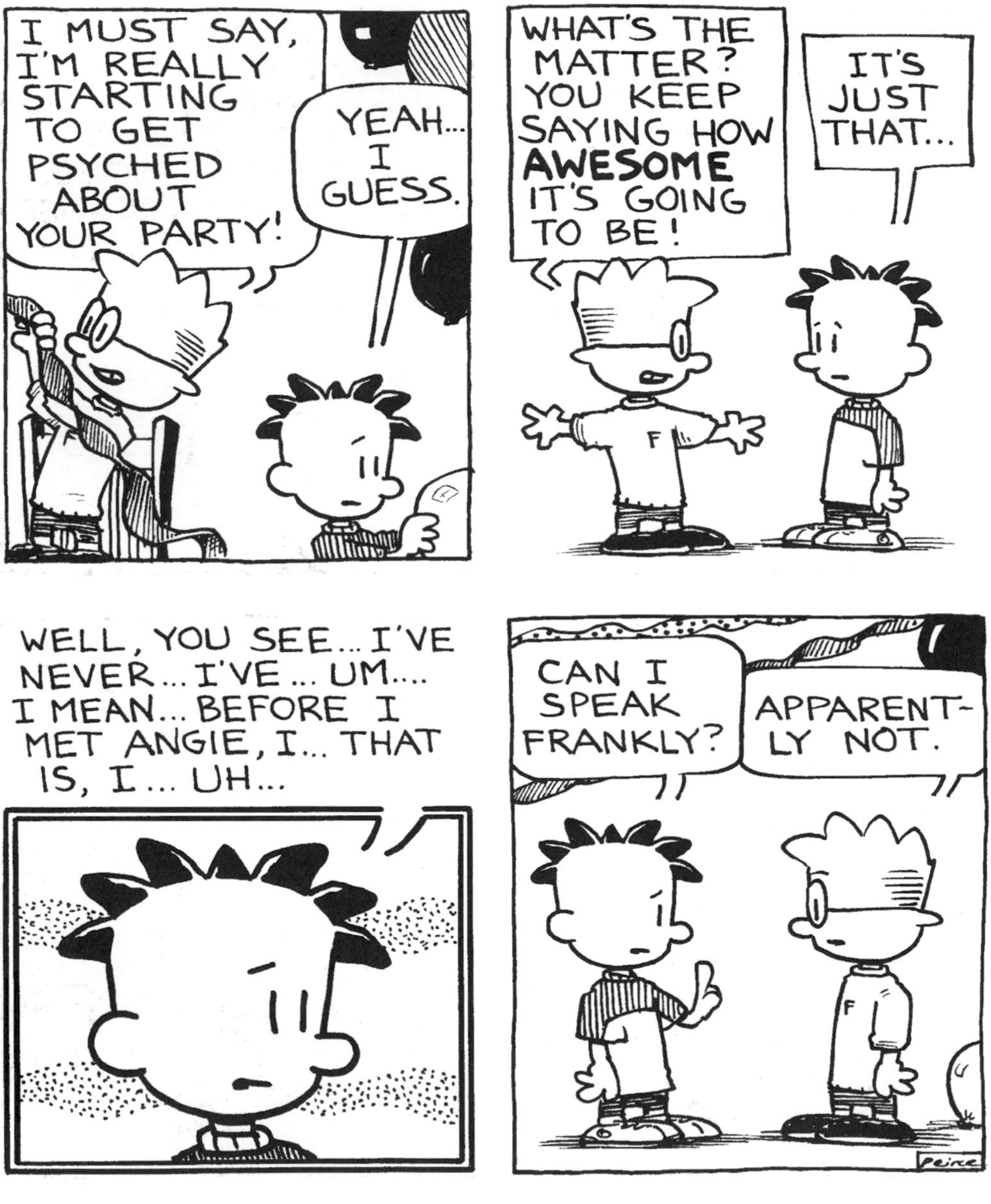
I MUST SAY, I'M REALLY STARTING TO GET PSYCHED ABOUT YOUR PARTY!
YEAH... I GUESS.
WHAT'S THE MATTER? YOU KEEP SAYING HOW **AWESOME** IT'S GOING TO BE!
IT'S JUST THAT...
WELL, YOU SEE... I'VE NEVER... I'VE... UM.... I MEAN... BEFORE I MET ANGIE, I... THAT IS, I... UH...
CAN I SPEAK FRANKLY?
APPARENT-LY NOT.
Peirce

THE TRUTH IS, I'M A LITTLE NERVOUS ABOUT THIS PARTY... YOU KNOW, THE WHOLE "COUPLES" THING... THE WHOLE "MAKING OUT" THING...
AM I SUPPOSED TO MAKE OUT WITH ANGIE? HOW DO I TELL IF SHE EVEN **WANTS** TO MAKE OUT?
MAYBE YOU COULD ASK YOUR DAD FOR ADVICE!
WA HA HA HA HA H
HA HA HA HA
OH HO HO HO
HEE HEE! GOOD ONE!
HIGH-FIVE ME!
SIGH...
Peirce

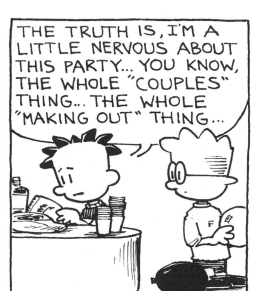

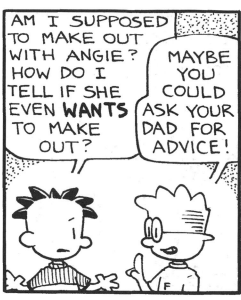

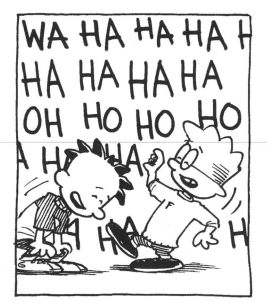

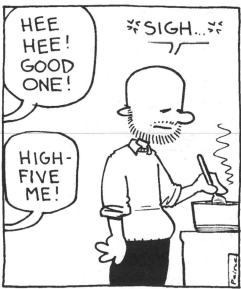

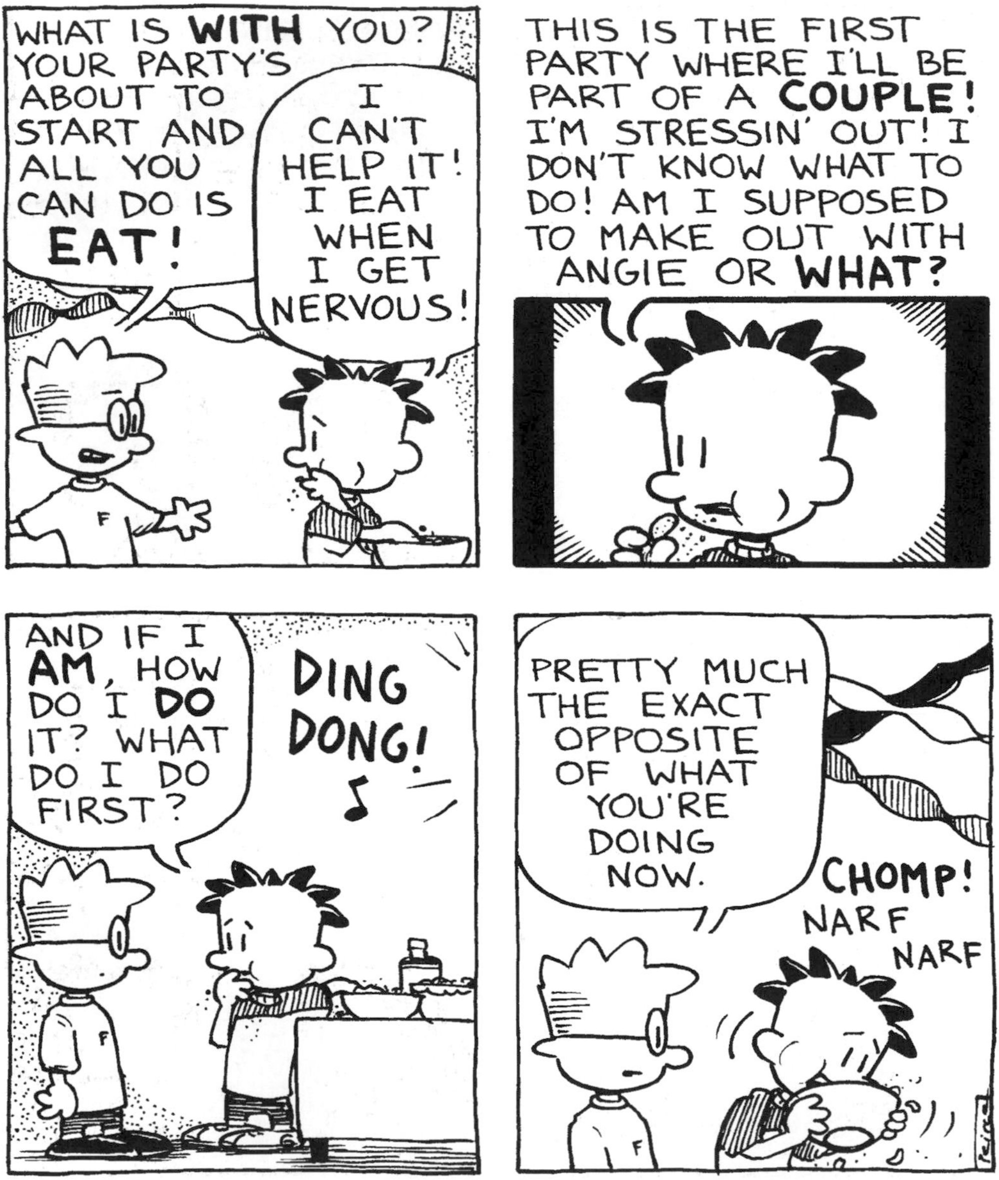
WHAT IS WITH YOU? YOUR PARTY'S ABOUT TO START AND ALL YOU CAN DO IS EAT!
I CAN'T HELP IT! I EAT WHEN I GET NERVOUS!
THIS IS THE FIRST PARTY WHERE I'LL BE PART OF A COUPLE! I'M STRESSIN' OUT! I DON'T KNOW WHAT TO DO! AM I SUPPOSED TO MAKE OUT WITH ANGIE OR WHAT?
AND IF I AM, HOW DO I DO IT? WHAT DO I DO FIRST?
DING DONG!
PRETTY MUCH THE EXACT OPPOSITE OF WHAT YOU'RE DOING NOW.
CHOMP!
NARF
NARF

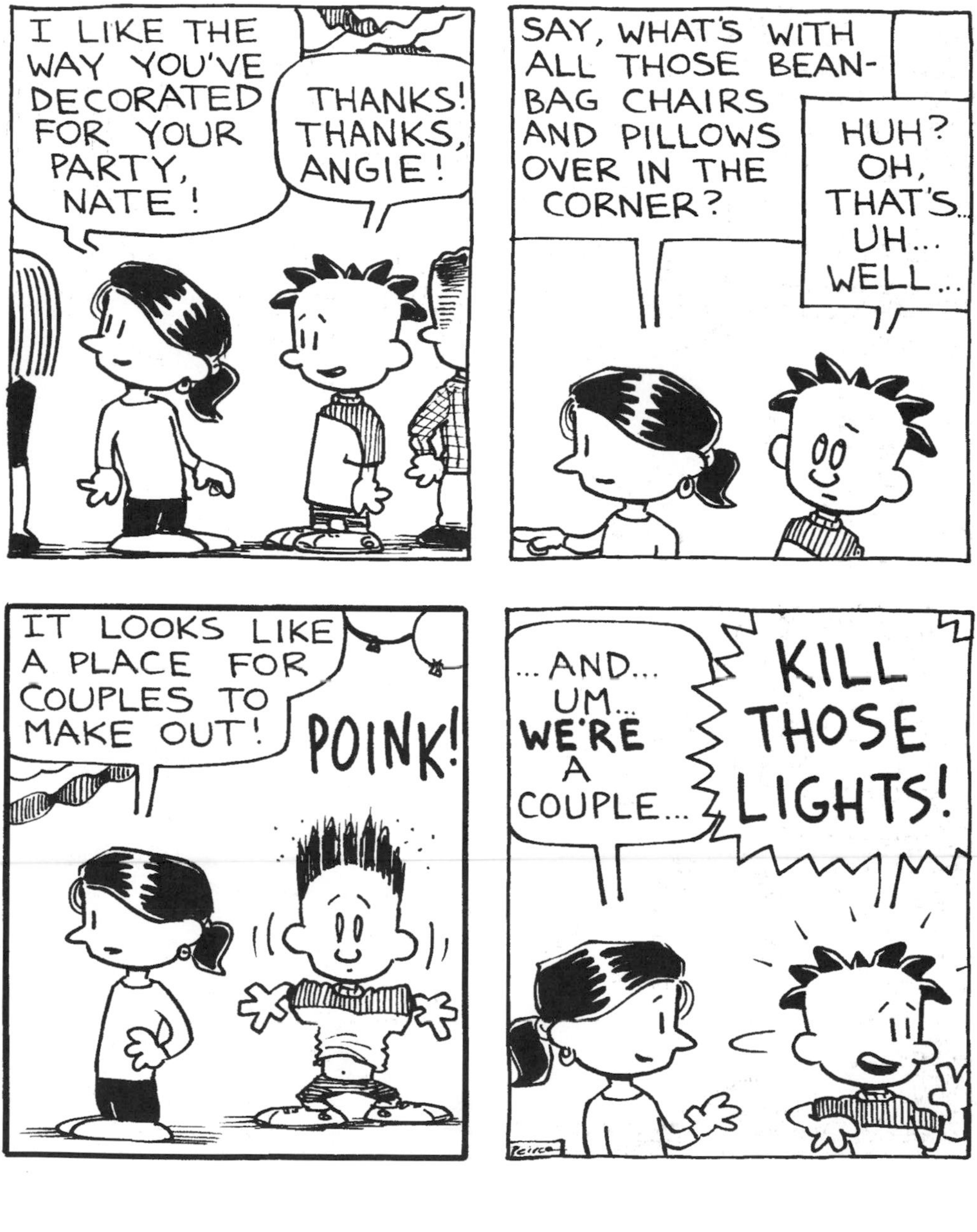
I LIKE THE WAY YOU'VE DECORATED FOR YOUR PARTY, NATE!
THANKS! THANKS, ANGIE!
SAY, WHAT'S WITH ALL THOSE BEAN-BAG CHAIRS AND PILLOWS OVER IN THE CORNER?
HUH? OH, THAT'S... UH... WELL...
IT LOOKS LIKE A PLACE FOR COUPLES TO MAKE OUT!
POINK!
...AND... UM... WE'RE A COUPLE...
KILL THOSE LIGHTS!
Peirce

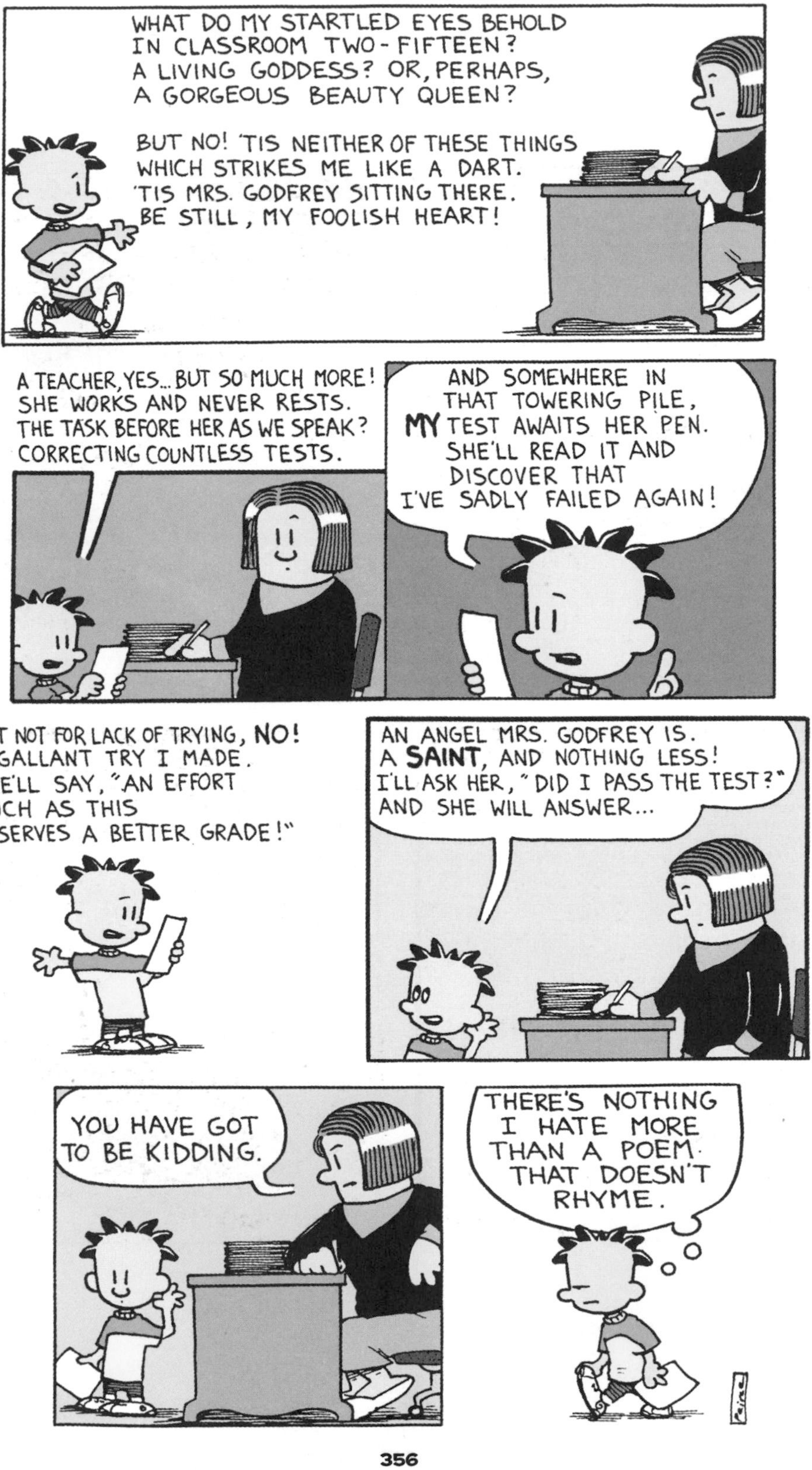
WHAT DO MY STARTLED EYES BEHOLD
IN CLASSROOM TWO-FIFTEEN?
A LIVING GODDESS? OR, PERHAPS,
A GORGEOUS BEAUTY QUEEN?
BUT NO! 'TIS NEITHER OF THESE THINGS
WHICH STRIKES ME LIKE A DART.
'TIS MRS. GODFREY SITTING THERE.
BE STILL, MY FOOLISH HEART!
A TEACHER, YES... BUT SO MUCH MORE!
SHE WORKS AND NEVER RESTS.
THE TASK BEFORE HER AS WE SPEAK?
CORRECTING COUNTLESS TESTS.
AND SOMEWHERE IN THAT TOWERING PILE, MY TEST AWAITS HER PEN. SHE'LL READ IT AND DISCOVER THAT I'VE SADLY FAILED AGAIN!
BUT NOT FOR LACK OF TRYING, NO!
A GALLANT TRY I MADE.
SHE'LL SAY, "AN EFFORT
SUCH AS THIS
DESERVES A BETTER GRADE!"
AN ANGEL MRS. GODFREY IS.
A SAINT, AND NOTHING LESS!
I'LL ASK HER, "DID I PASS THE TEST?"
AND SHE WILL ANSWER...
YOU HAVE GOT TO BE KIDDING.
THERE'S NOTHING I HATE MORE THAN A POEM THAT DOESN'T RHYME.
Peirce

OKAY, ANGIE'S GIVING OFF SOME POSITIVE VIBES HERE... SHE'S SUBTLY LETTING ME KNOW THAT SHE WANTS TO GET CLOSER...

NOW I'VE JUST GOT TO CASUALLY STEER HER OVER TOWARD "MAKE-OUT CORNER."

shuffa
shuffa
shuffa

GOTTA BE SUAVE ABOUT IT, THOUGH... JUST A LITTLE STROLL ACROSS THE ROOM... NO BIG DEAL... NOOOOOOO BIG DEAL...

WHA-? HEY!

SORRY. DIBS ON THIS CHAIR.

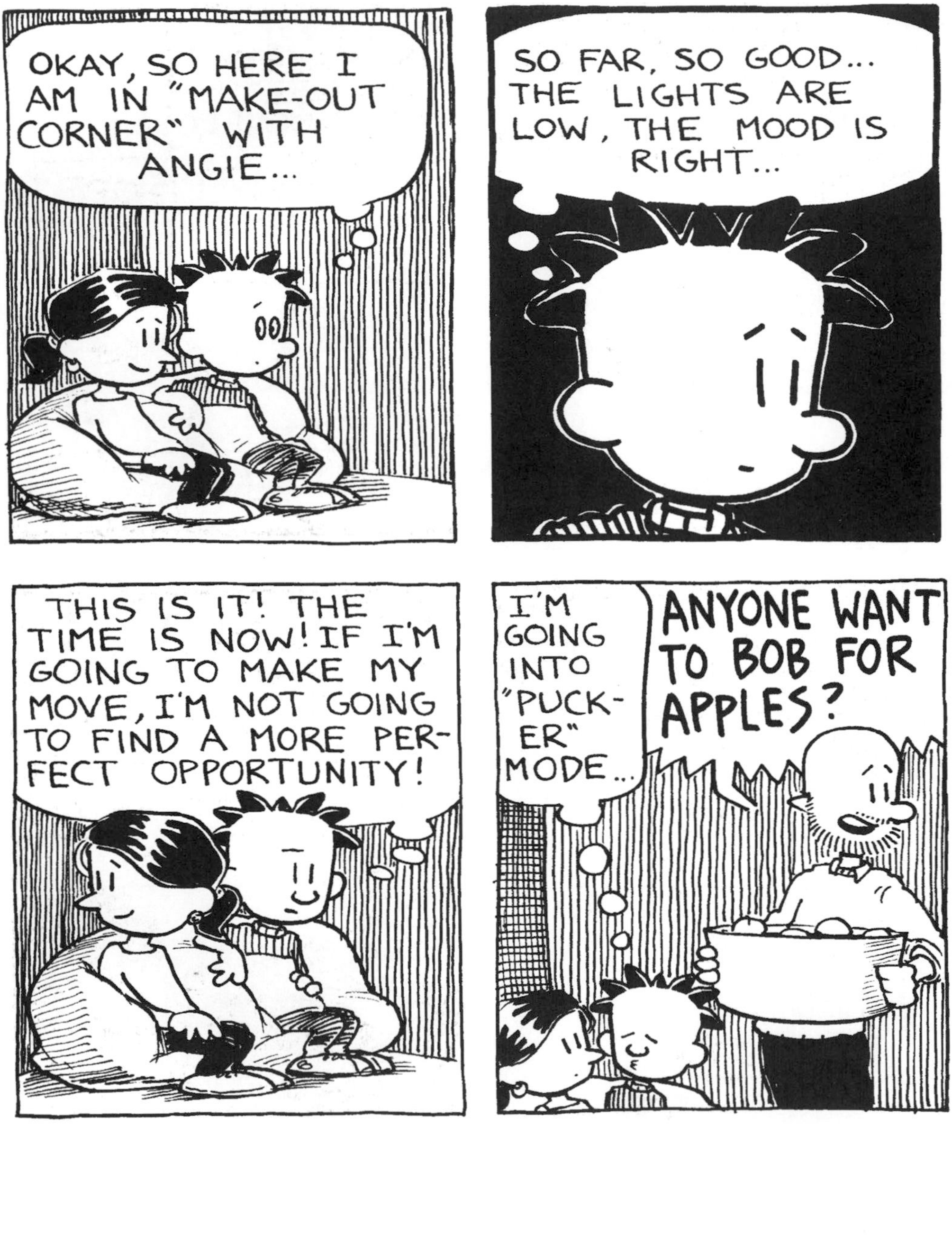
OKAY, SO HERE I AM IN "MAKE-OUT CORNER" WITH ANGIE...
SO FAR, SO GOOD... THE LIGHTS ARE LOW, THE MOOD IS RIGHT...
THIS IS IT! THE TIME IS NOW! IF I'M GOING TO MAKE MY MOVE, I'M NOT GOING TO FIND A MORE PERFECT OPPORTUNITY!
I'M GOING INTO "PUCKER" MODE...
ANYONE WANT TO BOB FOR APPLES?

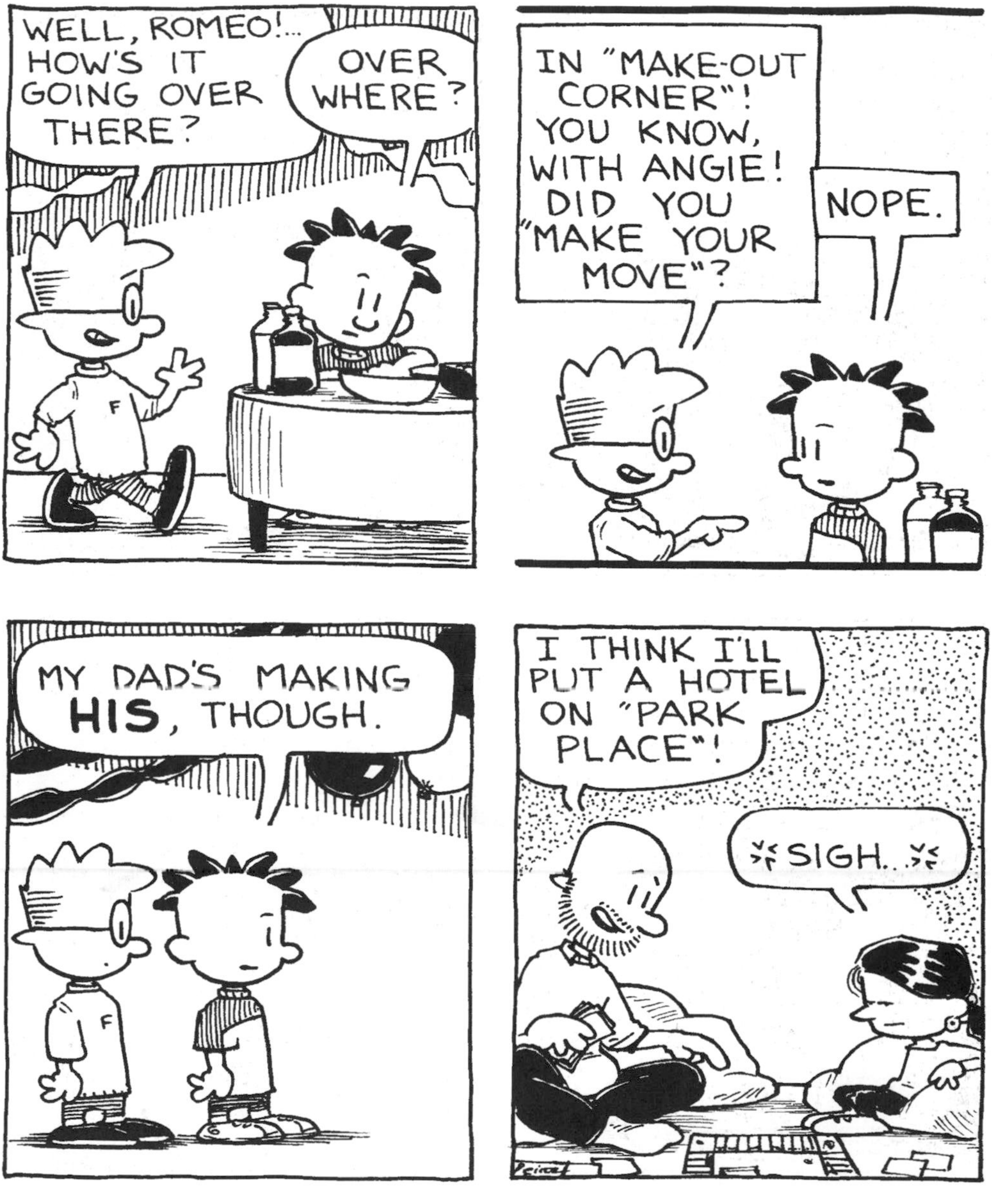
WELL, ROMEO!... HOW'S IT GOING OVER THERE?
OVER WHERE?
IN "MAKE-OUT CORNER"! YOU KNOW, WITH ANGIE! DID YOU "MAKE YOUR MOVE"?
NOPE.
MY DAD'S MAKING HIS, THOUGH.
I THINK I'LL PUT A HOTEL ON "PARK PLACE"!
SIGH.

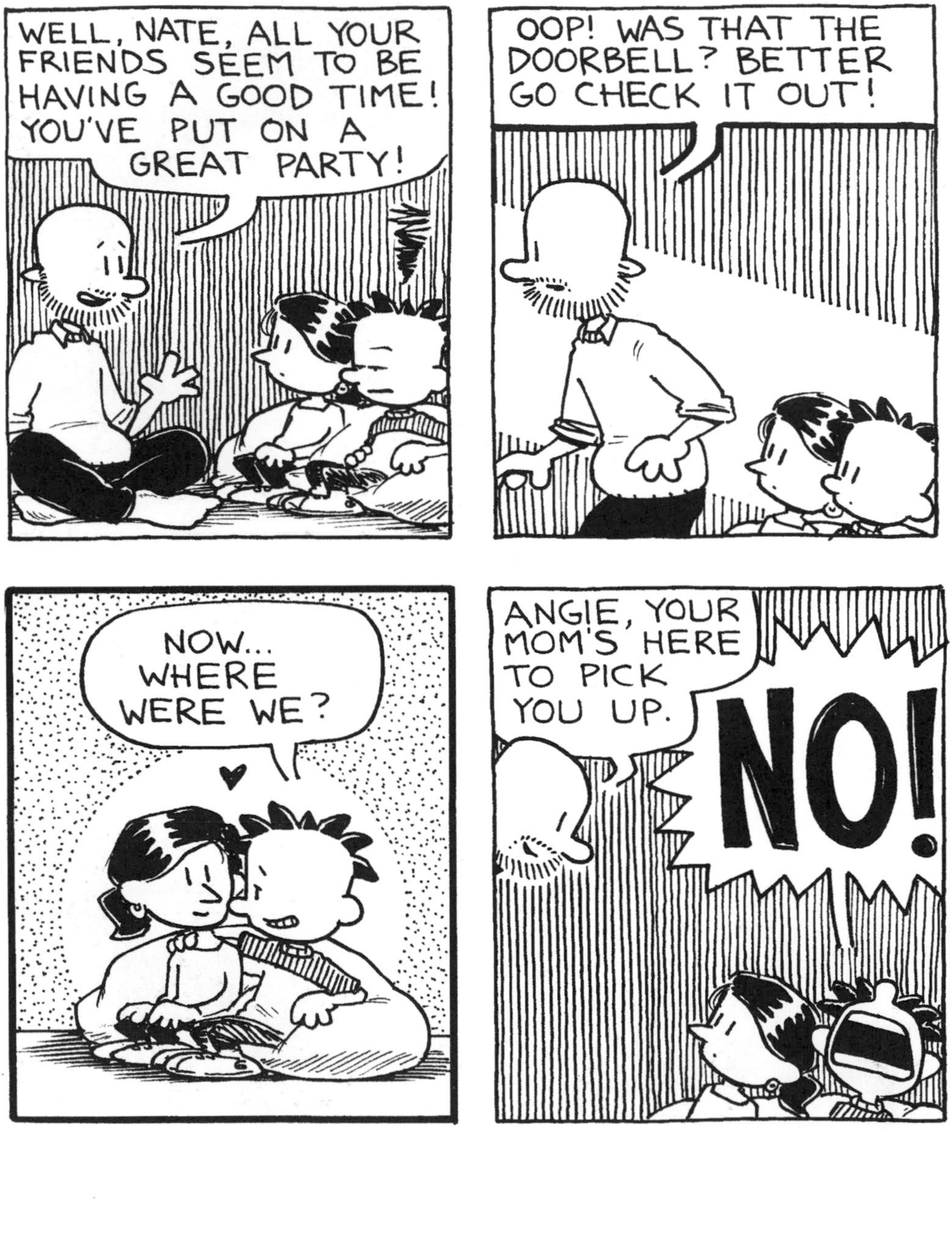
WELL, NATE, ALL YOUR FRIENDS SEEM TO BE HAVING A GOOD TIME! YOU'VE PUT ON A GREAT PARTY!
OOP! WAS THAT THE DOORBELL? BETTER GO CHECK IT OUT!
NOW... WHERE WERE WE?
ANGIE, YOUR MOM'S HERE TO PICK YOU UP.
NO!

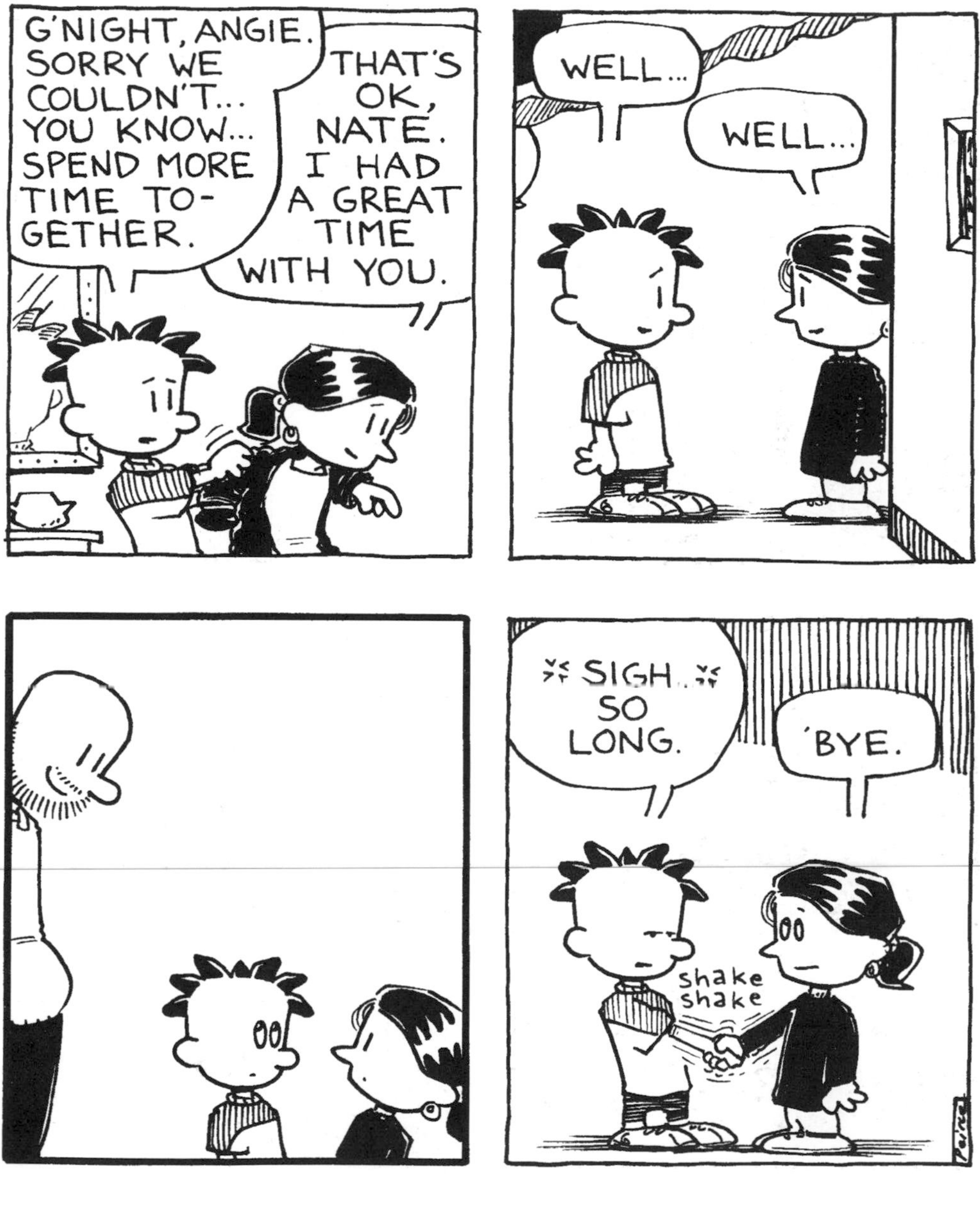
G'NIGHT, ANGIE. SORRY WE COULDN'T... YOU KNOW... SPEND MORE TIME TO-GETHER.
THAT'S OK, NATE. I HAD A GREAT TIME WITH YOU.
WELL...
WELL...
SIGH... SO LONG.
'BYE.
shake shake
Peirce

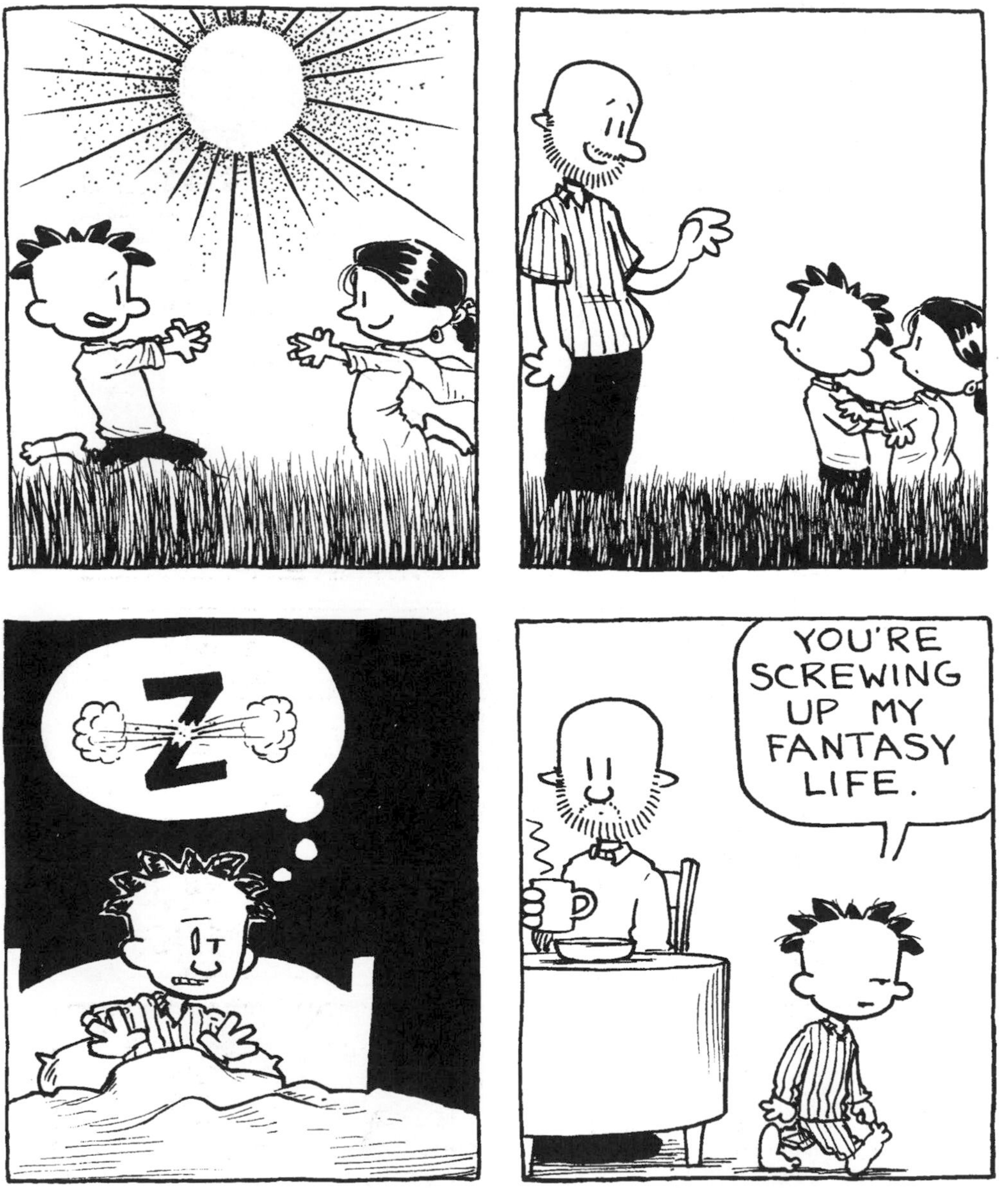
Z
YOU'RE SCREWING UP MY FANTASY LIFE.

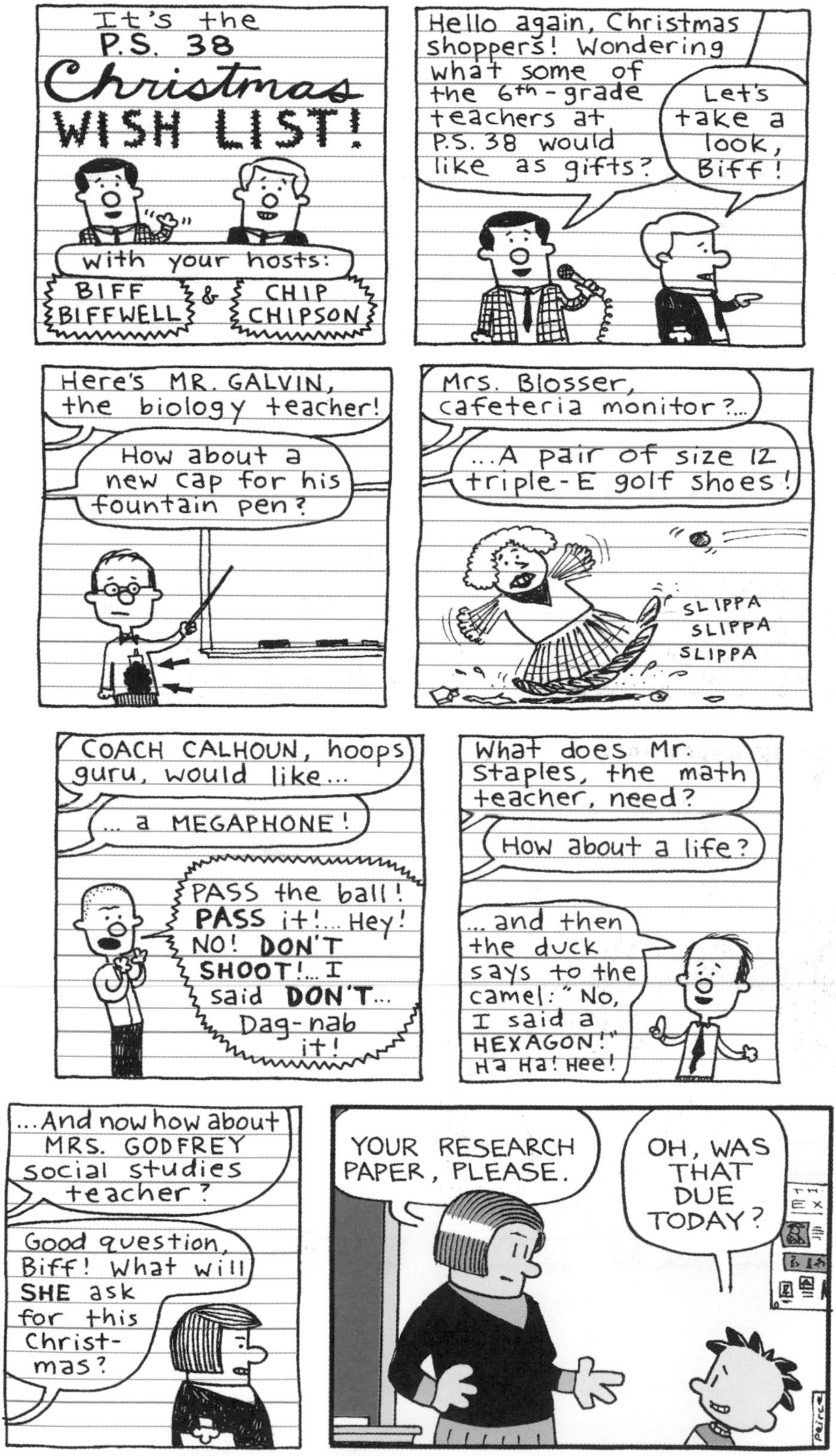
It's the P.S. 38 Christmas WISH LIST!
with your hosts:
BIFF BIFFWELL & CHIP CHIPSON
Hello again, Christmas shoppers! Wondering what some of the 6th-grade teachers at P.S. 38 would like as gifts?
Let's take a look, Biff!
Here's MR. GALVIN, the biology teacher!
How about a new cap for his fountain pen?
Mrs. Blosser, cafeteria monitor?...
...A pair of size 12 triple-E golf shoes!
SLIPPA SLIPPA SLIPPA
COACH CALHOUN, hoops guru, would like...
... a MEGAPHONE!
PASS the ball! PASS it!... Hey! NO! DON'T SHOOT!... I said DON'T... Dag-nab it!
What does Mr. Staples, the math teacher, need?
How about a life?
...and then the duck says to the camel: "No, I said a HEXAGON!" Ha Ha! Hee!
...And now how about MRS. GODFREY social studies teacher?
Good question, Biff! What will SHE ask for this Christmas?
YOUR RESEARCH PAPER, PLEASE.
OH, WAS THAT DUE TODAY?

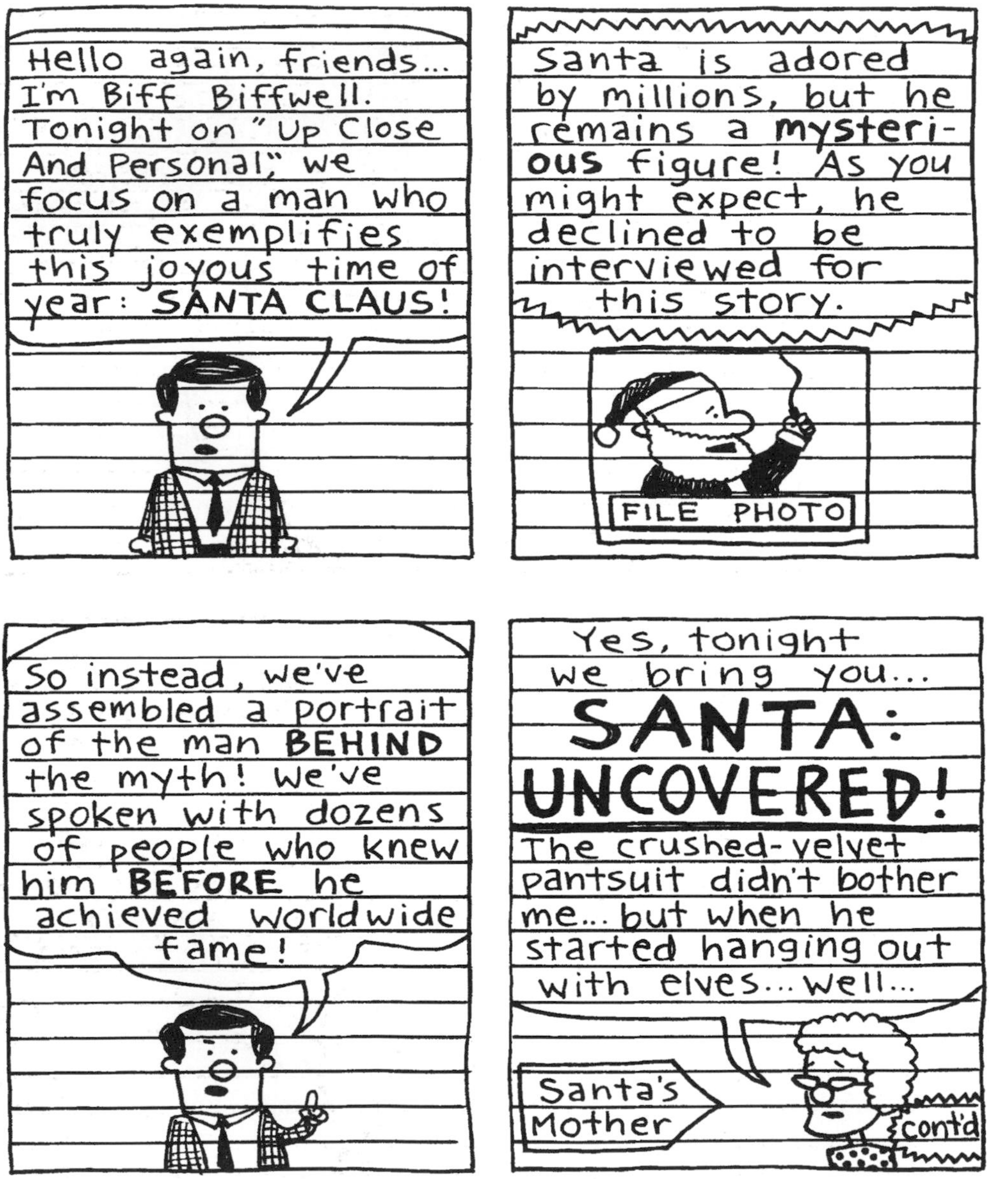
Hello again, friends... I'm Biff Biffwell. Tonight on "Up Close And Personal," we focus on a man who truly exemplifies this joyous time of year: SANTA CLAUS!
Santa is adored by millions, but he remains a mysterious figure! As you might expect, he declined to be interviewed for this story.
FILE PHOTO
So instead, we've assembled a portrait of the man BEHIND the myth! We've spoken with dozens of people who knew him BEFORE he achieved worldwide fame!
Yes, tonight we bring you... SANTA: UNCOVERED!
The crushed-velvet pantsuit didn't bother me... but when he started hanging out with elves... well...
Santa's Mother
cont'd

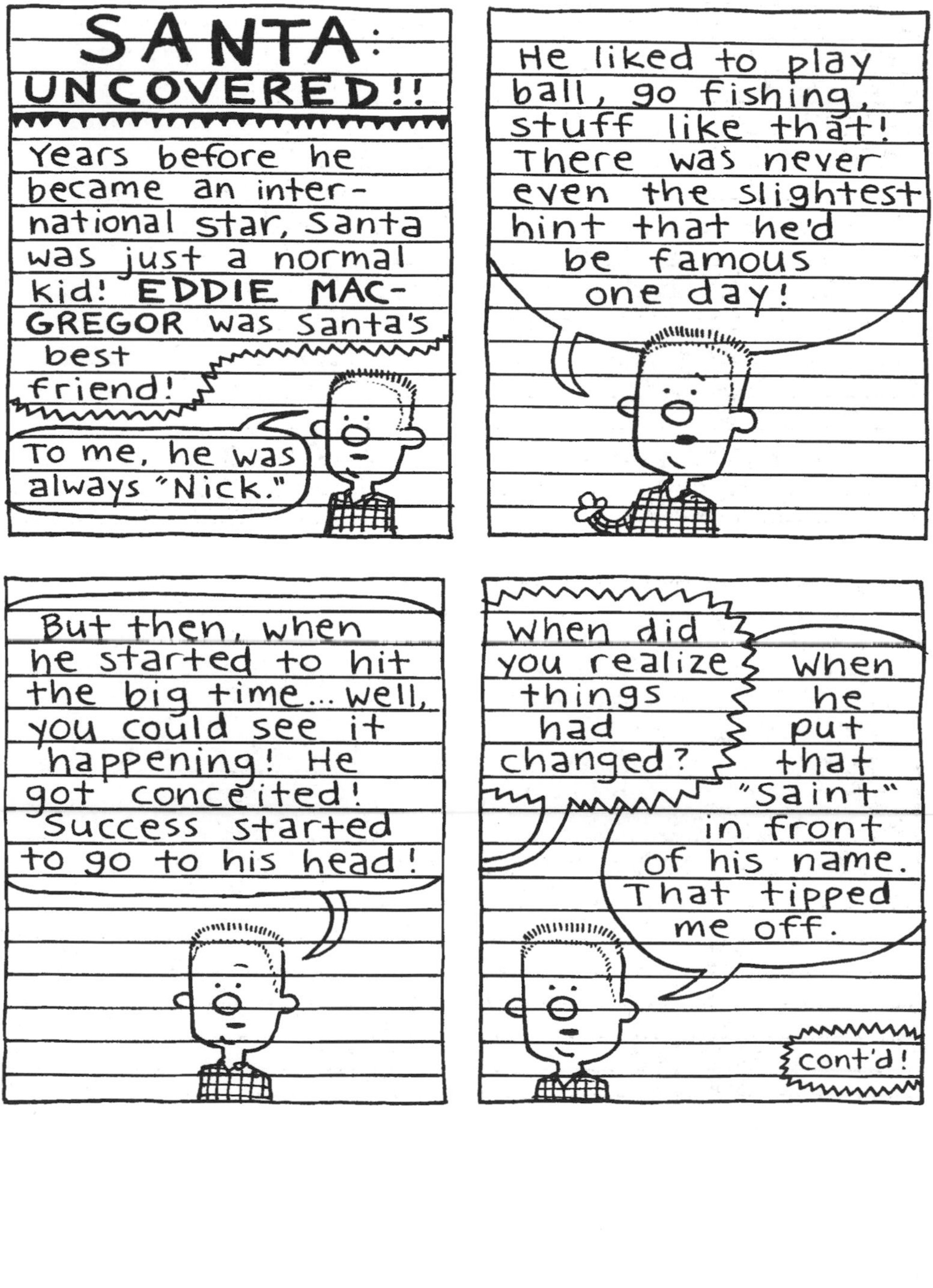
SANTA: UNCOVERED!!
Years before he became an inter-national star, Santa was just a normal kid! EDDIE MAC-GREGOR was Santa's best friend!
To me, he was always "Nick."
He liked to play ball, go fishing, stuff like that! There was never even the slightest hint that he'd be famous one day!
But then, when he started to hit the big time... well, you could see it happening! He got conceited! Success started to go to his head!
When did you realize things had changed?
When he put that "Saint" in front of his name. That tipped me off.
cont'd!

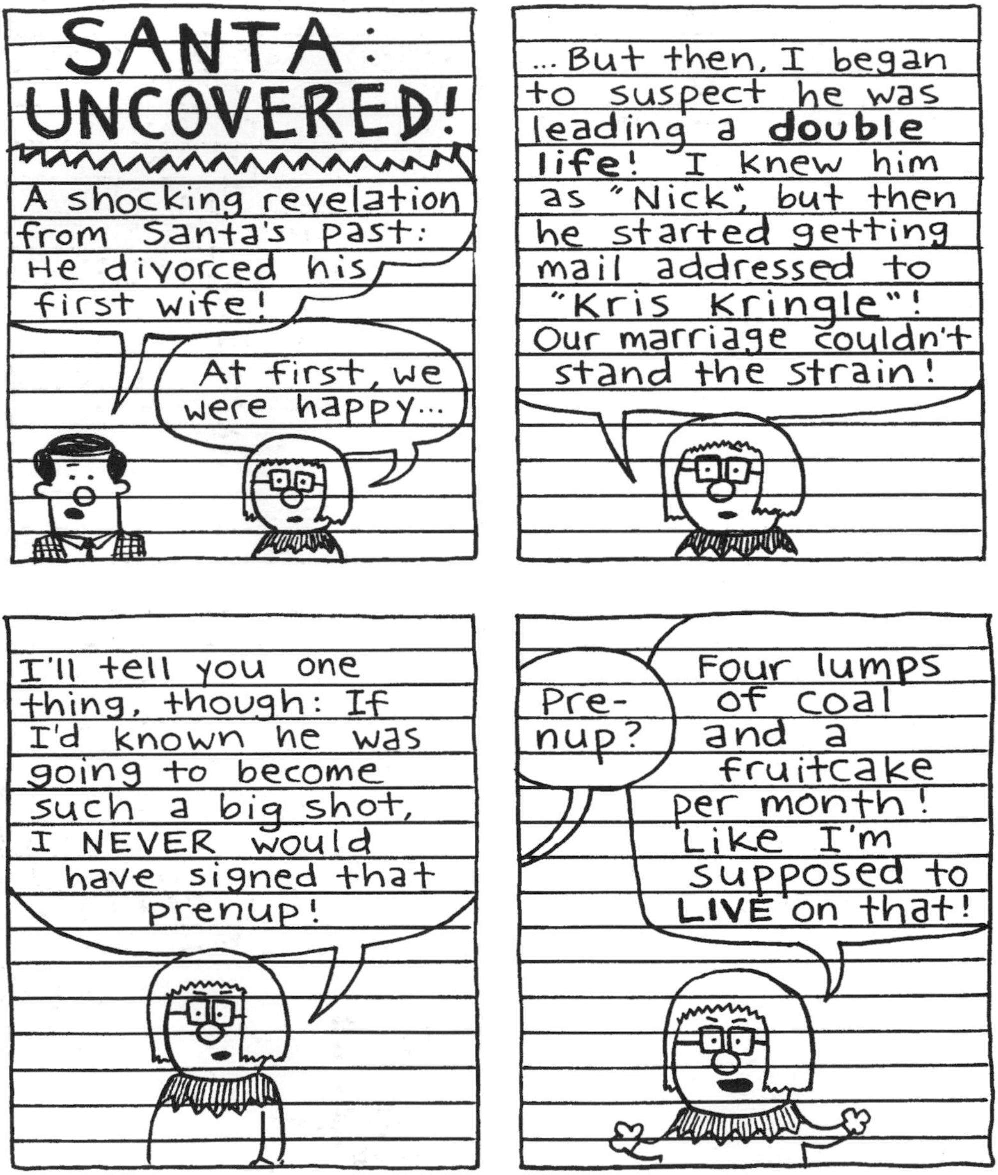
SANTA: UNCOVERED!
A shocking revelation from Santa's past: He divorced his first wife!
At first, we were happy...
...But then, I began to suspect he was leading a **double life**! I knew him as "Nick", but then he started getting mail addressed to "Kris Kringle"! Our marriage couldn't stand the strain!
I'll tell you one thing, though: If I'd known he was going to become such a big shot, I NEVER would have signed that prenup!
Pre-nup?
Four lumps of coal and a fruitcake per month! Like I'm supposed to **LIVE** on that!

SANTA: UNCOVERED!!
Tonight: a disgruntled reindeer speaks out!
Bitter? Yes, I'm bitter!
When Santa chose the reindeer to pull his precious sleigh, he took all the PRETTY BOYS and left ME out! Dancer... Prancer... Blitzen... what a bunch of LIGHTWEIGHTS!
He even picked my goody-two-shoes brother, DASHER! Apparently, I just didn't fit in with Santa's squeaky-clean IMAGE!
And your name is?...
Flasher. I tell you, it's not FAIR!

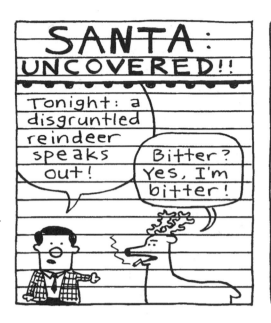

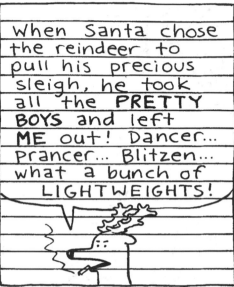

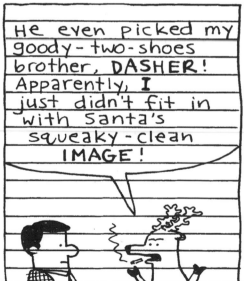

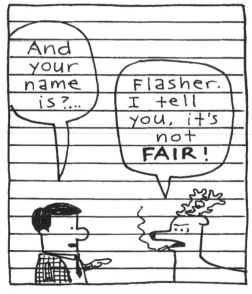

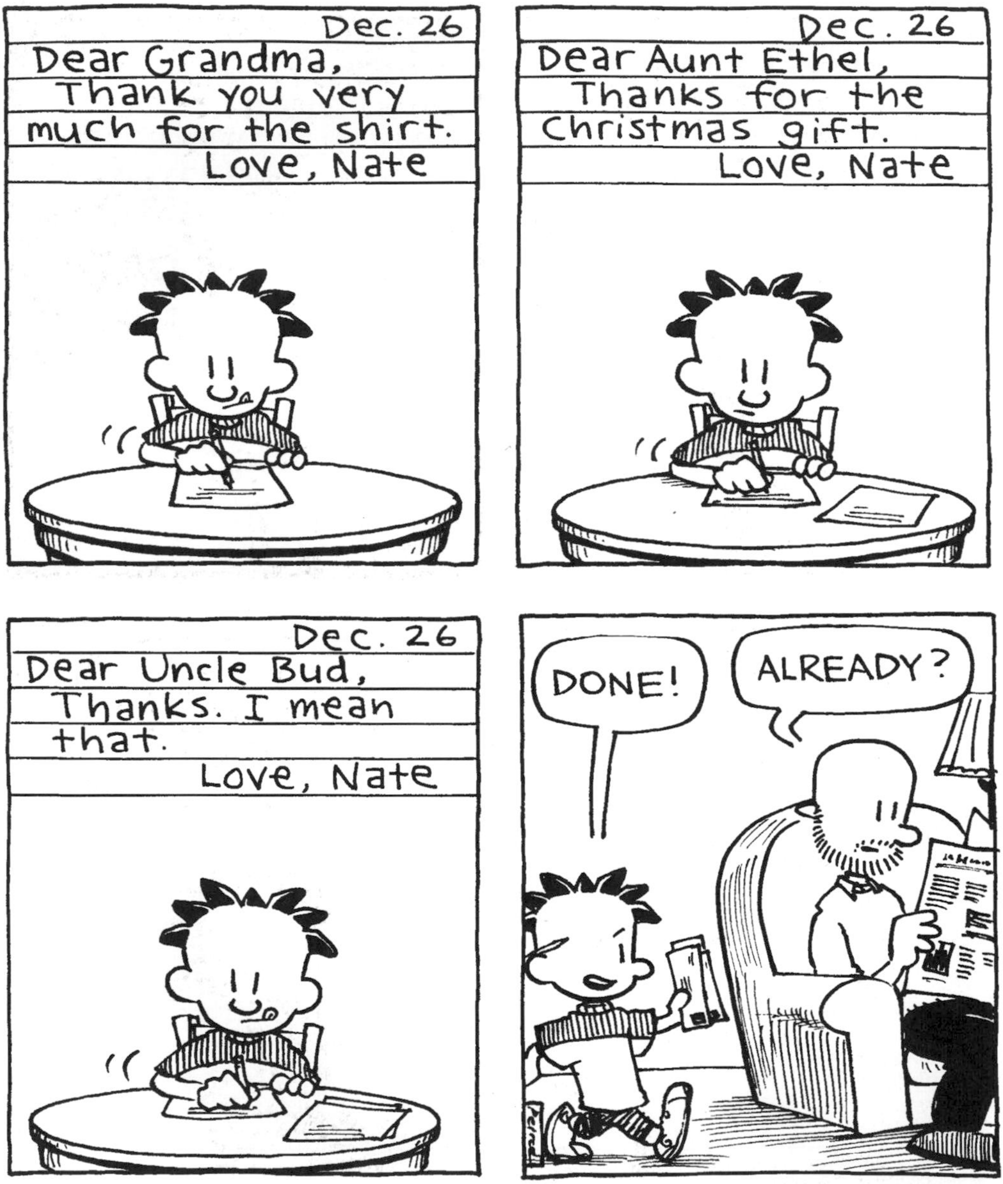
Dec. 26
Dear Grandma,
Thank you very much for the shirt.
Love, Nate
Dec. 26
Dear Aunt Ethel,
Thanks for the Christmas gift.
Love, Nate
Dec. 26
Dear Uncle Bud,
Thanks. I mean that.
Love, Nate
DONE!
ALREADY?

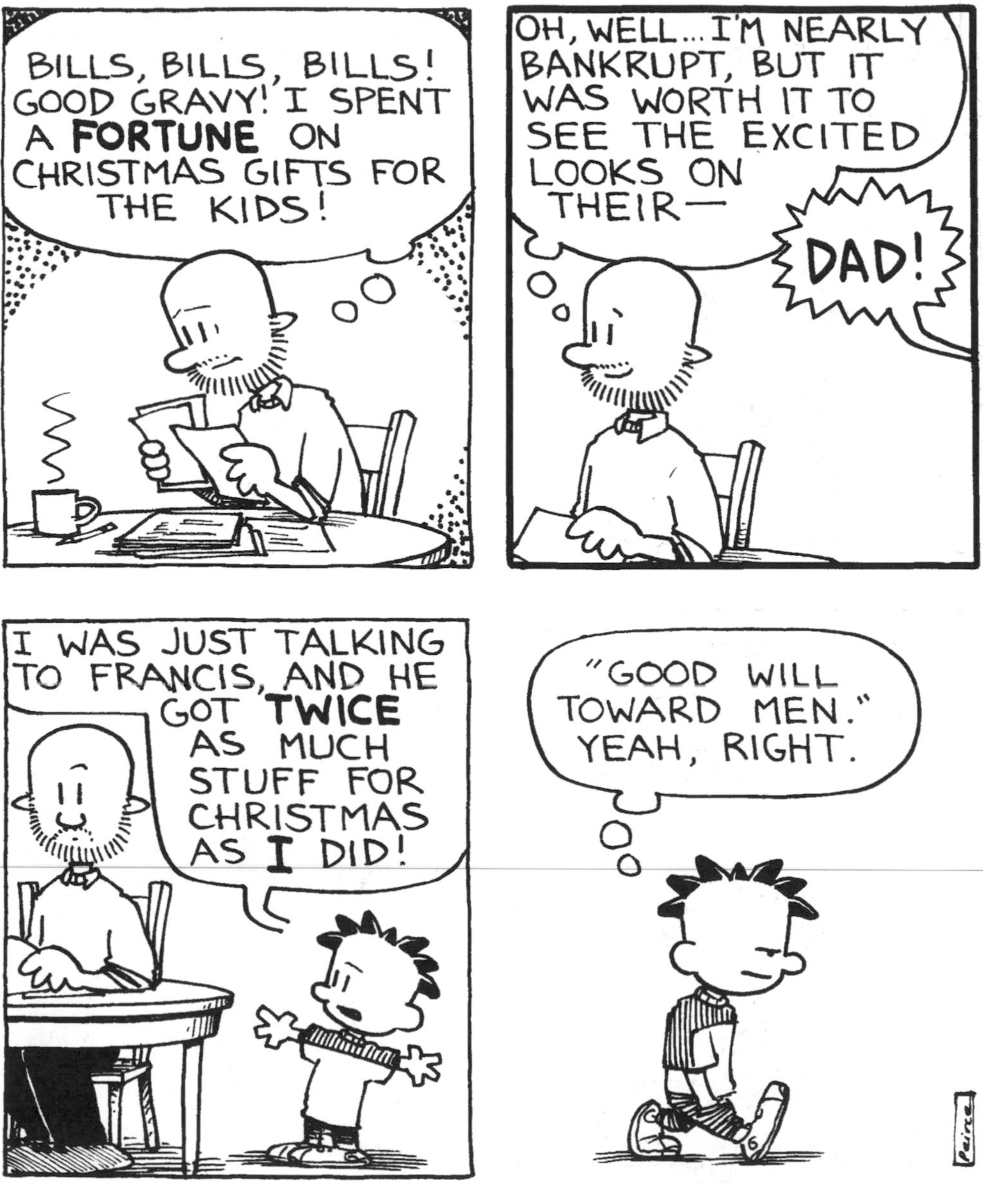
BILLS, BILLS, BILLS! GOOD GRAVY! I SPENT A **FORTUNE** ON CHRISTMAS GIFTS FOR THE KIDS!
OH, WELL... I'M NEARLY BANKRUPT, BUT IT WAS WORTH IT TO SEE THE EXCITED LOOKS ON THEIR—
DAD!
I WAS JUST TALKING TO FRANCIS, AND HE GOT **TWICE** AS MUCH STUFF FOR CHRISTMAS AS **I** DID!
"GOOD WILL TOWARD MEN." YEAH, RIGHT.
Peirce

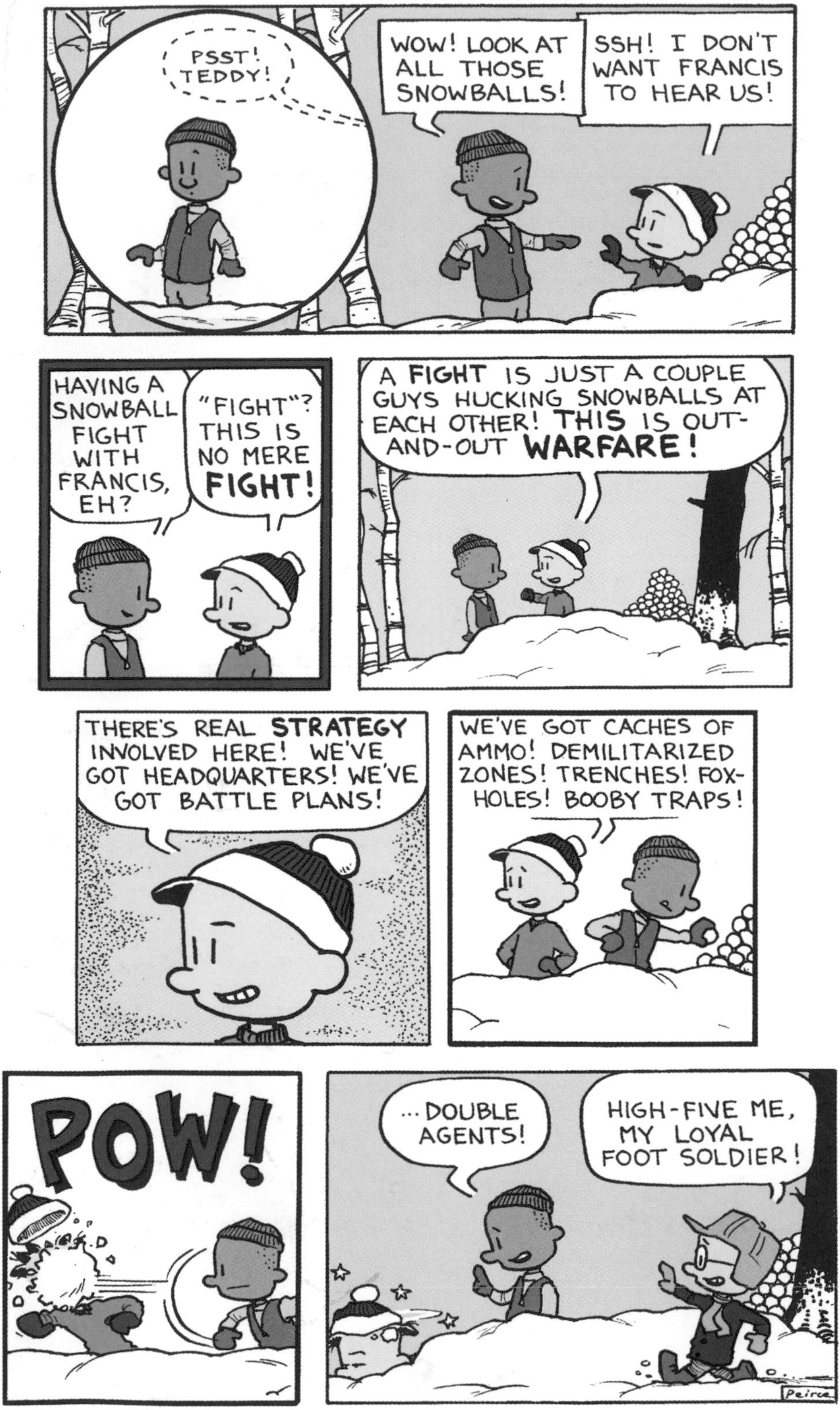
PSST! TEDDY!
WOW! LOOK AT ALL THOSE SNOWBALLS!
SSH! I DON'T WANT FRANCIS TO HEAR US!
HAVING A SNOWBALL FIGHT WITH FRANCIS, EH?
"FIGHT"? THIS IS NO MERE FIGHT!
A FIGHT IS JUST A COUPLE GUYS HUCKING SNOWBALLS AT EACH OTHER! THIS IS OUT-AND-OUT WARFARE!
THERE'S REAL STRATEGY INVOLVED HERE! WE'VE GOT HEADQUARTERS! WE'VE GOT BATTLE PLANS!
WE'VE GOT CACHES OF AMMO! DEMILITARIZED ZONES! TRENCHES! FOX-HOLES! BOOBY TRAPS!
POW!
...DOUBLE AGENTS!
HIGH-FIVE ME, MY LOYAL FOOT SOLDIER!
Peirce

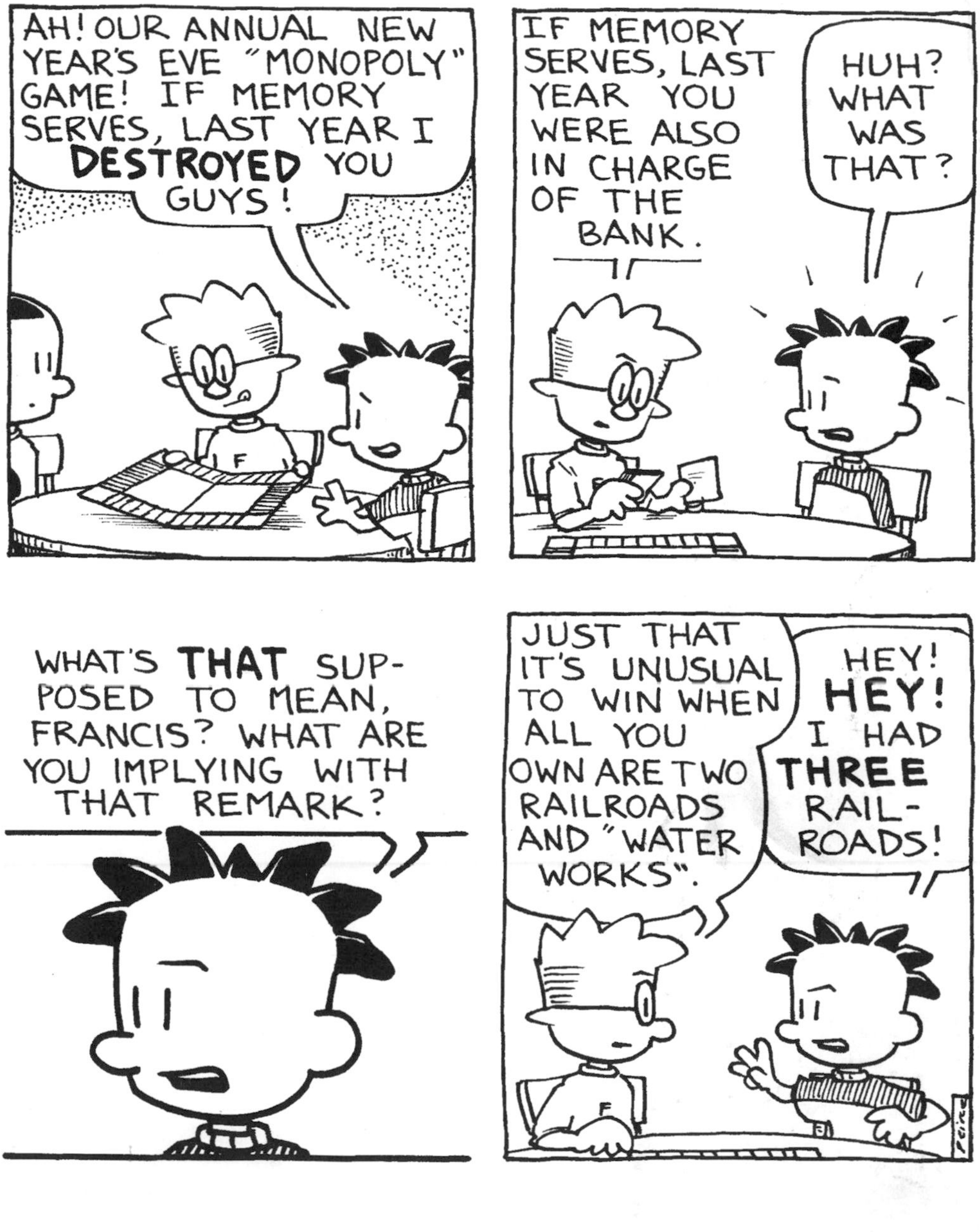
AH! OUR ANNUAL NEW YEAR'S EVE "MONOPOLY" GAME! IF MEMORY SERVES, LAST YEAR I **DESTROYED** YOU GUYS!
IF MEMORY SERVES, LAST YEAR YOU WERE ALSO IN CHARGE OF THE BANK.
HUH? WHAT WAS THAT?
WHAT'S **THAT** SUPPOSED TO MEAN, FRANCIS? WHAT ARE YOU IMPLYING WITH THAT REMARK?
JUST THAT IT'S UNUSUAL TO WIN WHEN ALL YOU OWN ARE TWO RAILROADS AND "WATER WORKS".
HEY! **HEY!** I HAD **THREE** RAILROADS!

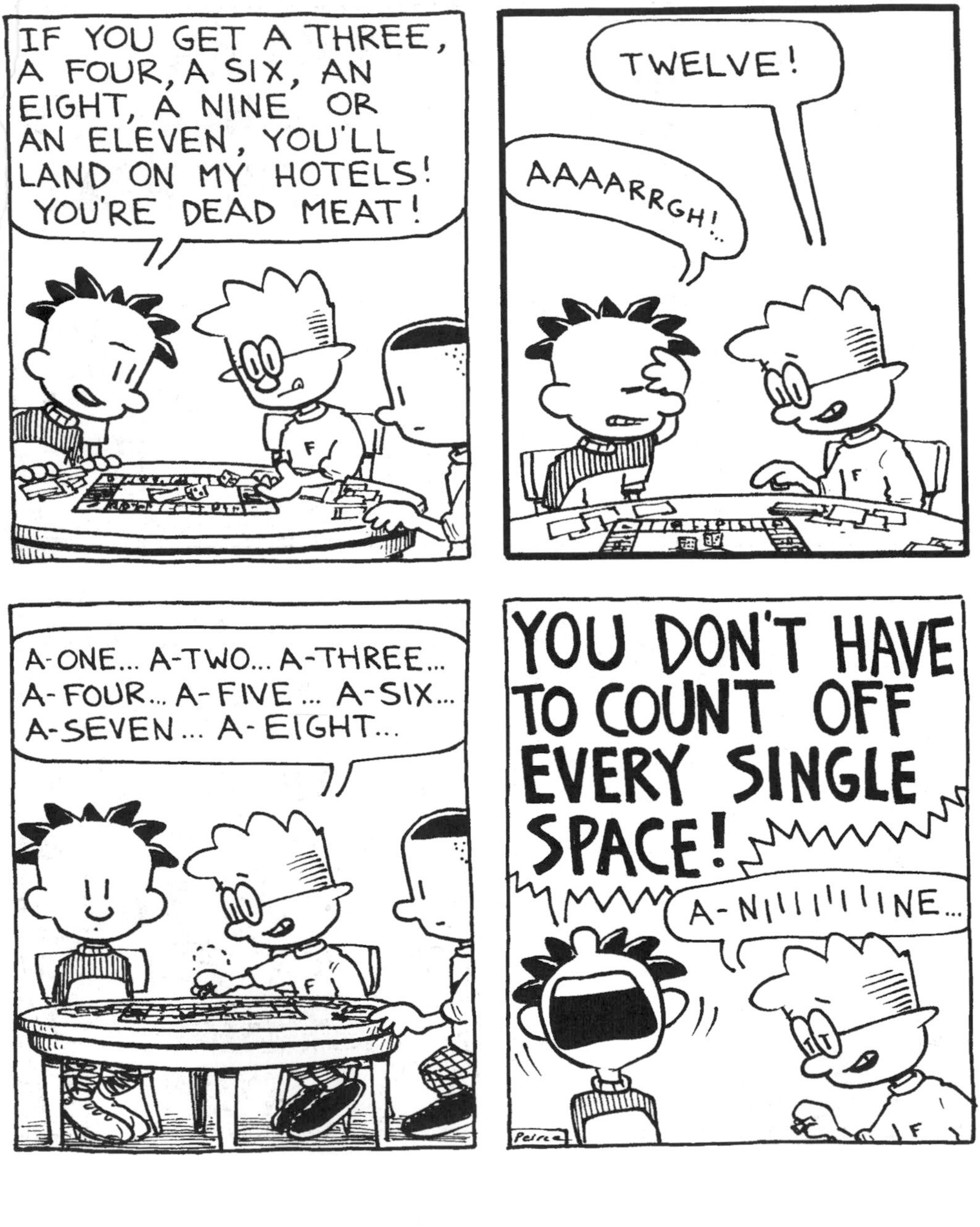
IF YOU GET A THREE, A FOUR, A SIX, AN EIGHT, A NINE OR AN ELEVEN, YOU'LL LAND ON MY HOTELS! YOU'RE DEAD MEAT!
TWELVE!
AAAARRGH!..
A-ONE... A-TWO... A-THREE... A-FOUR... A-FIVE... A-SIX... A-SEVEN... A-EIGHT...
YOU DON'T HAVE TO COUNT OFF EVERY SINGLE SPACE!
A-NIIIIIIINE...
Peirce

THE **ONLY** WAY YOU CAN ESCAPE MY PROPERTIES IS TO GET AN **ELEVEN**! YOU'RE GOIN' **DOWN**! NYA HA HA HA HA
BWA HA HA HA HA HA HA HA HA HA HA HA HAA!
NYA HYA HA HA HA HA HA HA HA —
ELEVEN!
WA HA HA HA HA HA HA HA HA HA HA

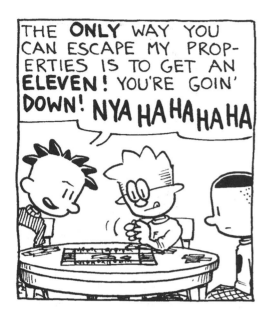

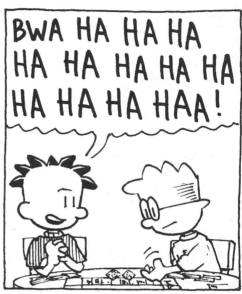

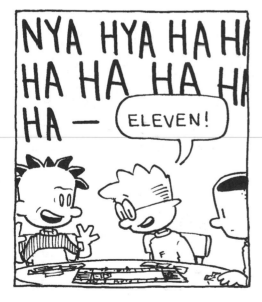

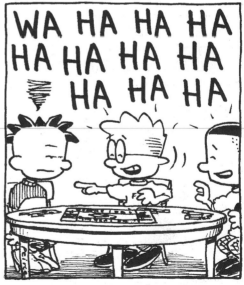